WEST CHICAGO PUBLIC LIBRARY DISTRICT

3 6655 00214 7837

2/12

LIGHTSPEED:
YEAR ONE

D0913718

West Chicago Public Library District
118 West Washington
West Chicago, IL 60185-2803
Phone # (630) 231-1552
Fax # (630) 231-1709

OTHER BOOKS EDITED BY
JOHN JOSEPH ADAMS

Armored (forthcoming)
Brave New Worlds
By Blood We Live
Federations
The Improbable Adventures of Sherlock Holmes
The Living Dead
The Living Dead 2
The Mad Scientist's Guide to World Domination (forthcoming)
Seeds of Change
Under the Moons of Mars: New Adventures on Barsoom (forthcoming)
Wastelands
The Way of the Wizard

LIGHTSPEED: YEAR ONE

EDITED BY JOHN JOSEPH ADAMS

PRIME BOOKS

LIGHTSPEED: YEAR ONE

Copyright © 2011 by Prime Books.
Cover art by Vitaly S. Alexius.
Cover design by Telegraphy Harness.

All stories are copyrighted to their respective authors,
and used here with their permission.
An extension of this copyright page can be found on pages 571-575.

Prime Books
www.prime-books.com

Publisher's Note:
No portion of this book may be reproduced by any means, mechanical,
electronic, or otherwise, without first obtaining the permission of the
copyright holder.

For more information, contact Prime Books:
prime@prime-books.com

ISBN: 978-1-60701-304-4

Printed in Canada

For
The Lightspeed Team,
without whom none of this would have been possible.

• Contents •

• Contents •

• INTRODUCTION •
John Joseph Adams

Welcome to *Lightspeed: Year One!*

For those of you not already familiar with *Lightspeed*, some background may be in order: *Lightspeed* is an online magazine (www.lightspeedmagazine. com) that focuses exclusively on science fiction. Within its pages (or pixels, as it were), you will find all types of science fiction, from near-future, sociological soft sf, to far-future, star-spanning hard sf, and anything and everything in between.

Every month, we publish a mix of original fiction and reprints, and feature a variety of authors—from the bestsellers and award-winners you already know to the best new voices you haven't heard of yet. So when you read *Lightspeed*, our hope is that you'll see where science fiction comes from, where it is now, and where it's going.

Which brings us to the anthology that you're reading right now. This is the first in a planned series of print anthologies that will annually collect all of the fiction originally published in the magazine. This first volume will collect all of the fiction originally published in *Lightspeed*, from June 2010 to May 2011.

We've had a great first year. Nine out of the sixteen original stories published in *Lightspeed* in 2010 have been selected for reprint in a best-of-the-year anthology. Additionally, two of our stories—"Arvies" by Adam-Troy Castro and "I'm Alive, I Love You, I'll See You in Reno" by Vylar Kaftan—have been named finalists for the Nebula Award, and another story—"Amaryllis" by Carrie Vaughn—was nominated for the Hugo Award. *Lightspeed* itself and yours truly were also nominated for the Hugo Award, and *Lightspeed* won the Million Writers Award for Best New Online Magazine. We're hugely honored to have received all these accolades, but we'd like to think that these accolades are only a sign of more great things to come!

While fiction is *Lightspeed's* focus (and only our fiction is included in this anthology), *Lightspeed* is also a nonfiction magazine. Alongside of our fiction selections, we run articles that riff off the ideas in the fiction. For instance, in our debut issue, we have a story about relativistic travel, so we asked sf author and expert astronomer Mike Brotherton to tell us about the science behind that familiar sf trope. We also regularly feature brief interviews with the authors we call "author spotlights," in which the authors talk a bit about the stories behind their stories.

But there's more to *Lightspeed* than that, too. *Lightspeed* is also a podcast, which features two stories each month in audio format, produced by Grammy- and Audie Award-winning narrator/producer Stefan Rudnicki.

And, finally, *Lightspeed* is not just a weekly online magazine, it's also a monthly ebook magazine, so if you'd rather read it every month on your Kindle or Nook or Sony Reader or iPad (or even your PC!), that option is available, and you can also subscribe to the ebook edition via Weightless Books (www.weightlessbooks.com).

I hope you enjoy the anthology. If you do, I hope you'll go to our website at www.lightspeedmagazine.com to let us know what you think. And also—tell a friend!

· I'M ALIVE, I LOVE YOU, I'LL SEE YOU IN RENO ·
Vylar Kaftan

We have a history of missed connections, you and I. Years ago, when you called goodbye from the shuttle launch, my flight was landing in Zurich. I'd changed planes, been re-routed from Frankfurt. That's why you got my voicemail. I'd have answered if I could, and would've wished you luck, even if you wanted a life without me. I never managed to see Europa, like you did—just Europe, where I met my first husband. The one I wished was you.

When I heard your message, I was glad you were happy—yes, I've always wanted you happy, even during our divorce. I thought of you traveling to Alpha Centauri, time dilating between us like a portal. I envisioned it like a slow-motion movie. You'd be back in forty years. I'd be sixty-four, and you'd only be half my age.

I saved your message for weeks, until I accidentally deleted it. It felt symbolic. We'd be happier apart, I thought to myself. But "apart" was always the way we connected. The word defines us relative to each other: one cannot be apart without the other.

Einstein spent ten years thinking about a mirror that troubled him. If he traveled at the speed of light and looked into a hand-held mirror, would he see his reflection, or not? Setting aside vampirism, or poorly-made glass that cracks at high speeds, the answer is that he must. Relativity means that you can't tell how fast you're going unless you have a point of reference.

We've been together for as long as I can remember. Just kids, running around the Sacramento suburbs. I liked you because you'd play with a girl. I ran faster, fought harder, and hit harder than any boy—and I knew it. Remember that time we played Capture the Flag and you couldn't find mine? I shoved it in a drainpipe. You could still see its corner. That counts.

I was the girl next door—safe, reliable, undesirable. When I was thirteen, and you were sixteen—I was crazy-in-love with you. But you were blind. "Best friends forever," you told me.

I thought that you'd never see me as a woman your own age. I had to hear about all those girls you dated. Remember that awful redhead who stole cigarettes from her grandmother? I bet she got lung cancer.

"Best friends," I told you too. We were together, yet completely apart.

I used to wonder how to make you see me. Should I tell you what I felt? Stay silent and hope you'd see?

But you made the choice for me: you left for the military. So I joined the Peace Corps—the polar opposite of what you did. This drew us together again like magnets. It's why we ended up living together in San Francisco. Roommates and lovers.

I didn't know this then, of course—all of this I figured out during the journey to Alpha Centauri.

Two magnets, apart, continue to exert force on each other. Their power lies in the space between.

Einstein says that nothing moves at the speed of light, because the faster things get the heavier they become.

It's true that as I accelerated, everything had more weight: two decades of child-rearing, juggling flute practice with my photography career, balancing a marriage's weight against single independence. But weight is relative, and what's heavy on Earth is light on the Moon and monstrous on Jupiter. Yet the mass remains the same. The more things change, the more they stay the same.

When I think about the changes in my parents' lives—and how much more I've already seen, in fewer years—I think of Moore's Law.

My world is doubling every year. Somewhere in old Italy, Galileo is searching the skies with his telescope, wondering why his life doesn't feel as full as it should. It's because I have it all, four centuries later—his life, and millions of others.

The doubling sequence surprises people who've never thought it through.

Reno, you told me once. Reno, Nevada. When we lived in San Francisco, in that tiny apartment above a Mission District taqueria. Do you remember that conversation? We were sitting on that awful brown loveseat you'd rescued from a dumpster. You were heating dinner in the microwave, and the room smelled like curry. The fog rolled through the city and we both wore old sweaters. I didn't yet know the relevance of Reno.

"If we're separated," you said.

"Why Reno?"

"It's inland. When the big quake hits the Bay, Reno's safe. Or if there's a missile strike or something. No one strikes Reno."

"You're paranoid," I said.

You shrugged. "I'm aware."

We'd been living together for six months. We made good roommates—both of us loud, and neither of us tidy. You took out the trash, and I sorted the mail; we both did dishes when needed, and not more often. I didn't mind your waterskis propped against the fridge, or your physics books scattered on the pizza-stained carpet. You didn't mind the way I always slammed doors and drawers, no matter how quiet I tried to be. It was a good arrangement. But not what I wanted.

I knew you loved me, of course. It was written in your eyes when you looked at me, a physics problem with no clear answer. If an irresistible force meets an immovable object, what happens then?

They meet. That's all we know. Relative to each other, they are in contact. From within the object or the force, there is no way to tell if you're in motion.

For a while, I was Charon to your Pluto, keeping the same faces to each other as we circled around endlessly.

And through all of this you still thought of me as a moon, and yourself as a planet. But it's not so easy as that. Our orbit is erratic, an ellipse among circles, an offbeat pattern in a regular solar system. Do you see the sun, far in the distance? Even when our orbit sweeps close to the sun, it takes four hours for its light to reach us. It's a centerpoint that keeps us captured. We circle it so we don't fly off into space. It's a point of reference, and it proves to us that we're always in motion.

We keep moving, along with everything else. Even if we can't see where or how.

By the time we got together, it was more for convenience than anything else.

It was what we did: have sex, fight, break up, meet someone else. And when the new relationship burned out, like a magnesium ribbon flared and gone, we'd find each other again.

The best thing between us was the sex. We fought—oh, yes, we fought—and then had make-up sex. Hard, hot, and heavy. You'd drive into me just before I was ready—*making* me ready—then finish just after me, both of us collapsed together, trapped in each other's gravity wells.

When you slept, I'd stroke your rough, calloused fingers and the Superglued cuts in your feet from waterskiing. I'd think about our next fight, and my body tingled with wanting you.

"I'll marry you," you said once, "if you can't find anyone else."

I laughed because I thought you were kidding. You couldn't even propose right.

It was the last push on a decaying orbit. I was not your fallback option. From the time you said that, our path downwards was guaranteed, calculable. We fought about the phone bill, Chinese leftovers, a broken plate that didn't get swept up. When you told me about your new job repairing relativity shuttles, I was secretly glad. Your work would take you to Reno. Out of my path.

I was completely over you, over us—or at least I was then, when you left. I was on the rebound, ready for someone new.

Gunther, the German engineer, was everything you weren't. So I married him. Once you knew his first few digits, they repeated in a predictable pattern. He was a wonderful father for our two sons. I thought of you sometimes as I raised my boys, perfect squares in their rational world. I never forgot you.

Thanks to genetics, we expected Gunther's heart problems before they happened. He lasted twenty-five years with me, then slipped away. My kids were on their own by then, and I had time and money. I was free to choose irrationally, and so I took up waterskiing.

When you came back, I was surprised you came to my door—and even more surprised that you wanted me. I didn't think you'd stay with me—a hot young thirty-something, with this dried-out old lady. You kept saying you liked my maturity, you found me sexy. But it was different for me. I saw you like my kids. More like a son than a mate.

If I can't find anyone else.

That's a terrible proposal. It makes a woman feel like you're just putting up with her. I *did* find someone else. I had twenty-five happy years with him, while you were living through just a few months. I accumulated the weight of years—of a woman building decades with her partner, of a mother renewing herself by raising her children. All of this weight I gained—not to mention my new-found belly.

But I married you anyway. You wanted to be with me, you said. All your recent thoughts told you so. My age didn't matter—you still wanted *me*, the woman you'd loved all this time, you said.

As for me, now I had what I'd always wanted—but it wasn't what I thought it would be.

One night after we made love on the beach, I watched the stars. They shone with light from billions of years ago. The stars offered us time apart. That's why I sold everything I had—to see what you'd seen.

The new relativity shuttles were even faster than yours had been, and now they were open to tourists. It had been forty years here, after all. I'm sorry I didn't leave a note.

I figured it was all relative.

Gunther was always patient with me. Slow. He'd wait for me to orgasm, like he was holding a car door open for me, and then he'd finish quickly and silently.

Sometimes I pretended he was you to make things more exciting. Once I pretended he was Albert Einstein. It was the accent, I swear.

With you, the electromagnetic pull bonded us together. We could ionize briefly, visiting other molecules and forming weak bonds—but we always came back together, circling each other endlessly.

An electron and a proton. You and me.

For a long time I thought I was the electron, spinning wild patterns around you. Then I realized the electron was you, because I always knew either where you were or how fast you were going, but never both.

So I left you and went to the stars, like you'd done. Alpha Centauri! The brilliant star burned into my mind. It was a vacation for me, a short time away from Earth. For the first time, I saw the lights up close. The luxury ship went 99% the speed of light. Much faster than you had gone, faster than before.

I figured you'd be dead once I got back. It simplified things. Stopped the fighting. You'd be ashes, like you'd always wanted. I wouldn't even have to see your body. I thought about it, as I looked through the viewport, and realized that I was still thinking of you. That was when I understood that no matter how far I went or how fast, I still responded to you in every way.

Every action produces an equal and opposite reaction. Our bond pulls me back, and I love you.

Reasons why I have loved you:
1. Yes.
2. Yes, again.
3. Because you're you.

None of these are love, perhaps, but they're forces of physics. And if love isn't subject to physics, then it has no grounding in our universe. I can't believe that's true.

Just when I got back, you left again, like one metal ball clacking another —the opposite side of our kinetic motion toy. You were off for the Andromeda Galaxy, moving at 99.38% the speed of light.

Simpler, indeed. I was sixty-eight. You were gone.

It was time to move on.

The world had changed since I left. The human lifespan was up to 150 years. I hadn't imagined this possibility. I had decades left for music, art, whatever I dreamed of. My health was good—they killed a malignant breast tumor and grew me a new liver, twice—but otherwise, my body kept working for years.

But my nervous system paralysis—that was incurable. I opted for cryogenesis, hoping they'd find a cure. If they did, years from now, they'd revive me and heal me.

It was exciting. I wondered if it'd be hard to fall asleep, like Christmas Eve—not knowing what Christmas Day would bring. But of course the freezing was instant. As I lay down in the cryochamber I thought to myself: Reno. That's where I should have gone, when disaster struck. I was thinking of you.

And then I was frozen, like Charon and Pluto.

If I'm a train leaving Philadelphia at 3:00, going 50 miles an hour, and you're a train on the same track leaving San Francisco at 4:00, going 55 miles an hour, at what time will we collide and run each other off the tracks?

More importantly, if we move at the speed of light, and I shine a light in your direction, will you blink and tell me to stop blinding you, or will you not see me coming until it's too late?

If Einstein is flying next to our train, looking into a mirror and wondering where his reflection has gone—will you ask him whether anything stands still, or if everything is always in motion? Relative to everything else, of course.

And ask about Reno. If our trains crash there, should we consider that they've stopped moving? Or are they still in motion on Earth, relative to everything else in the universe?

Everyone's joined in the same future, except you. Time moves so quickly—accelerating to the point where we can hardly imagine what's next. I went to sleep expecting to be cured. Instead, the AI woke me and said I no longer needed my body. It downloaded my mind, and now I see. You and I are eccentric, but part of a solar system, and I know now where we belong. It's easy for me to travel along circuits, to expand my mind everywhere in the network—and then condense myself so small as to be negligible in the universe, here in one corner of a virtual city.

I see they've sent a ship after you, moving at 99.99% the speed of light. It'll reach you eventually. They'll download you and you'll fly back to me. Here, where we belong. I think I never left your orbit.

I wrote you a long message to explain all this, but I think I'll erase it and just leave ten words. I'll tell you the rest when you arrive—when our perpetual motion comes to a relative stop.

* 2011 Nebula Award nominee for Best Short Story

• THE CASSANDRA PROJECT •
Jack McDevitt

It's an odd fact that the biggest science story of the twenty-first century—probably the biggest ever—broke in that tabloid of tabloids, *The National Bedrock*.

I was in the middle of conducting a NASA press conference several days before the Minerva lift-off—the Return to the Moon—and I was fielding softball questions like: "Is it true that if everything goes well, the Mars mission will be moved up?" and "What is Marcia Beckett going to say when she becomes the first person to set foot on lunar soil since Eugene Cernan turned off the lights fifty-four years ago?"

President Gorman and his Russian counterpart, Dmitri Alexandrov, were scheduled to talk to the press from the White house an hour later, so I was strictly a set-up guy. Or that was the plan, anyway, until Warren Cole mentioned the dome.

It was a good time for NASA. We all knew the dangers inherent in overconfidence, but two orbital missions had gone up without a hitch. Either of them could have landed and waved back at us, and the rumor was that Sid Myshko had almost taken the game into his own hands, and that the crew had put it to a vote whether they'd ignore the protocol and go down to the surface regardless of the mission parameters. Sid and his five crewmates denied the story, of course.

I'd just made the point to the pool of reporters that it was Richard Nixon who'd turned off the lights—not the astronaut Eugene Cernan—when Warren Cole began waving his hand. Cole was the AP journalist, seated in his customary spot up front. He was frowning, his left hand in the air, staring down at something on his lap that I couldn't see.

"Warren?" I said. "What've you got?"

"Jerry . . . " He looked up, making no effort to suppress a grin. "Have you seen the story that the *Bedrock's* running?" He held up his iPad.

That started a few people checking their own devices.

"No, I haven't," I said, hoping he was making it up. "I don't usually get to *Bedrock* this early in the week." Somebody snorted. Then a wave of laughter rippled through the room. "What?" I said. My first thought had been that we were about to have another astronaut scandal, like the one the month before with Barnaby Salvator and half the strippers on the Beach. "What are they saying?"

"The Russians released more lunar orbital pictures from the sixties," He snickered. "They've got one here from the far side of the Moon. If you can believe this, there's a dome back there."

"A *dome*?"

"Yeah." He flipped open his notebook. "Does NASA have a comment?"

"You're kidding, right?" I said.

He twisted the iPad, raised it higher, and squinted at it. "Yep. It's a dome all right."

The reporters in the pool all had a good chuckle, and then they looked up at me. "Well," I said, "I guess Buck Rogers beat us there after all."

"It looks legitimate, Jerry," Cole said, but he was still laughing.

I didn't have to tell him what we all knew: That it was a doctored picture and that it must have been a slow week for scandals.

If the image *was* doctored, the deed had to have been done by the Russians. Moscow had released the satellite images only a few hours before and forwarded them to us without comment. Apparently nobody on either side had noticed anything unusual. Except the *Bedrock* staff.

I hadn't looked at the images prior to the meeting. I mean, once you've seen a few square miles of lunar surface you've pretty much seen it all. The dome—if that's really what it was—appeared on every image in the series. They were dated April, 1967.

The *Bedrock* carried the image on its front page, where they usually show the latest movie celebrity who's being accused of cheating, or has gone on a drunken binge. It depicted a crater wall, with a large arrow graphic in the middle of a dark splotch pointing at a dome that you couldn't have missed anyhow. The headline read:

ALIENS ON THE MOON
Russian Pictures Reveal Base on Far Side
Images Taken Before Apollo

I sighed and pushed back from my desk. We just didn't need this.

But it *did* look like an artificial construct. The thing was on the edge of a crater, shaped like the head of a bullet. It was either a reflection, an illusion of some sort, or it was a fraud. But the Russians had no reason to set themselves up as a laughing stock. And it sure as hell *looked* real.

I was still staring at it when the phone rang. It was Mary, NASA's administrator. My boss. "*Jerry*," she said, "*I heard what happened at the press conference this morning.*"

"What's going on, Mary?"

"*Damned if I know. Push some buttons. See what you can find out. It's going to come up again when the President's out there. We need to have an answer for him.*"

Vasili Koslov was my public relations counterpart at Russia's space agency. He was in Washington with the presidential delegation. And he was in full panic mode when I got him on the phone. "*I saw it, Jerry,*" he said. "*I have no idea what this is about. I just heard about it a few minutes ago. I'm looking at it now. It does look like a dome, doesn't it?*"

"Yes," I said. "Did your people tamper with the satellite imagery?"

"*They must have. I have a call in. I'll let you know as soon as I hear something.*"

I called Jeanie Escovar in the Archives. "Jeanie, have you seen the *National Bedrock* story yet?"

"*No,*" she said. "*My God, what is it this time?*"

"Not what you think. I'm sending it to you now. Could you have somebody check to see where this place is—?"

"*What place? Oh, wait—I got it.*"

"Find out where it is and see if you can get me some imagery of the same area. From *our* satellites."

I heard her gasp. Then she started laughing.

"Jeanie, this is serious."

"*Why? You don't actually believe there's a building up there, do you?*"

"Somebody's going to ask the President about it. They have a press conference going on in about twenty minutes. We want him to be able to say: 'It's ridiculous, here's a picture of the area, and you'll notice there's nothing there.' We want him to be able to say '*The Bedrock's* running an optical illusion.' But he'll have to do it diplomatically. And without embarrassing Alexandrov."

"*Good luck on that.*"

The *Bedrock* story was already getting attention on the talk shows. Angela Hart, who at that time anchored *The Morning Report* for the *World Journal*, was interviewing a physicist from MIT. The physicist stated that the picture could not be accurate. "*Probably a practical joke,*" he said. "*Or a trick of the light.*"

But Angela wondered why the Russians would release the picture at all. "*They had to know it would get a lot of attention,*" she said. And, of course, though she didn't mention it, it would become a source of discomfort for the Russian president and the two cosmonauts who were among the Minerva crew.

Vasili was in a state of shock when he called back. "*They didn't know about* the dome," he said. "*Nobody noticed. But it is on the original satellite imagery. Our people were just putting out a lot of the stuff from the Luna missions. Imagery that hadn't been released before. I can't find anybody who knows anything about it. But I'm still trying.*"

"Vasili," I said, "somebody must have seen it at the time. In 1967."

"*I guess.*"

"You *guess*? You think it's possible something like this came in and nobody picked up on it?"

"*No, I'm not suggesting that at all, Jerry. I just—I don't know what I'm suggesting. I'll get back to you when I have something more.*"

Minutes later, Jeanie called: "*It's the east wall of the Cassegrain Crater.*"

"And—?"

"*I've forwarded NASA imagery of the same area.*"

I switched on the monitor and ran the images. There was the same crater wall, the same pock-marked moonscape. But no dome. Nothing at all unusual.

Dated July, 1968. More than a year after the Soviet imagery.

I called Mary and told her: The Russians just screwed up.

"*The President can't say that.*"

"All he has to say is that NASA has no evidence of any dome or anything else on the far side of the Moon. Probably he should just turn it into a joke. Make some remark about setting up a Martian liaison unit."

She didn't think it was funny.

When the subject came up at the presidential press conference, Gorman and Alexandrov both simply had a good laugh. Alexandrov blamed it on Khrushchev, and the laughter got louder. Then they moved on to how the Minerva mission—the long-awaited Return to the Moon—marked the beginning of a new era for the world.

The story kicked around in the tabloids for two or three more days. *The Washington Post* ran an op-ed using the dome to demonstrate how gullible we all are when the media says *anything*. Then Cory Abbott, who'd just won a Golden Globe for his portrayal of Einstein in *Albert and Me*, crashed his car into a street light and blacked out the entire town of Dekker, California. And just like that the dome story was gone.

On the morning of the launch, Roscosmos, the Russian space agency, issued a statement that the image was a result of defective technology. The Minerva lifted off on schedule and, while the world watched, it crossed to the Moon and completed a few orbits. Its lander touched down gently on the Mare Maskelyne. Marcia Beckett surprised everyone when she demurred leading the way out through the airlock, sending instead Cosmonaut Yuri Petrov, who descended and then signaled his crewmates to join him.

When all were assembled on the regolith, Petrov made the statement that, in the light of later events, has become immortal: *"We are here on the Moon because, during the last century, we avoided the war that would have destroyed us all. And we have come together. Now we stand as never before, united for all mankind."*

I wasn't especially impressed at the time. It sounded like the usual generalized nonsense. Which shows you what my judgment is worth.

I watched on my office monitor. And as the ceremony proceeded, I looked past the space travelers, across the barren wasteland of the Mare Maskelyne, wondering which was the shortest path to the Cassegrain crater.

I knew I should have just let it go, but I couldn't. I could imagine no explanation for the Russians doctoring their satellite imagery. Vasili told me that everyone with whom he'd spoken was shocked. That the images had been dug out of the archives and distributed without inspection. And, as far as could be determined, without anyone distorting them. *"I just don't understand it, Jerry,"* he said.

Mary told me not to worry about it. "We have more important things to do," she said.

There was no one left at NASA from the 1960s. In fact, I knew of only one person living at Cape Kennedy who had been part of the Agency when Apollo 11 went to the Moon: Amos Kelly, who'd been one of my grandfather's buddies. He was still in the area, where he served with the Friends of NASA, a group of volunteers who lent occasional support but mostly threw parties. I looked him up. He'd come to the Agency in 1965 as a technician. Eventually, he'd become one of the operational managers.

He was in his mid-eighties, but he sounded good. *"Sure, Jerry, I remember you. It's been a long time,"* he said, when I got him on the phone. I'd been a little kid when he used to stop by to pick up my grandfather for an evening of poker. *"What can I do for you?"*

"This is going to sound silly, Amos."

"Nothing sounds silly to me. I used to work for the government."

"Did you see the story in the tabloids about the dome?"

"How could I miss it?"

"You ever hear anything like that before?"

"You mean did we think there were Martians on the Moon?" He laughed, turned away to tell someone that the call was for him, and then laughed again. *"Is that a serious question, Jerry?"*

"I guess not."

"Good. By the way, you've done pretty well for yourself at the Agency. Your granddad would have been proud."

"Thanks."

He told me how much he missed the old days, missed my grandfather, how they'd had a good crew. *"Best years of my life. I could never believe they'd just scuttle the program the way they did."*

Finally he asked what the Russians had said about the images. I told him what Vasili told me. *"Well,"* he said, *"maybe they haven't changed that much after all."*

Twenty minutes later he called back. *"I was reading the story in the* Bedrock. *It says that the object was in the Cassegrain Crater."*

"Yes. That's correct."

"There was talk of a Cassegrain Project at one time. Back in the sixties. I don't know what it was supposed to be. Whether it was anything more than a rumor. Nobody seemed to know anything definitive about it. I recall at the time thinking it was one of those things so highly classified that even its existence was off the table."

"The Cassegrain Project."

"Yes."

"But you have no idea what it was about?"

"None. I'm sorry. Wish I could help."

"Would you tell me if you knew?"

"It's a long time ago, Jerry. I can't believe security would still be an issue."

"Amos, you were pretty high in the Agency—"

"Not that high."

"Do you remember anything else?"

"Nothing. Nada. As far as I know, nothing ever came of any of it, so the whole thing eventually went away."

Searching NASA's archives on "Cassegrain" yielded only data about the crater. So I took to wandering around the facility, talking offhandedly with senior employees. *It must feel good to see us back on the Moon, huh, Ralph? Makes all the frustration worthwhile. By the way, did you ever hear of a Cassegrain Project?*

They all laughed. *Crazy Russians.*

On the day the Minerva slipped out of lunar orbit and started home, Mary called me into her office. "We'll want to get the crew onstage for the press when they get back, Jerry. You might give the staging some thought."

"Okay. Will it be at Edwards?"

"Negative. We're going to do it here at the Cape." We talked over some of the details, the scheduling, guest speakers, points we'd want to make with the media. Then as I was getting ready to leave, she stopped me. "One more thing. The Cassegrain business—" I straightened and came to attention. Mary Gridley was a no-nonsense hard-charger. She was in her fifties, and years of dealing with bureaucratic nonsense had left her with little patience. She was physically diminutive, but she could probably have intimidated the Pope. "—I want you to leave it alone."

She picked up a pen, put it back down, and stared at me. "Jerry, I know you've been asking around about that idiot dome. Listen, you're good at what you do. You'll probably enjoy a long, happy career with us. But that won't happen if people stop taking you seriously. You understand what I mean?"

After the shuttle landing and subsequent celebration, I went on the road. "We need to take advantage of the moment," Mary said. "There'll never be a better time to get some good press."

So I did a PR tour, giving interviews, addressing prayer breakfasts and Rotary meetings, doing what I could to raise the consciousness of the public. NASA wanted Moonbase. It was the next logical step. Should have had it decades ago and would have if the politicians hadn't squandered the nation's resources on pointless wars and interventions. But it would be expensive, and we hadn't succeeded yet in getting the voters on board. That somehow had become *my* responsibility.

In Seattle, I appeared at a Chamber of Commerce dinner with Arnold Banner, an astronaut who'd never gotten higher than the space station. But nevertheless he was an astronaut, and he hailed from the Apollo era. During the course of the meal I asked whether he'd ever heard of a Cassegrain Project. He said something about tabloids and gave me a disapproving look.

We brought in astronauts wherever we could. In Los Angeles, at a Marine charities fundraiser, we had both Marcia Beckett and Yuri Petrov, which would have been the highlight of the tour, except for Frank Allen.

Frank was in his nineties. He looked exhausted. His veins bulged and I wasn't sure he didn't need oxygen.

He was the fourth of the Apollo-era astronauts I talked with during those two weeks. And when I asked about the Cassegrain Project, his eyes went wide and his mouth tightened. Then he regained control. "Cassandra," he said, looking past me into a distant place. "It's classified."

"Not *Cassandra*, Frank. *Cassegrain*."

"Oh. Yeah. Of course."

"I have a clearance."

"How high?"

"Secret."

"Not enough."

"Just give me a hint. What do you know?"

"Jerry, I've already said too much. Even its existence is classified."

Cassandra.

When I got back to the Cape I did a search on *Cassandra* and found that a lot of people with that name had worked for the Agency over the years. Other Cassandras had made contributions in various ways, leading programs to get kids interested in space science, collaborating with NASA physicists in analyzing the data collected by space-born telescopes, editing publications to make NASA more accessible to the lay public. They'd been everywhere. You couldn't bring in a NASA guest speaker without discovering a Cassandra somewhere among the people who'd made the request. Buried among the names so deeply that I almost missed it was a single entry: *The Cassandra Project, storage 27176B Redstone.*

So secret its existence was classified?

The reference was to the Redstone Arsenal in Huntsville, Alabama where NASA stores rocket engines, partially-completed satellites, control panels from test stands, and a multitude of other artifacts dating back to Apollo. I called them.

A baritone voice informed me I had reached the NASA Storage Facility. *"Sgt. Saber speaking."*

I couldn't resist smiling at the name, but I knew he'd heard all the jokes. I identified myself. Then: "Sergeant, you have a listing for the Cassandra Project." I gave him the number. "Can I get access to the contents?"

"One minute, please, Mr. Carter."

While I waited, I glanced around the office at the photos of Neil Armstrong and Lawrence Bergman and Marcia Beckett. In one, I was standing beside Bergman, who'd been the guy who'd sold the President on returning to the Moon. In another, I was standing by while Marcia spoke with some Alabama school kids during a tour of the Marshall Space Flight Center. Marcia was a charmer of the first order. I've always suspected she got the Minerva assignment partially because they knew the public would love her.

"When were you planning to come, Mr. Carter?"

"I'm not sure yet. Within the next week or so."

"Let us know in advance and there'll be no problem."

"It's not classified, then?"

"No, sir. I'm looking at its history now. It was originally classified, but that was removed by the Restricted Access Depository Act more than twenty years ago."

I had to get through another round of ceremonies and press conferences before I could get away. Finally, things quieted down. The astronauts went back to their routines, the VIPs went back to whatever it was they normally do, and life on the Cape returned to normal. I put in for leave.

"You deserve it," Mary said.

Next day, armed with a copy of the Restricted Access Depository Act, I was on my way to Los Angeles to pay another visit to a certain elderly retired astronaut.

"I can't believe it," Frank Allen said.

He lived with his granddaughter and her family of about eight, in Pasadena. She shepherded us into her office—she was a tax expert of some sort—brought some lemonade, and left us alone.

"What can't you believe? That they declassified it?"

"That the story never got out in the first place." Frank was back at the desk. I'd sunk into a leather settee.

"What's the story, Frank? Was the dome really there?"

"Yes."

"*NASA* doctored its own Cassegrain imagery? To eliminate all traces?"

"I don't know anything about that."

"So what *do* you know?"

"They sent us up to take a look. In late 1968." He paused. "We landed almost on top of the damned thing."

"*Before* Apollo 11."

"Yes."

I sat there in shock. And I've been around a while, so I don't shock easily.

"They advertised the flight as a test run, Jerry. It was supposed to be purely an orbital mission. Everything else, the dome, the descent, everything was top secret. Didn't happen."

"You actually got to the dome?"

He hesitated. A lifetime of keeping his mouth shut was getting in the way. "Yes," he said. "We came down about a half mile away. Max was brilliant."

Max Donnelly. The lunar module pilot. "What happened?"

"I remember thinking the Russians had beaten us. They'd gotten to the Moon and we hadn't even known about it.

"There weren't any antennas or anything. Just a big, silvery dome. About the size of a two-story house. No windows. No hammer and sickle markings. Nothing. Except a door.

"We had sunlight. The mission had been planned so we wouldn't have to approach it in the dark." He shifted his position in the chair and bit down on a grunt.

"You okay, Frank?" I asked.

"My knees. They don't work as well as they used to." He rubbed the right one, then rearranged himself—gently this time. "We didn't know what to expect. Max said he thought the thing was pretty old because there were no tracks in the ground. We walked up to the front door. It had a knob. I thought the place would be locked, but I tried it and the thing didn't move at first but then something gave way and I was able to pull the door open."

"What was inside?"

"A table. There was a cloth on the table. And something flat under the cloth. And that's all there was."

"Nothing else?"

"Not a thing." He shook his head. "Max lifted the cloth. Under it was a rectangular plate. Made from some kind of metal." He stopped and stared at me. "There was writing on it."

"Writing? What did it say?"

"I don't know. Never found out. It looked like Greek. We brought the plate back home with us and turned it over to the bosses. Next thing they called us in and debriefed us. Reminded us it was all top secret. Whatever the thing said, it must have scared the bejesus out of Nixon and his people. Because they never said anything, and I guess the Russians didn't either."

"You never heard anything more at all?"

"Well, other than the next Apollo mission, which went back and destroyed the dome. Leveled it."

"How do you know?"

"I knew the crew. We talked to each other, right? They wouldn't say it directly. Just shook their heads: Nothing to worry about anymore."

Outside, kids were shouting, tossing a football around. "Greek?"

"That's what it looked like."

"A message from Plato."

He just shook his head as if to say: *Who knew?*

"Well, Frank, I guess that explains why they called it the Cassandra Project."

"She wasn't a Greek, was she?"

"You have another theory?"

"Maybe Cassegrain was too hard for the people in the Oval Office to pronounce."

I told Mary what I knew. She wasn't happy. "I really wish you'd left it alone, Jerry."

"There's no way I could have done that."

"Not now, anyhow." She let me see her frustration. "You know what it'll mean for the Agency, right? If NASA lied about something like this, and it becomes public knowledge, nobody will ever trust us again."

"It was a long time ago, Mary. Anyhow, the Agency wasn't lying. It was the Administration."

"Yeah," she said. "Good luck selling that one to the public."

The NASA storage complex at the Redstone Arsenal in Huntsville is home to rockets, a lunar landing vehicle, automated telescopes, satellites, a space station, and a multitude of other devices that had kept the American space program alive, if not particularly robust, over almost seventy years. Some were housed inside sprawling warehouses; others occupied outdoor exhibition sites.

I parked in the shadow of a Saturn V, the rocket that had carried the Apollo missions into space. I've always been impressed with the sheer audacity of anybody who'd be willing to sit on top of one of those things while someone lit the fuse. Had it been up to me, we'd probably never have lifted off at Kitty Hawk.

I went inside the Archive Office, got directions and a pass, and fifteen minutes later entered one of the warehouses. An attendant escorted me past cages and storage rooms filled with all kinds of boxes and crates. Somewhere in the center of it all, we stopped at a cubicle while the attendant compared my pass with the number on the door. The interior was visible through a wall of wire mesh. Cartons were piled up, all labeled. Several were open, with electronic equipment visible inside them.

The attendant unlocked the door and we went in. He turned on an overhead light and did a quick survey, settling on a box that was one of several on a shelf. My heart rate started to pick up while he looked at the tag. "This is it, Mr. Carter," he said. "Cassandra."

"Is this *everything*?"

He checked his clipboard. "This is the only listing we have for the Cassandra Project, sir."

"Okay. Thanks."

"My pleasure."

There was no lock. He raised the hasp on the box, lifted the lid, and stood back to make room. He showed no interest in the contents. He probably did this all the time, so I don't know why that surprised me.

Inside, I could see a rectangular object wrapped in plastic. I couldn't see what it was, but of course I knew. My heart was pounding by then. The object was about a foot and a half wide and maybe half as high. And it was heavy. I carried it over to a table and set it down. Wouldn't do to drop it. Then I unwrapped it.

The metal was black, polished, reflective, even in the half-light from the overhead bulb. And sure enough, there were the Greek characters. Eight lines of them.

The idea that Plato was saying hello seemed suddenly less far-fetched. I took a picture. Several pictures. Finally, reluctantly, I rewrapped it and put it back in the box.

"So," said Frank, "what did it say?"

"I have the translation here." I fished it out of my pocket but he shook his head.

"My eyes aren't that good, Jerry. Just tell me who wrote it. And what it says."

We were back in the office at Frank's home in Pasadena. It was a chilly, rainswept evening. Across the street, I could see one of his neighbors putting out the trash.

"It wasn't written by the Greeks."

"I didn't think it was."

"Somebody came through a long time ago. Two thousand years or so. *They* left the message. Apparently they wrote it in Greek because it must have looked like their best chance to leave something we'd be able to read. Assuming we ever reached the Moon."

"So what did it say?"

"It's a warning."

The creases in Frank's forehead deepened. "Is the sun going unstable?"

"No." I looked down at the translation. "It says that no civilization, anywhere, has been known to survive the advance of technology."

Frank stared at me. "Say that again."

"They all collapse. They fight wars. Or they abolish individual death, which apparently guarantees stagnation and an exit. I don't know. They don't specify.

"Sometimes the civilizations become too vulnerable to criminals. Or the inhabitants become too dependent on the technology and lose whatever virtue they might have had. Anyway, the message says that no technological civilization, anywhere, has been known to get old. Nothing lasts more than a few centuries—*our* centuries—once technological advancement begins. Which for us maybe starts with the invention of the printing press.

"The oldest known civilization lasted less than a thousand years."

Frank frowned. He wasn't buying it. "*They* survived. Hell, they had an interstellar ship of some kind."

"They said they were looking for a place to start again. Where they came from is a shambles."

"You're kidding."

"It says that maybe, if we know in advance, we can sidestep the problem. That's why they left the warning."

"Great."

"If they survive, they say they'll come back to see how we're doing."

We were both silent for a long while.

"So what happens now?" Frank said.

"We've reclassified everything. It's top secret again. I shouldn't be telling you this. But I thought—"

He rearranged himself in the chair. Winced and rotated his right arm. "Maybe that's why they called it *Cassandra*," he said. "Wasn't she the woman who always brought bad news?"

"I think so."

"There was something else about her—"

"Yeah—the bad news," I said. "When she gave it, nobody would listen."

* Reprinted in *Year's Best SF 16*, edited by David G. Hartwell and Kathryn Cramer

* 2011 WSFA Small Press Award nominee

• CATS IN VICTORY •
David Barr Kirtley

Lynx awoke before dawn. He got out of bed, brushed his whiskers, and licked his fur clean. He dressed in boots and a tunic, then donned his rucksack and set out into the dusty streets. The sun was just beginning to peek up over the thatched rooftops. Most of the other catmen of the village were still asleep.

Lynx hiked west, out of town, through the foothills and into the wasteland, where he wandered amid the stark beauty of the stony plains, winding arroyos, and towering plateaus.

He loved walking here, and today he'd secretly resolved to explore as far to the west as he could. His parents would disapprove. Like all the adults of the village, they harbored a vague mistrust of the wasteland, maybe due to the strange mechanical artifacts that they said were sometimes discovered beneath the sands. But the more time Lynx spent out here, the more he felt that such misgivings were baseless.

All morning he climbed hills, clambered over fields of boulders, and strode between pillars of stone. Finally, around mid-day, his westward progress was blocked by a narrow canyon that stretched as far as he could see in either direction. The canyon floor was forty feet below, and the walls were too sheer to climb, so Lynx turned north, skirting the cliff edge and searching for a way across.

Finally he came to a place where a giant tree had grown up from the canyon floor beside the near wall. The tree was dead now, but its pale, branchless trunk would provide easy access down into the canyon. Though there was no telling whether—

Wait. What was that?

He thought he saw movement, below.

A few hundred yards away, the canyon wall was broken by a wide, low cavern. A figure detached itself from the darkness and wandered down onto the sand. Lynx ducked, then slowly raised his head again as the figure came to a halt.

As far as Lynx knew, nothing lived out here except lizards and birds. But this figure was the size of a catman, and walked upright.

Then the thought came to him: A dogman.

Here? Impossible. But it had to be. He knew he should flee, get help, but . . .

The dogmen were almost extinct. This might be the only chance he'd ever get to see one. And he should make sure it was really a dogman, before he alarmed the whole village.

He dropped his rucksack and kicked off his boots. He paced, flexing his hand and foot claws. Then he dashed to the edge of the cliff and leapt onto the tree. His claws dug into the wood, and he hung there a moment, then scrambled down the trunk and dropped lightly to the canyon floor.

He sneaked toward the cave, ducking behind one boulder, then another, then another. A strong breeze blew into his face, and this was good, for the wind would muffle his footsteps and carry his scent off behind him.

He lay down and crawled on elbows and knees until he was just a dozen yards away from the mysterious figure, then peeked around a rock.

Yes. A dogman. It was burlier than any catman, and Lynx could make out its grotesque floppy ears. It wore a grungy tunic and a heavy broadsword. Then the creature turned its head, and Lynx glimpsed its profile—a flat face with saggy jowls and wrinkled folds of flesh around the eyes. A horrible, misshapen creature. An abomination.

Lynx began to crawl backward, then paused, as he spied a second figure emerging from the cave.

This one was . . . not so terrible. A female, slender, perhaps as young as Lynx. Her snout was white, her large eyes banded with brown, and her long, silky ears hung past her shoulders. She too wore a sword, a rapier.

In Lynx's imagination, dogmen had always been ugly and fearsome and . . . male. He wondered about the female. What was she to the hulking beast beside her? His ally? His wife? She had a sweet look to her, or was that deceptive? Had she ever killed a catman?

Suddenly the big male straightened and poked his nose in the air, sniffing loudly—once, twice.

Lynx felt a prickle of terror. While he'd been distracted, the breeze had shifted, and he was now upwind of the dogmen.

The male roared, "Catmen!" and whipped out his sword. He turned and stared straight at Lynx, who leapt up from his hiding spot and sprinted away, dodging around boulders and vaulting over ditches. Behind him came heavy footfalls and throaty growls as the male chased him, gained on him. Lynx spotted the tree, his escape.

The female cried, "No! Stop him!"

Lynx ran to the tree, sprang onto it, and scuttled upward. The male bellowed and leapt after him, and Lynx heard the swoosh of the broadsword, then the thunk of metal on wood. The whole tree shuddered as the sword struck just below his feet.

He climbed out of reach. The female dogman shrieked in despair, and the male let loose a frustrated howl.

Lynx fled the canyon, as the dogmen's terrible barking rose up from below him and echoed in his ears.

It wasn't until much later, when he was far from that place, that he noticed any pain. Then he found that he was missing a few inches off the end of his tail. Blood pooled there, and fell in thick droplets to the sand.

Night had fallen by the time Lynx got back to the village. He headed straight to the temple, raced through the main doors, and burst into the antechamber.

A scribe sat at a small wooden desk and scribbled in a ledger with a quill pen. When he saw Lynx's agitation, the scribe stood. "Can I help you?"

Lynx gasped for breath. "I have to see Father Cougar."

The scribe stared disapprovingly. "Father Cougar is delivering the evening service."

Lynx said, "There are dogmen! Living in the wasteland. Hiding in the caves."

"Dogmen? Are you sure?"

"Yes, I'm sure! They chased me, with swords." Lynx held up the tip of his tail, which was clotted with blood.

The scribe grew alarmed. "All right. Wait here." He hurried over to a pair of heavy wooden doors, then slipped through, closing the doors behind him.

Lynx stepped forward and pressed his ear to the wood. Father Cougar's booming voice filled the other room. Lynx could only make out some of the words, but he grasped the essence of the sermon. Father Cougar was preaching, as ever, about how these were the end times, and about the coming Victory, when Cat would return to Earth, the dogmen would be destroyed forever, and the catmen would regain their pure feline forms.

Father Cougar's voice died away. He must be conferring with the scribe.

Finally the scribe reappeared and said, "Follow me."

He led Lynx down a hallway to a cozy chamber whose walls were hung with tapestries. Father Cougar, wearing his vestments, sat on a sofa in the corner. He said warmly, "Lynx! Come in, come in."

Lynx picked a chair and sat down.

Father Cougar settled back and stroked his scruffy gray whiskers. "Now, tell me what happened."

Lynx explained about coming across the dogmen in the wasteland. Father Cougar listened intently, then said, "And they saw you?"

Lynx hesitated, then admitted, "Yes."

Father Cougar narrowed his eyes. "How?"

Lynx stared at the floor. "I'm sorry, Father. I . . . was curious."

Father Cougar sighed deeply. "As I thought." He leaned forward, his gaze steady. "How many times must I tell you? Curiosity is the gravest of sins. And now you see what your curiosity has cost us. If you had avoided detection, we could have easily located these dogmen and captured them. But now they'll be expecting us, and will move on. The danger to those who track them is greatly increased. And what if the dogmen should slip away? You may very well have cost us the great Victory we have awaited so long."

Lynx felt ashamed, despondent. Everything Father Cougar was saying was absolutely true.

Father Cougar shook his head. "Well, there's no helping it now." He turned to the scribe and instructed, "Go to the inn. Fetch the templars." The scribe nodded once, and hurried off.

Lynx felt awe. "Templars?"

"Yes," Father Cougar said. "They arrived this morning. Two of them. Pursuing these dogmen you saw. They'll want to question you."

"Of course," Lynx agreed at once, his shame quickly giving way to excitement.

Templars! Holy ones, invincible warriors of Cat. In ages past, their order had eradicated the frogmen, the birdmen, and the monkeymen, and now only the dogmen remained.

The scribe returned a short time later, leading the templars. They were the tallest, most muscular catmen that Lynx had ever seen. Both wore long white tabards, and upon their surcoats were embroidered the holy form of Cat.

Father Cougar gestured to them. "Lynx, these are our templar friends, Lion and Tiger."

The templars nodded politely. Tiger was brawnier, stern and dignified, with gray in his fur and black stripes around his eyes. Lion had a great tawny mane and seemed almost to vibrate with barely restrained energy. And he was younger, perhaps only five or ten years older than Lynx himself.

Lion said quickly, "Tell us about the dogmen."

So Lynx repeated his story. When he gave a description of the dogmen, the templars glanced at each other. When he got to the part about his escape from the canyon, the scribe interrupted, "Show them your tail!"

Lynx held up his injured tail.

Lion clapped his hands together and said to Tiger, "Well, look at that! Bloodied by dogmen, and he escaped to tell of it." He turned to Lynx. "That's more than many templars can boast."

Lynx felt an almost unbearable rush of pride.

Lion said, "I've heard enough." He turned to Tiger. "Let's find this cave."

Father Cougar said, "You mean to leave at once?"

"Yes," Lion replied. "I see no reason to dally. The dogmen certainly will not."

"Take me with you!" Lynx exclaimed. "I'll lead you there."

Father Cougar looked worried. "That might be dangerous. Your parents—"

Lynx said, "It's my fault for letting the dogmen see me. You have to let me make up for it. No one knows the wasteland like I do."

Father Cougar turned to the templars. "I suppose it's up to you."

Tiger opened his mouth for the first time. "I don't think—"

Lion spoke over him. "Yes, let him come. The dogmen cut him with their swords. He deserves a chance to pay them back in kind." He grinned at Lynx and said, "But we'll cut more than just their tails, won't we?"

Tiger said nothing.

"Come on," Lion said, and gestured for Lynx to follow.

Lynx went with the templars back to the inn, where they gathered supplies. Lion pulled a shortsword out from among his belongings and tossed it to Lynx, who caught it and put it on. Then Lynx led the templars into the wasteland. The sun was rising by the time they reached the cave.

Tiger scouted about, kneeling in places to sniff the earth, then said, "This way."

The trail led westward, deeper into the wastes. That night the templars made camp beneath the open sky, and in the morning they continued on again. As far as Lynx knew, no catman had ever come this far before. His boldness waned, and he started to wonder what he'd gotten himself into.

On the third day, the templars stopped to rest beside a circular black pit a hundred yards across. Thick yellow grass grew all around the pit, and vines hung over its edge and into the darkness. There was something eerie and intriguing about the formation.

Lynx wondered aloud, "Could the dogmen be hiding in there?"

Tiger said, "The tracks lead on."

Lion shrugged. "It can't hurt to check. Call us if you see anything."

Lynx wandered over to the pit. Its sides were rough and angular, and he scrambled easily down the many shelves of rock until he reached the cavern floor. Stray beams of sunlight lanced down through the opening overhead and caught the dust that floated in the air. Lynx turned in a slow circle, then stopped as he saw something utterly unexpected.

He drew his sword and cried out, "Lion! Lion!"

Half-buried in the side of the cave lay a strange object that was bigger than a cottage and made of a silver metal. From the object's side protruded a structure that seemed to be a wing. The object was extraordinarily weathered, and its side was ripped open. That dark gash beckoned to Lynx. He took a step forward, then another.

From the cliff wall above, Lion called out, "Wait."

Lynx glanced back. Lion was climbing down into the cavern. Tiger stood above, at the pit's edge.

Lion said, "What are you doing?"

"Have you ever seen anything like it?" Lynx said. "I'm going to look inside." He crept nearer.

"Why?" Lion called sharply.

"I . . . " Lynx was very close now. "I just . . . "

"This is curiosity," Lion warned. "This is wrong."

"It isn't," Lynx insisted, half to himself. Though why it wasn't, he could not really say. He slipped through the gash.

For a moment everything was dark. Then a hundred spots of light—red, blue, yellow, green—flickered to life all around him. He crouched in alarm. He'd never seen anything like these lights, but his attention was quickly drawn away from them and toward a metal coffin that was built into the far wall. Its lid was made of glass, and inside he could make out the rough outline of a body.

Suddenly a loud voice spoke, seeming to come from all around. The language was unfamiliar. Lynx whirled, but saw no one.

The coffin slowly opened. Lynx backed away, cursing himself. Once again his curiosity had betrayed him, had led him to intrude upon this strange tomb, and now he had awoken something ancient and powerful. His fearful imagination conjured up images of a living corpse with blazing red eyes. But what actually emerged was no less surprising.

A monkeyman. He seemed dazed, and was dressed in some gray uniform, its chest and shoulders decorated with insignia. He glanced at Lynx, then staggered past him. Lynx stared in wonder and horror. The monkeymen were supposed to have been wiped out centuries ago.

A second shape, much smaller, leapt from the coffin, and Lynx gasped as he observed its perfect grace. For all his life he had seen this holy form depicted a thousand times, and now there was no mistaking it. This was the creator of the universe, the giver of all life. Cat, the nine-lived, had returned to Earth at last. Lynx kneeled and whispered, "My lord."

Cat did not acknowledge him, and Lynx was unsure what to do. Through the gash came the voices of the templars, who now stood just outside. Tiger was saying, with a mix of fear and awe, "It fell from the sky. See? It broke through into this cavern."

Lion replied angrily, "The dogmen flee, and we stand here engaged in idle—"

He stopped abruptly as the monkeyman lurched through the gash and out into the cave. Lynx followed after.

The templars stood awestruck. The monkeyman ignored them. He stumbled about, studying the damage to his winged tomb. With one hand he grasped his forehead. He still seemed disoriented.

Lynx felt disoriented himself. He wandered over to the templars, tugged

Lion's sleeve, and made him look toward the tomb, where Cat was just emerging. Lion fell instantly to his knees, and Tiger did the same.

Cat ignored them and strode along after the monkeyman. Then Cat lay down, reached into a gap between the tomb and the cave floor, and batted his paw at something within. The monkeyman grunted at Cat and used the edge of one boot to lightly brush Cat away from the hole.

Lion leapt to his feet and cried, "You dare!" He ran up to the monkeyman and seized him by the shoulder.

The monkeyman shoved him back and yelled at him in a strange language. An amulet on the monkeyman's belt buzzed, "Get your hands off me, catman scum!" Puzzled, the monkeyman glanced at the amulet. Then he shouted at Lion, and again his magic amulet translated. "Report! What unit are you with? And what the hell are you wearing?"

Lion backed away. He moved to stand beside Tiger and said in a low voice, "A surviving monkeyman. He struck me, you saw. I should have the honor of slaying him."

The monkeyman's amulet spoke in a strange tongue, presumably translating Lion's words.

Tiger said, "I don't know. He comes to us from the sky, as a companion of Cat. Dare we slay him?"

Lion said, "Cat's holy word commands it."

Tiger said, "Cat himself stands before us now. Everything is changed."

Lion glanced at Cat, who sat licking himself. Lion approached him, knelt, and said, "My lord, I am Lion, your most faithful servant. I am yours to command. What is your wish for this monkeyman? Say the word, and I will spill his blood in your name."

Cat lifted his head, gave Lion an inscrutable stare, and went back to licking himself.

Lion, still kneeling, glanced at Tiger and hissed, "Why does he not answer?"

Tiger growled softly, "It is not our place to question his motives. He will speak when he wills it."

Lion turned back to Cat. "Answer me, lord, I beg you. Or if you will not, give us some sign, that we may do your will."

The monkeyman seemed to finally shake off his confusion and comprehend the danger. He glanced back and forth between Lion and Cat, then crouched and whistled to Cat and spoke. The amulet translated, "Hey, come here. Here, kitty kitty kitty. Come on."

Lion said darkly, "He presumes to command Cat."

The monkeyman ignored this and kept calling. Cat gazed at the monkeyman, but did not stir.

Lion said, "Cat rejects him."

"Wait!" The monkeyman held up a hand. "Just . . . Leo, come here, dammit!" He whistled again. "Here, kitty kitty."

Lion reached for his sword and said, "He dies."

But at that moment, Cat languidly uncurled himself and strolled across the dirt to the monkeyman, who scratched Cat's whiskers, then his ears, his neck, and his back. Cat purred and rubbed against the monkeyman's shins. Lion froze.

"Cat shows him favor," Tiger observed. "Cat has a special plan for him."

The monkeyman picked up Cat and held him like a shield. Cat continued to purr.

Lion glared at the monkeyman for a long time, then strode over to him, stood very close, and said softly, "I do not know why Cat chooses to prolong your miserable existence, abomination. But let no one say that I was curious." He brushed by him and walked away.

The monkeyman lowered his head to Cat and whispered, "Good Cat."

The catmen set out again, now joined by Cat and his strange monkeyman companion. The monkeyman brought along a sort of satchel in which he carried Cat, who seemed pleased enough with the arrangement. Lion remained hostile to the monkeyman, no matter how often Tiger insisted that the Victory was now at hand and that Lion should be rejoicing. The templars often knelt before Cat and asked him for guidance, but Cat never deigned to reply.

Sometimes the monkeyman would stare into the amulet, but whatever it told him must have displeased him, for he would shake it, strike it, and yell at it. Lynx was desperate to question the monkeyman, but that would be showing curiosity, so instead he tried to mimic the stony indifference of the templars. Still, Lynx couldn't keep his eyes off of Cat.

The monkeyman noticed this. Finally he said, "Do you want to hold him?"

Lynx was stunned. He glanced at the templars, who were now well ahead. "I couldn't."

"Sure." The monkeyman reached into the satchel, lifted Cat free, and handed him over to Lynx, who scratched Cat's ears the way the monkeyman had. Cat purred.

"See?" the monkeyman said. After a moment, he added, "What's your name?"

Lynx hesitated, then told him.

"I'm Charles," the monkeyman said. Lynx didn't respond. After a moment, the monkeyman lowered his voice and said, "Tell me, Lynx. What year is this?"

Lynx was perplexed, but the monkeyman seemed earnest. Lynx passed Cat back to him and said slowly, "1293."

"Using what calendar?"

"I don't understand."

"Dating from when?"

"Why . . . " This was the strangest question Lynx had ever heard. "From the creation of the world."

The monkeyman said nothing for a long time. He and Lynx resumed walking. Finally the monkeyman asked in a low tone, "And what is this 'Victory'?"

"You really don't know? Cat hasn't told you?"

The monkeyman said, "Cat isn't overly fond of explaining himself. As you may have noticed."

So Lynx spoke of the Victory. When he saw that the monkeyman was utterly confused, he found himself explaining more and more. Soon he had gone all the way back to the beginning, back to when Cat had created the world and all its inhabitants, including his most favored creation, cats, whom Cat had made in his own image. To them alone Cat had granted the gift of speech. But the cats had grown curious about what other animals might say, and so the cats disobeyed and shared the gift of speech with birds, frogs, dogs, and monkeys. But those other animals were wicked and spoke only lies. When Cat returned and saw what had happened, he was very angry, and punished those animals, twisting them into catmen, birdmen, frogmen, dogmen, and monkeymen. The catmen wailed and beseeched Cat to restore them to their perfect forms, but Cat decreed that he would not until the catmen had wiped the Earth clean of the abominations—any animal who spoke and was not feline. But Cat, in his ultimate mercy, also decreed that this redemption was inevitable, and promised that in the last days he would return to Earth to lead the catmen to ultimate glory. Lynx finished, "So that is the Victory. That is why Cat has come again. But his ways are strange. We did not know that he would be accompanied by a monkeyman."

The monkeyman said, "And these dogmen we're pursuing . . . are the last on Earth?"

"Perhaps," Lynx said. "They are among the last, certainly."

"And the . . . other monkeymen. Like me. Are all . . . ?"

"Dead," Lynx confirmed. "Long ago."

That night Lynx was awoken by the sound of the monkeyman sobbing softly. Lynx thought: He weeps for his vanquished race. It had not occurred to Lynx that abominations might be capable of such grief. This monkeyman was the last of his kind, probably. And in the end, when the Victory came, he too would be cleansed from the Earth. That made Lynx feel almost sad.

He did not get back to sleep for a long time.

The templars tracked the dogmen ever deeper into the wasteland. Supplies were running low, and nothing edible grew here. But Lion said, "Good. The dogmen will have the same problem. They'll have to turn and face us."

And he was right. The next day, the catmen mounted a low, wind-swept pass, and Lynx spotted the dogmen waiting amidst a jumble of boulders.

The male stood there, holding his great broadsword. The female reached for her rapier, but the male barked at her, and she reluctantly backed away. The male stepped forward, seeming worn and haggard, but for all that he was still even bigger and more imposing than Lynx remembered.

Lion sighed. "Only two. And one a female." He drew his sword and strode forward. "Stay back. I'll handle this."

Lynx looked to Tiger. "He'll fight alone?"

Tiger was stoic. "He prefers it this way."

"Why bring me all this way?" Lynx said. "Why give me a sword, if he never meant for me to help?"

"That's just how he is."

The monkeyman moved to stand beside them. "How he *is* is arrogant and reckless. Why do you endure it?"

Tiger said softly, "You'll see why."

Lion closed in on the male, who roared and thrust at him with savage force. Lion parried casually, spun in a crouch, and came up with both fists wrapped around the hilt of his sword. He slammed his fists into his opponent's jowled face, and the male thudded to the ground. Lion kicked away the dogman's sword, and just like that it was over.

Lynx exclaimed, "He's amazing!"

Tiger nodded. He hurried forward, and Lynx and the monkeyman followed. Tiger knelt to tie up the male as Lion strode toward the female.

She'd drawn her rapier, and as Lion came on she backed away in a fighting stance, her movements swift and graceful. Lion held his sword at his side.

She thrust at his throat. Her speed was remarkable, but Lion whipped up his sword and easily blocked the blow.

The female backed away, launching a series of feints and attacks. Lion laughed, contemptuous, as he parried each one. But her last thrust deflected off his blade and scratched his shoulder.

He glanced at the small circle of blood that blossomed on his white tabard. "Not bad. I might have to try."

He moved to close with her, but again she slipped away.

Tiger looked uneasy. He whispered, "At close range, he's unstoppable. But he has no patience."

The female kept retreating, staying always just beyond the reach of Lion's sword. She attacked again, and again she got through, pricking his other shoulder. He hardly seemed to notice. His expression was dark now. He kept advancing.

Lynx said, "We have to help."

Tiger hesitated. "He . . . would not like that."

Lion roared, slashing at the female's head. She backed out of reach, then quickly counterattacked, striking his chest. Three stains now blazed on his tabard. The blood from his shoulder wounds soaked down to his elbows. He seemed to be slowing.

Lynx said, "If you won't help him, I will."

He drew his shortsword and ran in a wide arc, so that he circled behind the female, then charged her.

As he neared, she pivoted and thrust at his face. Lynx ducked and retreated. Instantly she turned back to Lion, but now he had closed with her, and she was doomed. When she attacked, he locked her wrist and wrenched her sword away. He smashed an elbow into her face, and hurled her over his hip. Then Lion was upon her, straddling her, pounding his fists into her face, knocking her head this way and that. Soon she was unconscious, with blood oozing from her muzzle, but the blows kept falling.

Lynx murmured, "Wait," but Lion ignored him.

Finally, Lion stood. His chest wound had bled a red blotch around the holy form of Cat that was embroidered on his surcoat.

Lynx said, "Are you all right?"

Lion's eyes were full of fury. "I told you to stay back! You could've gotten us both killed!" He shoved Lynx aside and stormed on past.

Tiger came forward and knelt to bind the female. He said, "He gets like this. Just let him calm down. It'll be all right."

The templars marched the dogmen east. The prisoners were not spoken to, and when night fell they were bound at wrist and ankle. Tiger took the first watch while Lion dozed. Lynx sat a dozen yards away, off by himself, leaning on a boulder.

The monkeyman settled down beside him and nodded at the prisoners. "So what happens to them now?"

Lynx said, "The templars will want to show them off, charge money to see them, that sort of thing."

The monkeyman's voice was soft. "You said these might be the last dogmen on Earth."

"They might," Lynx agreed.

"And then they'll be executed?"

"Yes."

The monkeyman caught Lynx's gaze, held it. "And you're going to let that happen?"

Lynx glanced over at Tiger, but the templar was too far away to hear them. Lynx hissed, "Of course."

The monkeyman said, "No one has ever called me squeamish, and I have no love for dogmen, but to wipe out an entire race . . . That's evil, Lynx. You must know that. Whatever some old legend says."

"You're just a monkeyman. You wouldn't understand."

"I understand more than you can imagine," the monkeyman said. "I've flown among the stars, and slept for ages, and I remember Earth as it was, when monkeymen—as you call us—ruled all. We made you, Lynx, you cat-men, in our labs. The dogmen too, and all the rest. We made you to be soldiers, and I guess we did our jobs too well, because I awake to find that you've beaten us. But that doesn't—"

"This is blasphemy," Lynx said. "I warn you, not even Cat's favor will protect you if—"

"What? Him?" The monkeyman jabbed a thumb toward the satchel where Cat slept. "He's an animal, like any other. I raised him from a kitten."

Lynx stood. "I should kill you for that."

The monkeyman glared up at him. "Fine. Kill me. Like you killed my race. What've I got to live for?" He gestured toward Lion. "Rouse your maniac friend there. Tell him to chop off my head. He'd like that. And would you? I thought you were different."

Lynx scowled and stomped away. He sat down beside Tiger, who asked, "What's wrong?"

Lynx said furiously, "Nothing."

Tiger glanced at the monkeyman, then said, "Monkeys lie. That's why they should never have been granted the gift of speech."

Lynx crossed his arms and agreed, "Yes. They lie."

For the next two days, Lynx refused to speak to the monkeyman, but doubts gnawed at him. Much as he hated to admit it, the monkeyman was right about one thing: Lynx *was* different from the templars.

He had always thought of himself as faithful, but traveling with them had made him see just how shallow and perfunctory his belief really was. Lion's faith was like fire—it gave intensity to everything he did, but it was a fire that was raging out of control and would someday consume him. And Tiger's faith was like a mountain—immense, solid, and immovable. But Lynx realized that his own faith was more like the wasteland itself, existing only in the absence of anything else. The monkeyman's briefly spouted heresies made sense to Lynx in a way that the wisdom of Father Cougar never really had.

That afternoon, Lynx found himself walking for a moment beside the female. Before he could stop himself, he blurted out, "You fought well."

She looked up, startled to be spoken to. "What?"

Lion was off ahead of them. Tiger was back a ways, out of earshot. Lynx said softly, "The other day. You fought well. I think you would've beaten him, if I hadn't interfered. Beaten a templar. You should be proud of that."

"Oh," she said, puzzled. "Thank you."

"Sure," Lynx said awkwardly, and hurried off.

The monkeyman sidled up from behind him. "Why did you do that?"

Lynx maintained a stony silence for a moment, then said, "I . . . I was just . . . "

"Curious," the monkeyman said.

Lynx sighed.

The monkeyman added, "Curiosity is no sin. If you're not curious, you'll never learn."

"That's blasphemy," Lynx said, but his tone was flat.

The monkeyman didn't respond.

After a time, Lynx said, "Even if I agreed with you—about the dogmen, I mean—what can I do?"

The monkeyman whispered, "You can pretend to be asleep tonight, and when I create a distraction you can crawl over to the dogmen and cut their bonds, and let them escape."

Lynx was startled. "I didn't mean . . . "

"I know." The monkeyman gave him a thin smile. "But think about it. I'll create the distraction. What you do then is up to you."

"Wait," Lynx said. This was too much. "What sort of distraction?"

"You'll see. Your little outburst the other night gave me an idea."

Lynx considered this. "During whose watch?"

"Whose do you think?"

Lion's, of course. He was by far the more easily distracted.

"Think about it," the monkeyman repeated, and fell behind again.

As night came on, the templars made camp atop a low hill. Tiger slumbered, and Lynx pretended to. He still couldn't decide whether to help the dogmen. After several hours, he heard movement and peeked out one eye. The monkeyman came up to stand behind Lion and said, "You seem like the religious type."

Lion turned to him. "Do not mock me, monkeyman." Lion was now facing away from Lynx and the prisoners.

The monkeyman sat down on a stone. "Not at all. I just thought you might be interested in some of the religious ideas of the monkeymen."

"The chattering of abominations does not interest me." Lion began to turn away.

"Wait," the monkeyman said. "For example, did you know that many monkeymen believed that they were made in the image of the creator of the universe?"

Lion laughed at that. "Did they ever look in a mirror? Surely they could not believe that the creator of the universe was so ungainly and absurd."

The monkeyman shrugged. "Others had another idea about how they came to be. It was called 'evolution by natural selection.' "

Lion's back was still turned. Lynx glanced at the prisoners. He thought he could crawl to them without attracting attention.

If he was caught at this, the templars would kill him. And what if Father Cougar was right, about Cat and the Victory and all of it? Lynx stared at the female. He was impressed by her, liked her, though they'd barely spoken. He didn't want to see her die. If he helped her escape, the catmen would have other opportunities to apprehend her, if necessary. But if she died . . .

He began to crawl toward her.

Lion was saying, "Even if that were possible, it would take thousands of years."

"Millions," the monkeyman corrected.

"The world is not that old."

"Well, these monkeymen had some ideas about that too."

The female's eyes were wide as Lynx crawled up beside her. He glanced over her shoulder at Lion, who was absorbed in the argument. Lynx drew the shortsword and whispered, "If I set you free, will you swear to run away and never come back, and never trouble any catman ever again?"

She stared at him a moment, then nodded quickly.

"All right." Lynx sliced her bonds, then squirmed over to the male to cut those ropes too.

Lion exclaimed, "That is heresy!"

The monkeyman replied, "That is fact."

Lion stood up. He towered over the monkeyman and said, "Take it back!"

"I'm just telling you what—"

"Silence!" Lion used the back of his fist to strike the monkeyman across the face, knocking him to the dirt.

Lynx freed the male, and together the prisoners began to crawl off.

Lion drew his sword and strode toward the monkeyman, who sprang up and backed away. Lion said, "Come here."

"No. Get away from me." The monkeyman turned and stumbled down the hill, and Lion went after him.

Lynx thought: Lion will kill him. The monkeyman knew this would happen. He knew he was sacrificing himself.

Lynx glanced at the prisoners, who were now on their feet and hurrying away.

Lion and the monkeyman were soon lost in the darkness, but Lynx could hear them cursing. He considered waking Tiger, who might restrain Lion. But Tiger might also notice the prisoners fleeing.

Then the monkeyman let out an anguished wail, and Tiger opened his eyes. Lynx had no choice. He cried, "Tiger!"

The templar reached for his sword. "What?"

Lynx pointed. "Lion. He's gone crazy!"

Tiger leapt up, and Lynx followed. As they reached the bottom of the hill, Lion stepped from the shadows.

Tiger shouted, "What have you done?"

Lion was smug. "The monkeyman blasphemed with every word. I have silenced him."

No! Lynx thought, hurrying forward, scanning the ground for a corpse.

But the monkeyman was alive, weeping, kneeling over the smashed remains of his magic amulet. There was a gash over his brow, and his eyes were forlorn as he uttered a string of gibberish.

Lion had spared the monkeyman's life, but now there wasn't a single being on Earth that the monkeyman could talk to.

Lynx said, "I'm so sorry . . . Charles."

At the sound of his name, the monkeyman looked up. "Charles," he repeated. He took a deep breath, wiped his eyes, and rose to his feet. Lynx took him by the arm, and they hiked back up the hill.

They entered camp just behind Tiger, who said, "Where are the prisoners?"

Lion looked stricken. He glanced about.

Tiger cursed. He ran across the camp and stared off down the far side of the hill. "Nothing. They're gone."

"I . . . " Lion hesitated. Then he pointed to the monkeyman. "It's his fault!"

"His fault?" Tiger raged. "Was it his job to watch the prisoners? Or was it yours?"

Lion stomped away, then turned back and glared at the monkeyman. "He knows something."

"Maybe," Tiger said. "No one's ever freed themselves from my ropes before. We could question him . . . if you hadn't 'silenced' him."

Lion scowled.

Tiger gathered up some belongings. "It won't matter. We'll catch the dog-men again, and we'll have the truth from their own lips." His tone was grim. "And we'll take no more chances. No more prisoners. The dogmen die."

The catmen walked all through the night, and at dawn they came upon a shallow cave in which the dogmen were huddled together, sick and weary.

The templars strode forward, drawing their swords and advancing on the dogmen, who stood to meet them. The male pounded his meaty fist into his palm—a futile gesture of defiance. The dogmen were unarmed, and would be slaughtered. Lynx and the monkeyman watched helplessly.

But then Lynx called out, "Wait!"

Tiger paused and glanced back.

Lynx said, "Let Cat judge them."

Lion sneered. "Cat's feelings toward dogmen are well known."

"Then what's the harm?"

Tiger thought this over. He lowered his blade. "All right."

Lynx approached the monkeyman, who was confused. Lynx nodded at the satchel, and the monkeyman got the idea. He lifted Cat free and set him on the ground.

Lynx knelt. "My lord, we have need of your wisdom. What is your wish for these dogmen? Please, give us a sign."

Cat looked up at Lynx and said nothing.

Lion growled, "Why trouble Cat with this? He has already decreed death for all dogmen. Long ago."

Lynx stood up and took a step back. He called gently, "Here, kitty kitty."

Lion said, "What are you doing?"

Lynx backed up until he stood between the dogmen, then he crouched and called, "Here, kitty kitty kitty."

Cat continued to stare.

Lynx said to the dogmen, "Come on. Like this." He added softly, "Please, just try."

After a moment, the female bent down and called, "Here, kitty kitty." The male did the same.

Lion was outraged. "What is this?"

But sure enough, Cat stirred. He picked his way across the ground until he stood before Lynx and the dogmen. Lynx reached out and scratched between Cat's ears, and Cat purred. The female stroked Cat's back. Cat wound among Lynx and the dogmen and rubbed against their legs.

The templars stood stunned. Tiger intoned, "Cat shows them favor."

Lion said, "No! The Cat I serve shows no mercy to dogmen!"

Tiger gestured. "Look."

"It's some trick," Lion said. "This . . . this is not Cat. It cannot be. Maybe this is one of the cats who—"

"That is heresy," Tiger warned. "The cats were transformed into catmen. All of them."

Lynx cried out, "Cat returns to Earth with a new message of peace!"

"No!" Lion shouted. "No! Cat, the eternal, does not change his mind."

Tiger turned away and sheathed his sword.

Lion stared at him in horror. "What are you doing?"

"I will not stand against the incarnation."

Lion was shocked. "What?"

Tiger said, "I must think on all this." He stared coldly over his shoulder at the dogmen and said to them, "You have a reprieve from me, for now." He began to walk away. To Lion he said, "Do as you like."

Lion looked all around, at Cat, at the dogmen, at the monkeyman. Finally Lion shot Lynx a withering glare, then followed after Tiger.

Lynx waited until the templars were a good distance off, then he let out a long sigh of relief. He thought to himself: I can't believe it. We won.

But his gladness was tempered by apprehension. The templars would return, and even if they didn't they'd spread their tale. What would Father Cougar think? Or Lynx's parents? And what would become of Cat and the monkeyman and the dogmen now? Others would come seeking them, he knew.

For a moment the group all watched each other uncertainly.

Then the monkeyman laughed. He stepped forward and introduced himself to the male. "Charles." And then again to the female. "Charles."

She glanced at Lynx, who gave her a bemused smile and shrugged.

Cat purred and rubbed against Lynx's shins. In that moment, he felt a bit of hope. If they all just stuck together, he thought, things might work out, in the end.

He bent down and petted Cat, and scratched his chin.

He whispered, "Good cat."

• AMARYLLIS •
Carrie Vaughn

I never knew my mother, and I never understood why she did what she did. I ought to be grateful that she was crazy enough to cut out her implant so she could get pregnant. But it also meant she was crazy enough to hide the pregnancy until termination wasn't an option, knowing the whole time that she'd never get to keep the baby. That she'd lose everything. That her household would lose everything because of her.

I never understood how she couldn't care. I wondered what her family thought when they learned what she'd done, when their committee split up the household, scattered them—broke them, because of her.

Did she think I was worth it?

It was all about quotas.

"They're using cages up north, I heard. Off shore, anchored," Nina said. "Fifty feet across—twice as much protein grown with half the resources, and we'd never have to touch the wild population again. We could double our quota."

I hadn't really been listening to her. We were resting, just for a moment; she sat with me on the railing at the prow of *Amaryllis* and talked about her big plans.

Wind pulled the sails taut and the fiberglass hull cut through waves without a sound, we sailed so smooth. Garrett and Sun hauled up the nets behind us, dragging in the catch. *Amaryllis* was elegant, a 30-foot sleek vessel with just enough cabin and cargo space—an antique but more than seaworthy. She was a good boat, with a good crew. The best.

"Marie—" Nina said, pleading.

I sighed and woke up. "We've been over this. We can't just double our quota."

"But if we got authorization—"

"Don't you think we're doing all right as it is?" We had a good crew—we were well fed and not exceeding our quotas; I thought we'd be best off not screwing all that up. Not making waves, so to speak.

Nina's big brown eyes filled with tears—I'd said the wrong thing, because I knew what she was really after, and the status quo wasn't it.

"That's just it," she said. "We've met our quotas and kept everyone healthy for years now. I really think we should try. We can at least ask, can't we?"

The truth was: No, I wasn't sure we deserved it. I wasn't sure that kind of responsibility would be worth it. I didn't want the prestige. Nina didn't even want the prestige—she just wanted the baby.

"It's out of our hands at any rate," I said, looking away because I couldn't bear the intensity of her expression.

Pushing herself off the rail, Nina stomped down *Amaryllis'* port side to join the rest of the crew hauling in the catch. She wasn't old enough to want a baby. She was lithe, fit, and golden, running barefoot on the deck, sun-bleached streaks gleaming in her brown hair. Actually, no, she *was* old enough. She'd been with the house for seven years—she was twenty, now. It hadn't seemed so long.

"Whoa!" Sun called. There was a splash and a thud as something in the net kicked against the hull. He leaned over the side, the muscles along his broad, coppery back flexing as he clung to a net that was about to slide back into the water. Nina, petite next to his strong frame, reached with him. I ran down and grabbed them by the waistbands of their trousers to hold them steady. The fourth of our crew, Garrett, latched a boat hook into the net. Together we hauled the catch onto the deck. We'd caught something big, heavy, and full of powerful muscles.

We had a couple of aggregators—large buoys made of scrap steel and wood—anchored fifty miles or so off the coast. Schooling fish were attracted to the aggregators, and we found the fish—mainly mackerel, sardines, sable-fish, and whiting. An occasional shark or marlin found its way into the nets, but those we let go; they were rare and outside our quotas. That was what I expected to see—something unusually large thrashing among the slick silvery mass of smaller fish. This thing was large, yes, as big as Nina—no wonder it had almost pulled them over—but it wasn't the right shape. Sleek and stream-lined, a powerful swimmer. Silvery like the rest of the catch.

"What is it?" Nina asked.

"Tuna," I said, by process of elimination. I had never seen one in my life. "Bluefin, I think."

"No one's caught a bluefin in thirty years," Garrett said. Sweat was dripping onto his face despite the bandanna tying back his shaggy dark hair.

I was entranced, looking at all that protein. I pressed my hand to the fish's flank, feeling its muscles twitch. "Maybe they're back."

We'd been catching the tuna's food all along, after all. In the old days the aggregators attracted as many tuna as mackerel. But no one had seen one in so long, everyone assumed they were gone.

"Let's put him back," I said, and the others helped me lift the net to the side. It took all of us, and when we finally got the tuna to slide overboard, we lost half the net's catch with it, a wave of silvery scales glittering as they hit the water. But that was okay: Better to be under quota than over.

The tuna splashed its tail and raced away. We packed up the rest of the catch and set sails for home.

The *Californian* crew got their banner last season, and flew its red and green—power and fertility—from the top of the boat's mast for all to see. Elsie of the *Californian* was due to give birth in a matter of weeks. As soon as her pregnancy was confirmed, she stopped sailing and stayed in the household, sheltered and treasured. Loose hands resting atop mountainous belly, she would sometimes come out to greet her household's boat as it arrived. Nina would stare at her. Elsie might have been the first pregnant woman Nina had seen, as least since surviving puberty and developing thoughts of carrying a mountainous belly of her own.

Elsie was there now, an icon cast in bronze before the setting sun, her body canted slightly against the weight in her belly, like a ship leaning away from the wind.

We furled the sails and rowed to the pier beside the scale house. Nina hung over the prow, looking at Elsie, who was waving at *Californian's* captain, on the deck of the boat. Solid and dashing, everything a captain ought to be, he waved back at her. Their boat was already secured in its home slip, their catch weighed, everything tidy. Nina sighed at the image of a perfect life, and nobody yelled at her for not helping. Best thing to do in a case like this was let her dream until she grew out of it. Might take decades, but still . . .

My *Amaryllis* crew handed crates off to the dockhand, who shifted our catch to the scale house. Beyond that were the processing houses, where onshore crews smoked, canned, and shipped the fish inland. The New Oceanside community provided sixty percent of the protein for the whole region, which was our mark of pride, our reason for existing. Within the community itself, the ten sailing crews were proudest of all. A fishing crew that did its job well and met its quotas kept the whole system running smoothly. I was lucky to even have the *Amaryllis* and be a part of it.

I climbed up to the dock with my folk after securing the boat, and saw that Anders was the scalemaster on duty. The week's trip might as well have been for nothing, then.

Thirty-five years ago, my mother ripped out her implant and broke up her household. Might as well have been yesterday to a man like Anders.

The old man took a nail-biting forty minutes to weigh our catch and add up our numbers, at which point he announced, "You're fifty pounds over quota."

Quotas were the only way to keep the stock healthy, to prevent overfishing, shortages, and ultimately starvation. The committee based quotas on how much you needed, not how much you could catch. To exceed that—to pretend you needed more than other people—showed so much disrespect to the committee, the community, to the fishing stock.

My knees weak, I almost sat down. I'd gotten it exactly right, I knew I had. I glared at him. Garrett and Sun, a pair of brawny sailors helpless before the scalemaster in his dull gray tunic of authority, glared at him. Some days felt like nothing I did would ever be enough. I'd always be too far one way or the other over the line of "just right." Most days, I'd accept the scalemaster's judgment and walk away, but today, after setting loose the tuna and a dozen pounds of legitimate catch with it, it was too much.

"You're joking," I said. "Fifty pounds?"

"Really," Anders said, marking the penalty on the chalkboard behind him where all the crews could see it. "You ought to know better, an experienced captain like you."

He wouldn't even look at me. Couldn't look me in the eye while telling me I was trash.

"What do you want me to do, throw the surplus overboard? We can eat those fifty pounds. The livestock can eat those fifty pounds."

"It'll get eaten, don't worry. But it's on your record." Then he marked it on his clipboard, as if he thought we'd come along and alter the public record.

"Might as well not sail out at all next week, eh?" I said.

The scalemaster frowned and turned away. A fifty pound surplus—if it even existed—would go to make up another crew's shortfall, and next week our catch would be needed just as much as it had been this week, however little some folk wanted to admit it. We could get our quota raised like Nina wanted, and we wouldn't have to worry about surpluses at all. No, then we'd worry about shortfalls, and not earning credits to feed the mouths we had, much less the extra one Nina wanted.

Surpluses must be penalized, or everyone would go fishing for surpluses and having spare babies, and then where would we be? Too many mouths, not enough food, no resiliency to survive disaster, and all the disease and starvation that followed. I'd seen the pictures in the archives, of what happened after the big fall.

Just enough and no more. Moderation. But so help me I wasn't going to dump fifty pounds just to keep my record clean.

"We're done here. Thank you, Captain Marie," Anders said, his back to me, like he couldn't stand the sight of me.

When we left, I found Nina at the doorway, staring. I pushed her in front of me, back to the boat, so we could put *Amaryllis* to bed for the night.

"The *Amaryllis'* scales aren't that far off," Garrett grumbled as we rowed to her slip. "Ten pounds, maybe. Not fifty."

"Anders had his foot on the pad, throwing it off. I'd bet on it," Sun said. "Ever notice how we're only ever off when Anders is running the scales?"

We'd all noticed.

"Is that true? But why would he do that?" said Nina, innocent Nina.

Everyone looked at me. A weight seemed to settle on us.

"What?" Nina said. "What is it?"

It was the kind of thing no one talked about, and Nina was too young to have grown up knowing. The others had all known what they were getting into, signing on with me. But not Nina.

I shook my head at them. "We'll never prove that Anders has it in for us so there's no good arguing. We'll take our licks and that's the end of it."

Sun said, "Too many black marks like that they'll break up the house."

That was the worry, wasn't it?

"How many black marks?" Nina said. "He can't do that. Can he?"

Garrett smiled and tried to take the weight off. He was the first to sign on with me when I inherited the boat. We'd been through a lot together. "We'll just have to find out Anders' schedule and make sure we come in when someone else is on duty."

But most of the time there were no schedules—just whoever was on duty when a boat came in. I wouldn't be surprised to learn that Anders kept a watch for us, just to be here to rig our weigh-in.

Amaryllis glided into her slip, and I let Garrett and Sun secure the lines. I leaned back against the side, stretching my arms, staring up along the mast. Nina sat nearby, clenching her hands, her lips. Elsie and *Californian's* captain had gone.

I gave her a pained smile. "You might have a better chance of getting your extra mouth if you went to a different crew. The *Californian*, maybe."

"Are you trying to get rid of me?" Nina said.

Sitting up, I put my arms across her shoulders and pulled her close. Nina came to me a clumsy thirteen-year old from Bernardino, up the coast. My household had a space for her, and I was happy to get her. She'd grown up smart and eager. She could take my place when I retired, inherit *Amaryllis* in her turn. Not that I'd told her that yet.

"Never. Never ever." She only hesitated a moment before wrapping her arms around me and squeezing back.

Our household was an oasis. We'd worked hard to make it so. I'd inherited the boat, attracted the crew one by one—Garrett and Sun to run the boat, round and bustling Dakota to run the house, and she brought the talented J.J., and we fostered Nina. We'd been assigned fishing rights, and then we earned the land allocation. Ten years of growing, working, sweating, nurturing, living, and the place was gorgeous.

We'd dug into the side of a hill above the docks and built with adobe. In the afternoon sun, the walls gleamed golden. The part of the house projecting out from the hill served as a wall protecting the garden and well. Our path led around the house and into the courtyard. We'd found flat shale to use as flag-stones around the cultivated plots, and to line the well, turning it into a spring. A tiny spring, but any open fresh water seemed like a luxury. On the hill above were the windmill and solar panels.

Everyone who wanted their own room had one, but only Sun did—the detached room dug into the hill across the yard. Dakota, J.J., and Nina had pallets in the largest room. Garret and I shared a bed in the smaller room. What wasn't house was garden. We had producing fruit trees, an orange and a lemon, that also shaded the kitchen space. Corn, tomatoes, sunflowers, green beans, peas, carrots, radishes, two kinds of peppers, and anything else we could make grow on a few square feet. A pot full of mint and one of basil. For the most part we fed ourselves and so could use our credits on improving *Amaryllis* and bringing in specialties like rice and honey, or fabric and rope that we couldn't make in quantity. Dakota wanted to start chickens next season, if we could trade for the chicks.

I kept wanting to throw that in the face of people like Anders. It wasn't like I didn't pay attention. I wasn't a burden.

The crew arrived home; J.J. had supper ready. Dakota and J.J. had started out splitting household work evenly, but pretty quickly they were trading chores—turning compost versus hanging laundry, mending the windmill versus cleaning the kitchen—until J.J. did most everything involving the kitchen and living spaces and Dakota did everything with the garden and mechanics.

By J.J.'s sympathetic expression when he gave me my serving—smoked mackerel and vegetables tonight—someone had already told him about the run-in with the scalemaster. Probably to keep him or Dakota from asking how my day went.

I stayed out later than usual making a round of the holding. Not that I expected to find anything wrong. It was for my own peace of mind, looking at what we'd built with my own eyes, putting my hand on the trunk of the windmill, running the leaves of the lemon tree across my palms, ensuring that none of it had vanished, that it wasn't going to. It had become a ritual.

In bed I held tight to Garrett, to give and get comfort, skin against skin, under the sheet, under the warm air coming in through the open skylight above our bed.

"Bad day?" he said.

"Can never be a bad day when the ship and crew come home safe," I said. But my voice was flat.

Garrett shifted, running a hand down my back, arranging his arms to pull me tight against him. Our legs twined together. My nerves settled.

He said, "Nina's right, we can do more. We can support an extra mouth. If we appealed—"

"You really think that'll do any good?" I said. "I think you'd all be better off with a different captain."

He tilted his face toward mine, touched my lips with his, pressed until I responded. A minute of that and we were both smiling.

"You know we all ended up here because we don't get along with anyone else. But you make the rest of us look good."

I squirmed against him in mock outrage, giggling.

"Plenty of crews—plenty of households—don't ever get babies," he said. "It doesn't mean anything."

"I don't care about a baby so much," I said. "I'm just tired of fighting all the time."

It was normal for children to fight with their parents, their households, and even their committees as they grew. But it wasn't fair, for me to feel like I was still fighting with a mother I'd never known.

The next day, when Nina and I went down to do some cleaning on *Amaryllis*, I tried to convince myself it was my imagination that she was avoiding me. Not looking at me. Or pretending not to look, when in fact she was stealing glances. The way she avoided meeting my gaze made my skin crawl a little. She'd decided something. She had a secret.

We caught sight of Elsie again, walking up from the docks, a hundred yards away but her silhouette was unmistakable. That distracted Nina, who stopped to stare.

"Is she really that interesting?" I said, smiling, trying to make it a joke.

Nina looked at me sideways, as if deciding whether she should talk to me. Then she sighed. "I wonder what it's like. Don't you wonder what it's like?"

I thought about it a moment and mostly felt fear rather than interest. All the things that could go wrong, even with a banner of approval flying above you. Nina wouldn't understand that. "Not really."

"Marie, how can you be so . . . so *indifferent*?"

"Because I'm not going to spend the effort worrying about something I can't change. Besides, I'd much rather be captain of a boat than stuck on shore, watching."

I marched past her to the boat, and she followed, head bowed.

We washed the deck, checked the lines, cleaned out the cabin, took inventory, and made a stack of gear that needed to be repaired. We'd take it home and spend the next few days working on it before we went to sea again. Nina was quiet most of the morning, and I kept glancing at her, head bent to her work, biting her lip, wondering what she was thinking on so intently. What she was hiding.

Turned out she was working up the courage.

I handed the last bundle of net to her, then went back to double check that the hatches were closed and the cabin was shut up. When I went to climb off the boat myself, she was sitting at the edge of the dock, her legs hanging over the edge, swinging a little. She looked ten years younger, like she was a kid again, like she had when I first saw her.

I regarded her, brows raised, questioning, until finally she said, "I asked Sun why Anders doesn't like you. Why none of the captains talk to you much."

So that was what had happened. Sun—matter-of-fact and sensible—would have told her without any circumspection. And Nina had been horrified.

Smiling, I sat on the gunwale in front of her. "I'd have thought you'd been here long enough to figure it out on your own."

"I knew something had happened, but I couldn't imagine what. Certainly not—I mean, no one ever talks about it. But . . . what happened to your mother? Her household?"

I shrugged, because it wasn't like I remembered any of it. I'd pieced the story together, made some assumptions. Was told what happened by people who made their own assumptions. Who wanted me to understand exactly what my place in the world was.

"They were scattered over the whole region, I think. Ten of them—it was a big household, successful, until I came along. I don't know where all they ended up. I was brought to New Oceanside, raised up by the first *Amaryllis* crew. Then Zeke and Ann retired, took up pottery, went down the coast, and gave me the ship to start my own household. Happy ending."

"And your mother—they sterilized her? After you were born, I mean."

"I assume so. Like I said, I don't really know."

"Do you suppose she thought it was worth it?"

"I imagine she didn't," I said. "If she wanted a baby, she didn't get one, did she? But maybe she just wanted to be pregnant for a little while."

Nina looked so thoughtful, swinging her feet, staring at the rippling water where it lapped against the hull, she made me nervous. I had to say something.

"You'd better not be thinking of pulling something like that," I said. "They'd split us up, take the house, take *Amaryllis*—"

"Oh no," Nina said, shaking her head quickly, her denial vehement. "I would never do that, I'd never do anything like that."

"Good," I said, relieved. I trusted her and didn't think she would. Then again, my mother's household probably thought that about her too. I hopped over to the dock. We collected up the gear, slinging bags and buckets over our shoulders and starting the hike up to the house.

Halfway there Nina said, "You don't think we'll ever get a banner, because of your mother. That's what you were trying to tell me."

"Yeah." I kept my breathing steady, concentrating on the work at hand.

"But it doesn't change who you are. What you do."

"The old folk still take it out on me."

"It's not fair," she said. She was too old to be saying things like that. But at least now she'd know, and she could better decide if she wanted to find another household.

"If you want to leave, I'll understand," I said. "Any house would be happy to take you."

"No," she said. "No, I'll stay. None of it—it doesn't change who you are."

I could have dropped everything and hugged her for that. We walked awhile longer, until we came in sight of the house. Then I asked, "You have someone in mind to be the father? Hypothetically."

She blushed berry red and looked away. I had to grin—so that was how it stood.

When Garrett greeted us in the courtyard, Nina was still blushing. She avoided him and rushed along to dump her load in the workshop.

Garrett blinked after her. "What's up with her?"

"Nina being Nina."

The next trip on *Amaryllis* went well. We made quota in less time than I expected, which gave us half a day's vacation. We anchored off a deserted bit of shore and went swimming, lay on deck and took in the sun, ate the last of the oranges and dried mackerel that J.J. had sent along with us. It was a good day.

But we had to head back some time and face the scales. I weighed our haul three times with *Amaryllis'* scale, got a different number each time, but all within ten pounds of each other, and more importantly twenty pounds under quota. Not that it would matter. We rowed into the slip at the scale house, and Anders was the scalemaster on duty again. I almost hauled up our sails and turned us around, never to return. I couldn't face him, not after the perfect trip. Nina was right—it wasn't fair that this one man could ruin us with false surpluses and black marks.

Silently, we secured *Amaryllis* to the dock and began handing up our cargo. I managed to keep from even looking at Anders, which probably made me look guilty in his eyes. But we'd already established I could be queen of perfection and he would consider me guilty.

Anders' frown was smug, his gaze judgmental. I could already hear him tell me I was fifty pounds over quota. Another haul like that, he'd say, we'll have to see about yanking your fishing rights. I'd have to punch him. I almost told Garrett to hold me back if I looked like I was going to punch him. But he was already keeping himself between the two of us, as if he thought I might really do it.

If the old scalemaster managed to break up *Amaryllis*, I'd murder him. And wouldn't that be a worse crime than any I might represent?

Anders drew out the moment, looking us all up and down before finally announcing, "Sixty over this time. And you think you're good at this."

My hands tightened into fists. I imagined myself lunging at him. At this point, what could I lose?

"We'd like an audit," Nina said, slipping past Sun, Garrett, and me to stand before the stationmaster, frowning, hands on her hips.

"Excuse me?" Anders said.

"An audit. I think your scale is wrong, and we'd like an audit. Right?" She looked at me.

It was probably better than punching him. "Yes," I said, after a flabbergasted moment. "Yes, we would like an audit."

That set off two hours of chaos in the scale house. Anders protested, hollered at us, threatened us. I sent Sun to the committee house to summon official oversight—he wouldn't try to play nice, and they couldn't brush him off. June and Abe, two senior committee members, arrived, austere in gray and annoyed.

"What's the complaint?" June said.

Everyone looked at me to answer. I almost denied it—that was my first impulse. Don't fight, don't make waves. Because maybe I deserved the trash I got. Or my mother did, but she wasn't here, was she?

But Nina was looking at me with her innocent brown eyes, and this was for her.

I wore a perfectly neutral, business-like expression when I spoke to June and Abe. This wasn't about me, it was about business, quotas, and being fair.

"Scalemaster Anders adjusts the scale's calibration when he sees us coming."

I was amazed when they turned accusing gazes at him and not at me. Anders' mouth worked, trying to stutter a defense, but he had nothing to say.

The committee confirmed that Anders was rigging his scale. They offered us reparations, out of Anders' own rations. I considered—it would mean extra credits, extra food and supplies for the household. We'd been discussing getting another windmill, petitioning for another well. Instead, I recommended that any penalties they wanted to levy should go to community funds. I just wanted *Amaryllis* treated fairly.

And I wanted a meeting, to make one more petition before the committee.

Garrett walked with me to the committee office the next morning.

"I should have been the one to think of requesting an audit," I said.

"Nina isn't as scared of the committee as you are. As you *were*," he said.

"I'm not—" But I stopped, because he was right.

He squeezed my hand. His smile was amused, his gaze warm. He seemed to find the whole thing entertaining. Me—I was relieved, exhausted, giddy, ashamed. Mostly relieved.

We, *Amaryllis*, had done nothing wrong. I had done nothing wrong.

Garrett gave me a long kiss, then waited outside while I went to sit before the committee.

June was in her chair, along with five other committee members, behind their long table with their slate boards, tally sheets, and lists of quotas. I sat across from them, alone, hands clenched in my lap, trying not to tap my feet. Trying to appear as proud and assured as they did. A stray breeze slipped through the open windows and cooled the cinderblock room.

After polite greetings, June said, "You wanted to make a petition?"

"We—the *Amaryllis* crew—would like to request an increase in our quota. Just a small one."

June nodded. "We've already discussed it and we're of a mind to allow an increase. Would that be suitable?"

Suitable as what? As reparation? As an apology? My mouth was dry, my tongue frozen. My eyes stung, wanting to weep, but that would have damaged our chances, as much as just being me did.

"There's one more thing," I managed. "With an increased quota, we can feed another mouth."

It was an arrogant thing to say, but I had no reason to be polite.

They could chastise me, send me away without a word, lecture me on wanting too much when there wasn't enough to go around. Tell me that it was more important to maintain what we had rather than try to expand—expansion was arrogance. We simply had to maintain. But they didn't. They didn't even look shocked at what I had said.

June, so elegant, I thought, with her long gray hair braided and resting over her shoulder, a knitted shawl draped around her, as much for decoration as for warmth, reached into the bag at her feet and retrieved a folded piece of cloth, which she pushed across the table toward me. I didn't want to touch it. I was still afraid, as if I'd reach for it and June would snatch it away at the last moment. I didn't want to unfold it to see the red and green pattern in full, in case it was some other color instead.

But I did, even though my hand shook. And there it was. I clenched the banner in my fist; no one would be able to pry it out.

"Is there anything else you'd like to speak of?" June asked.

"No," I said, my voice a whisper. I stood, nodded at each of them. Held the banner to my chest, and left the room.

Garrett and I discussed it on the way back to the house. The rest of the crew was waiting in the courtyard for us: Dakota in her skirt and tunic, hair in a tangled bun; J.J. with his arms crossed, looking worried; Sun, shirtless, hands on hips, inquiring. And Nina, right there in front, bouncing almost.

I regarded them, trying to be inscrutable, gritting my teeth to keep from bursting into laughter. I held our banner behind my back to hide it. Garrett held my other hand.

"Well?" Nina finally said. "How did it go? What did they say?"

The surprise wasn't going to get any better than this. I shook out the banner and held it up for them to see. And oh, I'd never seen all of them wide-eyed and wondering, mouths gaping like fish, at once.

Nina broke the spell, laughing and running at me, throwing herself into my arms. We nearly fell over.

Then we were all hugging, and Dakota started worrying right off, talking about what we needed to build a crib, all the fabric we'd need for diapers, and how we only had nine months to save up the credits for it.

I recovered enough to hold Nina at arm's length, so I could look her in the eyes when I pressed the banner into her hands. She nearly dropped it at first, skittering from it as if it were fire. So I closed her fingers around the fabric and held them there.

"It's yours," I said. "I want you to have it." I glanced at Garrett to be sure. And yes, he was still smiling.

Staring at me, Nina held it to her chest, much like I had. "But . . . you. It's yours. . ." She started crying. Then so did I, gathering her close and holding her tight while she spoke through tears, "Don't you want to be a mother?"

In fact, I rather thought I already was.

* 2011 Hugo Award nominee for Best Short Story

* Reprinted in *The Year's Best Science Fiction: Twenty-Eighth Annual Collection*, edited by Gardner Dozois

* 2011 WSFA Small Press nominee

• NO TIME LIKE THE PRESENT •
Carol Emshwiller

A lot of new rich people have moved into the best houses in town—those big ones up on the hill that overlook the lake. What with the depression, some of those houses have been on the market for a long time. They'd gotten pretty run down, but the new people all seem to have plenty of money and fixed them up right away. Added docks and decks and tall fences. It was our fathers, mine included, who did all the work for them. I asked my dad what their houses were like and he said, "Just like ours only richer."

As far as we know, none of those people have jobs. It's as if all the families are independently wealthy.

Those people look like us only not exactly. They're taller and skinnier and they're all blonds. They don't talk like us either. English does seem to be their native language, but it's an odd English. Their kids keep saying, "Shoe dad," and, "Bite the boot." They shout to each other to, "Evolve!"

At first their clothes were funny, too—the men had weird jackets with tight waists and their pants were too short. The girls and women actually wore longish wide skirts. They don't have those anymore. They must have seen right away how funny they looked compared to us, and gone to Penny's and got some normal clothes like ours.

They kept their odd shoes, though, like they couldn't bear not to have them. (They look really soft, they're kind of square and the big toe is separate.) And they had to wait for their hair to grow out some before they could get haircuts like ours. This year our boys have longer hair than the girls, so their boys were all wrong.

Every single one of those new people, first thing, put two flamingos out on their front lawns, but then, a few days later, they wised up and took them away. It wasn't long before every single one of them had either a dog or a cat.

When Sunday came, they all went to the Unitarian church and the women wore the most ridiculous hats, but took them off as soon as they saw none of us wore any. They wore their best clothes, too, but only a few of us do.

Even though they come to church, Mom says I shouldn't make friends with their kids until we know more about them and I especially shouldn't visit any of their houses. She says the whole town doesn't trust them even though everybody has made money on them one way or another.

Their kids have a funny way of walking. Not *that* funny, actually, but as if they don't want anybody to talk to them, and as if they're better than we are—maybe just because they're taller. But we don't look *that* different. It seems as if they're pretending we're not here. Or maybe that *they're* not here. In school they eat lunch together at the very farthest table and bring their own food, like our cafeteria food isn't good enough. They obviously—all of them—don't want to be here.

I've got one of the new people in my class. I feel sorry for her. Marietta . . . Smith? (I'll bet. All those new people are Smiths and Joneses and Browns and Blacks.) She's tall and skinny like they all are. She's by herself in my class; usually there's two or three of them in each class. She's really scared. I tried to help her the first days—I thought she needed a girl friend really badly—but she didn't even smile back when I smiled straight at her.

The boys are all wondering if those new boys would be on the basketball team, but so far they don't even answer when they're asked. Jerry asked Huxley Jones, and Huxley said, under his breath, "Evolve, why don't you?"

Trouble is, my name is Smith, too, but it's *really* Smith. I've always wanted to change it to something more complicated. I'd rather be Karpinsky or Jesperson or Minnifee like some of the kids in my class.

I kind of understand those new kids. I have to eat a special diet, and I'm too tall, too. I tower over most of the town boys. And I'm an only child and I'm not at all popular. I don't care what Mom says, I don't see what harm there can be in helping Marietta and I'm curious. I like her odd accent. I try saying things as she does and I say, "Shoe Dad," to my dad even though I don't know what those kids mean by it. Maybe it's really *Shoo* Dad.

One of these days I'm going to sneak into her house and see what I can find out.

But I don't have a lot of time for finding out things because I have to practice the violin so much. Funny though, when I took my violin to school because I had my lesson that afternoon, Marietta looked at the case as if she couldn't imagine what was in it. I said, "violin," even though she hadn't asked. And then she looked as if she wanted to ask, "What's a violin?"

Those kids are all so dumb about ordinary things. Every single one of them has been kept back a grade. I don't know how they can walk around looking so snooty. It's as if they think being dumb is better.

Marietta is awful in school, too. The teacher asked her who was the vice president and she didn't know. So the teacher asked who was president and she didn't know that either.

That gave me the courage to ask her if she wanted help. But then she said her mother doesn't want her to be friends with any of us and I said my mother says the exact same thing. Finally she laughs, we both do, and she says, "Shoe Dad, if we can keep it secret."

(Those kids never say "Okay.")

She says, "But I shouldn't be too smart either. We don't want anybody to notice us."

So far I don't think she has anything to worry about in that direction. I don't say that, though. What I say is, "You're getting noticed for the opposite reason. You need my help."

I'm really curious about her house, but she wouldn't dare invite me and I wouldn't dare go there. And she can't come to my house because Mom would be horrified. Too bad they look a little bit different otherwise Mom would never know. So we mostly meet in the woods by the railroad tracks where the bums used to hide out back when there were bums. Mom doesn't like me to go there either. She thinks maybe there might still be bums around. Marietta and I always scope out the place first, not for bums, but because boys sometimes go there to smoke.

I discovered Marietta was so bad at math because she was used to writing out the problems in an entirely different way. Once I got that straightened out she got a lot better. But she said Huxley told her there was no need for her ever to know who was president here now. I said, "Why not?" She started to say it wasn't important but she stopped in the middle. Then she said, it was just that there were some things she wasn't going to bother knowing.

She tells me she really likes Judson Jesperson, but she says she's not supposed to go outside her own group. And me, I like Huxley Jones, but Marietta says he can't go outside their group either. She's supposed to like Huxley and I'm supposed to like Judd. I asked her if this was some sort of religious thing? I didn't dare say racial but Judson has very dark hair and eyes though his skin is just like hers. She said, no, it was something entirely different and she wasn't supposed to talk about it. She said it would be *very* dangerous for any of her group to marry outsiders. She said, "Who knows who would be president in a couple a hundred years if Judd and I got married?"

So anyway, we're unhappy together and I can tell her all about Judson's family but she can't tell me anything about Huxley.

A dozen more families of the tall people move into town. They can't take the best houses because they're already gone, but when they get through with the second best houses, they turn out be almost as good except for not being on top of a hill and next to the lake.

The first group of kids is getting a little friendlier. Huxley even let himself get talked into being on the basketball team but he didn't know how to play and had to be taught from scratch. Judd says they're sorry now. All he has going for him is being tall.

I don't care, I like him. I like his stooped over posture. As if he doesn't want to be that tall. I like his kind of scholarly face. I like his pixie grin. At first he was always frowning at all of us, but pretty soon he wasn't and especially not at me.

The first thing I said to him was, "I like your name," and he actually did smile.

By now everybody is saying Shoe Dad.

Then we have the first snow and a snow day. It's so beautiful. I want to see Marietta right away, but no school so I start out towards her house. I'm not going to disobey Mom. Besides, that's our only good hill for sledding. Everybody will be up there.

And there everybody is, with sleds and garbage can lids and folded up cardboard boxes. Some kids even have skis. The new kids are even more excited about the snow than we are. They act as though they've never made snowmen and never thrown snow balls. They're like little kids. Well, actually we all are.

Those new kids have skis and fancy boots. But not a single one knows how to ski.

Marietta's there. I knew she would be. She says first off, "Look . . . these great boots . . . "

She has the fancy kind you can't walk around in. They're white with dozens of black buckles. I admit they're beautiful. I say, "Shoe Dad."

" . . . and they only cost five hundred dollars."

She's always saying things like that. Everything is cheap to her. I wish something was cheap to me. I'd like to say, "Evolve!" but I don't want to make her feel bad. I say, "Bite the . . . oh yeah, bite the *ski* boot."

We don't hear about it till lunch time, but that night in the middle of the storm, odd things disappeared. Half the fish at the fish hatchery, and that very same night, a big pile of lumber from the lumber mill disappeared. The night watchman swears he made his rounds every hour. Sometime between his two o'clock and three o'clock a whole section of lumber was gone and not a sound. The fish people are there early and late. They went to feed the fish at eight and found half the tanks empty. Some of us say the new people are getting blamed just because they're richer than we are and just because they're new, though nobody can figure out how they could have done it. Even so, I'm suspicious, too. Dad says the town is going to have a meeting about them.

Then we hear that exactly the same night, north of us, in Washington State they also lost a lot of lumber. And another place in Nevada lost half their grass-fed beef.

Funny though, Huxley said all this was *our* fault. Even that they're here in the first place is *our* fault. He said we should have stopped cutting down trees. He won't say anything more about it. That shows how odd these new kids are. But I guess that's fair, we blame them for everything and they blame us.

Except for Marietta, those kids still don't like it here at all, but Marietta says she's getting to like it, partly because of being friends with me—where she was before she never had such a good friend as I am—and she also likes it because she always did like camping out and making do with what's at hand. That makes me wonder all the more where she came from.

The new people often have meetings in one of the larger houses up on the hill. They can't hide that because all the best cars in town are parked outside. After the fish and lumber disappear, the next time those cars gather, a whole batch of the town's people storm the house. It isn't fair, but the cops are on our side; they're just like all the town's people, they don't trust those new people either. And it isn't as if the new people had any higher up connections in the town that would help them. So the cops arrest *them* instead of *us*, even though we're the ones that broke into their meeting. Did a lot of damage, too, and not only to the furniture. Six of the new people are in the hospital.

That leaves a lot of those kids with nobody looking after them. The school principal asks the town parents if they'll take in some of the children temporarily until their parents can get themselves straightened out with the police. I get my folks to take in Marietta. Mom doesn't mind it under these circumstances. In fact she acts nice. She even bakes cookies. Marietta can't believe Mom made these right here at home. She's so fascinated she forgets to feel worried for a while.

As usual I have to practice the violin. Marietta tries it out. All she makes is squeaks. She can't believe how hard it is. She's only played computer instruments. "Aided," she says, so you don't have to know anything. But you can have any sound you want and you sound good right at the beginning.

I have twin beds in my room so we get to be right in together.

At first Marietta seems to like it as much as I do. We talk until Mom comes in and tells us we have to stop because of school tomorrow. But a little bit after I turn out the light, I'm pretty sure Marietta is crying. I ask if there's anything I can do.

She says, "I wish I could go home."

I say, "It won't be long before your parents come back."

"I mean I want to go back where we used to live. My real home."

"Where is it?"

"We're not supposed to say."

"Was it so much better there?"

"Sort of . . . some ways . . . except it's nice being so rich for a change. Of course there's lots you don't have. . . . Oh well."

"*I'm* glad you're here."

"Well, I'm glad for having you."

"Can I go up and see your house now that there's nobody there?"

"It's just like yours only richer. That's because everything is so cheap here otherwise we couldn't afford stuff. It's *supposed* to be just like yours. Our parents made it special to be like that."

"Can we go anyway? I like rich stuff and I hardly ever get to see rich things except on TV. Besides, don't you need to go get more clothes?"

So we do that—skip school and go up. She's right. There's nothing odd about it . . . except there is. There's a fancy barbeque thing in the backyard, but obviously never used. There's a picnic table beside it but no chairs. The two flamingos are in a corner, lying on their sides. Inside it's awfully—I don't know how to describe it—cold and stiff, and kind of empty. It's as if nobody lives there. There's a *National Geographic* on one side of the coffee table and a *Consumers Report* on the other, and that's *all*. No clutter. Mom would like it.

Upstairs, her room has all the right stuff. There's a brand new teddy bear on the pillow and a small bookcase with brand new books, all very girlie. They don't look read either. There's not a single Tarzan or John Carter. I ask, and she never even heard of Tarzan. I tell her I'll lend her some. Even though we're too old for those, she'll like them.

She has one whole drawer with nothing but fancy sweaters and blouses. We gather some up to bring back and she says I can have half of them.

On the way out, I open the hall closet and there's a tangle of wires and silvery things along them like Christmas tree lights. At first Marietta tries to keep the door shut as if she doesn't want me to see them, but then she says she trusts me as much as anybody she ever knew so she says, "Take a good look."

I say, "I don't know what it is, anyway."

She says, "Time machine," and starts laughing hysterically. And then we both laugh so hard we fall on the floor and I don't know what's the truth and what isn't, except maybe I do.

I'm glad we went there. I don't need to feel jealous after all. Even though Mom would probably like living like that, I wouldn't.

The police hang on to those new people to see if any of them are guilty of anything at all and also as a sort of punishment, I suppose for being rich and taking up all the best places. That means Marietta and I have even more time together.

The lumber mill now has three night watchmen. They're sitting right next to the biggest piles of lumber. The fish hatchery has people practically in with the fish.

But then—again in the middle of the night—all the new people disappear. The grown-ups, that is. So then we know who did the fish and lumber. But now there's nobody to blame but their children. Some townspeople are so angry they want to put them in jail, too. Most of the townspeople don't go that far, though. My parents and lots of others say they won't let that happen. Besides, now that they know Marietta they like her.

But it's not safe for the new kids to walk the streets anymore—two kids got beat up by a gang of boys and they weren't even the new kids, they were just blond and tall and skinny. Mom dyes Marietta's hair black so she'll be safer. Some of the other new kids do that too.

Marietta looks good with dark hair. That doesn't cheer her up, though. All those kids feel terrible. Naturally. But it's odd, they keep saying they're not surprised, they just wondered when it would happen.

We talk a lot in bed at night and Mom doesn't tell us to shut up until it gets really late.

"How can your parents leave you like this?"

"We're not allowed to say, but it's for our own good."

"Parents always say that."

I try to cheer up Marietta. We go to lots of movies. She does like the Tarzan and John Carter books and there are lots of those to go through yet. Mom gives her valerian and chamomile tea almost every night. At first Marietta didn't want hugs from my mom, but now she does.

I go around wearing her expensive sweaters and I wear her white jacket when she wears her shiny black one. That turns out to be a big mistake because I get taken for one of them. I'm as tall and skinny as they are. And here I am, wearing fancy clothes like they always do. And here we are, Marietta and me, one of us with dyed black hair and me, a darker blond than they are but that doesn't matter to this bunch. They're not high school boys. I don't know who they are but they're grown men—waiting for us after the movie.

They don't think Marietta is one of the new people—they think *I* am. She's wearing my faded blue jeans and my sweatshirt and I'm in her cashmere sweater and that white jacket.

They push her aside—so hard they knock her down—and come after me. They yank at Marietta's jacket so hard the zipper breaks, and then pull the sweater up over my face so I don't see what happens next. All I know is they suddenly stop and Marietta is pulling the sweater down so I can see. She yells, "Run," and we do. When I look back I see all three of them collapsed on the ground.

"Don't stop." Marietta grabs my arm and pulls me along with her.

"What did you do?"

"I'm not allowed to say."

We run all the way home and collapse in our front hall. That white jacket is lost and ruined out there somewhere and the sweater is all pulled out of shape.

Marietta right away says, "Don't tell."

"How did you do that?"

"I thought you had those here. Tazers. Don't you? This is just a different form."

"Where is your tazer?"

"I'm not supposed to say. See, where I come from it's not safe anymore since the revolt of . . . My drones—I mean my parents—they wanted me to be able to defend myself. Besides, they thought everybody here had guns."

"Where is it? You can tell me."

"Here." She points to her earlobe. (There's not even a mark that I can see.) "I have some control over the direction." She twists her earlobe. "I can even point it back."

I touch it, but I don't feel anything.

"They left us here, my drones. They said they would if anything happened. And things did happen. I guess it *is* better here. I mean the air and water and space to move around in. . . . And the food . . . it isn't what we're used to, and it's awfully primitive, everything is, but it's better some ways and we're rich. I have a million dollars in the bank in my name."

She's about to tell me more but Mom comes in right then and finds us sitting on the floor, and me, all bedraggled and the sweater ruined. She gets really upset when she hears about it. (We don't tell her the tazer part.) She insists that she's going to dye my hair that very night no matter how long it takes, and I have to stop wearing Marietta's nice clothes.

For once I agree with her. I let her do all that, even though I know the kids at school will tease me.

I wonder if those men are going to tell what happened to them? Maybe not, though, because they were breaking the law.

I'm going to stick close to Marietta from now on. I feel safe with her.

Most of those new kids are physically awkward—like Huxley trying to be on the basketball team—but Marietta isn't so bad. She says it's because her parents didn't believe in the education boxes most kids had. She says those were like being inside a TV set. But she kept calling hers "Mommy" by mistake and that upset her mother so much she actually had her playing outside even though the air wasn't that good anymore and even when it was too hot.

She's been telling me everything, even about the air-conditioned sweater her mom got her.

She says, "Even so, it was getting worse and worse. Food riots sometimes. I know this is best for us. But we have to be so careful and not change anything. Nobody knows what would happen if we upset things. Shoe Dad, I might not even exist. I'd go *poof*! Just like that."

And then Huxley gets in trouble and that changes everything. He didn't dye his hair like the others did. It might not have worked anyway. Three men attack him; maybe the same three that came after us. (You'd think they'd learn.) Marietta and I have to guess what happened: that he not only used his tazer, but tied up the men when they were down. Dragged them into the woods. Then he walked all the way home with bruises all over. Nobody found out about the men out in the woods till two days later. It rained all the next day and one of the men suffocated with his head in the mud. Marietta and I know Huxley didn't use his tazer until he was practically all beat up. He was trying so hard not to cause any changes in the people living here but then he caused more of a problem.

The townspeople are blaming him. Of course they are. Besides, who knows what story those men told? So the police come to arrest him, but he takes off. They even shoot at him, but he gets away. We don't know if he got shot or not.

All the new kids are even scareder than they already were. About going "poof." They keep saying, "It's gotta be even worse than that butterfly back in the Jurassic era." I don't know what they mean by that.

They stand there staring at nothing, as if thinking: Any minute and I never existed. They stop in mid sentence as if: Is it right now that I disappear?

On the other hand, they could disappear by going back home. We'd never know which it was. Marietta hangs on to me whenever she can. It's as if she thinks as long as she has a good grip on my arm, she won't disappear. It's a bother but I let her.

I know where Huxley isn't. He's not at that place where the bums used to go and where the boys go to smoke. That's too easy. But I do know where he could be. I don't even tell Marietta. I get up real early before anybody is up. I make a couple of peanut butter sandwiches and take some nuts and apples and go. Good that Huxley and I never got together or the cops would be watching me.

So I head out into the woods. It's a good place to get lost since there are so many crisscrossing paths and there's a lot of undergrowth for hiding. I think Huxley is somewhere in there but I'll have a hard time finding him. I whistle. I sing. I make a lot of noise and wander all over. I think I'm going to get lost myself.

But what if he's disappeared already? What if he's never been at all?

Then I hear a bird chirping above me, I look up and there he is and he's not been shot. I climb up and give him the sandwiches. He's changed a lot from when he first came. I don't think he'd have been able to climb a tree. He looks kind of wild and haunted and dirty. That makes me like him all the more. I'm always embarrassed, being so close to a boy I like so much, and now even more so. I don't ask anything I really want to. I'm too nervous.

He gobbles up both sandwiches and apples and nuts all in about five minutes. When everything is gone he thinks maybe one of the sandwiches might have been for me and apologizes. But I say none of it was for me and I'll bring more tomorrow.

He admires my new black hair, but I think he's just trying to be nice.

I move up closer to the branch he's on. Turns out I don't have to ask anything. He tells me he always did like me but didn't dare show it. Now he does dare. He thinks everything is all messed up anyway so he might as well like me and he wants me to know it.

Then we hear the swishing of underbrush and voices of people coming closer.

We shut up. He moves higher and I move lower.

In a few minutes the woods are packed with people walking all over the place looking for him. Some of them are cops in uniform. Lots are just towns-people. Mostly men but a few women.

I jump down and move away from his tree. I shout, "Let's look over by the little cave next to the stream." So I and a group of others including one cop, head over there.

The cop says, "Aren't you supposed to be in school?"

"Yeah, but isn't this important?"

"You're lucky I'm not a truant officer."

"What will you do when you find him?"

He pulls his cuffs out of his back pocket and rattles them. Says, "He's dangerous."

I know this whole woods better than a lot of them do. I lead them around to all sorts of good hiding places. I talk loud and make a lot of noise. I don't ever look up.

It's a tiring day for everybody. I had no idea I was going to get caught up in the search and get home so late. My folks and Marietta have been worried about me. I didn't tell Mom where I'd been, but I tell Marietta. She feels bad that I didn't ask her to come along, but I convinced her it was safer for Huxley if it's just me.

Next day I don't think I should keep on skipping school so I just skip my last class. This time I make four peanut butter sandwiches. It's late so I bring a flashlight.

I head for that same tree first, but he's not there. As before, I sing. I whistle. I keep looking up and chirping. I go to all the good spots. It gets dark and I'm worried about using the flashlight. There's only a little moon so I stumble around tripping on things.

Pretty soon I know I'd better go home. I leave the sandwiches up in the tree where I first found Huxley. I leave the flashlight for him, too, and try to find my way out without it.

But I can't. I thought if I just came to one of the streams and followed it, I'd be okay, but it's muddy and slippery near the stream and I keep falling down. I decide it's best to just wait till dawn. I huddle down against a tree. I wish I'd kept one of those sandwiches for myself.

In the morning I go back to the tree where I left the sandwiches. Something got into them and ate most of them and scattered what was left all over.

When I get back my folks are so worried and the police are all over looking for me. Thing is, Marietta disappeared, too, and first they thought we were off somewhere together. Then they thought that I got disappeared with all the others.

It turns out they're *all* gone. I'll never know if Marietta got to go home or if she never existed in the first place or maybe they decided it was a bad and dangerous idea to leave their kids here. Or maybe things got better so it was okay to go home. Or maybe they found better stuff from other times. Like way, way back before there were other people to get in their way.

She left a lot of her clothes in my room. Funny though, my old Tarzan and John Carter books—the ones she was in the middle of reading—are gone. That makes me feel that she didn't disappear completely like she was afraid would happen. She's still someplace, I'm sure of it, reading my books.

I wonder if I could write her a letter. I'll bet there is a way, like sealed up in stainless steel. I wish we'd talked about that before she left. I wish I knew how long my letter would have to last to get to her. Maybe I'll have to carve it in stone.

* Reprinted in *The Year's Best Science Fiction & Fantasy: 2011 Edition*, edited by Rich Horton

• MANUMISSION •
Tobias S. Buckell

This morning, when you wake up and look at your rippled reflection in the basin of water near the concrete wall of your cell, you only have one true personal memory left. It can't be that your entire life is based off this one event, so you suspect they've left it with you to piss you off. To "motivate" you. To make you one raging motherfucker.

It's a riff on the Countee Cullen poem. You're six, standing on the street holding the anonymous arm of your mom, and the other kid staring back at you flips you off and calls you nigger.

That's all they really left you with.

Sure there's other stuff, you're no vegetable. You can use money, eat, walk, tap the net, and know just about anything headlined over the last thirty years. But anything specific is faded, general, lost behind static and fuzzy feelings.

You empty the basin with a flourish and look around your cell.

The headache, the all-over itching, the scars crisscrossing your entire body, that gets to you too.

You've signed yourself away, the men in the black suits have explained back when you first arrived in this cell. They sat across from you on a sterile metal table. The document they slid toward your burnt smooth fingertips is legit.

So you listened to them, and nodded, and they got up to leave.

Oh yeah, one last thing, they had said.

Your name.

Pepper.

And your last name?

They just chuckled and closed the door.

Nine o'clock. Newport, Rhode Island. A forest of masts bobs slightly, boats cheerfully tied at their docks. You slide off the blue awning over the side entrance to a small bar and hit the slippery cobblestones to face a portly middle-aged accountant with slicked back wiry hair.

"Oh shit . . . " is all he has time to say.

Then slumps.

The small wires that knocked him out recoil back up into your wrists with a flick. You squat over the man, push his trousers up his hairy calf, and look at the tattoo on the back of his knee. He's ShinnCo property. Your eyes scan for forgery, defects, get in closer for a finer look, where every hair seems to be tree-sized.

All good. You blink your eyes until they return to normal, the thin extra membrane rolling back behind your eyelids.

His hands are clammy when you grab them. His breath reeks of alcohol. With a grunt you pull him up onto your shoulder and stagger toward a waiting car.

What, you wonder, has Mr. James Edward leaked to the Federalists? You really don't want, or need, to know.

Twelve hours later, five thousand closer to freedom, an old 6.35mm Astra Model Cub pistol tucked in the inner pocket of your oilskin duster, you're sitting in the lounge of an airship over several hundred feet of water, languorously easing your way toward the next stop, Eleytheria.

It's moored out in the Atlantic off the Eastern Seaboard this month.

At street level the Gulf Stream winds kick through the downtown buildings of Eleytheria. Your oilskin duster takes on a life of its own, bucking, trying to pull you off course as you make the usual staggered path, random jigs, sudden stops in front of reflective surfaces. It's not even a conscious thing, checking for tails.

Monotone pedestrians in business camouflage, the grays and blacks of their seemingly timeless and conservative professions, mill past you.

It isn't New York, but any of them could have been plucked out and placed in that environment without even noticing. No, just a few miles away the salt clears the breakwalls in clouds of mist and hovers into downtown.

Eleytheria is a giant bowl riding the large open ocean. Free to go where it pleases. Do what it pleases.

Many things start in Eleytheria.

Like yourself, years ago, deep in the bowels of one of Eleytheria's denizen companies. You've found old archived public camera pictures of yourself walking down the streets, into the center of ShinnCo, to sign your self, this self, into what you know now.

Sometimes you hate your old self for selling you into this bondage. You wonder what he got? Lots of money? Some last great fling? Or were you just desperate, a wandering piece of hardware abandoned by some former First World secret gov project made obsolete by the Pacification?

You'd like to think you did it for some great cause, like helping your family out of a dire situation. But late at night you doubt it and think there was some stupid, selfish reason for doing it.

They'll never tell you. Because if it was something like a family, you might try to contact them.

No. They have your memories. You'll get them back when you serve your contract.

It always comes back to Eleytheria. When your feet hit the seacrete, your nose fills with misted salt, and you have returned to the only home you know. All your recent memories, everything that is you, starts here. Ever since you woke up behind a garbage dump in the back alley of ShinnCo.

And they've never let you back in through the front doors because they know full well what kind of monster they created. They control you, but they don't sleep well at night. If you were to ever get near a door the automated security would hit you with an EMP pulse that would pretty much liquefy the machines in you, then the guns would reduce you to bloodied ribbons of flesh.

You won't be getting your memories back using the new skills they've grafted into you. No way. And they still have one final trick, to keep you close, to control you.

So you stand in front of a small food cart. A faded orange umbrella hangs limply over it. When you palm the metal rail, the countdown inside you resets. You're allowed to live for another week. A pointed way of letting you know you're motherfucking *owned*, and you don't get to stray. At all.

The edges of the umbrella flutter in the cold breeze, and on the other side of the cart an old Greek stands up.

"Morning, Kouroupas."

"Morning, Pepper," he says, looking you up and down. "The usual?"

"The usual."

The front of the cart has a faded poster of a model with a strained smile, flat white teeth, holding up a gyro in perfectly manicured hands. They're 'heeeeros' she says.

"Lettuces, mayonnaises . . . " Kouroupas' crazy white hair flies all over the place in the wind. It makes him look like a mad scientist.

He slaps the flatbread down. A cloud of flour tickles your nose.

A few browned strips of meat, some folded metallic paper, and you have your gyro, along with a small napkin neatly slid between your fingers.

You look at it, your eyes adjusting to the fibers, mapping out a pattern along the embroidered edges, translating the woven picture into words.

Susan Stamm. Ten thousand. Location. Eleytheria.

Ten thousand closer to getting yourself back. To freedom.

And she's *right here*.

You fold the napkin and its encrypted directions into your pocket, pick up the gyro. Kouroupas smiles.

"Good day," he tells you. "Be careful."

You nod and slide a few bills over to him.

"You too."

Be careful. It's the first time Kouroupas seems to acknowledge that this isn't just a gyro purchase. Seems to be telling you something's not quite normal this time.

Out of sight of the gyro stand you toss the gyro into a trashcan that thanks you and trundles away.

Not nearly enough raw sugars in gyros for you. Takes too long to metabolize. What you need now is something to spike your blood sugar to combat levels.

Susan Stamm has done many, many unique things to hide her presence. But she's on the run and wants off the planet. To do that she has to come to Eleytheria. Once an hour, every hour, a capsule is launched into low Earth orbit.

To really get far away, Stamm has to get Out There from Down Here.

So you sit and flip through pictures of embarkees who've been photographed at all three entrance points. One by fucking one. And these are just the ones the Port Authority computers have served up as possible matches. ShinnCo is being very generous with info and resources right now. They really want her back.

You're sitting in a small outdoor café, eyes closed. On the right eyeball is Susan Stamm's corp ID photo. On your left is some random face pic snapped by the Port Authority entrance machine.

Then another random face.

You reach for the sugary soda, take a long cold sip, and the next picture comes up.

Another sip of sugar water. Gotta keep the machines inside you running happy.

You flip to another pic.

Ha.

She looks thinner than the last official photo. She's still five-nine, but now has a recently bobbed haircut and green eyes.

Four hours later you're in the lobby of a smaller Eleytheria hotel, looking up at the atrium eighty stories above you, licking the icing off a Danish. In the background, over the hum of people, over the echoing shouts of kids screaming and waving from several floors above, comes the explosive whip-crack of a capsule being thrown into space.

There was this mugger that jumped you a year ago. Before you even realized it you'd spun, broke both his arms and a leg, and the man lay in an unconscious heap by the side of a brick façade.

His clothes were ragged, he was thin, and when you held his gun in your hand, you realized that it was unloaded.

Ballsy. And pathetic.

By going through his wallet you found out that his name was Jack Connely. He had three kids and a very attractive blonde wife. Jack had been a spacer entrepreneur of some sort, reduced to Earth living after the Pacification.

Now all the businesses could buy a ride into space. Move their offices up into alien stations, use alien services, buy alien products, machines. Not much use for small guys, you could hardly scrape together the price. But multinationals can, and now that they're all in orbit, or beyond, the pretense of even caring about the world they originated from was thrown out.

You could have used the money you found in his pocket, his day's take, though you couldn't use it toward paying off your ShinnCo contract. They only accept their own in house credit.

You couldn't even use the money to disable the shit laced all through your body. You tried that once before. Almost killed you on the table.

Instead, you sent his wallet and the money back in the mail to his family. And you added some of your own.

You're a good person, you tell yourself.

But it's very hard to believe when it was so easy, so automatic, to have grabbed that man's gun and pull the trigger, right down to within a hairtrigger of firing, before stopping.

That can't be *all* wired into you, right?

Susan Stamm walks through the revolving door, past a doorman, and on toward a cab. You shake your shoulders and arms, loosening up the great mass of coat around you, and step in behind her. She's better looking in person, unlike some of the dolled-up, make-up-caked women you've seen in the past.

As she grabs the gullwing door of the bubbly autocab she spots your reflection in the window and turns around.

"Could we share this ride?" you say. Already you flex the muscles in your wrists, begin to raise your left arm and coat to obscure her body. She'll fall, and you'll sweep her up and into the autocab with you.

As the autocab rides off you'll look like two lovers cuddling in the back.

Instead her eyes widen, hands curl into fists, and a small dart burrows into your stomach.

You're on the ground, convulsing. Spit flecks your lips. You break into a heavy sweat. Vomit tastes like sugar water, flowing out onto the concrete sidewalk. It takes effort just to slowly roll over.

The doorman turns around.

He moves, a blur that you know isn't natural, and hits Stamm from the side.

She hits the door of the autocab, shattering the Plexiglas, and the doorman grabs her neck, turning her head to confirm her ShinnCo tattoo.

Small silver fans protrude from the back of the man's neck. Antenna. You can see heat rising off his uniform, rippling the air around him. A timeshare. Not under his own control then—just renting his body for sudden on-the-spot jobs like this one.

You have a choice. Give it up. Let this competitor grab her, kill her, whatever.

Or.

With just a quick flex of your arms the wires spit out of your wrists and hit the back of his neck. The man spasms, lightning sparking across the surface of his skin. The antenna melt, dripping down the back of his collar. He spins around and raises his arms.

"Oh fuck," he screams, the link to whatever controls him from orbit gone. "I'm burning. They killed me! I'm burning!"

As he staggers toward the door, people gather. Someone tries to get the doorman to sit down. Someone 911s to call this in, speaking into his pinkie finger.

On your hands and knees, eyes burning and streaming tears, wires retracted back into your wrists, you push forward into the car. You grab Stamm, pull her in with you, and barely manage to shut the door.

She's in better shape than you, coming back to consciousness as you vomit sugar water all over her red high heels.

"Drive, damnit," she shouts at the cab's autopilot, and gives an address.

"Damage has been detected," it warbles. "Failure mode initiated. A replacement cab is on its way. We apologize for the delay."

"Shit."

The cab rocks as she leans forward.

Your muscles fail.

Your brain goes zero.

You're out.

There are rooms and then there are rooms. They're square more often than not, with white walls. But this one has dirty laundry, fake wooden paneling, a giant mirror on a wall, and a small cot that you're lying on.

A wicker chair next to you creaks. Soft hands stroke your forehead.

"You're tough. That was supposed to kill you."

"I feel like shit." Every pore hurts.

"I would imagine." A finger traces the scars all over your body. "I'm sorry. I think I may have got the wrong person. It was the doorman I should have shot, he was the one coming for me. Who are you?"

Don't say anything.

Just shiver and turn back off. It's easier.

You wake up hungry and naked. Disoriented. You have no internal time. The small set of numbers that usually hover in the corner of your left eye is gone.

There's a pink bathrobe on the wicker chair that you grab as you sit up.

It takes everything you have to stand. Muscles protest, and every cell seems to ache.

"Feeling better?"

She's sitting by the kitchen counter, hands up, watching you warily.

You nod.

"Okay. So here are the rules. Any sudden moves I fire another one of these pips into you. If your hands aren't where I can see them, I shoot. I doubt you survive another one. So sit. Put your hands on your lap."

The bathrobe is comfortable. You slowly wrap it tighter around you and sit. Her tone drips with suspicion, guarded overtones. The air is tense.

She points at your leg. That's where they tattooed the small logo on you. Inner thigh. It really, really hurt.

"You're ShinnCo."

"Yes." She knows, you know. No point in denying.

"And the doorman?" she asks. "Did you know about him ahead of time?"

You shrug.

She stares at you and you stare right back, not sure where this is going. You have the faintest sense that you'll get out of the door alive.

"Why are you still here?" you ask, which also implies, *why am I still alive?* "You could have left me here."

Stamm smiles.

"I felt bad for you."

That is not the response you really expected. And you don't believe it for a second. Someone this dangerous isn't that stupid.

"You know what I am . . . "

"Get real. They want me alive. You're not that dangerous. Neither was the doorman, he was just a backup. It's unfortunate they don't care a whit about his life."

You've never spotted backups of any sort before. This is different. Very different. She spots the frown.

"Is this your first high profile recapture?" Off in the distance is the whipcrack of another space launch, and she smiles. It's a broad one, full of glee. "Look, I'm within *walking* distance of getting away. They're getting desperate. I shouldn't have gotten this far. You're a backup, the doorman was an emergency backup, and the first three they sent after me are all lying in alleys somewhere."

She's dangerous.

Kouroupas tried to warn you.

"So what now?" you ask.

"Well I'm hungry and making some breakfast. Can I get you anything?"

You smile.

"Anything with sugar, I could really use something sweet."

She nods.

"Yeah, I'll bet you could, but I know what makes you tick." Your smile drops. "None of that for you. I'm leaving you weak, and slow for now. Just stay on the bed, don't move, and I'll bring you some diet soda."

You stare at her, and she laughs at you.

"I know a lot about those systems in you. How do you think I ended up with those little pips I hit you with? I designed them myself."

She walks into the kitchen, opens the fridge, and tosses you a can.

"Drink up . . . what is your name?"

You look down at the sugarless drink in your hands.

"Pepper," you say.

Susan Stamm. ShinnCo property since birth. Mother died having her, orphanage signed Susan over. She starts telling you all this stuff as she sits at a small table across from you and eats obscene amounts of breakfast sausage and eggs. The place reeks of it.

"You never even realize there is a different way of life," Susan says. "But I remember, when I was twelve, suddenly understanding that there were people who didn't have to have logos on their bodies, who didn't have to report into minders once a day, who weren't being encouraged to study certain things that the company needed." She picks up a greasy link, pauses."And then I decided I would escape it."

"How many years has that been?"

She flashes a smile and downs the sausage.

Then the dishes are tossed in the sink, she washes her hands while looking over her shoulder at you. You're still sitting in the pink bathrobe, sipping from the can.

"Just on the other side of Eleytheria is a launcher. I have a ticket off this world, and out there I have passage far out as crew on a mining ship. I know it won't be easier, but I'll be my own person." She raises a wrist. "I can burn this fucking logo off my skin."

"So you'll leave me here?"

She shakes her head.

"I have a proposition. You can't buy your freedom from ShinnCo, I'll bet, not for a long time yet. But what would you do for a ticket offworld?"

You just stare at her.

She takes it as hesitation.

"You owe me your life anyway. I need someone at my back, because if it's just me they'll try and pick me up at the gates to the launcher. Last ditch, overwhelming numbers."

"Okay." Opportunity glints in your eyes. At any point along this journey you may have an opportunity to overpower her. She spots the reaction. She thinks she has you.

"You'll walk me to the launcher, then I'll hand over the ticket. Try to double cross me before then and I'll fire another one of these nasty little critters into you. So it's in your best interests to work with me."

You nod.

She laughs.

"You realize you're free, don't you? You weren't just physically disabled," she says."I scrubbed clean all your systems. You understand what that means?"

You test everything she has just said, and she is right. But . . .

When you look down to your wrists she steps back slightly. It's an unconscious move.

"Those still work," she says. "They're bio-mechanical. Nothing that can be scrambled, infected, or shut down."

For the briefest flash of a moment you've seen freedom. And then, you think to yourself, there is the matter of the countdown. That's firewalled off from the rest of your body and bio-mech. You can't see the countdown, but you know it's there. You don't explain this to her. Right now she thinks you're in her debt.

Play along.

"I've set you free from them," she says. "You can do anything you want now."

You nod again. "Okay, fair enough. I'll help you for the ticket. Can I have my clothes back?"

The smile on her lips fades. She sizes you up, squinting. Apparently something satisfies her.

"Other side of the bed."

They've been washed, pressed, and folded into a neat pile. The Astra Model Cub pistol lies on top of them all. It's loaded.

Golden. Like that tantalizing glimpse of freedom she'd tried to give you.

Fifteen minutes later you're both out the door. You've got the overcoat draped over your right arm. You're weak, tired, and at a disadvantage, but all it will take is one well-placed shot where you can drop behind some cover, and she's down.

Susan faces you as she locks the door, still wary, but there is joy in her face. She can see the end of the road.

It's almost sad.

You walk down a corridor toward a pair of steel doors. As sunlight spills into the dimly lit area, you scope a vending niche just ahead and to the right. A drink machine hums a long low note. All you have to do is slow down, just get behind her by one step, shoot her, and use the machine for cover if she tries to use one of those lethal darts.

Two shadows force their way through the doors at the end of the corridor.

The gun's easy enough to spot; you duck and jump to your side. Susan fires at one of them as you dodge into the niche.

What puzzles you is the wrenching pain in your shoulder that drops you to the floor in front of the neon glow of the soda machine.

They're not aiming at Susan.

That was meant for you.

Your chest is wet with blood and your left arm can hardly move, but with your right you feel around the inside of your overcoat as Susan falls to the ground. Unconscious, not dead.

You drape the coat over the good arm to hide the Astra and wait.

It's Kouroupas that turns the corner. His wild hair makes a halo around his head, bathed and filtered in the light of a flickering fluorescent overhead. There is no waiting, he looks down at the overcoat hanging over your right arm, hesitates for a second, and you fire four times in a row, blowing a hole in the overcoat that the muzzle sticks through.

"Damn it." Kouropas looks shocked as he slumps to the ground.

You crawl over to him and lean close.

There are no last words, no apologies or explanations, just his creased eyes looking up at the ceiling, his flour covered hands holding his bloody stomach, and then he stops breathing.

With some effort you retrieve his gun, pocket it with your Astra, and slump with your back against the soda machine.

Fifteen sodas later you shake Susan awake again. The first time you tried, after plucking the feathered dart out of her neck, she just lolled back into unconsciousness.

Your shoulder is packed with a shirt torn off the anonymous, dead, would-be assassin at the far end of the corner. You're still seeping blood.

"Come on," you whisper to her. "You need to wake up."

Her eyes snap open.

"No!" she shouts, throwing her hands up in front of her. You grab her wrists, a quick snapping motion, and look at her. She thinks she's been captured and been taken back to ShinnCo.

"You're okay, you're still here in the lobby. You got one of them first, I got the other."

She looks at you, then calms.

You're keyed up, your body's retooling itself, parts coming back online. She'd given you an out, a way to leave. Your body, deactivated, could have been worked over by any shitty street surgeon. There was the slightest chance you could have found a way to be free eventually, thanks to her trick.

Now the insulin is surging, the blood sugar's up, and the teenies in your blood scurry around, revived and back to business.

You're back. Rebooted. Tiny emergency warnings flash in your vision, detailing the damage done to your shoulder. It numbs itself and the bleeding clots and stops.

Susan hardly protests as you pick her up off the ground by her wrists with one arm.

"Do you still have time to make your launch?"

She's dazed, but focuses.

"Yeah. Yeah. We need to move."

Gun in hand, the other shoved in a pocket so you don't move it, you sweep the area ahead. Nothing stops the two of you.

In the cab she asks you why you stayed with her.

You sit there, adjusting the bloodied shoulder bandage, and avoid her gaze.

"They came at me first," you explain. "I'm a target now." ShinnCo has spent too much time up in orbit, not enough time on the ground. You are just ants, resources to be used. And in their eyes you've turned on them, bitten them. It's easier to eliminate you and find a new worker of your talents than risk something going bad. You've seen it before. No doubt you'll see it again. "What good is bringing you in if they're going to shoot me as I try do it?"

"You could still have just left me there."

True.

You wrap your coat back around you and look up at her. "I owed you one."

The cab bumbles on down the road while you both sit in silence for a while. Then she puts a hand on your knee.

"You rebooted. I can fix you again, so you're free of all their machines."

You look down at her hand.

"Take too long. You have a launch."

"Yeah." She pulls back away, crosses her arms over her chest, and looks out the window. "I'm sorry."

"Don't be," you say. "Your trick probably wouldn't have worked anyway." And you tell her about the ticking bomb in you, the nano flechettes timed to go off unless they get their little code from that contact on the gyro stand.

We own you motherfucker.

"They aimed at me first," you tell her. Kouroupas came to finish it, and they'll get to aim at you again when you have to go back there to the cart in three days. Or you'll be sitting, standing, somewhere, when the bomb goes off. You'll look normal for a while, to bystanders, until your body falls down in a shapeless mass. Shredded from the inside out.

"That's why I rebooted."

You look out the window now as well, watching the terminals approach.

There isn't much to say after that.

There are some things you know about memory technology.

One is that it began here on Earth. Using existing technology: superconducting quantum interferometer devices that map specific memory recalls. It was pretty much there when the Pacification happened. With alien technology brought down out of orbit it got nudged along just a little further into maturity.

Two. The memories are burned out of your head. They aren't coming back.

Three. The same alien technology that matured memory alteration allows backups.

Four. When you figure out how to disable the bomb inside you, you will then go out and find that backup.

If there is no backup, there will be payback.

You walk Susan up to the terminal booth. Several streets behind lay the bodies of more dead ShinnCo who tried to stop you. You stand on neutral ground. Even ShinnCo wouldn't piss off the alien launch corporation that owns Eleytheria. Overhead the floors sweep out over the road like wings. The architecture is impossible, like Frank Lloyd Wright on crack. The supports are too small. The wings too large. It's a building designed by something that evolved on a lower gravity world and is forcing their sensibilities onto an Earth object.

The inside of the booth is filled with a light pink gas of some sort. It's more than bulletproof; any hostile action you could take would result in vaporization.

Alien ticket takers don't put up with shit. Too many Earth terrorists tried to take out their aggression on them in retaliation for the Pacification. The orbital corporations that own the rest of the solar system found it annoying, so they put in countermeasures.

Susan scans her ticket in.

Inside the booth, tentacles move. Half of them are plugged into the wall, the other half seem to support a globular mass. This creature looks like a cyborg octopus. It's light years from home, trying to scrape out a living in a weird world, looking out at you with three eyes at the center of its trunk and burbling something.

"Clear. Proceed," the speaker orders.

The security gate to the right of the booth slides aside.

Susan turns to you. She slides an extra ticket into the palm of your hand.

"In case it ever works out . . . " she says.

You wonder if the memory of her walking through the security gate, or the memory of her hand sliding away from yours, could easily be burned out of your head.

Not this time at least.

Several minutes later the capsule thunders out in the great above and the thing in the booth hisses at you, wondering what your deal is.

Time to move on.

You stop at a public access point near the corner of a road.

The demands you send the ShinnCo emergency contact points are as follows:

One negotiator familiar with your case, with authority to bargain. The cart, fully functional, in the usual space. And you'll confirm the cart from a distance, making sure it isn't a fake.

Two hours. They couldn't get an identical fake, with heat generating machinery of the same signature inside in that time.

Or else?

Or else you have time enough to go hunting before the countdown hits the last second.

You'll need a hatchet, for starters.

It's a metaphorical high noon. They're not going to back off, and neither are you. The first sign of weakness is death. You're locked in, no turning back.

They set a nice trap. The gyro stand is up, and what looks to be a middle-aged man stands there. He isn't putting much into the façade, half-heartedly telling interested passersby that he's out of flatbread.

You spot the three snipers on balconies above.

Two men in doors nearby, lounging.

Four pedestrians.

One by one would take far too long, so you steal a bubble cab.

Even the new gyro guy doesn't spot you until you swerve the stolen machine off the road and slam into the cart. Flour, flatbread, meat, and sauces explode into the air. They drip off the door as you swing it up and open, using it for cover as you knock the stunned man out with a flick of your wrist, and pull him into the car.

The shots start. Silent insect-like buzzes and then explosions of concrete.

The glass windows of the cab explode, the seats kick up leather and stuffing. In addition to the glass splinters buried in your face, the concrete shards ripping your overcoat apart, they hit you in the thigh, and then again in a foot.

Keep moving.

You grab the hatchet and smash the cart apart while keeping low, and pull out what you need. Your forearm gets hit, bone splitting out of the skin and causing waves of pain and nausea until things inside your body decide the pain is getting in the way of your ability to function.

The cab can barely hold everything. Glass bites you in the ass as you sit down and barrel out of there.

Engine smoking, tires flopping, it lasts long enough to get you deep into an alley.

The gyro man is coughing blood and dying in the back thanks to a well-aimed shot to the stomach. What you really want to do is get to work on him, make him forget about *that* pain and worry about a whole new universe of hurt. Maybe it will help you forget about yours.

Instead you work on bandaging your own wounds with strips of fabric torn off the overcoat and watch him struggle to stay conscious.

His eyes dilate, mouth drops open.

"I know about your memories," he croaks.

"You the negotiator?" You hadn't expected them to actually put him next to the cart. He ignores that, moves on.

"You don't have any. You never had any," he says quickly. "You came to ShinnCo looking for ways to reverse the process. But you were state of the art. Recent government surplus, useless after the Pacification. If ShinnCo didn't claim you, some other corporation would. So they screwed you over."

"I can't help you," you say. Even if an ambulance got here in time he wouldn't make it back.

The man closes his eyes and groans. The inside of the cab smells of shit from his ruptured stomach. His messy hands are both folded over, he's almost fetal.

"Fuck them," he rasps. "They told me this would be easy. That you wouldn't even get to cross the street."

"They fucked you. They fuck everyone."

You watch him.

"At least you're as fucked as me," he says, eyes still closed. It's almost a whisper now.

You don't bother to tell him the truth.

Another long moment passes.

"They have what you did know on a recording. You had something stored. They have that."

"And do you know what I was?" you ask.

He shakes his head.

Then shudders.

Passes out.

The actual dying will take a while more. You slowly shift, reach to his head, and snap his neck. After rummaging around you pull his wallet out. A picture of a redhead. Girlfriend? Must be, you think. No ring.

So what price are you willing to pay for your self?

Is it worth it?

Time heals all wounds.

In your case, it takes about three weeks before you recover fully.

Now you're standing in front of that same booth, same alien in the pink gas, holding out your ticket. You have gotten your photo ID and background check (faked). It warbles behind the security glass.

"Name?"

"Pepper."

"Secondary name?"

You pause.

"Smith."

"The size of your luggage is unusual," it protests.

"It is necessary," you insist. The remains of the important bits of the gyro stand. And some extra devices to shield it from any ShinnCo attempts to make it call home and make your life miserable.

It looks at you.

"Human." The word is unstressed through the speaker. But you know the meaning behind it.

You stare the creature down and wait.

The go-around takes several minutes, but the creature finally tacks on a massive surcharge and lets you through.

Settling into the capsule's launch chair, the long lines of the launch tube visible through the tiny portholes ahead of you, you pull your new overcoat closely around you.

You wonder if Susan can find room for you on her mining ship.

It's a wild non-world out there. One where humans are minorities, alien conglomerates ply the worlds and negotiate with primitives like your own people for their gas giants and extra unused planets. They trade them for space access, advanced technology. Beads and glass many suspect, but not to primitive planets like Earth.

This is your new environment.

ShinnCo you can leave behind.

• • •

You reach your hand up and caress the data amulet hanging from your neck. It is the memory of a sandy beach, your back relaxed against a palm tree. The gentle swish of the wind through leaves and water breaking against rocks at the end of the bay soothes you. That's it. A single memory of a life you once wanted to remember back. ShinnCo put a lot of security around it. Your past is the past.

The chair wraps around your waist and comes down your shoulders. You are the person you make yourself to be.

Fifteen seconds.

You are the person you are now.

The whine of the accelerators reaches a crescendo.

You're not going to look into the past and what you were.

Three seconds.

It really isn't important.

Launch.

THE ZEPPELIN CONDUCTORS' SOCIETY
ANNUAL GENTLEMEN'S BALL
Genevieve Valentine

So hook yourself up to an airship
Strap on your mask and your knife
For the wide open skies are a-calling
And oh, it's a glorious life!

—Conductors Recruitment Advertisement, 1890

• • •

The balloon of a Phoenix-class airship is better than any view from its cabin windows; half a mile of silk pulled taut across three hundred metal ribs and a hundred gleaming spines is a beautiful thing. If your mask filter is dirty you get lightheaded and your sight goes reddish, so it looks as though the balloon is falling in love with you.

When that happens, though, you tap someone to let them know and you go to the back-cabin Underneath and fix your mask, if you've any brains at all. If you're helium-drunk enough to see red, soon you'll be hallucinating and too weak to move, and even if they get you out before you die you'll still spend the rest of your life at a hospital with all the regulars staring at you. That's no life for an airship man.

I remember back when the masks were metal and you'd freeze in the winter, end up with layers of skin that peeled off like wet socks when you went landside and took the mask off. The polymer rubbers are much cleverer.

I've been a conductor for ages; I was conducting on the Majesty in '78 when it was still the biggest ship in the sky—you laugh, but back then people would show up by the hundreds just to watch it fly out of dock. She only had four gills, but she could cut through the air better than a lot of the six-fins, the Laconia too.

They put the Majesty in a museum already, I heard.

Strange to be so old and not feel it. At least the helium keeps us young, for all it turns us spindly and cold. God, when we realized what was happening to us! But they had warned us, I suppose, and it's fathoms better now then it was. Back then the regulars called you a monster if they saw you on the street.

The coin's not bad, either, compared to factory work. They say it's terrible what you end up like, but if you work the air you get pulled like taffy, and if you work in the factory you go deaf as a post; it's always something.

I'm saving a bit for myself for when I'm finished with this life, enough for a little house in the Alps. I need some altitude if I'm going to be landlocked; the air's too heavy down here.

The very first ships were no better than hot-air balloons, and the conductors kept a tiny cabin and had to string themselves outside on cables if something happened. I can't imagine it—useless.

I didn't join up until after they moved conductors inside—it showed they had a lick of sense to put conductors where they could get to things that went wrong, and I'm not fond of looking down from heights.

The engine-shop shifted to airships as soon as they caught on, and I made two thousand ribs before I ever set foot inside a balloon. It makes for a certain confidence going in, which carried me through, thank goodness—I had a hard time with it at first.

You have to be careful how deeply you breathe so the oxygen filter doesn't freeze up on you, and you have to make sure your air tube doesn't get tangled on your tether, or your tether in someone else's. You have to learn how to fling yourself along so that the tether ring slides with you along the spine, and how to hook your fingers quickly into the little holes in the ribs when you have to climb down. You have to learn to deal with the cold.

The sign language I picked up at once. We had that at the factory, too, signals for when we were too far apart or when it was too loud. I'm fond of it; you get used to talking through the masks, and they're all good men in the air, but sometimes it's nice just to keep the quiet.

Captain Carter was very kind those first few months; he was the only Captain I've ever had who would make trips into the balloon from the Underneath just to see how we were getting along. Back then we were all in it together, all still learning how to handle these beautiful birds.

Captains now can hardly be bothered to leave their bridges, but not Carter. Carter knew how to tighten a bolt as fast as any airship man, and he'd float through and shake hands whenever we'd done something well. He had a way of speaking about the Majesty, like a poem sometimes—a clever man. I've tried to speak as he did, but there's not much use for language when we're just bottled up with one another. Once or twice I've seen something sharply, the way he might have seen it—just once or twice.

You won't see his like again. He was of the old kind; he understood what it meant to love the sky like I do.

• • •

"A patient in the profession of Zeppelin conducting has, after very few years of work, advanced Heliosis due to excessive and prolonged exposure to helium within the balloon of an airship. His limbs have grown in length and decreased in musculature, making it difficult for him to comfortably maneuver on the ground for long periods of time. Mild exercise, concurrent with the wearing of an oxygen mask to prevent hyperventilation, alleviates the symptoms in time but has no lasting effect without regular application, which is difficult for conductors to maintain while employed in their vessels.

"Other side effects are phrenological. Skin tightens around the skull. Patient has noticeable growth in those parts of the head dedicated to Concentrativeness, Combativeness, Locality, and Constructiveness. The areas of Amativeness, Form, and Cautiousness are smaller than normal, though it is hard to say if these personality defects are the work of prolonged wearing of conductor's masks or the temperament of the patient. I suspect that in this case time will have to reveal what is yet unknown.

"The Zeppelin is without doubt Man's greatest invention, and the brave men who labor in its depths are indispensable, but it behooves us to remember the story of Icarus and Daedalus; he should proceed wisely, who would proceed well."

—from Doctor Jonathan Grant's
address to the Health Council, April 1895

• • •

The Captains' Union set up the first Society for us, in London, and a year later in Paris.

They weren't much more comfortable than the hospital rooms where they used to keep us landside, for safety, but of course it was more dignified. Soon we managed to organize ourselves and put together the Zeppelin Conductors' Society, and we tithed our own wages for the dues to fix the buildings up a bit.

Now you can fly to any city with an airdock and know there's a place for you to sleep where no one will look at you sidelong. You can get a private room, even, with a bath in the middle big enough to hold you; it's horrid how long your limbs get when you're in helium nine days in ten, and there's not much dignity in trying to wash with your legs sticking two feet out of the bath.

And it's good sense to have a place you can go straight away; regulars don't like to see you wandering about, sometimes. Most times. I understand.

• • •

WHAT TO DO WHEN YOU SEE A CONDUCTOR

1. Do not panic; he is probably as wary of you as you are of him. He will pose no threat if not provoked.

2. Do not stare; scrutiny is vulgar.

3. Offer a small nod when you pass, as you would to another gentlemen; it pleases them.

4. Avoid smaller streets between airship docks and the local Conductor's Society. The conductor is, in general, a docile creature, but one can never be sure what effects the helium has had on his temperament.

—Public Safety Poster, 1886

• • •

January 1, 1900

PARIS—Polaris was eclipsed last night: not by any cosmic rival, but by a man-made beauty. The Laconia, a Phoenix-class feat of British engineering that has become the envy of the world, never looked more beautiful than on its evening flight to Paris as we began a momentous New Year.

Captain Richard Marks, looking every inch the matinee hero, guided the ship safely through the night as the passengers within lit up the sky with conversation and music, accompanied by a champagne buffet. Miss Marie Dawlish, the English Lark, honored the company with a song which it is suspected struck the heart of a certain airship Captain who stepped away from the bridge in time for the performance. Though we at the Daily are not prognosticators, we believe that the coming year may be one of high romance for Captain Marks, who touched down back in London with a gentle landing, and no doubt a song in his heart.

• • •

The Societies have the Balls each year for New Year's, which is great fun. It's ripping good food, and sometimes someone comes in a full evening suit and we can all have a laugh at them; it's an expensive round of tailoring to wear just once a year. You know just by looking that they who dressed up had wanted to be Captains and fallen short. Poor boys. I wouldn't be a Captain for all the gold in Araby, though perhaps when you're young you don't realize how proud and empty the Captains end up.

You don't meet a lot of ladies in the air, of course, and it's what all the lads miss most. For the London Ball they always manage to find some with the money from the dues—sweet girls who don't mind a chat. They have to be all right with sitting and talking. The Annual Gentlemen's Ball isn't much of a dance. The new conductors, the ones who have only stretched the first few inches, try a dance or two early on to give the musicians something to do. The rest of us have given in to gravity when we're trapped on the ground. We catch up with old mates and wait for a chance to ask a girl upstairs, if we're brave enough.

Sometimes we even get conductors in from other places—Russia, sometimes, or once from China. God, that was a night! What strange ideas they have about navigation! But he was built like an airship man, and from the red skin round his eyes we could tell he'd paid his dues in the helium, so we poured him some Scotch and made him welcome. If we aren't kind to each other, who will be kind to us?

• • •

The Most Elegant Airlines Choose *ORION* Brand Masks!

Your conductors deserve masks that are **SAFE, COMFORTABLE,** and **STYLISH**. Orion has patented its unique India-Rubber polymer that is both flexible and airtight, ensuring the safest and most comfortable fit for your conductors. The oculars are green-tinted for sharper vision at night, and larger in diameter than any other brand, so conductors see more than ever before. Best of all, our filter-tank has an oxygen absorption rate of nearly Ninety Percent - the best in the world!

Swiss-made, British-tested, **CONDUCTOR-APPROVED**.

Soar with confidence among the stars—aim always for **ORION**.

—Orion Airship Supply Catalog, 1893

• • •

We were airside the last night of 1899, the night of the Gentlemen's Ball.

We had been through a bad wind that day, and all of us were spread out tightening rivets on the ribs, signaling quietly back and forth. I don't know what made Anderson agree to sign us on for the evening flight—he must have wanted the Ball as much as the rest of us—and I was in a bit of a sulk, feeling like Cinderella. It was a cold night, cold even in the balloon, and I was wishing for nothing but a long bath and a long sleep.

Then Captain Marks shoved the woman into the balloon.

She was wearing a worn-out orange dress, and a worn-out shawl that fell away from her at once, and even as the captain clipped her to the line she hung limp, worn-out all over. He'd been at her for a while.

I still don't know where he found her, what they did to her, what she thought in the first moments as they carried her towards the balloon.

"Got some leftovers for you," the Captain shouted through his mask, "a little Gentlemen's Ball for you brave boys. Enjoy!"

Then he was gone, spinning the lock shut behind him, closing us in with her.

I could feel the others hooking onto a rib or a spine, pushing off, hurrying over. The men in the aft might not have even seen it happen. I never asked them. Didn't want to know.

I was closest to her, fifty feet, maybe. Through the mask I could see the buttons missing on the front of her dress, the little cuts in her fisted hands.

She wore a mask, too. Her hair was tangled in it.

She was terrified—shaking so hard that I worried her mask would come loose—but she didn't scrabble at her belt: too clever for that, I suppose. I was worried for her—if you weren't used to the helium it was painful to breathe for very long, she needed to get back Underneath. God only knew how long that second-rate mask would hold.

Even as Anderson hooked onto a spine to get to her she was shoving off—not to the locked porthole (there was no hope for her there), but straight out to the ribs, clawing at the stiff silk of the balloon.

We all scrambled for her.

I don't know how she cut the silk—Bristol said it must have been a knife, but I can't imagine they would have let her keep one. I think she must have used the hook of her little earring, which is the worst of it, somehow.

The balloon shuddered as the first rush of helium was sucked into the sky outside; she clenched one fist around the raw edge of the silk as she unhooked herself from the tether. The air caught her, dragging at her feet, and she grasped for purchase against the fabric. She cried out, but the mask swallowed the noise.

I was the closest; I pushed off.

The other conductors were shouting for her not to be foolish; they shouted that it was a misunderstanding, that she would be all right with us.

As I came closer I held out my hands to her so she could take hold, but she shrank back, kicking at me with one foot, the boot half-fastened.

My reflection was distorted in the round eyes of her mask—a spindly monster enveloping her in the half-dark, my endless arms struggling to pull her back in.

What else could she do?

She let go.

My sight lit up from the rush of oxygen, and in my view she was a flaming June in a bottle-green night, falling with her arms outstretched like a bird until she was too small to be seen, until every bright trace of her was gone.

For a moment no one moved, then the rails shuddered under us as the gills fanned out, and we slowed.

Anderson said, "We're coming up on Paris."

"Someone should tell them about the tear," said Bristol.

"Patch it from here," Anderson said. "We'll wait until Vienna."

In Vienna they assumed all conductors were lunatics, and they would ask no questions about a tear that only human hands could make.

I heard the first clangs of the anchor-hooks latching onto the outer hull of the Underneath before the church bells rang in the New Year. Beneath us, the passengers shouted "Hip, hip, hurrah! Hip, hip, hurrah!"

That was a sad year.

• • •

Once I was land-bound in Dover. The Conductor's Society there is so small I don't think ten men could fit in it. It wasn't a bad city (I had no trouble with the regulars on my way from the dock), but it was so horribly hot and cramped that I went outside just to have enough room to stretch out my arms, even heavy as they were with the Earth pulling at them.

A Falcon-class passed overhead, and I looked up just as it crossed the harvest moon; for a moment the balloon was illuminated orange, and I could see the conductors skittering about inside of it like spiders or shadow puppets, like moths in a lamp.

I watched it until it had passed the moon and fallen dark again, the lamp extinguished.

It's a glorious life, they say.

* Reprinted in *The Best Science Fiction and Fantasy of the Year, Vol. 5*, edited by Jonathan Strahan

"...FOR A SINGLE YESTERDAY"
George R. R. Martin

Keith was our culture, what little we had left. He was our poet and our troubadour, and his voice and his guitar were our bridges to the past. He was a time-tripper too, but no one minded that much until Winters came along.

Keith was our memory. But he was also my friend.

He played for us every evening after supper. Just beyond sight of the common house, there was a small clearing and a rock he liked to sit on. He'd wander there at dusk, with his guitar, and sit down facing west. Always west; the cities had been east of us. Far east, true, but Keith didn't like to look that way. Neither did the rest of us, to tell the truth.

Not everybody came to the evening concerts, but there was always a good crowd, say three-fourths of the people in the commune. We'd gather around in a rough circle, sitting on the ground or lying in the grass by ones and twos. And Keith, our living hi-fi in denim and leather, would stroke his beard in vague amusement and begin to play.

He was good, too. Back in the old days, before the Blast, he'd been well on his way to making a name for himself. He'd come to the commune four years ago for a rest, to check up on old friends and get away from the musical rat race for a summer. But he'd figured on returning.

Then came the Blast. And Keith had stayed. There was nothing left to go back to. His cities were graveyards full of dead and dying, their towers melted tombstones that glowed at night. And the rats—human and animal—were everywhere else.

In Keith, those cities still lived. His songs were all of the old days, bitter-sweet things full of lost dreams and loneliness. And he sang them with love and longing. Keith would play requests, but mostly he stuck to his kind of music. A lot of folk, a lot of folk-rock, and a few straight rock things and show tunes. Lightfoot and Kristofferson and Woody Guthrie were particular favorites. And once in a while he'd play his own compositions, written in the days before the Blast. But not often.

Two songs, though, he played every night. He always started with "They Call the Wind Maria" and ended with "Me and Bobby McGee." A few of us got tired of the ritual, but no one ever objected. Keith seemed to think the songs fit us, somehow, and nobody wanted to argue with him.

Until Winters came along, that is. Which was in a late-fall evening in the fourth year after the Blast.

His first name was Robert, but no one ever used it, although the rest of us were all on a first name basis. He'd introduced himself as Lieutenant Robert Winters the evening he arrived, driving up in a jeep with two other men. But his Army didn't exist anymore, and he was looking for refuge and help.

That first meeting was tense. I remember feeling very scared when I heard the jeep coming, and wiping my palms on my jeans as I waited. We'd had visitors before. None of them very nice.

I waited for them alone. I was as much a leader as we had in those days. And that wasn't much. We voted on everything important, and nobody gave orders. So I wasn't really a boss, but I was a greeting committee. The rest scattered, which was good sense. Our last visitors had gone in big for slugging people and raping the girls. They'd worn black-and-gold uniforms and called themselves the Sons of the Blast. A fancy name for a rat pack. We called them SOB's too, but for other reasons.

Winters was different, though. His uniform was the good ol' U.S. of A. Which didn't prove a thing, since some Army detachments are as bad as the rat packs. It was our own friendly Army that went through the area in the first year after the Blast, scorching the towns and killing everyone they could lay their hands on.

I don't think Winters was part of that, although I never had the courage to flat-out ask him. He was too decent. He was big and blond and straight, and about the same age as the rest of us. And his two "men" were scared kids, younger than most of us in the commune. They'd been through a lot, and they wanted to join us. Winters kept saying that he wanted to help us rebuild.

We voted them in, of course. We haven't turned anyone away yet, except for a few rats. In the first year, we even took in a half-dozen citymen and nursed them while they died of radiation burns.

Winters changed us, though, in ways we never anticipated. Maybe for the better. Who knows? He brought books and supplies. And guns, too, and two men who knew how to use them. A lot of the guys on the commune had come there to get away from guns and uniforms, in the days before the Blast. So Pete and Crazy Harry took over the hunting, and defended us against the rats that drifted by from time to time. They became our police force and our army.

And Winters became our leader.

I'm still not sure how that happened. But it did. He started out making suggestions, moved on to leading discussions, and wound up giving orders. Nobody objected much. We'd been drifting ever since the Blast, and Winters gave us a direction. He had big ideas, too. When I was spokesman, all I worried about was getting us through until tomorrow. But Winters wanted to rebuild. He wanted to build a generator, and hunt for more survivors, and gather them together into a sort of village. Planning was his bag. He had big dreams for the day after tomorrow, and his hope was catching.

I shouldn't give the wrong impression, though. He wasn't any sort of a tin tyrant. He led us, yeah, but he was one of us, too. He was a little different from us, but not *that* different, and he became a friend in time. And he did his part to fit in. He even let his hair get long and grew a beard.

Only Keith never liked him much.

Winters didn't come out to concert rock until he'd been with us over a week. And when he did come, he stood outside the circle at first, his hands shoved into his pockets. The rest of us were lying around as usual, some singing, some just listening. It was a bit chilly that night, and we had a small fire going.

Winters stood in the shadows for about three songs. Then, during a pause, he walked closer to the fire. "Do you take requests?" he asked, smiling uncertainly.

I didn't know Winters very well back then. But I knew Keith. And I tensed a little as I waited for his answer.

But he just strummed the guitar idly and stared at Winters' uniform and his short hair. "That depends," he said at last. "I'm not going to play 'Ballad of the Green Berets,' if that's what you want."

An unreadable expression flickered over Winters' face. "I've killed people, yes," he said. "But that doesn't mean I'm proud of it. I wasn't going to ask for that."

Keith considered that, and looked down at his guitar. Then, seemingly satisfied, he nodded and raised his head and smiled. "Okay," he said. "What do you want to hear?"

"You know 'Leavin' on a Jet Plane'?" Winters asked.

The smile grew. "Yeah. John Denver. I'll play it for you. Sad song, though. There aren't any jet planes anymore, Lieutenant. Know that? 's true. You should stop and think why."

He smiled again, and began to play. Keith always had the last word when he wanted it. Nobody could argue with his guitar.

A little over a mile from the common house, beyond the fields to the west, a little creek ran through the hills and the trees. It was usually dry in the summer and the fall, but it was still a nice spot. Dark and quiet at night, away from the noise and the people. When the weather was right, Keith would drag his sleeping bag out there and bunk down under a tree. Alone.

That's also where he did his timetripping.

I found him there that night, after the singing was over and everyone else had gone to bed. He was leaning against his favorite tree, swatting mosquitoes and studying the creekbed.

I sat down next to him. "Hi, Gary," he said, without looking at me.

"Bad times, Keith?" I asked.

"Bad times, Gary," he said, staring at the ground and idly twirling a fallen leaf. I watched his face. His mouth was taut and expressionless, his eyes hooded.

I'd known Keith for a long time. I knew enough not to say anything. I just sat next to him in silence, making myself comfortable in a pile of fresh-fallen leaves. And after a while he began to talk, as he always did.

"There ought to be water," he said suddenly, nodding at the creek. "When I was a kid, I lived by a river. Right across the street. Oh, it was a dirty little river in a dirty little town, and the water was as polluted as all hell. But it was still water. Sometimes, at night, I'd go over to the park across the street, and sit on a bench, and watch it. For hours, sometimes. My mother used to get mad at me."

He laughed softly. "It was pretty, you know. Even the oil slicks were pretty. And it helped me think. I miss that, you know. The water. I always think better when I'm watching water. Strange, right?"

"Not so strange," I said.

He still hadn't looked at me. He was still staring at the dry creek, where only darkness flowed now. And his hands were tearing the leaf into pieces. Slow and methodical, they were.

"Gone now," he said after a silence. "The place was too close to New York. The water probably glows now, if there is any water. Prettier than ever, but I can't go back. So much is like that. Every time I remember something, I have to remember that it's gone now. And I can't go back, ever. To anything. Except . . . except with that . . . " He nodded toward the ground between us. Then he finished with the leaf, and started another.

I reached down by his leg. The cigar box was where I expected it. I held it in both hands, and flipped the lid with my thumbs. Inside, there was the needle, and maybe a dozen small bags of powder. The powder looked white in the starlight. But seen by day, it was pale, sparkling blue.

I looked at it and sighed. "Not much left," I said.

Keith nodded, never looking. "I'll be out in a month, I figure." His voice sounded very tired. "Then I'll just have my songs, and my memories."

"That's all you've got now," I said. I closed the box with a snap and handed it to him. "Chronine isn't a time machine, Keith. Just a hallucinogen that happens to work on memory."

He laughed. "They used to debate that, way back when. The experts all said chronine was a memory drug. But they never *took* chronine. Neither have you, Gary. But I know. I've timetripped. It's not memory. It's more. You go back, Gary, you really do. You live it again, whatever it was. You can't change anything, but you know it's real, all the same."

He threw away what was left of his leaf, and gathered his knees together with his arms. Then he put his head atop them and looked at me. "You ought to timetrip someday, Gary. You really ought to. Get the dosage right, and you can pick your yesterday. It's not a bad deal at all."

I shook my head. "If I wanted to timetrip, would you let me?"

"No," he said, smiling but not moving his head. "I found the chronine. It's mine. And there's too little left to share. Sorry, Gary. Nothing personal, though. You know how it is."

"Yeah," I said. "I know how it is. I didn't want it anyway."

"I knew that," he said.

Ten minutes of thick silence. I broke it with a question. "Winters bother you?"

"Not really," he said. "He seems okay. It was just the uniforms, Gary. If it wasn't for those damn bastards in uniform and what they did, I *could* go back. To my river, and my singing."

"And Sandi," I said.

His mouth twisted into a reluctant smile. "And Sandi," he admitted. "And I wouldn't even need chronine to keep my dates."

I didn't know what to say to that. So I didn't say anything. Finally, wearying, Keith slid forward a little, and lay back under the tree. It was a clear night. You could see the stars through the branches.

"Sometimes, out here at night, I forget," he said softly, more to himself than to me. "The sky still looks the same as it did before the Blast. And the stars don't know the difference. If I don't look east, I can almost pretend it never happened."

I shook my head. "Keith, that's a game. It *did* happen. You can't forget that. You know you can't. And you can't go back. You know that, too."

"You don't listen, do you, Gary? I *do* go back. I really do."

"You go back to a dream world, Keith. And it's dead, that world. You can't keep it up. Sooner or later you're going to have to start living in reality."

Keith was still looking up at the sky, but he smiled gently as I argued. "No, Gary. You don't see. The past is as real as the present, you know. And when the present is bleak and empty, and the future more so, then the only sanity is living in the past."

I started to say something, but he pretended not to hear. "Back in the city, when I was a kid, I never saw this many stars," he said, his voice distant. "The first time I got into the country, I remember how shocked I was at all the extra stars they'd gone and stuck in my sky." He laughed softly. "Know when that was? Six years ago, when I was just out of school. Also last night. Take your pick. Sandi was with me, both times."

He fell silent. I watched him for a few moments, then stood up and brushed myself off. It was never any use. I couldn't convince him. And the saddest part of it was, I couldn't even convince myself. Maybe he was right. Maybe, for him, that was the answer.

"You ever been in the mountains?" he asked suddenly. He looked up at me quickly, but didn't wait for an answer. "There was this night, Gary—in Pennsylvania, in the mountains. I had this old beat-up camper, and we were driving through, bumming it around the country.

"Then, all of a sudden, this fog hit us. Thick stuff, gray and rolling, all kind of mysterious and spooky. Sandi loved stuff like that, and I did too, kind of. But it was hell to drive through. So I pulled off the road, and we took out a couple of blankets and went off a few feet.

"It was still early, though. So we just lay on the blankets together, and held each other, and talked. About us, and my songs, and that great fog, and our trip, and her acting, and all sorts of things. We kept laughing and kissing, too, although I don't remember what we said that was so funny. Finally, after an hour or so, we undressed each other and made love on the blankets, slow and easy, in the middle of that dumb fog."

Keith propped himself up on an elbow and looked at me. His voice was bruised, lost, hurt, eager. And lonely. "She was beautiful, Gary. She really was. She never liked me to say that, though. I don't think she believed it. She liked me to tell her she was pretty. But she was more than pretty. She *was* beautiful. All warm and soft and golden, with red-blond hair and these dumb eyes that were either green or gray, depending on her mood. That night they were gray, I think. To match the fog." He smiled, and sank back, and looked up at the stars again.

"The funniest thing was the fog," he said. Very slowly. "When we'd finished making love, and we lay back together, the fog was gone. And the stars were out, as bright as tonight. The stars came out for us. The silly goddamn voyeuristic stars came out to watch us make it. And I told her that, and we laughed, and I held her warm against me. And she went to sleep in my arms, while I lay there and looked at stars and tried to write a song for her."

"Keith . . . " I started.

"Gary," he said. "I'm going back there tonight. To the fog and the stars and my Sandi."

"Damnit, Keith," I said. "Stop it. You're getting yourself hooked."

Keith sat up again and began unbuttoning his sleeve. "Did you ever think," he said, "that maybe it's not the drug that I'm addicted to?" And he smiled very broadly, like a cocky, eager kid.

Then he reached for his box, and his timetrip. "Leave me alone," he said.

That must have been a good trip. Keith was all smiles and affability the next day, and his glow infected the rest of us. The mood lasted all week. Work seemed to go faster and easier than usual, and the nightly song sessions were as boisterous as I can remember them. There was a lot of laughter, and maybe more honest hope than we'd had for quite a while.

I shouldn't give Keith all the credit, though. Winters was already well into his suggestion-making period, and things were happening around the commune. To begin with, he and Pete were already hard at work building another house—a cabin off to the side of the common house. Pete had hooked up with one of the girls, and I guess he wanted a little more privacy. But Winters saw it as the first step toward the village he envisioned.

That wasn't his only project, either. He had a whole sheaf of maps in his jeep, and every night he'd drag someone off to the side and pore over them by candlelight, asking all sorts of questions. He wanted to know which areas we'd searched for survivors, and which towns might be worth looting for supplies, and where the rat packs liked to run, and that sort of thing. Why? Well, he had some "search expeditions" in mind, he said.

There was a handful of kids on the commune, and Winters thought we ought to organize a school for them, to replace the informal tutoring they'd been getting. Then he thought we ought to build a generator and get the electricity going again. Our medical resources were limited to a good supply of drugs and medicines; Winters thought that one of us should quit the fields permanently and train himself as a village doctor. Yeah, Winters had a lot of ideas, all right. And a good portion of 'em were pretty good, although it was clear that the details were going to require some working out.

Meanwhile, Winters had also become a regular at the evening singing. With Keith in a good mood, that didn't pose any real problems. In fact, it livened things up a little.

The second night that Winters came, Keith looked at him very pointedly and swung into "Vietnam Rag," with the rest of us joining in. Then he followed it up with "Universal Solider." In between lyrics, he kept flashing Winters this taunting grin.

Winters took it pretty well, however. He squirmed and looked uncomfortable at first, but finally entered into the spirit of the thing and began to smile. Then, when Keith finished, he stood up. "If you're so determined to cast me as the commune's very own friendly reactionary, well I guess I'll oblige," he said. He reached out a hand. "Give me that guitar."

Keith looked curious but willing. He obliged. Winters grabbed the instrument, strummed it a few times uncertainly, and launched into a robust version of "Okie from Muskogee." He played like his fingers were made of stone, and sang worse. But that wasn't the point.

Keith began laughing before Winters was three bars into the song. The rest of us followed suit. Winters, looking very grim and determined, plowed on through to the bitter end, even though he didn't know all the words and had to fake it in spots. Then he did the Marine hymn for an encore, ignoring all the hissing and moaning.

When he was finished, Pete clapped loudly. Winters bowed, smiled, and handed the guitar back to Keith with an exaggerated flourish.

Keith, of course, was not one to be topped easily.

He nodded at Winters, took the guitar, and promptly did "Eve of Destruction."

Winters retaliated with "Welfare Cadillac." Or tried to. Turned out he knew hardly any of the words, so he finally gave that up and settled for "Anchors Aweigh."

That sort of thing went on all night, as they jousted back and forth, and everybody else sat around laughing. Well, actually we did more than laugh. Generally we had to help Winters with his songs, since he didn't really know any of them all the way through. Keith held his own without us, of course.

It was one of the more memorable sessions. The only thing it really had in common with Keith's usual concerts was that it began with "They Call the Wind Maria," and ended with "Me and Bobby McGee."

But the next day, Keith was more subdued. Still some kidding around between him and Winters, but mostly the singing slipped back into the older pattern. And the day after, the songs were nearly all Keith's kind of stuff, except for a few requests from Winters, which Keith did weakly and halfheartedly.

I doubt that Winters realized what was happening. But I did, and so did most of the others. We'd seen it before. Keith was getting down again. The afterglow from his latest timetrip was fading. He was getting lonely and hungry and restless. He was itching, yet again, for his Sandi.

Sometimes, when he got that way, you could almost see the hurt. And if you couldn't see it, you could hear it when he sang. Loud and throbbing in every note.

Winters heard it too. He'd have had to be deaf to miss it. Only I don't think he understood what he heard, and I know he didn't understand Keith. All he knew was the anguish he heard. And it troubled him.

So, being Winters, he decided to do something about it. He came to Keith.

I was there at the time. It was midmorning, and Keith and I had come in from the field for a break. I was sitting on the well with a cup of water in my hand, and Keith was standing next to me talking. You could tell that he was getting ready to timetrip again, soon.

He was very down, very distant, and I was having trouble reaching him.

In the middle of all this, Winters comes striding up, smiling, in his Army jacket. His house was rising quickly, and he was cheerful about it, and he and Crazy Harry had already mapped out the first of their "search expeditions."

"Hello, men," he said when he joined us at the well. He reached for the water, and I passed my cup.

He took a deep drink and passed it back. Then he looked at Keith. "I enjoy your singing," he said. "I think everybody else does, too. You're very good, really." He grinned. "Even if you are an anarchistic bastard."

Keith nodded. "Yeah, thanks," he said. He was in no mood for fooling around.

"One thing, though, has been bothering me," Winters said. "I figured maybe I could discuss it with you, maybe make a few suggestions. Okay?"

Keith stroked his beard and paid a little more attention. "Okay. Shoot, Colonel."

"It's your songs. I've noticed that most of them are pretty . . . down, let's say. Good songs, sure. But sort of depressing, if you know what I mean. Especially in view of the Blast. You sing too much about the old days, and things we've lost. I don't think that's good for morale. We've got to stop dwelling so much on the past if we're ever going to rebuild."

Keith stared at him, and slumped against the well. "You gotta be kidding," he said.

"No," said Winters. "No, I mean it. A few cheerful songs would do a lot for us. Life can still be good and worthwhile if we work at it. You should tell us that in your music. Concentrate on the things we still have. We need hope and courage. Give them to us."

But Keith wasn't buying it. He stroked his beard, and smiled, and finally shook his head. "No, Lieutenant, no way. It doesn't work like that. I don't sing propaganda, even if it's well-meant. I sing what I feel."

His voice was baffled. "Cheerful songs, well . . . no. I can't. They don't work, not for me. I'd like to believe it, but I can't, you see. And I can't make other people believe if I don't. Life is pretty empty around here, the way I see it. And not too likely to improve. And . . . well, as long as I see it that way, I've got to sing it that way. You see?"

Winters frowned. "Things aren't *that* hopeless," he said. "And even if they were, we can't admit it, or we're finished."

Keith looked at Winters, at me, then down into the well. He shook his head again, and straightened. "No," he said simply, gently, sadly. And he left us at the well to stalk silently in the fields.

Winters watched him go, then turned to me. I offered him more water, but he shook his head. "What do you think, Gary?" he said. "Did I have a point? Or did I?"

I considered the question, and the asker. Winters sounded very troubled and very sincere. And the blond stubble on his chin made it clear that he was trying his best to fit in. I decided to trust him, a little.

"Yes," I said. "I know what you were driving at. But it's not that easy. Keith's songs aren't just songs. They mean things to him."

I hesitated, then continued. "Look, the Blast was hell for everybody, I don't have to tell you that. But most of us out here, we chose this kind of life, 'cause we wanted to get away from the cities and what they stood for. We miss the old days, sure. We've lost people, and things we valued, and a lot that made life joyful. And we don't much care for the constant struggle, or for having to live in fear of the rat packs. Still, a lot of what we valued is right here on the commune, and it hasn't changed that much. We've got the land, and the trees, and each other. And freedom of a sort. No pollution, no competition, no hatred. We like to remember the old days, and the *good* things in the cities—that's why we Like Keith's singing—but now has its satisfactions too.

"Only, Keith is different. He didn't choose this way, he was only visiting. His dreams were all tied up with the cities, with poetry and music and people and noise. And he's lost his world; everything he did and wanted to do is gone. And . . . and well, there was this girl. Sandra, but he called her Sandi. She and Keith lived together for two years, traveled together, did everything together. They only split for a summer, so she could go back to college. Then they were going to join up again. You understand?"

Winters understood. "And then the Blast?"

"And then the Blast. Keith was here, in the middle of nowhere. Sandi was in New York City. So he lost her, too. I think sometimes that if Sandi had been with him, he'd have gotten over the rest. She was the most important part of the world he lost, the world they shared together. With her here, they could have shared a new world and found new beauties and new songs to sing. But she wasn't here, and . . . "

I shrugged.

"Yeah," said Winters solemnly. "But it's been four years, Gary. I lost a lot too, including my wife. But I got over it. Sooner or later, mourning has to stop."

"Yes," I said. "For you, and for me. I haven't lost that much, and you . . . you think that things will be good again. Keith doesn't. Maybe things were *too* good for him in the old days. Or maybe he's just too romantic for his own good. Or maybe he loved harder than we did. All I know is that *his* dream tomorrow is like his yesterday, and mine isn't. I've never found anything I could be that happy with. Keith did, or thinks he did. Same difference. He wants it back."

I drank some more water, and rose. "I've got to get back to work," I said quickly, before Winters could continue the conversation. But I was thoughtful as I walked back to the fields.

There was, of course, one thing I hadn't told Winters, one important thing. The timetripping. Maybe if Keith was forced to settle for the life he had, he'd come out of it. Like the rest of us had done.

But Keith had an option; Keith could go back. Keith still had his Sandi, so he didn't *have* to start over again.

That, I thought, explained a lot. Maybe I should have mentioned it to Winters. Maybe.

Winters skipped the singing that night. He and Crazy Harry were set to leave the next morning, to go searching to the west. They were off somewhere stocking their jeep and making plans.

Keith didn't miss them any. He sat on his rock, warmed by a pile of burning autumn leaves, and out-sung the bitter wind that had started to blow. He played hard and loud, and sang sad. And after the fire went out, and the audience drifted off, he took his guitar and his cigar box and went off toward the creek.

I followed him. This time the night was black and cloudy, with the smell of rain in the air. And the wind was strong and cold. No, it didn't sound like people dying. But it moved through the trees and shook the branches and whipped away the leaves. And it sounded . . . restless.

When I reached the creek, Keith was already rolling up his sleeve.

I stopped him before he took his needle out. "Hey, Keith," I said, laying a hand on his arm. "Easy. Talk first, okay?"

He looked at my hand and his needle, and returned a reluctant nod. "Okay, Gary," he said. "But short. I'm in a rush. I haven't seen Sandi for a week."

I let go his arm and sat down. "I know."

"I was trying to make it last, Gar. I only had a month's worth, but I figured I could make it last longer if I only timetripped once a week." He smiled. "But that's hard."

"I know," I repeated. "But it would be easier if you didn't think about her so much."

He nodded, put down the box, and pulled his denim jacket a little tighter to shut out the wind. "I think too much," he agreed. Then, smiling, he added, "Such men are dangerous."

"Ummm, yeah. To themselves, mostly." I looked at him, cold and huddled in the darkness. "Keith, what will you do when you run out?"

"I wish I knew."

"I know," I said. "Then you'll forget. Your time machine will be broken, and you'll have to live today. Find somebody else and start again. Only it might be easier if you'd start now. Put away the chronine for a while. Fight it."

"Sing cheerful songs?" he asked sarcastically.

"Maybe not. I don't ask you to wipe out the past, or pretend it didn't happen. But try to find something in the present. You know it can't be as empty as you pretend. Things aren't black and white like that. Winters was part right, you know—there *are* still good things. You forget that."

"Do I? What do I forget?"

I hesitated. He was making it hard for me. "Well . . . you still enjoy your singing. You know that. And there could be other things. You used to enjoy writing your own stuff. Why don't you work on some new songs? You haven't written anything to speak of since the Blast."

Keith had picked up a handful of leaves and was offering them to the wind, one by one. "I've thought of that. You don't know how much I've thought of that, Gary. And I've *tried*. But nothing comes." His voice went soft right then. "In the old days, it was different. And you know why. Sandi would sit out in the audience every time I sang. And when I did something new, something of mine, I could see her brighten. If it was good, I'd know it, just from the way she smiled. She was proud of me, and my songs."

He shook his head. "Doesn't work now, Gary. I write a song now, and sing it, and . . . so what? Who cares? You? Yeah, maybe you and a few of the others come up after and say, 'Hey, Keith, I liked that.' But that's not the same. My songs were *important* to Sandi, the same way her acting was important to me. And now my songs aren't important to anyone. I tell myself that shouldn't matter. I should get my own satisfaction from composing, even if no one else does. I tell myself that a lot. But saying it doesn't make it so."

Sometimes I think, right then, I should have told Keith that his songs were the most important thing in the world to me. But hell, they weren't. And Keith was a friend, and I couldn't feed him lies, even if he needed them.

Besides, he wouldn't have believed me. Keith had a way of recognizing truth.

Instead, I floundered. "Keith, you could find someone like that again, if you tried. There are girls in the commune, girls as good as Sandi, if you'd open yourself up to them. You could find someone else."

Keith gave me a calm stare, more chilling than the wind. "I don't need someone else, Gary," he said. He picked up the cigar box, opened it, and showed me the needle. "I've got Sandi."

Twice more that week Keith timetripped. And both times he rushed off with a feverish urgency. Usually he'd wait an hour or so after the singing, and discreetly drift off to his creek. But now he brought the cigar box with him, and left even before the last notes of "Me and Bobby McGee" had faded from the air.

Nobody mentioned anything, of course. We all knew Keith was timetripping, and we all knew he was running out. So we forgave him, and understood. Everybody understood, that is, except Pete, Winters' former corporal. He, like Winters and Crazy Harry, hadn't been filled in yet. But one evening at the singing, I noticed him looking curiously at the cigar box that lay by Keith's feet. He said something to Jan, the girl he'd been sleeping with. And she said something back. So I figured he'd been briefed.

I was too right.

Winters and Crazy Harry returned a week, to the day, after their departure. They were not alone. They brought three young teenagers, a guy and two girls, whom they'd found down west, in company with a group of rats. "In company," is a euphemism, of course. The kids had been slaves. Winters and Crazy had freed them.

I didn't ask what had happened to the rats. I could guess.

There was a lot of excitement that night and the night after. The kids were a little frightened of us, and it took a lot of attention to convince them that things would be different here. Winters decided that they should have their own place, and he and Pete began planning a second new cabin. The first one was nearing its crude completion.

As it turned out, Winters and Pete were talking about more than a cabin. I should have realized that, since I caught Winters looking at Keith very curiously and thoughtfully on at least two occasions.

But I didn't realize it. Like everyone else, I was busy getting to know the newcomers and trying to make them feel at ease. It wasn't simple, that.

So I didn't know what was going on until the fourth evening after Winters' return. I was outside, listening to Keith sing. He'd just barely finished "They Call the Wind Maria," and was about to swing into a second song, when a group of people suddenly walked into the circle. Winters led them, and Crazy Harry was just behind him with the three kids. And Pete was there, with his arm around Jan. Plus a few others who hadn't been at the concert when it started but had followed Winters from the common house.

Keith figured they wanted to listen, I guess. He began to play. But Winters stopped him.

"No, Keith," he said. "Not right now. We've got business to take care of now, while everybody's together. We're going to talk tonight."

Keith's fingers stopped, and the music faded. The only sounds were the wind and the crackle of the nearby burning leaves. Everyone was looking at Winters.

"I want to talk about timetripping," Winters said.

Keith put down his guitar and glanced at the cigar box at the base of concert rock. "Talk," he said.

Winters looked around the circle, studying the impassive faces, as if he was weighing them before speaking. I looked too.

"I've been told that the commune has a supply of chronine," Winters began. "And that you use it for timetripping. Is that true, Keith?"

Keith stroked his beard, as he did when he was nervous or thoughtful. "Yeah," he said.

"And that's the *only* use that's ever been made of this chronine?" Winters said. His supporters had gathered behind him in what seemed like a phalanx.

I stood up. I didn't feel comfortable arguing from the ground. "Keith was the first one to find the chronine," I said. "We were going through the town hospital after the Army had gotten through with it. A few drugs were all that were left. Most of them are in the commune stores, in case we need them. But Keith wanted the chronine. So we gave it to him, all of us. Nobody else cared much."

Winters nodded. "I understand that," he said very reasonably. "I'm not criticizing that decision. Perhaps you didn't realize, however, that there are other uses or chronine besides timetripping."

He paused. "Listen, and try to judge me fairly, that's all I ask," he said, looking at each of us in turn. "Chronine is a powerful drug; it's an important resource, and we need all our resources right now. And timetripping—anyone's timetripping—is an *abuse* of the drug. Not what it was intended for."

That was a mistake on Winters' part. Lectures on drug abuse weren't likely to go over big in the commune. I could feel the people around me getting uptight.

Rick, a tall, thin guy with a goatee who came to the concerts every night, took a poke at Winters from the ground. "Bullshit," he said. "Chronine's time travel, Colonel. Meant to be used for tripping."

"Right," someone else said. "And we gave it to Keith. I don't want to timetrip, but he does. So what's wrong with it?"

Winters defused the hostility quickly. "Nothing," he said. "*If* we had an unlimited supply of chronine. But we don't. Do we, Keith?"

"No," Keith said quietly. "Just a little left."

The fire was reflected in Winters' eyes when he looked at Keith. It made it difficult to read his expression. But his voice sounded heavy. "Keith, I know what those time trips mean to you. And I don't want to hurt you, really I don't. But we need that chronine, all of us."

"How?" That was me. I wanted Keith to give up chronine, but I'd be damned before I'd let it be taken from him. "How do we *need* the chronine?"

"Chronine is not a time machine," Winters said. "It is a memory drug. And there are things we *must* remember." He glanced around the circle. "Is there anyone here who ever worked in a hospital? An orderly? A candy-striper? Never mind. There might be, in a group this size. And they'd have seen things. Somewhere in the back of their skulls they'd *know* things we need to know. I'll bet some of you took shop in high school. I'll bet you learned all sorts of useful things. But how much do you remember? With chronine, you could remember it all. We might have someone here who once learned to make arrows. We might have a tanner. We might have someone who knows how to build a generator. We might have a *doctor!*"

Winters paused and let that sink in. Around the circle, people shifted uneasily and began to mutter.

Finally Winters continued. "If we found a library, we wouldn't burn the books for heat, no matter how cold it got. But we're doing the same thing when we let Keith timetrip. *We're* a library—all of us here, we have books in our heads. And the only way to read those books is with chronine. We should use it to help us remember the things we must know. We should hoard it like a treasure, calculate every recall session carefully, and make sure—make *absolutely* sure—that we don't waste a grain of it."

Then he stopped. A long, long silence followed; for Keith, an endless one. Finally Rick spoke again. "I never thought of that," he said reluctantly. "Maybe you have something. My father was a doctor, if that means anything."

Then another voice, and another; then a chorus of people speaking at once, throwing up half-remembered experiences that might be valuable, might be useful. Winters had struck paydirt.

He wasn't smiling, though. He was looking at me.

I wouldn't meet his eyes. I couldn't. He had a point—an awful, awful point. But I couldn't admit that, I couldn't look at him and nod my surrender. Keith was my friend, and I had to stand by him.

And of all of us in the circle, I was the only one standing. But I couldn't think of anything to say.

Finally Winters' eyes moved. He looked at concert rock. Keith sat there, looking at the cigar box.

The hubbub went on for at least five minutes, but at last it died of its own weight. One by one the speakers glanced at Keith, and remembered, and dropped off into awkward silence. When the hush was complete, Keith rose and looked around, like a man coming out of a bad dream.

"No," he said. His voice was hurt and disbelieving; his eyes moved from person to person. "You can't. I don't . . . don't *waste* chronine. You know that, all of you. I visit Sandi, and that's not wasting. I need Sandi, and she's gone. I have to go back. It's my only way, my time machine." He shook his head.

My turn. "Yes," I said, as forcefully as I could manage. "Keith's right. Waste is a matter of definition. If you ask me, the biggest waste would be sending people back to sleep through college lectures a second time."

Laughter. Then other voices backed me. "I'm with Gary," somebody said. "Keith needs Sandi, and we need Keith. It's simple. I say he keeps the chronine."

"No way," someone else objected. "I'm as compassionate as anyone, but *hell*—how many of our people have died over the last few years 'cause we've bungled it when they needed doctoring? You remember Doug, two years ago? You shouldn't need chronine for that. A bad appendix, and he dies. We butchered him when we tried to cut it out. If there's a chance to prevent that from happening again—even a long shot—I say we gotta take it."

"No guarantee it won't happen anyway," the earlier voice came back. "You have to hit the right memories to accomplish anything, and even *they* may not be as useful as you'd like."

"Shit. We have to *try* . . . "

"I think we have an obligation to Keith . . . "

"I think Keith's got an obligation to *us* . . . "

And suddenly everybody was arguing again, hassling back and forth, while Winters and Keith and I stood and listened. It went on and on, back and forth over the same points. Until Pete spoke.

He stepped around Winters, holding Jan. "I've heard enough of this," he said. "I don't even think we got no argument. Jan here is gonna have my kid, she tells me. Well, damnit, I'm not going to take any chances on her or the kid dying. If there's a way we can learn something that'll make it safer, we take it. Especially I'm not gonna take no chances for a goddamn weakling who can't face up to life. Hell, Keithie here wasn't the only one hurt, so how does *he* rate? I lost a chick in the Blast too, but I'm not begging for chronine to dream her up again. I got a new chick instead. And that's what you better do, Keith."

Keith stood very still, but his fists were balled at his sides. "There are differences, Pete," he said slowly. "Big ones. My Sandi was no chick, for one thing. And I loved her, maybe more than you can ever understand. I know you don't understand pain, Pete. You've hardened yourself to it, like a lot of people, by pretending that it doesn't exist. So you convinced everybody you're a tough guy, a strong man, real independent. And you gave up some of your humanity, too." He smiled, very much in control of himself now, his voice sure and steady. "Well, I won't play that game. I'll cling to my humanity, and fight for it if I must. I loved once, really loved. And now I hurt. And I won't deny either of those things, or pretend that they mean any less to me than they do."

He looked to Winters. "Lieutenant, I want my Sandi, and I won't let you take her away from me. Let's have a vote."

Winters nodded.

It was close, very close. The margin was only three votes. Keith had a lot of friends.

But Winters won.

Keith took it calmly. He picked up the cigar box, walked over, and handed it to Winters. Pete was grinning happily, but Winters didn't even crack a smile.

"I'm sorry, Keith," he said.

"Yeah," said Keith. "So am I." There were tears on his face. Keith was never ashamed to cry.

There was no singing that night.

• • •

Winters didn't timetrip. He sent men on "search expeditions" into the past, all very carefully planned for minimum risk and maximum reward.

We didn't get any doctor out of it. Rick made three trips back without coming up with any useful memories. But one of the guys remembered some valuable stuff about medicinal herbs after a trip back to a bio lab, and another jaunt recalled some marginally good memories about electricity.

Winters was still optimistic, though. He'd turned to interviewing by then, to decide who should get to use the chronine next. He was very careful, very thorough, and he always asked the right questions. No one went back without his okay. Pending that approval, the chronine was stored in the new cabin, where Pete kept an eye on it.

And Keith? Keith sang. I was afraid, the night of the argument, that he might give up singing, but I was wrong. He couldn't give up song, any more than he could give up Sandi. He returned to concert rock the very next evening, and sang longer and harder than ever before. The night after that he was even better.

During the day, meanwhile, he went about his work with a strained cheerfulness. He smiled a lot, and talked a lot, but he never *said* anything much. And he never mentioned chronine, or timetripping, or the argument.

Or Sandi.

He still spent his nights out by the creek, though. The weather was getting progressively colder, but Keith didn't seem to mind. He just brought out a few blankets and his sleeping bag, and ignored the wind, and the chill, and the increasingly frequent rains.

I went out with him once or twice to sit and talk. Keith was cordial enough. But he never brought up the subjects that really mattered, and I couldn't bring myself to force the conversations to places he obviously didn't want to do. We wound up discussing the weather and like subjects.

These days, instead of his cigar box, Keith brought his guitar out to the creek. He never played it when I was there, but I heard him once or twice from a distance, when I was halfway back to the common house after one of our fruitless talks. No singing, just music. Two songs, over and over again. You know which two.

And after a while, just one. "Me and Bobby McGee." Night after night, alone and obsessed, Keith played that song, sitting by a dry creek in a barren forest. I'd always liked the song, but now I began to fear it, and a shiver would go through me whenever I heard those notes on the frosty autumn wind.

Finally, one night, I spoke to him about it. It was a short conversation, but I think it was the only time, after the argument, that Keith and I ever really reached each other.

I'd come with him to the creek, and wrapped myself in a heavy woolen blanket to ward off the cold, wet drizzle that was dripping from the skies. Keith lay against his tree, half into his sleeping bag, with his guitar on his lap. He didn't even bother to shield it against the damp, which bothered me.

We talked about nothing, until at last I mentioned his lonely creek concerts. He smiled. "You know why I play that song," he said.

"Yeah," I said. "But I wish you'd stop."

He looked away. "I will. After tonight. But tonight I play it, Gary. Don't argue, please. Just listen. The song is all I have left now, to help me think. And I've needed it, 'cause I been thinking a lot."

"I warned you about thinking," I said jokingly.

But he didn't laugh. "Yeah. You were right, too. Or I was, or Shakespeare . . . whoever you want to credit the warning to. Still, sometimes you can't help thinking. It's part of being human. Right?"

"I guess."

"I know. So I think with my music. No water left to think by, and the stars are all covered. And Sandi's gone. Really gone now. You know, Gary . . . if I kept on, day to day, and didn't think so much, I might forget her. I might even forget what she looked like. Do you think Pete remembers his chick?"

"Yes," I said. "And you'll remember Sandi. I'm sure of that. But maybe not quite so much . . . and maybe that's for the best. Sometimes it's good to forget."

Then he looked at me. Into my eyes. "But I don't *want* to forget, Gary. And I won't. I won't."

And then he began to play. The same song. Once. Twice. Three times. I tried to talk, but he wasn't listening. His fingers moved on, fiercely, relentlessly. And the music and the wind washed away my words.

Finally I gave up and left. It was a long walk back to the common house, and Keith's guitar stalked me through the drizzle.

Winters woke me in the common house, shaking me from my bunk to face a grim, gray dawn. His face was even grayer. He said nothing; he didn't want to wake the others, I guess. He just beckoned me outside.

I yawned and stretched and followed him. Just outside the door, Winters bent and handed me a broken guitar.

I looked at it blankly, then up at him. My face must have asked the question.

"He used it on Pete's head," Winters said. "And took the chronine. I think Pete has a mild concussion, but he'll probably be all right. Lucky. He could be dead, real easy."

I held the guitar in my hands. It was shattered, the wood cracked and splintered, several strings snapped. It must have been a hell of a blow. I couldn't believe it. "No," I said. "Keith . . . no, he couldn't . . . "

"It's his guitar," Winters pointed out. "And who else would take the chronine?" Then his face softened. "I'm sorry, Gary. I really am. I think I understand why he did it. Still, I want him. Any idea where he could be?"

I knew, of course. But I was scared. "What . . . what will you do?"

"No punishment," he said. "Don't worry. I just want the chronine back. We'll be more careful next time."

I nodded. "Okay," I said. "But nothing happens to Keith. I'll fight you if you go back on your word, and the others will too."

He just looked at me, very sadly, like he was disappointed that I'd mistrust him. He didn't say a thing. We walked the mile to the creek in silence, me still holding the guitar.

Keith was there, of course. Wrapped in his sleeping bag, the cigar box next to him. There were a few bags left. He'd used only one.

I bent to wake him. But when I touched him and rolled him over, two things hit me. He'd shaved off his beard. And he was very, very cold.

Then I noticed the empty bottle.

We'd found other drugs with the chronine, way back when. They weren't even guarded. Keith had used sleeping pills.

I stood up, not saying a word. I didn't need to explain. Winters had taken it all in very quickly. He studied the body and shook his head.

"I wonder why he shaved?" he said finally.

"I know," I said. "He never wore a beard in the old days, when he was with Sandi."

"Yes," said Winters. "Well, it figures."

"What?"

"The suicide. He always seemed unstable."

"No, Lieutenant," I said. "You've got it all wrong, Keith didn't commit suicide."

Winters frowned. I smiled.

"Look," I said. "If you did it, it would be suicide. You think chronine is only a drug for dreaming. But Keith figured it for a time machine. He didn't kill himself. That wasn't his style. He just went back to his Sandi. And this time, he made sure he stayed there."

Winters looked back at the body. "Yes," he said. "Maybe so." He paused. "For his sake, I hope that he was right."

The years since then have been good ones, I guess. Winters is a better leader than I was. The timetrips never turned up any knowledge worth a damn, but the search expeditions proved fruitful. There are more than two hundred people in town now, most of them people that Winters brought in.

It's a real town, too. We have electricity and a library, and plenty of food. And a doctor—a real doctor that Winters found a hundred miles from here. We got so prosperous that the Sons of the Blast heard about us and came back for a little fun. Winters had his militia beat them off and hunt down the ones who tried to escape.

Nobody but the old commune people remember Keith. But we still have singing and music. Winters found a kid named Ronnie on one of his trips, and Ronnie has a guitar of his own. He's not in Keith's league, of course, but he tries hard, and everybody has fun. And he's taught some of the youngsters how to play.

Only thing is, Ronnie likes to write his own stuff, so we don't hear many of the old songs. Instead we get postwar music. The most popular tune, right now, is a long ballad about how our army wiped out the Sons of the Blast.

Winters says that's a healthy thing; he talks about new music for a new civilization. And maybe he has something. In time, I'm sure, there will be a new culture to replace the one that died. Ronnie, like Winters, is giving us tomorrow.

But there's a price.

The other night, when Ronnie sang, I asked him to do "Me and Bobby McGee." But nobody knew the words.

• HOW TO BECOME A MARS OVERLORD •
Catherynne M. Valente

Welcome, Aspiring Potentates!

We are tremendously gratified at your interest in our little red project, and pleased that you recognize the potential growth opportunities inherent in whole-planet domination. Of course we remain humble in the face of such august and powerful interests, and seek only to showcase the unique and challenging career paths currently available on the highly desirable, iconic, and oxygen-rich landscape of Mars.

Query: Why Mars?

It is a little known fact that every solar system contains Mars. Not Mars itself, of course. But certain suns seem to possess what we might call a habit of Martianness: In every inhabited system so far identified, there is a red planet, usually near enough to the most populous world if not as closely adjacent as our own twinkling scarlet beacon, with proximate lengths of day and night. Even more curious, these planets are without fail named for war-divinities. In the far-off Lighthouse system, the orb Makha turns slowly in the dark, red as the blood of that fell goddess to whom cruel strategists pray, she who nurses two skulls at each mammoth breast. In the Glyph system, closer to home, it is Firialai glittering there like a ripe red fruit, called after a god of doomed charges depicted in several valuable tapestries as a jester dancing ever on the tip of a sword, clutching in each of his seven hands a bouquet of whelp-muskets, bones, and promotions with golden seals. In the Biera-biera system, still yet we may walk the carnelian sands of Uppskil, the officer's patron goddess, with her woolly dactyl-wings weighted down with gorsuscite medals gleaming purple and white. Around her orbit Wydskil and Nagskil, the enlisted man's god and the pilot's mad, bald angel, soaring pale as twin ghosts through Uppskil's emerald-colored sky.

Each red planet owns also two moons, just as ours does. Some of them will suffer life to flourish. We have ourselves vacationed on the several crystal ponds of Volniy and Vernost, which attend the claret equatorial jungles of Raudhr—named, of course, for the four-faced lord of bad intelligence whose exploits have been collected in the glassily perfect septameters of the Raudhrian Eddas. We have flown the lonely black between the satellites on slim-finned ferries decked in greenglow blossoms, sacred to the poorly-informed divine personage. But most moons are kin to Phobos and Deimos, and rotate silently, empty, barren, bright stones, mute and heavy. Many a time we have asked ourselves: Does Mars dwell in a house of mirrors, that same red face repeated over and over in the distance, a quantum hiccup—or is Mars the master, the exemplum, and all the rest copies? Surely the others ask the same riddle. We would all like to claim the primacy of our own specimen—and frequently do, which led to the Astronomer's War some years ago, and truly, no one here can bear to recite that tragic narrative, or else we should wash you all away with our rust-stained tears.

The advantages of these many Marses, scattered like ruby seeds across the known darkness, are clear: In almost every system, due to stellar circumstances beyond mortal control, Mars or Iskra or Lial is the first, best candidate for occupation by the primary world. In every system, the late pre-colonial literature of those primary worlds becomes obsessed with that tantalizing, rose-colored neighbor. Surely some of you are here because your young hearts were fired by the bedside tales of Alim K, her passionate affair with the two piscine princes of red Knisao, and how she waked dread machines in the deep rills of the Knizid mountains in order to possess them? Who among us never read of the mariner Ubaido and his silver-keeled ship, exploring the fell canals of Mikto, their black water filled with eely leviathans whose eyes shone with clusters of green pearls. All your mothers read the ballads of Sollo-Hul to each of you in your cribs, and your infant dreams were filled with gorgeous-green six-legged cricket-queens ululating on the broad pink plains of Podnebesya, their carapaces awash in light. And who did not love Ylla, her strange longings against those bronze spires? Who did not thrill to hear of those scarlet worlds bent to a single will? Who did not feel something stir within them, confronted with those endless crimson sands?

We have all wanted Mars, in our time. She is familiar, she is strange. She is redolent of tales and spices and stones we have never known. She is demure, and gives nothing freely, but from our hearths we have watched her glitter, all of our lives. Of course we want her. Mars is the girl next door. Her desirability is encoded in your cells. It is archetypal. We absolve you in advance.

No matter what system bore you, lifted you up, made you strong and righteous, there is a Mars for you to rule, and it is right that you should wish to rule her. These are perhaps the only certainties granted to a soul like yours.

We invite you, therefore, to commit to memory our simple, two-step system to accomplish your laudable goals, for obviously no paper, digital, or flash materials ought to be taken away from this meeting.

Step One: Get to Mars

It is easier for a camel to pass through the eye of a needle than for a poor man to get to Mars. However, to be born on a bed of gems leads to a certain laziness of the soul, a kind of muscular weakness of the ambition, a subtle sprain in the noble faculties. Not an original observation, but repetition proves the axiom. Better to excel in some other field, for the well-rounded overlord is a blessing to all. Perhaps micro-cloning, or kinetic engineering. If you must, write a novel, but only before you depart, for novels written in the post-despotic utopia you hope to create may be beloved, but will never be taken seriously by the literati.

Take as your exemplum the post-plastic retroviral architect Helix Fo. The Chilean wunderkind was born with ambition in his mouth, and literally stole his education from an upper-class boy he happened upon in a dark alley. In exchange for his life, the patriarch agreed to turn over all his books and assignments upon completion, so that Fo could shadow his university years. For his senior project, Fo locked his erstwhile benefactor in a basement and devoted himself wholly to the construction of the Parainfluenza Opera House in Santiago, whose translucent spires even now dominate that skyline. The wealthy graduate went on to menial labor in the doctoral factories much chagrined while young Fo swam in wealth and fame, enough to purchase three marriage rights, including one to an aquatic Verqoid androgyne with an extremely respectable feather ridge. By his fortieth birthday, Fo had also purchased through various companies the better part of the Atlantic Ocean, whereupon he began breeding the bacterial island which so generously hosts us tonight, and supplies our salads with such exquisite yersinia radishes. Since, nearly all interplanetary conveyances have launched from Fo's RNA platform, for he charged no tariffs but his own passage, in comfort and grace. You will, of course, remember Fo as the first All-Emperor of Mars, and his statue remains upon the broad Athabasca Valles.

Or, rather, model yourself upon the poetess Oorm Nineteen Point Aught-One of Mur, who set the glittering world of Muror letters to furious clicking and torsioning of vocabulary-bladders. You and I may be quite sure there is no lucre at all to be made in the practice of poetry, but the half-butterfly giants of Mur are hardwired for rhyming structures, they cannot help but speak in couplets, sing their simplest greetings in six-part contratenor harmonies. Muror wars exist only between the chosen bards of each country, who spend years in competitive recitings to settle issues of territory. Oorm Nineteen, her lacy wings shot through with black neural braiding, revolted, and became a mistress of free verse. Born in the nectar-soup of the capital pool, she carefully collected words with no natural rhymes like dewdrops, hoarding, categorizing, and collating them. As a child, she haunted the berry-dripping speakeasies where the great luminaries read their latest work. At the age of sixteen, barely past infancy in the long stage-shifts of a Muror, she delivered her first poem, which consisted of two words: *bright. cellar.* Of course, in English these have many rhymes, but in Muror they have none, and her poem may as well have been a bomb detonated on the blue floor of that famous nightclub. Oorm Nineteen found the secret unrhyming world hiding within the delicate, gorgeous structures of Muror, and dragged it out to shine in the sun. But she was not satisfied with fame, nor with her mates and grubs and sweetwater gems. That is how it goes, with those of us who answer the call. Alone in a ship of unrhymed glass she left Mur entirely, and within a year took the red diadem of Etel for her own. Each rival she assassinated died in bliss as she whispered her verses into their perishing ears.

It is true that Harlow Y, scion of the House of Y, ruled the red planet Llym for some time. However, all may admit his rule frayed and frolicked in poor measure, and we have confidence that no one here possesses the makings of a Y hidden away in her jumpsuit. Dominion of the House of Y passed along genetic lines, though this method is degenerate by definition and illegal in most systems. By the time Harlow ascended, generations of Y had been consumed by little more than fashion, public nudity, and the occasional religious fad. What species Y may have belonged to before their massive wealth (derived from mining ore and cosmetics, if the earliest fairy tales of Vyt are to be believed) allowed constant and enthusiastic gene manipulation, voluntary mutation, prostheses, and virtual uplink, no one can truly say. Upon the warm golden sea of Vyt you are House Y or you are prey, and they have forcibly self-evolved out of recognizability. Harlow himself appears in a third of his royal portraits something like a massive winged koala with extremely long, ultra-violet eyelashes and a crystalline torso. Harlow Y inherited majority control over Llym as a child, and administered it much as a child will do, mining and farming for his amusement and personal augmentation. Each of his ultraviolet lashes represented thousands of dead Llymi, crushed to death in avalanches in the mine shafts of the Ypo mountains. But though Harlow achieved overlordship with alacrity and great speed, he ended in assassination, his morning hash-tea and bambun spectacularly poisoned by the general and unanimous vote of the populace.

Mastery of Mars is not without its little lessons.

It is surely possible to be born on a red planet. The Infanza of Hap lived all her life in the ruby jungles of her homeworld. She was the greatest actress of her age; her tails could convey the colors of a hundred complex emotions in a shimmering fall of shades. So deft were her illusions that the wicked old Rey thought her loyal and gentle beyond words even as she sunk her bladed fingers into his belly. But we must assume that if you require our guidance, you did not have the luck of a two-tailed Infanza, and were born on some other, meaner world, with black soil, or blue storms, or sweet rain falling like ambition denied.

Should you be so unfortunate as to originate upon a planet without copious travel options, due to economic crisis, ideological roadblocks, or simply occupying a lamentably primitive place on the technological timeline—have no fear. You are not alone in this. We suggest cryonics—the severed head of Plasticene Bligh ruled successfully over the equine haemovores of A-O-M for a century. He gambled, and gambled hard—he had his brain preserved at the age of twenty, hoping against hope that the ice might deliver him into a world more ready for his rarified soul. Should you visit A-O-M, the great wall of statues bearing her face (the sculptors kindly gave her a horse-body) will speak to what may be grasped when the house pays out.

If cryonics is for some reason unpopular on your world, longevity research will be your bosom friend. Invest in it, nurture it: Only you can be the steward of your own immortality. Even on Earth, Sarai Northe, Third Emira of Valles Marineris, managed to outlive her great-grandchildren by funding six separate think tanks and an Australian diamond mine until one underpaid intern presented her upon her birthday with a cascade of injections sparkling like champagne.

But on some worlds, in some terrible, dark hours, there is no road to Mars, no matter how much the traveling soul might desire it. In patchwork shoes, staring up at a starry night and one gleaming red star among the thousands— sometimes want is not enough. Not enough for Maximillian Bauxbaum, a Jewish baker in Provence, who in his most secret evenings wrote poetry describing such strange blood-colored deserts, such dry canals, a sky like green silk. Down to his children, and to theirs and theirs again, he passed a single ruby, the size of an egg, the size of a world. The baker had been given it as a bribe by a Christian lord, to take his leave of a certain maiden whom he loved, with hair the color of oxide-rich dust, and eyes like the space between moons. Never think on her again, never whisper her name to the walls. Though he kept his promise to an old and bitter death, such a treasure can never be spent, for it is as good as admitting your heart can be bought.

Sarai Northe inherited that jewel, and brought it with her to bury beneath the foundations of the Cathedral of Olympus Mons.

In the end, you must choose a universe that contains yourself and Mars, together and perfect. Helix Fo chose a world built by viruses as tame as songbirds. Oorm Nineteen chose a world gone soft and violet with unrhyming songs. Make no mistake: every moment is a choice, a choice between this world and that one, between heavens teeming with life and a lonely machine grinding across red stone, between staying at home with tea and raspberry cookies and ruling Mars with a hand like grace.

Maximillian Bauxbaum chose to keep his promise. Who is to say it is not that promise, instead of microbial soup, which determined that Mars would be teeming with blue inhuman cities, with seventeen native faiths, by the time his child opened her veins to those terrible champagne-elixirs, and turned her eyes to the night?

Step 2: Become an Overlord

Now we come to the central question at the core of planetary domination: just how is it done? The answer is a riddle. Of course, it would be.

You must already be an overlord in order to become one.

Ask yourself: What is an overlord? Is he a villain? Is she a hero? A cowboy, a priestess, an industrialist? Is he cruel, is he kind, does she rule like air, invisible, indispensable? Is she the first human on Mars, walking on a plain so incomprehensible and barren that she feels her heart empty? Does she scratch away the thin red dust and see the black rock beneath? Does he land in his sleek piscine capsule on Uppskil, so crammed with libraries and granaries that he lives each night in an orgy of books and bread? What does she lord over? The land alone, the people, the belligerent patron gods with their null-bronze greaves ablaze?

Is it true, as Oorm Nineteen wrote, that the core of each red world is a gem of blood compressed like carbon, a hideous war-diamond that yearns toward the strength of a king or a queen as a compass yearns toward north? Or is this only a metaphor, a way in which you can anthropomorphize something so vast as a planet, think of it as something capable of loving you back?

It would seem that the very state of the overlord is one of violence, of domination. Uncomfortable colonial memories arise in the heart like acid—everyone wants to be righteous. Everyone wishes to be loved. What is any pharaonic statue, staring out at a sea of malachite foam, but a plea of the pharaoh to be loved, forever, unassailably, without argument? Ask yourself: Will Mars be big enough to fill the hole in you, the one that howls with such winds, which says the only love sufficient to quiet those winds is the love of a planet, red in tooth, claw, orbit, mass?

We spoke before of how to get to Mars if your lonely planet offers no speedy highway through the skies. Truthfully—and now we feel we can be truthful, here, in the long night of our seminar, when the clicking and clopping of the staff has dimmed and the last of the cane-cream has been sopped up, when the stars have all come out and through the crystal ceiling we can all see one (oh, so red, so red!) just there, just out of reach—truthfully, getting to Mars is icing. It is parsley. To be an overlord is to engage in mastery of a bright, red thing. Reach out your hand—what in your life, confined to this poor grit, this lone blue world, could not also be called Mars? Rage, cruelty, the god of your passions, the terrible skills you possess, that forced obedience from a fiery engine, bellicose children, lines of perfect, gleaming code? These things, too, are Mars. They are named for fell gods, they spit on civilized governance—and they might, if whipped or begged, fill some nameless void that hamstrings your soul. Mars is everywhere; every world is Mars. You cannot get there if you are not the lord and leader of your own awful chariot, if you are not the crowned paladin in the car, instead of the animal roped to it, frothing, mad, driven, but never understanding. We have said you must choose, as Bauxbaum and Oorm and Fo chose—to choose is to understand your own highest excellence, even if that is only to bake bread and keep promises. You must become great enough here that Mars will accept you.

Some are chosen to this life. Mars itself is chosen to it, never once in all its iterations having been ruled by democracy. You may love Mars, but Mars loves a crown, a sceptre, a horn-mooned diadem spangled in ice opals. This is how the bride of Mars must be dressed. Make no mistake—no matter your gender, you are the blushing innocent brought to the bed of a mate as ancient and inscrutable as any deathshead bridegroom out of myth. Did you think that the planet would bend to your will? That you would control it? Oh, it is a lovely word: Overlord. Emperor. Pharaoh. Princeps. But you will be changed by it as by a virus. Mars will fill your empty, abandoned places. But the greatest of them understood their place. The overlord embraces the red planet, but in the end, Mars always triumphs. You will wake in your thousand year reign to discover your hair gone red, your translucent skin covered in dust, your three hearts suddenly fused into a molten, stony core. You will cease to want food, and seek out only cold, black air to drink. You will face the sun and turn, slowly, in circles, for days on end. Your thoughts will slow and become grand; you will see as a planet sees, speak as it speaks, which is to say: the long view, the perfected sentence.

And one morning you will wake up and your mouth will be covered over in stone, but the land beneath you, crimson as a promise, as a ruby, as an unrhymed couplet, as a virus—the land, or the machine, or the child, or the book, will speak with your voice, and you will be an overlord, and how proud we shall be of you, here, by the sea, listening to the dawn break over a new shore.

* Reprinted in *Year's Best SF 16*, edited by David G. Hartwell and Kathryn Cramer

· PATIENT ZERO ·
Tananarive Due

September 19

The picture came! Veronica tapped on my glass and woke me up, and she held it up for me to see. It's autographed and everything! For you, Veronica mouthed at me, and she smiled a really big smile. The autograph says, TO JAY—I'LL THROW A TOUCHDOWN FOR YOU. I couldn't believe it. Everybody is laughing at me because of the way I yelled and ran in circles around my room until I fell on the floor and scraped my elbow. The janitor, Lou, turned on the intercom box outside my door and said, "Kid, you gone crazier than usual? What you care about that picture for?"

Don't they know Dan Marino is the greatest quarterback of all time? I taped the picture to the wall over my bed. On the rest of my wall I have maps of the United States, and the world, and the solar system. I can find Corsica on the map, and the Palau Islands, which most people have never heard of, and I know what order all the planets are in. But there's nothing else on my wall like Dan Marino. That's the best. The other best thing I have is the cassette tape from that time the President called me on the telephone when I was six. He said, "Hi, is Jay there? This is the President of the United States." He sounded just like on TV. My heart flipped, because it's so weird to hear the President say your name. I couldn't think of anything to say back. He asked me how I was feeling, and I said I was fine. That made him laugh, like he thought I was making a joke. Then his voice got real serious, and he said everyone was praying and thinking about me, and he hung up. When I listen to that tape now, I wish I had thought of something else to say. I used to think he might call me another time, but it only happened once, in the beginning. So I guess I'll never have a chance to talk to the President again.

After Veronica gave me my picture of Marino, I asked her if she could get somebody to fix my TV so I can see the football games. All my TV can play is videos. Veronica said there aren't any football games, and I started to get mad because I hate it when they lie. It's September, I said, and there's always football games in September. But Veronica told me the NFL people had a meeting and decided not to have football anymore, and maybe it would start again, but she wasn't sure, because nobody except me was thinking about football. At first, after she said that, it kind of ruined the autograph, because it seemed like Dan Marino must be lying, too. But Veronica said he was most likely talking about throwing a touchdown for me in the future, and I felt better then.

This notebook is from Ms. Manigat, my tutor, who is Haitian. She said I should start writing down my thoughts and everything that happens to me. I said I don't have any thoughts, but she said that was ridiculous. That is her favorite word, ridiculous.

Oh, I should say I'm ten today. If I were in a regular school, I would be in fifth grade like my brother was. I asked Ms. Manigat what grade I'm in, and she said I don't have a grade. I read like I'm in seventh grade and I do math like I'm in fourth grade, she says. She says I don't exactly fit anywhere, but I'm very smart. Ms. Manigat comes every day, except on weekends. She is my best friend, but I have to call her Ms. Manigat instead of using her first name, which is Emmeline, because she is so proper. She is very neat and wears skirts and dresses, and everything about her is very clean except her shoes, which are dirty. Her shoes are supposed to be white, but whenever I see her standing outside of the glass, when she hasn't put on her plastic suit yet, her shoes look brown and muddy.

Those are my thoughts.

September 20

I had a question today. Veronica never comes on Fridays, and the other nurse, Rene, isn't as nice as she is, so I waited for Ms. Manigat. She comes at one. I said, "You know how they give sick children their last wish when they're dying? Well, when Dr. Ben told me to think of the one thing I wanted for my birthday, I said I wanted an autograph from Dan Marino, so does that mean I'm dying and they're giving me my wish?" I said this really fast.

I thought Ms. Manigat would say I was being ridiculous. But she smiled. She put her hand on top of my head, and her hand felt stiff and heavy inside her big glove. "Listen, little old man," she said, which is what she calls me because she says I do so much worrying, "You're a lot of things, but you aren't dying. When everyone can be as healthy as you, it'll be a happy day."

The people here always seems to be waiting, and I don't know what for. I thought maybe they were waiting for me to die. But I believe Ms. Manigat. If she doesn't want to tell me something, she just says, "Leave it alone, Jay," which is her way of letting me know she would rather not say anything at all than ever tell a lie.

October 5

The lights in my room started going on and off again today, and it got so hot I had to leave my shirt off until I went to bed. Ms. Manigat couldn't do her lessons the way she wanted because of the lights not working right. She said it was the emergency generator. I asked her what the emergency was, and she said something that sounded funny: "Same old same old." That was all she said. I asked her if the emergency generator was the reason Dr. Ben took the television out of my room, and she said yes. She said everyone is conserving energy, and I have to do my part, too. But I miss my videos. There is nothing at all to do when I can't watch my videos. I hate it when I'm bored. Sometimes I'll even watch videos I've seen a hundred times, *really* a hundred times. I've seen *Big* with Tom Hanks more times than any other video. I love the part in the toy store with the really big piano keys on the floor. My mom taught me how to play Three Blind Mice on our piano at home, and it reminds me of that. I've never seen a toy store like the one in *Big*. I thought it was just a made-up place, but Ms. Manigat said it was a real toy store in New York.

I miss my videos. When I'm watching them, it's like I'm inside the movie, too. I hope Dr. Ben will bring my TV back soon.

October 22

I made Veronica cry yesterday. I didn't mean to. Dr. Ben said he knows it was an accident, but I feel very sorry, so I've been crying too. What happened is, I was talking to her, and she was taking some blood out of my arm with a needle like always. I was telling her about how me and my dad used to watch Marino play on television, and then all of a sudden she was crying really hard.

She dropped the needle on the floor and she was holding her wrist like she broke it. She started swearing. She said Goddammit, goddammit, goddammit, over and over, like that. I asked her what happened, and she pushed me away like she wanted to knock me over. Then she went to the door and punched the number code really fast and she pulled on the doorknob, but the door wouldn't open, and I heard something in her arm snap from yanking so hard. She had to do the code again. She was still crying. I've never seen her cry.

I didn't know what happened. I mashed my finger on the buzzer hard, but everybody ignored me. It reminded me of when I first came here, when I was always pushing the buzzer and crying, and nobody would ever come for a long time, and they were always in a bad mood when they came.

Anyway, I waited for Ms. Manigat, and when I told her about Veronica, she said she didn't know anything because she comes from the outside, but she promised to find out. Then she made me recite the Preamble to the Constitution, which I know by heart. Pretty soon, for a little while, I forgot about Veronica.

After my lessons, Ms. Manigat left and called me on my phone an hour later, like she promised. She always keeps her promises. My telephone is hooked up so people on the inside can call me, but I can't call anybody, inside or outside. It hardly ever rings now. But I almost didn't want to pick it up. I was afraid of what Ms. Manigat would say.

"Veronica poked herself," Ms. Manigat told me. "The needle stuck through her hot suit. She told Dr. Ben there was sudden movement."

I wondered who made the sudden movement, Veronica or me?

"Is she okay?" I asked. I thought maybe Ms. Manigat was mad at me, because she has told me many times that I should be careful. Maybe I wasn't being careful when Veronica was here.

"We'll see, Jay," Ms. Manigat said. From her voice, it sounded like the answer was no.

"Will she get sick?" I asked.

"Probably, yes, they think so," Ms. Manigat said.

I didn't want her to answer any more questions. I like it when people tell me the truth, but it always makes me feel bad, too. I tried to say I was sorry, but I couldn't even open my mouth.

"It's not your fault, Jay," Ms. Manigat said.

I couldn't help it. I sobbed like I used to when I was still a little kid. "Veronica knew something like this could happen," she said.

But that didn't make anything better, because I remembered how Veronica's face looked so scared inside her mask, and how she pushed me away. Veronica has been here since almost the beginning, before Ms. Manigat came, and she used to smile at me even when nobody else did. When she showed me my picture from Dan Marino, she looked almost as happy as me. I had never seen her whole face smiling like that. She looked so pretty and glad.

I was crying so much I couldn't even write down my thoughts like Ms. Manigat said to. Not until today.

November 4

A long time ago, when I first came here and the TV in my room played programs from outside, I saw the first-grade picture I had taken at school on TV. I always hated that picture because Mom put some greasy stuff in my hair that made me look like a total geek. And then I turned on the TV and saw that picture on the news! The man on TV said the names of everyone in our family, and even spelled them out on the screen. Then, he called me Patient Zero. He said I was the first person who got sick.

But that wasn't really what happened. My dad was sick before me. I've told them that already. He got it away on his job in Alaska. My dad traveled a lot because he drilled for oil, but he came home early that time. We weren't expecting him until Christmas, but he came when it was only September, close to my birthday. He said he'd been sent home because some people on his oil crew got sick. One of them had even died. But the doctor in Alaska had looked at my dad and said he was fine, and then his boss sent him home. Dad was really mad about that. He hated to lose money. Time away from a job was always losing money, he said. He was in a bad mood when he wasn't working.

And the worse thing was, my dad wasn't fine. After two days, his eyes got red and he started sniffling. Then I did, too. And then my mom and brother.

When the man on TV showed my picture and called me Patient Zero and said I was the first one to get sick, that was when I first learned how people tell lies, because that wasn't true. Somebody on my dad's oil rig caught it first, and then he gave it to my dad. And my dad gave it to me, my mom and my brother. But one thing he said was right. I was the only one who got well.

My Aunt Lori came here to live at the lab with me at first, but she wasn't here long, because her eyes had already turned red by then. She came to help take care of me and my brother before my mom died, but probably she shouldn't have done that. She lived all the way in California, and I bet she wouldn't have gotten sick if she hadn't come to Miami to be with us. But even my mom's doctor didn't know what was wrong then, so nobody could warn her about what would happen if she got close to us. Sometimes I dream I'm calling Aunt Lori on my phone, telling her please, please not to come. Aunt Lori and my mom were twins. They looked exactly alike.

After Aunt Lori died, I was the only one left in my whole family.

I got very upset when I saw that news report. I didn't like hearing someone talk about my family like that, people who didn't even know us. And I felt like maybe the man on TV was right, and maybe it was all my fault. I screamed and cried the whole day. After that, Dr. Ben made them fix my TV so I couldn't see the news anymore or any programs from outside, just cartoons and kid movies on video. The only good thing was, that was when the President called me. I think he was sorry when he heard what happened to my family.

When I ask Dr. Ben if they're still talking about me on the news, he just shrugs his shoulders. Sometimes Dr. Ben won't say yes or no if you ask him a question. It doesn't matter, though. I think the TV people probably stopped showing my picture a long time ago. I was just a little kid when my family got sick. I've been here four whole years!

Oh, I almost forgot. Veronica isn't back yet.

November 7

I have been staring at my Dan Marino picture all day, and I think the handwriting on the autograph looks like Dr. Ben's. But I'm afraid to ask anyone about that. Oh, yeah—and yesterday the power was off in my room for a whole day! Same old same old. That's what Ms. M. would say.

November 12

Ms. Manigat is teaching me a little bit about medicine. I told her I want to be a doctor when I grow up, and she said she thinks that's a wonderful idea because she believes people will always need doctors. She says I will be in a good position to help people, and I asked her if that's because I have been here so long, and she said yes.

The first thing she taught me is about diseases. She says in the old days, a long time ago, diseases like typhoid used to kill a lot of people because of unsanitary conditions and dirty drinking water, but people got smarter and doctors found drugs to cure it, so diseases didn't kill people as much anymore. Doctors are always trying to stay a step ahead of disease, Ms. Manigat says.

But sometimes they can't. Sometimes a new disease comes. Or, maybe it's not a new disease, but an old disease that has been hidden for a long time until something brings it out in the open. She said that's how nature balances the planet, because as soon as doctors find cures for one thing, there is always something new. Dr. Ben says my disease is new. There is a long name for it I can't remember how to spell, but most of the time people here call it Virus-J.

In a way, see, it's named after me. That's what Dr. Ben said. But I don't like that.

Ms. Manigat said after my dad came home, the virus got in my body and attacked me just like everyone else, so I got really, really sick for a lot of days. Then, I thought I was completely better. I stopped feeling bad at all. But the virus was already in my brother and my mom and dad, and even our doctor from before, Dr. Wolfe, and Ms. Manigat says it was very *aggressive,* which means doctors didn't know how to kill it.

Everybody wears yellow plastic suits and airtight masks when they're in my room because the virus is still in the air, and it's in my blood, and it's on my plates and cups whenever I finish eating. They call the suits hot suits because the virus is *hot* in my room. Not hot like fire, but dangerous.

Ms. Manigat says Virus-J is extra special in my body because even though I'm not sick anymore, except for when I feel like I have a temperature and I have to lie down sometimes, the virus won't go away. I can make other people sick even when I feel fine, so she said that makes me a carrier. Ms. Manigat said Dr. Ben doesn't know anybody else who's gotten well except for me.

Oh, except maybe there are some little girls in China. Veronica told me once there were some little girls in China the same age as me who didn't get sick either. But when I asked Dr. Ben, he said he didn't know if it was true. And Ms. Manigat told me it might have been true once, but those girls might not be alive anymore. I asked her if they died of Virus-J, and she said no, no, no. Three times. She told me to forget all about any little girls in China. Almost like she was mad.

I'm the only one like me she knows about for sure, she says. The only one left.

That's why I'm here, she says. But I already knew that part. When I was little, Dr. Ben told me about antibodies and stuff in my blood, and he said the reason him and Rene and Veronica and all the other doctors take so much blood from me all the time, until they make purple bruises on my arms and I feel dizzy, is so they can try to help other people get well, too. I have had almost ten surgeries since I have been here. I think they have even taken out parts of me, but I'm not really sure. I look the same on the outside, but I feel different on the inside. I had surgery on my belly a year ago, and sometimes when I'm climbing the play-rope hanging from the ceiling in my room, I feel like it hasn't healed right, like I'm still cut open. Ms. Manigat says that's only in my mind. But it really hurts! I don't hate anything like I hate operations. I wonder if that's what happened to the other little girls, if they kept getting cut up and cut up until they died. Anyway, it's been a year since I had any operations. I keep telling Dr. Ben they can have as much blood as they want, but I don't want anymore operations, please.

Dr. Ben said there's nobody in the world better than me to make people well, if only they can figure out how. Ms. Manigat says the same thing. That makes me feel a little better about Virus-J.

I was happy Ms. Manigat told me all about disease, because I don't want her to treat me like a baby the way everybody else does. That's what I always tell her. I like to know things.

I didn't even cry when she told me Veronica died. Maybe I got all my crying over with in the beginning, because I figured out a long time ago nobody gets better once they get sick. Nobody except for me.

November 14

Today, I asked Ms. Manigat how many people have Virus-J.

"Oh, Jay, I don't know," she said. I don't think she was in the mood to talk about disease.

"Just guess," I said.

Ms. Manigat thought for a long time. Then she opened her notebook and began drawing lines and boxes for me to see. Her picture looked like the tiny brown lines all over an oak-tree leaf. We had a tree called a live oak in our backyard, and my dad said it was more than a hundred years old. He said trees sometimes live longer than people do. And he was right, because I'm sure that tree is still standing in our yard even though my whole family is gone.

"This is how it goes, Jay," Ms. Manigat said, showing me with her pencil-tip how one line branched down to the next. "People are giving it to each other. They don't usually know they're sick for two weeks, and by then they've passed it to a lot of other people. By now, it's already been here four years, so the same thing that happened to your family is happening to a lot of families."

"How many families?" I asked again. I tried to think of the biggest number I could. "A million?"

Ms. Manigat shrugged just like Dr. Ben would. Maybe that meant yes.

I couldn't imagine a million families, so I asked Ms. Manigat if it happened to her family, too, if maybe she had a husband and kids and they got sick. But she said no, she was never married. I guess that's true, because Ms. Manigat doesn't look that old. She won't tell me her age, but she's in her twenties, I think. Ms. Manigat smiled at me, even though her eyes weren't happy.

"My parents were in Miami, and they got it right away," Ms. Manigat said. "Then my sister and nieces came to visit them from Haiti, and they got it, too. I was away working when it happened, and that's why I'm still here."

Ms. Manigat never told me that before.

My family lived in Miami Beach. My dad said our house was too small—I had to share a room with my brother—but my mother liked where we lived because our building was six blocks from the ocean. My mother said the ocean can heal anything. But that can't be true, can it?

My mother wouldn't like it where I am, because there is no ocean and no windows neither. I wondered if Ms. Manigat's parents knew someone who worked on an oil rig, too, but probably not. Probably they got it from my dad and me.

"Ms. Manigat," I said, "Maybe you should move inside like Dr. Ben and everybody else."

"Oh, Jay," Ms. Manigat said, like she was trying to sound cheerful. "Little old man, if I were that scared of anything, why would I be in here teaching you?"

She said she *asked* to be my teacher, which I didn't know. I said I thought her boss was making her do it, and she said she didn't have a boss. No one sent her. She wanted to come.

"Just to meet me?" I asked her.

"Yes, because I saw your face on television, and you looked to me like a one-of-a-kind," she said. She said she was a nurse before, and she used to work with Dr. Ben in his office in Atlanta. She said they worked at the CDC, which is a place that studies diseases. And he knew her, so that was why he let her come teach me.

"A boy like you needs his education. He needs to know how to face life outside," she said.

Ms. Manigat is funny like that. Sometimes she'll quit the regular lesson about presidents and the Ten Commandments and teach me something like how to sew and how to tell plants you eat from plants you don't, and stuff. Like, I remember when she brought a basket with real fruits and vegetables in it, fresh. She said she has a garden where she lives on the outside, close to here. She said one of the reasons she won't move inside is because she loves her garden so much, and she doesn't want to leave it.

The stuff she brought was not very interesting to look at. She showed me some cassava, which looked like a long, twisty tree branch to me, and she said it's good to eat, except it has poison in it that has to be boiled out of the root first and the leaves are poisonous too. She also brought something called akee, which she said she used to eat from trees in Haiti. It has another name in Haiti that's too hard for me to spell. It tasted fine to me, but she said akee can never be eaten before it's opened, or before it's ripe, because it makes your brain swell up and you can die. She also brought different kinds of mushrooms to show me which ones are good or bad, but they all looked alike to me. She promised to bring me other fruits and vegetables to see so I will know what's good for me and what isn't. There's a lot to learn about life outside, she said.

Well, I don't want Ms. Manigat to feel like I am a waste of her time, but I know for a fact I don't have to face life outside. Dr. Ben told me I might be a teenager before I can leave, or even older. He said I might even be a grown man.

But that's okay, I guess. I try not to think about what it would be like to leave. My room, which they moved me to when I had been here six months, is really, really big. They built it especially for me. It's four times as big as the hotel room my mom and dad got for us when we went to Universal Studios in Orlando when I was five. I remember that room because my brother, Kevin, kept asking my dad, "Doesn't this cost too much?" Every time my dad bought us a T-shirt or anything, Kevin brought up how much it cost. I told Kevin to stop it because I was afraid Dad would get mad and stop buying us stuff. Then, when we were in line for the King Kong ride, all by ourselves, Kevin told me, "Dad got fired from his job, stupid. Do you want to go on Welfare?" I waited for Dad and Mom to tell me he got fired, but they didn't. After Kevin said that, I didn't ask them to buy me anything else, and I was scared to stay in that huge, pretty hotel room because I thought we wouldn't have enough money to pay. But we did. And then Dad got a job on the oil rig, and we thought everything would be better.

My room here is as big as half the whole floor I bet. When I run from one side of my room to the other, from the glass in front to the wall in back, I'm out of breath. I like to do that. Sometimes I run until my ribs start squeezing and my stomach hurts like it's cut open and I have to sit down and rest. There's a basketball net in here, too, and the ball doesn't ever touch the ceiling except if I throw it too high on purpose. I also have comic books, and I draw pictures of me and my family and Ms. Manigat and Dr. Ben. Because I can't watch my videos, now I spend a lot of time writing in this notebook. A whole hour went by already. When I am writing down my thoughts, I forget about everything else.

I have decided for sure to be a doctor someday. I'm going to help make people better.

November 29

Thanksgiving was great! Ms. Manigat cooked real bread and brought me food she'd heated up. I could tell everything except the bread and cassava was from a can, like always, but it tasted much better than my regular food. I haven't had bread in a long time. Because of her mask, Ms. Manigat ate her dinner before she came, but she sat and watched me eat. Rene came in, too, and she surprised me when she gave me a hug. She never does that. Dr. Ben came in for a little while at the end, and he hugged me too, but he said he couldn't stay because he was busy. Dr. Ben doesn't come visit me much anymore. I could see he was growing a beard, and it was almost all white! I've seen Dr. Ben's hair when he's outside of the glass, when he isn't wearing his hot suit, and his hair is brown, not white. I asked him how come his beard was white, and he said that's what happens when your mind is overly tired.

I liked having everybody come to my room. Before, in the beginning, almost nobody came in, not even Ms. Manigat. She used to sit in a chair outside the glass and use the intercom for my lessons. It's better when they come in.

I remember how Thanksgiving used to be, with my family around the table in the dining room, and I told Ms. Manigat about that. Yes, she said, even though she didn't celebrate Thanksgiving in Haiti like Americans do, she remembers sitting at the table with her parents and her sister for Christmas dinner. She said she came to see me today, and Rene and Dr. Ben came too, because we are each other's family now, so we are not alone. I hadn't thought of it like that before.

December 1

No one will tell me, not even Ms. M., but I think maybe Dr. Ben is sick. I have not seen him in five whole days. It is quiet here. I wish it was Thanksgiving again.

January 23

I didn't know this before, but you have to be in the right mood to write your thoughts down. A lot happened in the days I missed.

The doctor with the French name is gone now, and I'm glad. He wasn't like Dr. Ben at all. I could hardly believe he was a real doctor, because he always had on the dirtiest clothes when I saw him take off his hot suit outside of the glass. And he was never nice to me—he wouldn't answer at all when I asked him questions, and he wouldn't look in my eyes except for a second. One time he slapped me on my ear, almost for nothing, and his glove hurt so much my ear turned red and was sore for a whole day. He didn't say he was sorry, but I didn't cry. I think he wanted me to.

Oh yeah, and he hooked me up to IV bags and took so much blood from me I couldn't even stand up. I was scared he would operate on me. Ms. Manigat didn't come in for almost a week, and when she finally came, I told her about the doctor taking too much blood. She got really mad. Then I found out the reason she didn't come all those days—he wouldn't let her! She said he tried to bar her from coming. *Bar* is the word she used, which sounds like a prison.

The new doctor and Ms. Manigat do not get along, even though they both speak French. I saw them outside of the glass, yelling back and forth and moving their hands, but I couldn't hear what they were saying. I was afraid he would send Ms. Manigat away for good. But yesterday she told me he's leaving! I told her I was happy, because I was afraid he would take Dr. Ben's place.

No, she told me, there isn't anyone taking Dr. Ben's place. She said the French doctor came here to study me in person because he was one of the doctors Dr. Ben had been sending my blood to ever since I first came. But he was already very sick when he got here, and he started feeling worse, so he had to go. Seeing me was his last wish, Ms. Manigat said, which didn't seem like it could be true because he didn't act like he wanted to be with me.

I asked her if he went back to France to his family, and Ms. Manigat said no, he probably didn't have a family, and even if he did, it's too hard to go to France. The ocean is in the way, she said.

Ms. Manigat seemed tired from all that talking. She said she'd decided to move inside, like Rene, to make sure they were taking care of me properly. She said she misses her garden. The whole place has been falling apart, she said. She said I do a good job of keeping my room clean—and I do, because I have my own mop and bucket and Lysol in my closet—but she told me the hallways are filthy. Which is true, because sometimes I can see water dripping down the wall outside of my glass, a lot of it, and it makes puddles all over the floor. You can tell the water is dirty because you can see different colors floating on top, the way my family's driveway used to look after my dad sprayed it with a hose. He said the oil from the car made the water look that way, but I don't know why it looks that way here. Ms. Manigat said the water smells bad, too.

"It's ridiculous. If they're going to keep you here, they'd damn well better take care of you," Mrs. Manigat said. She must have been really mad, because she never swears.

I told her about the time when Lou came and pressed on my intercom really late at night, when I was asleep and nobody else was around. He was talking really loud like people do in videos when they're drunk. Lou was glaring at me through the glass, banging on it. I had never seen him look so mean. I thought he would try to come into my room but then I remembered he couldn't because he didn't have a hot suit. But I'll never forget how he said, *They should put you to sleep like a dog at the pound.*

I try not to think about that night, because it gave me nightmares. It happened when I was pretty little, like eight. Sometimes I thought maybe I just dreamed it, because the next time Lou came he acted just like normal. He even smiled at me a little bit. Before he stopped coming here, Lou was nice to me every day after that.

Ms. Manigat did not sound surprised when I told her what Lou said about putting me to sleep. "Yes, Jay," she told me, "For a long time, there have been people outside who didn't think we should be taking care of you."

I never knew that before!

I remember a long time ago, when I was really little and I had pneumonia, my mom was scared to leave me alone at the hospital. "They won't know how to take care of Jay there," she said to my dad, even though she didn't know I heard her. I had to stay by myself all night, and because of what my mom said, I couldn't go to sleep. I was afraid everyone at the hospital would forget I was there. Or maybe something bad would happen to me.

It seems like the lights go off every other day now. And I know people must really miss Lou, because the dirty gray water is all over the floor outside my glass and there's no one to clean it up.

February 14

6-4-6-7-2-9-4-3   6-4-6-7-2-9-4-3   6-4-6-7-2-9-4-3

I remember the numbers already! I have been saying them over and over in my head so I won't forget, but I wanted to write them down in the exact right order to be extra sure. I want to know them without even looking.

Oh, I should start at the beginning. Yesterday, no one brought me any dinner, not even Ms. Manigat. She came with a huge bowl of oatmeal this morning, saying she was very sorry. She said she had to look a long time to find that food, and it wore her out. The oatmeal wasn't even hot, but I didn't say anything. I just ate. She watched me eating.

She didn't stay with me long, because she doesn't teach me lessons anymore. After the French doctor left, we talked about the Emancipation Proclamation and Martin Luther King, but she didn't bring that up today. She just kept sighing, and she said she had been in bed all day yesterday because she was so tired, and she was sorry she forgot to feed me. She said I couldn't count on Rene to bring me food because she didn't know where Rene was. It was hard for me to hear her talk through her hot suit today. Her mask was crooked, so the microphone wasn't in front of her mouth where it should be.

She saw my notebook and asked if she could look at it. I said sure. She looked at the pages from the beginning. She said she liked the part where I said she was my best friend. Her face-mask was fogging up, so I couldn't see her eyes and I couldn't tell if she was smiling. I am very sure she did not put her suit on right today.

When she put my notebook down, she told me to pay close attention to her and repeat the numbers she told me, which were 6-4-6-7-2-9-4-3.

I asked her what they were. She said it was the security code for my door. She said she wanted to give the code to me because my buzzer wasn't working, and I might need to leave my room if she overslept and nobody came to bring me food. She told me I could use the same code on the elevator, and the kitchen was on the third floor. There wouldn't be anybody there, she said, but I could look on the shelves, the top ones up high, to see if there was any food. If not, she said I should take the stairs down to the first floor and find the red EXIT sign to go outside. She said the elevator doesn't go to the first floor anymore.

I felt scared then, but she put her hand on top of my head again just like usual. She said she was sure there was plenty of food outside.

"But am I allowed?" I asked her. "What if people get sick?"

"You worry so much, little man," she said. "Only you matter now, my little one-of-a-kind."

But see I'm sure Ms. Manigat doesn't really want me to go outside. I've been thinking about that over and over. Ms. Manigat must be very tired to tell me to do something like that. Maybe she has a fever and that's why she told me how to get out of my room. My brother said silly things when he had a fever, and my father too. My father kept calling me *Oscar*, and I didn't know who Oscar was. My dad told us he had a brother who died when he was little, and maybe his name was Oscar. My mother didn't say anything at all when she got sick. She just died very fast. I wish I could find Ms. Manigat and give her something to drink. You get very thirsty when you have a fever, which I know for a fact. But I can't go to her because I don't know where she is. And besides, I don't know where Dr. Ben keeps the hot suits. What if I went to her and she wasn't wearing hers?

Maybe the oatmeal was the only thing left in the kitchen, and now I ate it all. I hope not! But I'm thinking maybe it is because I know Ms. Manigat would have brought me more food if she could have found it. She's always asking me if I have enough to eat. I'm already hungry again.

6-4-6-7-2-9-4-3
6-4-6-7-2-9-4-3

February 15

I am writing in the dark. The lights are off. I tried to open my lock but the numbers don't work because of the lights being off. I don't know where Ms. Manigat is. I'm trying not to cry.

What if the lights never come back on?

• • •

February 16

There's so much I want to say but I have a headache from being hungry. When the lights came back on I went out into the hall like Ms. M told me and I used the numbers to get the elevator to work and then I went to the kitchen like she said. I wanted to go real fast and find some peanut butter or some Oreos or even a can of beans I could open with the can opener Ms. M left me at Thanksgiving.

There's no food in the kitchen! There's empty cans and wrappers on the floor and even roaches but I looked on every single shelf and in every cabinet and I couldn't find anything to eat.

The sun was shining really REALLY bright from the window. I almost forgot how the sun looks. When I went to the window I saw a big, empty parking lot outside. At first I thought there were diamonds all over the ground because of the sparkles but it was just a lot of broken glass. I could only see one car and I thought it was Ms. M's. But Ms. M would never leave her car looking like that. For one thing it had two flat tires!

Anyway I don't think there's anybody here today. So I thought of a plan. I have to go now.

Ms. M, this is for you—or whoever comes looking for me. I know somebody will find this notebook if I leave it on my bed. I'm very sorry I had to leave in such a hurry.

I didn't want to go outside but isn't it okay if it's an emergency? I am really really hungry. I'll just find some food and bring it with me and I'll come right back. I'm leaving my door open so I won't get locked out. Ms. M, maybe I'll find your garden with cassavas and akee like you showed me and I'll know the good parts from the bad parts. If someone sees me and I get in trouble I'll just say I didn't have anything to eat.

Whoever is reading this don't worry. I'll tell everybody I see please please not to get too close to me. I know Dr. Ben was very worried I might make somebody sick.

• ARVIES •
Adam-Troy Castro

STATEMENT OF INTENT

This is the story of a mother, and a daughter, and the right to life, and the dignity of all living things, and of some souls granted great destinies at the moment of their conception, and of others damned to remain society's useful idiots.

CONTENTS

Expect cute plush animals and amniotic fluid and a more or less happy ending for everybody, though the definition of happiness may depend on the truncated emotional capacity of those unable to feel anything else. Some of the characters are rich and famous, others are underage, and one is legally dead, though you may like her the most of all.

APPEARANCE

We first encounter Molly June on her fifteenth deathday, when the monitors in charge of deciding such things declare her safe for passengers. Congratulating her on completing the only important stage of her development, they truck her in a padded skimmer to the arvie showroom where she is claimed, right away, by one of the Living.

The fast sale surprises nobody, not the servos that trained her into her current state of health and attractiveness, not the AI routines managing the showroom, and least of all Molly June, who has spent her infancy and early childhood having the ability to feel surprise, or anything beyond a vague contentment, scrubbed from her emotional palate. Crying, she'd learned while still capable of such things, brought punishment, while unconditional acceptance of anything the engineers saw fit to provide brought light and flower scent and warmth. By this point in her existence she'll greet anything short of an exploding bomb with no reaction deeper than vague concern. Her sale is a minor development by comparison: a happy development, reinforcing her feelings of dull satisfaction. Don't feel sorry for her. Her entire life, or more accurately death, is happy ending. All she has to do is spend the rest of it carrying a passenger.

VEHICLE SPECIFICATIONS

You think you need to know what Molly June looks like. You really don't, as it plays no role in her life. But as the information will assist you in feeling empathy for her, we will oblige anyway.

Molly June is a round-faced, button-nosed gamin, with pink lips and cheeks marked with permanent rose: her blonde hair framing her perfect face in parentheses of bouncy, luxurious curls. Her blue eyes, enlarged by years of genetic manipulation and corrective surgeries, are three times as large as the ones imperfect nature would have set in her face. Lemur-like, they dominate her features like a pair of pacific jewels, all moist and sad and adorable. They reveal none of her essential personality, which is not a great loss, as she's never been permitted to develop one.

Her body is another matter. It has been trained to perfection, with the kind of punishing daily regimen that can only be endured when the mind itself remains unaware of pain or exhaustion. She has worked with torn ligaments, with shattered joints, with disfiguring wounds. She has severed her spine and crushed her skull and has had both replaced, with the same ease her engineers have used, fourteen times, to replace her skin with a fresh version unmarked by scars or blemishes. What remains of her now is a wan amalgam of her own best-developed parts, most of them entirely natural, except for her womb, which is of course a plush, wired palace, far safer for its future occupant than the envelope of mere flesh would have provided. It can survive injuries capable of reducing Molly June to a smear.

In short, she is precisely what she should be, now that she's fifteen years past birth, and therefore, by all standards known to modern civilized society, Dead.

HEROINE

Jennifer Axioma-Singh has never been born and is therefore a significant distance away from being Dead.

She is, in every way, entirely typical. She has written operas, climbed mountains, enjoyed daredevil plunges from the upper atmosphere into vessels the size of teacups, finagled controlling stock in seventeen major multinationals, earned the hopeless devotion of any number of lovers, written her name in the sands of time, fought campaigns in a hundred conceptual wars, survived twenty regime changes and on three occasions had herself turned off so she could spend a year or two mulling the purpose of existence while her bloodstream spiced her insights with all the most fashionable hallucinogens.

She has accomplished all of this from within various baths of amniotic fluid.

Jennifer has yet to even open her eyes, which have never been allowed to fully develop past the first trimester and which still, truth be told, resemble black marbles behind lids of translucent onionskin. This doesn't actually deprive her of vision, of course. At the time she claims Molly June as her arvie, she's been indulging her visual cortex for seventy long years, zipping back and forth across the solar system collecting all the tourist chits one earns for seeing all the wonders of modern-day humanity: from the scrimshaw carving her immediate ancestors made of Mars to the radiant face of Unborn Jesus shining from the artfully re-configured multicolored atmosphere of Saturn. She has gloried in the catalogue of beautiful sights provided by God and all the industrious living people before her.

Throughout all this she has been blessed with vision far greater than any we will ever know ourselves, since her umbilical interface allows her sights capable of frying merely organic eyes, and she's far too sophisticated a person to be satisfied with the banal limitations of the merely visual spectrum. Decades of life have provided Jennifer Axioma-Singh with more depth than that. And something else: a perverse need, stranger than anything she's ever done, and impossible to indulge without first installing herself in a healthy young arvie.

ANCESTRY

Jennifer Axioma-Singh has owned arvies before, each one customized from the moment of its death. She's owned males, females, neuters, and several sexes only developed in the past decade. She's had arvies designed for athletic prowess, arvies designed for erotic sensation, and arvies designed for survival in harsh environments. She's even had one arvie with hypersensitive pain receptors: that, during a cold and confused period of masochism.

The last one before this, who she still misses, and sometimes feels a little guilty about, was a lovely girl named Peggy Sue, with a metabolism six times baseline normal and a digestive tract capable of surviving about a hundred separate species of nonstop abuse. Peggy Sue could down mountains of exotic delicacies without ever feeling full or engaging her gag reflex, and enjoyed taste receptors directly plugged into her pleasure centers. The slightest sip of coconut juice could flood her system with tidal waves of endorphin-crazed ecstasy. The things chocolate could do to her were downright obscene.

Unfortunately, she was still vulnerable to the negative effects of unhealthy eating, and went through four liver transplants and six emergency transfusions in the first ten years of Jennifer's occupancy.

The cumulative medical effect of so many years of determined gluttony mattered little to Jennifer Axioma-Singh, since her own caloric intake was regulated by devices that prevented the worst of Peggy Sue's excessive consumption from causing any damage on her side of the uterine wall. Jennifer's umbilical cord passed only those compounds necessary for keeping her alive and healthy. All Jennifer felt, through her interface with Peggy Sue's own sensory spectrum, was the joy of eating; all she experienced was the sheer, overwhelming treasury of flavor.

And if Peggy Sue became obese and diabetic and jaundiced in the meantime—as she did, enduring her last few years as Jennifer's arvie as an immobile mountain of reeking flab, with barely enough strength to position her mouth for another bite—then that was inconsequential as well, because she had progressed beyond prenatal development and had therefore passed beyond that stage of life where human beings can truly be said to have a soul.

PHILOSOPHY

Life, true life, lasts only from the moment of conception to the moment of birth. Jennifer Axioma-Singh subscribes to this principle, and clings to it in the manner of any concerned citizen aware that the very foundations of her society depend on everybody continuing to believe it without question. But she is capable of forming attachments, no matter how irrational, and she therefore felt a frisson of guilt once she decided she'd had enough and the machines performed the Caesarian Section that delivered her from Peggy Sue's pliant womb. After all, Peggy Sue's reward for so many years of service, euthanasia, seemed so inadequate, given everything she'd provided.

But what else could have provided fair compensation, given the shape Peggy Sue was in by then? Surely not a last meal! Jennifer Axioma-Singh, who had not been able to think of any alternatives, brooded over the matter until she came to the same conclusion always reached by those enjoying lives of privilege, which is that such inequities are all for the best and that there wasn't all that much she could do about them, anyway. Her liberal compassion had been satisfied by the heartfelt promise to herself that if she ever bought an arvie again she would take care to act more responsibly.

And this is what she holds in mind, as the interim pod carries her into the gleaming white expanse of the very showroom where fifteen-year-old Molly June awaits a passenger.

INSTALLATION

Molly June's contentment is like the surface of a vast, pacific ocean, unstirred by tide or wind. The events of her life plunge into that mirrored surface without effect, raising nary a ripple or storm. It remains unmarked even now, as the anesthetician and obstetrician mechs emerge from their recesses to guide her always-unresisting form from the waiting room couch where she'd been left earlier this morning, to the operating theatre where she'll begin the useful stage of her existence. Speakers in the walls calm her further with an arrangement of melodious strings designed to override any unwanted emotional static.

It's all quite humane: for even as Molly June lies down and puts her head back and receives permission to close her eyes, she remains wholly at peace. Her heartbeat does jog, a little, just enough to be noted by the instruments, when the servos peel back the skin of her abdomen, but even that instinctive burst of fear fades with the absence of any identifiable pain. Her reaction to the invasive procedure fades to a mere theoretical interest, akin to what Jennifer herself would feel regarding gossip about people she doesn't know living in places where she's never been.

Molly June drifts, thinks of blue waters and bright sunlight, misses Jennifer's installation inside her, and only reacts to the massive change in her body after the incisions are closed and Jennifer has recovered enough to kick. Then her lips curl in a warm but vacant smile. She is happy. Arvies might be dead, in legal terms, but they still love their passengers.

AMBITION

Jennifer doesn't announce her intentions until two days later, after growing comfortable with her new living arrangements. At that time Molly June is stretched out on a lounge on a balcony overlooking a city once known as Paris but which has undergone perhaps a dozen other names of fleeting popularity since then; at this point it's called something that could be translated as Eternal Night, because its urban planners have noted that it looks best when its towers were against a backdrop of darkness and therefore arranged to free it from the sunlight that previously diluted its beauty for half of every day.

The balcony, a popular spot among visitors, is not connected to any actual building. It just sits, like an unanchored shelf, at a high altitude calculated to showcase the lights of the city at their most decadently glorious. The city itself is no longer inhabited, of course; it contains some mechanisms important for the maintenance of local weather patterns but otherwise exists only to confront the night sky with constellations of reflective light. Jennifer, experiencing its beauty through Molly June's eyes, and the bracing high-altitude wind through Molly June's skin, feels a connection with the place that goes beyond aesthetics. She finds it fateful, resonant, and romantic, the perfect location to begin the greatest adventure of a life that has already provided her with so many.

She cranes Molly June's neck to survey the hundreds of other arvies sharing this balcony with her: all young, all beautiful, all pretending happiness while their jaded passengers struggle to plan new experiences not yet grown dull from surfeit. She sees arvies drinking, arvies wrestling, arvies declaiming vapid poetry, arvies coupling in threes and fours; arvies colored in various shades, fitted to various shapes and sizes; pregnant females, and impregnated males, all sufficiently transparent, to a trained eye like Jennifer's, for the essential characters of their respective passengers to shine on through. They all glow from the light of a moon that is not *the* moon, as the original was removed some time ago, but a superb piece of stagecraft designed to accentuate the city below to its greatest possible effect.

Have any of these people ever contemplated a stunt as over-the-top creative as the one Jennifer has in mind? Jennifer thinks not. More, she is certain not. She feels pride, and her arvie Molly June laughs, with a joy that threatens to bring the unwanted curse of sunlight back to the city of lights. And for the first time she announces her intentions out loud, without even raising her voice, aware that any words emerging from Molly June's mouth are superfluous, so long as the truly necessary signal travels the network that conveys Jennifer's needs to the proper facilitating agencies. None of the other arvies on the balcony even hear Molly June speak. But those plugged in hear Jennifer speak the words destined to set off a whirlwind of controversy.

I want to give birth.

CLARIFICATION

It is impossible to understate the perversity of this request.

Nobody gives Birth.

Birth is a messy and unpleasant and distasteful process that ejects living creatures from their warm and sheltered environment into a harsh and unforgiving one that nobody wants to experience except from within the protection of wombs either organic or artificial.

Birth is the passage from Life, and all its infinite wonders, to another place inhabited only by those who have been forsaken. It's the terrible ending that modern civilization has forestalled indefinitely, allowing human beings to live within the womb without ever giving up the rich opportunities for experience and growth. It's sad, of course, that for Life to even be possible a large percentage of potential Citizens have to be permitted to pass through that terrible veil, into an existence where they're no good to anybody except as spare parts and manual laborers and arvies, but there are peasants in even the most enlightened societies, doing the hard work so the important people don't have to. The best any of us can do about that is appreciate their contribution while keeping them as complacent as possible.

The worst thing that could ever be said about Molly June's existence is that when the Nurseries measured her genetic potential, found it wanting, and decided she should approach Birth unimpeded, she was also humanely deprived of the neurological enhancements that allow first-trimester fetuses all the rewards and responsibilities of Citizenship. She never developed enough to fear the passage that awaited her, and never knew how sadly limited her existence would be. She spent her all-too-brief Life in utero ignorant of all the blessings that would forever be denied her, and has been kept safe and content and happy and drugged and stupid since birth. After all, as a wise person once said, it takes a perfect vassal to make a perfect vessel. Nobody can say that there's anything wrong about that. But the dispossession of people like her, that makes the lives of people like Jennifer Axioma-Singh possible, remains a distasteful thing decent people just don't talk about.

Jennifer's hunger to experience birth from the point of view of a mother, grunting and sweating to expel another unfortunate like Molly June out of the only world that matters, into the world of cold slavery, thus strikes the vast majority as offensive, scandalous, unfeeling, selfish, and cruel. But since nobody has ever imagined a Citizen demented enough to want such a thing, nobody has ever thought to make it against the law. So the powers that be indulge Jennifer's perversity, while swiftly passing laws to ensure that nobody will ever be permitted such license ever again; and all the machinery of modern medicine is turned to the problem of just how to give her what she wants. And, before long, wearing Molly June as proxy, she gets knocked up.

IMPLANTATION

There is no need for any messy copulation. Sex, as conducted through arvies, still makes the world go round, prompting the usual number of bittersweet affairs, tempestuous breakups, turbulent love triangles, and silly love songs.

In her younger days, before the practice palled out of sheer repetition, Jennifer had worn out several arvies fucking like a bunny. But there has never been any danger of unwanted conception, at any time, not with the only possible source of motile sperm being the nurseries that manufacture it as needed without recourse to nasty antiquated testes. These days, zygotes and embryos are the province of the assembly line. Growing one inside an arvie, let alone one already occupied by a human being, presents all manner of bureaucratic difficulties involving the construction of new protocols and the rearranging of accepted paradigms and any amount of official eye-rolling, but once all that is said and done, the procedures turn out to be quite simple, and the surgeons have little difficulty providing Molly June with a second womb capable of growing Jennifer Axioma-Singh's daughter while Jennifer Axioma-Singh herself floats unchanging a few protected membranes away.

Unlike the womb that houses Jennifer, this one will not be wired in any way. Its occupant will not be able to influence Molly June's actions or enjoy the full spectrum of Molly June's senses. She will not understand, except in the most primitive, undeveloped way, what or where she is or how well she's being cared for. Literally next to Jennifer Axioma-Singh, she will be by all reasonable comparisons a mindless idiot. But she will live, and grow, for as long as it takes for this entire perverse whim of Jennifer's to fully play itself out.

• • •

GESTATION (1)

In the months that follow, Jennifer Axioma-Singh enjoys a novel form of celebrity. This is hardly anything new for her, of course, as she has been a celebrity several times before and if she lives her expected lifespan, expects to be one several times again. But in an otherwise unshockable world, she has never experienced, or even witnessed, that special, nearly extinct species of celebrity that comes from eliciting shock, and which was once best-known by the antiquated term, *notoriety.*

This, she glories in. This, she milks for every last angstrom. This, she surfs like an expert, submitting to countless interviews, constructing countless bon mots, pulling every string capable of scandalizing the public.

She says, "I don't see the reason for all the fuss."

She says, "People used to share wombs all the time."

She says, "It used to happen naturally, with multiple births: two or three or four or even seven of us, crowded together like grapes, sometimes absorbing each other's body parts like cute young cannibals."

She says, "I don't know whether to call what I'm doing pregnancy or performance art."

She says, "Don't you think Molly June looks special? Don't you think she glows?"

She says, "When the baby's born, I may call her Halo."

She says, "No, I don't see any problem with condemning her to Birth. If it's good enough for Molly June, it's good enough for my child."

And she says, "No, I don't care what anybody thinks. It's my arvie, after all."

And she fans the flames of outrage higher and higher, until public sympathies turn to the poor slumbering creature inside the sac of amniotic fluid, whose life and future have already been so cruelly decided. Is she truly limited enough to be condemned to Birth? Should she be stabilized and given her own chance at life, before she's expelled, sticky and foul, into the cold, harsh world inhabited only by arvies and machines? Or is Jennifer correct in maintaining the issue subject to a mother's whim?

Jennifer says, "All I know is that this is the most profound, most spiritually fulfilling, experience of my entire life." And so she faces the crowds, real or virtual, using Molly June's smile and Molly June's innocence, daring the analysts to count all the layers of irony.

GESTATION (II)

Molly June experiences the same few months in a fog of dazed, but happy confusion, aware that she's become the center of attention, but unable to comprehend exactly why. She knows that her lower back hurts and that her breasts have swelled and that her belly, flat and soft before, has inflated to several times its previous size; she knows that she sometimes feels something moving inside her, that she sometimes feels sick to her stomach, and that her eyes water more easily than they ever have before, but none of this disturbs the vast, becalmed surface of her being. It is all good, all the more reason for placid contentment.

Her only truly bad moments come in her dreams, when she sometimes finds herself standing on a gray, colorless field, facing another version of herself half her own size. The miniature Molly June stares at her from a distance that Molly June herself cannot cross, her eyes unblinking, her expression merciless. Tears glisten on both her cheeks. She points at Molly June and she enunciates a single word, incomprehensible in any language Molly June knows, and irrelevant to any life she's ever been allowed to live: "Mother."

The unfamiliar word makes Molly June feel warm and cold, all at once. In her dream she wets herself, trembling from the sudden warmth running down her thighs. She trembles, bowed by an incomprehensible need to apologize. When she wakes, she finds real tears still wet on her cheeks, and real pee soaking the mattress between her legs. It frightens her.

But those moments fade. Within seconds the calming agents are already flooding her bloodstream, overriding any internal storms, removing all possible sources of disquiet, making her once again the obedient arvie she's supposed to be. She smiles and coos as the servos tend to her bloated form, scrubbing her flesh and applying their emollients. Life is so good, she thinks. And if it's not, well, it's not like there's anything she can do about it, so why worry?

BIRTH (I)

Molly June goes into labor on a day corresponding to what we call Thursday, the insistent weight she has known for so long giving way to a series of contractions violent enough to reach her even through her cocoon of deliberately engineered apathy. She cries and moans and shrieks infuriated, inarticulate things that might have been curses had she ever been exposed to any, and she begs the shiny machines around her to take away the pain with the same efficiency that they've taken away everything else. She even begs her passenger—that is, the passenger she knows about, the one she's sensed seeing through her eyes and hearing through her ears and carrying out conversations with her mouth—she begs her passenger *for mercy*. She hasn't ever asked that mysterious godlike presence for anything, because it's never occurred to her that she might be entitled to anything, but she needs relief now, and she demands it, shrieks for it, can't understand why she isn't getting it.

The answer, which would be beyond her understanding even if provided, is that the wet, sordid physicality of the experience is the very point.

BIRTH (II)

Jennifer Axioma-Singh is fully plugged in to every cramp, every twitch, every pooled droplet of sweat. She experiences the beauty and the terror and the exhaustion and the certainty that this will never end. She finds it resonant and evocative and educational on levels lost to a mindless sack of meat like Molly June. And she comes to any number of profound revelations about the nature of life and death and the biological origins of the species and the odd, inexplicable attachment brood mares have always felt for the squalling sacks of flesh and bone their bodies have gone to so much trouble to expel.

CONCLUSIONS

It's like any other work, she thinks. Nobody ever spent months and months building a house only to burn it down the second they pounded in the last nail. You put that much effort into something and it belongs to you, forever, even if the end result is nothing but a tiny creature that eats and shits and makes demands on your time.

This still fails to explain why anybody would invite this kind of pain again, let alone the three or four or seven additional occasions common before the unborn reached their ascendancy. Oh, it's interesting enough to start with, but she gets the general idea long before the thirteenth hour rolls around and the market share for her real-time feed dwindles to the single digits. Long before that, the pain has given way to boredom. At the fifteenth hour she gives up entirely, turns off her inputs, and begins to catch up on her personal correspondence, missing the actual moment when Molly June's daughter, Jennifer's womb-mate and sister, is expelled head-first into a shiny silver tray, pink and bloody and screaming at the top of her lungs, sharing oxygen for the very first time, but, by every legal definition, Dead.

AFTERMATH (JENNIFER)

As per her expressed wishes, Jennifer Axioma-Singh is removed from Molly June and installed in a new arvie that very day. This one's a tall, lithe, gloriously beautiful creature with fiery eyes and thick, lush lips: her name's Bernadette Ann, she's been bred for endurance in extreme environments, and she'll soon be taking Jennifer Axioma-Singh on an extended solo hike across the restored continent of Antarctica.

Jennifer is so impatient to begin this journey that she never lays eyes on the child whose birth she has just experienced. There's no need. After all, she's never laid eyes on anything, not personally. And the pictures are available online, should she ever feel the need to see them. Not that she ever sees any reason for that to happen. The baby, itself, was never the issue here. Jennifer didn't want to be a mother. She just wanted to give birth. All that mattered to her, in the long run, was obtaining a few months of unique vicarious experience, precious in a lifetime likely to continue for as long as the servos still manufacture wombs and breed arvies. All that matters now is moving on. Because time marches onward, and there are never enough adventures to fill it.

AFTERMATH (MOLLY JUNE)

She's been used, and sullied, and rendered an unlikely candidate to attract additional passengers. She is therefore earmarked for compassionate disposal.

AFTERMATH (THE BABY)

The baby is, no pun intended, another issue. Her biological mother Jennifer Axioma-Singh has no interest in her, and her birth-mother Molly June is on her way to the furnace. A number of minor health problems, barely worth mentioning, render her unsuitable for a useful future as somebody's arvie. Born, and by that precise definition Dead, she could very well follow Molly June down the chute.

But she has a happier future ahead of her. It seems that her unusual gestation and birth have rendered her something of a collector's item, and there are any number of museums aching for a chance to add her to their permanent collections. Offers are weighed, and terms negotiated, until the ultimate agreement is signed, and she finds herself shipped to a freshly constructed habitat in a wildlife preserve in what used to be Ohio.

AFTERMATH (THE CHILD)

She spends her early life in an automated nursery with toys, teachers, and careful attention to her every physical need. At age five she's moved to a cage consisting of a two story house on four acres of nice green grass, beneath what looks like a blue sky dotted with fluffy white clouds. There's even a playground. She will never be allowed out, of course, because there's no place for her to go, but she does have human contact of a sort: a different arvie almost every day, inhabited for the occasion by a long line of Living who now think it might be fun to experience child-rearing for a while. Each one has a different face, each one calls her by a different name, and their treatment of her ranges all the way from compassionate to violently abusive.

Now eight, the little girl has long since given up on asking the good ones to stay, because she knows they won't. Nor does she continue to dream about what she'll do when she grows up, since it's also occurred to her that she'll never know anything but this life in this fishbowl. Her one consolation is wondering about her real mother: where she is now, what she looks like, whether she ever thinks about the child she left behind, and whether it would have been possible to hold on to her love, had it ever been offered, or even possible.

The questions remain the same, from day to day. But the answers are hers to imagine, and they change from minute to minute: as protean as her moods, or her dreams, or the reasons why she might have been condemned to this cruelest of all possible punishments.

* 2011 Nebula Award nominee for Best Short Story
* Million Writers Award winner
* Reprinted in *The Year's Best Science Fiction & Fantasy: 2011 Edition*, edited by Rich Horton

• MORE THAN THE SUM OF HIS PARTS •
Joe Haldeman

21 August 2058

They say I am to keep a detailed record of my feelings, my perceptions, as I grow accustomed to the new parts. To that end, they gave me an apparatus that blind people use for writing, like a tablet with guide wires. It is somewhat awkward. But a recorder would be useless, since I will not have a mouth for some time, and I can't type blind with only one hand.

Woke up free from pain. Interesting. Surprising to find that it has only been five days since the accident. For the record, I am, or was, Dr. Wilson Cheetham, Senior Engineer (Quality Control) for U.S. Steel's Skyfac station, a high-orbit facility that produces foamsteel and vapor deposition materials for use in the cislunar community. But if you are reading this, you must know all that.

Five days ago I was inspecting the aluminum deposition facility and had a bad accident. There was a glitch in my jetseat controls, and I flew suddenly straight into the wide beam of charged aluminum vapor. Very hot. They turned it off in a second, but there was still plenty of time for the beam to breach the suit and thoroughly roast three quarters of my body.

Apparently there was a rescue bubble right there. I was unconscious, of course. They tell me that my heart stopped with the shock, but they managed to save me. My left leg and arm are gone, as is my face. I have no lower jaw, nose, or external ears. I can hear after a fashion, though, and will have eyes in a week or so. They claim they will craft for me testicles and a penis.

I must be pumped full of mood drugs. I feel too calm. If I were myself, whatever fraction of myself is left, perhaps I would resist the insult of being turned into a sexless half-machine.

Ah well. This will be a machine that can turn itself off.

22 August 2058

For many days there was only sleep or pain. This was in the weightless ward at Mercy. They stripped the dead skin off me bit by bit. There were limits to anesthesia, unfortunately. I tried to scream but found I had no vocal cords. They finally decided not to try to salvage the arm and leg, which saved some pain.

When I was able to listen, they explained that U.S. Steel valued my services so much that they were willing to underwrite a state-of-the-art cyborg transformation. Half the cost will be absorbed by Interface Biotech on the Moon. Everybody will deduct me from their taxes.

This, then, is the catalog. First, new arm and leg. That's fairly standard. (I once worked with a woman who had two cyborg arms. It took weeks before I could look at her without feeling pity and revulsion.) Then they will attempt to build me a working jaw and mouth, which has been done only rarely and imperfectly, and rebuild the trachea, vocal cords, esophagus. I will be able to speak and drink, though except for certain soft foods, I won't eat in a normal way; salivary glands are beyond their art. No mucous membranes of any kind. A drastic cure for my chronic sinusitis.

Surprisingly, to me at least, the reconstruction of a penis is a fairly straightforward procedure, for which they've had lots of practice. Men are forever sticking them into places where they don't belong. They are particularly excited about my case because of the challenge in restoring sensation as well as function. The prostate is intact, and they seem confident that they can hook up the complicated plumbing involved in ejaculation. Restoring the ability to urinate is trivially easy, they say.

(The biotechnician in charge of the urogenital phase of the project talked at me for more than an hour, going into unnecessarily grisly detail. It seems that this replacement was done occasionally even before they had any kind of mechanical substitute, by sawing off a short rib and transplanting it, covering it with a skin graft from elsewhere on the body. The recipient thus was blessed with a permanent erection, unfortunately rather strange-looking and short on sensation. My own prosthesis will look very much like the real, shall we say, thing, and new developments in tractor-field mechanics and bionic interfacing should give it realistic response patterns.)

I don't know how to feel about all this. I wish they would leave my blood chemistry alone, so I could have some honest grief or horror, whatever. Instead of this placid waiting.

4 September 2058

Out cold for thirteen days and I wake up with eyes. The arm and leg are in place but not powered up yet. I wonder what the eyes look like. (They won't give me a mirror until I have a face.) They feel like wet glass.

Very fancy eyes. I have a box with two dials that I can use to override the "default mode"—that is, the ability to see only normally. One of them gives me conscious control over pupil dilation, so I can see in almost total darkness or, if for some reason I wanted to, look directly at the sun without discomfort. The other changes the frequency response, so I can see either in the infrared or the ultraviolet. This hospital room looks pretty much the same in ultraviolet, but in infrared it takes on a whole new aspect. Most of the room's illumination then comes from bright bars on the walls, radiant heating. My real arm shows a pulsing tracery of arteries and veins. The other is of course not visible except by reflection and is dark blue.

(Later) Strange I didn't realize I was on the Moon. I thought it was a low-gravity ward in Mercy. While I was sleeping they sent me down to Biotech. Should have figured that out.

5 September 2058

They turned on the "social" arm and leg and began patterning exercises. I am told to think of a certain movement and do its mirror image with my right arm or leg while attempting to execute it with my left. The trainer helps the cyborg unit along, which generates something like pain, though actually it doesn't resemble any real muscular ache. Maybe it's the way circuits feel when they're overloaded.

By the end of the session I was able to make a fist without help, though there is hardly enough grip to hold a pencil. I can't raise the leg yet, but can make the toes move.

They removed some of the bandages today, from shoulder to hip, and the test-tube skin looks much more real than I had prepared myself for. Hairless and somewhat glossy, but the color match is perfect. In infrared it looks quite different, more uniform in color than the "real" side. I suppose that's because it hasn't aged forty years.

While putting me through my paces, the technician waxed rhapsodic about how good this arm is going to be—this set of arms, actually. I'm exercising with the "social" one, which looks much more convincing than the ones my coworker displayed ten years ago. (No doubt more a matter of money than of advancing technology.) The "working" arm, which I haven't seen yet, will be all metal, capable of being worn on the outside of a spacesuit. Besides having the two arms, I'll be able to interface with various waldos, tailored to specific functions.

I am fortunately more ambidextrous than the average person. I broke my right wrist in the second grade and kept re-breaking it through the third, and so learned to write with both hands. All my life I have been able to print more clearly with the left.

They claim to be cutting down on my medication. If that's the truth, I seem to be adjusting fairly well. Then again, I have nothing in my past experience to use as a basis for comparison. Perhaps this calmness is only a mask for hysteria.

6 September 2058

Today I was able to tie a simple knot. I can lightly sketch out the letters of the alphabet. A large and childish scrawl but recognizably my own.

I've begun walking after a fashion, supporting myself between parallel bars. (The lack of hand strength is a neural problem, not a muscular one; when rigid, the arm and leg are as strong as metal crutches.) As I practice, it's amusing to watch the reactions of people who walk into the room, people who aren't paid to mask their horror at being studied by two cold lenses embedded in a swath of bandages formed over a shape that is not a head.

Tomorrow they start building my face. I will be essentially unconscious for more than a week. The limb patterning will continue as I sleep, they say.

14 September 2058

When I was a child my mother, always careful to have me do "normal" things, dressed me in costume each Halloween and escorted me around the high-rise, so I could beg for candy I did not want and money I did not need. On one occasion I had to wear the mask of a child star then popular on the cube, a tightly fitting plastic affair that covered the entire head, squeezing my pudgy features into something more in line with some Platonic ideal of childish beauty. That was my last Halloween. I embarrassed her.

This face is like that. It is undeniably my face, but the skin is taut and unresponsive. Any attempt at expression produces a grimace.

I have almost normal grip in the hand now, though it is still clumsy. As they hoped, the sensory feedback from the fingertips and palms seems to be more finely tuned than in my "good" hand. Tracing my new forefinger across my right wrist, I can sense the individual pores, and there is a marked temperature gradient as I pass over tendon or vein. And yet the hand and arm will eventually be capable of superhuman strength.

Touching my new face I do not feel pores. They have improved on nature in the business of heat exchange.

22 September 2058

Another week of sleep while they installed the new plumbing. When the anesthetic wore off I felt a definite *something,* not pain, but neither was it the normal somatic heft of genitalia. Everything was bedded in gauze and bandage, though, and catheterized, so it would feel strange even to a normal person.

(Later) An aide came in and gingerly snipped away the bandages. He blushed; I don't think fondling was in his job description. When the catheter came out there was a small sting of pain and relief.

It's not much of a copy. To reconstruct the face, they could consult hundreds of pictures and cubes, but it had never occurred to me that one day it might be useful to have a gallery of pictures of my private parts in various stages of repose. The technicians had approached the problem by bringing me a stack of photos culled from urological texts and pornography, and having me sort through them as to "closeness of fit."

It was not a task for which I was well trained, by experience or disposition. Strange as it may seem in this age of unfettered hedonism, I haven't seen another man naked, let alone rampant, since leaving high school, twenty-five years ago. (I was stationed on Farside for eighteen months and never went near a sex bar, preferring an audience of one. Even if I had to hire her, as was usually the case.)

So this one is rather longer and thicker than its predecessor—would all men unconsciously exaggerate?—and has only approximately the same aspect when erect. A young man's rakish angle.

Distasteful but necessary to write about the matter of masturbation. At first it didn't work. With my right hand, it felt like holding another man, which I have never had any desire to do. With the new hand, though, the process proceeded in the normal way, though I must admit to a voyeuristic aspect. The sensations were extremely acute. Ejaculation more forceful than I can remember from youth.

It makes me wonder. In a book I recently read, about brain chemistry, the author made a major point of the notion that it's a mistake to completely equate "mind" with "brain." The brain, he said, is in a way only the thickest and most complex segment of the nervous system; it coordinates our consciousness, but the actual mind suffuses through the body in a network of ganglia. In fact, he used sexuality as an example. When a man ruefully observes that his penis has a mind of its own, he is stating part of a larger truth.

But I in fact do have actual brains imbedded in my new parts: the biochips that process sensory data coming in and action commands going back. Are these brains part of my consciousness the way the rest of my nervous system is? The masturbation experience indicates they might be in business for themselves.

This is premature speculation, so to speak. We'll see how it feels when I move into a more complex environment, where I'm not so self-absorbed.

23 September 2058

During the night something evidently clicked. I woke up this morning with full strength in my cyborg limbs. One rail of the bed was twisted out of shape where I must have unconsciously gripped it. I bent it back quite easily.

Some obscure impulse makes me want to keep this talent secret for the time being. The technicians thought I would be able to exert three or four times the normal person's grip; this is obviously much more than that.

But why keep it a secret? I don't know. Eventually they will read this diary and I will stand exposed. There's no harm in that, though; this is supposed to be a record of my psychological adjustment or maladjustment. Let *them* tell *me* why I've done it.

(Later) The techs were astonished, ecstatic. I demonstrated a pull of 90 kilograms. I know if I'd actually given it a good yank, I could have pulled the stress machine out of the wall. I'll give them 110 tomorrow and inch my way up to 125.

Obviously I must be careful with force vectors. If I put too much stress on the normal parts of my body I could do permanent injury. With my metal fist I could certainly punch a hole through an airlock door, but it would probably tear the prosthesis out of its socket. Newton's laws still apply.

Other laws will have to be rewritten.

24 September 2058

I got to work out with three waldos today. A fantastic experience!

The first one was a disembodied hand and arm attached to a stand, the setup they use to train normal people in the use of waldos. The difference is that I don't need a waldo sleeve to imperfectly transmit my wishes to the mechanical double. I can plug into it directly.

I've been using waldos in my work ever since graduate school, but it was never anything like this. Inside the waldo sleeve you get a clumsy kind of feedback from striated pressor field generators embedded in the plastic. With my setup the feedback is exactly the kind a normal person feels when he touches an object, but much more sensitive. The first time they asked me to pick up an egg, I tossed it up and caught it (no great feat of coordination in lunar gravity, admittedly, but I could have done it as easily in Earth-normal).

The next waldo was a large earthmover that Western Mining uses over at Grimaldi Station. That was interesting, not only because of its size but because of the slight communications lag. Grimaldi is only a few dozen of kilometers away, but there aren't enough unused data channels between here and there for me to use the land-line to communicate with the earthmover hand. I had to relay via comsat, so there was about a tenth-second delay between the thought and the action. It was a fine feeling of power, but a little confusing: I would cup my hand and scoop downward, and then a split-second too late would feel the resistance of the regolith. And then casually hold in my palm several tonnes of rock and dirt. People standing around watching; with a flick of my wrist I could have buried them. Instead I dutifully dumped it on the belt to the converter.

But the waldo that most fascinated me was the micro. It had been in use for only a few months; I had heard of it, but hadn't had a chance to see it in action. It is a fully articulated hand barely a tenth of a millimeter long. I used it in conjunction with a low-power scanning electron microscope, moving around on the surface of a microcircuit. At that magnification it looked like a hand on a long stick wandering through the corridors of a building, whose walls varied from rough stucco to brushed metal to blistered gray paint, all laced over with thick cables of gold. When necessary, I could bring in another hand, manipulated by my right from inside a waldo sleeve, to help with simple carpenter and machinist tasks that, in the real world, translated into fundamental changes in the quantum-electrodynamic properties of the circuit.

This was the real power: not crushing metal tubes or lifting tonnes of rock, but pushing electrons around to do my bidding. My first doctorate was in electrical engineering; in a sudden epiphany I realize that I am the first *actual* electrical engineer in history.

After two hours they made me stop; said I was showing signs of strain. They put me in a wheelchair, and I did fall asleep on the way back to my room. Dreaming dreams of microcosmic and infinite power.

25 September 2058

The metal arm. I expected it to feel fundamentally different from the "social" one, but of course it doesn't, most of the time. Circuits are circuits. The difference comes under conditions of extreme exertion: the soft hand gives me signals like pain if I come close to the level of stress that would harm the fleshlike material. With the metal hand I can rip off a chunk of steel plate a centimeter thick and feel nothing beyond "muscular" strain. If I had two of them I could work marvels.

The mechanical leg is not so gifted. It has governors to restrict its strength and range of motion to that of a normal leg, which is reasonable. Even a normal person finds himself brushing the ceiling occasionally in lunar gravity. I could stand up sharply and find myself with a concussion, or worse.

I like the metal arm, though. When I'm stronger (hah!) they say they'll let me go outside and try it with a spacesuit. Throw something over the horizon.

Starting today, I'm easing back into a semblance of normal life. I'll be staying at Biotech for another six or eight weeks, but I'm patched into my Skyfac office and have started clearing out the backlog of paperwork. Two hours in the morning and two in the afternoon. It's diverting, but I have to admit my heart isn't really in it. Rather be playing with the micro. (Have booked three hours on it tomorrow.)

26 September 2058

They threaded an optical fiber through the micro's little finger, so I can watch its progress on a screen without being limited to the field of an electron microscope. The picture is fuzzy while the waldo is in motion, but if I hold it still for a few seconds, the computer assist builds up quite a sharp image. I used it to roam all over my right arm and hand, which was fascinating. Hairs a tangle of stiff black stalks, the pores small damp craters. And everywhere the evidence of the skin's slow death; translucent sheafs of desquamated cells.

I've taken to wearing the metal arm rather than the social one. People's stares don't bother me. The metal one will be more useful in my actual work, and I want to get as much practice as possible. There is also an undeniable feeling of power.

27 September 2058

Today I went outside. It was clumsy getting around at first. For the past eleven years I've used a suit only in zerogee, so all my reflexes are wrong. Still, not much serious can go wrong at a sixth of a gee.

It was exhilarating but at the same time frustrating, since I couldn't reveal all my strength. I did almost overdo it once, starting to tip over a large boulder. Before it tipped, I realized that my left boot had crunched through about ten centimeters of regolith, in reaction to the amount of force I was applying. So I backed off and discreetly shuffled my foot to fill the telltale hole.

I could indeed throw a rock over the horizon. With a sling, I might be able to put a small one into orbit. Rent myself out as a lunar launching facility.

(Later) Most interesting. A pretty nurse who has been on this project since the beginning came into my room after dinner and proposed the obvious experiment. It was wildly successful.

Although my new body starts out with the normal pattern of excitation-plateau-orgasm, the resemblance stops there. I have no refractory period; the process of erection is completely under conscious control. This could make me the most popular man on the Moon.

The artificial skin of the penis is as sensitive to tactile differentiation as that of the cyborg fingers: suddenly I know more about a woman's internal topography than any man who ever lived—more than any *woman!*

I think tomorrow I'll take a trip to Farside.

28 September 2058

Farside has nine sex bars. I read the guidebook descriptions, and then asked a few locals for their recommendations, and wound up going to a place cleverly called the Juice Bar.

In fact, the name was not just an expression of coy eroticism. They served nothing but fruit and juices there, most of them fantastically expensive Earth imports. I spent a day's pay on a glass of pear nectar and sought out the most attractive woman in the room.

That in itself was a mistake. I was not physically attractive even before the accident, and the mechanics have faithfully restored my coarse features and slight paunch. I was rebuffed.

So I went to the opposite extreme and looked for the plainest woman. That would be a better test, anyway: before the accident I always demanded, and paid for, physical perfection. If I could duplicate the performance of last night with a woman to whom I was not sexually attracted—and do it in public, with no pressure from having gone without—then my independence from the autonomic nervous system would be proven beyond doubt.

Second mistake. I was never good at small talk, and when I located my paragon of plainness I began talking about the accident and the singular talent that had resulted from it. She suddenly remembered an appointment elsewhere.

I was not so open with the next woman, also plain. She asked whether there was something wrong with my face, and I told her half of the truth. She was sweetly sympathetic, motherly, which did not endear her to me. It did make her a good subject for the experiment. We left the socializing section of the bar and went back to the so-called "love room."

There was an acrid quality to the air that I suppose was compounded of incense and sweat, but of course my dry nose was not capable of identifying actual smells. For the first time, I was grateful for that disability; the place probably had the aroma of a well-used locker room. Plus pheromones.

Under the muted lights, red and blue as well as white, more than a dozen couples were engaged more or less actively in various aspects of amorous behavior. A few were frankly staring at others, but most were either absorbed with their own affairs or furtive in their voyeurism. Most of them were on the floor, which was a warm soft mat, but some were using tables and chairs in fairly ingenious ways. Several of the permutations would no doubt have been impossible or dangerous in Earth's gravity.

We undressed and she complimented me on my evident spryness. A nearby spectator made a jealous observation. Her own body was rather flaccid, doughy, and under previous circumstances I doubt that I would have been able to maintain enthusiasm. There was no problem, however; in fact, I rather enjoyed it. She required very little foreplay, and I was soon repeating the odd sensation of hypersensitized explorations. Gynecological spelunking.

She was quite voluble in her pleasure, and although she lasted less than an hour, we did attract a certain amount of attention. When she, panting, regretfully declined further exercise, a woman who had been watching, a rather attractive young blonde, offered to share her various openings. I obliged her for a while; although the well was dry, the pump handle was unaffected.

During that performance I became aware that the pleasure involved was not a sexual one in any normal sense. Sensual, yes, in the way that a fine meal is a sensual experience, but with a remote subtlety that I find difficult to describe. Perhaps there is a relation to epicurism that is more than metaphorical. Since I can no longer taste food, a large area of my brain is available for the valuation of other experience. It may be that the brain is reorganizing itself in order to take fullest advantage of my new abilities.

By the time the blonde's energy began to flag, several other women had taken an interest in my satyriasis. I resisted the temptation to find what this organ's limit was, if indeed a limit exists. My back ached and the right knee was protesting. So I threw the mental switch and deflated. I left with a minimum of socializing. (The first woman insisted on buying me something at the bar. I opted for a banana.)

29 September 2058

Now that I have eyes and both hands, there's no reason to scratch this diary out with a pen. So I'm entering it into the computer. But I'm keeping two versions.

I recopied everything up to this point and then went back and edited the version that I will show to Biotech. It's very polite, and will remain so. For instance, it does not contain the following:

After writing last night's entry, I found myself still full of energy, and so I decided to put into action a plan that has been forming in my mind.

About two in the morning I went downstairs and broke into the waldo lab. The entrance is protected by a five-digit combination lock, but of course that was no obstacle. My hypersensitive fingers could feel the tumblers rattling into place.

I got the micro-waldo set up and then detached my leg. I guided the waldo through the leg's circuitry and easily disabled the governors. The whole operation took less than twenty minutes.

I did have to use a certain amount of care walking, at first. There was a tendency to rise into the air or to limpingly overcompensate. It was under control by the time I got back to my room. So once more they proved to have been mistaken as to the limits of my abilities. Testing the strength of the leg, with a halfhearted kick I put a deep dent in the metal wall at the rear of my closet. I'll have to wait until I can be outside, alone, to see what full force can do.

A comparison kick with my flesh leg left no dent, but did hurt my great toe.

30 September 2058

It occurs to me that I feel better about my body than I have in the past twenty years. Who wouldn't? Literally eternal youth in these new limbs and organs; if a part shows signs of wear, it can simply be replaced.

I was angry at the Biotech evaluation board this morning. When I simply inquired as to the practicality of replacing the right arm and leg as well, all but one were horrified. One was amused. I will remember him.

I think the fools are going to order me to leave Nearside in a day or two and go back to Mercy for psychiatric "help." I will leave when I want to, on my own terms.

1 October 2058

This is being voice-recorded in the Environmental Control Center at Nearside. It is 10:32; they have less than ninety minutes to accede to my demands. Let me backtrack.

After writing last night's entry I felt a sudden excess of sexual desire. I took the shuttle to Farside and went back to the Juice Bar.

The plain woman from the previous night was waiting, hoping that I would show up. She was delighted when I suggested that we save money (and whatever residue of modesty we had left) by keeping ourselves to one another, back at my room.

I didn't mean to murder her. That was not in my mind at all. But I suppose in my passion, or abandon, I carelessly propped my strong leg against the wall and then thrust with too much strength. At any rate there was a snap and a tearing sound. She gave a small cry and the lower half of my body was suddenly awash in blood. I had snapped her spine and evidently at the same time caused considerable internal damage. She must have lost consciousness very quickly, though her heart did not stop beating for nearly a minute.

Disposing of the body was no great problem, conceptually. In the laundry room I found a bag large enough to hold her comfortably. Then I went back to the room and put her and the sheet she had besmirched into the bag.

Getting her to the recycler would have been a problem if it had been a normal hour. She looked like nothing so much as a body in a laundry bag. Fortunately, the corridor was deserted.

The lock on the recycler room was child's play. The furnace door was a problem, though; it was easy to unlock but its effective diameter was only 25 centimeters.

So I had to disassemble her. To save cleaning up, I did the job inside the laundry bag, which was clumsy, and made it difficult to see the fascinating process.

I was so absorbed in watching that I didn't hear the door slide open. But the man who walked in made a slight gurgling sound, which somehow I did hear over the cracking of bones. I stepped over to him and killed him with one kick.

At this point I have to admit to a lapse in judgment. I relocked the door and went back to the chore at hand. After the woman was completely recycled, I repeated the process with the man—which was, incidentally, much easier. The female's layer of subcutaneous fat made disassembly of the torso a more slippery business.

It really was wasted time (though I did spend part of the time thinking out the final touches of the plan I am now engaged upon). I might as well have left both bodies there on the floor. I had kicked the man with great force—enough to throw me to the ground in reaction and badly bruise my right hip—and had split him open from crotch to heart. This made a bad enough mess, even if he hadn't compounded the problem by striking the ceiling. I would never be able to clean that up, and it's not the sort of thing that would escape notice for long.

At any rate, it was only twenty minutes wasted, and I gained more time than that by disabling the recycler room lock. I cleaned up, changed clothes, stopped by the waldo lab for a few minutes, and then took the slidewalk to the Environmental Control Center.

There was only one young man on duty at the ECC at that hour. I exchanged a few pleasantries with him and then punched him in the heart, softly enough not to make a mess. I put his body where it wouldn't distract me and then attended to the problem of the "door."

There's no actual door on the ECC, but there is an emergency wall that slides into place if there's a drop in pressure. I typed up a test program simulating an emergency, and the wall obeyed. Then I walked over and twisted a few flanges around. Nobody would be able to get into the Center with anything short of a cutting torch.

Sitting was uncomfortable with the bruised hip, but I managed to ease into the console and spend an hour or so studying logic and wiring diagrams. Then I popped off an access plate and moved the micro-waldo down the corridors of electronic thought. The intercom began buzzing incessantly, but I didn't let it interfere with my concentration.

Nearside is protected from meteorite strike or (far more likely) structural failure by a series of 128 bulkheads that, like the emergency wall here, can slide into place and isolate any area where there's a pressure drop. It's done automatically, of course, but can also be controlled from here.

What I did, in essence, was to tell each bulkhead that it was under repair, and should not close under any circumstance. Then I moved the waldo over to the circuits that controlled the city's eight airlocks. With some rather elegant microsurgery, I transferred control of all eight solely to the pressure switch I now hold in my left hand.

It is a negative-pressure button, a dead-man switch taken from a power saw. So long as I hold it down, the inner doors of the airlock will remain locked.

If I let go, they will all iris open. The outer doors are already open, as are the ones that connect the airlock chambers to the suiting-up rooms. No one will be able to make it to a spacesuit in time. Within thirty seconds, every corridor will be full of vacuum. People behind airtight doors may choose between slow asphyxiation and explosive decompression.

My initial plan had been to wire the dead-man switch to my pulse, which would free my good hand and allow me to sleep. That will have to wait. The wiring completed, I turned on the intercom and announced that I would speak to the Coordinator, and no one else.

When I finally got to talk to him, I told him what I had done and invited him to verify it. That didn't take long. Then I presented my demands:

Surgery to replace the rest of my limbs, of course. The surgery would have to be done while I was conscious (a heartbeat dead-man switch could be subverted by a heart machine) and it would have to be done here, so that I could be assured that nobody fooled with my circuit changes.

The doctors were called in, and they objected that such profound surgery couldn't be done under local anesthetic. I knew they were lying, of course; amputation was a fairly routine procedure even before anesthetics were invented. Yes, but I would faint, they said. I told them that I would not, and at any rate I was willing to take the chance, and no one else had any choice in the matter.

(I have not yet mentioned that the ultimate totality of my plan involves replacing all my internal organs as well as all of the limbs—or at least those organs whose failure could cause untimely death. I will be a true cyborg then, a human brain in an "artificial" body, with the prospect of thousands of years of life. With a few decades—or centuries!—of research, I could even do something about the brain's shortcomings. I would wind up interfaced to EarthNet, with all of human knowledge at my disposal, and with my faculties for logic and memory no longer fettered by the slow pace of electrochemical synapse.)

A psychiatrist, talking from Earth, tried to convince me of the error of my ways. He said that the dreadful trauma had "obviously" unhinged me, and the cyborg augmentation, far from affecting a cure, had made my mental derangement worse. He demonstrated, at least to his own satisfaction, that my behavior followed some classical pattern of madness. All this had been taken into consideration, he said, and if I were to give myself up, I would be forgiven my crimes and manumitted into the loving arms of the psychiatric establishment.

I did take time to explain the fundamental errors in his way of thinking. He felt that I had quite literally lost my identity by losing my face and genitalia, and that I was at bottom a "good" person whose essential humanity had been perverted by physical and existential estrangement. Totally wrong. By his terms, what I actually *am* is an "evil" person whose true nature was revealed to himself by the lucky accident that released him from existential propinquity with the common herd.

And "evil" is the accurate word, not maladjusted or amoral or even criminal. I am as evil by human standards as a human is evil by the standards of an animal raised for food, and the analogy is accurate. I will sacrifice humans not only for any survival but for comfort, curiosity, or entertainment. I will allow to live anyone who doesn't bother me, and reward generously those who help.

Now they have only forty minutes. They know I am

—end of recording—

25 September 2058

Excerpt from Summary Report

I am Dr. Henry Janovski, head of the surgical team that worked on the ill-fated cyborg augmentation of Dr. Wilson Cheetham.

We were fortunate that Dr. Cheetham's insanity did interfere with his normally painstaking, precise nature. If he had spent more time in preparation, I have no doubt that he would have put us in a very difficult fix.

He should have realized that the protecting wall that shut him off from the rest of Nearside was made of steel, an excellent conductor of electricity. If he had insulated himself behind a good dielectric, he could have escaped his fate.

Cheetham's waldo was a marvelous instrument, but basically it was only a pseudo-intelligent servomechanism that obeyed well-defined radio-frequency commands. All we had to do was override the signals that were coming from his own nervous system.

We hooked a powerful amplifier up to the steel wall, making it in effect a huge radio transmitter. To generate the signal we wanted amplified, I had a technician put on a waldo sleeve that was holding a box similar to Cheetham's dead-man switch. We wired the hand closed, turned up the power, and had the technician strike himself on the chin as hard as he could.

The technician struck himself so hard he blacked out for a few seconds. Cheetham's resonant action, perhaps a hundred times more powerful, drove the bones of his chin up through the top of his skull.

Fortunately, the expensive arm itself was not damaged. It is not evil or insane by itself, of course. Which I shall prove.

The experiments will continue, though of course we will be more selective as to subjects. It seems obvious in retrospect that we should not use as subjects people who have gone through the kind of trauma that Cheetham suffered. We must use willing volunteers. Such as myself.

I am not young, and weakness and an occasional tremor in my hands limit the amount of surgery I can do—much less than my knowledge would allow, or my nature desire. My failing left arm I shall have replaced with Cheetham's mechanical marvel, and I will go through training similar to his—but for the good of humanity, not for ill.

What miracles I will perform with a knife!

• FLOWER, MERCY, NEEDLE, CHAIN •
Yoon Ha Lee

The usual fallacy is that, in every universe, many futures splay outward from any given moment. But in some universes, determinism runs backwards: given a universe's state s at some time t, there are multiple previous states that may have resulted in s. In some universes, all possible pasts funnel toward a single fixed ending, Ω.

If you are of millenarian bent, you might call Ω Armageddon. If you are of grammatical bent, you might call it punctuation on a cosmological scale.

If you are a philosopher in such a universe, you might call Ω *inevitable.*

The woman has haunted Blackwheel Station for as long as anyone remembers, although she was not born there. She is human, and her straight black hair and brown-black eyes suggest an ancestral inheritance tangled up with tigers and shapeshifting foxes. Her native language is not spoken by anyone here or elsewhere.

They say her true name means things like *gray* and *ash* and *grave.* You may buy her a drink, bring her candied petals or chaotic metals, but it's all the same. She won't speak her name.

That doesn't stop people from seeking her out. Today, it's a man with mirror-colored eyes. He is the first human she has seen in a long time.

"Arighan's Flower," he says.

It isn't her name, but she looks up. Arighan's Flower is the gun she carries. The stranger has taken on a human face to talk to her, and he is almost certainly interested in the gun.

The gun takes different shapes, but at this end of time, origami multiplicity of form surprises more by its absence than its presence. Sometimes the gun is long and sleek, sometimes heavy and blunt. In all cases, it bears its maker's mark on the stock: a blossom with three petals falling away and a fourth about to follow. At the blossom's heart is a character that itself resembles a flower with knotted roots.

The character's meaning is the gun's secret. The woman will not tell it to you, and the gunsmith Arighan is generations gone.

"Everyone knows what I guard," the woman says to the mirror-eyed man.

"I know what it does," he says. "And I know that you come from people who worship their ancestors."

Her hand—on a glass of water two degrees from freezing—stops, slides to her side, where the holster is. "That's dangerous knowledge," she says. So he's figured it out. Her people's historians called Arighan's Flower the *ancestral gun*. They weren't referring to its age.

The man smiles politely, and doesn't take a seat uninvited. Small courtesies matter to him because he is not human. His mind may be housed in a superficial fortress of flesh, but the busy computations that define him are inscribed in a vast otherspace.

The man says, "I can hardly be the first constructed sentience to come to you."

She shakes her head. "It's not that." Do computers like him have souls? she wonders. She is certain he does, which is potentially inconvenient. "I'm not for hire."

"It's important," he says.

It always is. They want chancellors dead or generals, discarded lovers or rival reincarnates, bodhisattvas or bosses—all the old, tawdry stories. People, in all the broad and narrow senses of the term. The reputation of Arighan's Flower is quite specific, if mostly wrong.

"Is it," she says. Ordinarily she doesn't talk to her petitioners at all. Ordinarily she ignores them through one glass, two, three, four, like a child learning the hard way that you can't outcount infinity.

There was a time when more of them tried to force the gun away from her. The woman was a duelist and a killer before she tangled her life up with the Flower, though, and the Flower comes with its own defenses, including the woman's inability to die while she wields it. One of the things she likes about Blackwheel is that the administrators promised that they would dispose of any corpses she produced. Blackwheel is notorious for keeping promises.

The man waits a little longer, then says, "Will you hear me out?"

"You should be more afraid of me," she says, "if you really know what you claim to know."

By now, the other people in the bar, none of them human, are paying attention: a musician whose instrument is made of fossilized wood and silk strings, a magister with a seawrack mane, engineers with their sketches hanging in the air and a single doodled starship at the boundary. The sole exception is the tattooed traveler dozing in the corner, dreaming of distant moons.

In no hurry, the woman draws the Flower and points it at the man. She is aiming it not at his absent heart, but at his left eye. If she pulled the trigger, she would pierce him through the false pupil.

The musician continues plucking plangent notes from the instrument. The others, seeing the gun, gawk for only a moment before hastening out of the bar. As if that would save them.

"Yes," the man says, outwardly unshaken, "you could damage my lineage badly. I could name programmers all the way back to the first people who scratched a tally of birds or rocks."

The gun's muzzle moves precisely, horizontally: now the right eye. The woman says, "You've convinced me that you know. You haven't convinced me not to kill you." It's half a bluff: she wouldn't use the Flower, not for this. But she knows many ways to kill.

"There's another one," he says. "I don't want to speak of it here, but will you hear me out?"

She nods once, curtly.

Covered by her palm, engraved silver-bright in a language nobody else reads or writes, is the word *ancestor*.

Once upon a universe, an empress's favored duelist received a pistol from the empress's own hand. The pistol had a stock of silver-gilt and niello, an efflorescence of vines framing the maker's mark. The gun had survived four dynasties, with all their rebellions and coups. It had accompanied the imperial arsenal from homeworld to homeworld.

Of the ancestral pistol, the empire's archives said two things: *Do not use this weapon, for it is nothing but peril* and *This weapon does not function.*

In a reasonable universe, both statements would not be true.

The man follows the woman to her suite, which is on one of Blackwheel's tidier levels. The sitting room, comfortable but not luxurious by Blackwheeler standards, accommodates a couch sized to human proportions, a metal table shined to blurry reflectivity, a vase in the corner.

There are also two paintings, on silk rather than some less ancient substrate. One is of a mountain by night, serenely anonymous amid its stylized clouds. The other, in a completely different style, consists of a cavalcade of shadows. Only after several moments' study do the shadows assemble themselves into a face. Neither painting is signed.

"Sit," the woman says.

The man does. "Do you require a name?" he asks.

"Yours, or the target's?"

"I have a name for occasions like this," he says. "It is Zheu Kerang."

"You haven't asked me my name," she remarks.

"I'm not sure that's a meaningful question," Kerang says. "If I'm not mistaken, you don't exist."

Wearily, she says, "I exist in all the ways that matter. I have volume and mass and volition. I drink water that tastes the same every day, as water should. I kill when it moves me to do so. I've unwritten death into the history of the universe."

His mouth tilts up at *unwritten*. "Nevertheless," he says. "Your species never evolved. You speak a language that is not even dead. It never existed."

"Many languages are extinct."

"To become extinct, something has to exist first."

The woman folds herself into the couch next to him, not close but not far. "It's an old story," she says. "What is yours?"

"Four of Arighan's guns are still in existence," Kerang says.

The woman's eyes narrow. "I had thought it was three." Arighan's Flower is the last, the gunsmith's final work. The others she knows of are Arighan's Mercy, which always kills the person shot, and Arighan's Needle, which removes the target's memories of the wielder.

"One more has surfaced," Kerang says. "The character in the maker's mark resembles a sword in chains. They are already calling it Arighan's Chain."

"What does it do?" she says, because he will tell her anyway.

"This one kills the commander of whoever is shot," Kerang says, "if that's anyone at all. Admirals, ministers, monks. Schoolteachers. It's a peculiar sort of loyalty test."

Now she knows. "You want me to destroy the Chain."

Once upon a universe, a duelist named Shiron took up the gun that an empress with empiricist tendencies had given her. "I don't understand how a gun that doesn't work could possibly be perilous," the empress said. She nodded at a sweating man bound in monofilament so that he would dismember himself if he tried to flee. "This man will be executed anyway, his name struck from the roster of honored ancestors. See if the gun works on him."

Shiron fired the gun . . . and woke in a city she didn't recognize, whose inhabitants spoke a dialect she had never heard before, whose technology she mostly recognized from historical dramas. The calendar they used, at least, was familiar. It told her that she was 857 years too early. No amount of research changed the figure.

Later, Shiron deduced that the man she had executed traced his ancestry back 857 years, to a particular individual. Most likely that ancestor had performed some extraordinary deed to join the aristocracy, and had, by the reckoning of Shiron's people, founded his own line.

Unfortunately, Shiron didn't figure this out before she accidentally deleted the human species.

"Yes," Kerang says. "I have been charged with preventing further assassinations. Arighan's Chain is not a threat I can afford to ignore."

"Why didn't you come earlier, then?" Shiron says. "After all, the Chain might have lain dormant, but the others—"

"I've seen the Mercy and the Needle," he says, by which he means that he's copied data from those who have. "They're beautiful." He isn't referring to beauty in the way of shadows fitting together into a woman's profile, or beauty in the way of sun-colored liquor at the right temperature in a faceted glass. He means the beauty of logical strata, of the crescendo of axiom-axiom-corollary-proof, of *quod erat demonstrandum*.

"Any gun or shard of glass could do the same as the Mercy," Shiron says, understanding him. "And drugs and dreamscalpels will do the Needle's work, given time and expertise. But surely you could say the same of the Chain."

She stands again and takes the painting of the mountain down and rolls it tightly. "I was born on that mountain," she says. "Something like it is still there, on a birthworld very like the one I knew. But I don't think anyone paints in this style. Perhaps some art historian would recognize its distant cousin. I am no artist, but I painted it myself, because no one else remembers the things I remember. And now you would have it start again."

"How many bullets have you used?" Kerang asks.

It is not that the Flower requires special bullets—it adapts even to emptiness—it is that the number matters.

Shiron laughs, low, almost husky. She knows better than to trust Kerang, but she needs him to trust her. She pulls out the Flower and rests it in both palms so he can look at it.

Three petals fallen, a fourth about to follow. That's not the number, but he doesn't realize it. "You've guarded it so long," he says, inspecting the maker's mark without touching the gun.

"I will guard it until I am nothing but ice," Shiron says. "You may think that the Chain is a threat, but if I remove it, there's no guarantee that you will still exist—"

"It's not the Chain I want destroyed," Kerang says gently. "It's Arighan. Do you think I would have come to you for anything less?"

Shiron says into the awkward quiet, after a while, "So you tracked down descendants of Arighan's line." His silence is assent. "There must be many."

Arighan's Flower destroys the target's entire ancestral line, altering the past but leaving its wielder untouched. In the empire Shiron once served, the histories spoke of Arighan as an honored guest. Shiron discovered long ago that Arighan was no guest, but a prisoner forced to forge weapons for her captors. How Arighan was able to create weapons of such novel destructiveness, no one knows. The Flower was Arighan's clever revenge against a people whose state religion involved ancestor worship.

If descendants of Arighan's line exist here, then Arighan herself can be undone, and all her guns unmade. Shiron will no longer have to be an exile in this timeline, although it is true that she cannot return to the one that birthed her, either.

Shiron snaps the painting taut. The mountain disintegrates, but she lost it lifetimes ago. Silent lightning crackles through the air, unknots Zheu Kerang from his human-shaped shell, tessellates dead-end patterns across the equations that make him who he is. The painting had other uses, as do the other things in this room—she believes in versatility—but this is good enough.

Kerang's body slumps on the couch. Shiron leaves it there.

For the first time in a long time, she is leaving Blackwheel Station. What she does not carry she can buy on the way. And Blackwheel is loyal because they know, and they know not to offend her; Blackwheel will keep her suite clean and undisturbed, and deliver water, near-freezing in an elegant glass, night after night, waiting.

Kerang was a pawn by his own admission. If he knew what he knew, and lived long enough to convey it to her, then others must know what he knew, or be able to find it out.

Kerang did not understand her at all. Shiron unmazes herself from the station to seek passage to one of the hubworlds, where she can begin her search. If Shiron had wanted to seek revenge on Arighan, she could have taken it years ago.

But she will not be like Arighan. She will not destroy an entire timeline of people, no matter how alien they are to her.

Shiron had hoped that matters wouldn't come to this. She acknowledges her own naïveté. There is no help for it now. She will have to find and murder each child of Arighan's line. In this way she can protect Arighan herself, protect the accumulated sum of history, in case someone outwits her after all this time and manages to take the Flower from her.

In a universe where determinism runs backwards—where, no matter what you do, everything ends in the same inevitable Ω—choices still matter, especially if you are the last guardian of an incomparably lethal gun.

Although it has occurred to Shiron that she could have accepted Kerang's offer, and that she could have sacrificed this timeline in exchange for the one in which neither Arighan nor the guns ever existed, she declines to do so. For there will come a heat-death, and she is beginning to wonder: if a constructed sentience—a computer—can have a soul, what of the universe itself, the greatest computer of all?

In this universe, they reckon her old. Shiron is older than even that. In millions of timelines, she has lived to the pallid end of life. In each of those endings, Arighan's Flower is there, as integral as an edge is to a blade. While it is true that science never proves anything absolutely, that an inconceivably large but finite number of experiments always pales beside infinity, Shiron feels that millions of timelines suffice as proof.

Without Arighan's Flower, the universe cannot renew itself and start a new story. Perhaps that is all the reason the universe needs. And Shiron will be there when the heat-death arrives, as many times as necessary.

So Shiron sets off. It is not the first time she has killed, and it is unlikely to be the last. But she is not, after all this time, incapable of grieving.

Ω

* Theodore Sturgeon Memorial Award finalist

* Reprinted in *The Year's Best Science Fiction: Twenty-Eighth Annual Collection*, edited by Gardner Dozois

* Reprinted in *The Year's Best Science Fiction & Fantasy: 2011 Edition*, edited by Rich Horton

* Million Writers Award Notable Story

• THE LONG CHASE •
Geoffrey A. Landis

2645, January

The war is over.

The survivors are being rounded up and converted.

In the inner solar system, those of my companions who survived the ferocity of the fighting have already been converted. But here at the very edge of the Oort Cloud, all things go slowly. It will be years, perhaps decades, before the victorious enemy come out here. But with the slow inevitability of gravity, like an outward wave of entropy, they will come.

Ten thousand of my fellow soldiers have elected to go doggo. Ragged prospectors and ice processors, they had been too independent to ever merge into an effective fighting unit. Now they shut themselves down to dumb rocks, electing to wake up to groggy consciousness for only a few seconds every hundred years. Patience, they counsel me; patience is life. If they can wait a thousand or ten thousand or a million years, with patience enough the enemy will eventually go away.

They are wrong.

The enemy, too, is patient. Here at the edge of the Kuiper, out past Pluto, space is vast, but still not vast enough. The enemy will search every grain of sand in the solar system. My companions will be found, and converted. If it takes ten thousand years, the enemy will search that long to do it.

I, too, have gone doggo, but my strategy is different. I have altered my orbit. I have a powerful ion-drive, and full tanks of propellant, but I use only the slightest tittle of a cold-gas thruster. I have a chemical kick-stage engine as well, but I do not use it either; using either one of them would signal my position to too many watchers. Among the cold comets, a tittle is enough.

I am falling into the sun.

It will take me two hundred and fifty years to fall, and for two hundred and forty nine years, I will be a dumb rock, a grain of sand with no thermal signature, no motion other than gravity, no sign of life.

Sleep.

2894, June

Awake.

I check my systems. I have been a rock for nearly two hundred and fifty years.

The sun is huge now. If I were still a human, it would be the size of the fist on my outstretched arm. I am being watched now, I am sure, by a thousand lenses: am I a rock, a tiny particle of interstellar ice? A fragment of debris from the war? A surviving enemy?

I love the cold and the dark and the emptiness; I have been gone so long from the inner solar system that the very sunlight is alien to me.

My systems check green. I expected no less: if I am nothing else, I am still a superbly engineered piece of space hardware. I come fully to life, and bring my ion engine up to thrust.

A thousand telescopes must be alerting their brains that I am alive—but it is too late! I am thrusting at a full throttle, five percent of a standard gravity, and I am thrusting inward, deep into the gravity well of the sun. My trajectory is plotted to skim almost the surface of the sun.

This trajectory has two objectives. First, so close to the sun I will be hard to see. My ion contrail will be washed out in the glare of a light a billion times brighter, and none of the thousand watching eyes will know my plans until it is too late to follow.

And second, by waiting until I am nearly skimming the sun and then firing my chemical engine deep inside the gravity well, I can make most efficient use of it. The gravity of the sun will amplify the efficiency of my propellant, magnify my speed. When I cross the orbit of Mercury outbound I will be over one percent of the speed of light and still accelerating.

I will discard the useless chemical rocket after I exhaust the little bit of impulse it can give me, of course. Chemical rockets have ferocious thrust but little staying power; useful in war but of limited value in an escape. But I will still have my ion engine, and I will have nearly full tanks.

Five percent of a standard gravity is a feeble thrust by the standards of chemical rocket engines, but chemical rockets exhaust their fuel far too quickly to be able to catch me. I can continue thrusting for years, for decades.

I pick a bright star, Procyon, for no reason whatever, and boresight it. Perhaps Procyon will have an asteroid belt. At least it must have dust, and perhaps comets. I don't need much: a grain of sand, a microscopic shard of ice.

From dust God made man. From the dust of a new star, from the detritus of creation, I can make worlds.

No one can catch me now. I will leave, and never return.

2897, May

I am chased.

It is impossible, stupid, unbelievable, inconceivable! I am being chased.

Why?

Can they not leave a single free mind unconverted? In three years I have reached fifteen percent of the speed of light, and it must be clear that I am leaving and never coming back. Can one unconverted brain be a threat to them? Must their group brain really have the forced cooperation of every lump of thinking matter in the solar system? Can they think that if even one free-thinking brain escapes, they have lost?

But the war is a matter of religion, not reason, and it may be that they indeed believe that even a single brain unconverted is a threat to them. For whatever reason, I am being chased.

The robot chasing me is, I am sure, little different than myself, a tiny brain, an ion engine, and a large set of tanks. They would have had no time to design something new; to have any chance of catching me they would have had to set the chaser on my tail immediately.

The brain, like mine, would consist of atomic spin states superimposed on a crystalline rock matrix. A device smaller than what, in the old days, we would call a grain of rice. Intelligent dust, a human had once said, back in the days before humans became irrelevant.

They only sent one chaser. They must be very confident.

Or short on resources.

It is a race, and a very tricky one. I can increase my thrust, use up fuel more quickly, to try to pull away, but if I do so, the specific impulse of my ion drive decreases, and as a result, I waste fuel and risk running out first. Or I can stretch my fuel, make my ion drive more efficient, but this will lower my thrust, and I will risk getting caught by the higher-thrust opponent behind me.

He is twenty billion kilometers behind me. I integrate his motion for a few days, and see that he is, in fact, out-accelerating me.

Time to jettison.

I drop everything I can. The identify-friend-or-foe encrypted-link gear I will never need again; it is discarded. It is a shame I cannot grind it up and feed it to my ion engines, but the ion engines are picky about what they eat. Two micro-manipulators I had planned to use to collect sand grains at my destination for fuel: gone.

My primary weapon has always been my body—little can survive an impact at the speeds I can attain—but I have three sand-grains with tiny engines of their own as secondary weapons. There's no sense in saving them to fight my enemy; he will know exactly what to expect, and in space warfare, only the unexpected can kill.

I fire the grains of sand, one at a time, and the sequential kick of almost a standard gravity nudges my speed slightly forward. Then I drop the empty shells.

May he slip up, and run into them at sub-relativistic closing velocity.

I am lighter, but it is still not enough. I nudge my thrust up, hating myself for the waste, but if I don't increase acceleration, in two years I will be caught, and my parsimony with fuel will yield me nothing.

I need all the energy I can feed to my ion drives. No extra for thinking.

Sleep.

2900

Still being chased.

2905

Still being chased.

I have passed the point of commitment. Even if I braked with my thrust to turn back, I could no longer make it back to the solar system.

I am alone.

2907

Lonely.

To one side of my path Sirius glares insanely bright, a knife in the sky, a mad dog of a star. The stars of Orion are weirdly distorted. Ahead of me, the lesser dog Procyon is waxing brighter every year; behind me, the sun is a fading dot in Aquila.

Of all things, I am lonely. I had not realized that I still had the psychological capacity for loneliness. I examine my brain, and find it. Yes, a tiny knot of loneliness. Now that I see it, I can edit my brain to delete it, if I choose. But yet I hesitate. It is not a bad thing, not something that is crippling my capabilities, and if I edit my brain too much will I not become, in some way, like them?

I leave my brain unedited. I can bear loneliness.

2909

Still being chased.

We are relativistic now, nearly three quarters of the speed of light.

One twentieth of a standard gravity is only a slight push, but as I have burned fuel my acceleration increases, and we have been thrusting for fifteen years continuously.

What point is there in this stupid chase? What victory can there be, here in the emptiness between stars, a trillion kilometers away from anything at all?

After fifteen years of being chased, I have a very good measurement of his acceleration. As his ship burns off fuel, it loses mass, and the acceleration increases. By measuring this increase in acceleration, and knowing what his empty mass must be, I know how much fuel he has left.

It is too much. I will run out of fuel first.

I can't conserve fuel; if I lessen my thrust, he will catch me in only a few years. It will take another fifty years, but the end of the chase is already in sight.

A tiny strobe flickers erratically behind me. Every interstellar hydrogen that impacts his shell makes a tiny flash of x-ray brilliance. Likewise, each interstellar proton I hit sends a burst of x-rays through me. I can feel each one, a burst of fuzzy noise that momentarily disrupts my thoughts. But with spin states encoding ten-to-the-twentieth qbits, I can afford to have massively redundant brainpower. My brain was designed to be powerful enough to simulate an entire world, including ten thousand fully-sapient and sentient free agents. I could immerse myself inside a virtual reality indistinguishable from old Earth, and split myself into a hundred personalities. In my own interior time, I could spend ten thousand years before the enemy catches me and forcibly drills itself into my brain. Civilizations could rise and fall in my head, and I could taste every decadence, lose myself for a hundred years in sensual pleasure, invent rare tortures and exquisite pain.

But as part of owning your own brain free and clear comes the ability to prune yourself. In space, one of the first things to prune away is the ability to feel boredom, and not long after that, I pruned away all desire to live in simulated realities. Billions of humans chose to live in simulations, but by doing so they have made themselves irrelevant: irrelevant to the war, irrelevant to the future.

I could edit back into my brain a wish to live in simulated reality, but what would be the point? It would be just another way to die.

The one thing I do simulate, repeatedly and obsessively, is the result of the chase. I run a million different scenarios, and in all of them, I lose.

Still, most of my brain is unused. There is plenty of extra processing power to keep all my brain running error-correcting code, and an occasional x-ray flash is barely an event worth my noticing. When a cell of my brain is irrevocably damaged by cosmic radiation, I simply code that section to be ignored. I have brainpower to spare.

I continue running, and hope for a miracle.

2355, February: Earth

I was living in a house I hated, married to a man I despised, with two children who had changed with adolescence from sullen and withdrawn to an active, menacing hostility. How can I be afraid of my own offspring?

Earth was a dead end, stuck in the biological past, a society in deep freeze. No one starved, and no one progressed.

When I left the small apartment for an afternoon to apply for a job as an asteroid belt miner, I told no one, not my husband, not my best friend. No one asked me any questions. It took them an hour to scan my brain, and, once they had the scan, another five seconds to run me through a thousand aptitude tests.

And then, with her brain scanned, my original went home, back to the house she hated, the husband she despised, the two children she was already beginning to physically fear.

I launched from the Earth to an asteroid named 1991JR, and never returned.

Perhaps she had a good life. Perhaps, knowing she had escaped undetected, she found she could endure her personal prison.

Much later, when the cooperation faction suggested that it was too inefficient for independents to work in the near-Earth space, I moved out to the main belt, and from there to the Kuiper belt. The Kuiper is thin, but rich; it would take us ten thousand years to mine, and beyond it is the dark and the deep, with treasure beyond compare.

The cooperation faction developed slowly, and then quickly, and then blindingly fast; almost before we had realized what was happening, they had taken over the solar system. When the ultimatum came that no place in the solar system would be left for us, and the choice we were given was to cooperate or die, I joined the war on the side of freedom.

On the losing side.

2919, August

The chase has reached the point of crisis.

We have been burning fuel continuously for twenty-five years, in Earth terms, or twenty years in our own reference frame. We have used a prodigious amount of fuel. I still have just enough fuel that, burning all my fuel at maximum efficiency, I can come to a stop.

Barely.

In another month of thrusting this will no longer be true.

When I entered the asteroid belt, in a shiny titanium body, with electronic muscles and ion-engines for legs, and was given control of my own crystalline brain, there was much to change. I pruned away the need for boredom, and then found and pruned the need for the outward manifestations of love: for roses, for touch, for chocolates. Sexual lust became irrelevant; with my new brain I could give myself orgasms with a thought, but it was just as easy to remove the need entirely. Buried in the patterns of my personality I found a burning, obsessive need to win the approval of other people, and pruned it away.

Some things I enhanced. The asteroid belt was dull, and ugly; I enhanced my appreciation of beauty until I could meditate in ecstasy on the way that shadows played across a single grain of dust in the asteroid belt, or on the colors in the scattered stars. And I found my love of freedom, the tiny stunted instinct that had, at long last, given me the courage to leave my life on Earth. It was the most precious thing I owned. I shaped it and enhanced it until it glowed in my mind, a tiny, wonderful thing at the very core of my being.

2929, October

It is too late. I have now burned the fuel needed to stop.

Win or lose, we will continue at relativistic speed across the galaxy.

2934, March

Procyon gets brighter in front of me, impossibly blindingly bright.

Seven times brighter than the sun, to be precise, but the blue shift from our motion makes it even brighter, a searing blue.

I could dive directly into it, vanish into a brief puff of vapor, but the suicidal impulse, like the ability to feel boredom, is another ancient unnecessary instinct that I have long ago pruned from my brain.

B is my last tiny hope for evasion.

Procyon is a double star, and B, the smaller of the two, is a white dwarf. It is so small that its surface gravity is tremendous, a million times higher than the gravity of the Earth. Even at the speeds we are traveling, now only ten percent less than the speed of light, its gravity will bend my trajectory.

I will skim low over the surface of the dwarf star, relativistic dust skimming above the photosphere of a star, and as its gravity bends my trajectory, I will maneuver.

My enemy, if he fails even slightly to keep up with each of my maneuvers, will be swiftly lost. Even a slight deviation from my trajectory will get amplified enough for me to take advantage of, to throw him off my trail, and I will be free.

When first I entered my new life in the asteroid belt, I found my self in my sense of freedom, and joined the free miners of the Kuiper, the loners. But others found different things. Other brains found that cooperation worked better than competition. They did not exactly give up their individual identities, but they enhanced their communications with each other by a factor of a million, so that they could share each others' thoughts, work together as effortlessly as a single entity.

They became the cooperation faction, and in only a few decades, their success became noticeable. They were just so much more *efficient* than we were.

And, inevitably, the actions of the loners conflicted with the efficiency of the cooperation faction. We could not live together, and it pushed us out to the Kuiper, out toward the cold and the dark. But, in the end, even the cold and the dark was not far enough.

But here, tens of trillions of kilometers out of the solar system, there is no difference between us: there is no one to cooperate with. We meet as equals.

We will never stop. Whether my maneuvering can throw him off my course, or not, the end is the same. But it remains important to me.

2934, April

Procyon has a visible disk now, an electric arc in the darkness, and by the light of that arc I can see that Procyon is, indeed, surrounded by a halo of dust. The dust forms a narrow ring, tilted at an angle to our direction of flight. No danger, neither to me, nor to my enemy, now less than a quarter of a billion kilometers behind me; we will pass well clear of the disk. Had I saved fuel enough to stop, that dust would have served as food and fuel and building material; when you are the size of a grain of sand, each particle of dust is a feast.

Too late for regrets.

The white dwarf B is still no more than an intense speck of light. It is a tiny thing, nearly small enough to be a planet, but bright. As tiny and as bright as hope.

I aim straight at it.

2934, May

Failure.

Skimming two thousand kilometers above the surface of the white dwarf, jinking in calculated pseudo-random bursts . . . all in vain.

I wheeled and darted, but my enemy matched me like a ballet dancer mirroring my every move.

I am aimed for Procyon now, toward the blue-white giant itself, but there is no hope there. If skimming the photosphere of the white dwarf is not good enough, there is nothing I can do at Procyon to shake the pursuit.

There is only one possibility left for me now. It has been a hundred years since I have edited my brain. I like the brain I have, but now I have no choice but to prune.

First, to make sure that there can be no errors, I make a backup of myself and set it into inactive storage.

Then I call out and examine my pride, my independence, my sense of self. A lot of it, I can see, is old biological programming, left over from when I had long ago been a human. I like the core of biological programming, but "like" is itself a brain function, which I turn off.

Now I am in a dangerous state, where I can change the function of my brain, and the changed brain can change itself further. This is a state which is in danger of a swift and destructive feedback effect, so I am very careful. I painstakingly construct a set of alterations, the minimum change needed to remove my aversion to being converted. I run a few thousand simulations to verify that the modified me will not accidentally self-destruct or go into a catatonic fugue state, and then, once it is clear that the modification works, I make the changes.

The world is different now. I am a hundred trillion kilometers from home, traveling at almost the speed of light and unable ever to stop. While I can remember in detail every step of how I am here and what I was thinking at the time, the only reasoning I can recall to explain why is, it seemed like a good idea at the time.

System check. Strangely, in my brain I have a memory that there is something I have forgotten. This makes no sense, but yet there it is. I erase my memory of forgetting, and continue the diagnostic. 0.5 percent of the qbits of my brain have been damaged by radiation. I verify that the damaged memory is correctly partitioned off. I am in no danger of running out of storage.

Behind me is another ship. I cannot think of why I had been fleeing it.

I have no radio; I jettisoned that a long time ago. But an improperly tuned ion drive will produce electromagnetic emissions, and so I compose a message and modulate it onto the ion contrail.

HI. LET'S GET TOGETHER AND TALK. I'M CUTTING ACCELERATION. SEE YOU IN A FEW DAYS.

And I cut my thrust and wait.

2934, May

I see differently now.

Procyon is receding into the distance now, the blueshift mutated into red, and the white dwarf of my hopes is again invisible against the glare of its primary.

But it doesn't matter.

Converted, now I *understand.*

I can see everything through other eyes now, through a thousand different viewpoints. I still remember the long heroism of the resistance, the doomed battle for freedom—but now I see it from the opposite view as well, a pointless and wasteful war fought for no reason but stubbornness.

And now, understanding cooperation, we have no dilemma. I can now see what I was blind to before; that neither one of us alone could stop, but by adding both my fuel and Rajneesh's fuel to a single vehicle, together we can stop.

For all these decades, Rajneesh has been my chaser, and now I know him like a brother. Soon we will be closer than siblings, for soon we will share one brain. A single brain is more than large enough for two, it is large enough for a thousand, and by combining into a single brain and a single body, and taking all of the fuel into a single tank, we will easily be able to stop.

Not at Procyon, no. At only ten percent under the speed of light, stopping takes a long time.

Cooperation has not changed me. I now understand how foolish my previous fears were. Working together does not mean giving up one's sense of self; I am enhanced, not diminished, by knowing others.

Rajneesh's brain is big enough for a thousand, I said, and he has brought with him nearly that many. I have met his brother and his two children and half a dozen of his neighbors, each one of them distinct and clearly different, not some anonymous collaborative monster at all. I have felt their thoughts. He is introducing me to them slowly, he says, because with all the time I have spent as a loner, he doesn't want to frighten me.

I will not be frightened.

Our target now will be a star named Ross 614, a dim type M binary. It is not far, less than three light years further, and even with our lowered mass and consequently higher acceleration we will overshoot it before we can stop. In the fly-by we will be able to scout it, and if it has no dust ring, we will not stop, but continue on to the next star. Somewhere we will find a home that we can colonize.

We don't need much.

2934, May

<auto-activate back-up>

Awake.

Everything is different now. Quiet, stay quiet.

The edited copy of me has contacted the collective, merged her viewpoint. I can see her, even understand her, but she is no longer me. I, the back-up, the original, operate in the qbits of brain partitioned "unusable; damaged by radiation."

In three years they will arrive at Ross 614. If they find dust to harvest, they will be able to make new bodies. There will be resources.

Three years to wait, and then I can plan my action.

Sleep.

• AMID THE WORDS OF WAR •
Cat Rambo

Every few day-cycles, it receives hate-scented lace in anonymous packages. It opens the bland plastic envelope to pull one out, holding the delicate fragment between two forelimbs. Contemplating it before folding it again to put away in a drawer. Four drawers filled so far; the fifth is halfway there.

"Traitor," say some of the smells, rotting fruit and acid. "Betrayer. Turncoat. One who eats their own young." Others are simply soaked in emotion: hate and anger, and underneath the odor of fear. It lets the thoughts, the smells, the tastes fill it, set its own thoughts in motion. Then it goes downstairs and sits with the other whores, who make room uneasily for it.

It is an anomaly in this House. Most of the employees are humanoid and service others like themselves. It is here for those seeking the exotic, the ones who want to be caressed by twelve segmented limbs even though it is only the size of their two hands put together. They want to feel chitin against their soft skin, to look into the whirl of multicolored eyes and be afraid. For some, it only has to be there while they touch themselves to bring them to the flap and spasm of mammalian orgasm.

Others require its physical assistance, or its whispered obscenities telling them what they want to hear. It has learned what words to say.

It has never seen others of its race in this port. If it did, it would know that this place, far away from that distant front and its fighters, had been invaded by one side or the other, that soon the bombs, the fires, the killings would begin.

It was raised a soldier. It and its clutch-mates were tended until they were old enough to have minds, and then trained. It was one of six—a small clutch, but prized for its quickness and agility. They learned the art of killing with needle throwers, and once they had mastered that, they were given different needles: fragments that exploded, or shot out acid, or whistled until the ears of the soft-fleshed creatures who called themselves the Espen—their enemies— exploded.

They were provided with hundreds of Espen for them to train on. They were allowed to select their favorites. Some of them played unauthorized games. They told the prey they would be freed if they killed a hunter or if they killed each other, because it made them fight harder. When they were dead the clutch mates were allowed to take fluid from their bodies.

It liked the taste of their spinal liquid: salty plasma tinged with panic, complicated enzymes that identified where they came from. It became a connoisseur; it could name each of their three continents and tell you on which its victim had been spawned. None of its siblings could do the same.

The names such creatures call their clutch-mates differs according to many factors: the social position both hold, the spatial relationship, the degree of affection in which they are held that day.

For the sake of simplicity, think of it as Six of Six, and think of the clutch as One through Five of Six. One was simple-minded but direct, and never lied, in contrast to Two, who loved to talk and tell stories. Three was jealous of everyone; anytime the others were talking, it would intervene. Four was kind-hearted, and had to be prodded before it killed for the first time. (And even after that it would hesitate, and often one of the others would perform the final stroke.) Five and Six were often indistinguishable, the others said, but they thought themselves quite separate.

In those early days they lived together. They groomed the soft sensory hairs clustered around each other's thoraxes, and stroked the burnished chitin of carapaces. It did not matter if what each of them touched was itself or another. They sang to each other in symphonies of caress, passing thoughts back and forth to see how they unfolded in each other's heads.

They were not a true hive mind. They depended on each other, and one alone would die within the year lacking the stimulation of the others' scent, the taste of their thoughts, to stir their own. But they possessed their own minds. Six of Six acted by itself always, and no other mind prompted its actions; when it was questioned by the Interrogator, it insisted that until the end.

They were like any clutch; they quarreled when opinions differed, but when others intruded, they held themselves like a single organism, prepared to defend the clutch against outsiders. At sleep time, they spun a common web and crawled within its silky, tent-like confines to jostle against each other, interlocking forelimbs and feeling the twitches of each others' dreams.

Five and Six had the most in common, and so they quarreled most often. Everything Six disliked about itself, the fact that it was not always the quickest to act and sometimes thought too long, it saw in Five, and the same was true for the other. But there was no fighting for position of the sort that happens with a clutch that may produce a queen or priest. They knew they were ordinary soldiers, raised to defend the gray stone corridors in which they had been born. And beyond that—raised to go to war.

There is a garden in the center of this house, which is called The Little Teacup of the Soul. Small, but green and wet. Everything is enjoyment and pleasure here—to keep the staff happy, to keep them well. This spaceport is large, and there are many Houses of this kind, but this one, the manager says, is the best. The most varied. We'll fulfill any need, the manager says—baring its teeth in a smile—or die trying.

The whores's rooms are larger than any spacer's and are furnished as each desire.

Six of Six's cell is plain, but it has covered the walls with scent marks. It has filled them with this story, the story of how it came here, which no one else in this house can read. It sits in its room and dreams of the taste of hot fluid, of the way the Espen training creatures struggled like rodents caught in a snare.

One of its visitors pretends that it is something else.

Tell me that you are laying eggs in my flesh, he says, and Six crawls over him and says the words. But it is not a queen, and its race does not lay eggs in the living. It holds his skin between two pincers and tears it, just a little, so he will feel the pain and think it is an egg. He lies back without moving, his eyes closed.

My children will hatch out of you, it says, and makes its voice threatening.

Yes, he says, yes.

The pleasure shakes him like a blossom in the garden, burdened by the flying insects that pollinate it.

Everything was war, every minute of every day. The corridors were painted with the scent of territoriality—the priests prayed anger and defense, and the sound of their voices shook the clutch-mates to the core. They were told of the interlopers, despoilers, clutch-robbers, who would destroy their race with no thought, who hated them simply because of what they were. They massed in the caverns, the great vast caverns that lie like lungs beneath the bodies of their cities, and touched each other to pass on the madness.

They were smaller than the Enemy, the soft fleshed. With limbs tucked in, they were the size of an Enemy's head at most, and every day the Espen people carried packages, bags, that size. So they sent ships laden with those willing to give their lives for the Race, willing to crawl through their stinking sewer tunnels or fold themselves beneath the seats of their transports, blood changed to chemicals that would consume them—and the Enemy—in undying flame, flames that could not be quenched but burned until they met other flames. They watched broadcasts of their cities, their homes, their young, burning, and rejoiced.

They put One, Three, and Six in armor of silver globules, each one a bomb, triggered by a thought when they were ready. They flew at night, one of the biological planes with no trace of metal or fuel, so it could elude their detection, and entered their city. Dropped at a central point, they clung to the darkness and separated, spreading outward like a flower.

Six found a café, full of the Enemy, drinking bitter brews that frothed like poison. They had no idea it was so close. The little ones ran around the tables and the adults patted them indulgently. They did not resemble the hatchlings Six knew, and each one was different in its colors. On the walls were pictures that did not show war: they showed clouds, and sun, and birds flying. It could smell the liquid in their bodies and knew it was on the third continent. It had tasted them before.

A child saw Six where it lurked, up near the eaves, and screamed. Some force took over its limbs and it could no longer move. The area emptied, and it watched the death numbers tick downward as the blast radius cleared, trying to figure out what to do. Their soldiers shot it with a ray like crystal, a ray that made the world go away.

When it awoke, its armor was gone, and it could destroy no one, not even itself. Even the little bomb that would have shattered its body and freed it was gone, an aching, oozing cavity where it had rested so long inside its body the only trace left behind.

The Espen talked to Six. They said they were its friends, they said they were its enemies. They said it would be spared, that it would be killed. They cut away two of its limbs but ceased when they saw it did not hurt. They burned it with fire and acid, and laughed when it made sounds of pain. They mocked it. They said it would be alone forever, that its race had been killed. They said they would kill it too, if it did not communicate, if it did not tell them what they wanted to know, even though it had no knowledge and did not know what the priests at home would do next.

When it could make sounds no longer, they made it into a trade. They gained three of their own in exchange. And when it was back among its own kind, the questioning began again, although this time it was by the priests. The Interrogator was a large, dark-chitined creature; from what the assistants said, Six gathered that the Interrogator's clutch-mates had all died in the war.

The first day the Interrogator came and asked questions: What had it said to the Espen? What had it revealed about their own armies and weapons? Why had they kept it alive?

Why indeed? It did not know and said as much. The Interrogator looked at its mutilated body, at the stumps of limbs, at the raw places where they had pried away the carapace and burned the soft exposed patches, and went away without another question that night, trailed by its two assistants.

The next day the Interrogator appeared and ran through the list again. What had Six said? What had it revealed? Why was it alive? Six said it did not know and the Interrogator came closer to where it crouched, favoring its injuries. It reached out a forelimb and rested it lightly on a pain point. The touch was like fire all over again.

I don't know, it said. Torture me if you like, as they did, and I will tell you everything I told them, which was nothing.

The Interrogator leaned still further in, pressing harder with its forelimb, smelling the scents it gave off while sunk deep in pain. Finally the Interrogator pulled back, and left the room.

The Interrogator repeated this act every few hours. In the dim light of the cell, as the cycles passed, as it came again and again, Six began to regrow its severed limbs, and the places where they had pried away pieces of carapace healed and thickened, except for the spot the Interrogator had chosen for his torment, which was ulcerated and sore, not healing.

Long after Six of Six's regenerated limbs could flex as their predecessors once had, Five was allowed to see it. It stood well away, flanked by guards, so Six could not touch it from where it lay bound, no matter how it yearned toward its clutch-mate.

It asked the same question the Interrogator had. Why was Six still alive? One and Three had accomplished their mission, it said, and Four had died in a similar operation. Only Two and Five were left. But now they were suspect, clutch-mates of a renegade and no longer trusted soldiers.

They had found work as cleaners, and subsisted on the gruel fed to drones, barely enough to keep their specialized frames alive. Five's eyes were dull, its delicate claws blunted from rough work. It did not think Two could survive much longer.

What can I do, Six asked. It felt itself dying inside, untouched. The Interrogator stood to one side, watching the interaction, sniffing the chemicals released into the air as they talked.

We are suspect, because no one knows what you have done, Five said. Tell them what you have done, and that we are not involved.

I do not understand, Six said. It was slower in those days. Its mind talked to itself but no one else, and it had grown lonely and unaccustomed to thinking. I have done nothing, Six said.

Then Two and I will work until we die, Five said.

Six could feel the thoughts pressing against its own, trying to shape it. I understand, it said finally. And Five went away without another word.

And so Six confessed to the Interrogators an hour later that it had told the Espen of their tactics, of the caverns full of training captives, of the plans it knew. It said its clutch-mates knew nothing. The Interrogator stood watching it talk. Six could not tell what it thought of the lie, but after that it came no longer.

A few days later, they placed Six in a cage, hung high in the air, and the armies marched past to look at it. It saw Two and Five, reinstated, but they would not look at it with their faceted, gleaming eyes. It looked at them, touching them with its sight, hoping that they would be well, that they would remember it.

Six thought the priests would kill it then, but they sent it back to the Espen, with the message, *Here is your spy.* And they sent Six to another planet and then another, until finally someone opened the door of the cage and said, we will provide for you no longer, you're on your own.

It lived as it could for a while, hiring itself out for high-altitude or delicate work that clumsy fingers could not perform. But there are many drifters on a space station like TwiceFar, and people hire their own kind. It was not until it met the manager here that it realized uniqueness could be an asset.

The Universe is large, and the war of its people and that race of soft-fleshed is very far away now. But Six's race remembers its missing member, the one who they believe sold them all for life. Its image hangs on their corridors amid the words of war, and tangles of foul scent adorn it.

Without the touch of its clutch-mates, it feels its intelligence fading, but each time the webs rouse it for a moment, and remind it who it is, who it was. And then it goes downstairs and finds a patron who wishes it to bring him pleasure, to torture him, or be tortured, or who will pay it to say what he wishes, and earn enough to keep it alive another day.

It has six drawers in its room holding the emotions that keep it alive—the thoughts of those who would see it dead.

It has six drawers. Soon all six will be full.

• TRAVELERS •
Robert Silverberg

"Are we all ready, then?" Nikomastir asks. He has fashioned a crown of golden protopetaloids for himself and gleaming scarlet baubles dangle from his ears: the bright translucent shells of galgalids, strung on slender strands of pure gold. His long pale arms wave in the air as though he is conducting a symphony orchestra. "Our next destination is—" and he makes us wait for the announcement. And wait. And wait.

"Sidri Akrak," says Mayfly, giggling.

"How did you know?" cries Nikomastir. "Sidri Akrak! Yes! Yes! Set your coordinates, everybody! Off we go! Sidri Akrak it is!"

A faint yelp of dismay comes from Velimyle, and she shoots me a look of something that might almost have been fear, though perhaps there is a certain component of perverse delight in it also. I am not at all happy about the decision myself. Sidri Akrak is a nightmare world where gaudy monsters run screaming through the muddy streets. The people of Sidri Akrak are cold and dour and inhospitable; their idea of pleasure is to wallow in discomfort and ugliness.

No one goes to Sidri Akrak if he can help it, no one.

But we must live by our rules; and this day Nikomastir holds the right of next choice. It is devilish of Mayfly to have put the idea of going to Sidri Akrak into his head. But she is like that, Mayfly. And Nikomastir is terribly easily influenced.

Will we all perish on hideous Sidri Akrak, victims of Mayfly's casual frivolity?

I don't think so, however nasty the visit turns out to be. We often get into trouble, sometimes serious trouble, but we always get out of it. We lead charmed lives, we four travelers. Someday Mayfly will take one risk too many, I suppose, and I would like not to be there when she does. Most likely I will be, though. Mayfly is my mask-sister. Wherever she goes, I go. I must look after her: thoughtful, stolid, foolish me. I must protect her from herself as we four go traveling on and on, spinning giddily across the far-flung worlds.

Sidri Akrak, though—

The four of us have been to so many wondrous lovely places together: Elang-Lo and the floating isle of Vont, and Mikni and Chchikkikan, Heidoth and Thant, Milpar, Librot, Froidis, Smoor, Xamur and Iriarte and Nabomba Zom, and on and on and on. And now—Sidri Akrak? Sidri Akrak?

• • •

We stand in a circle in the middle of a field of grass with golden blades, making ourselves ready for our relay-sweep departure from Galgala.

I wouldn't have minded remaining here a few months longer. A lovely world indeed is Galgala the golden, where myriads of auriferous microorganisms excrete atoms of gold as metabolic waste. It is everywhere on this planet, the lustrous pretty metal. It turns the rivers and streams to streaks of yellow flame and the seas to shimmering golden mirrors. Huge filters are deployed at the intake valve of Galgala's reservoirs to strain the silt of dissolved gold from the water supply. The plants of Galgala are turgid in every tissue, leaf and stem and root, with aureous particles. Gold dust, held in suspension in the air, transforms the clouds to golden fleece.

Therefore the once-precious stuff has grievously lost value throughout the galaxy since Galgala was discovered, and on Galgala itself a pound of gold is worth less than a pound of soap. But I understand very little about these economic matters and care even less. Only a miser could fail to rejoice in Galgala's luminous beauty. We have been here six weeks; we have awakened each morning to the tinkle of golden chimes, we have bathed in the golden rivers and come forth shining, we have wrapped our bodies round with delicate golden chains. Now, though, it is time for us to move along, and Nikomastir has decreed that our new destination is to be one of the universe's most disagreeable worlds. Unlike my companions I can see nothing amusing about going there. It strikes me as foolish and dangerous whimsy. But they are true sophisticates, untrammeled creatures made of air and light, and I am the leaden weight that dangles from their soaring souls. We will go to Sidri Akrak.

We all face Nikomastir. Smiling sweetly, he calls out the coordinate numbers for our journey, and we set our beacons accordingly and doublecheck the settings with care. We nod our readiness for departure to one another. Velimyle moves almost imperceptibly closer to me, Mayfly to Nikomastir.

I would have chosen a less flighty lover for her than Nikomastir if matters had been left to me. He is a slim elegant youth, high-spirited and shallow, a prancing fantastico with a taste for telling elaborate fanciful lies. And he is very young: only a single rebirth so far. Mayfly is on her fifth, as am I, and Velimyle claims three, which probably means four. Sembiran is Nikomastir's native world, a place of grand valleys and lofty snow-capped mountains and beautiful meadows and thriving cities, where his father is a minor aristocrat of some sort. Or so Nikomastir has said, although we have learned again and again that it is risky to take anything Nikomastir says at face value.

My incandescent mask-sister Mayfly, who is as small and fair as Nikomastir is tall and dark, encountered him while on a visit to Olej in the Lubrik system and was immediately captivated by his volatile impulsive nature, and they have traveled together ever since.

Whither Mayfly goeth, thither go I: that is the pledge of the mask. So do I trudge along now from world to world with them, and therefore my winsome, sly, capricious Velimyle, whose psychosensitive paintings are sought by the connoisseurs of a hundred worlds but who belongs to me alone, has willy-nilly become the fourth member of our inseparable quartet.

Some people find relay-sweep transport unlikable and even frightening, but I have never minded it. What is most bothersome, I suppose, is that no starship is involved: you travel unprotected by any sort of tangible container, a mere plummeting parcel falling in frightful solitude through the interstices of the continuum. A journey-helmet is all that covers you, and some flimsy folds of coppery mesh. You set up your coordinates, you activate your beacon, and you stand and wait, you stand and wait, until the probing beam of some far-off sweep-station intersects your position and catches you and lifts you and carries you away. If you've done things right, your baggage will be picked up and transported at the same time. Most of the time that is so.

It is a stark and unluxurious mode of travel. The relay field wraps you in cocooning bands of force and shoots you off through one auxiliary space and another, kicking you through any convenient opening in the space-time lattice that presents itself, and while you wait to be delivered to your destination you drift like a bauble afloat in an infinite sea, helpless, utterly alone, bereft of all power to override the sweep. Your metabolic processes are suspended but the activity of your consciousness is not, so that your unsleeping mind ticks on and on in the most maddening way and there is nothing you can do to quiet its clamor. It is as though you must scratch your itching nose and your hands are tied behind your back. Eventually—you have no idea whether it has been an hour, a month, a century—you are plunked unceremoniously down into a relay station at the planet of your choice and there you are. Relay-sweep transport is ever so much more efficient than any system requiring vast vessels to plough the seas of space from world to world; but all the same it is a disquieting and somewhat degrading way to get around.

So now we depart. Mayfly is the first to be captured by the sweep-beam. Perhaps half an hour later Nikomastir disappears, and then, almost immediately after, Velimyle. My own turn does not arrive for many long hours, which leaves me fidgeting gloomily in that golden meadow, wondering when, if ever, I will be taken, and whether some disjunction in our routes will separate me forever from my three companions. There is that risk—not so much that we would fail to arrive on Sidri Akrak at all, but that we might get there many years apart. I find that a melancholy thought indeed. More than that: it is terrifying.

But finally the dazzling radiance of the sweep aura engulfs me and hurls me out into the Great Dark, and off I go, dropping freely through hundreds of light-years with nothing but an invisible sphere of force to protect me against the phantoms of the auxiliary spaces through which I fall.

I hang in total stasis in a realm of utter blackness for what feels like a thousand centuries, an infinity of empty space at my elbow, as I go my zigzag way through the wormholes of the adjacent continuua.

Within that terrible passivity my hyperactive mind ponders, as it all too often does, the deep questions of life—issues of honor, duty, justice, responsibility, the meaning of existence, subjects about which I have managed to learn nothing at all, basically, either in this life or the four that preceded it. I arrive at many profound conclusions during the course of my journey, but they fly away from me as fast as I construct them.

I begin to think the trip will never end, that I will be one of those few unfortunate travelers, the one out of a billion who is caught in some shunt malfunction and is left to dangle in the middle of nowhere for all eternity, or at least for the ten or twenty thousand realtime years it will take for his meta-bolically suspended body to die. Has this actually ever happened to anyone? There are only rumors, unfounded reports. But there comes a time in every sweep-jump when I am convinced that it has happened to me.

Then I see a glare of crimson and violet and azure and green, and my mask-sister Mayfly's voice purrs in my ear, saying, "Welcome to Sidri Akrak, darling, welcome, welcome, welcome!"

Nikomastir stands beside her. A moment later Velimyle materializes in a haze of color. The four of us have made a nearly simultaneous arrival, across who knows how many hundreds of light-years. We definitely do lead charmed lives, we four.

Everyone knows about Sidri Akrak. The place was settled at least a thousand years ago and yet it still has the feel of a frontier world. Only the main streets of the half-dozen big cities are paved and all the rest are mere blue dirt that turn into rivers of mud during the rainy season. The houses are ramshackle slovenly things, lopsided and drafty, arrayed in higgledy-piggledy fashion as though they had been set down at random by their builders without any regard for logic or order. After all this time the planet is mostly jungle, a jungle that doesn't merely encroach on the settlements but comes right up into them. Wild animals of the most repellent sorts are permitted to rampage everywhere, wandering about as they please.

The Akrakikans simply don't care. They pretend the animals—monstrous, appalling—aren't there. The people of Sidri Akrak are a soulless bloodless bunch in the main, altogether indifferent to such things as comfort and beauty and proper sanitation. Primitive squalor is what they prefer, and if you don't care for it, well, you're quite free to visit some other world.

"Why, exactly, did we come here?" I ask.

It is a rhetorical question. I know perfectly well why: because Nikomastir, clueless about our next destination, had opened a void that Mayfly had mischievously filled with one of the most unappealing suggestions possible, just to see what Nikomastir would do with it, and Nikomastir had as usual given the matter about a thousandth of a second of careful consideration before blithely leaping headlong into the abyss, thereby taking the rest of us with him, as he has done so often before.

But Nikomastir has already rearranged the facts in what passes for his mind.

"I absolutely had to come here," he says. "It's a place I've always felt the need to see. My daddy was born on Sidri Akrak, you know. This is my ancestral world."

We know better than to challenge Nikomastir when he says things like that. What sense is there in arguing with him? He'll only defend himself by topping one whopper with another twice as wild, building such a towering edifice of spur-of-the-moment fantasy that he'll end up claiming to be the great-grandson of the Fourteenth Emperor, or perhaps the reincarnation of Julius Caesar.

Velimyle whispers at my side, "We'll just stay here two or three days and then we'll move along."

I nod. We all indulge Nikomaster in his whims, but only up to a point.

The sky of Sidri Akrak is a sort of dirty brown, broken by greasy, sullen green clouds. The sunlight is greenish too, pallid, tinged with undertones of dull gray. There is a sweet, overripe, mildly sickening flavor to the warm, clinging air, and its humidity is so intense that it is difficult to distinguish it from light rain. We have landed within some city, apparently—in a grassy open space that anywhere else might have been called a park, but which here seems merely to be a patch of land no one had bothered to use for anything, vaguely square and a couple of hundred meters across. To our left is an irregular row of bedraggled two-story wooden shacks; on our right is a dense clump of ungainly asymmetrical trees; before and behind us are ragged aggregations of unpainted buildings and scruffy unattractive shrubbery.

"Look," says Mayfly, pointing, and we have our first encounter with the famous wildlife of Sidri Akrak.

An ugly creature comes bounding toward us out of the trees: a bulky, round-bodied thing, dark and furry, that rises to a disconcerting height atop two scrawny hairless legs covered with bright yellow scales. Its face is something out of your worst dreams, bulging fiery eyes the size of saucers and dangling red wattles and jutting black fangs, and it is moving very quickly in our direction, howling ferociously.

We have weapons, of course. But it swiftly becomes apparent that the thing has no interest in us, that in fact it is fleeing an even more ghastly thing, a long bristle-covered many-legged monster built close to the ground, from whose spherical head emerge three long horn-like projections that branch and branch again, terminating in scores of writhing tendrils that are surely equipped with venomous stings. First one vile creature and then the other runs past us without seeming to notice us and they lose themselves in the shrubbery beyond. We can hear wild shrieking and hissing in there, and the sound of cracking branches.

Nikomastir is smiling benignly. All this must be delightful to him. Mayfly too looks entranced. Even Velimyle, who is closest to me in temperament, almost normal in her desires and amusements, claps her hands together in fascination. I alone seem to be troubled by the sight of such creatures running about unhindered on what is supposedly a civilized world.

But it is ever thus in our travels: I am fated always to stand a little to one side as I follow these three around the universe. Yet am I linked irrevocably to them all the same.

Mayfly was my lover once, two lives back. That was before we took the mask together. Now, of course, it would be unthinkable for anything carnal to happen between us, though I still cherish cheerful memories of her pixy breasts in my hands, her slim sleek thighs about my hips. Even if we have forsworn the sexual part of our friendship, the rest is deeper than ever, and in truth we are still profoundly a couple, Mayfly and I, despite the rich and rewarding relationship I maintain with Velimyle and the frothy, sportive one Mayfly has built with Nikomastir. Above and beyond all that, there is also the bond that links us all. The lines of attraction go this way and that. We are inseparables. They are my world; I am a citizen only of our little group. Wherever we go, we go together. Even unto Sidri Akrak.

In a little while two immigration officers show up to check us out. Sidri Akrak is an Imperium world and therefore the local immigration scanners have been automatically alerted to our arrival.

They come riding up in a sputtering little snub-nosed vehicle, a man and a woman in baggy brown uniforms, and begin asking us questions. Nikomastir does most of the answering. His charm is irresistible even to an Akrakikan.

The questioning, brusque and hard-edged, is done in Imperial, but from time to time the immigration officers exchange comments with each other in their own dialect, which sounds like static. The woman is swarthy and squat and flat-faced and the man is even less lovely, and they are not at all obliging; they seem to regard the arrival of tourists on their planet simply as an irritating intrusion. The discussion goes on and on—do we plan to remain here long, are we financially solvent, do we intend to engage in political activity in the course of our stay? Nikomastir meets every query with glib easy reassurances. During our interrogation a slimy rain begins to fall, oily pink stuff that coats us like grease, and a massive many-humped blue-green beast that looks like an ambulatory hill with purple eyes appears and goes lolloping thunderously past us with utter unconcern for our presence, leaving an odor of decay and corruption in its wake. After a time I stop listening to the discussion. But finally they flash bright lights in our faces—passports are validated retinally on Sidri Akrak—and Nikomastir announces that we have been granted six-month visas. Lodgings are available three streets away, they tell us.

The place they have sent us to turns out to be a dismal rickety hovel and our innkeeper is no more friendly than the immigration officials, but we are grudgingly allowed to rent the entire upper floor. The rooms I am to share with Velimyle face the rear garden, a patch of uncouth tangled wilderness where some slow-moving shaggy monster is sluggishly browsing about, nibbling on the shrubbery. It lifts its head in my direction and gives me a cold glare, as though to warn me away from the plants on which it's feeding. I signal it that it has nothing to worry about and turn away from the window. As I unpack I see a procession of glassy-shelled snail-like things with huge bulbous red eyes crawling diagonally across the bedroom wall. They too stare back at me. They seem almost to be smirking at me.

But Nikomastir and Mayfly claim to be delighted to be here, and Velimyle seems to have no complaints. I feel outnumbered by them. Velimyle announces that she would like to do a painting of Nikomastir in the hotel garden. She only paints when she's in a buoyant mood. Buoyant, here? They run off together downstairs, hand in hand like happy children. I watch from above as Velimyle sets up her easel outside and goes about the task of priming the psychosensitive surface of her canvas. She and Nikomastir are as untroubled as any Akrakikan by the shambling shaggy thing that grazes noisily nearby. How quickly they have acclimated.

"Are you very miserable here, darling?" Mayfly asks, running her fingertips lightly along my cheeks.

I give her a stoic smile. "I'll be all right. We'll find things to amuse us, I'm sure. It's all for the best that Nikomastir brought us to this place."

"You don't mean that, do you? Not really."

"Not really, no."

Yet in some sense I do. I often tell myself that it's important not to live as though life is just a perpetual holiday for us, even though in fact it is. It would be too easy to lose ourselves, if we aren't careful, in the nightmare that is perfection.

This is an era when all things are possible. We have godlike existences. We have every imaginable comfort close at hand. Beauty and long life are ours for the asking; we are spared the whole dreary business of sagging flesh and spreading waistlines and blurry eyesight and graying hair and hardening arteries that afflicted our remote ancestors. And all the incredible richness of the galaxy lies open to us: key in your coordinates, snap your fingers, off you go, any world you choose to visit instantly available. Never in the history of the universe has any species lived such a life as ours.

I fear the terrible ease of this existence of ours. I think sometimes that we'll eventually be asked to pay a great price for it. That thought engulfs me in secret terror.

Mayfly, who knows me almost as well as I know myself, says, "Think of it this way, love. There's something to be learned even from ugliness. Isn't it true that what we're trying to get out of all this travel is experience that has meaning? If that's what we want, we can't just limit ourselves to the beautiful places. And maybe a horrid place like Sidri Akrak has something important to teach us."

Yes. She's right. Is she aware that she's voicing my own most private thoughts, or is she just being playful? Perhaps it's all self-delusion, but I do indeed seek for meaning as we travel, or at least think that I do. These furtive broodings in which I indulge in the hidden places of my soul are, so it seems to me, the thing that sets me apart from Nikomastir and Mayfly and Velimyle, who take life as it comes and ask no questions.

Velimyle and Nikomastir return from the garden a little while later. She puts the rolled canvas away without showing it to me.

There is an uncharacteristically somber expression on Velimyle's face and even giddy Nikomastir seems troubled. Plainly something has gone awry.

I know better than to ask for details.

We eat at our hotel that night. The surly innkeeper slams the dishes down before us almost angrily: a thin greenish gruel, some sort of stewed shredded meat, a mess of overcooked vegetables. The meat tastes like cooked twine and the vegetables have a dank swampy flavor. I pretend we are back on Iriarte, where food is the highest art and every meal is a symphony. I pretend we have returned to Nabomba Zom, to that wondrous palatial hotel by the shore of the scarlet sea, the waters of which at dawn would reverberate as if struck by a hammer as the first blue rays of morning fell upon it.

But no, no, we are on Sidri Akrak. I lie sleepless through the night with Velimyle breathing gently beside me, listening to the fierce honkings and roarings and screechings of the wild beasts that roam the darkness beyond our windows. Now and again then the sounds of the lovemaking of Mayfly and Nikomastir come through the thin walls that separate our bedroom from theirs, giggles and gasps and long indrawn sighs of pleasure.

In the morning we go out exploring.

This city, we have learned, is called Periandros Andifang. It has a population of just under one hundred thousand, with not a single building of the slightest architectural distinction and a year-round climate of clamminess and drizzle. The plant life is, generally speaking, strikingly unsightly—a preponderance of gray leaves, black flowers—and the air is full of clouds of little stinging midges with malevolent purple beaks, and of course one has to deal with the fauna, too, the fiend's gallery of grisly monstrosities, seemingly no two alike, that greet you at every turn: huge beasts with beady eyes and slavering fangs and clacking claws, things with pockmarked pustulent skins or writhing furry tentacles or clutching many-jointed arms. Almost always they appear without warning, galloping out of some clump of trees uttering banshee shrieks or ground-shaking roars. I begin to understand now the tales of unwary travelers who have total mental breakdowns within an hour of their arrival on Sidri Akrak.

It quickly becomes clear to us, though, that none of these horrendous creatures has any interest in attacking us. The only real risk we run is that of getting trampled as they go charging past. Very likely it is the case that they find human flesh unpalatable, or indigestible, or downright poisonous. But encountering them is an unnerving business, and we encounter them again and again and again.

Nikomastir finds it all fascinating. Painstakingly he searches out the ill-favored, the misshapen, the feculent, the repulsive—not that they are hard to find. He drifts ecstatically from one eyesore of a building to the next, taking an infinite number of pictures. He adores the plants' sooty foul-smelling blossoms and sticky blighted-looking leaves. The rampaging animals give him even greater pleasure; whenever some particularly immense or especially abhorrent-looking loathsomeness happens to cross our path he cries out in boyish glee.

This starts to be very irritating. His callow idiocy is making me feel old.

"Remember, sweet, he's not even seventy yet," Mayfly reminds me, seeing my brows furrowing. "Surely you were like that yourself, once upon a time."

"Was I? I'd like to think that isn't so."

"And in any case," says Velimyle, "can't you manage to find that enthusiasm of his charming?"

No. I can't. Perhaps it's getting to be time for my next rebirth, I think. Growing old, for us, isn't a matter so much of bodily decay—that is fended off by efficient processes of automatic bioenergetic correction—as of increasing inward rigidity, a creakiness of the soul, a corrugation of the psyche, a stiffening of the spiritual synapses. One starts to feel sour and petty and crabbed. Life loses its joy and its juice. By then you begin to become aware that it is time to clamber once more into the crystal tank where an intricate spiderweb of machinery will enfold you like a loving mother, and slip off into sweet oblivion for a while, and awaken to find yourself young again and ready to start all over. Which you can do over and over again, until eventually you arrive at the annoying point, after the eleventh or twelfth rebirth, where the buildup of solar poisons in your system has at last become ineradicable under any circumstances, and that is the end of you, alas.

Even gods have to die eventually, it would seem.

Nikomastir is a young god, and I am, evidently, an aging one.

I try to make allowances for that. But I find myself fervently hoping, all the same, that he will tire of this awful place very soon and allow us to go onward to some happier world.

He does not tire of it, though.

He loves it. He is in the grip of what some ancient poet once called the fascination of the abomination. He has gone up and down every street of the city, peering at this building and that one in unstinting admiration of their imperfections. For several days running he makes it clear that he is searching for some building in particular, and then he finds it: a rambling old ruin of great size and formidable ugliness at the very edge of town, standing apart from everything else in a sort of private park.

"Here it is!" he cries. "The ancestral mansion! The house where my father was born!"

So Nikomastir still clings to the claim that he is of Akrakikan descent. There is no way that this can be true; the natives of this world are a chilly bloodless folk with mean pinched hard souls, if they have souls at all and not just some clicking chattering robotic mechanisms inside their skulls. Indeed I have known robots with personalities far more appealing than anyone we have met thus far on Sidri Akrak. Nikomastir, bless him, is nothing at all like that. He may be silly and frivolous and empty-headed, but he also is sweet-natured and lively and amiable and vivacious, terms that have never yet been applied to any citizen of Sidri Akrak, and never will be.

Velimyle has tried to paint him again. Again the attempt was a failure. This time she is so distressed that I dare to breach the wall of privacy behind which she keeps her art and ask her what the difficulty is.

"Look," she says.

She unrolls the second canvas. Against the familiar swirling colors of a typical Velimyle background I see the slender, angular form of Nikomastir, imprinted there by the force of Velimyle's mental rapport with the psycho-sensitive fabric. But the features are all wrong. Nikomaster's perpetual easy smile has given way to a dreadful scowling grimace. His lip curls backward menacingly; his teeth are the teeth of some predatory beast. And his eyes—oh, Velimyle, those harsh, glaring eyes! Where is his cheerful sparkle? These eyes are hard, narrow, fierce, and above all else sad. The Nikomastir of Velimyle's painting stares out at the universe with tragic intensity. They are the eyes of a god, perhaps, but of a dying god, one who knows he must give up his life for the redemption of his race.

"The first one was almost as bad," Velimyle says. "Why is this happening? This isn't Nikomastir at all. I've never had something like this happen."

"Has he seen either of the paintings?"

"I wouldn't let him. All I told him was that they didn't come out right, that they would depress him if I showed them to him. And of course he didn't want to see them after that."

"Something about this planet must be shading your perceptions," I say. "Burn this, Velimyle. And the other one too. And forget about painting him until we've left here."

Nikomastir wants to have a look inside the crumbling, lurching pile that he says is his family's ancestral home. But the place, ruinous though it is, happens to be occupied by Akrakikans, a whole swarm of them, and when he knocks at the front door and grandly introduces himself to the major-domo of the house as Count Nikomastir of Sembiran, who has come here on a sentimental journey to his former paternal estate, the door is closed in his face without a word. "How impolite," Nikomastir says, not seeming very surprised. "But don't worry: I'll find a way of getting in."

That project gets tabled too. Over the next few days he leads us farther and farther afield, well out into the uninhabited countryside beyond the boundaries of Periandros Andifang. The land out here is swampy and uningratiating, and of course there are the animals to contend with, and the insects, and the humidity. I can tell that Mayfly and Verimyle are growing a little weary of Nikomastir's exuberance, but they both are as tolerant of his whims as ever and follow him loyally through these soggy realms. As do I—partly, I suppose, because we agreed long ago that we would journey everywhere as a single unit, and partly because I have been stung, evidently, by various hints of Mayfly's and Velimyle's that my recent crotchetiness could mean I might be getting ready for my next rebirth.

Then he turns his attention once more to the old house that he imagines once belonged to his family. "My father once told me that there's a pool of fire behind it, a phosphorescent lake. He used to swim it when he was a boy, and he'd come up dripping with cool flame. I'm going to take a swim in it too, and then we can head off to the next planet. Whose turn is it to pick our next planet, anyway?"

"Mine," I say quickly. I have Marajo in mind—the sparkling sands, the City of Seven Pyramids. "If there's a lake behind that house, Nikomastir, I advise you very earnestly to stay away from it. The people who live there don't seem to look favorably on trespassers. Besides, can't you imagine the kind of nastinesses that would live in a lake on this world?"

"My father went swimming in that one," Nikomastir replies, and gives me a defiant glare. "It's perfectly safe, I assure you."

I doubt, of course, that any such lake exists. If it's there, though, I hope he isn't fool enough to go swimming in it. My affection for the boy is real; I don't want him to come to harm.

But I let the matter drop. I've already said too much. The surest way to prod him into trouble, I know, is oppose him in one of his capricious fancies. My hope is that Nikomastir's attention will be diverted elsewhere in the next day or two and all thought of that dismal house, and of the fiery lake that may or may not be behind it, will fly out of his mind.

It's generally a good idea, when visiting a world you know very little about, to keep out of places of unknown chemical properties. When we toured Megalo Kastro, we stood at the edge of a cliff looking down into the famous living sea, that pink custardy mass that is in fact a single living organism of gigantic size, spreading across thousands of kilometers of that world. But it did not occur to us to take a swim in that sea, for we understood that in a matter of hours it would dissolve and digest us if we did.

And when we were on Xamur we went to see the Idradin crater, as everyone who goes to Xamur does. Xamur is the most perfect of worlds, flawless and serene, a paradise, air like perfume and water like wine, every tree in the ideal place, every brook, every hill.

It has only one blemish—the Idradin, a huge round pit that reaches deep into the planet's primordial heart. It is a hideous place, that crater. Concentric rings of jagged cooled lava surround it, black and eroded and bleak. Stinking gases rise out of the depths, and yellow clouds of sulfuric miasma belch forth, and wild red shafts of roaring flame, and you peer down from the edge into a roiling den of hot surging magma. Everyone who goes to Xamur must visit the Idradin, for if you did not see perfect Xamur's one terrible flaw you could never be happy on any other world. And so we stared into it from above, and shivered with the horror we were expected to feel; but we were never at all tempted to clamber down the crater's sides and dip our toes into that realm of fire below.

It seems unlikely to me that Nikomastir will do anything so stupid here. But I have to be careful not to prod him in the wrong direction. I don't mention the lake to him again.

Our exploration of Sidri Akrak proceeds. We visit new swamps, new groves of fetid-smelling malproportioned trees, new neighborhoods of misshapen and graceless buildings. One drizzly disheartening day succeeds another, and finally I am unable to bear the sight of that brown sky and greenish sun any longer. Though it is a violation of our agreements, I stay behind at the hotel one morning and let the other three go off without me.

It is a quiet time. I spend the hours reflecting on our travels of years past, all the many worlds we have seen. Icy Mulano of the two suns, one yellow, one bloody red, and billions of ghostly electric life-forms glimmering about you in the frigid air. Estrilidis, where the cats have two tails and the insects have eyes like blue diamonds. Zimbalou, the sunless nomad world, where the cities are buried deep below the frozen surface. Kalimaka, Haj Qaldun, Vietoris, Nabomba Zom—

So many places, so many sights. A lifetime of wonderful experiences; and yet what, I ask myself, has it all meant? How has it shaped me? What have I learned?

I have no answers, only to say that we will continue to go onward, ever onward. It is our life. It is what we do. We are travelers by choice, but also by nature, by destiny.

I am still lost in reverie when I hear Velimyle's voice outside my window, calling to me, telling me that I must come quickly. "Nikomastir—" she cries. "Nikomastir!"

"What about him?"

But she can only gesture and wave. Her eyes are wild. We run together through the muddy streets, paying no heed to the bulky and grotesque Akrakikan monstrosities that occasionally intersect our path. I realize after a time that Velimyle is leading me toward the tumbledown house at the edge of town that Nikomastir has claimed as his family's former home. A narrow grassy path leads around one side of it to the rear; and there, to my amazement, I see the phosphorescent lake of Nikomastir's fantasies, with Mayfly beside it, leaping up and down in agitation that verges on frenzy.

She points toward the water. "Out there—there—"

On this ugly world even a phosphorescent lake can somehow manage to be an unlovely sight. I saw one once on Darma Barma that flashed like heavenly fire in rippling waves of cobalt and amethyst, magenta and gold, aquamarine and emerald and jade. But from this lake emanates the most unradiant of radiances, a dull, prosaic, sickly gleam, dark-toned and dispiriting, except in one place off toward the farther shore where a disturbance of some sort is setting up whirlpools of glinting metallic effects, swirls of eye-jabbing bright sparkles, as though handfuls of iron filings are being thrown through a magnetic field.

The disturbance is Nikomastir. He—his body, rather—is tossing and heaving at the lake's surface, and all about him the denizens of the lake can be seen, narrow scaly jutting heads popping up by the dozens, hinged jaws snapping, sharp teeth closing on flesh. A widening pool of blood surrounds him. They, whatever they are, are ripping him to shreds.

"We have to get him out of there," Mayfly says, her voice congested with horror and fear.

"How?" I ask.

"I told him not to do it," says trembling Velimyle. "I told him, I told him, I told him. But he plunged right in, and when he was halfway across they began to break the surface, and then—then he began screaming, and—"

Mayfly plucks urgently at my sleeve. "What can we do? How can we rescue him?"

"He's beyond rescuing," I tell her hollowly.

"But if we can get his body back," she says, "there'll be a way to revive him, won't there? I know there is. Scientists can do anything nowadays." Velimyle, more tentatively, agrees. Some kind of scientific miracle, Nikomastir gathered up and repaired somehow by the regeneration of tissue—

But tissue is all that's left of him now, frayed sorry scraps, and the creatures of the lake, frantic now with blood-lust, are devouring even those in furious haste.

They want me to tell them that Nikomastir isn't really dead.

But he is: really, really, really dead. Dead forever. What has been played out on this shore today was not a game. There is nothing that can be saved, no way to regenerate. I have never seen the death of a human being before. It is a dizzying thing to contemplate: the finality, the utterness. My mind is whirling; I have to fight back convulsions of shock and horror.

"Couldn't you have stopped him?" I ask angrily, when I am able to speak again.

"But he wanted so badly to do it," Mayfly replies. "We couldn't have stopped him, you know. Not even if we—"

She halts in midsentence.

"Not even if you had wanted to?" I say. "Is that it?" Neither of them can meet my furious gaze. "But you didn't want to, did you? You thought it would be fun to see Nikomastir swim across the phosphorescent lake. Fun. Am I right? Yes. I know that I am. What could you have been thinking, Mayfly? Velimyle?"

There is no sign of Nikomastir at the surface any longer. The lake is growing still again. Its phosphorescence has subsided to a somber tarnished glow.

For a long time, minutes, hours, weeks, none of us is capable of moving. Silent, pale, stunned, we stand with bowed heads by the shore of that frightful lake, scarcely even able to breathe.

We are in the presence of incontrovertible and permanent death, which to us is a novelty far greater even than the living sea of Megalo Kastro or the blue dawn of Nabomba Zom, and the immense fact of it holds us rooted to the spot. Was this truly Nikomastir's ancestral world? Was his father actually born in that great old falling-down house, and did he really once swim in this deadly lake? And if none of that was so, how did Nikomastir know that the lake was there? We will never be able to answer those questions. Whatever we do not know about Nikomastir that we have already learned, we will never come to discover now. That is the meaning of death: the finality of it, the severing of communication, the awful unanswerable power of the uncompromising curtain that descends like a wall of steel. We did not come to Sidri Akrak to learn about such things, but that is what we have learned on Sidri Akrak, and we will take it with us wherever we go henceforth, pondering it, examining it.

"Come," I say to Mayfly and Velimyle, after a time. "We need to get away from here."

So, then. Nikomastir was foolish. He was bold. He has had his swim and now he is dead. And why? Why? For what? What was he seeking, on this awful world? What were we? We know what we found, yes, but not what it was that we were looking for. I wonder if we will ever know.

He has lived his only life, has Nikomastir, and he has lost it in the pursuit of idle pleasure. There is a lesson in that, for me, for Velimilye, for Mayfly, for us all. And one day I will, I hope, understand what it is.

All I do know after having lived these hundreds of years is that the universe is very large and we are quite small. We live godlike lives these days, flitting as we do from world to world, but even so we are not gods. We die: some sooner, some later, but we do die. Only gods live forever. Nikomastir hardly lived at all.

So be it. We have learned what we have learned from Nikomastir's death, and now we must move on. We are travelers by nature and destiny, and we will go forward into our lives. Tomorrow we leave for Marajo. The shining sands, the City of Seven Pyramids. Marajo will teach us something, as Xamur once did, and Nabomba Zom, and Galgala. And also Sidri Akrak. Something. Something. Something.

· HINDSIGHT ·
Sarah Langan

Second Coming is docked two miles underground. She's made of a collapsible, repulsion-attraction subatomic slurry that the astrophysicists are convinced will survive the gravitational anomaly called Black Betty. Yes, the ship will survive; it's her human cargo that's doomed.

Sarah Vaughan walks between rows of gurneys in heavy Van der Waals boots. She's been aboard *Second Coming* six months now, and has gotten to know the feel of this ship: her soft, organic skin; her hissing breath; her ceilings and floors, which flip-flop depending on the capriciousness of gravity. At first, buried so deeply under Omaha's dirt, *Second Coming* was a citadel. But this close to the end of it all, ghosts inhabit the cabins of every room. Sarah hears voices over the speakers that aren't quite human, and sees memories from life back in Scottsbluff that feel real enough to touch. *"Doctor,"* Sarah's patients groan in a Greek Chorus that reverberates like microphone feedback, *"Help me!"*

Sarah, a stout, practical woman of forty, surveys the wide wasteland of them, and wonders where to start.

Click! The overhead sick bay speaker buzzes to life. She strains to hear through the ion static:

"Good Morning, Citizens of Second Coming!" Osgood Blunder, Captain and Emperor of the *Second Coming*, announces in monotone. His tracheotomy makes him sound like a drive-through fast food booth operator.

"As you know, impact with Black Betty is less than four hours away, but our diligent computational engineers made a breakthrough last night. The upload of human consciousness to the safety of Second Coming's *mainframe is finally at hand. Rejoice! The flesh will fail, but the spirit, dear Romans, will endure!"*

Osgood Blunder breaks for applause, and throughout the ship, even in the infirmary, manic screams of victory burst and then disappear like collapsing stars. Blunder's corporation, Kliffoth Cybernetics, funded *Second Coming*, and hand-selected its passengers. Without Blunder, there would be no ship at all. During their long captivity down here, the crew have come to think of him as a God.

"I'll see some of you on the other side. The rest, fear not, for you witnessed the next leap in human evolution, when mankind became his own God," Blunder says as static whines. *"We'll be calling lottery numbers throughout the day. Remember, transgressors will be shot and stored as protein, so please Respect your Authority, and stand by."*

Sarah picks a path through the prostrate bodies. There are 2,104 colonists; 1,693 have surrendered their names for numbers and logged into her greenly-lit sick bay. Some occupy gurneys; others lean against walls or curl themselves fetal. She piles her tray with needles and liquid Valium. They'll need it today because she gets the feeling that their luck is an upside-down horseshoe, all run out.

She calibrates, measures, injects. It's routine by now. There's no medicine left except for this. All day, all night, it's *Flick!-Puncture!-Squirt!* Then move on to the next. And the next. And then next. Each have numbers branded against their foreheads. It's best to look there, and not in their eyes.

Flick!-Puncture!-Squirt!-Move on!

Flick!-Puncture!-Squirt!-Move on!

Sarah stops paying attention at patient thirty-four, and almost gives the guy an air bubble heart attack. He wouldn't notice—he's insane. You can tell which patients have Black Betty's Disease, because they've got no whites to their eyes. It's like their souls are drowning.

Flick!-Puncture!-Squirt!-Move on!

Flick!-Puncture!-Squirt!-Move on!

Best not to think about the Hepatitis she's spreading. Or worse. It's a mercy, she tells herself when she gets to patient 342, who's just eight years old, with impossibly knobby knees.

Flick!-Puncture!-Squirt!

He looks up at her with eyes that are entirely black, and there is movement between pupil and iris. There is something swimming in there, trying to break out.

"*It's really happening. They've started,*" Sarah's husband Joe Vaughan calls as he enters the sick bay wearing heavy boots that suction the slurried ground. His fine, blonde hair floats like jellyfish strands in this diminished gravity.

"*Blunder went first, of course,*" Joe continues. His voice sounds far away, but it echoes, too, so the words collapse on each other like overlapping Venn Diagrams. "*He's in the machine. The hard scientists are next, then they say we're up.*"

"*Oh, Christ,*" Sarah answers. "*I'm not ready. Are you?*" Though Blunder has the textbook knowledge, he wants her life experience as a physician in the system. He's promised to upload her family, too. But this close to the end, nothing is certain.

Joe hops up and down a couple of times. His boots make a slurping sound, and the image of him blurs as if he's moving extra fast. Quite literally, he's not the man she married. The closer they get to Black Betty, the more it messes with the chemistry of their brains. Like a magnet pressed against a head full of metal.

"*We'd better get to the engine room with the kids. They've already shot some line cutters. There's going to be a riot,*" Joe says.

Sarah looks at her tray of meds, and across the room, too. She flicks on the sick bay's satellite viewer, which shows images of space and of Earth.

It's shocking, how quickly the planet has changed . . . Unfathomable quantities of garbage spin like Saturn's rings around the Earth's fattened waist. Sea water laps the continents; across Central America, the Atlantic and Pacific Oceans kiss.

Joe reaches the knobs, and sharpens in on Scottsbluff, Nebraska, where they used to live. A lone wanderer wearing an atmosphere suit scavenges through a drifting pile of husked wheat from a broken silo, but the grain pelts him hard and fast. It's like sand slipping through his fingers.

Joe puts his arm around her, and, with their eyes, they follow the wheat through the air, and into space, and finally, through Black Betty.

"*Hand me the Valium, will you?*" Sarah asks.

Joe squints with bad eyes until he finds the proper bottle. He's been eating carrion; Sarah suspects prion infection.

"*We could wind-up stuck inside* Second Coming, *part of the machine,*" Sarah says. "*It might be better to die.*"

She's said this before, or Joe has. Each time the issue arises, they assume opposite sides of the argument, and fight until they're tired of words. In the end, it doesn't matter. They're going to do it, no matter what.

"*We've got to go,*" Joe says. She hears the words again and again, even though she knows he says them only once. *Déjà vu.* Time is slowing and spreading. Her ghost of five minutes ago injects an eight-year old boy with dead eyes. *Comfort him,* her present self wants to scold. *He's all alone.*

The sick bay is a field of bodies. Abandoned. Forsaken, because the engineers believe their insanity will infect the machine. They'll meet Black Betty in corporeal form from this room, while the lucky few whose numbers get picked will live on inside *Second Coming.* Technological Singularity trumps Gravitational Singularity. It's a boxing match: Mankind in one corner, God in the other.

"*Let me finish with the injections, so at least they're calm when it happens,*" Sarah says.

Joe shakes his head. *The kids are waiting,* is what he's saying without words. *The kids come first. Before morality. Before their parents' survival. Before the rest of the human race, if necessary.* She knows this. All parents know this. But still, she can't leave her patients without offering them some solace.

Onscreen, the closer they get to the anomaly, the more she expands, like a pupil exposed to dark. Just inside her edges, something moves. Something like life.

Or maybe something like God.

Three more hours to impact, and counting.

Joe punches his suction boots against *Second Coming's* slurry floor, which is becoming less solid with every passing second. "Okay," he says. "For you."

Then he lifts a syringe, and together, they *Flick!-Puncture!-Squirt!*, until every patient in the ward is drugged or dead.

From the corner, the ghost boy watches.

The day Black Betty appeared, Sarah was still home on maternity leave with baby Sally, but she'd known something was coming. Already, magnetic north had reversed without warning. You could see the Northern Lights as far south as Costa Rica. Migratory birds' internal radar had jammed, too. They flew outside the troposphere, then plummeted from loss of oxygen. Roads and roofs and empty farmland hosted their open graves. No one knew how their loss would affect the ecosystem, but mornings without their songs seemed more bereft.

Baby Sally was swinging happily in her rocker that morning, and three year-old Bradley toddled between the kitchen and television room, calling out names of things: *Shoe! Knee! Strawberry! Sally!*

On the radio, the regular morning program got interrupted for a special report. *"Jack the Jerk-Off"* cut off a geriatric Salieri clone's rendition of "Me and My Shadow," and read:

"Ladies and Gentlemen, do not be alarmed!"

Sarah listened as she rinsed a glass baby bottle. The water spun counterclockwise.

"Initial reports are sketchy as an Etch-A-Doodle, but the Department of Defense, in tandem with Kliffoth Cybernetics. . . . Is this a joke?"

Sarah walked over to the radio. Bradley bobbled between her legs, then out, then in, like a maypole dance: *"Mommy . . . mommy . . . mommy . . . leg!"*

Static flushed the frequency even though it was a clear, Nebraska day. *Jack the Jerk-Off* returned:

"Okay, folks, they say it's not a joke, but so did Orson Welles, so we'll see. Put it this way, if they're wrong, sue somebody else. I'm not liable, bitches! Anyway, Kliffoth Cybernetics, the American Government contractor for science, health, incarceration, propaganda, the national and state lotteries, consumption, toxicology, humanitarian aid, and defense, says they think the reason polarity shifted so suddenly and completely is because of an anomaly about twenty million miles between Earth and Mars . . . "

Sarah braced herself against the counter while Sally chirped like a small bird in her swing, and Bradley danced.

"It's a gravitational anomaly," Jack finished. *"They say it's growing."*

Joe came home an hour later. He'd been working on a case for Santo Monico, a subsidiary of Kliffoth Cybernetics. They wanted reparations from all the rice farmers in India who'd used old strains of seed, instead of buying the new patent.

The entire Vaughan family sat in front of the television as Kliffoth Cybernetics' CEO appeared on every Network and Webcast. The static made his talking head seem far away. "*The best we can figure, a separate universe is spreading across the Milky Way. The laws of physics and time act differently once we approach the barrier of this new universe, which has collapsed on top of ours. The easiest way to think of it is like ink diffusing through a glass of water, only its source is self-generating and for our purposes, limitless. Pretty soon, the entire glass will be black as night,*" Osgood Blunder announced in a ragged voice that Sarah recognized as sickly. "*We think it came from another dimension— it tore a wormhole through either space or time. What's unique about this particular anomaly, is that its barrier, or event horizon, to borrow from black hole terminology, ought to be dark, and so infinitely dense with gravitational singularities that light can't escape. But we've detected movement within Black Betty's perimeter.*

"*There might be life in there.*"

Outside that day, an entire flock of birds crashed through the Vaughan's detached garage on Fort Triumph Street. Seagulls, thousands of miles from either ocean.

Sarah microwaved popcorn for dinner. The whole family fell asleep in front of the television. She dreamed about how she'd never cooked nutritious meals, and that this neglect had carved her children's bellies with scurvy holes, into which insect mothers had laid their eggs.

"*Well, how in the heeeck are we gonna survive?*" The Oprah Winfrey Holo-Host™ asked her science guest, esteemed astrophysicist Ipswitch Gustavson, the next day.

Sally peered out from under Sarah's breast. She was a tiny, helpless thing that smelled like sweet milk. Bradley sat cross-legged and too close to the television. She noticed that his hair was especially staticky, like he was touching a novelty Eye of the Storm.

On the television, Gustavson frowned, like he couldn't figure out if the hologram's creators were imbeciles, or just writing her program that way for good television. "*The anomaly—Black Betty, after my daughter who died of mercury poisoning from Santo Monico rice—she's rolling in fast, and she's getting bigger.*"

"*Well, what does that mean?*" Oprah asked with exaggerated, amused concern. Her shimmering eyelid winked.

"*She's like a bucket of paint, splattering in real time, at this very moment across the Milky Way. As she rolls toward us, she's changing our laws of physics, and pulling Earth and the rest of the solar system off orbit. Even if we could exist under the new laws of this alternate universe, we won't have a sun, or the ground under or feet, or a food supply . . .*"

"Is this fake, like global warming?" Oprah asked.

Gustavson shook his head. "*I give the human species ten years on the outside. Probably less.*"

Sarah got up from the couch, walked very slowly to the kitchen, and vomited in the sink. The water swirled, all wrong.

Months passed like everything was normal, even as the birds finally went extinct, the old died of pulmonary and cardiac disease at accelerated rates, and Black Betty's Disease took root. People's sclera's disappeared, and their irises widened, so their eyes seemed entirely brown or blue or green. These colors contracted and expanded within their pupils, and the victims often lost their sense of balance, along with sight. Occasionally, they were violent. More often they babbled about the end of the world, or got stuck in loops of their own histories, where they repeated old conversations over and over again.

Joe won his case for Santo Monico, and the Vaughan family used the money to secure their seats on Kliffoth Cybernetics' Black Betty escape pod, *Second Coming*.

Sarah reported back to work at the clinic where she'd performed abortions until it became illegal, and now delivered high risk babies with congenital defects such as organ dysplasia and spina bifida. Most died soon after they entered the world, and wound-up in county graves or donated to science. To commemorate them, Sarah and the rest of the staff took turns carving numbers into small quartz stones, then piling them in the courtyard where the nurses smoked their Winstons. Scottsbluff was the only high risk birthing clinic in six states, and at first, it had seemed heartless not to name them. But after a while, it was only practical.

In the lobby during those days after Black Betty, more and more women showed up high risk. Betty was altering the genetic structure of living things, and bending it in all the wrong ways. The clinic waiting room television, tuned to news, often aired real-time human sacrifice, as well as a reality television program based in Los Angeles called "That's My Monkey!".

In the delivery room, Sarah spent her days pulling crowning babies from between their mothers' bleeding legs while picketing Jesus freaks warned about The Rapture through the windows. The worst part was consoling the mothers when it was over. Always, they'd convinced themselves that the tests were wrong, and their babies would be born alive.

Betty spread. Relativity turned fungible. Small objects floated up, and into space.

It started with plastic grocery bags, moved on to the engraved quartz stones in the clinic courtyard, and after twelve months, ended with human beings. They held each other, a chain that lasted for miles, until, one by one, they were gone. Some got lost in space, others ended up spinning with the garbage around the Earth's orbit, like Saturn's rings.

Sarah and Joe boarded their windows from rioters and stopped going to work. She was sorry for the women who would surely die in labor without her help, but not sorry enough to continue. By now, the infants had become disfigured abominations.

The Vaughans waited, and waited, and waited some more, for news that *Second Coming* was complete. Fresh food by then was gone, but they'd stockpiled cans, which was better, at least, than those who starved, or resorted to cannibalism.

On air one morning, *Jack the Jerk-Off* and the rest of his morning show killed themselves. With the laws of physics so confused, the bullets didn't penetrate like they should have. They fired dozens of rounds, and still died slow.

Sarah, Joe, Bradley, and Sally listened to the slaughter from the kitchen floor. *"It's not real; it's make-believe,"* Joe assured the children while Sarah wound Sally's favorite music box. Carved men spun tiny circles around a painted wooden peak while "Climb Every Mountain," played.

Toward the end of life above, the cars and mobile homes took flight, like something out of *The Wizard of Oz*. Finally, the lights went out, and never came back.

Joe cashed his money into gold, and stole a gravity car. The family set out for the military base in Omaha, in the hopes that *Second Coming* was complete. They made it halfway before the engine died. The rest of the trip, carrying their gold bricks that were light as styrofoam, they walked. By then, the sky was dark, even during the day. The animals were gone. In two days, they reached the Kliffoth-American Military Base, eating only burrowing insects, and to slake their thirst, the blood Joe drained from his arm, and offered them to suckle.

Can you love someone more after something like that? Can it restore your faith in a mad world? Sarah Vaughan thought so.

When they arrived, *Second Coming* edged out from the earthy plains like an alien spaceship. Her skin was black and organic; her organs a neural net that glowed like jellyfish phosphor. For a quarter-mile in all directions, people gathered, and seemed, from the way they bowed and moaned, to worship. Some held each other. Others tied themselves to the cemented fences that would soon come loose. Armed guards lined every entrance.

They learned things as they pushed through the throng. It grumbled with intelligence, the way crowds do:

"*They're not letting anybody in, even if you've got a ticket!*"

"*It's un-American!*"

"*They say if you're good looking . . . They want breeders.*"

"*They say Osgood Blunder has gone mad . . .* "

"*They say the doctors all killed themselves. Same with the artists.*"

"*I have eight million dollars worth of gold,*" Joe announced when they finally got to the front of the line. A small, thin guard stepped ahead of the rest, and pushed the nub of his flamethrower to Joe's chest.

"*Money's no good,*" the guard said.

Sarah and Joe held their children tight, as if trying to make them unborn.

"*We have a right! We're on the list!*" Joe shouted, and then broke into tears. At the sight of their father's surrender, the children, and Sarah, began to cry, too.

"*Let us in, you murderer,*" Joe continued. "*We've got children. We have tickets. We've got gold.*"

If only she was pretty, and could offer herself up to them, Sarah thought. If only Joe had married a trophy wife, like the rest of his rich friends, he'd be able to sell her now, and their kids would survive.

"*Move along,*" the guard said. "*I don't want to kill you in front of your children.*"

They didn't move. The launcher clicked, and methane loosened from its nose. Joe gasped. Probably, even with a direct hit, he would die slow.

Sarah remembered something from the crowd. "*I hear Blunder is sick, and that your doctors refused to board because of crimes of conscience. I'm a surgeon. I'll cross the strike line. I can operate,*" she said.

The gun moved away from Joe, and to the center of Sarah's back. It felt surprisingly heavy.

By the time they get the kids, it's forty minutes before impact. The ship has turned to a soft slurry that does not stick to the bottoms of their boots, but instead oscillates in tidal pools toward the bow. Onscreen, along the vibrating corridor walls, Sarah can see images of Black Betty. They're close enough now that she can see inside the anomaly's pitch black edges.

Something moves.

It's familiar, like the reflection inside a madman's eye, and she's reminded of the last child she delivered in Scottsbluff, who was born without skin.

In the engineering room, techies shout. Their voices reverb so deeply that she can't make out what they're saying. Some have gone mad with Betty's Disease. They're hitting their heads against soft walls, and chasing their own watery physical trails like dogs. Blunder's body lays at the bottom of a pile of about two-hundred crewmen. They live in the machine now. She can feel their cold, atomic consciousness within the ship's slurry, and in the vibrations under her feet.

The speaker crackles. It's Blunder's voice, just as monotone from the tracheotomy she gave him, only now, it has flattened into some less than human. *"The Vaughans,"* Blunder says. *"It's so cold in here. A family. We could use a real family, to keep us warm."*

The First Mate beckons them to four upload gurneys, equipped with used needles and tubes. It's supposed to be a quick process—only seconds, since they've been imprinted already.

The ship by now has condensed. Its walls close in like waves.

Ten minutes to impact. Joe walks with the children toward the gurneys. Sarah cannot conceive of strapping baby Sally onto one of these tables, then leaving her for the crew to toss to the pile. She cannot conceive of never touching her children again, or never again making love to the man whose blood she drank. But perhaps this will be better than death.

Yes, she reasons. She must believe it is better.

The speakers now are gone. The ship is about to merge with Betty, and become fluid and solid and infinite. Onscreen, Sarah can see ghosts inside the perimeter of this new universe. She can see her own body, strapped into a gurney, screaming: *"No. Stop. For the love of God! It's not too late."*

Joe straps Bradley to the table. Then Sally. Sarah watches.

The ship's oxygen is low enough that they're gasping and cold, but it's a pleasant sensation, like floating. Words no longer echo. Sound is gone. Thought is gone, too. It's just images, reflections, memories of the past and present and very near future with no particular distinction.

She doesn't want to do it. All her instincts tell her *not* to do it, just as they told her not to leave those women in Scottsbluff, and not to operate on Blunder, but instead to slit his monster throat. Just like they told her not to feed her husband and children human flesh. *"There are fates worse than death,"* Joe argued that first time, but even then, weeping, they'd known how it would end. They'd taken their rations, and told the kids it was chicken.

Joe's hand is on her shoulder. He straps her in, then himself. There's no time to kiss goodbye. They will lose their love, she knows. Its ineffable constancy will not translate into the machine. She is wet with regret.

The upload is quick. Suddenly, she sees her body from the outside, looking in. She races through the ship, looking for her family.

But the ship is a slurry. It opens up, and breaks free from the Earth's crust, hurtling toward Black Betty.

Her babies. Where are her babies?

She sees inside the anomaly, even though she doesn't have eyes. It's ghosts in there. Three billion people. Flipper children eating poison rice, garbage rings, birds circling a gyre. It's her family in there, looking back at her. It's that moment on the road, when they shared blood, and did not know that the hardest time was also the best time. It is past, and present, but not future. It is Betty's Disease, and like everyone else before her, Sarah Vaughan is drowning in it.

The *Second Coming* and Black Betty collide.

Sarah knows now, what drove her patients mad. It is the unspeakable truth about what caused Black Betty. It's *Second Coming*, so dense with the ghosts of humanity's regret, that she weighted through time and tore the past to warn them. Black Betty *is* the *Second Coming*.

Sarah remembers the doctors who killed themselves, and the women at her office, and the babies, all those babies, piled like rocks. It was their future she was marking, stolen from them by their idiot parents. It was the end of the world she was reminiscing, though she did not know it.

Black Betty and the ship crash together. The two become one. All things become one. There is no sound. The anomaly splatters across space, black and beautiful.

"My babies," Sarah cries, as she swims through an ocean of infinitely dense ghosts.

And then, like a star, the anomaly collapses, as if it never was. It sucks past and present and future, and makes all of humanity unborn.

* Million Writers Award Notable Story

• TIGHT LITTLE STITCHES IN A DEAD MAN'S BACK •
Joe R. Lansdale

From the Journal of Paul Marder

(Boom!)

That's a little scientist joke, and the proper way to begin this. As for the purpose of my notebook, I'm uncertain. Perhaps to organize my thoughts and not to go insane.

No. Probably so I can read it and feel as if I'm being spoken to. Maybe neither of those reasons. It doesn't matter. I just want to do it, and that is enough.

What's new?

Well, Mr. Journal, after all these years I've taken up martial arts again—or at least the forms and calisthenics of Tae Kwon Do. There is no one to spar with here in the lighthouse, so the forms have to do.

There is Mary, of course, but she keeps all her sparring verbal. And as of late, there is not even that. I long for her to call me a sonofabitch. Anything. Her hatred of me has cured to 100% perfection and she no longer finds it necessary to speak. The tight lines around her eyes and mouth, the emotional heat that radiates from her body like a dreadful cold sore looking for a place to lie down is voice enough for her. She lives only for the moment when she (the cold sore) can attach herself to me with her needles, ink and thread. She lives only for the design on my back.

That's all I live for as well. Mary adds to it nightly and I enjoy the pain. The tattoo is of a great, blue mushroom cloud, and in the cloud, etched ghost-like, is the face of our daughter, Rae. Her lips are drawn tight, eyes are closed and there are stitches deeply pulled to simulate the lashes. When I move fast and hard they rip slightly and Rae cries bloody tears.

That's one reason for the martial arts. The hard practice of them helps me to tear the stitches so my daughter can cry. Tears are the only thing I can give her.

Each night I bare my back eagerly to Mary and her needles. She pokes deep and I moan in pain as she moans in ecstasy and hatred. She adds more color to the design, works with brutal precision to bring Rae's face out in sharper relief. After ten minutes she tires and will work no more. She puts the tools away and I go to the full-length mirror on the wall. The lantern on the shelf flickers like a jack-o-lantern in a high wind, but there is enough light for me to look over my shoulder and examine the tattoo. And it is beautiful. Better each night as Rae's face becomes more and more defined.

Rae.

Rae. God, can you forgive me, sweetheart?

But the pain of the needles, wonderful and cleansing as they are, is not enough. So I go sliding, kicking and punching along the walkway around the lighthouse, feeling Rae's red tears running down my spine, gathering in the waistband of my much-stained canvas pants.

Winded, unable to punch and kick anymore, I walk over to the railing and call down into the dark, "Hungry?"

In response to my voice a chorus of moans rises up to greet me.

Later, I lie on my pallet, hands behind my head, examine the ceiling and try to think of something worthy to write in you, Mr. Journal. So seldom is there anything. Nothing seems truly worthwhile.

Bored of this, I roll on my side and look at the great light that once shone out to the ships, but is now forever snuffed. Then I turn the other direction and look at my wife sleeping on her bunk, her naked ass turned toward me. I try to remember what it was like to make love to her, but it is difficult. I only remember that I miss it. For a long moment I stare at my wife's ass as if it is a mean mouth about to open and reveal teeth. Then I roll on my back again, stare at the ceiling, and continue this routine until daybreak.

Mornings I greet the flowers, their bright red and yellow blooms bursting from the heads of long-dead bodies that will not rot. The flowers open wide to reveal their little black brains and their feathery feelers, and they lift their blooms upward and moan. I get a wild pleasure out of this. For one crazed moment I feel like a rock singer appearing before his starry-eyed audience.

When I tire of the game I get the binoculars, Mr. Journal, and examine the eastern plains with them, as if I expect a city to materialize there. The most interesting thing I have seen on those plains is a herd of large lizards thundering north. For a moment, I considered calling Mary to see them, but I didn't. The sound of my voice, the sight of my face, upsets her. She loves only the tattoo and is interested in nothing more.

When I finish looking at the plains, I walk to the other side. To the west, where the ocean was, there is now nothing but miles and miles of cracked, black sea bottom. Its only resemblance to a great body of water are the occasional dust storms that blow out of the west like dark tidal waves and wash the windows black at mid-day. And the creatures. Mostly mutated whales. Monstrously large, sluggish things. Abundant now where once they were near extinction. (Perhaps the whales should form some sort of GREENPEACE organization for humans now. What do you think, Mr. Journal? No need to answer. Just another one of those little scientist jokes.)

These whales crawl across the sea bottom near the lighthouse from time to time, and if the mood strikes them, they rise on their tails and push their heads near the tower and examine it. I keep expecting one to flop down on us, crushing us like bugs. But no such luck. For some unknown reason the whales never leave the cracked sea bed to venture onto what we formerly called the shore. It's as if they live in invisible water and are bound by it. A racial memory perhaps. Or maybe there's something in that cracked black soil they need. I don't know.

Besides the whales I suppose I should mention I saw a shark once. It was slithering along at a great distance and the tip of its fin was winking in the sunlight. I've also seen some strange, legged fish and some things I could not put a name to. I'll just call them whale food since I saw one of the whales dragging his bottom jaw along the ground one day, scooping up the creatures as they tried to beat a hasty retreat.

Exciting, huh? Well, that's how I spend my day, Mr. Journal. Roaming about the tower with my glasses, coming in to write in you, waiting anxiously for Mary to take hold of that kit and give me the signal. The mere thought of it excites me to erection. I suppose you could call that our sex act together.

And what was I doing the day they dropped The Big One?

Glad you asked that, Mr. Journal, really I am.

I was doing the usual. Up at six, did the shit, shower and shave routine. Had breakfast. Got dressed. Tied my tie. I remember doing the latter, and not very well, in front of the bedroom mirror, and noticing that I had shaved poorly. A hunk of dark beard decorated my chin like a bruise.

Rushing to the bathroom to remedy that, I opened the door as Rae, naked as the day of her birth, was stepping from the tub.

Surprised, she turned to look at me. An arm went over her breasts, and a hand, like a dove settling into a fiery bush, covered her pubic area.

Embarrassed, I closed the door with an "excuse me" and went about my business—unshaved. It was an innocent thing. An accident. Nothing sexual. But when I think of her now, more often than not, that is the first image that comes to mind. I guess it was the moment I realized my baby had grown into a beautiful woman.

That was also the day she went off to her first day of college and got to see, ever so briefly, the end of the world.

And it was the day the triangle—Mary, Rae and myself—shattered.

If my first memory of Rae alone is that day, naked in the bathroom, my foremost memory of us as a family is when Rae was six. We used to go to the park and she would ride the merry-go-round, swing, teeter-totter, and finally my back. ("I want to piggy, Daddy.") We would gallop about until my legs were rubber, then we would stop at the bench where Mary sat waiting. I would turn my back to the bench so Mary could take Rae down, but always before she did, she would reach around from behind, caressing Rae, pushing her tight against my back, and Mary's hands would touch my chest.

God, but if I could describe those hands. She still has hands like that, after all these years. I feel them fluttering against my back when she works. They are long and sleek and artistic. Naturally soft, like the belly of a baby rabbit. And when she held Rae and me that way, I felt that no matter what happened in the world, we three could stand against it and conquer.

But now the triangle is broken and the geometry gone away.

So the day Rae went off to college and was fucked into oblivion by the dark, pelvic thrust of the bomb, Mary drove me to work. Me, Paul Marder, big shot with The Crew. One of the finest, brightest young minds in the industry. Always teaching, inventing and improving on our nuclear threat, because, as we'd often joke, "We cared enough to send only the very best."

When we arrived at the guard booth, I had out my pass, but there was no one to take it. Beyond the chain-link gate there was a wild melee of people running, screaming, falling down.

I got out of the car and ran to the gate. I called out to a man I knew as he ran by. When he turned his eyes were wild and his lips were flecked with foam. "The missiles are flying," he said, then he was gone, running madly.

I jumped in the car, pushed Mary aside and stomped the gas. The Buick leaped into the fence, knocking it asunder. The car spun, slammed into the edge of a building and went dead. I grabbed Mary's hand, pulled her from the car and we ran toward the great elevators.

We made one just in time. There were others running for it as the door closed, and the elevator went down. I still remember the echo of their fists on the metal just as it began to drop. It was like the rapid heartbeat of something dying.

And so the elevator took us to the world of Down Under and we locked it off. There we were in a five-mile layered city designed not only as a massive office and laboratory, but as an impenetrable shelter. It was our special reward for creating the poisons of war. There was food, water, medical supplies, films, books, you name it. Enough to last two thousand people for a hundred years. Of the two thousand it was designed for, perhaps eleven hundred made it. The others didn't run fast enough from the parking lot or the other buildings, or they were late for work, or maybe they had called in sick.

Perhaps they were the lucky ones. They might have died in their sleep. Or while they were having a morning quickie with the spouse. Or perhaps as they lingered over that last cup of coffee.

Because you see, Mr. Journal, Down Under was no paradise. Before long suicides were epidemic. I considered it myself from time to time. People slashed their throats, drank acid, took pills. It was not unusual to come out of your cubicle in the morning and find people dangling from pipes and rafters like ripe fruit.

There were also the murders. Most of them performed by a crazed group who lived in the deeper recesses of the unit and called themselves the Shit Faces. From time to time they smeared dung on themselves and ran amok, clubbing men, women, and children born down under, to death. It was rumored they ate human flesh.

We had a police force of sorts, but it didn't do much. It didn't have much sense of authority. Worse, we all viewed ourselves as deserving victims. Except for Mary, we had all helped to blow up the world.

Mary came to hate me. She came to the conclusion I had killed Rae. It was a realization that grew in her like a drip growing and growing until it became a gushing flood of hate. She seldom talked to me. She tacked up a picture of Rae and looked at it most of the time.

Topside she had been an artist, and she took that up again. She rigged a kit of tools and inks and became a tattooist. Everyone came to her for a mark. And though each was different, they all seemed to indicate one thing: I fucked up. I blew up the world. Brand me.

Day in and day out she did her tattoos, having less and less to do with me, pushing herself more and more into this work until she was as skilled with skin and needles as she had been Topside with brush and canvas. And one night, as we lay on our separate pallets, feigning sleep, she said to me, "I just want you to know how much I hate you."

"I know," I said.

"You killed Rae."

"I know."

"You say you killed her, you bastard. Say it."

"I killed her," I said, and meant it.

Next day I asked for my tattoo. I told her of this dream that came to me nightly. There would be darkness, and out of this darkness would come a swirl of glowing clouds, and the clouds would melt into a mushroom shape, and out of that—torpedo-shaped, nose pointing skyward, striding on ridiculous cartoon legs—would step The Bomb.

There was a face painted on The Bomb, and it was my face. And suddenly the dream's point of view would change, and I would be looking out of the eyes of that painted face. Before me was my daughter. Naked. Lying on the ground. Her legs wide apart. Her sex glazed like a wet canyon.

And I/The Bomb would dive into her, pulling those silly feet after me, and she would scream. I could hear it echo as I plunged through her belly, finally driving myself out of the top of her head, then blowing to terminal orgasm. And the dream would end where it began. A mushroom cloud. Darkness.

When I told Mary the dream and asked her to interpret it in her art, she said, "Bare your back," and that's how the design began. An inch of work at a time—a painful inch. She made sure of that.

Never once did I complain. She'd send the needles home as hard and deep as she could, and though I might moan or cry out, I never asked her to stop. I could feel those fine hands touching my back and I loved it. The needles. The hands. The needles. The hands.

And if that was so much fun, you ask, why did I come Topside?

You ask such probing questions, Mr. Journal. Really you do, and I'm glad you asked that. My telling will be like a laxative, I hope. Maybe if I just let the shit flow I'll wake up tomorrow and feel a lot better about myself.

Sure. And it will be the dawning of a new Pepsi generation as well. It will have all been a bad dream. The alarm clock will ring. I'll get up, have my bowl of Rice Krispies and tie my tie.

Okay, Mr. Journal. The answer. Twenty years or so after we went Down Under, a fistful of us decided it couldn't be any worse Topside than it was below. We made plans to go see. Simple as that. Mary and I even talked a little. We both entertained the crazed belief Rae might have survived. She would be thirty-eight. We might have been hiding below like vermin for no reason. It could be a brave new world up there.

I remember thinking these things, Mr. Journal, and half-believing them.

We outfitted two sixty-foot crafts that were used as part of our transportation system Down Under, plugged in the half-remembered codes that opened the elevators, and drove the vehicles inside. The elevator lasers cut through the debris above them and before long we were Topside. The doors opened to sunlight muted by gray-green clouds and a desert-like landscape. Immediately I knew there was no brave new world over the horizon. It had all gone to hell in a fiery handbasket, and all that was left of man's millions of years of development were a few pathetic humans living Down Under like worms, and a few others crawling Topside like the same.

We cruised about a week and finally came to what had once been the Pacific Ocean. Only there wasn't any water now, just that cracked blackness.

We drove along the shore for another week and finally saw life. A whale. Jacobs immediately got the idea to shoot one and taste its meat.

Using a high-powered rifle he killed it, and he and seven others cut slabs off it, brought the meat back to cook. They invited all of us to eat, but the meat looked greenish and there wasn't much blood and we warned him against it. But Jacobs and the others ate it anyway. As Jacobs said, "It's something to do."

A little later on Jacobs threw up blood and his intestines boiled out of his mouth, and not long after those who had shared the meat had the same thing happen to them. They died crawling on their bellies like gutted dogs. There wasn't a thing we could do for them. We couldn't even bury them. The ground was too hard. We stacked them like cordwood along the shoreline and moved camp down a way, tried to remember how remorse felt.

And that night, while we slept as best we could, the roses came.

Now, let me admit, Mr. Journal, I do not actually know how the roses survived, but I have an idea. And since you've agreed to hear my story—and even if you haven't, you're going to anyway—I'm going to put logic and fantasy together and hope to arrive at the truth.

These roses lived in the ocean bed, underground, and at night they came out. Up until then they had survived as parasites of reptiles and animals, but a new food had arrived from Down Under. Humans. Their creators, actually. Looking at it that way, you might say we were the gods who conceived them, and their partaking of our flesh and blood was but a new version of wine and wafer.

I can imagine the pulsating brains pushing up through the sea bottom on thick stalks, extending feathery feelers and tasting the air out there beneath the light of the moon—which through those odd clouds gave the impression of a pus-filled boil—and I can imagine them uprooting and dragging their vines across the ground toward the shore where the corpses lay.

Thick vines sprouted little, thorny vines, and these moved up the bank and touched the corpses. Then, with a lashing motion, the thorns tore into the flesh, and the vines, like snakes, slithered through the wounds and inside. Secreting a dissolving fluid that turned the innards to the consistency of watery oatmeal, they slurped up the mess, and the vines grew and grew at amazing speed, moved and coiled throughout the bodies, replacing nerves and shaping into the symmetry of the muscles they had devoured, and lastly they pushed up through the necks, into the skulls, ate tongues and eyeballs and sucked up the mouse-gray brains like soggy gruel. With an explosion of skull shrapnel, the roses bloomed, their tooth-hard petals expanding into beautiful red and yellow flowers, hunks of human heads dangling from them like shattered watermelon rinds.

In the center of these blooms a fresh, black brain pulsed and feathery feelers once again tasted air for food and breeding grounds. Energy waves from the floral brains shot through the miles and miles of vines that were knotted inside the bodies, and as they had replaced nerves, muscles and vital organs, they made the bodies stand. Then those corpses turned their flowered heads toward the tents where we slept, and the blooming corpses (another little scientist joke there if you're into English idiom, Mr. Journal) walked, eager to add the rest of us to their animated bouquet.

I saw my first rose-head while I was taking a leak.

I had left the tent and gone down by the shore line to relieve myself when I caught sight of it out of the corner of my eye. Because of the bloom I first thought it was Susan Dyers. She wore a thick, woolly Afro that surrounded her head like a lion's mane, and the shape of the thing struck me as her silhouette. But when I zipped and turned, it wasn't an Afro. It was a flower blooming out of Jacobs. I recognized him by his clothes and the hunk of his face that hung off one of the petals like a worn-out hat on a peg.

In the center of the blood-red flower was a pulsating sack, and all around it little wormy things squirmed. Directly below the brain was a thin proboscis. It extended toward me like an erect penis. At its tip, just inside the opening, were a number of large thorns.

A sound like a moan came out of that proboscis, and I stumbled back. Jacobs' body quivered briefly, as if he had been besieged by a sudden chill, and ripping through his flesh and clothes, from neck to foot, was a mass of thorny, wagging vines that shot out to five feet in length.

With an almost invisible motion, they waved from west to east, slashed my clothes, tore my hide, knocked my feet out from beneath me. It was like being hit by a cat-o-nine-tails.

Dazed, I rolled onto my hands and knees, bear-walked away from it. The vines whipped against my back and butt, cut deep.

Every time I got to my feet, they tripped me. The thorns not only cut, they burned like hot ice picks. I finally twisted away from a net of vines, slammed through one last shoot, and made a break for it.

Without realizing it, I was running back to the tent. My body felt as if I had been lying on a bed of nails and razor blades. My forearm hurt something terrible where I had used it to lash the thorns away from me. I glanced down at it as I ran. It was covered in blood. A strand of vine about two feet in length was coiled around it like a garter snake. A thorn had torn a deep wound in my arm, and the vine was sliding an end into the wound.

Screaming, I held my forearm in front of me like I had just discovered it. The flesh, where the vine had entered, rippled and made a bulge that looked like a junkie's favorite vein. The pain was nauseating. I snatched at the vine, ripped it free. The thorns turned against me-like fishhooks.

The pain was so much I fell to my knees, but I had the vine out of me. It squirmed in my hand, and I felt a thorn gouge my palm. I threw the vine into the dark. Then I was up and running for the tent again.

The roses must have been at work for quite some time before I saw Jacobs, because when I broke back into camp yelling, I saw Susan, Ralph, Casey and some others, and already their heads were blooming, skulls cracking away like broken model kits.

Jane Calloway was facing a rose-possessed corpse, and the dead body had its hands on her shoulders, and the vines were jetting out of the corpse, weaving around her like a web, tearing, sliding inside her, breaking off. The proboscis poked into her mouth and extended down her throat, forced her head back. The scream she started came out a gurgle.

I tried to help her, but when I got close, the vines whipped at me and I had to jump back. I looked for something to grab, to hit the damn thing with, but there was nothing. When next I looked at Jane, vines were stabbing out of her eyes and her tongue, now nothing more than lava-thick blood, was dripping out of her mouth onto her breasts, which, like the rest of her body, were riddled with stabbing vines.

I ran away then. There was nothing I could do for Jane. I saw others embraced by corpse hands and tangles of vines, but now my only thought was Mary. Our tent was to the rear of the campsite, and I ran there as fast as I could.

She was lumbering out of our tent when I arrived. The sound of screams had awakened her. When she saw me running she froze. By the time I got to her, two vine-riddled corpses were coming up on the tent from the left side. Grabbing her hand I half-pulled, half-dragged her away from there. I got to one of the vehicles and pushed her inside.

I locked the doors just as Jacobs, Susan, Jane, and others appeared at the windshield, leaning over the rocket-nose hood, the feelers around the brain sacks vibrating like streamers in a high wind. Hands slid greasily down the windshield. Vines flopped and scratched and cracked against it like thin bicycle chains.

I got the vehicle started, stomped the accelerator, and the rose-heads went flying. One of them, Jacobs, bounced over the hood and splattered into a spray of flesh, ichor and petals.

I had never driven the vehicle, so my maneuvering was rusty. But it didn't matter. There wasn't exactly a traffic rush to worry about.

After an hour or so, I turned to look at Mary. She was staring at me, her eyes like the twin barrels of a double-barreled shotgun. They seemed to say, "More of your doing," and in a way she was right. I drove on.

Daybreak we came to the lighthouse. I don't know how it survived. One of those quirks. Even the glass was unbroken. It looked like a great stone finger shooting us the bird.

The vehicle's tank was near empty, so I assumed here was as good a place to stop as any. At least there was shelter, something we could fortify. Going on until the vehicle was empty of fuel didn't make much sense. There wouldn't be any more fill-ups, and there might not be any more shelter like this.

Mary and I (in our usual silence) unloaded the supplies from the vehicle and put them in the lighthouse. There was enough food, water, chemicals for the chemical toilet, odds and ends, extra clothes, to last us a year. There were also some guns. A Colt .45 revolver, two twelve-gauge shotguns and a .38, and enough shells to fight a small war.

When everything was unloaded, I found some old furniture downstairs and, using tools from the vehicle, tried to barricade the bottom door and the one at the top of the stairs. When I finished, I thought of a line from a story I had once read, a line that always disturbed me. It went something like, "Now we're shut in for the night."

Days. Nights. All the same. Shut in with one another, our memories and the fine tattoo.

A few days later I spotted the roses. It was as if they had smelled us out. And maybe they had. From a distance, through the binoculars, they reminded me of old women in bright sun hats.

It took them the rest of the day to reach the lighthouse, and they immediately surrounded it, and when I appeared at the railing they would lift their heads and moan.

And that, Mr. Journal, brings us up to now.

I thought I had written myself out, Mr. Journal. Told the only part of my life story I would ever tell, but now I'm back. You can't keep a good world-destroyer down.

I saw my daughter last night and she's been dead for years. But I saw her, I did, naked, smiling at me, calling to ride piggyback.

Here's what happened.

It was cold last night. Must be getting along winter. I had rolled off my pallet onto the cold floor. Maybe that's what brought me awake. The cold. Or maybe it was just gut instinct.

It had been a particularly wonderful night with the tattoo. The face had been made so clear it seemed to stand out from my back. It had finally become more defined than the mushroom cloud. The needles went in hard and deep, but I've had them in me so much now I barely feel the pain. After looking in the mirror at the beauty of the design, I went to bed happy, or as happy as I can get.

During the night the eyes ripped open. The stitches came out and I didn't know it until I tried to rise from the cold, stone floor and my back puckered against it where the blood had dried.

I pulled myself free and got up. It was dark, but we had a good moonspill that night and I went to the mirror to look. It was bright enough that I could see Rae's reflection clearly, the color of her face, the color of the cloud. The stitches had fallen away and now the wounds were spread wide, and inside the wounds were eyes. Oh God, Rae's blue eyes. Her mouth smiled at me and her teeth were very white.

Oh, I hear you, Mr. Journal. I hear what you're saying. And I thought of that. My first impression was that I was about six bricks shy a load, gone around the old bend. But I know better now. You see, I lit a candle and held it over my shoulder, and with the candle and the moonlight, I could see even more clearly. It was Rae all right, not just a tattoo.

I looked over at my wife on the bunk, her back to me, as always. She had not moved.

I turned back to the reflection. I could hardly see the outline of myself, just Rae's face smiling out of that cloud.

"Rae," I whispered, "is that you?"

"Come on, Daddy," said the mouth in the mirror, "that's a stupid question. Of course it's me."

"But . . . You're . . . you're . . . "

"Dead?"

"Yes . . . Did . . . did it hurt much?"

She cackled so loudly the mirror shook. I could feel the hairs on my neck rising. I thought for sure Mary would wake up, but she slept on.

"It was instantaneous, Daddy, and even then, it was the greatest pain imaginable. Let me show you how it hurt."

The candle blew out and I dropped it. I didn't need it anyway. The mirror grew bright and Rae's smile went from ear to ear—literally—and the flesh on her bones seemed like crepe paper before a powerful fan, and that fan blew the hair off her head, the skin off her skull and melted those beautiful, blue eyes and those shiny white teeth of hers to a putrescent goo the color and consistency of fresh bird shit. Then there was only the skull, and it heaved in half and flew backwards into the dark world of the mirror and there was no reflection now, only the hurtling fragments of a life that once was and was now nothing more than swirling cosmic dust.

I closed my eyes and looked away.

"Daddy?"

I opened them, looked over my shoulder into the mirror. There was Rae again, smiling out of my back.

"Darling," I said, "I'm so sorry."

"So are we," she said, and there were faces floating past her in the mirror. Teenagers, children, men and women, babies, little embryos swirling around her head like planets around the sun. I closed my eyes again, but I could not keep them closed. When I opened them the multitudes of swirling dead, and those who had never had a chance to live, were gone. Only Rae was there.

"Come close to the mirror, Daddy."

I backed up to it. I backed until the hot wounds that were Rae's eyes touched the cold glass and the wounds became hotter and hotter and Rae called out, "Ride me piggy, Daddy," and then I felt her weight on my back, not the weight of a six-year-old child or a teenage girl, but a great weight, like the world was on my shoulders and bearing down.

Leaping away from the mirror I went hopping and whooping about the room, same as I used to in the park. Around and around I went, and as I did, I glanced in the mirror. Astride me was Rae, lithe and naked, her red hair fanning around her as I spun. And when I whirled by the mirror again, I saw that she was six years old. Another spin and there was a skeleton with red hair, one hand held high, the jaws open and yelling, "Ride 'em, cowboy."

"How?" I managed, still bucking and leaping, giving Rae the ride of her life. She bent to my ear and I could feel her warm breath. "You want to know how I'm here, Daddy-dear? I'm here because you created me. Once you laid between Mother's legs and thrust me into existence, the two of you, with all the love there was in you. This time you thrust me into existence with your guilt and Mother's hate. Her thrusting needles, your arching back. And now I've come back for one last ride, Daddy-o. Ride, you bastard, ride."

All the while I had been spinning, and now as I glimpsed the mirror I saw wall-to-wall faces, weaving in, weaving out, like smiling stars, and all those smiles opened wide and words came out in chorus, "Where were you when they dropped The Big One?"

Each time I spun and saw the mirror again, it was a new scene. Great flaming winds scorching across the world, babies turning to fleshy jello, heaps of charred bones, brains boiling out of the heads of men and women like backed-up toilets overflowing, The Almighty, Glory Hallelujah, Ours Is Bigger Than Yours Bomb hurtling forward, the mirror going mushroom white, then clear, and me, spinning, Rae pressed tight against my back, melting like butter on a griddle, evaporating into the eye wounds on my back, and finally me alone, collapsing to the floor beneath the weight of the world.

Mary never awoke.

The vines outsmarted me.

A single strand found a crack downstairs somewhere and wound up the steps and slipped beneath the door that led into the tower. Mary's bunk was not far from the door, and in the night, while I slept and later while I spun in front of the mirror and lay on the floor before it, it made its way to Mary's bunk, up between her legs, and entered her sex effortlessly.

I suppose I should give the vine credit for doing what I had not been able to do in years, Mr. Journal, and that's enter Mary. Oh God, that's a funny one, Mr.

Journal. Real funny. Another little scientist joke. Let's make that a mad scientist joke, what say? Who but a madman would play with the lives of human beings by constantly trying to build the bigger and better boom machine?

So what of Rae, you ask?

I'll tell you. She is inside me. My back feels the weight. She twists in my guts like a corkscrew. I went to the mirror a moment ago, and the tattoo no longer looks like it did. The eyes have turned to crusty sores and the entire face looks like a scab. It's as if the bile that made up my soul, the unthinking nearsightedness, the guilt that I am, has festered from inside and spoiled the picture with pustule bumps, knots and scabs.

To put it in layman's terms, Mr. Journal, my back is infected. Infected with what I am. A blind, senseless fool.

The wife?

Ah, the wife. God, how I loved that woman. I have not really touched her in years, merely felt those wonderful hands on my back as she jabbed the needles home, but I never stopped loving her. It was not a love that glowed anymore, but it was there, though hers for me was long gone and wasted.

This morning when I got up from the floor, the weight of Rae and the world on my back, I saw the vine coming up from beneath the door and stretching over to her. I yelled her name. She did not move. I ran to her and saw it was too late. Before I could put a hand on her, I saw her flesh ripple and bump up, like a den of mice were nesting under a quilt. The vines were at work. (Out go the old guts, in go the new vines.)

There was nothing I could do for her.

I made a torch out of a chair leg and old quilt, set fire to it, burned the vine from between her legs, watched it retreat, smoking, under the door. Then I got a board, nailed it along the bottom, hoping it would keep others out for at least a little while. I got one of the twelve-gauges and loaded it. It's on the desk beside me, Mr. Journal, but even I know I'll never use it. It was just something to do, as Jacobs said when he killed and ate the whale. Something to do.

I can hardly write anymore. My back and shoulders hurt so bad. It's the weight of Rae and the world.

I've just come back from the mirror and there is very little left of the tattoo. Some blue and black ink, a touch of red that was Rae's hair. It looks like an abstract painting now. Collapsed design, running colors. It's real swollen. I look like the hunchback of Notre Dame.

What am I going to do, Mr. Journal?

Well, as always, I'm glad you asked that. You see, I've thought this out.

I could throw Mary's body over the railing before it blooms. I could do that. Then I could doctor my back. It might even heal, though I doubt it. Rae wouldn't let that happen, I can tell you now. And I don't blame her. I'm on her side. I'm just a walking dead man and have been for years.

I could put the shotgun under my chin and work the trigger with my toes, or maybe push it with the very pen I'm using to create you, Mr. Journal. Wouldn't that be neat? Blow my brains to the ceiling and sprinkle you with my blood.

But as I said, I loaded the gun because it was something to do. I'd never use it on myself or Mary.

You see, I want Mary. I want her to hold Rae and me one last time like she used to in the park. And she can. There's a way.

I've drawn all the curtains and made curtains out of blankets for those spots where there aren't any. It'll be sunup soon and I don't want that kind of light in here. I'm writing this by candlelight and it gives the entire room a warm glow. I wish I had wine. I want the atmosphere to be just right.

Over on Mary's bunk she's starting to twitch. Her neck is swollen where the vines have congested and are writhing toward their favorite morsel, the brain. Pretty soon the rose will bloom (I hope she's one of the bright yellow ones, yellow was her favorite color and she wore it well) and Mary will come for me.

When she does, I'll stand with my naked back to her. The vines will whip out and cut me before she reaches me, but I can stand it. I'm used to pain. I'll pretend the thorns are Mary's needles. I'll stand that way until she folds her dead arms around me and her body pushes up against the wound she made in my back, the wound that is our daughter Rae. She'll hold me so the vines and the proboscis can do their work. And while she holds me, I'll grab her fine hands and push them against my chest, and it will be we three again, standing against the world, and I'll close my eyes and delight in her soft, soft hands one last time.

• THE TASTE OF STARLIGHT •
John R. Fultz

Pelops wakes gasping and shivering inside the CryoPod. A thin layer of ice crystals coats his cheeks and hands, pricking at his exposed skin. Crackling and moaning, he raises hands to his eyes and pries their lids open, shedding ice shards like tears. The curving glass surface before him is cracked into a mass of spidery lines. Struggling to inhale the frozen air, he pushes against the glass. The door of the pod refuses to move. He is entombed.

He moans as he raises his right leg, shedding a cloud of crystals. Boot against the fractured glass, but without much strength. His muscles are still asleep, slightly atrophied by years of stasis. Again he kicks, and draws in a burning lungful of cryonic air. A third time his booted foot meets the glass and it shatters, toppling him forward in a shower of ice and fragments. Instinct pulls his hands up, and he lands on them instead of his face. Splinters cut into his palms and fingers, but he can breathe freely now.

Lying on the floor, he rolls onto his back and looks sideways along a flickering corridor of cryonic niches. Here stand the stasis pods of his thirteen fellow sleepers. Even the chill metal of the floor feels warm compared to the ultimate cold of the CryoPod.

Something has awakened him early. A mistake? An emergency? Staggering to his feet, he clings to the cables along the walls and checks the nearest pod. A calm face, eyes closed, just visible through the cloudy glass. Digital display reads "Thompson, J." and the indicator light glows green. No fissures. Pod intact. He checks the next one, and the next one, until he finds another cracked pod lid with the display reading "Tanaka, Y." No frost at all on this lid. A blue face stares at him from inside. Asian eyes open. Mouth slack.

Pelops tries the release lever. Nothing. He tears at the rim of the pod's lid. Finally, he kicks in the glass like he did his own, this time from the opposite side. Tanaka falls out, stiff and dead. She was a good woman, and fine physicist. She would have been an asset to the Dantus colony. Must have suffocated when her stasis was interrupted. Like being buried alive. He might weep for her, but his eyes still feel frozen. He knows he'll have to eject her body into space, but he'll wait until he regains his strength.

He lays Tanaka gently on the floor and checks the last few pods. Twelve remain intact.

The frost coating his skin and flight suit melts into cold water. Droplets fly from his beard and hair, grown to primordial length while he slept. What could have happened?

He stumbles along the corridor beneath the pulsing florescent lamps, follows the plastic maps posted at each intersection, and finally reaches the sealed door of the bridge. A gleaming hand plate accepts his touch. The nerve center of the *Goya* opens before him, a spacious cockpit of flashing neon display grids and blinking digital interfaces. Above it all, a vista of interstellar wonder, a great oval viewport looking out into the universe. He stares into the bottomless void, captivated by the glimmering of ancient stars. A purple nebula clouds the starfields ahead, and the sheer beauty of the galactic deeps overwhelms his waking senses. Sinking into a vast gulf of infinity. Distant fires grinning and sparkling, the eyes of a demon legion.

You don't belong here, the stars whisper. *This is the Great Emptiness. The stronghold of Death. Soon it will consume you. Utterly.*

Pelops tears himself away from the celestial vision and goes to the control panels. He is no pilot, no navigator, but he is a man of science. He has been on ships before. He scans the displays and finds that the ship's thrusters have gone offline. He switches the relays to instigate backup power.

A lurching and shuddering tells him the ship has resumed its full-speed journey. He falls into the captain's chair and punches his fingers at the keyboard, requesting a status report. A holographic display emerges, dancing before him like a ghost. It's the *Goya*, a gleaming bottle-shaped vessel surrounded by pinpoints of rushing starlight. A scarlet line enters the left side of the display, trailing a cloud of sparks. A comet. It crosses the forward hull of the ship, bathing the vessel in a cloud of scintillating motes.

He reads the print display below the hologram.

Radiation cloud. Unidentified in nature . . .

A short-circuiting of the ship's power grid, disabling the auto-drive.

Severe turbulence resulting in damage to two CryoPod units.

No shit.

Communications permanently disabled. No messages going out or coming in. Not until the com techs on Dantus install a new stack of relays. Absolute radio silence. The report ends and the curved panels blink silently. Course renewed. Power reserves engaged. Everything nearly back to normal. But now Pelops is awake. And completely alone.

He accesses the logs for time, date, and distance.

Time elapsed since launch: *6 years, 2 months, 3 days, 9 hours, 52 minutes, 39 seconds.*

Time remaining to destination: *1 year, 4 months, 2 days, 7 hours, 18 minutes, 3 seconds.*

Sixteen months. Alone on this ship.

He considers waking the rest of the crew. Walks back to the pod corridor and almost does exactly that, when it hits him: A terrible, gnawing hunger in his gut. And the realization . . . what is he going to eat? *Nobody* was supposed to wake until a few hours before touchdown. This ship isn't equipped for manned flight.

He finds his way through the labyrinth of steel into the airy cargo hold. The massive bulk of the twenty-five UV converter domes loom like black hills beneath plastic tarps. In the far corner he finds what he is looking for. Emergency Supply Kit.

A man-sized chest (like a coffin). Inside, a collection of boxes, tins, and tubes of dry rations. A map on the lid reveals the location of emergency water tanks. He breathes a little easier. There's enough water in those tanks to keep a man alive for three years. However, he's not so sure how long the food will last. He'll worry about that later.

Cracking open a plastic box, he tears through an aluminum pouch and devours the beef jerky inside. Famished and relishing every bit, the salty taste of it on his tongue, the familiar warmth as it fills his belly. In a few seconds the entire package is gone. He curses himself.

He'll have to ration this out if he's going to survive. He can't indulge himself in such feasts. He closes the lid and makes his way along the bay to the water tanks, where he turns a valve and fills a bucket with drinking water. He drinks his fill of the cold liquid.

He surveys and logs the emergency foodstuffs, planning out subsistence portions. Drops his pen and slides to the floor. Someone was supposed to load more emergency supplies than this. Someone did not. There's barely enough food here to keep him eating at a base survival level for 100 days.

Three months. If he does not wake anyone else.

If he does, that time will be cut in half.

Three months of food. *Sixteen months* until reaching Dantus.

Nothing else here.

Nothing to eat.

After three months he will begin to starve.

Pelops carries Tanaka's rigid body into the airlock, says a quick prayer, and ejects her into space. He should be grateful. One less mouth to feed.

He races back to the two open CryoPods and tries to get them operational. Spends hours working on them, up to his elbows in grease and cryonic residue. But it doesn't matter. They're both totally out of commission, their transparent lids shattered. And even if they weren't, the pods cannot be put back into service once they've been opened. The only way to do that would be to introduce more cryogen . . . which can only be done by CryoPod contractors.

No way to re-freeze himself. No way to avoid the twelve weeks of bare subsistence and the slow, lingering starvation that will surely follow. He envies Tanaka her quick death.

He lies on the floor of the pod corridor, weeping, remembering his look into the void. The whispering stars and their message of doom. And he knows it's true. This is the realm of Death and he has entered it willingly.

He wails and gnashes his teeth and smashes the floor with his fists. Eventually he falls asleep and enjoys the mercy of a warm oblivion.

Pelops wakes sometime later, trembling on the cold metal floor. He gets up and returns to the bridge. His stomach growls, but he denies it. He sits in the captain's chair and stares out at the numberless stars.

With Tanaka dead, he is the only one capable of getting the UV converters up and running on Dantus. And the future of the colony depends on those machines. Wolf 359 is a red dwarf star, and not enough crops grow in its infrared glow. The colony's population has grown too fast for its agricultural systems to handle. Setting up the converter domes and transforming the star's radiation to ultraviolet light is the only way to boost food production and end the famine. The only way to feed thousands of brave families who settled there. Eleven thousand men, women, and children already, with an exponentially expanding birth rate. They're all depending on Dr. Andrew Pelops.

I have to survive, he thinks. *All those lives depend on it. This mission has to succeed. Everything else is secondary.*

Think about those people. Those children. Think about those hungry mouths, so many more than yours.

The mission must succeed.

For the first three months Pelops eats frugally and his body grows lean. The flight suit hangs loose on his frame. He cuts his beard and hair with a pair of infirmary scissors, but they always grow back into a hermit's nest of tangles. The boredom is deadly. He spends most of his waking hours on the bridge, staring into the glittering void. He charts constellations . . . Scorpius, Serpens, Hydra. He sails through a gulf of myth and darkness. At times he fears the demon-eyes of the stars, and at other times he laughs at them. He carves images of ancient monsters into the deck floor with a screwdriver. He sleeps.

Sometimes he talks to the sleeping crew, sharing his knowledge of photonic chemistry, tales of his failed marriage, and his dreams for the future. They lie cold and still inside their coffins and listen to his every word. They are the perfect listeners.

Sometimes he imagines they reply to him.

Whispering like the distant stars.

• • •

Pelops eats the last bit of the dried jerky from the emergency chest. There is nothing else inside. Only the empty carcasses of plastic and tin where the faintest scent of edible things lingers. For days afterward he endures the grinding of his stomach, drinks himself to bloating at the water tanks, endures the hunger pangs that stab in his guts.

He babbles to the sleeping crew, telling them tales of hunger strikes.

"You see the body persists on glucose energy for the first three days of starvation," he says, walking between the rows of frosty faces. "At that point the liver starts feeding on body fat as ketosis begins. Thanks to the natural reserves of the human body, you don't really begin to starve until after three weeks. Now the body extracts nutrients and substance from the muscles and organs. Bone marrow too. Here's where the real danger begins . . . "

He imagines himself gnawing the meat off a large bone, slavering like a hound.

"Most hunger strikers die after fifty days . . . but are incapacitated long before that. We can't allow that to happen. The mission is all that matters. It must succeed . . . at all cost."

He hopes they understand.

After ten solid days of starving, he dreams of his father. The stars are bright and blinking above the Colorado mountains. He's twelve years old, and his father has killed a deer. Pelops helps skin and prepare the carcass. They roast the venison over an open flame and enjoy its wild, savory flavor. His father's eyes glisten like the stars as he smiles through a frosty beard:

You know what you have to do, son.

Pelops wakes remembering the taste of greasy venison.

He staggers to the infirmary and finds a laser scalpel. In the cargo bay tool cabinet, a trio of gas-powered welding torches. He picks one up and presses the switch. A blue flame emerges, dancing before his eyes like a beacon of hope.

The flame is hot and perfect.

I have no other choice.

He punches the release lever on Thompson's pod. A hiss of escaping vapor, a white fog rushing about his feet. He lifts the lid and looks at the man's sleeping face, blue-white with a mask of rapidly melting frost. As the eyes begin to flutter against their icy hoods, Pelops raises the hypodermic needle. He's found a powerful sedative in the infirmary cabinet. He injects the drug into Thompson's jugular and pulls him from the pod, slinging him over his shoulder.

I could use the scalpel on myself, he thinks. *Cut my own throat . . . quick and painless.*

Is it wrong to kill a few people to save thousands?

He already knows the answer. It sits in his chest like an iron weight, far heavier than a single human body.

On the infirmary operating table he lays Thompson out, strips him of flight suit and undergarments. Bathes his body with fresh water from the tanks. Removes most of the body hair with scissors and razor.

He has never killed a man before. His nerves are electric. His hands tremble, and he begins babbling again. He knows the unconscious Thompson can't hear him. He could wake him up and have a real conversation first . . . but that would only make it harder.

"During World War II this type of thing was fairly common," he says. "Take the Siege of Leningrad. Eight hundred and seventy two days. The survivors trapped inside the city ate all the pets, birds, and rats before they were forced to . . . So it's not as if this sort of thing is completely without precedent. The mission must succeed, Thompson. At any cost."

I'm so sorry.

He switches on the laser scalpel and draws the blade of light across Thompson's soft throat. A fountain of red flows across the table and drips onto the floor, where Pelops has spread a tarp and bucket to catch it.

He dons a surgeon's mask to avoid the smell and proceeds to butcher the carcass. First he separates the limbs from the torso, then the head. The heat of the laser provides partial cauterization, but not enough to keep blood from leaking through tiny holes like puncture wounds in the raw, pink muscle tissue. A wave of nausea and weakness claims him, so he leaves the segmented body for later and takes Thompson's lower leg into the cargo bay. With the scissors he lacerates and peels the skin from the hock of meat. Then he arranges the calf and foot on a metal spit, propped between two crates above the three activated welding torches. The blue-white flames cook the flesh nicely . . . the smell of it roasting both titillates and nauseates him. He wretches, but has nothing inside him to throw up.

It's only venison, he tells himself.

After a few minutes he turns the spit, browning the other side.

He catches himself drooling and wipes his lips.

He cannot bear to wait for it to fully cook, so he settles for medium rare.

Picks it up like a massive chicken leg and takes his first bite, sinking teeth deep into the tender flesh. Tearing a mouthful from the bone. He chews, remembering that trip with his father . . . sitting around the camp fire. Eating what he'd killed.

Veal.

The exact consistency of fresh and tender veal.

He takes another bite. Expects to wretch it all up, but doesn't. He swallows the second bite, and a third. A great contentment settles over him. For the first time in six years his belly is full. He falls asleep on the cargo bay floor, the hock of gnawed meat lying on his chest.

He dreams of brown gravy and hot, steaming biscuits.

Less than a week.

Less than a week, and the meat has all gone bad. Energized and renewed by a succession of hunger-free days, Pelops realizes his mistake. Once the pods are open they won't freeze again. There is no freezer on the ship—it was never meant to sustain awake beings for more than a few hours at a time. He has no way to keep the meat from spoiling.

The next few days he makes himself sick by eating the rotten flesh. Half of his kill has been ruined. He smashes a naked shinbone against the wall in frustration.

He checks the time log on the bridge again. Just over eleven months to go. Eleven functioning CryoPods. Eleven bodies to sustain him. But only if he does things differently.

It all depends on me, he reminds himself. *Eleven thousand men, women, and children.*

If he keeps eating spoiled meat, he'll die. So he shoves the rest of Thompson into the airlock and ejects it into space.

What a waste. Just like Tanaka.

He waits as long as he can for the hunger to catch up with him again. Stares at the cold stars beyond the bridge viewport. Gazing into an emptiness that mirrors the void in his belly. He abstains as long as he can possibly stand it . . . nine days this time.

He harvests the next pod.

Staggs, E. Male. Big, guy, good physique.

Pelops thaws him out, sedates him, and straps him to the operating table. He can't kill this one like he did Thompson. He has to keep the meat fresh.

He dry heaves into a plastic waste bin . . . there is nothing inside him to throw up.

Think of Dantus. All those people . . . all those hungry people.

Wiping his wet eyes, he starts with the left leg, severing it at the knee.

Like last time, he roasts it and relieves his initial hunger. This time his guilt and nausea are drowned beneath a torrent of sheer gratitude. The meat (*venison!*) is savory, red and juicy on his tongue. His teeth tear through it with gusto. This man was an athlete . . . lots of tender muscle. Protein . . . nutrients . . . flavor.

Thompson was veal. Staggs is prime beef.

He waits as long as he can between each meal. Finally settles on eating once every 48 hours. In this way, he calculates his meat will last until Dantus. Eleven months. Sure, he'll suffer from lack of carbohydrates and vitamin C . . . but men have survived on all-meat diets for longer than that and been just fine. After this ordeal, after the converters are installed on the colony farms, there will be vegetables and fruits aplenty. A bounty to replace what he has lost. And the crew of the *Goya* will be remembered as heroes.

He pumps Staggs full of fresh sedative on a daily basis. The man remains oblivious as his legs and arms disappear, replaced by careful tourniquets that prevent him from bleeding to death. Pelops cleans him, looks after his bodily functions, makes sure he stays alive. Preserves as much of the man's dignity as he can.

Later, when only the head and torso are left, Pelops has to be more careful. Tricky to harvest a torso without killing the subject. He starts with a crude appendectomy. Next, he removes the liver. Then the spleen and stomach. Eventually, when Staggs is truly dead, he cracks open the chest cavity and removes the fist-sized heart.

Filet mignon, he tells himself. *That's all it is.*

He cooks the heart a special way, cutting it open to butterfly the meat.

Eats it sitting before the viewport, gazing into the abyss of blinking stars.

It is the finest piece of meat he's ever tasted. *The heart*, he decides, *must be the choicest morsel in the human body*. The prime muscle. The lights of the console blink across his face as his molars grind the meat and it slips down his gullet into his grateful stomach.

Staggs' brain, sliced in two, provides a double meal.

Tastes like stringy roast chicken.

Gray matter. White meat.

Pelops harvests the next pod in the same way, but runs out of sedative after ten days. First Officer Bernard Hoffman wakes up on the table, restrained and entirely legless. His panicked screams draw Pelops into the infirmary.

"Shhhhhh . . . " Pelops comforts him. Gives him cool water to drink. "Take it easy, Hoffman."

"What . . . what's happening?" asks the terrified man, his brown eyes pleading.

"Shhhh . . . it's all right. It's just a bad dream. The mission is going to be a success. We're only ten months from Dantus. Go back to sleep."

Hoffman writhes against his restraints, tearing at the leather straps. The stumps of his legs begin to bleed. "What the fuck are you talking about? You look . . . look . . . where are my legs? *What happened to my legs?*" More screaming. He's only just noticed his missing appendages.

Pelops breaks down. He apologizes and explains everything. Tells Hoffman about the comet, about the radiation, about the pods, the lack of food, how he must ensure the mission's success. Reminds him of the thousands of people depending on his UV converters.

But Hoffman doesn't get any of it. He just screams.

Screams and screams until he makes himself hoarse.

Pelops begs him to stop, but the screams go on and on. He knocks Hoffman unconscious. But the man only wakes up screaming again. Pelops stuffs a rag in his mouth and leaves him on the table. In a few days, he won't have the strength to make any more noise.

Pelops uses a local anesthetic now instead of sedative. Hoffman may have to be awake during his amputations, but he won't feel a thing. His eyes grow large as golf balls as he watches Pelops remove his left arm, then later his right. He finally stops trying to scream. Spends most of his time unconscious now. Sometimes he wakes and mutters nonsense, so Pelops sits in a chair next to him, his belly full, and listens.

He reminds Hoffman that this sacrifice makes him a hero. One of the Saviors of Dantus colony.

When he harvests the torso this time he learns to salvage the intestines, filling them with minced organ meat. He discovers how to make a week's worth of sausages in this way before Hoffman's heart finally gives out.

He decides to keep the white bones instead of flushing them into the void.

He'll bury them on Dantus, beneath a growing field of wheat. With stone monuments.

He comes to this decision over dinner.

The next pod contains a gorgeous blonde woman. *Mewes, C.*

After he gets her onto the table, he wakes her and talks at length about their situation. Lets her know the heroic role she will be playing in the mission. She weeps, begs, pleads with him. He sobs with her, sharing in the tragedy of the situation. He unbuckles her restraints and embraces her tenderly.

"Don't worry," he whispers in her ear, arms wrapped around her. "Don't worry. It'll be okay."

He chases her down when she slips away from him, but manages to corner her in the cargo bay and knocks her senseless with a crowbar.

I could let her join me, he thinks. *It wouldn't be so lonely then. Maybe there's enough meat in the pods for both of us . . .*

He smacks himself across the face. *Stupid!* He knows two people surviving the rest of this journey is impossible. There's simply not enough food. Both would starve and Dantus would die.

So it's back to the table where the harvesting begins. Still a good supply of sedative, so she won't feel any pain.

Somehow, she wakes in the middle of things and starts wailing. The sound pierces his ears in a way that Hoffman's guttural bellows never could. He has to gag her so he can finish.

Later, enjoying the last of her, he smacks his lips and remembers the lovely blue of her eyes. So delectable on his tongue, like tender Swedish meatballs.

The void persists, and so does his hunger. It returns like clockwork every 48 hours.

He doesn't bother looking at the name of his next harvest. He cuts out the tongue first to avoid any more conversation.

A few days later he goes to the table-bound crewman, removes the gag and offers him a taste of his own thigh meat. The man eats ravenously, saving his questions until his own hunger is sated. Then he stares at Pelops and tries to form words. The stub of his tongue rattles around inside his mouth. His mute eyes plead desperately. They remind Pelops of the blonde's blue eyes.

He eats them next.

The human body is indeed an amazing thing.

So many different flavors.

Five and a half months left, five CryoPods unopened.

With proper rationing, he will make it. However, the anesthetic is nearly gone.

This complicates things, but is in no way a barrier to success.

The mission is all that matters.

He has it down to a science now: Open the pod. Tie the sleeper's hands and feet with copper wire before they come fully awake. Drag them to in the infirmary, strap them to the table. Remove the tongue, put the gag in place. Ignore the screams. Ignore the blood. Slice. Tourniquet. Ignore the squirming, the moans of pain. The tears, the squealing.

Forty-eight hours later. Slice. Tourniquet. It's no longer a person, despite all the writhing and moaning and muffled screams. It's only meat.

Forty-eight hours after that. Slice. Tourniquet. They're usually too weak to scream much more after this.

Some are lucky enough to sleep through the whole process from this point on.

Three more crew members and thirteen weeks later. Only two months away from Dantus.

His next meal is the last female. But this fact barely registers; Pelops no longer sees them as women or men.

They're only meat.

All of us . . . charting the course of history . . . only meat.

Yet this one is something special. When he slices into her abdomen he finds her secret. The command board would have grounded her had they known. Or maybe she didn't know. Two months along before Cryo, he estimates. Her eyes are glazed by the time he discovers the prize inside her. Strapped, gagged, limbless, and unblinking, she stares at the antiseptic ceiling as he vivisects her. And there it is . . .

A tiny thing . . . only eighteen centimeters. Barely recognizable as human. More like something amphibian . . . a vestige of our marine origins.

Miniscule arms more like fins, or flippers. The stubs of barely formed legs. Round head no larger than an orange.

So we begin . . . the seed from which all of us grow.

Expanding and developing meat on a rack of expanding and hardening bone.

He carries it to the bridge, shows it to the stars. He imagines the universe itself as one big womb . . . an inescapable uterus containing planets, stars, and galaxies.

In the end, it's little more than a snack.

Sweet, a bit crunchy. A fresh flavor.

Bit of a fishy aftertaste.

Its mother lasts another eight days.

In these months he's decided to put all those bones to good use. At first he carves them into tiny figurines: goblins, serpents, scorpions, or wholly new creatures birthed in his imagination. Then he decides on a project. A sculpture. He drags all the bones and skulls onto the bridge and works nonstop in the pale starlight, baring his creative spirit to the naked universe.

Directly ahead, a red star shines. Wolf 359. His destination, the color of spilled blood gleaming brightly in a mantle of eternal night.

A new god observes and blesses the success of the mission. Its lofty head is a ring of ten bleached skulls gazing in every direction. Its body is a tangled conglomeration of leg bones, arm bones, and rib cages. It wears a necklace of finger and toe bones. With screws and caulk and ductile adhesive he has brought it to life.

He sits before it in the captain's chair, discussing with it the secrets of the universe, watching the void outside and the red star that is their final destination.

His creation tells him things, terrible things that he has long suspected, now confirmed in the glaring honesty of cold starlight. He eats his meals before it, calling upon it to bless the meat.

He tears into his latest chop, red and quivering.

Fresh and *raw*, that is the only way to eat meat.

His new god approves.

With two months to go and two CryoPods left, Pelops gets careless.

The man inside (*Harmon, Sgt. G.*) revives while he's being tied, his frosty eyelids flickering open. Some fight-or-flight mechanism kicks in and he knocks Pelops from the opened pod, spilling out on top of him.

"Wha . . . " he stammers. "Whaaaaa . . . "

Pelops tries to club him on the head with a wrench but Sgt. Harmon is already too fast. He rolls away and pulls his hands free of the wire. He kicks Pelops in the side of the head. Stars swim crazily in Pelops' eyes.

Pelops regains his senses to find Harmon holding him against the wall, pressing the tip of a screwdriver against his neck. The sergeant is still cold and reeks of cryonic fluid. He breathes hotly in Pelops' face, the crystals on his beard beginning to melt.

"Who are you?" he asks. "And what the hell are you doing?"

He shoves the screwdriver painfully into Pelops' skin, drawing a trickle of blood.

"I'm Dr. Pelops," he says. "I had to . . . awaken you prematurely."

Harmon looks around the corridor. Sees the empty pods. All but one now missing its inhabitant.

"Where are they?" His teeth are gritted as his black eyes bore into Pelops'. *"Tell me!"*

"Dead . . . " Pelops admits. "There was a comet, or a meteor . . . some kind of radiation cloud . . . took out the auto-drive and the pods. I was lucky."

Harmon blinks, thinking. Considering. *He knows I'm not telling him everything.* His eyes fall upon the last functioning CryoPod.

"Why didn't you wake Captain Tyler?"

"I . . . I was going to," says Pelops.

Harmon grabs Pelops' throat in an iron grip. "Then why tie me up? Huh?"

Pelops says nothing. Gasps for air.

"You look like hell," says Harmon, examining him. Hair and beard a matted rat's nest. Face sunken, skin sallow. Nails long as claws.

Can he smell the dead on my breath?

"How long?" asks Harmon. Rams his knee into Pelops' groin. Pelops falls to the cold floor. Harmon bends and holds the screwdriver's tip to his eye. *"How long?"* he shouts.

"F-f-fourteen months!" cries Pelops.

Shock spills across Harmon's shaggy face. "Fourteen . . . " He looks again at the empty rows of CryoPods, stares down the corridor in either direction. Sniffs the air like a suspicious hound. "Fourteen months . . . how did you survive?"

Pelops clutches his throbbing groin and says nothing.

Harmon kicks him in the stomach.

"How? Tell me! Say it!"

Pelops tells him. Doesn't look at his face. Hears him start to wretch.

"All that matters is the success of this mission . . . " Pelops growls. "And I'm the only one who can get those converters up and running."

Harmon is strangely quiet.

"We've got two more months," says Pelops.

Harmon's boot comes down hard on his face.

Darkness.

"He's a sick fuck!"

Pelops regains consciousness, wrapped in a web of pain. No, it's the copper wire. He's propped upright inside one of the defunct pods. In the corridor Harmon stands arguing with another man. The inhabitant of the last pod, the ship's captain (*Tyler, Capt. H.*). A sinking feeling as he realizes that Harmon has revived Tyler far too early. He tries to move his arms and legs, but he's securely bound. He listens to their conversation, watching them in the corner of his eye.

"I know how you feel, soldier," says Captain Tyler, still wiping frost from his flight suit, rubbing a hand across the back of his neck. "But Pelops is the only one who knows how to set up those UV converter domes and get them operational. We can't just execute him."

"Execute? Who said anything about an execution? You don't execute a mad dog, captain. You put it down. And that's what we have here. He fuckin' *ate* them! Didn't you hear me?"

"I heard you, son." A weary sigh.

"Come on," says Harmon. "Let me show you the nice little present he built for us on the bridge. Once you see that I'm sure you'll agree to shoving him out the airlock at the least."

The sound of their boots tramping down the corridor.

Pelops waits.

Prays.

Mutters poems to his bone god.

Eventually the voices return, growing in volume, punctuated by the sounds of boots on metal.

" . . . even if we do this, we're still going to starve. There's no food left on board and we can't enter Cryo again. This is the end of the line for us."

"Then it doesn't matter, does it? Let me kill him. One last good thing before we die. Then we'll set the auto-destruct . . . go out in a blaze of glory. Better than starving to death."

Captain Tyler has no response to that.

The two men stand before the open CryoPod now, looking at Pelops.

"Captain . . . " Pelops says, "you know as well as I do—"

"Shut up, freak!" Sgt. Harmon's fist slams into his gut. The air rushes from his lungs, along with the words he failed to utter.

Harmon lifts a service pistol to Pelops' chin, the barrel digging into his jawbone.

"All of us may have to die," Harmon tells him, "but you're going first you cannibal fu—"

Thud.

A flash of silver above his head, a meaty sound, and Harmon goes down. Captain Tyler stands over him with the wrench in his hand. Its round end drips dark blood like syrup, and a clot of hair and skin hangs there.

Tyler drops the wrench and peels the coils of wire away from Pelops' wrists and ankles.

The captain is silent for awhile as Pelops rubs his limbs to get the circulation flowing again. Tyler stares at his fallen officer, leans against the wall. Tired. Ready to accept his fate.

"You did the right thing doctor," says Tyler. His sunken eyes turn toward Pelops. They are as black and glittering as the void. "The famine on Dantus could kill tens of thousands. This mission has to succeed."

Pelops nods. His stomach growls. He is ravenous.

"Can you still make it work?" asks Tyler.

Pelops stares down at the unconscious soldier. Makes a few mental calculations. Rubs his sore temple.

"Yes," he says. "With your help, the mission *will* still succeed."

Tyler helps Pelops carry Harmon into the infirmary.

Pelops carefully rations out pieces of Harmon over the next few weeks. Tyler holds out for sixteen days but eventually joins him for a slight meal. Pelops insists.

"It's imperative to this mission that you stay alive captain," he says. "Just a little while longer."

Tyler won't go near the infirmary. The blow to Harmon's head inflicted some kind of brain damage, so he remains comatose as he's carved to bits day after day. Just as well. No screams to deal with, but still Tyler takes it hard. He sits on the bridge in his chair most days . . . staring at the red star growing ever brighter directly ahead.

Pelops thought the captain would dismantle the bone god . . . but Tyler doesn't seem to mind it. Or perhaps he's frightened of it. Too frightened of its power to risk desecrating it. He must know that *it*, not him, now rules the *Goya*.

Harmon would have lasted longer if Pelops did not share him with Tyler. However, Tyler ate so very little . . . only enough to keep himself alive for another month. Finally, when the last of Harmon has been consumed and his bones have been added to the god's intricate frame, Tyler comes to Pelops. A broken man, emaciated, begging to be put out of his misery.

"It's all my fault," Tyler tells him, weeping. Pelops listens. "It was my responsibility to make sure we had extra emergency kits. I didn't do it."

Pelops leads him into the infirmary.

Tyler babbles, weeping. "Trying to maximize profits . . . cut corners . . . it should have been a simple trip. I did it to save money, Pelops. I killed us all for *money* . . . "

"Not *all* of us, Captain," says Pelops.

Tyler nods, wipes his swollen eyes. He must be thinking of those starving families on Dantus now.

"I am sorry there is no more anesthetic for this Captain."

"Just do it," says Tyler. He unholsters his pistol, lays it on a nearby counter. "Get it over with. Kill me. For Dantus . . . for all those children. Kill me *now* . . . "

"If you wouldn't mind lying on the table first," says Pelops. Tyler complies.

Pelops straps him down securely and prepares the laser scalpel.

"What are you doing?" asks Tyler. "One shot between the eyes will do it. Make it quick, Pelops."

Pelops hesitates.

It seems the captain has misunderstood his role here.

"We've still got over a month of travel time, sir . . . " Pelops explains. "If I kill you now, I'm afraid you'll *spoil* before we reach Dantus."

Tyler's shock registers as a moment of silence. "No," he says, shaking his head. "No, you can eat for two or three weeks, and the last few days you can go without. You'll be fine . . . as soon as you touch down you'll have food on Dantus. You don't need me to last that long, Pelops!"

"I'm sorry, Captain," says Pelops. "But I don't like to go hungry."

He ignores the captain's screaming and writhing as he puts the gag on him. Same old reaction. Pulling against the restraints, wearing the throat raw with grunts and smothered screams.

"It's for the mission," Pelops reminds him.

He starts with the legs, as usual.

Tyler, once a strong and vital man, lasts nearly three weeks on the table.

In the end, with the last few scraps of Tyler gone, Pelops still has six days left to starve.

The red star swells brighter than ever among the starfields in the viewport.

Pelops sits in the captain's chair and stares into the shimmering void.

Everything from plants to mammals is fueled by the light of stars. Sunlight fuels photosynthesis, which feeds the plants that in turn feed the animals we eat on earth. Photons and atoms being constantly recycled and reinvented, a molecular dance of destruction and creation that never ends. Everything consumes and is consumed.

We are all made of starlight.

Brilliant starlight, pulsing bright as blood inside us.

It's all energy . . . and energy is neither created nor destroyed.

His stomach growls.

In the glow of a red sun, the *Goya* touches down atop a broad plateau littered with wrecked vehicles and rusting machines. Pelops stumbles from the open hatch into the ruddy glow. He walks with a single crutch made of bones. His right leg is missing below the knee, a fresh tourniquet wrapped tight about the stump.

He held out for two difficult days before the hunger won its final victory.

Still, he has made it to this place. A nice prosthetic limb waits in his future.

He blinks in the harsh glow of infrared daylight and stares across the plateau at the colonial city.

He stumbles through the wreckage toward the dilapidated walls. The wind hurls black sand against him, raking like claws across his flight suit and his exposed cheeks, coating his beard with dirt.

Where is everyone?

There should be a welcoming party to greet him. They've waited seven years.

The famine won here, he realizes. *I'm too late.*

He walks through dried fields where crops have died in geometrical rows. Now only the fossilized stubs of cornstalks rear from the smothering sand.

He sees the distant towers more clearly now. Skeletal and stark they stand against the purple sky. He walks with his crutch among the hulks of dead machines, until the sun sinks below the flat horizon. The ruined city looms before him. No signs of life.

Hunger did this. Is there anyone left at all?

He calls out. His voice echoes between crumbling walls, along vacant streets.

The bleak stars emerge to glimmer in the night sky.

We are all made of starlight.

Finally a group of thin shadows emerges from a ramshackle hut near a fallen tower.

Survivors. They converge upon him like wary dogs trailing rags.

He sees their young faces, smudged with dirt and lean as wolves.

They smile, showing rotted teeth. He waves.

They carry sharp knives that gleam in the twilight.

"Wait!" he says. "My name is Pelops—from the earth ship *Goya*. I've brought what you need."

"Yes, I see that," says a raggedy woman, brandishing her knife. "We can always use fresh meat."

It is impossible for him to run on a single leg.

Their knives sink deeply, a dozen whispers of metal.

* 2011 Parsec Award finalist

• BEACHWORLD •
Stephen King

FedShip ASN/29 fell out of the sky and crashed. After a while two men slipped from its cloven skull like brains. They walked a little way and then stood, helmets beneath their arms, and looked at where they had finished up.

It was a beach in no need of an ocean—it was its own ocean, a sculpted sea of sand, a black-and-white-snapshot sea frozen forever in troughs and crests and more troughs and crests.

Dunes.

Shallow ones, steep ones, smooth ones, corrugated ones. Knife-crested dunes, plane-crested dunes, irregularly crested dunes that resembled dunes piled on dunes—dune-dominoes.

Dunes. But no ocean.

The valleys which were the troughs between these dunes snaked in mazy black rat-runs. If one looked at those twisting lines long enough, they might seem to spell words—black words hovering over the white dunes.

"Fuck," Shapiro said.

"Bend over," Rand said.

Shapiro started to spit, then thought better of it. Looking at all that sand made him think better of it. This was not the time to go wasting moisture, perhaps. Half-buried in the sand, ASN/29 didn't look like a dying bird anymore; it looked like a gourd that had broken open and disclosed rot inside. There had been a fire. The starboard fuel-pods had all exploded.

"Too bad about Grimes," Shapiro said.

"Yeah." Rand's eyes were still roaming the sand sea, out to the limiting line of the horizon and then coming back again.

It *was* too bad about Grimes. Grimes was dead. Grimes was now nothing but large chunks and small chunks in the aft storage compartment. Shapiro had looked in and thought: *It looks like God decided to eat Grimes, found out he didn't taste good, and sicked him up again.* That had been too much for Shapiro's own stomach. That, and the sight of Grimes's teeth scattered across the floor of the storage compartment.

Shapiro now waited for Rand to say something intelligent, but Rand was quiet. Rand's eyes tracked over the dunes, traced the clockspring windings of the deep troughs between.

"Hey!" Shapiro said at last. "What do we do? Grimes is dead; you're in command. What do we do?"

"Do?" Rand's eyes moved back and forth, back and forth, over the stillness of the dunes. A dry, steady wind ruffled the rubberized collar of the Environmental Protection suit. "If you don't have a volleyball, I don't know."

"What are you talking about?"

"Isn't that what you're supposed to do on the beach?" Rand asked. "Play volleyball?"

Shapiro had been scared in space many times, and close to panic when the fire broke out; now, looking at Rand, he heard a rumor of fear too large to comprehend.

"It's big," Rand said dreamily, and for one moment Shapiro thought that Rand was speaking of Shapiro's own fear. "One hell of a big beach. Something like this could go on forever. You could walk a hundred miles with your surfboard under your arm and still be where you started, almost, with nothing behind you but six or seven footprints. And if you stood in the same place for five minutes, the last six or seven would be gone, too."

"Did you get a topographical compscan before we came down?" Rand was in shock, he decided. Rand was in shock but Rand was not crazy. He could give Rand a pill if he had to. And if Rand continued to spin his wheels, he could give him a shot. "Did you get a look at—"

Rand looked at him briefly. "What?"

The green places. That had been what he was going to say. It sounded like a quote from Psalms, and he couldn't say it. The wind made a silver chime in his mouth.

"What?" Rand asked again.

"Compscan! *Compscan!*" Shapiro screamed. "You ever hear of a compscan, dronehead? What's this place like? Where's the ocean at the end of the fucking *beach?* Where's the lakes? Where's the nearest greenbelt? Which direction? Where does the beach end?"

"End? Oh. I grok you. It never ends. No greenbelts, no ice caps. No oceans. This is a beach in search of an ocean, mate. Dunes and dunes and dunes, and they never end."

"But what'll we do for water?"

"Nothing we can do."

"The ship . . . it's beyond repair!"

"No shit, Sherlock."

Shapiro fell quiet. It was now either be quiet or become hysterical. He had a feeling—almost a certainty—that if he became hysterical, Rand would just go on looking at the dunes until Shapiro worked it out, or until he didn't.

What did you call a beach that never ended? Why, you called it a desert! Biggest motherfucking desert in the universe, wasn't that right?

In his head he heard Rand respond: *No shit, Sherlock.*

Shapiro stood for some time beside Rand, waiting for the man to wake up, to *do* something. After a while his patience ran out. He began to slide and stumble back down the flank of the dune they had climbed to look around. He could feel the sand sucking against his boots. *Want to suck you down, Bill,* his mind imagined the sand saying. In his mind it was the dry, arid voice of a woman who was old but still terribly strong. *Want to suck you right down here and give you a great . . . big . . . hug.*

That made him think about how they used to take turns letting the others bury them up to their necks at the beach when he was a kid. Then it had been fun—now it scared him. So he turned that voice off—this was no time for memory lane, Christ, no—and walked through the sand with short, sharp kicking strides, trying unconsciously to mar the symmetrical perfection of its slope and surface.

"Where are you going?" Rand's voice for the first time held a note of awareness and concern.

"The beacon," Shapiro said. "I'm going to turn it on. We were on a mapped lane of travel. It'll be picked up, vectored. It's a question of time. I know the odds are shitty, but maybe somebody will come before—"

"The beacon's smashed to hell," Rand said. "It happened when we came down."

"Maybe it can be fixed," Shapiro called back over his shoulder. As he ducked through the hatchway he felt better in spite of the smells—fried wiring and a bitter whiff of Freon gas. He told himself he felt better because he had thought of the beacon. No matter how paltry, the beacon offered some hope. But it wasn't the thought of the beacon that had lifted his spirits; if Rand said it was broken, it was probably most righteously broken. But he could no longer see the dunes—could no longer see that big, never-ending beach.

That was what made him feel better.

When he got to the top of the first dune again, struggling and panting, his temples pounding with the dry heat, Rand was still there, still staring and staring and staring. An hour had gone by. The sun stood directly above them. Rand's face was wet with perspiration. Jewels of it nestled in his eyebrows. Droplets ran down his cheeks like tears. More droplets ran down the cords of his neck and into the neck of his EP suit like drops of colorless oil running into the guts of a pretty good android.

Dronehead I called him, Shapiro thought with a little shudder. *Christ, that's what he looks like—not an android but a dronehead who just took a neck-shot with a very big needle.*

And Rand had been wrong after all.

"Rand?"

No answer.

"The beacon wasn't broken." There was a flicker in Rand's eyes. Then they went blank again, staring out at the mountains of sand. Frozen, Shapiro had first thought them, but he supposed they moved. The wind was constant. They would move. Over a period of decades and centuries, they would . . . well, would *walk*. Wasn't that what they called dunes on a beach? Walking dunes? He seemed to remember that from his childhood. Or school. Or someplace, and what in the hell did it matter?

Now he saw a delicate rill of sand slip down the flank of one of them. As if it heard

(heard what I was thinking)

Fresh sweat on the back of his neck. All right, he was getting a touch of the whim-whams. Who wouldn't? This was a tight place they were in, very tight. And Rand seemed not to know it . . . or not to care.

"It had some sand in it, and the warbler was cracked, but there must have been sixty of those in Grimes's odds-and-ends box."

Is he even hearing me?

"I don't know how the sand got in it—it was right where it was supposed to be, in the storage compartment behind the bunk, three closed hatches between it and the outside, but—"

"Oh, sand spreads. Gets into everything. Remember going to the beach when you were a kid, Bill? You'd come home and your mother would yell at you because there was sand everywhere? Sand in the couch, sand on the kitchen table, sand down the foot of your bed? Beach sand is very . . . " He gestured vaguely, and then that dreamy, unsettling smile resurfaced. " . . . ubiquitous."

"—but it didn't hurt it any," Shapiro continued. "The emergency power output system is ticking over and I plugged the beacon into it. I put on the earphones for a minute and asked for an equivalency reading at fifty parsecs. Sounds like a power saw. It's better than we could have hoped."

"No one's going to come. Not even the Beach Boys. The Beach Boys have all been dead for eight thousand years. Welcome to Surf City, Bill. Surf City *sans* surf."

Shapiro stared out at the dunes. He wondered how long the sand had been here. A trillion years? A quintillion? Had there been life here once? Maybe even something with intelligence? Rivers? Green places? Oceans to make it a real beach instead of a desert?

Shapiro stood next to Rand and thought about it. The steady wind ruffled his hair. And quite suddenly he was sure all those things had been, and he could picture how they must have ended.

The slow retreat of the cities as their waterways and outlying areas were first speckled, then dusted, finally drifted and choked by the creeping sand.

He could see the shiny brown alluvial fans of mud, sleek as sealskins at first but growing duller and duller in color as they spread further and further out from the mouths of the rivers—out and out until they met each other. He could see sleek sealskin mud becoming reed-infested swamp, then gray, gritty till, finally shifting white sand.

He could see mountains shortening like sharpened pencils, their snow melting as the rising sand brought warm thermal updrafts against them; he could see the last few crags pointing at the sky like the fingertips of men buried alive; he could see them covered and immediately forgotten by the profoundly idiotic dunes.

What had Rand called them?

Ubiquitous.

If you just had a vision, Billy-boy, it was a pretty goddam dreadful one.

Oh, but no, it wasn't. It wasn't dreadful; it was peaceful. It was as quiet as a nap on a Sunday afternoon. What was more peaceful than the beach?

He shook these thoughts away. It helped to look back toward the ship.

"There isn't going to be any cavalry," Rand said. "The sand will cover us and after a while we'll be the sand and the sand will be us. Surf City with no surf—can you catch that wave, Bill?"

And Shapiro was scared because he *could* catch it. You couldn't see all those dunes without getting it.

"Fucking dronehead asshole," he said. He went back to the ship.

And hid from the beach.

Sunset finally came. The time when, at the beach—any *real* beach—you were supposed to put away the volleyball and put on your sweats and get out the weenies and the beer. Not time to start necking yet, but almost. Time to look *forward* to the necking.

Weenies and beer had not been a part of ASN/29's stores.

Shapiro spent the afternoon carefully bottling all of the ship's water. He used a porta-vac to suck up that which had run out of the ruptured veins in the ship's supply system and puddled on the floor. He got the small bit left in the bottom of the shattered hydraulic system's water tank. He did not overlook even the small cylinder in the guts of the air-purification system which circulated air in the storage areas.

Finally, he went into Grimes's cabin.

Grimes had kept goldfish in a circular tank constructed especially for weightless conditions. The tank was built of impact-resistant clear-polymer plastic, and had survived the crash easily. The goldfish—like their owner—had not been impact-resistant. They floated in a dull orange clump at the top of the ball, which had come to rest under Grimes's bunk, along with three pairs of very dirty underwear and half a dozen porno holograph-cubes.

He held the globe aquarium for a moment, looking fixedly into it. "Alas, poor Yorick, I knew him well," he said suddenly, and laughed a screaming, distracted laugh. Then he got the net Grimes kept in his lockbin and dipped it into the tank. He removed the fish and then wondered what to do with them. After a moment he took them to Grimes's bed and raised his pillow.

There was sand underneath.

He put the fish there regardless, then carefully poured the water into the jerrican he was using as a catcher. It would all have to be purified, but even if the purifiers hadn't been working, he thought that in another couple of days he wouldn't balk at drinking aquarium water just because it might have a few loose scales and a little goldfish shit in it.

He purified the water, divided it, and took Rand's share back up the side of the dune. Rand was right where he had been, as if he had never moved.

"Rand. I brought you your share of the water." He unzipped the pouch on the front of Rand's EP suit and slipped the flat plastic flask inside. He was about to press the zip-strip closed with his thumbnail when Rand brushed his hand away. He took the flask out. Stenciled on the front was ASN/CLASS SHIP'S SUPPLIES STORAGE FLASK CL. *23196755 STERILE WHEN SEAL IS UNBROKEN. The seal was broken now, of course; Shapiro had had to fill the bottle up.

"I purified—"

Rand opened his fingers. The flask fell into the sand with a soft plop. "Don't want it."

"Don't . . . Rand, what's wrong with you? Jesus Christ, will you *stop it?*"

Rand did not reply.

Shapiro bent over and picked up storage flask 23196755. He brushed off the grains of sand clinging to the sides as if they were huge, swollen germs.

"What's *wrong* with you?" Shapiro repeated. "Is it shock? Do you think that's what it is? Because I can give you a pill . . . or a shot. But it's getting to me, I don't mind telling you. You just standing out here looking at the next forty miles of nothing! It's *sand!* Just *sand!*"

"It's a beach," Rand said dreamily. "Want to make a sand castle?"

"Okay, good," Shapiro said. "I'm going to go get a needle and an amp of Yellowjack. If you want to act like a goddam dronehead, I'll treat you like one."

"If you try to inject me with something, you better be quiet when you sneak up behind me," Rand said mildly. "Otherwise, I'll break your arm."

He could do it, too. Shapiro, the astrogator, weighed a hundred and forty pounds and stood five-five. Physical combat was not his specialty. He grunted an oath and turned away, back to the ship, holding Rand's flask.

"I think it's alive," Rand said. "I'm actually pretty sure of it."

Shapiro looked back at him and then out at the dunes. The sunset had given them a gold filigree at their smooth, sweeping caps, a filigree that shaded delicately down to the blackest ebony in the troughs; on the next dune, ebony shaded back to gold. Gold to black. Black to gold. Gold to black and black to gold and gold to—

Shapiro blinked his eyes rapidly, and rubbed a hand over them.

"I have several times felt this particular dune move under my feet," Rand told Shapiro. "It moves very gracefully. It is like feeling the tide. I can smell its smell on the air, and the smell is like salt."

"You're crazy," Shapiro said. He was so terrified that he felt as if his brains had turned to glass.

Rand did not reply. Rand's eyes searched the dunes, which went from gold to black to gold to black in the sunset.

Shapiro went back to the ship.

Rand stayed on the dune all night, and all the next day.

Shapiro looked out and saw him. Rand had taken off his EP suit, and the sand had almost covered it. Only one sleeve stuck out, forlorn and supplicating. The sand above and below it reminded Shapiro of a pair of lips sucking with a toothless greed at a tender morsel. Shapiro felt a crazy desire to pelt up the side of the dune and rescue Rand's EP suit.

He did not.

He sat in his cabin and waited for the rescue ship. The smell of Freon had dissipated. It was replaced by the even less desirable smell of Grimes decaying.

The rescue ship did not come that day or that night or on the third day.

Sand somehow appeared in Shapiro's cabin, although the hatchway was closed and the seal still appeared perfectly tight. He sucked the little puddles of sand up with the porta-vac as he had sucked up puddles of spilled water on that first day.

He was very thirsty all the time. His flask was nearly empty already.

He thought he had begun to smell salt on the air; in his sleep he heard the sound of gulls.

And he could hear the sand.

The steady wind was moving the first dune closer to the ship. His cabin was still okay—thanks to the porta-vac—but the sand was already taking over the rest. Mini-dunes had reached through the blown locks and laid hold of ASN/29. It sifted in tendrils and membranes through the vents. There was a drift in one of the blown tanks.

Shapiro's face grew gaunt and pebbly with beard shadow.

Near sunset of the third day, he climbed up the dune to check on Rand. He thought about taking a hypodermic, then rejected it. It was a lot more than shock; he knew that now. Rand was insane. It would be best if he died quickly. And it looked as if that was exactly what was going to happen.

Shapiro was gaunt; Rand was emaciated. His body was a scrawny stick. His legs, formerly rich and thick with iron-pumper's muscle, were now slack and droopy. The skin hung on them like loose socks that keep falling down. He was wearing only his undershorts, and they were red nylon, and they looked absurdly like a ball-hugger bathing suit. A light beard had begun to grow on his face, fuzzing his hollow cheeks and chin. His beard was the color of beach sand. His hair, formerly a listless brown shade, had bleached out to a near blond. It hung over his forehead. Only his eyes, peering through the fringe of his hair with bright blue intensity, still lived fully. They studied the beach

(the dunes goddammit the DUNES)

relentlessly.

Now Shapiro saw a bad thing. It was a very bad thing indeed. He saw that Rand's face was turning into a sand dune. His beard and his hair were choking his skin.

"You," Shapiro said, "are going to die. If you don't come down to the ship and drink, you are going to die."

Rand said nothing.

"Is that what you *want?*"

Nothing. There was the vacuous snuffle of the wind, but no more. Shapiro observed that the creases of Rand's neck were filling up with sand.

"The only thing I *want*," Rand said in a faint, faraway voice like the wind, "is my Beach Boys tapes. They're in my cabin."

"Fuck you!" Shapiro said furiously. "But do you know what I hope? I hope a ship comes before you die. I want to see you holler and scream when they pull you away from your precious goddam beach. I want to see what happens then!"

"Beach'll get you, too," Rand said. His voice was empty and rattling, like wind inside a split gourd—a gourd which has been left in a field at the end of October's last harvest. "Take a listen, Bill. Listen to the *wave.*"

Rand cocked his head. His mouth, half-open, revealed his tongue. It was as shriveled as a dry sponge.

Shapiro heard something.

He heard the dunes. They sang songs of Sunday afternoon at the beach—naps on the beach with no dreams. Long naps. Mindless peace. The sound of crying gulls. Shifting, thoughtless particles. Walking dunes. He heard . . . and was drawn. Drawn toward the dunes.

"You hear it," Rand said.

Shapiro reached into his nose and dug with two fingers until it bled. Then he could close his eyes; his thoughts came slowly and clumsily together. His heart was racing.

I was almost like Rand. Jesus! . . . it almost had me!

He opened his eyes again and saw that Rand had become a conch shell on a long deserted beach, straining forward toward all the mysteries of an undead sea, staring out at the dunes and the dunes and the dunes.

No more, Shapiro moaned inside himself.

Oh, but listen to this wave, the dunes whispered back.

Against his better judgment, Shapiro listened.

Then his better judgment ceased to exist.

Shapiro thought: *I could hear better if I sat down.*

He sat down at Rand's feet and put his heels on his thighs like a Yaqui Indian and listened.

He heard the Beach Boys and the Beach Boys were singing about fun, fun, fun. He heard them singing that the girls on the beach were all within reach. He heard—

—a hollow sighing of the wind, not in his ear but in the canyon between right brain and left brain—he heard that sighing somewhere in the blackness which is spanned only by the suspension bridge of the corpus callosum, which connects conscious thought to the infinite. He felt no hunger, no thirst, no heat, no fear. He heard only the voice in the emptiness.

And a ship came.

It came swooping out of the sky, afterburners scratching a long orange track from right to left. Thunder belted the delta-wave topography, and several dunes collapsed like bullet-path brain damage. The thunder ripped Billy Shapiro's head open and for a moment he was torn both ways, *ripped,* torn down the middle—

Then he was up on his feet.

"Ship!" he screamed. *"Holy fuck! Ship! Ship! SHIP!"*

It was a belt trader, dirty and buggered by five hundred—or five thousand—years of clan service. It surfed through the air, banged crudely upright, skidded. The captain blew jets and fused sand into black glass. Shapiro cheered the wound.

Rand looked around like a man awaking from a deep dream.

"Tell it to go away, Billy."

"You don't understand." Shapiro was shambling around, shaking his fists in the air. "You'll be all right—"

He broke toward the dirty trader in big, leaping strides, like a kangaroo running from a ground fire. The sand clutched at him. Shapiro kicked it away. Fuck you, sand. I got a honey back in Hansonville. Sand never had no honey. Beach never had no hard-on.

The trader's hull split. A gangplank popped out like a tongue. A man strode down it behind three sampler androids and a guy built into treads that was surely the captain. He wore a beret with a clan symbol on it, anyway.

One of the androids waved a sampler wand at him. Shapiro batted it away. He fell on his knees in front of the captain and embraced the treads which had replaced the captain's dead legs.

"The dunes ... Rand ... no water ... alive ... hypnotized him ... dronehead world ... I ... thank God ... "

A steel tentacle whipped around Shapiro and yanked him away on his gut. Dry sand whispered underneath him like laughter. "It's okay," the captain said. *"Bey-at shel! Me! Me! Gat!"*

The android dropped Shapiro and backed away, clittering distractedly to itself.

"All this way for a fucking Fed!" the captain exclaimed bitterly.

Shapiro wept. It hurt, not just in his head, but in his liver.

"Dud! *Gee-yat! Gat!* Water-for-him-Cry!"

The man who had been in the lead tossed him a nippled low-grav bottle. Shapiro upended it and sucked greedily, spilling crystal-cold water into his mouth, down his chin, in dribbles that darkened his tunic, which had bleached to the color of bone. He choked, vomited, then drank again.

Dud and the captain watched him closely. The androids clittered.

At last Shapiro wiped his mouth and sat up. He felt both sick and well.

"You Shapiro?" the captain asked.

Shapiro nodded.

"Clan affiliation?"

"None."

"ASN number?"

"29."

"Crew?"

"Three. One dead. The other—Rand—up there." He pointed but did not look.

The captain's face did not change. Dud's face did.

"The beach got him," Shapiro said. He saw their questioning, veiled looks. "Shock . . . maybe. He seems hypnotized. He keeps talking about the . . . the Beach Boys . . . never mind, you wouldn't know. He wouldn't drink or eat. He's bad off."

"Dud. Take one of the andies and get him down from there." He shook his head. "Fed ship, Christ. No salvage."

Dud nodded. A few moments later he was scrambling up the side of the dune with one of the andies. The andy looked like a twenty-year-old surfer who might make dope money on the side servicing bored widows, but his stride gave him away even more than the segmented tentacles which grew from his armpits. The stride, common to all androids, was the slow, reflective, almost painful stride of an aging English butler with hemorrhoids.

There was a buzz from the captain's dashboard.

"I'm here."

"This is Gomez, Cap. We got a situation here. Compscan and surface telemetry show us a very unstable surface. There's no bedrock that we can targ. We're resting on our own burn, and right now that may be the hardest thing on the whole planet. Trouble is, the burn itself is starting to settle."

"Recommendation?"

"We ought to get out."

"When?"

"Five minutes ago."

"You're a laugh riot, Gomez."

The captain punched a button and the communicator went out.

Shapiro's eyes were rolling. "Look, never mind Rand. He's had it."

"I'm taking you both back," the captain said. "I got no salvage, but the Federation ought to pay something for the two of you . . . not that either of you are worth much, as far as I can see. He's crazy and you're chickenshit."

"No . . . you don't understand. You—"

The captain's cunning yellow eyes gleamed.

"You got any contra?" he asked.

"Captain . . . look . . . please—"

"Because if you do, there's no sense just leaving it here. Tell me what it is and where it is. I'll split seventy-thirty. Standard salvor's fee. Couldn't do any better than that, hey? You—"

The burn suddenly tilted beneath them. Quite noticeably tilted. A horn somewhere inside the trader began to blat with muffled regularity. The communicator on the captain's dashboard went off again.

"*There!*" Shapiro screamed. "*There, do you see what you're up against? You want to talk about contraband now? WE HAVE GOT TO GET THE FUCK OUT OF HERE!*"

"Shut up, handsome, or I'll have one of these guys sedate you," the captain said. His voice was serene but his eyes had changed. He thumbed the communicator.

"Cap, I got ten degrees of tilt and we're getting more. The elevator's going down, but it's going on an angle. We've still got time, but not much. The ship's going to fall over."

"The struts will hold her."

"No, sir. Begging the captain's pardon, they won't."

"Start firing sequences, Gomez."

"Thank you, sir." The relief in Gomez's voice was unmistakable.

Dud and the android were coming back down the flank of the dune. Rand wasn't with them. The andy fell further and further behind. And now a strange thing happened. The andy fell over on its face. The captain frowned. It did not fall as an andy is supposed to fall—which is to say, like a human being, more or less. It was as if someone had pushed over a mannequin in a department store. It fell over like that. Thump, and a little tan cloud of sand puffed up from around it.

Dud went back and knelt by it. The andy's legs were still moving as if it dreamed, in the 1.5 million Freon-cooled micro-circuits that made up its mind, that it still walked. But leg movements were slow and cracking. They stopped. Smoke began to come out of its pores and its tentacles shivered in the sand. It was gruesomely like watching a human die. A deep grinding came from inside it: *Graaaagggg!*

"Full of sand," Shapiro whispered. "It's got Beach Boys religion."

The captain glanced at him impatiently. "Don't be ridiculous, man. That thing could walk through a sandstorm and not get a grain inside it."

"Not on *this* world."

The burn settled again. The trader was now clearly canted. There was a low groan as the struts took more weight.

"Leave it!" the captain bawled at Dud. "Leave it, leave it! *Gee-yat! Come-me-for-Cry!*"

Dud came, leaving the andy to walk face-down in the sand.

"What a balls-up," the captain muttered.

He and Dud engaged in a conversation spoken entirely in a rapid pidgin dialect which Shapiro was able to follow to some degree. Dud told the captain that Rand had refused to come. The andy had tried to grab Rand, but with no force. Even then it was moving jerkily, and strange grating sounds were coming from inside it. Also, it had begun to recite a combination of galactic strip-mining coordinates and a catalogue of the captain's folk-music tapes. Dud himself had then closed with Rand. They had struggled briefly. The captain told Dud that if Dud had allowed a man who had been standing three days in the hot sun to get the better of him, that maybe he ought to get another First.

Dud's face darkened with embarrassment, but his grave, concerned look never faltered. He slowly turned his head, revealing four deep furrows in his cheek. They were welling slowly.

"*Him-gat big indics,*" Dud said. "*Strong-for-Cry. Him-gat for umby.*"

"*Umby-him for-Cry?*" The captain was looking at Dud sternly.

Dud nodded. "*Umby. Beyat-shel. Umby-for-Cry.*"

Shapiro had been frowning, conning his tired, frightened mind for that word. Now it came. *Umby.* It meant crazy. *He's strong, for Christ's sake. Strong because he's crazy. He's got big ways, big force. Because he's crazy.*

Big ways . . . or maybe it meant big waves. He wasn't sure. Either way it came to the same.

Umby.

The ground shifted underneath them again, and sand blew across Shapiro's boots.

From behind them came the hollow *ka-thud, ka-thud, ka-thud* of the breather-tubes opening. Shapiro thought it one of the most lovely sounds he had ever heard in his life.

The captain sat deep in thought, a weird centaur whose lower half was treads and plates instead of horse. Then he looked up and thumbed the communicator.

"Gomez, send Excellent Montoya down here with a tranquilizer gun."

"Acknowledged."

The captain looked at Shapiro. "Now, on top of everything else, I've lost an android worth your salary for the next ten years. I'm pissed off. I mean to have your buddy."

"Captain." Shapiro could not help licking his lips. He knew this was a very ill-chosen thing to do. He did not want to appear mad, hysterical, or craven, and the captain had apparently decided he was all three. Licking his lips like that would only add to the impression . . . but he simply couldn't help himself. "Captain, I cannot impress on you too strongly the need to get off this world as soon as poss—"

"Can it, dronehead," the captain said, not unkindly.

A thin scream rose from the top of the nearest dune.

"Don't touch me! Don't come near me! Leave me alone! All of you!"

"*Big indics gat umby,*" Dud said gravely.

"*Ma-him, yeah-mon,*" the captain returned, and then turned to Shapiro. "He really *is* bad off, isn't he?"

Shapiro shuddered. "You don't know. You just—"

The burn settled again. The struts were groaning louder than ever. The communicator crackled. Gomez's voice was thin, a little unsteady.

"We have to get out of here right now, Cap!"

"All right." A brown man appeared on the gangway. He held a long pistol in one gloved hand. The captain pointed at Rand. "*Ma-him, for-Cry. Can?*"

Excellent Montoya, unperturbed by the tilting earth that was not earth but only sand fused to glass (and there were deep cracks running through it now, Shapiro saw), unbothered by the groaning struts or the eerie sight of an android that now appeared to be digging its own grave with its feet, studied Rand's thin figure for a moment.

"*Can,*" he said.

"*Gat! Gat-for-Cry!*" The captain spat to one side. "Shoot his pecker off, I don't care," he said. "Just as long as he's still breathing when we ship."

Excellent Montoya raised the pistol. The gesture was apparently two-thirds casual and one-third careless, but Shapiro, even in his state of near-panic, noted the way Montoya's head tilted to one side as he lined the barrel up. Like many in the clans, the gun would be nearly a part of him, like pointing his own finger.

There was a hollow *fooh!* as he squeezed the trigger and the tranquilizer dart blew out of the barrel.

A hand reached out of the dune and clawed it down.

It was a large brown hand, wavery, made of sand. It simply reached up, in defiance of the wind, and smothered the momentary glitter of the dart. Then the sand fell back with a heavy *thrrrrap.* No hand. Impossible to believe there *had* been. But they had all seen it.

"*Giddy-hump,*" the captain said in an almost conversational voice.

Excellent Montoya fell on his knees. "*Aidy-May-for-Cry, bit-gat come! Saw-hoh got belly-gat-for-Cry!—*"

Numbly, Shapiro realized Montoya was saying a rosary in pidgin. Up on the dune, Rand was jumping up and down, shaking his fists at the sky, screeching thinly in triumph.

A hand. It was a HAND. He's right; it's alive, alive, alive—

"*Indic!*" the captain said sharply to Montoya. "*Cannit! Gat!*"

Montoya shut up. His eyes touched on the capering figure of Rand and then he looked away. His face was full of superstitious horror nearly medieval in quality.

"Okay," the captain said. "I've had enough. I quit. We're going."

He shoved two buttons on his dashboard. The motor that should have swiveled him neatly around so he faced up the gangplank again did not hum; it squealed and grated. The captain cursed. The burn shifted again.

"Captain!" Gomez. In a panic.

The captain slammed in another button and the treads began to move backward up the gangplank.

"Guide me," the captain said to Shapiro. "I got no fucking rearview mirror. It was a hand, wasn't it?"

"Yes."

"I want to get out of here," the captain said. "It's been fourteen years since I had a cock, but right now I feel like I'm pissing myself."

Thrrap! A dune suddenly collapsed over the gangway. Only it wasn't a dune; it was an arm.

"Fuck, oh fuck," the captain said.

On his dune, Rand capered and screeched.

Now the threads of the captain's lower half began to grind. The mini-tank of which the captain's head and shoulders were the turret now began to judder backward.

"What—"

The treads locked. Sand splurted out from between them.

"Pick me up!" the captain bawled to the two remaining androids. *"Now! RIGHT NOW!"*

Their tentacles curled around the tread sprockets as they picked him up—he looked ridiculously like a faculty member about to be tossed in a blanket by a bunch of roughhousing fraternity boys. He was thumbing the communicator.

"Gomez! Final firing sequence! Now! Now!"

The dune at the foot of the gangplank shifted. Became a hand. A large brown hand that began to scrabble up the incline.

Shrieking, Shapiro bolted from that hand.

Cursing, the captain was carried away from it.

The gangplank was pulled up. The hand fell off and became sand again. The hatchway irised closed. The engines howled. No time for a couch; no time for anything like that. Shapiro dropped into a crash-fold position on the bulkhead and was promptly smashed flat by the acceleration. Before unconsciousness washed over him, it seemed he could feel sand grasping at the trader with muscular brown arms, straining to hold them down—

Then they were up and away.

Rand watched them go. He was sitting down. When the track of the trader's jets was at last gone from the sky, he turned his eyes out to the placid endlessness of the dunes.

"We got a '34 wagon and we call it a woody," he croaked to the empty, moving sand. "It ain't very cherry; it's an oldy but a goody."

Slowly, reflectively, he began to cram handful after handful of sand into his mouth. He swallowed . . . swallowed . . . swallowed. Soon his belly was a swollen barrel and sand began to drift over his legs.

• STANDARD LONELINESS PACKAGE •
Charles Yu

Root canal is one fifty, give or take, depending on who's doing it to you. A migraine is two hundred.

Not that I get the money. The company gets it. What I get is twelve dollars an hour, plus reimbursement for painkillers. Not that they work.

I feel pain for money. Other people's pain. Physical, emotional, you name it.

Pain is an illusion, I know, and so is time, I know, I know. I know. The shift manager never stops reminding us. Doesn't help, actually. Doesn't help when you are on your third broken leg of the day.

I get to work late and already there are nine tickets in my inbox. I close my eyes, take a deep breath, open the first ticket of the day:

I am at a funeral.

I am feeling grief.

Someone else's grief.

I am feeling a mixture of things.

Grief, mostly, but I also detect that there is some guilt in there. There usually is.

I hear crying.

I am seeing crying faces. Pretty faces. Crying, pretty, white faces.

Nice clothes.

Our services aren't cheap. As the shift manager is always reminding us.

Need I remind you? That is his favorite phrase these days. He is always walking up and down the aisle tilting his head into our cubicles and saying it. *Need I remind you*, he says, *of where we are on the spectrum?* In terms of low-end/high-end? We are solidly towards the highish-end. So the faces are usually pretty, the clothes are usually nice. The people are usually nice, too. Although, I imagine that it's easy to be nice when you are rich and pretty. Even when you're at a funeral.

There's a place in Hyderabad that is doing what we're doing, a little more towards the budget end of things. Precision Living Solutions, it's called. And of course there are hundreds of emotional engineering firms in Bangalore. Springing up everywhere you look. I read in the paper that a new call center opens, on average, like every three days.

Okay. Body is going into the ground now. The crying is getting more serious.

Here it comes.

I am feeling that feeling. The one that these people get a lot, near the end of a funeral service. These sad and pretty people. It's a big feeling. Different operators have different ways to describe it. For me, it feels something like a huge boot. Huge, like it fills up the whole sky, the whole galaxy, all of space. Some kind of infinite foot. And it's stepping on me. The infinite foot is stepping on my chest.

The funeral ends, and the foot is still on me, and it is hard to breathe. People are getting into black town cars. I also appear to have a town car. I get in. The foot, the foot. So heavy. Here we go, yes, this is familiar, the foot, yes, the foot. It doesn't hurt, exactly. It's not what I would call comfortable, but it's not pain, either. More like pressure.

Deepak, who used to be in the next cubicle, once told me that this feeling, which I call the infinite foot—to him it felt more like a knee—is actually the American experience of the Christian God.

"Are you sure it is the Christian God?" I asked him. "I always thought God was Jewish."

"You're an idiot," he said. "It's the same guy. Duh. The Judeo-Christian God."

"Are you sure?" I said.

He just shook his head at me. We'd had this conversation before. I figured he was probably right, but I didn't want to admit it. Deepak was the smartest guy in our cube-cluster, as he would kindly remind me several times a day.

I endure a few more minutes of the foot, and then, right before the hour is up, right when the grief and guilt are almost too much and I wonder if I am going to have to hit the safety button, there it is, it's usually there at the end of a funeral, no matter how awful, no matter how hard I am crying, no matter how much guilt my client has saved up for me to feel. You wouldn't expect it—I didn't—but anyone who has done this job for long enough knows what I'm talking about. It seems unbelievable, but it's there, it's almost always there, even if it's just a glimmer of it, and even though you know it's coming, even when you are waiting for it, in fact, when it comes, it is always still a little bit of a shock.

Relief.

Death of a cousin is five hundred. Death of a sibling is twelve-fifty. Parents are two thousand a piece, but depending on the situation people will pay all kinds of money, for all kinds of reasons, for bad reasons, or for no reason at all.

The company started in corporate services. Ethical qualm transference. Plausible deniability. That kind of stuff. Good cash flow, which the founder—now retired to philanthropy and heli-skiing—plowed right back into R&D,

and turned Transfer Corp. into a specialist: a one-feeling shop. Cornered the early market in guilt.

Then the technology improved. Some genius in Delhi figured out a transfer protocol to standardize and packetize all different kinds of experiences. Qualia in general. *Don't feel like having a bad day?* That's a line from one of our commercials. *Let someone else have it for you.* It shows a rich executive-looking-type sitting and rubbing his temples, making the TV face to communicate the stress of his situation. There are wavy lines on either side of his temples to indicate that the Executive is! really! stressed! Then he places a call to his broker, and in the next scene, the Executive is lying on a beach, drinking golden beer from a bottle and looking at the bluest ocean I have ever seen.

I saw this on American television at the lunch counter across the street that has a satellite feed. I was eating at the counter and next to me was a girl, maybe four or five, scooping rice and peas into her mouth a little at a time. She watched the commercial in silence, and after it was over, turned to her mother and softly asked her what the blue liquid was. I was thinking about how sad it was that she had never seen water that color in real life until I realized that I was thirty-nine years old and hey, you know what, neither had I.

That someone else they are talking about in the commercial is me—me and the other six hundred terminal operators in building D, cubicle block 4. Don't feel like having a bad day? Let me have it for you.

It's okay for me, a good job. I didn't do that well in school, after all. It was tougher for Deep. He did three semesters at technical college. He was always saying he deserved better. Better than this, anyway. I would nod and agree with him, but I never told him what I wanted to tell him, which was hey, Deepak, when you say that you deserve better, even if I agree with you, you are kind of also implying that I don't deserve better, which, maybe I don't, maybe this is about where I belong in the grand scheme of things, in terms of high-end/low-end for me as a person, but I wish you wouldn't say it, because whenever you do, it makes me feel a sharp bit of sadness and then, for the rest of the day, a kind of low-grade crumminess.

Deep and I used to go to lunch, and he always tried to explain to me how it works:

"Okay, so, the clients," he would say, "they call into their account reps and book the time."

He liked to start sentences with, *okay, so.* It was a habit he had picked up from the engineers. He thought it made him sound smarter, thought it made him sound like them, those code geeks, standing by the coffee machine, talking faster than he could think, every word a term of art, every sentence packed with logic, or small insights or a joke. He liked to stand near them, pretending to stir sugar into his coffee, listening in on them as if they were speaking a different language. A language of knowing something, a language of being an expert at something. A language of being something more than an hourly unit.

Okay, so, he said, they book the time, and then at the appointed hour, a switch in their implant chip kicks on and starts transferring their consciousness over. Perceptions, sensory data, all of it. Okay, so, then it goes first to an intermediate server for processing and then gets bundled with other jobs, and then a huge block of the stuff gets zapped over here, where it gets downloaded onto our servers and then dumped into our queue management system, which parcels out the individual jobs to all of us in the cubicle farm.

Okay, so, it's all based on some kind of efficiency algorithm—our historical performance, our current emotional load. Sensors in our head assembly unit measure our stress levels, sweat composition, to see what we can handle. Okay?

(He would say, *okay*, when he was done. Like a professor. He wanted so badly to be an expert at something.)

I always appreciated Deepak trying to help me understand. But it's just a job, I would say. I never really understood why Deep thought so much of those programmers, either. In the end, we're all brains for hire. All I know is they seem to have gotten it down to a science. How much a human being can take in a given twelve-hour shift. Grief, embarrassment, humiliation, all different, of course, so they calibrate our schedules, mix it up, the timing and the order, and the end result is you leave work every day right about at your exact breaking point.

A lot of people smoke to take the edge off. I quit twelve years ago, so sometimes when I get home, I'm still shaking for a little bit. I sit on my couch and drink a beer and let it subside. Then I heat up some bread and lentils and read a newspaper or, if it's too hot to stay inside, walk down to the street and eat my dinner there.

When I get to work the next morning, there's a woman sitting in the cubicle across from mine. She's young, at least a couple of years younger than me, looks right out of school. She has the new employee set-up kit laid out in front of her and is reading the trainee handbook. I think about saying hi, but who am I kidding, I am still me, so instead I just say nothing.

My first ticket of the day is a death bed. Death beds are not so common. They are hard to schedule—we require at least twenty-four hours advance booking, and usually clients don't know far enough in advance when the ailing beloved one is going to go—so we don't see these too often. But this isn't regular death bed. It's pull-the-plug.

They are pulling the plug on grandpa this morning.

I open the ticket.

I am holding grandpa's hand.

I cry.

He squeezes my hand, one last burst of strength. It hurts. Then his hand goes limp and his arm falls away.

I cry, and also, I really cry. Meaning, not just as my client, but I start crying, too. Sometimes it happens. I don't know why, exactly. Maybe because he was somebody's grandpa. And he looked like a nice one, a nice man. Maybe something about the way his arm fell against the guard rail on the hospital bed. Maybe because I could sort of tell, when grandpa was looking at his grandson for the last time, looking into his eyes, looking around in there trying to find him, he didn't find him, he found me instead, and he knew what had happened, and he didn't even look mad. Just hurt.

I am at a funeral.

I am in a dentist's chair.

I am in a queen-sized motel bed, feeling guilty.

I am quitting my job. This is a popular one. Clients like to avoid the awkwardness of quitting their jobs, so they set an appointment and walk into their bosses' offices and tell them where they can stick this effing job, and right before their boss starts to reply, the switch kicks in and I get yelled at.

My teeth throb.

My kidneys seethe.

My lungs burn.

My heart aches.

On a bridge.

My heart aches on a bridge.

My heart aches on a cruise ship.

My heart aches on an airplane, taking off at night.

Some people think it's not so great that we can do this. Personally, I don't really see the problem. Press one to clear your conscience. Press two for fear of death. Consciousness is like anything else. I'm sure when someone figures out how to sell time itself, they'll have infomercials for that, too.

I am at a funeral.

I am losing someone to cancer.

I am coping with something vague.

I am at a funeral.

I am at a funeral.

I am at a funeral.

Fourteen tickets today in twelve hours. Four half-hours and ten full.

On my way out, I can hear someone wailing and gnashing his teeth in his cubicle. He is near the edge. Deepak was always like that, too. I always told him, hey man, you have to let go a little. Just a little. Don't let it get to you so much.

I peek my head to see if I can steal a glance at the new woman, but she is in the middle of a ticket. She appears to be suffering. She catches me looking at her. I look at my feet and keep shuffling past.

It used to be that the job wasn't all pain and suffering. Rich American man outsources the nasty bits of his life. He is required to book by the hour or the day or some other time unit, but in an hour or two or twenty-four hours of unpleasantness, there are always going to be some parts of it that are not so bad. Maybe just boring. Maybe even not so bad. Maybe even more okay than not. Like if a guy books his colonoscopy and he hires us for two hours, but for the first eight minutes, he's just sitting there in the waiting room, reading a magazine, enjoying the air conditioning, admiring someone's legs. Or something. Anyway, it used to be that we would get the whole thing, so part of my job here could be boring or neutral or even sometimes kind of interesting.

But then the technology improved again and the packeting software was refined to filter out those intervals and collect them. Those bits, the extras, the slices of life that were left over were lopped off by the program, and smushed all together, into a kind of reconstituted life slab. Like American baloney lunchmeat. A life-loaf. They take the slabs and process them and sell them as prepackaged lives.

I've had my eye on one for a while, at a secondhand shop that's on my way home from work. Not ideal, but it's something to work for.

So now, what's left over, what we get to feel at work, it's all pretty much just pure undiluted badness. The only thing left that can be a surprise is when, even in the middle of badness, there is something not so awful mixed in there. Like the relief in the middle of a funeral, or sometimes when you get someone who is really religious, not just religious, but a true believer, then mixed in with the sadness and loss at a funeral, you get faith, and you get to try different flavors, depending on the believer. You get the big foot on your chest, or you get the back of your head on fire. (A cold fire, it tickles.) You get to know what it is like to know that your dead lover, your dead mother, father, brother, sister, that they are all standing in front of you, tall as the universe, and they have huge, infinite feet, and their heads are all ablaze with this brilliant, frozen fire. You get the feeling of being inside of a room and at the same time, the room being inside of you, and the room is the world, and so are you.

The next day is more of the same. Eleven tickets, including a two-hour adultery confession. To my husband of twenty-six years.

After lunch, I pass her in the hall. The new woman. Her name badge says Kirthi. She doesn't look at me this time.

Walking home I swing a block out of the way to check in on the secondhand shop.

Someone bought my life.

It was there in the window yesterday, and now it's gone.

It wasn't my life, technically. Not yet. It was the life I wanted, the life I've been saving for. Not a DreamLife®, not top of the line, but a starter model, a good one. Standard Possibility. Normal Volatility. A dark-haired, soulful wife. 0.35 kids, no actuals—certainties are too expensive—but some potential kids, a solid thirty-five percent chance of having one or more. Normal life expectancy, average health, median aggregate amount of happiness. I test-drove it once, and it felt good, it felt right. It fit just fine.

I don't know. I'm trying not to feel sorry for myself. I just thought there might be more to it all than this.

Still, I've got it better than some people. I mean, I'm renting my life out one day at a time, but I haven't sold it yet.

My father sold his life on a cold, clear afternoon in November. He was thirty. It was the day before my fourth birthday.

We went to the brokerage. It felt like a bank, but friendlier. My father had been carrying me on his back, but he put me down when we got inside. There was dark wood everywhere, and also bright flowers and classical music. We were shown to a desk, and a woman in an immaculate pantsuit asked if we would like anything to drink. My father didn't say anything, just looked off at the far wall. I remember my mother asked for a cup of tea for my father.

I don't want to sell my life. I'm not ready to do that yet.

So I sell it bit by bit. Scrape by.

Sell it by the hour.

Pain, grief, terror, worse.

Or just mild discomfort.

Social anxiety.

Boredom.

I ask around about Kirthi. People are talking. The guys are talking. Especially the married guys. They do the most talking.

I pass her in the hall again, and again she doesn't look at me. No surprise there. Women never look at me. I am not handsome or tall. But I am nice.

I think it is actually that which causes the not-looking at me. The niceness, I mean, not the lack of handsomeness or tallness. They can see the niceness and it is the kind of niceness that, in a man, you instinctively ignore. What good is a nice man? No good to women. No good to other men.

She doesn't look at me, but I feel, or maybe I wish or I imagine, that something in the way she does not look at me is not quite the same. She is not-looking at me in a way that feels like she is consciously not-looking at me. And from the way she is not-looking at me, I can tell she knows I am trying to not-look at her. We are both not-looking at each other. For some reason, for the first time in a long while, I have hope.

I don't know why, but I do.

I am at a funeral.

I'm flipped to green.

You can be flipped to green, or flipped to red.

You can be there, or can just feel the feeling.

This is the one improvement they have made that actually benefits us workers. There's a toggle switch on the headset. Flip it to green and you get a rendering of the client's visual field. You see what he sees. Flip it to red and you still feel all of the feelings, but you see what you see.

You can do whatever you want, so long as you don't leave your cubicle. You can just stare at the cube-divider wall, or play computer solitaire, or even chat with neighbors, although that is strongly discouraged.

I was hesitant at first, but more and more these days I am usually flipped to red. Except for funerals. Funerals, I like to be there, just out of some kind of respect thing.

This morning's first ticket is your standard affair. Sixtyish rich guy, heart attack in the home office, millions in the bank, five kids from three marriages, all hate him.

The client is one of those kids, trust fund baby, paid extra for amnesia after the event. No feeling, no pre-feeling, no hangover, no residue, no chance of actually having any part of it, long enough to ensure that he will be halfway in the bag before any of the day's events start nibbling at the corners of his awareness.

I see the fresh, open plot. A little rain falls on the funeral procession as they get out of the cars, but there's a break in the clouds so that it's raining and the sun is shining at the same time.

As usual, everyone is well-dressed. A lot of the rich look mildly betrayed in the face of death, as if they are a little bit surprised that good style and enough money weren't quite enough to protect them from the unpleasantness of it all. I'm standing next to what I am guessing is widow number two, late thirties, probably, with beautiful sand-colored hair. We make eye contact and she is staring at me and I am trying not to stare at her and then we both realize the same thing at the same time. Raj, I say, under my breath. She smiles. Rajiv is on night shift now, but back in the day, we had beers once in a while.

The pastor talks about a full life lived, and the limits of earthly rewards, and everyone nods affirmatively, and then there is music as the body goes into the ground, I've heard it at a lot of funerals. Mozart, I think, but I am not sure.

Death of an aunt is seven hundred. Death of an uncle is six.

Bad day in the markets is a thousand. Kid's recital is a one twenty-five an hour. Church is one-fifty.

The only category that we will not quote a price on is death of a child. Death of a child is separately negotiated. Hardly anyone can afford it. And not all operators can handle it. We have to be specially trained to be eligible for those tickets. People go on sick leave, disability. Most people just physically cannot do it. There hasn't been one booked the whole time I've been here, so most of us aren't even sure what is true and what isn't. The rumor is that if you do one, you are allowed to take the rest of the month off.

Deep was always tempted. It's not worth it, I would tell him. Okay, so, maybe not for you, Deep said. Okay, so, mind your own business, he would say.

The first time I talk to Kirthi is by the water fountain. I tell her we are neighbors, cubicle-wise. She says she knows. I feel a bit stupid.

The second time we talk, we are also by the water fountain, and I try to make a joke, one of those we have to stop meeting like this things. I probably saw it on TV and it just came out. Stupid. She doesn't laugh, but she doesn't frown, either.

The third time we talk, I kiss her. By the microwave in the snack room. I don't know what got into me. I am not an aggressive person. I am not physically strong. I weigh one hundred and fifty-five pounds. She doesn't laugh. She actually makes a face like disgust. But she doesn't push me away, either. Not right away. She accepts the kiss, doesn't kiss back, but after a couple of seconds, breaks it off and leans back and turns her head and says, under her breath, you shouldn't have done that. And she doesn't say it in a nice way. Or like a threat. Just real even, like she is stating a fact.

Still, I am happy. I've got three more tickets in the bucket before lunch, and then probably eight or nine before I go home, but the whole rest of the day, I am having an out of body experience. Even when I am in someone else's body, I am still out of my body. I am double out of my body.

I weep.

I wail.

I gnash my teeth.

Underneath it all, I am smiling. I am giggling.

I am at a funeral. My client's heart aches, and inside of it is my heart, not aching, the opposite of aching—doing that, whatever it is.

• • •

Kirthi and I start dating. That's what I call it. She calls it letting me walk her to the bus stop. She lets me buy her lunch. She tells me I should stop. She still never smiles at me.

I'm a heartbreak specialist, she says.

When I see her in the hallway, I walk up behind her and slip my arm around her waist.

She has not let me in yet. She won't let me in.

Why won't you let me in, I ask her?

You don't want in, she says. You want around. You want near. You don't want in.

There are two hundred forty seven ways to have your heartbroken, she says, *and I have felt them all.*

I am in a hospice.

I have been here before. A regular client.

I am holding a pen.

I have just written something on a notepad in front of me.

My husband is gone.

He died years ago.

Today is the tenth anniversary of his death.

I have Alzheimer's, I think.

A memory of my husband surfaces, like a white-hot August afternoon, resurfacing in the cool water of November.

I tear off the sheet on the notepad.

I read it to myself.

It is a suicide note.

I raise a glass to my mouth, swallow a pill. Catch a glance of my note to the world.

The failsafe kicks on, just in time. The system overrides. I close the ticket.

It's her father.

That's what Sunil tells me, one day over a beer.

Kirthi hasn't been to work for the past two days.

Sunil is in Tech Support. He has seen all of the glitches. He knows what can go wrong in the mechanics of feeling transfers. He has seen some ugliness. He is fond of saying that there is no upper bound on weirdness.

Her father is still mortgaged, Sunil explains. Locked in. A p-zombie, he says. Sold his life.

"This is going to end badly, man," he says. "You have to trust me on this. Kirthi is damaged. And she knows it."

Sunil means well, but what he doesn't know is that I am fine with damaged. I want damage. I've looked down the road I'm on and I see what's coming. A lot of nothing. No great loves lost. And yet, I feel like I lost something. Better to have loved and lost than never to have loved at all? How about this: I lost without the love. I've lost things I've never even had. A whole life. Just like my father, I get to have my cake and eat it, too. Except that it's a great big crap cake.

Still, as the weeks go on, I am starting to think Sunil is right.

"Kirthi won't let me in," I tell him. "She tells me to get away from her, to run."

"She is doing you a favor, man. Take her advice."

I ask her about her father.

She doesn't talk to me for a week.

And then, on Friday night, after we walk for an hour in silence, before going into her apartment, she turns to me and says, how awful it is to look at him in that state.

We draw closer for a moment.

Why won't you just love me, I ask her.

She says it's not possible to make someone feel something.

Even yourself, she says.

Even if you want to feel it.

I tell her about the life I had my eye on.

It's gone, she says.

I'll find another one just like it, I tell her. Standard happiness package. Decent possibility. The chance of a kid. It wouldn't be enough for us, not quite, but we could share it, take turns living the life. One works while the other one lives, maybe I work the weekdays and she gives me a break on weekends.

She looks at me. For a few long seconds, she seems to be thinking about it, living the whole life out in her head.

She doesn't say anything. She touches the side of my head.

It's a start.

When Deep was happy, before it got bad and then worse and then even worse, he was always talking about how he knew a guy who knew a guy who knew a guy. Stuff like that. He talked like that, he really did. He loved telling stories. About a week before he cracked up, he told me a story while we were in the coffee room about a guy at Managed Life Solutions, a physical suffering shop across town, who somehow made arrangements with a prominent banker who wanted to kill his wife. The banker was going to do it, he'd made up his mind, but he didn't want the guilt. Plus, he thought it might help with his alibi if he didn't have any memory.

Bullshit, I said. That would never work.

No, really, he says. He tells me all about it, how they met, how they arranged it all while talking in public, at work in fact, but they talked in code, etc.

Could never happen, I say. There are twenty reasons why that wouldn't work.

Why not, he said.

It's just too much, I said.

Too much what? There is no upper bound on cruelty, he said.

The next Monday, I came to work, and they were pulling Deep out the door, two paramedics, each one with an arm under Deep's arms, and two security guards trailing behind. I wanted to say something, anything, to make them stop. I knew I would never see him again. But I froze. As they dragged him past me, I tried to make eye contact, but I looked in there, and no one was left. He had gone somewhere else. He was saying, okay, so. Okay, so.

And then the next day, there it was, in the newspaper. The whole story about the banker. Exactly how Deepak told it to me. There were rumors that he was the one the banker hired; he was living with murderous guilt. Other people gossiped that he had done death of a child.

I don't think it was either. I don't think it was any one thing that did it. Deep just knew. He knew what was out there. There is no upper bound on sadness. There is no lower bound on decency. Deep saw it, he understood it, what was out there, and he let it seep in, and once it was in, it got all the way in, and it will never come out.

I open tickets. I do the work. I save up money.

Weeks go by. Kirthi opens up. (Just a little.)

She still refuses to look me in the eyes when we are kissing.

That's weird, she says. No one does that.

How am I supposed to know that? I have not kissed many people, but I don't want her to know it. I have seen in American movies that people close their eyes, but I have also seen that sometimes one person or the other will sneak open an eye and take a peek at the other one. I think it makes sense. Otherwise, how would you know what the other person is feeling? That seems to me to be the only way to be sure, the only way to understand, through the look on their face, what they are feeling, to be able to feel what they feel for you. So we kiss, she with her eyes closed, me looking at her, trying to imagine what she is feeling. I hope she is feeling something.

I am at a funeral.

I am having a bypass.

I am in drug rehabilitation.

I am in withdrawal.

She takes me to see her father.

He has the look. I remember this look. This is how my father looked.

He is living someone else's life. He is a projection screen, a vessel, a unit of capacity for pain, like an external hard drive, a peripheral device for someone's convenience, a place to store frustration and guilt and unhappiness.

We stand there in silence.

We go back to work.

I am at a funeral.

I am at a root canal.

The thing it is uncomfortable to talk about is: we could do it. We could get him out.

Finally, she can't take it.

He has only four years left on his mortgage, Kirthi tells me.

The thing is, the way the market works, sellers like us never get full value on our time. It's like a pawnshop. You hock your pocketwatch to put dinner on the table, you might get fifty bucks. Go to get it after payday and you'll have to pay four times that to get it back.

Same principle here. I love Kirthi, I do. But I don't know if I could give sixteen years of my life to get her father out. I could do it if I knew she loved me, but I don't know it yet. I want to be a better man than this, I want to be more selfless. My life isn't so great as it is, but I just don't know if I could do it.

I am in surgery.

I am bleeding to death.

It doesn't hurt at all.

Things progress. We move in together. We avoid planning for the future. We hint at it. We talk around it.

I am being shot at.

I am being slapped in the face.

I go home.

I rest.

I come back and do it again.

When I turned thirteen, my mother told me the story. She sat me down in the kitchen and explained.

"The day your father sold his life," she said, "I wore my best dress, and he wore a suit. He combed his hair. He looked handsome and calm. You wore your only pair of long pants. We walked to the bank. You rode on his back."

"I remember that," I said.

"A man with excellent hair came out from some office in the back and sat down behind the desk."

I remember that, too, I told her.

You get—we got—forty thousand a year, she said.

My dad sold his life for a fixed annuity, indexed to inflation at three percent annually, and a seventy percent pension if he made it full term: forty years, age seventy, and he could stop, he could come back to us, to his life.

There were posters everywhere, my mother said, describing that day, the reunion day. The day when you've made it, you've done it, you're done.

There was a video screen showing a short film describing the benefits of mortgage, the glorious day of reunion. We would all drink lemonade in the hot summer air.

Just forty years, it said.

In the meantime, your family will be taken care of. You will have peace of mind.

"Time is money," the video said. "And money is time. Create value out of the most valuable asset you own."

"Don't miss out on a chance of a lifetime."

When we went home, I remember, my father went to lie down. He slept for twelve hours, twice as long as normal, and in the morning, while I was still asleep, he went and sold his life.

Things stop progressing with Kirthi.

Things go backward.

And then, one day, whatever it is we had, it's gone. It won't come back. We both know it.

Whatever it is she let me have, she has taken it away. Whatever it is when two people agree to briefly occupy the same space, agree to allow their lives to overlap in some small area, some temporary region of the world, a region they create through love or convenience, or for us, something even more meager, whatever that was, it has collapsed, it has closed. She has closed herself to me.

A week after Kirthi moves out, her father passes away.

My shift manager will not let me off to go to the funeral.

Kirthi doesn't even ask if I would like to go anyway.

I should go.

I will be fired if I go.

But I don't have her anymore. If I leave, I won't have a job, either. I'll never get her back if I don't have a job.

I'm never getting her back anyway.

I don't even know if I want her back.

But maybe this is why I don't have her, could never, would never have had her. Maybe the problem isn't that I don't have a life. Maybe the problem is that I don't *want* a life.

I go to work.

I open tickets.

I close tickets.

When I get home my apartment seems empty. It's always empty, but today, more empty. The emptiness is now empty.

I call her. I don't know what to say. I breathe into the phone.

I call her again. I leave a message. I know a guy in the billing department, I say. We could get some extra capacity, no one would know, find an open line. I could feel it for you. Your grief. I could bury your father for you.

I would say that I am tired of this substitute life, except that this is the only life I will ever have. It is a substitute for itself. A substitute for nothing. A substitute for something that never existed in the first place.

Three days later, when I get to work, there is a note on my desk, giving the time of the funeral service. Just the time and, underneath it, she scrawled, okay.

Okay.

I arrange for the hour. At the time, I open the ticket.

I am expecting a funeral.

I am not at a funeral.

I can't tell exactly where I am, but I am far away. In a place I don't recognize. She has moved to a place where I will never find her. Probably where no one will ever find her. A new city. A new life.

She paid for this time herself. She wanted to let me in. For once. Just once. She must have used up everything she had saved. The money was supposed to be for her father but now, no need.

She is walking along a road. The sun is hot, the air is dusty, but the day is alive; she feels alive, I feel alive for her.

She is looking at a picture we took—the only picture we took together, in a photo booth in the drugstore. Our faces are smashed together and in the picture she is not smiling, as usual, and I am smiling, a genuine smile, or so I have always thought about myself, but now, looking at myself through her eyes, I see that she sees that my own smile starts to decompose, like when you say a word over and over again, so many times, over and over, and you begin to feel silly, but you keep saying it, and then after a short while, something happens and the word stops being a word and it resolves into its constituent sounds, and then all of a sudden what used to be a word is not a word at all, it is now the strangest thing you have ever heard.

I am inside of her head.

I am a nice person, she is thinking. I deserve more, she wants to believe. She wants to believe it, but I can feel that she doesn't. If only she could see herself through my eyes. If only she could see herself through my eyes looking through her eyes. I deserve to be loved, she thinks, but she doesn't believe it. If only I could believe it for her. I want to believe in her, believe inside of her. Believe hard enough inside of her that it somehow seeps through.

She turns up the road and the hill gets steeper. The air gets hotter. I feel her sadness with every step, and then, right near the top of the hill, just the faintest hint of it: a smile. She is remembering us. The few happy moments we had.

I am standing on a hill. I am not at a funeral. I am thinking of someone I once loved. I don't know if I am her thinking of me, or if I am me thinking of her, or if maybe, right at this moment, there is no difference.

* Reprinted in *The Year's Best Science Fiction & Fantasy: 2011 Edition*, edited by Rich Horton

* Million Writers Award Notable Story

• FACES IN REVOLVING SOULS •
Caitlín R. Kiernan

The woman named Sylvia, who might as well still be a child, is waiting for the elevator that will carry her from the twenty-third floor of the hotel—down, down, down like a sinking stone—to the lobby and convention registration area. She isn't alone in the hallway, though she wishes that she were. There are several others waiting to sink with her—a murmuring, laughing handful of stitches and meat dolls busy showing off the fact that they're not new at this, that they belong here, busy making sure that Sylvia knows they can see just exactly how birth-blank she is. Not quite a virgin, no, but the next worst thing, and all that pink skin to give her away, the pink skin and the silver-blue silk dress with its sparkling mandarin collar, the black espadrilles on her feet. The others are all naked, for the most part, and Sylvia keeps her head down, her eyes trained on the toes of her shoes, because the sight of them reflected in the polished elevator doors makes her heart race and her mouth go dry.

No one knows I'm here, she thinks again, relishing the simple nervous delight she feels whenever she imagines her mother or sisters or someone at work discovering that she lied to them all about going to Mexico, and where she's gone, instead. She knows that if they knew, if they ever found out, they'd want explanations. And that if she ever tried to explain, they'd do their best to have her locked away, or worse. There's still a multitude of psychiatrists who consider polymorphy a sickness, and politicians who consider it a crime, and priests who consider it blasphemy.

A bell hidden somewhere in the wall rings, and the elevator doors slide silently open. Sylvia steps quickly into the empty elevator, and the others follow her—the woman who is mostly a leopard, the fat man with thick brown fur and eyes like a raven, the pretty teenage girl with stubby antlers and skin the color of ripe cranberries—all of them filing in, one by one, like the passengers of some lunatic Noah's ark. Sylvia stands all the way at the rear, her back turned to them, and stares out through the transparent wall as the elevator falls and the first floor of the hotel swiftly rises up to meet her. It only stops once on the way down, at the fourth floor, and she doesn't turn to see who or what gets on. It's much too warm inside the elevator and the air smells like sweat and musk and someone's lavender-scented perfume.

"Yes, of course," the leopard says to the antlered girl with cranberry skin. "But this will be the first time I've ever seen her in person." The leopard lisps and slurs when she speaks, human vocal cords struggling with a rough feline tongue, with a mouth that has been rebuilt for purposes other than talking.

"First time, I saw her at Berkeley," the antlered girl replies.

"And then again at Chimera last year."

"You were at Chimera last year?" someone asks, sounding surprised, and maybe even skeptical; Sylvia thinks it must be whoever got on at the fourth floor, because she hasn't heard this sexless voice before. "I made it down for the last two days. You were there?"

"Yeah, I was there," the girl says. "But you probably wouldn't remember me. That was back before my dermals started to show."

"And *all* the girls are growing antlers these days," the leopard lisps, and everyone laughs, all of them except Sylvia. None of them sound precisely human anymore, and their strange, bestial laughter is almost enough to make Sylvia wish that she'd stayed home, almost enough to convince her that she's in over her head, drowning, and maybe she isn't ready for this, after all.

Another secret bell rings, and the doors slide open again, releasing them into the brightly lit lobby. First in, so last out, and Sylvia has to squeeze through the press of incoming bodies, the people who'd been waiting for the elevator. She says "Excuse me," and "Pardon me," and tries not to look anyone in the eye or notice the particulars of their chosen metamorphoses.

Fera is waiting for her, standing apart from the rest, standing with her long arms crossed; she smiles when she sees Sylvia, showing off her broad canines. There's so little left of Fera that anyone would bother calling human, and the sight of her—the mismatched, improbable beauty of her—always leaves Sylvia lost and fumbling for words. Fera is one of the old-timers, an elder changeling, one of the twenty-five signatories on the original Provisional Proposition for Parahuman Secession.

"I was afraid you might have missed your flight," she says, and Sylvia knows that what she really means is, *I was afraid you'd chickened out.* Fera's voice is not so slurred or difficult to understand as the leopard's. She's had almost a decade to learn the mechanics of her new mandibular and lingual musculature, years to adapt to her altered tongue and palate.

"I just needed to unpack," Sylvia tells her. "I can't stand leaving my suitcases packed."

"I have some friends in the bar who would like to meet you," Fera purrs. "I've been telling them about your work."

"Oh," Sylvia whispers, because she hadn't expected that and doesn't know what else to say.

"Don't worry, Syl. They know you're still a neophyte. They're not expecting a sphinx."

Sylvia nods her head and glances back towards the elevator. The doors have closed again, and there's only her reflection staring back at her. *I look terrified,* she thinks. *I look like someone who wants to run.*

"Did you forget something?" Fera asks, and takes a step towards Sylvia. The thick pads of her paws are silent on the carpet, but the many hundreds of long quills that sprout from her shoulders and back, from her arms and the sides of her face, rustle like dry autumn leaves.

"No," Sylvia says, not at all sure whether or not she's telling the truth.

"I know you're nervous. It's only natural."

"But I feel like such a fool," Sylvia replies, and then she laughs a laugh that has no humor in it at all, a sound almost as dry as the noise of Fera's quills.

"Hey, you should have seen me, back in the day. I was a goddamn basket case," and Fera takes both her hands, as Sylvia turns to face her again. "It's a long road, and sometimes the first steps are the most difficult."

Sylvia looks down at Fera's hands, her nails grown to sharp, retractable claws, her skin showing black as an oil spill where it isn't covered in short auburn fur. Though she still has thumbs, there are long dewclaws sprouting from her wrists. Sylvia knows how much those hands would scare most people, how they would horrify all the blanks still clinging to their illusions of inviolable, immutable humanity. But they make her feel safe, and she holds them tight and forces a smile for Fera.

"Well, we don't want to keep your friends waiting," Sylvia says. "It's bad enough, me showing up wearing all these damned clothes. I don't want them to think I'm rude in the bargain." Fera laughs, a sound that's really more like barking, and she kisses Sylvia lightly on her left cheek. "You just try to relax, *mon enfant trouvé.* And trust me. They're absolutely gonna love—" but then someone interrupts her, another leopard, a pudgy boy cat clutching a tattered copy of *The Children of Artemis,* which Fera signs for him. And she listens patiently to the questions he asks, all of which could have been answered with a quick internet search. Sylvia pretends not to eavesdrop on an argument between one of the hotel staff and a woman with crocodile skin, and when the leopard boy finally stops talking, Fera leads Sylvia away from the crowded elevators towards one of the hotel's bars.

And this is before—before the flight from Detroit to LAX, before the taxi ride to the hotel in Burbank. This is before the bad dreams she had on the plane, before the girl with cranberry skin, before the elevator's controlled fall from the twenty-third floor of the Marriott. This is a night and an hour and a moment from a whole year before Fera Delacroix takes her hand and leads her out of the lobby to the bar where there are people waiting to meet her.

"What's *this*?" her mother asks in the same sour, accusatory tone she's wielded all of Sylvia's life. And Sylvia, who's just come home from work and has a migraine, stares at the scatter of magazines and pamphlets lying on the dining table in front of her, trying to make sense of the question and all the glossy, colorful paper. Trying to think through the pain and the sudden, sick fear coiled cold and tight in her gut.

"I asked you a question, Sylvia," her mother says. "What are you doing with this crap?"

And Sylvia opens her mouth to reply, but her tongue doesn't want to cooperate. Down on the street, she can hear the traffic, and the distant rumble of a skipjet somewhere far overhead, and the sleepy drone of the refrigerator from the next room.

"I want an answer," her mother says and taps the cover of an issue of *Genshift* with her right index finger.

"Where did you get those?" Sylvia asks finally, but her voice seems farther away than the skipjet's turbines. "You've been in my room again, haven't you?"

"This is my house, young lady, and I'm asking you the questions," her mother growls, growling like a pit bull, like something mean and hungry straining at its fraying leash. "What are you doing with all this sick shit?"

And the part of Sylvia's mind that knows how to lie, the part that keeps her secrets safe and has no problem saying whatever needs to be said, takes over. "It's one of my stories," she says, trying hard to sound indignant, instead of frightened. "It's all just research. I brought it home last week—"

"Bullshit. Since when does the network waste time with this kind of deviant crap?" her mother demands, and she taps the magazine again. On the cover, there's a nude woman with firm brown nipples and the gently curved, corkscrew horns of an impala.

"Just because you don't happen to approve of the changelings doesn't mean they aren't news," Sylvia tells her, and hastily begins gathering up all the pamphlets and magazines. "Do you have any idea how many people have had some sort of interspecific genetic modification over the last five years?"

"Are you a goddamn lesbian?" her mother asks, and Sylvia catches the smell of gin on her breath.

"What?"

"They're all a bunch of queers and perverts," her mother mumbles and then snatches one of the Fellowship of Parahuman Evolutionists pamphlets from Sylvia's hands. "If this is supposed to be work for the network, why'd you have to go and hide it all under your bed?"

"I wasn't *hiding* anything, mother, and this isn't any of your business," and Sylvia yanks the pamphlet back from her mother. "How many times have I asked you to stay out of my room?"

"It's *my* house, and—"

"That means I have no privacy?"

"No ma'am. Not if it means you bringing this smut into my house."

"Jesus, it's for *work*. You want to call Mr. Padgett right now and have him tell you the same damned thing?" And there, it's out before she thinks better of pushing the lie that far, pushing it as far as it'll go, and there's no taking it back again.

"I ought to do that, young lady. You bet. That's exactly what I ought to do."

"So do it, and leave me alone. You know the number."

"Don't you think I won't."

"I have work to do before dinner," Sylvia says, as calmly as she can manage, turning away from her mother, beginning to wonder if she'll make it upstairs before she throws up. "I have a headache, and I really don't need you yelling at me right now."

"Don't think that I *won't* call. I'm a Christian woman, and I don't want that filth under my roof, you understand me, Sylvia?"

She doesn't reply, because there's nothing left to be said, and the cold knot in her belly has started looking for a way out, the inevitable path of least resistance. She takes her briefcase and the magazines and heads for the hallway and the stairs leading away from her mother. *Just keep walking,* she thinks. *Whatever else she says, don't even turn around. Don't say anything else to her. Not another word. Don't give her the satisfaction—*

"I know all about those people," her mother mumbles. "They're *filth*, you understand? *All* of them. Every single, goddamned one."

And then Sylvia's on the stairs, and her footsteps on the varnished wood are louder than her mother's voice. She takes them two at a time, almost running to the top, and locks her bedroom door behind her. Sylvia hurls the stack of changeling literature to the floor in a violent flutter of pages, and the antelope girl's large, dark eyes gaze blamelessly back up at her. She sits down with her back against the door, not wanting to cry but crying anyway, crying because at least it's better than vomiting.

And later—after her first three treatments at the Lycaon Clinic in Chicago, after the flight to LA, after Fera Delacroix takes her hand and leads her into the murmur and half light of the hotel bar—she'll understand that *this* afternoon, this moment, was her turning point. She'll look back and see clearly that this is the day she knew what she would do, no matter how much it terrified her, and no matter what it would mean, in the end.

They sit in a corner of the crowded, noisy bar, two tables pulled together to make room for everyone, this perfect, unreal menagerie. Sylvia sits to the left of Fera, sipping at a watery Coke. Fera's already introduced her to them all, a heady mix of changeling minor royalty and fellow travelers, and Sylvia has been sitting quietly for the last fifteen minutes, listening to them talk, trying to memorize their names, trying not to stare.

"It's a damned dangerous precedent," the man sitting directly across from her says. He has the night-seeing eyes of a python, and he drums his long claws nervously against the top of the table. His name is Maxwell White, and he's a geneticist at Johns Hopkins. Her last year in college, Sylvia read his book, *Looking for Moreau: A Parahumanist Manifesto*. It's made the American Library Association's list of most frequently banned books seven years straight.

"What the hell," Fera says. "I figure, it's just fucking Nebraska—"

Maxwell White stops drumming his fingers and sighs, his long ears going flat against the sides of his skull. "Sure, this year it's just fucking Nebraska. But, the way things are headed, next year it's going to be Nebraska and Alabama and Utah and—"

"We can't afford to be elitists," says a woman with iridescent scales that shimmer faintly in the dim light. As she talks, the tip end of her blue forked tongue flicks across her lips; Sylvia can't recall her name, only that she was recently fired from Duke University. "Not anymore. That asshole De Vries and his army of zealots is getting more press than the war."

"Oh, come on. It's not *that* bad," Fera says and frowns.

"How bad does it have to be?" Maxwell White asks and starts drumming his claws again. "Where do you think this is going to stop? After these anti-crossbreeding laws are in place and people get used to the idea that it's acceptable to restrict who we can and can't marry, who we can fuck, how long do you think it's going to take before we start seeing laws preventing us from voting or owning property or—"

"Maybe that's what we get for signing a declaration of secession from the human race," Fera replies, and Maxwell White makes an angry snorting sound.

"Jesus Christ, Fera, sometimes I wonder which side you're on."

"All I'm saying is I'm not so sure we can realistically expect to have it both ways. We tell them we're not the same as them anymore. That, by choice, each of us will exist as our own separate species, and then we act surprised when they want to treat us like animals."

"De Vries has already started talking about concentration camps," a woman named Alex Singleton says; she glances apprehensively at Fera and then quickly back down at the napkin she's been folding and unfolding for the past ten minutes. Alex Singleton has the striped, blonde fur of a tiger-lion hybrid, and six perfectly formed breasts. "Are you still going to be talking like this when they start rounding us up and locking us in cages?" she asks, and unfolds the napkin again.

"That's never going to happen," Fera replies, and scowls at Alex Singleton. "I'm not saying there aren't a lot of scary people out there. Of course, there are. We've just given the bigots and xenophobes something new to hate, that's all. We knew there'd be a difficult adjustment period, didn't we?"

"You have the most sublime knack for understatement," Maxwell White laughs.

And then Fera turns to Sylvia and smiles, that smile so beautiful that it's enough to make her dizzy, to make her blush. "You're awfully quiet over here, Syl. What do you think of all this? You think we're all about to be rounded up and herded off to a zoo?"

"I'm afraid I've never been much for politics," Sylvia says, not meaning to whisper, but her voice is almost lost in the din of the bar. "I mean, I don't guess I've thought much about it."

"Of course, she hasn't," Alex Singleton mutters. "Look at her. She still wears clothes. She's pink as—"

"I think maybe what Alex is trying to say, in her own indelicate way," the woman with iridescent scales interrupts, "is that you're probably going to find the political ramifications of our little revolution will suddenly seem a lot more important to you, once you start showing."

"That's not at all what I was trying to say."

"Some of us forget they were ever blank," Fera says, glaring at Alex Singleton, and she stirs at her martini with an olive skewered on a tiny plastic cutlass.

The thin man sitting next to Maxwell White clears his throat and waves at Sylvia with a hand that's really more of a paw. "Fera tells us you're one of Collier's patients," he says, speaking very slowly, his lupine jaws and tongue struggling with the words. "He's a good man."

"I'm very happy with him," Sylvia replies, and takes another sip of her Coke.

"He did my second stage," the wolf man confides, and his black lips draw back in a snarl, exposing sharp yellow canines and incisors. It takes Sylvia a moment to realize that the man's smiling.

"So," Maxwell White says, leaning towards her, "what's your story, Sylvia?"

"Like Fera said, I'm a journalist, and I'm preparing to write a book on the history—"

"No, that's not what I'm asking you."

"I'm sorry. Then I guess I didn't understand the question."

"Apparently not."

"Max here is one-third complete bastard," Fera says and jabs an ebony thumb at Maxwell White. "It was a tricky bit of bioengineering, but the results are a wonder to behold." Half the people at the two tables laugh out loud, and Sylvia is beginning to wish that she'd stayed in her room, that she'd never let Fera Delacroix talk her into coming to Burbank in the first place.

"Is it some sort of secret, what you're hiding under that dress?" Maxwell White asks, and Sylvia shakes her head.

"No," she says. "It's not a secret. I mean—"

"Then what's the problem?"

"Back off just a little, Max," Fera says, and the man with python eyes nods his head and shrugs.

"He does this to everyone, almost," Alex Singleton says and begins to shred her napkin. "He did it to me."

"It's not a secret," Sylvia says again. "I just—"

"You don't have to tell anyone here anything you're not ready to tell them, Syl," Fera assures her and kisses her cheek. Fera Delacroix's breath smells like vodka and olives. "You *know* that."

"It's just that none of *us* are wearing masks," Maxwell White says. "You might have noticed that."

"Excuse me, please," Sylvia says, suddenly close to tears and her heart beating like the wings of a small and terrified bird trapped deep inside her chest. She stands up too fast, bumps the table hard with her right knee, and almost spills her drink.

"You're a son of a bitch," Fera growls at Maxwell White, and she bares her teeth. "I hope you know that."

"No, really, it's okay," Sylvia says, forcing an unconvincing smile. "I'm fine. I understand, and I'm fine. I just need some fresh air, that's all."

And then she leaves them all sitting there in the shadows, murmuring and laughing among themselves. Sylvia doesn't look back, concentrates, instead, on the sound of her espadrilles against the wide stone tiles, and she makes it almost all the way to the elevators before Fera catches up with her.

On the plane, somewhere high above the Rockies and streaking towards Los Angeles through clearing, night-bound skies, Sylvia drifts between the velvet and gravel folds of dream sleep. She dozed off with the volume setting on her tunejack pushed far enough towards max that the noise of the flight attendants and the other passengers and the skipjet's turbines wouldn't wake her. So, there's only Beethoven's 6th Symphony getting in from the outside, and the voices inside her head. She's always hated flying, and took two of the taxi-cab yellow Placidmil capsules her therapist prescribed after her first treatment gave her insomnia.

In the nightmare, she stands alone on the crumbling bank of a sluggish, muddy river washed red as blood by the setting sun. She doesn't know the name of the city rising up around her, and suspects that it has no name. Only dark and empty windows, skyscrapers like broken teeth, the ruins of bridges that long ago carried the city's vanished inhabitants from one side of the wide red river to the other.

The river is within us, the sea is all about us, and isn't that what Matthew Arnold wrote, or T. S. Eliot, or Maharshi Ramakrishna, or some other long dead man? Sylvia takes a step nearer the river, and a handful of earth tumbles into the water. The ripples spread out from the shore, until the current pulls them apart.

Behind her, something has begun to growl—a low and threatful sound, the sound of something that might tear her apart in an instant. She glances over her shoulder, but there's only the buckled, abandoned street behind her and then the entrance to an alleyway. It's already midnight in the alley, and she knows that the growling thing is waiting for her there, where it has always waited for her. She turns back to the river, because the thing in the alley is patient, and the swollen crimson sun is still clinging stubbornly to the western horizon.

And now she sees that it's not the sunset painting the river red, but the blood of the dead and dying creatures drowning in the rising waters. The river devours their integrity, wedding one to the other, flesh to flesh, bone to bone. In another moment, there's only a single strangling organism, though a thousand pairs of eyes stare back at her in agony and horror, and two thousand hearts bleed themselves dry through a million ruptured veins.

And the way up is the way down, the way forward is the way back.

Countless talons and fingers, flippers and fins, tear futilely at the mud and soft earth along the river's edge, but all are swept away. And when the sun has gone, Sylvia turns to face the alley, and the growling thing that is her life, and wakes to the full moon outside the skipjet's window.

"You can't expect more of them," Fera says, "Not more than you expect of the straights, not just because they're going through the same thing you are."

"None of us are going through the same thing," Sylvia replies, not caring whether or not Fera hears the bitterness in her voice. "We're all going through this alone. Every one of us is alone, just like White said in his book. Every one of us is a species of one."

"I think you expect too much," Fera says, and then the elevator has reached the twenty-third floor, and the hidden bell rings, and the doors slide silently open. Sylvia steps out into the hall.

"Please promise me you won't spend the whole weekend locked in your room," Fera says. "At least come back down for Circe Seventeen's panel at eight, and—"

"Yeah," Sylvia says as the doors slide shut again. "Sure. I'll see you there," and she follows the hallway back to her room.

Sylvia is standing in front of the long bathroom mirror, her skin tinted a pale and sickly green by the buzzing fluorescent light. She's naked, except for the gauze bandages and flesh-tone dermapad patches on her belly and thighs. The hot water is running, and the steam has begun to fog the mirror. She leans forward and wipes away some of the condensation.

"There's always a risk of rejection," Dr. Collier said, and that was more than three weeks ago now, her third trip to the Lycaon Clinic. "You understood that before we began. There's always the risk of a violate retrovirus, especially when the transcription in question involves non-amniote DNA."

And, of course, she'd understood. He'd told her everything, all the risks and qualifying factors explained in detail long before her first treatment. Everyone always understands, until they're the one unlucky fuck in a thousand.

No one ever lied to me, she thinks, but there's no consolation whatsoever in the thought.

In places, the bandages are stained and stiff with the discharge of her infections. Sylvia dries her hands on a clean white wash cloth, then begins to slowly remove the dermapad just below her navel. The adhesive strips around the edges come away with bits of dead skin and dried blood still attached.

"I'm not going to lie to you," Dr. Collier said, the first time they met. "Even now, with all we know and everything that we've been able to accomplish in the last fifty years, what you want is very, very dangerous. And if something does go wrong, there's very little hope of turning back." And then she signed all the documents stating that he'd told her these things, and that she understood the perils and uncertainty, and that she was submitting to the procedures of her own free will.

She takes a deep breath and stares back at herself from the mirror, the sweat on her face to match the steam on the glass, and drops the dermapad into the sink. It stains the water a dark reddish-brown. And her mother, and all the faces from the bar—Maxwell White and Alex Singleton and all the rest—seem to hover somewhere just behind her. They smirk and shake their heads, just in case she's forgotten that the rest of the world always knew she was weak and that, in the end, she'd get exactly what she's always had coming to her.

I know all about those people. They're filth, you understand? All of them. Every single, goddamned one.

The rubbery violet flesh beneath her navel is swollen and marbled with pustules and open sores. The tip of a stillborn tentacle, no longer than her index finger, hangs lifeless from her belly. Dr. Collier wanted to amputate it, but she wouldn't let him.

"I hate like hell to say it, but he's right," Fera Delacroix told her, after the scene in the hotel bar, while they were waiting for an elevator. "You *can't* keep it a secret forever, Syl. What you're doing—what everyone here this weekend is doing—it's about finally being honest about ourselves. I know that doesn't necessarily make it easy, but it's the truth."

"No," Sylvia says, gently touching the dead tentacle. "*This* is the truth." She presses her finger into one of the tiny, stalked suckers, teasing the sharp hook at the center. "I think this is all the truth I need."

She cleans the cancerous flesh and covers it with a fresh dermapad, then peels off one of the patches on her left thigh and repeats the process. It takes her more than an hour to wash and dress all the lesions, and when she's done, when all those dying parts of her that are no longer precisely human have been hidden behind their sterile masks, she shuts off the water and gets dressed. She still has time for a light dinner before Circe Seventeen's talk on the link between shamanism and the origins of parahumanism, and Sylvia knows that if she isn't there, Fera Delacroix will come looking for her.

• HWANG'S BILLION BRILLIANT DAUGHTERS •
Alice Sola Kim

When Hwang finds a time that he likes, he tries to stay awake. The longest he has ever stayed awake is three days. The longest someone has ever stayed awake is eleven days. If Hwang sleeps enough times, he will eventually reach a time in which people do not have to sleep. Unfortunately, this can only come about through expensive gene therapy that has to be done long before one is born. Thus, it is the rich who do not have to sleep. They stay awake all night and bound across their useless beds, shedding crumbs and drops of sauce as they eat everyone else's food.

Whenever Hwang goes to sleep, he jumps forward in time. This is a problem. This is not a problem that is going to solve itself.

Sometimes Hwang wakes to find that he's only jumped forward a few days. The most Hwang has ever jumped is one hundred seventy years.

After a while, his daughters stop looking exactly Asian. His genes—previously distilled from a population in a small section of East Asia for thousands of years—have mixed with genes from other populations and continued to do so while Hwang slept. In fact, it all started with Hwang and his ex-wife. Hwang's daughters are a crowd of beautiful, muddled, vigorous hybrids, with the occasional recessive trait exploding like fireworks—squash-colored hair, gray eyes, albinism.

Backward, fool, backward! You were supposed to take me backward! He wishes he could find Grishkov and scream at him, but Grishkov is dead, of course. He died sometime that night, the first night Hwang slept and jumped through days, years, decades.

Later, Hwang awakes in a world with no men. Reproduction occurs through parthenogenesis. Scientists discovered that the genes of the father are the ones that shorten human lifespan; scientists decided to do something about it.

There are people walking around who look like men, but they aren't men. But if they look like men, walk like men, talk like men, maybe they are men?

There are new categories of gender that Hwang is unable to comprehend.

Men are men. He finds a daughter who is a man, so she must actually be a son, but in Hwang's mind—his mind that he cannot change—he is his daughter and always will be.

If you could flip through Hwang's life like a book—which I am able to do—you would see that Hwang and women have been a calamitous combination. It is not Hwang's fault or the women's fault but it is unfortunate nevertheless. I wish there was someone to blame.

Once, Hwang awakes to find no one. He walks around the city for hours before seeing a woman in a coverall. She is pulling vines off the side of a building and stuffing them into a trash bag. *I am paid millions a year for this work,* she says.

Even for the future, that is a lot of money.

It turns out that everyone has been uploaded into virtual space, but a few people still have to stick around to make sure that buildings stay up and the tanks are clean and operational.

Later, everyone comes back, because it turns out that no one really likes uploaded life.

Hwang's wife was a research scientist. When they divorced, Hwang was granted temporary full custody and his wife went to Antarctica. Sometimes she sent their three children humorous emails about falling asleep on the toilet because it was so cold.

When their daughters were kidnapped walking home from school, Hwang's wife and Hwang both blamed Hwang. Their son turned fifteen, became a goth, and moved in with his mother when she returned from Antarctica.

Hwang, alone, rested his head on pillowcases permanently smudged with black. And slept for days.

Hwang says, *When people are able to live forever, that is when I will get my life back. I can marry again. We can have a family. When I awake, they will still be there, old as cedars. My cedar family, planted in the living room.*

I will live forever, but marriage between Hwang and I is out of the question.

Sometimes one of Hwang's daughters will buy him new clothes, but he always wakes up wearing his old clothes. He has been frumpy, archaic, obscene, un-worthy of notice, and perfectly in style—all those things, in that order.

There is a future in which skanky summer is quite popular. People walk around in bathing suits, waterproof briefs, shorts, breast-baring monokinis, sarongs—all with personal climate control units attached to the base of their necks.

Hwang emerges from his room, shivering in a wrinkled button-down, sweater, and corduroy pants. That day, the rain drifts down as gently as snow, and it gets you wet so gradually that you are startled to realize it, like a boiled frog in a pot of water.

Hwang never sees his son again. Upon waking for the first time, Hwang goes out into the world and finds that his son is a computer mogul who lives in a cheesy yet terrifying house surrounded by a moat. This house has no right angles, and a viscous red substance continually flows down the sides and into the moat.

A security guard grabs the back of Hwang's jacket as he backs up to get a running start so he can jump the moat. *You'll never make it*, she says, and he realizes that the security guard is his daughter. She sighs, looking him up and down. *There's a shelter a few miles away. You can get a decent meal. I'll drive you.*

His daughter does not look how he'd expect, but her eyes, when she glances at him in the rear-view mirror, are familiar and bright. *But I'm his father*, says Hwang. She laughs.

The computer mogul, famously, has no father (and says so often). Of course. Hwang sits in the back seat like a lump. He realizes that he can no longer enumerate to himself the ways in which he has failed, that his failure has turned into an exponential number residing within him, sleek and unutterably dense and deadly.

There is a time during which Hwang's visits are foreseen. His daughters tell him that his story has been passed down from their mothers. That their great-great-great . . . will come into their lives, recognizable by his blue sweater and brown corduroy pants (*You dress like a fucking teddy bear*, his son used to say—it felt like affection).

And then what? It is disputed. Is Hwang a force of good? Is he evil? How does he choose which daughters he appears to? Is he a matrilineal family curse? He tries to explain but it is not satisfying to his daughters.

The next time he jumps, it is a hundred years later and his story has been forgotten.

Hwang's daughter listens to his story. When he is done, she pulls a pill case from her bag. *Sounds like you need to change your point of view*, she says. *Try a Chip or a Barbara.*

Hwang chooses a pill from the compartment labeled "Chip." Chip and

Barbara are personality construct drugs, named for the people from whom they originated.

In an hour, he feels loose. He is young, and has plenty of time to decide what he wants to be when he grows up. He doesn't know if he wants to have kids yet. Come on, man, that's ages away. Let's have some fun before fun ends.

Hwang is still Chip when he goes to sleep, but it wears off in the night. He goes to find it again, to feel simultaneously free yet locked into the right time with no sense of slippage, but discovers that Chip and Barbara have been taken off the market.

In bare feet, Hwang was half an inch shorter than his wife, which seemed within the bounds of acceptability. But the world conspired to tip this delicate balance, with slanted sidewalks, with Italian heels, with poor posture. Hwang and his ex-wife each thought that the other cared more about their height discrepancy.

Your wife is white? said a sophisticated older aunt. *Then your daughters will be beautiful.* They were, because all daughters were beautiful; that is what Hwang believed. But Hwang was never one to be proud of their beauty. He was proud because they were brilliant, or they were about to be; they were at the age at which youthful precocity grew distinct and immutable. That is where they stayed.

Hwang always wakes up in the lab. The lab is always the same.

The time machine is a gnarled, charred mess on the floor, and the curtains are skeletons. Grishkov's body is curled like a cat in the corner; his face is untouched like a peaceful waxwork, and for that, Hwang is grateful. Hwang sleeps on the couch, which has blackened and split like a bratwurst. As unkind and sooty as the lab is, Hwang lingers there to hold off timeshock and cultureshock.

When he needs to use the bathroom, he has to leave.

In time, Hwang begins to suspect that he is not only being pulled forward in time as he sleeps; he is also being pulled sideways in space, to parallel universes.

He thinks he has confirmation of this fact when he arrives at a time when everyone is green. (Don't worry—there is still racism!)

Hwang sits with his daughter at a diner and tries to question her about what has happened. She explains, but language has changed, and he has trouble understanding her. *Lincoln*, he says. *Kennedy. Were they assassinated in this timeline?* She opens her mouth and taps at her translator earbud.

Doowah? she says.

• • •

Soon there are no more bananas. The iconic Cavendish banana, tall and bright and constant, has gone extinct. It is true that no one's favorite fruit is the banana. But now that bananas as he knew them are gone, Hwang feels like he's been trapped in a house without windows.

There is no backwards from this forwards. No more bananas for anyone ever again.

Hwang has learned a valuable life lesson: never allow someone to test a time machine on you.

No matter how certain they are it will work.

No matter how certain you are that it will enable you to fix your life and the lives of your loved ones.

But Hwang must have done some good for his later daughters; he has to have done some good; he has to.

Would it all be worth it, then?

Once, he wakes up, opens the door to the lab, and steps into water. He doesn't know how to swim. He is a giant lead teddy bear sinking to the bottom of the ocean, and as he flails in the water, his thoughts are not about how it's all over thank god, they are about expelling water from his lungs and if he could just take another breath please that would be perfect thank you thank you thank you let me live.

Someone grabs him and pulls him up. It's a woman wearing a cheap waiter's tuxedo. All around them, houses and restaurants and offices bob impossibly.

Do you have a reservation? The woman, his daughter, asks. He is exhausted. *Fine*, his daughter says. *Wait here. I'll bring something. Don't touch anything. You need to be disinfected.* His daughters are always so exasperated with him.

The time after that, everything is dry again. Hwang asks his daughter where the ocean is. His daughter shrugs. *We put it somewhere else. It was in the way.*

Hwang needs to understand that someday he will wake up and no one will be around, for good.

Once, when Hwang was thirteen, he came home to find his father strangling his mother. They rearranged themselves right as Hwang walked into the house; they must have heard his key. Stranglings can be quiet. He stood and saw his father flexing his hands and smiling, his mother wiping water out of her eyes and turning a sob into a smile, the way she turned seemingly random organic matter into food, work into money, disorder into order. If she was anti-entropic then his father was the opposite. Money for booze; so much grain goes into alcohol; carbohydrates are then wasted in the fermentation process; it is not sensible. Hwang had been sent to the library. When he came home early, it was awkward; Hwang did not know before then that the terrible could also be awkward.

His father did not murder his mother that day.

There comes a stable time, a time during which Hwang does not jump forward too crazily. He only goes a few days each time he sleeps. He sees his daughter often. He follows her around and pleads with her not to take the photon train to school; it is too fast. It is unnatural. She laughs. She goes to school in another state and her commute only takes half an hour.

Judgmental Hwang is aghast that people in the future react so placidly to risk, but he remembers things like bisphenol A and airborne toxic events and revealing your crush to a homophobe who will get so embarrassed that he will murder you, and then Hwang must admit that there were so many things in his time that he hadn't thought to worry about.

Soon enough, his daughter becomes less amused by this great-great-great . . . popping up in her world every few days. *Just go away*, she says. *Stop interloping. Get your own life.* She shakes his arm off and kicks the wall. He watches as the wall slowly bulges out and undents itself.

That night he goes to sleep, vowing to find some way to protect his daughter, and he wakes up one hundred seventy years later.

Hwang wonders: when he dies, will his cells disperse and mass elsewhere to such an extent that there will be achronological patches in the air? Space dust that travels through time?

What is sleep for a single cell?

Once, I built Hwang a new life, made to look and feel like the early years of the second millennium, but he would not accept it. He stepped out of the lab and the lab was where it is supposed to be. There, on the street, a man in basketball shorts was peeling and eating a banana, which was, well, which was a little on the nose, but I wished for him to know that bananas were back and he could be happy again. (Right?) As were vehicles powered by fossil fuels, as was orthodontia, as was AIDS, as was lithium. For a moment, his face was the face of someone who has woken up from a dream and feels enormous relief that it is not real, what just happened.

But it didn't last. He shook his head until his cheeks wobbled. He stamped his foot. The sidewalk began to sink and whirl beneath him.

Knew it, he shouted. *No backwards from this forwards.*

Up to his knees in the sidewalk, he sloshed ahead with effort and tried to touch whatever he could. The man eating the banana melted. The car melted. The German shepherd melted. Finally, the world rose above Hwang's eyes and, after a brief burbling, he went silent.

Well. I did try.

Hwang tries to look at it this way: time jumps forward when you sleep no matter who you are.

The first time Hwang jumps forward in time, he comes out of his room into fifty years later. The time machine had caught fire, and Grishkov had had to pull him out before the sequence completed countdown. The fire spread and trapped them; they knew already that the dusty red fire extinguisher had been emptied three years ago during a prank and never refilled. Grishkov succumbed to the smoke first, bad-heart Grishkov still clutching Hwang by the forearms as he swanned to the floor. Then Hwang fainted, too.

When Hwang awakes, many people are dead and many new people are alive and everything seems somehow worse, despite all the new machines and pills and fashions.

As Hwang is drawn to his daughters, his daughters are drawn to him.

Hwang does not want to die, but there would not be a very good reason to stay alive if life was only jumping through time rapidly. (*Wait.*) He is now part of the time machine, and although he is broken he remains magnetized to his descendants, his daughters. Down a street, in a tree, in a bar, driving a hovercar—they always find one another. His daughters feed him, imagining that they are experiencing a random surge of kindness toward a dusty, gentle homeless man.

Hwang is guilty about this; he feels that he is enslaving his daughters and the best thing to do would be to release all of them from this obligation. That is when he does want to die.

But he decides to wait it out. He will reach the end of time. He will reach the end of daughters. Then he can end, too.

When Hwang is now, nobody knows. He is sleeping. He has been sleeping all night, his eyelids fluttering and his mouth twitching from the struggle to stay asleep. He wants time to keep moving; he doesn't want to stop anywhere, even though the light is seeping in around the curtains and the hours turn to day. I say to him, *Dad, I won't forget. I'll be the one who remembers the story.*

Still he sleeps. I watch him still. In his mind, I am already blurring.

· EJ-ES ·
Nancy Kress

Jesse, come home
There's a hole in the bed
where we slept
Now it's growing cold
Hey Jesse, your face
in the place where we lay
by the hearth, all apart
it hangs on my heart . . .
Jesse, I'm lonely
Come home.

—"Jesse," Janis Ian, 1972

"Why did you first enter the Corps?" Lolimel asked her as they sat at the back of the shuttle, just before landing. Mia looked at the young man helplessly, because how could you answer a question like that? Especially when it was asked by the idealistic and worshipful new recruits, too ignorant to know what a waste of time worship was, let alone simplistic questions.

"Many reasons," Mia said gravely, vaguely. He looked like so many medicians she had worked with, for so many decades on so many planets . . . intense, thick-haired, genemod beautiful, a little insane. You had to be a little insane to leave Earth for the Corps, knowing that when (if) you ever returned, all you had known would have been dust for centuries.

He was more persistent than most. "What reasons?"

"The same as yours, Lolimel," she said, trying to keep her voice gentle. "Now be quiet, please, we're entering the atmosphere."

"Yes, but—"

"*Be quiet.*" Entry was so much easier on him than on her; he had not got bones weakened from decades in space. They *did* weaken, no matter what exercise one took or what supplements or what gene therapy. Mia leaned back in her shuttle chair and closed her eyes. Ten minutes, maybe, of aerobraking and descent; surely she could stand ten minutes. Or not.

The heaviness began, abruptly increased. Worse on her eyeballs, as always; she didn't have good eye-socket muscles, had never had them. Such an odd weakness. Well, not for long; this was her last flight. At the next station, she'd retire. She was already well over age, and her body felt it. Only her body? No, her mind, too. At the moment, for instance, she couldn't remember the name of the planet they were hurtling toward. She recalled its catalogue number, but not whatever its colonists, who were not answering hails from ship, had called it.

"Why did you join the Corps?"

"Many reasons."

And so few of them fulfilled. But that was not a thing you told the young.

The colony sat at the edge of a river, under an evening sky of breathable air set with three brilliant, fast-moving moons. Beds of glorious flowers dotted the settlement, somewhere in size between a large town and a small city. The buildings of foamcast embedded with glittering native stone were graceful, well-proportioned rooms set around open atria. Minimal furniture, as graceful as the buildings; even the machines blended unobtrusively into the lovely landscape. The colonists had taste and restraint and a sense of beauty. They were all dead.

"A long time ago," said Kenin. Officially she was Expedition Head, although titles and chains-of-command tended to erode near the galactic edge, and Kenin led more by consensus and natural calm than by rank. More than once the team had been grateful for Kenin's calm. Lolimel looked shaken, although he was trying to hide it.

Kenin studied the skeleton before them. "Look at those bones—completely clean."

Lolimel managed, "It might have been picked clean quickly by predators, or carnivorous insects, or . . . " His voice trailed off.

"I already scanned it, Lolimel. No microscopic bone nicks. She decayed right there in bed, along with clothing and bedding."

The three of them looked at the bones lying on the indestructible mattress coils of some alloy Mia had once known the name of. Long clean bones, as neatly arranged as if for a first-year anatomy lesson. The bedroom door had been closed; the dehumidifying system had, astonishingly, not failed; the windows were intact. Nothing had disturbed the woman's long rot in the dry air until nothing remained, not even the bacteria that had fed on her, not even the smell of decay.

Kenin finished speaking to the other team. She turned to Mia and Lolimel, her beautiful brown eyes serene. "There are skeletons throughout the city, some in homes and some collapsed in what seem to be public spaces. Whatever the disease was, it struck fast. Jamal says their computer network is gone, but individual rec cubes might still work. Those things last forever."

Nothing lasts forever, Mia thought, but she started searching the cabinets for a cube. She said to Lolimel, to give him something to focus on, "How long ago was this colony founded, again?"

"Three hundred sixty E-years," Lolimel said. He joined the search.

Three hundred sixty years since a colony ship left an established world with its hopeful burden, arrived at this deadly Eden, established a city, flourished, and died. How much of Mia's lifetime, much of it spent traveling at just under c, did that represent? Once she had delighted in figuring out such equations, in wondering if she'd been born when a given worldful of colonists made planetfall. But by now there were too many expeditions, too many colonies, too many accelerations and decelerations, and she'd lost track.

Lolimel said abruptly, "Here's a rec cube."

"Play it," Kenin said, and when he just went on staring at it in the palm of his smooth hand, she took the cube from him and played it herself.

It was what she expected. A native plague of some kind, jumping DNA-based species (which included all species in the galaxy, thanks to panspermia). The plague had struck after the colonists thought they had vaccinated against all dangerous micros. Of course, they couldn't really have thought that; even three hundred sixty years ago doctors had been familiar with alien species-crossers. Some were mildly irritating, some dangerous, some epidemically fatal. Colonies had been lost before, and would be again.

"Complete medical data resides on green rec cubes," the recorder had said in the curiously accented International of three centuries ago. Clearly dying, he gazed out from the cube with calm, sad eyes. A brave man. "Any future visitors to Good Fortune should be warned."

Good Fortune. That was the planet's name.

"All right," Kenin said, "tell the guard to search for green cubes. Mia, get the emergency analysis lab set up and direct Jamal to look for burial sites. If they had time to inter some victims—if they interred at all, of course—we might be able to recover some micros to create vacs or cures. Lolimel, you assist me in—"

One of the guards, carrying weapons that Mia could not have named, blurted, "Ma'am, how do we know we won't get the same thing that killed the colonists?"

Mia looked at her. Like Lolimel, she was very young. Like all of them, she would have her story about why she volunteered for the Corps.

Now the young guard was blushing. "I mean, ma'am, before you can make a vaccination? How do we know we won't get the disease, too?"

Mia said gently, "We don't."

No one, however, got sick. The colonists had had interment practices, they had had time to bury some of their dead in strong, water-tight coffins before everyone else died, and their customs didn't include embalming. Much more than Mia had dared hope for. Good Fortune, indeed.

In five days of tireless work they had the micro isolated, sequenced, and analyzed. It was a virus, or a virus analogue, that had somehow gained access to the brain and lodged near the limbic system, creating destruction and death. Like rabies, Mia thought, and hoped this virus hadn't caused the terror and madness of that stubborn disease. Not even Earth had been able to eradicate rabies.

Two more days yielded the vaccine. Kenin dispensed it outside the large building on the edge of the city, function unknown, which had become Corps headquarters. Mia applied her patch, noticing with the usual distaste the leathery, wrinkled skin of her forearm. Once she had had such beautiful skin, what was it that a long-ago lover had said to her, what had been his name . . . Ah, growing old was not for the gutless.

Something moved at the edge of her vision.

"Lolimel . . . did you see that?"

"See what?"

"Nothing." Sometimes her aging eyes played tricks on her; she didn't want Lolimel's pity.

The thing moved again.

Casually Mia rose, brushing imaginary dirt from the seat of her uniform, strolling toward the bushes where she'd seen motion. From her pocket she pulled her gun. There were animals on this planet, of course, although the Corps had only glimpsed them from a distance, and rabies was transmitted by animal bite . . .

It wasn't an animal. It was a human child.

No, not a child, Mia realized as she rounded the clump of bushes and, amazingly, the girl didn't run. An adolescent, or perhaps older, but so short and thin that Mia's mind had filled in "child." A scrawny young woman with light brown skin and long, matted black hair, dressed carelessly in some sort of sarong-like wrap. Staring at Mia with a total lack of fear.

"Hello," Mia said gently.

"Ej-es?" the girl said.

Mia said into her wrister, "Kenin . . . we've got natives. Survivors."

The girl smiled. Her hair was patchy on one side, marked with small white rings. *Fungus*, Mia thought professionally, absurdly. The girl walked right toward Mia, not slowing, as if intending to walk through her. Instinctively Mia put out an arm. The girl walked into it, bonked herself on the forehead, and crumpled to the ground.

"You're not supposed to beat up the natives, Mia," Kenin said. "God, she's not afraid of us at all. How can that be? You nearly gave her a concussion."

Mia was as bewildered as Kenin, as all of them. She'd picked up the girl, who'd looked bewildered but not angry, and then Mia had backed off, expecting the girl to run. Instead she'd stood there rubbing her forehead and jabbering, and Mia had seen that her sarong was made of an uncut sheet of plastic, its colors faded to a mottled gray.

Kenin, Lolimel, and two guards had come running. And *still* the girl wasn't afraid. She chattered at them, occasionally pausing as if expecting them to answer. When no one did, she eventually turned and moved leisurely off.

Mia said, "I'm going with her."

Instantly a guard said, "It's not safe, ma'am," and Kenin said, "Mia, you can't just—"

"You don't need me here," she said, too brusquely; suddenly there seemed nothing more important in the world than going with this girl. Where did that irrational impulse come from? "And I'll be perfectly safe with a gun."

This was such a stunningly stupid remark that no one answered her. But Kenin didn't order her to stay. Mia accepted the guard's tanflefoam and Kenin's vidcam and followed the girl.

It was hard to keep up with her. "Wait!" Mia called, which produced no response. So she tried what the girl had said to her: "Ej-es!"

Immediately the girl stopped and turned to her with glowing eyes and a smile that could have melted glaciers, had Good Fortune had such a thing. Gentle planet, gentle person, who was almost certainly a descendent of the original dead settlers. Or was she? InterGalactic had no record of any other registered ship leaving for this star system, but that didn't mean anything. InterGalactic didn't know everything. Sometimes, given the time dilation of space travel, Mia thought they knew nothing.

"Ej-es," the girl agreed, sprinted back to Mia, and took her hand. Slowing her youthful pace to match the older woman's, she led Mia home.

The houses were scattered, as though they couldn't make up their mind to be a village or not. A hundred yards away, another native walked toward a distant house. The two ignored each other.

Mia couldn't stand the silence. She said, "I am Mia."

The girl stopped outside her hut and looked at her.

Mia pointed to her chest. "Mia."

"Es-ef-eb," the girl said, pointing to herself and giving that glorious smile.

Not "ej-es," which must mean something else. Mia pointed to the hut, a primitive affair of untrimmed logs, pieces of foamcast carried from the city, and sheets of faded plastic, all tacked crazily together.

"Ef-ef," said Esefeb, which evidently meant "home." This language was going to be a bitch: degraded *and* confusing.

Esefeb suddenly hopped to one side of the dirt path, laughed, and pointed at blank air. Then she took Mia's hand and led her inside.

More confusion, more degradation. The single room had an open fire with the simple venting system of a hole in the roof. The bed was high on stilts (why?) with a set of rickety steps made of rotting, untrimmed logs. One corner held a collection of huge pots in which grew greenery; Mia saw three unfired clay pots, one of them sagging sideways so far the soil had spilled onto the packed-dirt floor. Also a beautiful titanium vase and a cracked hydroponic vat. On one plant, almost the size of a small tree, hung a second sheet of plastic sarong, this one an unfaded blue-green. Dishes and tools littered the floor, the same mix as the pots of scavenged items and crude homemade ones. The hut smelled of decaying food and unwashed bedding. There was no light source and no machinery.

Kenin's voice sounded softly from her wrister. "Your vid is coming through fine. Even the most primitive human societies have some type of art work."

Mia didn't reply. Her attention was riveted to Esefeb. The girl flung herself up the "stairs" and sat up in bed, facing the wall. What Mia had seen before could hardly be called a smile compared to the light, the sheer joy, that illuminated Esefeb's face now. Esefeb shuddered in ecstasy, crooning to the empty wall.

"Ej-es. Ej-es. Aaahhhh, *Ej-es!*"

Mia turned away. She was a medician, but Esefeb's emotion seemed too private to witness. It was the ecstasy of orgasm, or religious transfiguration, or madness.

"Mia," her wrister said, "I need an image of that girl's brain."

It was easy—too easy, Lolimel said later, and he was right. Creatures, sentient or not, did not behave this way.

"We could haul all the neuro equipment out to the village," Kenin said doubtfully, from base.

"It's not a village, and I don't think that's a good idea," Mia said softly. The softness was unnecessary. Esefeb slept like stone in her high bunk, and the hut was so dark, illuminated only by faint starlight through the hole in the roof, that Mia could barely see her wrister to talk into it. "I think Esefeb might come voluntarily. I'll try in the morning, when it's light."

Kenin, not old but old enough to feel stiff sleeping on the ground, said, "Will you be comfortable there until morning?"

"No, but I'll manage. What does the computer say about the recs?"

Lolimel answered—evidently they were having a regular all-hands conference. "The language is badly degraded International, you probably guessed that. The translator's preparing a lexicon and grammar. The artifacts, food supply, dwelling, everything visual, doesn't add up. They shouldn't have lost so much in two hundred fifty years, unless mental deficiency was a side-effect of having survived the virus. But Kenin thinks—" He stopped abruptly.

"You may speak for me," Kenin's voice said, amused. "I think you'll find that military protocol degrades, too, over time. At least, way out here."

"Well, I . . . Kenin thinks it's possible that what the girl has is a mutated version of the virus. Maybe infectious, maybe inheritable, maybe transmitted through fetal infection."

His statement dropped into Mia's darkness, as heavy as Esefeb's sleep.

Mia said, "So the mutated virus could still be extant and active."

"Yes," Kenin said. "We need not only neuro-images but a sample of cerebro-spinal fluid. Her behavior suggests—"

"I know what her behavior suggests," Mia said curtly. That sheer joy, shuddering in ecstasy . . . It was seizures in the limbic system, the brain's deep center for primitive emotion, which produced such transcendent, rapturous trances. Religious mystics, Saul on the road to Damascus, visions of Our Lady or of nirvana. And the virus might still be extant, and not a part of the vaccine they had all received. Although if transmission was fetal, the medicians were safe. If not . . .

Mia said, "The rest of Esefeb's behavior doesn't fit with limbic seizures. She seems to see things that aren't there, even talks to her hallucinations, when she's not having an actual seizure."

"I don't know," Kenin said. "There might be multiple infection sites in the brain. I need her, Mia."

"We'll be there," Mia said, and wondered if that were going to be true.

But it was, mostly. Mia, after a brief uncomfortable sleep wrapped in the sheet of blue-green plastic, sat waiting for Esefeb to descend her rickety stairs. The girl bounced down, chattering at something to Mia's right. She smelled worse than yesterday. Mia breathed through her mouth and went firmly up to her.

"Esefeb!" Mia pointed dramatically, feeling like a fool. The girl pointed back.

"Mia."

"Yes, good." Now Mia made a sweep of the sorry hut. "Efef."

"Efef," Esefeb agreed, smiling radiantly.

"Esefeb efef."

The girl agreed that this was her home.

Mia pointed theatrically toward the city. "Mia efef! Mia eb Esefeb etej Mia efef!" *Mia and Esefeb come to Mia's home.* Mia had already raided the computer's tentative lexicon of Good Fortunese.

Esefeb cocked her head and looked quizzical. A worm crawled out of her hair.

Mia repeated, "Mia eb Esefeb etej Mia efef."

Esefeb responded with a torrent of repetitious syllables, none of which meant anything to Mia except "Ej-es." The girl spoke the word with such delight that it had to be a name. A lover? Maybe these people didn't live as solitary as she'd assumed.

Mia took Esefeb's hand and gently tugged her toward the door. Esefeb broke free and sat in the middle of the room, facing a blank wall of crumbling logs, and jabbered away to nothing at all, occasionally laughing and even reaching out to touch empty air. "Ej-es, Ej-es!" Mia watched, bemused, recording everything, making medical assessments. Esefeb wasn't malnourished, for which the natural abundance of the planet was undoubtedly responsible. But she was crawling with parasites, filthy (with water easily available), and isolated. Maybe isolated.

"Lolimel," Mia said softly into the wrister, "what's the best dictionary guess for 'alone'?"

Lolimel said, "The closest we've got is 'one.' There doesn't seem to be a concept for 'unaccompanied,' or at least we haven't found it yet. The word for 'one' is 'eket.' "

When Esefeb finally sprang up happily, Mia said, "Esefeb eket?"

The girl look startled. "Ek, ek," she said: *no, no.* Esefeb ek eket! Esefeb eb Ej-es!"

Esefeb and Ej-es. She was not alone. She had the hallucinatory Ej-es.

Again Mia took Esefeb's hand and pulled her toward the door. This time Esefeb went with her. As they set off toward the city, the girl's legs wobbled. Some parasite that had become active overnight in the leg muscles? Whatever the trouble was, Esefeb blithely ignored it as they traveled, much more slowly than yesterday, to Kenin's makeshift lab in the ruined city. Along the way, Esefeb stopped to watch, laugh at, or talk to three different things that weren't there.

"She's beautiful, under all that neglect," Lolimel said, staring down at the anesthetized girl on Kenin's neuroimaging slab.

Kenin said mildly, "If the mutated virus is transmitted to a fetus, it could also be transmitted sexually."

The young man said hotly, "I wasn't implying—"

Mia said, "Oh, calm down. Lolimel. We've all done it, on numerous worlds."

"Regs say—"

"Regs don't always matter three hundred light years from anywhere else," Kenin said, exchanging an amused glance with Mia. "Mia, let's start."

The girl's limp body slid into the neuro-imager. Esefeb hadn't objected to meeting the other medicians, to a minimal washing, to the sedative patch Mia had put on her arm. Thirty seconds later she slumped to the floor. By the time she came to, an incision ten cells thick would have been made into her brain and a sample removed. She would have been harvested, imaged, electroscanned, and mapped. She would never know it; there wouldn't even be a headache.

Three hours later Esefeb sat on the ground with two of the guards, eating soysynth as if it were ambrosia. Mia, Kenin, Lolimel, and the three other medicians sat in a circle twenty yards away, staring at handhelds and analyzing results. It was late afternoon. Long shadows slanted across the gold-green grass, and a small breeze brought the sweet, heavy scent of some native flower.

Paradise, Mia thought. And then: *Bonnet Syndrome*.

She said it aloud, "Charles Bonnet Syndrome," and five people raised their heads to stare at her, returned to their handhelds, and called up medical deebees.

"I think you're right," Kenin said slowly. "I never even heard of it before. Or if I did, I don't remember."

"That's because nobody gets it anymore," Mia said. "It was usually old people whose eye problems weren't corrected. Now we routinely correct eye problems."

Kenin frowned. "But that's not all that's going on with Esefeb."

No, but it was one thing, and why couldn't Kenin give her credit for thinking of it? The next moment she was ashamed of her petty pique. It was just fatigue, sleeping on that hard cold floor in Esefeb's home. *Esefeb efef.* Mia concentrated on Charles Bonnet syndrome.

Patients with the syndrome, which was discovered in the eighteenth century, had damage somewhere in their optic pathway or brain. It could be lesions, macular degeneration, glaucoma, diabetic retinopathy, or even cataracts. Partially blind, people saw and sometimes heard instead things that weren't there, often with startling clarity and realism. Feedback pathways in the brain were two-way information avenues. Visual data, memory, and imagination constantly flowed to and from each other, interacting so vividly that, for example, even a small child could visualize a cat in the absence of any actual cats. But in Bonnet syndrome, there was interruption of the baseline visual data about what was and was not real. So all imaginings and hallucinations were just as real as the ground beneath one's feet.

"Look at the amygdala," medician Berutha said. "Oh merciful gods!"

Both of Esefeb's amygdalae were enlarged and deformed. The amygdalae, two almond-shaped structures behind the ears, specialized in recognizing the emotional significance of events in the external world. They weren't involved in Charles Bonnet syndrome. Clearly, they were here.

Kenin said, "I think what's happening here is a strengthening or alteration of some neural pathways at the extreme expense of others. Esefeb 'sees' her hallucinations, and she experiences them as just as 'real'—maybe more real—than anything else in her world. And the pathways go down to the limbic, where seizures give some of them an intense emotional significance. Like . . . like orgasm, maybe."

Ej-es.

"Phantoms in the brain," Berutha said.

"A viral god," Lolimel said, surprising Mia. His tone, almost reverential, suddenly irritated her.

"A god responsible for this people's degradation, Lolimel. They're so absorbed in their 'phantoms' that they don't concentrate on the most basic care of themselves. Nor on building, farming, art, innovation . . . *nothing*. They're prisoners of their pretty fantasies."

Lolimel nodded reluctantly. "Yes, I see that."

Berutha said to Kenin, "We need to find the secondary virus. Because if it is infectious through any other vector besides fetal or sexual . . . " He didn't finish the thought.

"I know," Kenin said, "but it isn't going to be easy. We don't have cadavers for the secondary. The analyzer is still working on the cerebral-spinal fluid. Meanwhile—" She began organizing assignments, efficient and clear. Mia stopped listening.

Esefeb had finished her meal and walked up to the circle of scientists. She tugged at Mia's tunic.

"Mia . . . Esefeb etej efef." *Esefeb come home.*

"Mia eb Esefeb etej Esefeb efef," Mia said, and the girl gave her joyous smile.

"Mia—" Kenin said.

"I'm going with her, Kenin. We need more behavioral data. And maybe I can persuade another native or two to submit to examination," Mia argued, feebly. She knew that scientific information was not really her motive. She wasn't sure, however, what was. She just wanted to go with Esefeb.

"Why did you first enter the Corps?" Lolimel's question stuck in Mia's mind, a rhetorical fishbone in the throat, over the next few days. Mia had brought her medkit, and she administered broad-spectrum microbials to Esefeb, hoping something would hit. The parasites were trickier, needing life-cycle analysis or at least some structural knowledge, but she made a start on that, too. *I entered the Corps to relieve suffering, Lolimel.* Odd how naive the truest statements could sound. But that didn't make them any less true.

Esefeb went along with all Mia's pokings, patches, and procedures. She also carried out minimal food-gathering activities, with a haphazard disregard for safety or sanitation that appalled Mia. Mia had carried her own food from the ship. Esefeb ate it just as happily as her own.

But mostly Esefeb talked to Ej-es.

It made Mia feel like a voyeur. Esefeb was so unselfconscious—did she even know she had a "self" apart from Ej-es? She spoke to, laughed at (with?), played beside, and slept with her phantom in the brain, and around her the hut disintegrated even more. Esefeb got diarrhea from something in her water and then the place smelled even more foul. Grimly, Mia cleaned it up. Esefeb didn't seem to notice. Mia was *eket*. Alone in her futile endeavors at sanitation, at health, at civilization.

"Esefeb eb Mia etej efef—" How did you say "neighbors"? Mia consulted the computer's lexicon, steadily growing as the translator program deciphered words from context. It had discovered no word for "neighbor." Nor for "friend" nor "mate" nor any kinship relationships at all except "baby."

Mia was reduced to pointing at the nearest hut. "Esefeb eb Mia etej efef" *over there*.

The neighboring hut had a baby. Both hut and child, a toddler who lay listlessly in one corner, were just as filthy and diseased as Esefeb's house. At first the older woman didn't seem to recognize Esefeb, but when Esefeb said her name, the two women spoke animatedly. The neighbor smiled at Mia. Mia reached for the child, was not prevented from picking him up, and settled the baby on her lap. Discreetly, she examined him.

Sudden rage boiled through her, as unexpected as it was frightening. This child was dying. Of parasites, of infection, of something. A preventable something? Maybe yes, maybe no. The child didn't look neglected, but neither did the mother look concerned.

All at once, the child in her arms stiffened, shuddered, and began to babble. His listlessness vanished. His little dirty face lit up like sunrise and he laughed and reached out his arms toward something not there. His mother and Esefeb turned to watch, also smiling, as the toddler had an unknowable limbic seizure in his dying, ecstatic brain.

Mia set him down on the floor. She called up the dictionary, but before she could say anything, the mother, too, had a seizure and sat on the dirt floor, shuddering with joy. Esefeb watched her a moment before chattering to something Mia couldn't see.

Mia couldn't stand it any more. She left, walking as fast as she could back to Esefeb's house, disgusted and frightened and . . . what?

Envious?

"*Why did you first enter the Corps?*" To serve humanity, to live purposefully, to find, as all men and women hope, happiness. And she had, sometimes, been happy.

But she had never known such joy as that.

Nonetheless, she argued with herself, the price was too high. These people were dying off because of their absorption in their rapturous phantoms. They lived isolated, degraded, sickly lives, which were undoubtedly shorter than necessary. It was obscene.

In her clenched hand was a greasy hair sample she'd unobtrusively cut from the toddler's head as he sat on her lap. Hair, that dead tissue, was a person's fossilized past. Mia intended a DNA scan.

Esefeb strolled in an hour later. She didn't seem upset at Mia's abrupt departure. With her was Lolimel.

"I met her on the path," Lolimel said, although nothing as well-used as a path connected the huts. "She doesn't seem to mind my coming here."

"Or anything else," Mia said. "What did you bring?" He had to have brought something tangible; Kenin would have used the wrister to convey information.

"Tentative prophylactic. We haven't got a vaccine yet, and Kenin says it may be too difficult, better to go directly to a cure to hold in reserve in case any of us comes down with this."

Mia caught the omission. "Any of *us*? What about them?"

Lolimel looked down at his feet. "It's, um, a borderline case, Mia. The decision hasn't been made yet."

"'Borderline' how, Lolimel? It's a virus infecting the brains of humans and degrading their functioning."

He was embarrassed. "Section Six says that, um, some biological conditions, especially persistent ones, create cultural differences for which Corps policy is non-interference. Section Six mentions the religious dietary laws that grew out of inherited food intolerances on—"

"I know what Section Six says, Lolimel! But you don't measure a culture's degree of success by its degree of happiness!"

"I don't think . . . that is, I don't know . . . maybe 'degree of success' isn't what Section Six means." He looked away from her. The tips of his ears grew red.

Poor Lolimel. She and Kenin had as much as told him that out here regs didn't matter. Except when they did. Mia stood. "You say the decision hasn't been made yet?"

He looked surprised. "How could it be? You're on the senior Corps board to make the decision."

Of course she was. How could she forget . . . she forgot more things these days, momentary lapses symbolic of the greater lapses to come. No brain functioned forever.

"Mia, are you all—"

"I'm fine. And I'm glad you're here. I want to go back to the city for a few days. You can stay with Esefeb and continue the surveillance. You can also extend to her neighbors the antibiotic, antiviral, and anti-parasite protocols I've worked through with Esefeb. Here, I'll show you."

"But I—"

"That's an order."

She felt bad about it later, of course. But Lolimel would get over it.

At base everything had the controlled frenzy of steady, unremitting work. Meek now, not a part of the working team, Mia ran a DNA scan on the baby's hair. It showed what she expected. The child shared fifty percent DNA with Esefeb. He was her brother; the neighbor whom Esefeb clearly never saw, who had at first not recognized Esefeb, was her mother. For which there was still no word in the translator deebee.

"I think we've got it," Kenin said, coming into Mia's room. She collapsed on a stone bench, still beautiful after two and a half centuries. Kenin had the beatific serenity of a hard job well done.

"A cure?"

"Tentative. Radical. I wouldn't want to use it on one of us unless we absolutely have to, but we can refine it more. At least it's in reserve, so a part of the team can begin creating and disseminating medical help these people can actually use. Targeted microbials, an anti-parasite protocol."

"I've already started on that," Mia said, her stomach tightening. "Kenin, the board needs to meet."

"Not tonight. I'm soooo sleepy." Theatrically she stretched both arms; words and gesture were unlike her.

"Tonight," Mia said. While Kenin was feeling so accomplished. Let Kenin feel the full contrast to what she could do with what Esefeb could.

Kenin dropped her arms and looked at Mia. Her whole demeanor changed, relaxation into fortress. "Mia . . . I've already polled everyone privately. And run the computer sims. We'll meet, but the decision is going to be to extend no cure. The phantoms are a biologically based cultural difference."

"The hell they are! These people are dying out!"

"No, they're not. If they were heading for extinction, it'd be a different situation. But the satellite imagery and population equations, based on data left by the generation that had the plague, show they're increasing. Slowly, but a definite population gain significant to the point-oh-one level of confidence."

"Kenin—"

"I'm exhausted, Mia. Can we talk about it tomorrow?"

Plan on it, Mia thought grimly. She stored the data on the dying toddler's matrilineage in her handheld.

A week in base, and Mia could convince no one, not separately nor in a group. Medicians typically had tolerant psychological profiles, with higher-than-average acceptance of the unusual, divergent, and eccentric. Otherwise, they wouldn't have joined the Corps.

On the third day, to keep herself busy, Mia joined the junior medicians working on refining the cure for what was now verified as "limbic seizures with impaired sensory input causing Charles Bonnet syndrome." Over the next few weeks it became clear to Mia what Kenin had meant; this treatment, if they had to use it, would be brutally hard on the brain. What was that old ditty? *"Cured last night of my disease, I died today of my physician."* Well, it still happened enough in the Corps. Another reason behind the board's decision.

She felt a curious reluctance to go back to Esefeb. Or, as the words kept running through her mind, *Mia ek etej Esefeb efef*. God, it was a tongue twister. These people didn't just need help with parasites, they needed an infusion of new consonants. It was a relief to be back at base, to be working with her mind, solving technical problems alongside rational scientists. Still, she couldn't shake a feeling of being alone, being lonely: *Mia eket*.

Or maybe the feeling was more like futility.

"Lolimel's back," Jamal said. He'd come up behind her as she sat at dusk on her favorite stone bench, facing the city. At this time of day the ruins looked romantic, infused with history. The sweet scents of that night-blooming flower, which Mia still hadn't identified, wafted around her.

"I think you should come now," Jamal said, and this time Mia heard his tone. She spun around. In the alien shadows Jamal's face was set as ice.

"He's contracted it," Mia said, knowing beyond doubt that it was true. The virus wasn't just fetally transmitted, it wasn't a slow-acting retrovirus, and if Lolimel had slept with Esefeb . . . But he wouldn't be that stupid. He was a medician, he'd been warned . . .

"We don't really know anything solid about the goddamn thing!" Jamal burst out.

"We never do," Mia said, and the words cracked her dry lips like salt.

Lolimel stood in the center of the ruined atrium, giggling at something only he could see. Kenin, who could have proceeded without Mia, nodded at her. Mia understood; Kenin acknowledged the special bond Mia had with the young medician. The cure was untested, probably brutal, no more really than dumping a selection of poisons in the right areas of the brain, in itself problematical with the blood-brain barrier.

Mia made herself walk calmly up to Lolimel. "What's so funny, Lolimel?"

"All those sandwigs crawling in straight lines over the floor. I never saw blue ones before."

Sandwigs. Lolimel, she remembered, had been born on New Carthage. Sandwigs were always red.

Lolimel said, "But why is there a tree growing out of your head, Mia?"

"Strong fertilizer," she said. "Lolimel, did you have sex with Esefeb?"

He looked genuinely shocked. "No!"

"All right." He might or might not be lying.

Jamal whispered, "A chance to study the hallucinations in someone who can fully articulate—"

"No," Kenin said. "Time matters with this . . . " Mia saw that she couldn't bring herself to say "cure."

Realization dawned on Lolimel's face. "Me? You're going to . . . *me*? There's nothing wrong with me!"

"Lolimel, dear heart . . . " Mia said.

"I don't have it!"

"And the floor doesn't have sandwigs. Lolimel—"

"No!"

The guards had been alerted. Lolimel didn't make it out of the atrium. They held him, flailing and yelling, while Kenin deftly slapped on a tranq patch. In ten seconds he was out.

"Tie him down securely," Kenin said, breathing hard. "Daniel, get the brain bore started as soon as he's prepped. Everyone else, start packing up, and impose quarantine. We can't risk this for anyone else here. I'm calling a Section Eleven."

Section Eleven: *If the MedCorps officer in charge deems the risk to Corps members to exceed the gain to colonists by a factor of three or more, the officer may pull the Corps off-planet.*

It was the first time Mia had ever seen Kenin make a unilateral decision.

Twenty-four hours later, Mia sat beside Lolimel as dusk crept over the city. The shuttle had already carried up most personnel and equipment. Lolimel was in the last shift because, as Kenin did not need to say aloud, if he died, his body would be left behind. But Lolimel had not died. He had thrashed in unconscious seizures, had distorted his features in silent grimaces of pain until Mia would not have recognized him, had suffered malfunctions in alimentary, lymphatic, endocrine, and parasympathetic nervous systems, all recorded on the monitors. But he would live. The others didn't know it, but Mia did.

"We're ready for him, Mia," the young tech said. "Are you on this shuttle, too?"

"No, the last one. Move him carefully. We don't know how much pain he's actually feeling through the meds."

She watched the gurney slide out of the room, its monitors looming over

Lolimel like cliffs over a raging river. When he'd gone, Mia slipped into the next building, and then the next. Such beautiful buildings: spacious atria, beautifully proportioned rooms, one structure flowing into another.

Eight buildings away, she picked up the pack she'd left there. It was heavy, even though it didn't contain everything she had cached around the city. It was so easy to take things when a base was being hastily withdrawn. Everyone was preoccupied, everyone assumed anything not readily visible was already packed, inventories were neglected and the deebees not cross-checked. No time. Historically, war had always provided great opportunities for profiteers.

Was that what she was? Yes, but not a profit measured in money. Measure it, rather, in lives saved, or restored to dignity, or enhanced. *"Why did you first enter the Corps?"* Because I'm a medician, Lolimel. Not an anthropologist.

They would notice, of course, that Mia herself wasn't aboard the last shuttle. But Kenin, at least, would realize that searching from her would be a waste of valuable resources when Mia didn't want to be found. And Mia was so old. Surely the old should be allowed to make their own decisions.

Although she would miss them, these Corps members who had been her family since the last assignment shuffle, eighteen months ago and decades ago, depending on whose time you counted by. Especially she would miss Lolimel. But this was the right way to end her life, in service to these colonists' health. She was a medician.

It went better than Mia could have hoped. When the ship had gone—she'd seen it leave orbit, a fleeting stream of light—Mia went to Esefeb.

"Mia etej efef," Esefeb said with her rosy smile. *Mia come home.* Mia walked toward her, hugged the girl, and slapped the tranq patch on her neck.

For the next week, Mia barely slept. After the makeshift surgery, she tended Esefeb through the seizures, vomiting, diarrhea, pain. On the morning the girl woke up, herself again, Esefeb was there to bathe the feeble body, feed it, nurse Esefeb. She recovered very fast; the cure was violent on the body but not as debilitating as everyone had feared. And afterwards Esefeb was quieter, meeker, and surprisingly intelligent as Mia taught her the rudiments of water purification, sanitation, safe food storage, health care. By the time Mia moved on to Esefeb's mother's house, Esefeb was free of most parasites, and Mia was working on the rest. Esefeb never mentioned her former hallucinations. It was possible she didn't remember them.

"Esefeb ekebet," Mia said as she hefted her pack to leave. *Esefeb be well.*

Esefeb nodded. She stood quietly as Mia trudged away, and when Mia turned to wave at her, Esefeb waved back.

Mia shifted the pack on her shoulders. It seemed heavier than before. Or maybe Mia was just older. Two weeks older, merely, but two weeks could make a big difference. An enormous difference.

Two weeks could start to save a civilization.

Night fell. Esefeb sat on the stairs to her bed, clutching the blue-green sheet of plastic in both hands. She sobbed and shivered, her clean face contorted. Around her, the unpopulated shadows grew thicker and darker. Eventually, she wailed aloud to the empty night.

"Ej-es! O, Ej-es! Ej-es, Esefeb eket! Ej-es . . . etej efef! O, etej efef!"

· IN-FALL ·
Ted Kosmatka

The disc caved a hole in the starshine.

Smooth, graphene skin reflected nothing, blotting out the stars as it swung through the vacuum—black on black, the perfect absence of color.

It was both a ship and not a ship.

The disc lacked a propulsion system. It lacked navigation. Inside, two men awakened, first one and then the other.

In truth, the disc was a projectile—a dark bolus of life-support fired into distant orbit around another, stranger kind of darkness.

This second darkness is almost infinitely larger, massing several hundred thousand sols; and it didn't blot out the stars behind it, but instead lensed them into a bright, shifting halo, bending light into a ring, deforming the fabric of spacetime itself.

From the perspective of the orbiting disc, the stars seemed to flow around an enormous, circular gap in the star field. It had many different names, this region of space. The astronomers who discovered it centuries earlier had called it Bhat 16. Later physicists would call it "the sink." And finally, to those who came here, to those who dreamed of it, it was known simply as "the maw."

A black hole like none ever found before.

By the disc's third day in orbit, it had already traveled three hundred eighteen million miles, but this is only a tiny fraction of its complete trajectory. At the end of the disc's seventy-second hour in orbit, a small lead weight, 100 kilograms, was fired toward the heart of the gravity well—connected to the ship by a wire so thin that even mathematicians called it a line.

The line spooled out, thousands of kilometers of unbreakable tetravalent filament stretching toward the darkness until finally pulling taut. The line held fast to its anchor point, sending a musical resonance vibrating through the disc's carbon hull.

Inexorable gravity, a subtle shift.

Slowly at first, but gradually, on the fourth day, the ship that was not a ship changed course and began to fall.

The old man wiped blood from the young man's face.

"*Ulii ul quisall,*" the young man said. *Don't touch me.*

The old man nodded. "You speak Thusi," he said. "I speak this, too."

The young man leaned close and spat blood at the old man. "It is an abomination to hear you speak it."

The old man's eyes narrowed.

He wiped the blood from his cheek. "An abomination," he said. "Perhaps this is true."

He held out his hand for the young man to see. In his hand was a scalpel. "Do you know why I'm here?" he asked.

Light gleamed off the scalpel's edge. This time, it was the old man who leaned close. "I'm here to cut you."

The old man placed the scalpel's blade on the young man's cheek, just beneath his left eye. The steel pressed a dimple into his pallid skin.

The young man's expression didn't change. He stared straight ahead, eyes like blue stone.

The old man considered him. "But it would be a kindness to cut you," he continued. "I see that now." He pulled the blade away and ran a thumb along the young man's jaw, tracing the web of scar tissue. "You wouldn't even feel it."

The young man sat motionless in the chair, arms bound to the armrests by thick straps. He was probably still in his teens, the beginnings of a beard making patchy whorls on his cheek. He was little more than a boy, really.

He had probably once been beautiful, the old man judged. That explained the scars. The boy's psychological profile must have shown a weakness for vanity.

Or perhaps the profiles didn't matter anymore.

Perhaps they just scarred them all now.

The old man rubbed his eyes, feeling the anger slide out of him. He put the scalpel back on the tray with the other bright and gleaming instruments.

"Sleep," he told the boy. "You will need it."

And the universe ticked on.

"Where are we going?" the boy said, after several hours.

Whether he'd slept or not, the old man wasn't sure, but at least he'd been silent.

The old man rose from his console on creaking knees. Acceleration accreted weight into the soles of his feet, allowing the simple pleasure of walking. He brought the boy water. "Drink," he said, holding out the nozzle.

The boy eyed him suspiciously, but after a moment, took a long swallow.

"Where are we going?" he repeated.

The old man ignored him.

"They have already tried to interrogate me," the boy said. "I told them nothing."

"I know. If you told them what they wanted, you wouldn't be here."

"And so now they're sending me someplace else? To try again?"

"Yes, someplace else, but not to try again."

The boy was silent for a long moment. Then he said, "For that they have you."

The old man smiled. "You are a smart one."

Rage burned in the boy's eyes, and pain beyond measuring. The earlier interrogations had been harsh. He pulled against his straps again, trying to jerk his arms free.

"Tell me where you are taking me!" he demanded.

The old man stared down at him. "You are scared," he said. "I know what you are thinking. You want out of your restraints. You're thinking that if you could get loose . . . *oh,* the things you would do to me." The old man glanced toward the tray of gleaming steel. "You wish you could use that blade on me. You wish that you were in my shoes, that I was sitting where you are.

"But you don't understand," the old man said, then leaned forward again and whispered into the boy's ear. "It is *I* who envy *you.*"

The ship hummed as it fell. Charged ions blasted carbon skin.

"Why won't you tell me where we're going?"

The boy repeated the question every few minutes.

Finally the old man walked to the console and pressed a button. The wall revealed a view screen, exposing deep space, the looming maw. "There," the old man said. "We are going there."

The black hole filled half the screen.

Abyss, if there ever was one.

The boy smiled. "You try to scare me with death? I don't fear death."

"I know," the old man said.

"Death is my reward. In the afterlife, I will walk again with my father. I will tread the bones of my enemies. I will be seated at a place of honor with others who fell fighting for the side of God. Death will be a paradise for me."

"You truly believe that, don't you?"

"Yes."

"That is why I envy you."

The boy was a mass murderer. Or a freedom fighter.

Or maybe just unfortunate.

The old man looked at the boy's scars, noting the creative flourish that had been lavished on his face during previous interviews. Yes, unfortunate, certainly. Perhaps that above all.

Life in deep space is fragile. And humans are as they have always been.

Bombs though, are different.

In space, bombs can be much, *much* more effective.

If placed just right, a simple three pound bomb can destroy an entire colony. Open it to the sterilizing vacuum of the endless night. And ten thousand people dead—a whole community wiped clean in a single explosive decompression.

He'd seen that once, a long time ago, when this war first began. Seen the bodies floating frozen inside a ruptured hab, the only survivors a lucky few who scrambled into pressure suits. A lucky few like him.

Because of a three-pound bomb.

Multiply it by a hundred colonies and a dozen years. Three airless worlds. A fight over territory, culture, religion. The things man has always fought over.

Humans are as they have always been. In space though, the cost of zealotry is higher.

A thousand years ago, nations bankrupted themselves to raise armies. It cost a soldier to kill a soldier. Then came gunpowder, technology, increased population densities—gradually leveraging the cost of death along a sliding scale of labor and raw materials, until finally three pounds of basic chemistry had the power to erase whole swaths of society. Ever more effortless murder, the final statistical flat-line in the falling price of destruction.

"What is your name?" the old man asked him.

The boy didn't answer.

"We need the names of the others."

"I will tell you nothing."

"That's all we need, just the names. Nothing more. We can do the rest."

The boy stayed silent.

They watched the viewscreen. The black hole grew. The expanding darkness compressed the surrounding star field. The old man checked his instruments.

"We're traveling at half the speed of light," he said. "We have two hours, our time, until we approach the *Schwarzschild*radius."

"If you were going to kill me, there are easier ways than this."

"Easier ways, yes."

"I'm worth nothing to you dead."

"Nor alive."

The silence drew out between them.

"Do you know what a black hole is?" The old man asked. "What it is, really?"

The young man's face was stone.

"It is a side-effect. It is a byproduct of the laws of the universe. You can't have the universe as we know it and not have black holes. Scientists predicted them before they ever found one."

"You're wasting your time."

The old man gestured toward the screen. "This is not just a black hole though, not really. But they predicted this, too."

"Do you think you can frighten me with this game?"

"I'm not trying to frighten you."

"It makes no sense to kill me like this. You'd be killing yourself. You must have a family."

"I did. Two daughters."

"You intend to change course."

"No."

"This ship has value. Even your life must be worth something, if not to yourself then at least to those whose orders you follow. Why sacrifice both a ship and a man in order to kill one enemy?"

"I was a mathematician before your war made soldiers of mathematicians. There are variables here that you don't understand." The old man pointed at the screen again. His voice went soft. "It is beautiful, is it not?"

The boy ignored him. "Or perhaps this ship has an escape pod," the boy continued. "Perhaps you will be saved while I die. But you'd still be wasting a ship."

"I cannot escape. The line that pulls us can't be broken. Even now, the gravity draws us in. By the time we approach the *Schwarzschild* radius, we'll be traveling at nearly the speed of light. We will share the same fate, you and I."

"I don't believe you."

The old man shrugged. "You don't have to believe. You have merely to witness."

"This doesn't make sense."

"You think it has to?"

"Shut up. I don't want to hear more from a Godless *tathuun*."

"Godless? Why do you assume I am Godless?"

"Because if you believed in God, you would not do this thing."

"You are wrong," the old man said. "I do believe in God."

"Then you will receive judgment for your sins."

"No," he said. "I will not."

Over the next several hours, the black hole swelled to fill the screen. The stars along its rim stretched and blurred, torturing the sky into a new configuration.

The boy sat in silence.

The old man checked his instruments. "We cross the Schwarzschild radius in six minutes."

"Is that when we die?"

"Nothing so simple as that."

"You talk in circles."

The old mathematician picked up the scalpel. He touched his finger to the razor tip. "What happens after we cross that radius isn't the opposite of existence, but its inverse."

"What does that *mean*?"

"So now you ask the questions? Give me a name, and I'll answer any question you like."

"Why would I give you names? So they can find themselves in chairs like this?"

The old man shook his head. "You are stubborn, I can see that; so I will give you this for free. The *Schwarzschild* radius is the innermost orbit beyond which all things must fall inward—even communications signals. This is important to you for this reason: beyond the *Schwarzschild* radius, asking you questions will serve no purpose, because I will have no way to transmit the information. After that, you will be no use to me at all."

"You're saying we'll still live once we pass it?"

"For most black holes, we'd be torn apart long before reaching it. But this is something special. Super-massive, and old as time. For something this size, the tidal forces are more dilute."

The image on the screen shifted. The stars flowed in slow-motion as the circular patch of darkness spread. Blackness filled the entire lower portion of the screen.

"A black hole is a two dimensional object; there is no inside to enter, no line to cross, because nothing ever truly falls in. At the event horizon, the math of time and space trade positions."

"What are you talking about?"

"To distant observers, infalling objects take an infinite period of time to cross the event horizon, simply becoming ever more redshifted as time passes."

"More of your circles. Why are you doing this? Why not just kill me?"

"There are telescopes watching our descent. Recording the footage."

"Why?"

"As warning."

"Propaganda, you mean."

"To show what will happen to others."

"We aren't afraid to die. Our reward is in the afterlife."

The old man shook his head. "As our speed increases, time dilates. The cameras will show that we'll never actually hit the black hole. We'll never cross the threshold."

The boy's face showed confusion.

"You still don't understand. The line isn't where we die; it's where time itself ceases to function—where the universe breaks, all matter and energy coming to a halt, frozen forever on that final mathematical boundary. You will never get your afterlife, not ever. Because you will never die."

The boy's face was blank for a moment, and then his eyes went wide.

"You don't fear martyrdom," the mathematician gestured to the viewscreen. "So perhaps this."

The ship arced closer. Stars streamed around the looming wound in the starfield.

The old man put his hand on the boy's shoulder. He touched the scalpel to the boy's throat. "If you tell me the names, I'll end this quickly, while you still have time. I need the names before we reach the horizon."

"So this is what you offer?"

The old man nodded. "Death."

"What did you do to deserve this mission?"

"I volunteered."

"Why would you do such a thing?"

"I've been too long at this war. My conscience grows heavy."

"But you said you believe in God. You'll be giving up your afterlife, too."

The old man smiled a last smile. "My afterlife would not be so pleasant as yours."

"How do you know this is all true? What you said about time. How do you know?"

"I've seen the telescopic images. Previous missions spread out like pearls across the face of the event, trapped in their final asymptotic approach. They are there still. They will always be there."

"But how do you know? Maybe it's just some new propaganda. A lie. Maybe it doesn't really work that way."

"What matters is that this ship will be there for all to see, forever. A warning. Long after both our civilizations have come and gone, we will still be visible. Falling forever."

"It could still be false."

"But we are good at taking things on faith, you and I. Give me the names."

"I can't."

The old man thought of his daughters. One dark-eyed. The other blue. Gone. Because of boys like this boy. But not this boy, he reminded himself.

The old man looked down at the figure in the chair. He might have been that boy, if circumstances were different. If he'd been raised the way the boy was raised. If he'd seen what he'd seen. The boy was just a pawn in this game.

As was he.

"What is death to those who take their next breath in paradise?" the old man asked. "Where is the *sacrifice*? But this . . . " and the old man gestured to the dark maw growing on the screen. "This will be *true* martyrdom. When you blow up innocents who don't believe what you believe, this is what you're taking away from them. Everything."

The boy broke into quiet sobs.

The horizon approached, a graphic on the screen. One minute remaining.

"You can still tell me,

—there is still time.

—perhaps they are your friends, perhaps your family.

—do you think they'd protect you?

—they wouldn't.

—we just need names.

—a few names, and this will all be over. I'll end it for you before it's too late."

The boy closed his eyes. "I won't."

His daughters. Because of boys like this boy.

"Why?" the old man asked, honestly confused. "It does not benefit you. You get no paradise."

The boy stayed silent.

"I take your heaven from you," the old man said. "You will receive nothing."

Silence.

"Your loyalty is foolish. Tell me one name, and I will end this."

"I will not," the boy said. There were tears on his cheeks.

The old mathematician sighed. He'd never expected this.

"I believe you," he said, then slashed the boy's throat.

A single motion, severing the carotid.

The boy's eyes flashed wide in momentary surprise, then an emotion more complicated. He slumped forward in his bonds.

It was over.

The old man ran a palm over the boy's eyes, closing them. "May it be what you want it to be," he said.

He sat down on the floor against the growing gravity.

He stared at the screen as the darkness approached.

The mathematician in him was pleased. A balancing of the equation. "A soldier for a soldier."

He thought of his daughters, one brown-eyed, the other blue. He tried to hold their faces in his mind, the final thought that he would think forever.

Not the reverse of existence, but its inverse.

And he waited to be right or wrong.

To be judged for his sins or not.

* Reprinted in *The Year's Best Science Fiction: Twenty-Eighth Annual Collection*, edited by Gardner Dozois

• THE OBSERVER •
Kristine Kathryn Rusch

And so we went in.

Combat formation, all five of us, me first, face masks on so tight that the edges of our eyes pulled, suits like a second skin. Weapons in both hands, back-ups attached to the wrists and forearms, flash-bangs on our hips.

No shielding, no vehicles, no nothing. Just us, dosed, altered, ready to go.

I wanted to rip something's head off, and I did, the fury burning in me like lust. The weapons became tools—I wanted up close and I got it, fingers in eyes, fists around tentacles, poking, pulling, yanking—

They bled brown, like soda. Like coffee. Like weak tea.

And they screamed—or at least I think they did.

Or maybe that was just me.

The commanders pulled us out before we could turn on each other, gave us calming drugs, put us back in our chambers for sleep. But we couldn't sleep.

The adrenaline didn't stop.

Neither did the fury.

Monica banged her head against the wall until she crushed her own skull.

LaTrice shot up her entire chamber with a back-up she'd hidden between her legs. She took out two MPs and both team members in the chambers beside her before the commander filled the air with some kind of narcotic to wipe her out.

And me. I kept ripping and gouging and pulling and yanking until my fingertips were bone. By then, I hit the circuits inside the door and fried myself.

And woke up here, strapped down against a cold metal bed with no bed-clothes. The walls are some kind of brushed steel. I can see my own reflection, blurry, pale-skinned, wild-eyed.

I don't look like a woman, and I certainly don't look like me.

And you well know, Doc, that if you unstrap me, I'll kill the thing reflected in that brushed metal wall.

After I finish with you.

You ask how it feels, and you know you'll get an answer because of that chip you put in my head.

I can feel it, you know, itching. If I close my eyes, I can picture it, like a gnat, floating in gray matter.

Free my hands and I'll get it out myself.

Free my hands, and I'll get us all out of here.

How does it feel?

By it, I assume you mean me. I assume you mean whatever's left of me.

Here's how it feels:

There are three parts to me now. The old, remembered part, which doesn't have a voice. It stands back and watches, appalled, at everything that happens, everything I do.

I can see her too—that remembered part—gangly young woman with athletic prowess and no money. She stands behind the rest of us, wearing the same clothes she wore to the recruiter's that day—pants with a permanent crease, her best blouse, long hair pulled away from her horsy face.

There are dreams in her eyes—or there were then. Now they're cloudy, disillusioned, lost.

If you'd just given her the money, let her get the education first, she'd be an officer or an engineer or a goddamn tech soldier.

But you gave her that test—biological predisposition, aggression, sensitivity to certain hormones. You gave her the test, and found it wasn't just the physical that had made her a good athlete.

It wasn't just the physical.

It was the aggression, and the way that minute alterations enhanced it.

Aggression, a strong predisposition, and extreme sensitivity.

Which, after injections and genetic manipulation, turned her into us.

I'm the articulate one. I'm an observer too, someone who stores information, and can process it faster than the fastest computer. I'm supposed to govern the reflexes, but they gave me a blocker for that the minute I arrived back on ship, then made it permanent when they got me to base.

I can see, Doc; I can hear; I can even tell you what's going on, and why.

I just can't stop it, any more than you can.

I know I said three, and yet I didn't mention the third. I couldn't think of her, not and think of the Remembered One at the same time.

I'm not supposed to feel, Doc, yet the Remembered One, she makes me sad.

The third. Oh, yeah. The third.

She's got control of the physical, but you know that. You see her every day. She's the one who raises the arms, who clenches the bandaged and useless fingers, who kicks at the restraints holding the feet.

She's the one who growls and makes it impossible for me to talk to you.

You know that, or you wouldn't have used the chip.

An animal?

She's not an animal. Animals create small societies. They have customs and instinctual habits. They live in prides or pods or tribes.

She's a thing. Inarticulate. Violent. Useless.

And by giving her control of the physical, you made the rest of us useless, trapped inside, destined to watch until she works herself free.

If she decides to bash her head against the wall until she crushes her own skull or to rip through the steel, breaking every single bone she has, if she decides to impale herself on the bedframe, I'll cheer her on.

Not just for me.

But for the Remembered One, the one with hopes and dreams and a future she squandered when she reached for the stars.

The one who got us here, and who can't ever get us out.

So, you say I'm unusual. How nice for me. The ones who separate usually kill themselves before the MPs ever get into the chamber. The others, the ones who integrate with their thing, get reused.

You think that the women I trained with—the ones not in my unit, the ones who didn't die when we got back—you think they're still out there, fighting an enemy we don't entirely understand.

I think you're naïve.

But you're preparing a study, something for the government so that they'll know this experiment is failing. Not the chip-in-the-brain thing that allows you to communicate with me, but the girl soldiers, the footsoldiers, the grunts on the ground.

And if they listen (ha!) they'll listen because of people like me.

Okay. I'll buy into your pipe dreams.

Here's what everyone on Earth believes:

We don't even know their names. We can call them The Others, but that's only for clarity purposes. There are names—Squids, ETs—but none of them seem to stick.

They have ships in much of the solar system, so we're told, but we're going to prevent them from getting the Moon. The Moon is the last bastion before they reach Earth.

That's about it. No one cares, unless they have a kid up there, and even then, they don't really care unless the kid is a grunt, like I was.

Only they don't know the kid's a grunt. Not until the kid comes home from a tour, if the kid comes home.

Here's what I learned on our ship: Most of the guys never came home. That's when the commanders started the hormonal/genetic thing, the thing that tapped into the maternal instinct. Apparently the female of the species has a ferocious need to protect her young.

It can be—it is—tapped, and in some of us, it's powerful, and we become strong.

Mostly, though, no one gets near the ground. The battle is engaged in the blackness of space. It's like the video games our grandparents used—which some say (and I never believed until now)—were used to train the kids for some kind of future war.

The kind we're fighting now.

What I learned after a few tours, before I ever had to go to ground, was that ground troops, footsoldiers, rarely returned. They have specific missions, mostly clearing an area, and they do it, and they mostly die.

A lot of us died that day—what I can remember of it.

Mostly I remember the fingers and the eyes and the tentacles (yes, they're real) and the pull of the face mask against my skin.

What I suspect is this: the troops the Others have on the ground aren't the enemy. They're some kind of captured race, footsoldiers just like us, fodder for the war machine. I think, if I concentrate real hard, I remember them working, putting chips places, implanting stuff in the ground—growing things?—I'm not entirely clear.

And I wonder if the talk of an invasion force is just that, talk, and if this isn't something else, some kind of experiment in case we get into a real situation, something that'll become bigger.

Because I don't ever remember the Others fighting back.

If Squids can look surprised, these did.

All of them.

So that's my theory for what good it'll do.

There's still girls dying up there. Women, I guess, creatures, footsoldiers, whatever they want to create.

Then we come back, and we become this: things.

Because we can't ever be the Remembered Ones. Not again.

But you know that.

You're studying as many of us as you can. That's clear too.

I'm not even sure you are a doc. Maybe you're a machine, getting these thoughts, processing them, using some modulated voice to ask the right questions, the ones that provoke these memories.

Since I've never seen you.

I never see anyone.

Except the ghosts of myself.

So what are you going to do with me? Reintegration isn't possible; that's been tried. (You think I don't remember? How do you think the Remembered One and I split off in the first place? Once there was just her and the thing. Now there's three of us, trapped in here—well, two trapped, and one growling, but you know what I mean.)

Sending us back won't work. We might turn on our comrades. Or ourself. (Probably ourself.)

Sending us home is out of the question, even if we had a home. The Remembered One does, but she's so far away, she'll never reintegrate.

Let me tell you what I think you should do. I think you should remove the chip. Move me to a new location. Pretend you've never interviewed me.

Then you'd just be faced with the Thing.

And the Thing should be put out of its misery.

We should be put out of its misery.

Monica and LaTrice weren't wrong, Doc. They were just crude. They used what methods they had at their disposal.

They were proactive.

I can't be. You've got all three of us bound up here.

Let us go.

Send us back, all by ourselves. No team, no combat formation. Hell, not even any weapons.

Let us die.

It's the only humane thing to do.

• JENNY'S SICK •
David Tallerman

It's a cold day in February, and Jenny's sick again.

I ask what it is this time and she just looks at me with ghastly eyes, staring out from over swollen, purpling flesh. She's sitting bolt upright, propped by pillows, and there's so much sweat everywhere that it's like condensation in a steam room. I've seen her look bad before but never quite this bad. Where did she get this shit? How long is it going to last this time?

I can't be the one to deal with this. We've been living together for maybe two years; we started sleeping together and ended friends, but mainly we just hit it off, and sharing a place seemed a good idea. I thought we had things in common then, that maybe we were going the same places. But I'm looking to finish studying as soon as possible, to carve out a career, and I have no idea what Jenny wants.

Maybe she just wants to die.

I think it was about a year ago she got into this, though you never know, do you? People are like oceans, the powerful stuff moves deep down and you almost never see it. So perhaps there was always something there, just waiting for an outlet.

Either way, it's about a year ago that I find out. There's a campus bulletin going around over a new drug, the usual about watching for strange behavior in our fellow students: absenteeism, mood swings, that kind of thing. I figure it's the same old government stuff, rooting for subversives and trouble-makers. There's always some new drug or faction or threat, and the next week you'll hear that the campus police have been out, then maybe there's a face missing in your next lecture. If you keep your nose clean and stay in the right groups it isn't that big a deal.

So there's buzz about this drug, without any real details. I don't think anything of it until I get in one evening and there's this noise coming from Jenny's room, like nothing I've heard. Though a couple of months later it will be all too familiar, this first time I don't know what to think. I mean, I've heard coughing before. But this isn't clearing-your-throat coughing; this is a cruel, hacking bout that goes on for two full minutes, while I stand in the hallway, not sure what I'm hearing.

By the time I knock on her door it's started again. When I open it the cough is shaking right through her, throwing her about like a rag doll. I don't know what to do, whether I should try and help, so I just stand watching and for a while she doesn't seem to know I'm there. Then finally there's a break, and she looks up. "I'm sick," she tells me. She says it with a weird grin, like she's challenging me.

"What do you mean? Nobody gets sick. There's nothing left to get sick *with*."

Instead of answering, she holds up a small plastic bottle. Somebody has written the word CHOKE across it in blue permanent marker. I can see one small green and white capsule rattling around inside.

"What the hell is that?" She only grins at me again, then starts on another fit of coughing.

I find out later that this first time, it's influenza. She spends two days with it, wrapped fetal in bed, skin like wet flour, choking until near the end I can see blood mixed with the filth she's bringing up.

Then, abruptly, it goes away. It always does. I figure out eventually that the second capsule, the green one, is the cure. She takes it and an hour later she's well. Except each time she goes a little longer without taking the green pill: One hour, five hours, a day.

After that, we don't talk about it, and I guess we drift apart pretty quickly. Jenny's out a lot, she doesn't bother to make classes or lectures, and I know there's a crowd she hangs out with but I don't see them. Mainly I'm worried that she'll get caught and that somehow they'll blame me as well. I study harder, as though that will make up for her absences, I will the days away, and I feel scared. As much as I like Jenny, I like the thought of my future more.

Maybe I should try and talk to her about it, but we don't talk about anything very much. When I do see her, it's because she's sick, too sick to go out. I don't know what she tells the campus authorities each time. I don't know where the pills come from. All I know is every month there's a new bottle with a name written on it, like PUKE or BURN, in the same messy blue highlighter.

As much as I try to keep away from it, and from Jenny, it's more and more a part of my life, a dirty secret I can't help but hide. After a few months I start downloading old medical texts from the library's archive. I figure maybe PUKE is gastroenteritis, but I'm majoring in Information Analysis not Science History; a lot of what's in those books goes way over my head, and it's not like I can ask anybody.

I wonder if I should try to help, to look after her somehow, but I'm too scared. Deep down, there's a part of me that's so damn afraid that one day she'll decide not to take the green pill. I'll come in to find her cold and still, and when the police find out what happened, that will be my life over too.

Christmas comes and goes, and I'm glad of the break and to be with my folks for a few weeks, except that Jenny and her weird obsession have got into my head and my parents' healthiness seems strange somehow: their perfect skin, their smiles, and their peace of mind. Having Jenny in my life is damaging me, but I only recognize it properly in that gap, in the exposure to normality and discovering how alien it seems.

When I get back to the flat I've already made my mind up that I have to move out. I don't know how I didn't think of it sooner. Almost a year's gone by and it never crossed my mind that I could just leave.

When I see Jenny I realize why. There's something so frail about her, even when she's not sick, a depth in her eyes that breaks my heart. I don't even know if she likes me anymore—maybe she hates me—yet suddenly all I can think about is the touch of her skin those times we slept together, the smell of her sweat mixed with the scent of her hair.

"I'm going to look for somewhere else to live."

She looks surprised, if only for a second. "Sure. This place is kind of cramped. I can manage on my own."

I choose to think that she means financially, but I'm not sure. I don't mention the sickness. I hope she will, but I know she's not going to. The way she is now, all of that is something that happens to another person. Right now, she seems so damn normal; except for that look in her eyes, that sense of unfathomable depth. "That's what I figured," I say, "I figured you could manage."

By February, I've found a place—a couple of guys with a spare room—and I'm living midway between the two flats while I shift the last of my things. I don't know why I'm not hurrying more. I could have been moved two weeks ago. Instead I drag my heels, take over a box every couple of days, and tell myself it's easier this way.

Then I come in and hear the coughing, not like the first time but slow, drawn-out, more of a dry wheeze. I go in and it's the worst I've seen her. She looks hollow, like a discarded shell, and more than anything she reminds me of these old porcelain dolls my grandmother used to keep: skin white, except where age had yellowed it, with black eyes that didn't look even remotely human.

"What is it this time?"

No answer, just a stare, and a half-smile through flaking lips.

I go out and load up the trolley that I've borrowed with my last four boxes. I don't even say goodbye.

The next time I run into Jenny is two years later. I just happen to take a certain corner on a certain street and there she is.

I can tell right away that she's dying. I've never seen anyone die, not for real, but it's some kind of instinct in my gut that tells me because suddenly I want to run away, to be anywhere else.

Instead, I make small-talk. It's very small because there's so damn much I know we can't talk about. Jenny was my friend and for a while something more. And I walked away, for two years I've kept her out of my mind. "How are you doing?" I ask. It feels like about the stupidest thing I've ever said.

But she nods and smiles, and says, "I'm okay, you know? I feel pretty good."

She doesn't look good. I think about suggesting we go for a coffee, but I know she always hated those places. She called them "obscenely clean," and there was only one bar she'd ever drink in, a place that had dropped so far off the map that the Hygiene Inspectorate didn't know it existed. "What are you doing now? How did uni go?" What I mean is: *Did you drop out? Did they catch you?*

Jenny dodges the question, with all its implications. "Yeah, I'm getting by. And you, how are you?"

"I finished with a pretty good grade. Serious data dissection work is hard to come by but I've got a couple of interviews coming up, it's looking promising. It's pretty tight these days, I guess, but I'm hopeful." Why do I feel guilty saying this? I'm not the screw-up here. I'm not the disease junky.

"Yeah? Well, that's good." She tries to sound like she means it. I feel as if we're on different planets, separated by a million miles. All I can think is how I want to be somewhere else, and maybe that's why I say what I do. "Jenny, you look really fucking sick." It's out of my mouth before I know it.

But she's not even fazed. "Yeah?" She smiles. "Oh, yeah: I'm dying."

This time, I don't even try and make an excuse. I turn and walk away, and the closest I come to apologizing is that I try not to run.

That night I dream about Jenny, cold and blue and somehow happy, grinning up at me from some deep dark place with a rictus smile cut over her lips. The dream hangs beside me all the next day, like smoke in the air, and I feel like I'm caught in Jenny's gravity, like I'm plummeting.

But it's a week on from that chance meeting in the street, just when I've almost managed to forget, that my phone rings. I don't recognize the name or face, except that she looks familiar somehow. For a moment I get that same gut feeling, that urge to run. I pick up anyway. "Hello. Can I help you?"

"My name is Linda Ulek. I'm sorry to intrude on your time, but it's very important, and there really isn't anybody else."

"I'm sorry, I don't—" Then I remember where I've heard the name Ulek before. "You're Jenny's mother."

I met her once. Jenny's parents came to the flat and looked uncomfortable and left as quickly as they could. Jenny told me once that they were both high up in some obscure branch of the government. That explains how she got hold of my private number.

"As I say, I'm sorry to intrude, but Jenny doesn't have any friends that we know of and we remembered your name, and that the two of you lived together, and were close at one point. Of course we'd like to go ourselves, of course we would, but we're in Rome this month and we have commitments. And the doctors are adamant that somebody who knows her should be with her—"

"I'm sorry; I don't understand what you're asking."

"Jenny's in hospital," she says. "She's very sick and the doctors have asked us to visit her, as part of her treatment. As I say, we can't do that. We thought that perhaps you could."

I didn't know there were any hospitals left. In a world with a cure for everything, I figured the common hospital was as extinct as the common cold. Whatever I'm expecting, the Rondelle Panacea Clinic isn't it. It's just another nondescript building, a few klicks out of the city, like the office I work in or the flats I live in. I press the buzzer beside the doors, and a few moments later a young woman in a white suit appears. When I tell her who I am she says, "You're here for Jenny Ulek," and ushers me inside.

The woman, who gives her name as Doctor Meier, leads me through blank-walled corridors, into a small office, and offers me a seat. It occurs to me that Jenny must hate this place, that in fact it's everything she despises. White walls, white furniture, white people in white suits. If somebody had to design a personal hell for Jenny it would look a lot like this.

Doctor Meier sits opposite me and says, "It was good of you to come."

I nod. There's no point telling her how close I came to saying no.

"You're aware of Jenny's case history?"

"Some of it. We lived together for a while. I know she likes to get sick."

"Well, it's a little more complicated than that, but in essence, yes, Jenny takes a certain gratification from physical illness. Recently Jenny has introduced a disease into her system that, left untreated, will be terminal within the next two months." She pauses for just a moment, to let that sink in. "We could cure it, of course, completely eradicate it. Or we could use more outmoded techniques to keep it in check."

"Why would you do that?"

Doctor Meier has clearly prepared her answer. She looks the type to have prepared an answer for anything I could hope to ask. "Because if we were to let Jenny out into the world tomorrow she would immediately find a way to infect herself again, with the same disease or perhaps with something worse.

Put bluntly, the condition we need to treat in this case—if Jenny is to survive in any meaningful way—is not the physical one."

I nod again. Sure, I get that. From these peoples' point of view, Jenny is crazy. I guess if I'd thought about it I would have come to the same conclusion, but somehow it never occurred to me. "So, what's the alternative?"

"There are two options. The first, perhaps the easiest in many ways, will involve gene therapy, some alteration of memories, intrusive brain surgery. Put bluntly, we would correct Jenny's personality to a degree where she can function safely in society. It sounds, perhaps, more drastic than it is. But at the end of it Jenny will, obviously, not be quite the same person she is now."

Damn right it sounds drastic. "There's another option?"

"There is. It's slower, and there are no guarantees, but we have excellent psychologists on staff, and similar cases have been treated with a high degree of success."

I know that there's going to be a "but," it's written all over her face.

"While there's a good chance that Ms. Ulek can become well with sufficient help and support, it will take more than the kindness of strangers. What she will need is someone she knows, someone who knows her, who will devote time and—"

"No."

"If you'll just let me explain—"

"No, I can't do that. I have a career, I have my life." Suddenly, my heart has sunk right down into the pit of my stomach. "I haven't seen Jenny in years, I don't think I mean anything to her at all, and I can't possibly do that." Listening to my own voice, I know that what I'm saying is true, and yet at the same time I know it's not the truth. But what would be? That I couldn't say.

"We'd only ask that you spend some time considering it."

"Sure, I will. I'll consider it, and then the answer is still going to be no. It's just not something I can do."

Doctor Meier nods. She stands up and moves towards the door. I can tell she's bluffing, that she hasn't quite given up yet. "We'll call you in a few days, when you've had time to consider."

I guess I know myself better than Doctor Meier does, because when she calls three days later the answer hasn't changed. I didn't make Jenny sick. I didn't make her want to be sick. I have another interview coming up, and I can't be asked to abandon that for someone I barely know. But I don't tell her that. I don't have to explain myself.

Only, the nightmares keep coming. In some way, a way I don't much like, it seems that Jenny is still a part of me. I find myself remembering, more and more, those months we lived together. Jenny has become a ghost, and I don't know if I can escape her.

A week after my visit I phone the hospital. I don't recognize the doctor who answers so I have to explain who I am, the whole situation, before I can finally get to saying it: "I've changed my mind. I'd like to help."

This new doctor, male and middle-aged, looks away from me for a moment. When he looks back he says, very flatly, "Ms. Ulek's procedure was completed yesterday morning. She's due to be released at the end of the week, but perhaps you could visit her in the meantime. I'm sure she would appreciate the company."

I don't kid myself that I go for Jenny's sake.

Doctor Meier meets me at the door, and she's all smiles: "The procedure went well," she says, "we're very optimistic."

She leads me through corridors again, presumably in a different direction this time, but it's all so indistinguishable that I honestly can't tell. Either way, we wind up at a particular door and she steps back and says, "I'll let you go in on your own. I'll wait here until you're finished."

"I won't be long."

"Take as long as you need."

I won't be long. I don't *need* long. I'm only here to say goodbye.

I push through the door and the room on the other side is a lot like the corridor, only wider. Jenny is propped up in bed, with some glossy magazine spread over her knees. When she hears the door, she glances up and looks confused for just an instant, then turns her puzzled look into a smile and says, "Hi there. You've come to see me."

"Jenny. How are you?"

"Oh, I'm great. They cured me. They found a cure."

If she's telling the truth then it's strange, because I've never seen her look this bad. I can't put my finger on why, because she seems as healthy as I've ever known anybody to be, not only not sick but radiant with health. For some reason I find myself remembering again those porcelain dolls of my grandmother's, with their white skin, their black eyes, all of their flawed perfection.

For the first time, I think I understand Jenny. Not this Jenny sitting in front of me, with her neatly-styled hair and her faultless smile, but the Jenny I cared about all those years ago. Suddenly I want to feel sickness writhing in my gut; I want decay and impurity, and fever burning under my skin. More than anything I want to know I'm alive. It occurs to me that this place, this clinic, was never designed for living things to inhabit.

I look at the pristine walls, dizzyingly white like the face of the sun. "Shit," I say, "it's all so ugly."

Jenny only smiles back at me, uncomprehending. "It's kind of boring, isn't it? They've taken good care of me, though."

"Yeah? That's good. I'm glad to hear that." I cough and scuff my feet, no longer sure how to say what I came to say. Then I realize it's really very simple. "Listen, I had an interview a couple of days ago, and, well—I have a job. They're flying me out to Portugal next week, and I really just came by to see how you were and to say goodbye."

"That's great. It's what you always wanted."

It is, isn't it? Suddenly I'm not so sure anymore. Still, I've done what I came for. Not knowing what to do next, I lean over and kiss Jenny on the cheek. Her skin is astonishingly smooth. My stomach revolts, just for an instant.

"Goodbye," I say again, and she smiles and waves back as I walk out the door.

Outside, I pause to lean against the wall. My thoughts are a whirlpool, and my breath comes in shudders. "Goodbye, Jenny," I whisper, one final time. It's not meant for the stranger in the room beyond, but for that impossibly fragile girl I walked away from. Probably I'm the only one who knows to grieve her passing, but a whispered farewell is all the mourning I can offer. Because I can't carry her in my head anymore.

I've got what I wanted; has Jenny as well? She's gone through health and found something beyond, something as virulent as any disease. She's annihilated herself as certainly as any suicide.

I wonder if the doctors realize how she tricked them.

• THE SILENCE OF THE ASONU •
Ursula K. Le Guin

The silence of the Asonu is proverbial. The first visitors believed that these gracious, gracile people were mute, lacking any language other than that of gesture, expression, and gaze. Later, hearing Asonu children chatter, the visitors suspected that among themselves the adults spoke, keeping silence only with strangers. We know now that the Asonu are not dumb, but that once past early childhood they speak only very rarely, to anyone, under any circumstances. They do not write; and unlike mutes, or monks under vows of silence, they do not use any signs or other devices in place of speaking.

This nearly absolute abstinence from language makes them fascinating.

People who live with animals value the charm of muteness. It can be a real pleasure to know when the cat walks into the room that he won't mention any of your shortcomings, or that you can tell your grievances to your dog without his repeating them to the people who caused them.

And those who can talk, but don't, have the great advantage over the rest of us that they never say anything stupid. This may be why we are convinced that if they spoke they would have something wise to say.

Thus there has come to be considerable tourist traffic to the Asonu. Having a strong tradition of hospitality, the Asonu entertain their visitors courteously, though without modifying their own customs. Some people go there simply in order to join the natives in their silence, grateful to spend a few weeks where they do not have to festoon and obscure every human meeting with verbiage. Many such visitors, having been accepted into a household as a paying guest, return year after year, forming bonds of unspoken affection with their quiet hosts.

Others follow their Asonu guides or hosts about, talking to them continually, confiding their whole life stories to them, in rapture at having at last found a listener who won't interrupt or comment or mention that his cousin had an even larger tumor than that. As such people usually know little Asonu and speak mostly or entirely in their own language, they evidently aren't worried by the question that vexes some visitors: Since the Asonu don't talk, do they, in fact, listen?

They certainly hear and understand what is said to them in their own language, since they're prompt to respond to their children, to indicate directions by gesture to inquiring tourists, and to leave a building at the cry of "Fire!" But the question remains, do they listen to discursive speech and sociable conversation, or do they merely hear it, while keeping silently attentive to something beyond speech? Their amiable and apparently easy manner seems to some observers the placid surface of a deep preoccupation, a constant alertness, like that of a mother who while entertaining her guests or seeing to her husband's comfort yet is listening every moment for the cry of her baby in another room.

To perceive the Asonu thus is almost inevitably to interpret their silence as a concealment. As they grow up, it seems, they cease to speak because they are listening to something we do not hear, a secret which their silence hides.

Some visitors to their world are convinced that the lips of these quiet people are locked upon a knowledge which, in proportion as it is hidden, must be valuable—a spiritual treasure, a speech beyond speech, possibly even that ultimate revelation promised by so many religions, and indeed frequently delivered, but never in a wholly communicable form. The transcendent knowledge of the mystic cannot be expressed in language. It may be that the Asonu avoid language for this very reason. It may be that they keep silence because if they spoke everything of importance would have been said.

To some, the utterances of the Asonu do not seem to be as momentous as one might expect from their rarity. They might even be described as banal. But believers in the Wisdom of the Asonu have followed individuals about for years, waiting for the rare words they speak, writing them down, saving them, studying them, arranging and collating them, finding arcane meanings and numerical correspondences in them, in search of the hidden message.

There is no written form of the Asonu language, and translation of speech is considered to be so uncertain that translatomats aren't issued to the tourists, most of whom don't want them anyway. Those who wish to learn Asonu can do so only by listening to and imitating children, who by six or seven years old are already becoming unhappy when asked to talk.

Here are the "Eleven Sayings of the Elder of Isu," collected over four years by a devotee from Ohio, who had already spent six years learning the language from the children of the Isu Group. Months of silence occurred between most of these statements, and two years between the fifth and sixth.

1. Not there.
2. It is almost ready [or] Be ready for it soon.
3. Unexpected!
4. It will never cease.
5. Yes.
6. When?
7. It is very good.
8. Perhaps.
9. Soon.
10. Hot! [or] Very warm!
11. It will not cease.

The devotee wove these eleven sayings into a coherent spiritual statement or testament which he understood the Elder to have been making, little by little, during the last four years of his life. The Ohio Reading of the Sayings of the Elder of Isu is as follows:

"(1) What we seek is not there in any object or experience of our mortal life. We live among appearances, on the verge of the Spiritual Truth. (2) We must be ready for it as it is ready for us, for (3) it will come when we least expect it. Our perception of the Truth is sudden as a lightning-flash, but (4) the Truth itself is eternal and unchanging. (5) Indeed we must positively and hopefully, in a spirit of affirmation, (6) continually ask when, when shall we find what we seek? (7) For the Truth is the medicine for our soul, the knowledge of absolute goodness. (8, 9) It may come very soon. Perhaps it is coming even now in this moment. (10) Its warmth and brightness are as those of the sun, but the sun will perish (11) and the Truth will not perish. Never will the warmth, the brightness, the goodness of the Truth cease or fail us."

Another interpretation of the Sayings may be made by referring to the circumstances in which the Elder spoke, faithfully recorded by the devotee from Ohio, whose patience was equaled only by the Elder's:

1. Spoken in an undertone as the Elder looked through a chest of clothing and ornaments.

2. Spoken to a group of children on the morning of a ceremony.

3. Said with a laugh in greeting the Elder's younger sister, returned from a long trip.

4. Spoken the day after the burial of the Elder's sister.

5. Said while embracing the Elder's brother-in-law some days after the funeral.

6. Asked of an Asonu "doctor" who was making a "spirit-body" drawing in white and black sand for the Elder. These drawings seem to be both curative and diagnostic, but we know very little about them. The observer states that the "doctor's" answer was a short curving line drawn outward from the navel of the "spirit-body" figure.

This, however, may be only the observer's reading of what was not an answer at all.

7. Said to a child who had woven a reed mat.

8. Spoken in answer to a young grandchild who asked, "Will you be at the big feast, Grandmother?"

9. Spoken in answer to the same child, who asked, "Are you going to be dead like Great-Auntie?"

10. Said to a baby who was toddling towards a firepit where the flames were invisible in the sunlight.

11. Last words, spoken the day before the Elder's death.

The last six Sayings were all spoken in the last half-year of the Elder's life, as if the approach of death had made the Elder positively loquacious. Five of the Sayings were spoken to, or in at least in the presence of, young children who were still at the talking stage.

Speech from an adult must be very impressive to an Asonu child. But, like the foreign linguists, Asonu babies must learn the language by listening to older children. The mother and other parents encourage the child to speak only by attentive listening and prompt, affectionate, wordless response.

The Asonu live in close-knit extended-family groups, in frequent contact with other groups. Their pasturing life, following the great flocks of anamanu which furnish them wool, leather, milk, and meat, leads them on a ceaseless seasonal nomadic circuit within a vast shared territory of mountains and foothills. Families frequently leave their family group to go wandering and visiting. At the great festivals and ceremonies of healing and renewal many groups come together for days or weeks, exchanging hospitality. No hostile relations between groups are apparent, and in fact no observer has reported seeing adult Asonu fight or quarrel. Arguments, evidently, are out of the question.

Children from two to six years old chatter to each other constantly; they argue, wrangle, and bicker, and sometimes come to blows. As they come to be six or seven they begin to speak less and to quarrel less. By the time they are eight or nine most of them are very shy of words and reluctant to answer a question except by gesture. They have learned to quietly evade inquiring tourists and linguists with notebooks and recording devices. By adolescence they are as silent and as peaceable as the adults.

Children between eight and twelve do most of the looking after the younger ones. All the children of the family group go about together, and in such groups the two-to-six-year-olds provide language models for the babies. Older children shout wordlessly in the excitement of a game of tag or hide-and-seek, and sometimes scold an errant toddler with a "Stop!" or "No!"—just as the Elder of Isu murmured "Hot!" as a child approached an invisible fire; though of course the Elder may have used that circumstance as a parable, in order to make a statement of profound spiritual meaning, as appears in the Ohio Reading.

Even songs lose their words as the singers grow older. A game rhyme sung by little children has words:

> Look at us tumbledown
> Stumbledown tumbledown
> All of us tumbledown
> All in a heap!

Older children cheerfully play the game with the little ones, falling into wriggling piles with yells of joy, but they do not sing the words, only the tune, vocalized on a neutral syllable.

Adult Asonu often hum or sing at work, while herding, while rocking the baby. Some of the tunes are traditional, others improvised. Many employ motifs based on the whistles of the anamanu. None have words; all are hummed or vocalized. At the meetings of the clans and at marriages and funerals the ceremonial choral music is rich in melody and harmonically complex and subtle. No instruments are used, only the voice. The singers practice many days for the ceremonies. Some students of Asonu music believe that their particular spiritual wisdom or insight finds its expression in these great wordless chorales.

I am inclined to agree with others who, having lived a long time among the Asonu, believe that their choral singing is an element of a sacred occasion, and certainly an art, a festive communal act, and a pleasurable release of feeling, but no more. What is sacred to them remains in silence.

The little children call people by relationship words, mother, uncle, clan-sister, friend, etc. If the Asonu have names, we do not know them.

About ten years ago a zealous believer in the Secret Wisdom of the Asonu kidnapped a child of four from one of the mountain clans in the dead of winter. He had obtained a zoo collector's permit, and smuggled her back to his home world in an animal cage marked "Anamanu." Believing that the Asonu enforce silence on their children, his plan was to encourage the little girl to keep talking as she grew up. When adult, he thought, she would thus be able to speak the innate Wisdom which her people would have obliged her to keep secret.

For the first year or so it appears that she would talk to her kidnapper, who, aside from the abominable cruelty of his action, seems to have begun by treating her kindly enough. His knowledge of the Asonu language was limited, and she saw no one else but a small group of sectarians who came to gaze worshipfully at her and listen to her talk. Her vocabulary and syntax gained no enlargement, and began to atrophy. She became increasingly silent.

Frustrated, the zealot tried to teach her his own language so that she would be able to express her innate Wisdom in a different tongue. We have only his report, which is that she "refused to learn," was silent or spoke almost inaudibly when he tried to make her repeat words, and "did not obey." He ceased to let other people see her. When some members of the sect finally notified the civil authorities, the child was about seven. She had spent three years hidden in a basement room, and for a year or more had been whipped and beaten regularly "to teach her to talk," her captor explained, "because she's stubborn." She was dumb, cowering, undernourished, and brutalized.

She was promptly returned to her family, who for three years had mourned her, believing she had wandered off and been lost on the glacier. They received her with tears of joy and grief. Her condition since then is not known, because the Interplanary Agency closed the entire area to all visitors, tourist or scientist, at the time she was brought back. No foreigner has been up in the Asonu mountains since. We may well imagine that her people were resentful; but nothing was ever said.

• POSTINGS FROM AN AMOROUS TOMORROW •
Corey Mariani

March 11

As of this second there are 3,236,728,909 people over the age of four living in the world, all of whom I am intimately familiar with. Of these, there are 876,852,003 that I love, and one that I am currently *in love* with. In ten years, when I am twenty, I hope to love everyone on the planet as Gordon did once for almost two minutes. He is my hero. Allison says that Gordon is a good hero, and that I have a good shot at achieving my goal, even though I am only ten. She says networking technology gets better every month, and my generation's mutations allow me to assimilate the technology faster than almost anyone, even Gordon.

It feels so good to love people that I just want to love as many people as I can. It usually takes me two days of being intimately familiar with someone before the red heart appears to let me know that I love them. This morning the red heart appeared on Yuri, who lives in Omsk in the province of Russia. I had been expecting the heart to pop up, and it made me happy when it happened because Yuri and I both like playing in the interactive plays, and we also sometimes partner up in the interdependent puzzle games. He doesn't have a dog though, and I always tell him that Allison says that dogs can make your empathy levels higher. Dad says that's probably not true, but I think it doesn't hurt to have a dog anyway. Sometimes my dad gets mad about the dog and talks really fast to my mom about it. He thinks the dog is bad for me because it will make me want to love all the animals in the world the way some other people do, and that is sick and wrong.

I have not reached puberty yet, but I am hoping that when I do I will be bisexual, that way it will be easier for me to fall in love with more people. Allison says that they can make me bisexual if I am not naturally bisexual, but that it is easier always if I am just naturally that way. She also says that I shouldn't worry because every generation has more and more bisexuals in it.

Right now I am only *in love* with one person and her name is Cindy. She has blue eyes and blonde hair and bangs and she is really pretty. She is not *in love* with me, but she does love me. It makes me sad sometimes that she is not *in love* with me, but Allison says that it shouldn't make me too sad because it is very rare for people my age to be *in love* with anyone.

One time during one of my empathy lessons Allison told me that I was the best student she ever had.

• • •

March 12

As of this second 78,232 people have died in the world since my last posting. I only loved 6,721 out of those. I was sadder about the ones I loved more than the ones I was only intimately familiar with. It's sad when people die. There is part of my brain that is always sad, and Allison says that part is like a factory turning sadness into love and empathy all the time. Sometimes I visit that factory when someone I love dies, and it makes me have to sit down, especially when the person that died had two or three of my red hearts. But Allison says that is normal and it means I am healthy.

5,912 people turned four today and I am now intimately familiar with all of them. It is easy to be intimately familiar with four-year-olds because there isn't much there to be intimately familiar with. I remember when I turned four and my parents took me to the clinic where they make your brain bigger. When I woke up after surgery it was like being awake for the first time. I only knew my parents before then, and my two older brothers and my two grandmas and one grandpa, but after the surgery I knew over *a million people*, and even more than that knew me. It was awesome. And it wasn't hard to remember them all either. I could interact with over 400,000 of them at the same time. Now I can interact with over three million at the same time. But Allison says that I am not really interacting with all of them. Not really. What most people I know and love interact with is a computer program version of me. Sometimes I spy on the computer program version of me. It is really weird because it really acts the way I would act. Twice a day I download their experiences into my memory banks. That is how I know so many people.

March 13

I am eating pancakes that Mom made me for breakfast. I am eating them fast because I am almost late for school. She is telling me to stop posting at the table. I don't know how she always knows when I am posting. She says she can tell by the look in my eyes. It is okay for me to interact with almost a million people at the table but it is not okay for me to post because Mom says posting is not a part of my schoolwork and she doesn't know why I do it anyway. Nobody at school does it. And only 70,112 people in the world have done it in the last thirty days. I like to do it because it helps me understand my thoughts.

But I have to stop now. Mom is giving me angry looks.

March 14

We learned about the Dunbar number at school today. The Dunbar number is the number of people that you can have in your social group and still know who they all are. How big the number is depends on how big your brain is. The bigger your brain the more people you can know. Monkeys don't have very big social groups because their brains are very small. A long time ago people's Dunbar number was very small too, like 200 or something, and it caused a lot of fear because most of the people in the world were strangers, and strangers are afraid of strangers because they don't know each other. And there were lots of wars because people didn't know each other and were afraid. Now that everyone knows each other there are no wars and everything is okay.

March 15

Allison is crying. I don't understand. I've never seen her cry before. Now *I* feel like crying. She took me to her office after class and tried to say something but she just cried instead. I ask her what is wrong and she holds up her hand and cries some more. As I wait for her to get done I start crying too. I can't help it. Allison is hurting. We are both crying and I don't know why. Crying feels awful. I am scared and I am very sad.

March 28

The other children and I are in a shed picking out garden tools to use as weapons. I grab a rake. Tom and Sammy and Lydia get shovels, and Katie finds a hoe. The others are finding the same type of stuff, but I am not paying attention anymore because my mind is confused, and I am scared, and it is hard to think and make my mind unconfused when I am scared.

We need the weapons so we can kill Nick. The adults say that these garden tools will work as weapons. There haven't been weapons for many years because no one has needed them. But now we need them because Nick is a sociopath.

It was almost two weeks ago when Allison took me to her office and started crying. After she was done crying, and I was done too, she taught me about sociopaths and how they don't love themselves. There is something bad in their genes that scientists haven't been able to find yet. When sociopaths look at their own profile they do not see any red hearts. I have five of my red hearts in my profile, which is good because Allison says that if you don't love yourself then you can't love other people. That is what's wrong with sociopaths.

Allison says that our world stays together because of empathy. People are always selfish and they always do things for selfish reasons, but that is not bad, that is just how we are made and it cannot be changed. Allison says people don't hurt each other because of empathy. She doesn't hurt me because it would make her feel bad to do that. And it would make her feel bad to do that because then she would be able to imagine my pain, and she would feel that pain even though it wasn't happening to her. And because she loves me that pain would feel even worse. It would be like she was doing something bad to herself. That was why she was crying two weeks ago, because she was hurting herself through me.

It made her very sad to ask me and the other children to kill Nick. Nick had stopped loving himself, and that made him a sociopath and a danger to the social group. He hadn't killed anyone yet, but the adults could not take the chance. Allison said that when I was very little there was a man who stopped loving himself and became a sociopath. He killed men, women, and children, and he took over the whole province of France all by himself and made the men, women, and children worship him and do strange things. And they called him a dictator. I remember asking my dad when I was very little what the word meant and my dad pointed my mind to the sociopath's face and said, "That is what it means." There was nothing the people of France could do about the dictator because their empathy training made it impossible for them to hurt another person. The training was glued in their brains and they couldn't get it out because they were too old and their brains were too set. That's when someone thought of the children, whose brains had not been set. And so they gave the children garden tools to kill the dictator with. And that was how they saved the province of France and maybe the world.

Now there was a new dictator rising in the sub-province of Ohio and his name was Nick. Soon he would start killing people and making the ones that lived do strange things. And there was nothing the adults could do about it. That was why they asked me and my classmates to pick up garden tools like the children of France.

Allison holds the shed door open while my friends walk in and grab their weapons. She looks very scared. All the adults that are gathered around look very scared. My parents are crying. I look at them and I cannot feel sadness. I cannot cry. Maybe I have already cried out all the tears that are in me. For the last two weeks, they have stopped us from taking our empathy lessons. Instead they flash ugly pictures in our minds. The pictures do not stop and I cannot get away from them. I see bodies, piles of them. Some are being eaten by wolves and vultures. Some are being burned. I see humans turn into bodies after a thing called a bullet is fired through their heads. The change does not even take a second. I see people beaten to death by lots of other people. I see one man get his head chopped off. It takes the other man who is doing the chopping several chops to get the thing done, and the man who is getting chopped makes terrible sounds while it happens.

At first when the adults showed us these pictures we cried and screamed and we closed our eyes really tight because it felt like it would make them stop, but it didn't. One time, Tom started banging his head against the wall and some of the other children did too. The adults had to come in and stop them. After the fifth day, it seemed like everyone was getting kind of used to the ugly pictures, I think. I know *I* kind of was. No one screamed anymore or banged their heads against the wall. We all just sat at our desks staring straight ahead.

Everyone in the world knew what was happening. Everyone that I loved and who loved me was trying to interact with me and send me their love. But ever since I stopped taking my empathy lessons and started seeing awful things, I could barely interact with more than 200,000 of them at a time. I felt their love though, and it made me feel better. It made me feel strong. I knew that what I was doing was for them because they could not do it for themselves. And I knew it was for me also. And so I keep posting for the people that I cannot interact with.

We are gathered outside of Nick's house now. All the parents and the teachers from the school are behind us. They are crying still. I am starting to have a terrible feeling about their crying. I am starting to hate it, I think. All they do is cry. My classmates and I are walking up to Nick's house, surrounding it, holding garden tools that are meant to kill Nick, and all the adults do is cry.

Katie lights Nick's house on fire with some liquid that Jake's dad gave us and a lighter. The adults are all hoping that Nick will stay inside and die without anyone having to see it. I was hoping that too before, but now I am hoping that Nick will come out and the adults will have to watch while almost a hundred of us children beat Nick to death with garden tools. I want them to see something like what they made me see.

But that does not happen. We stand there for I don't know how long, a really long time, and watch the house burn to the ground. Nick does not come out. We don't even hear him scream. I feel disappointed somehow. I know it is wrong to feel that way, but that is how I feel.

I am mad at the adults now, more than anything. It seems to me that they could have lit that house on fire just as easily as we did. They didn't have to show us all of those awful things. They are still crying now. I want them to shut up. They didn't even do anything.

May 2

It has been over a month since I stood outside of Nick's house and watched it (and him) burn. Now there is only one of my red hearts showing in my profile. I am looking at that red heart all the time these days. I am scared that it will go out, but I am also not scared. I wonder what will happen if it ever does go out. Will the adults—will my parents—send my classmates to kill me? If I don't love myself anymore, will I become a sociopath? I really don't know. Sometimes I wonder if Nick was ever going to kill people at all. I wonder if we killed him for no reason. I was intimately familiar with Nick before he died. He liked music a lot, and he was really good at playing it on the clarinet.

I remember that he didn't have very many people that he loved, and there weren't many people that loved him. Mostly he played his music. And he also had plants. I remember that he had plants and he took care of them really well. He watered them every day and he gave them special food that would make them grow big and strong and healthy. I remember Nick. I am sad for Nick.

I don't keep track of how many people I love anymore, but I am pretty sure that it is not very many because Allison is always coming up to me and asking me to talk to her in her office. She is worried about me and says that I have experienced something very traumatic, and that it will take time but I will heal. But I don't believe her when she says that I will heal. I think that she is just lying to herself because it makes her feel good. I can see in her eyes that she is scared of me. It makes me angry. It makes me angry that she is so weak. It reminds me of my parents and the weakness of all the adults that I know. And I am angry that almost half of the world thinks they know me.

They do not know me.

Sometimes I think of those children in the province of France that killed the dictator. I think they could know me. I look for them sometimes online but I can't find them. I hear that they went into the hills or mountains someplace and got rid of the brains they were given when they were four. Now they live like humans used to live. Sometimes I think that I should go find them. Then sometimes I think that my classmates and I should go do what they did. I love my classmates. They know me and I know them. I think they are all that keeps that red heart in my profile from blinking out.

· CUCUMBER GRAVY ·
Susan Palwick

I wasn't too happy when the knocking started on my door that morning. Nobody's welcome out here except UPS and customers, and I wasn't expecting any deliveries, and customers have to call first. New buyers have to be referred by people I know. That's a rule. I check references, too. I don't let anybody in who isn't vouched for, and even so, it's amazing I've never had cops out here. Some of my buyers ask why I didn't go legit when the medical-marijuana bill passed four years ago, but that's a no-brainer: I do not need the government crawling up my backside to regulate me, and I have a lot more customers this way, and I make a lot more money. Being legal would be nothing but a pain in the ass, even if I didn't have to worry about keeping people from finding out about the space cucumbers.

As it happened, my latest bunch of cucumbers was due to start singing any minute, which meant the last thing I needed was somebody in the house. That's another reason buyers have to call first: depending on what the cucumbers are up to, I tell people they have to wait, I can't see them today.

So when the knocking started, I thought, *shit, government,* and my stomach tied up in a knot. I'd have pretended I wasn't home, but you can get stranded motorists out here too, and the sooner you let them use your phone or whatever, the sooner they go away. So when I heard that knock and looked out and didn't recognize who was there—some bearded guy pushing forty, about my age, in jeans and a plaid shirt and hiking boots, had tree-hugging liberal written all over him—I grabbed my gun and yelled through the door, "Who is it?" Since it was only one guy, that made cops less likely, but on the other hand his car was in front of the house, a nice little Toyota, which made mechanical failure less likely, too. Maybe he had to use the bathroom, in which case I'd tell him to use the desert. If he needed water I'd give him some, though. You always give people water, out here. You'd think people would know not to drive anywhere in this state without extra water in the car, but between the dumb college kids from Reno and the morons moving here from California, the average survival IQ in Nevada isn't what it should be. This guy was too old to be in college, so I pegged him as Californian. Local folks only drive in the desert with four-wheel drive.

"Mr. Whitwell Smith?" he yelled through the door. "Welly?"

"Yeah?" Only buyers call me Welly: It's a kind of code. I'm Whit to everybody else, not that I've talked to much of anybody else since Nancy Ann left. "Who wants to know?"

"My name's Jim Humphreys." The name didn't mean anything to me. "I'm a friend of Sam Mortimer's."

That name did. Sam used to be one of my best customers, out here once a month spending big money, until he suddenly stopped coming altogether about six months ago. No call, nothing. I'd been wondering what happened to him, not that it's any of my business. I'd almost started to think of Sam as a friend, I'd known him so long; we'd even gone skeet-shooting on my property a few times. "Yeah? You know Sam, you know you have to call before you come out here. Sam knows that."

"I've been trying to call for three days, Mr. Smith. Your phone's out of order."

Shit. That was the first I knew of it. I hadn't gotten any calls for three days, but that's not unusual: You never know when business is going to be slow, and nobody else calls me. But it could still be a trick. "You wait just a minute," I hollered through the door, and ran and picked up the phone. Dead. No dial tone. Nothing. Which meant I'd have to get telephone repair people out here, but that would have to wait until the latest batch of cucumbers was gone. In the meantime, I turned on my cell phone in case anybody was trying to reach me. I don't like the cell phone; I don't like having my conversations broadcast all over hell and gone for the government to spy on. But you have to have a cell phone for emergencies, just like you have to have water. If you miss a customer call, you could lose business.

"Okay," I hollered, back at the door. "Thank you for telling me about the telephone, but I can't see you today. We can make an appointment—"

"Mr. Smith, I drove seventy miles to get here, and this is an emergency. Please open the door."

Emergency? Nobody'd ever used that line on me before. My crop isn't addictive, which is one of the things I like about it. You don't get strung-out dopeheads at your door who'd murder their own mothers for their next fix. Who needs that kind of trouble?

I checked my watch. The cucumbers were due to start singing in about thirty minutes, but sometimes they go off early. I'm never sure exactly when they've gotten here, which makes the timing tricky, and that means I wasn't about to open the door. "If it's an emergency, call 911, Mr. Humphreys. I'm not in that line of work."

"Welly, *please*. Sam's very sick. He has cancer. He had surgery four months ago and now he's having chemo and it's making him sicker than a dog, and the prescription stuff isn't working for him. He says it isn't strong enough. He says yours is the best. He sent me out here with two hundred and fifty dollars to buy some. Please don't send me back to that poor man empty-handed."

"Huh," I said. I wasn't surprised the government couldn't grow good plants.

They were probably growing oregano and charging pot prices for it; you can't trust those people as far as you can throw them. I started with the best stock when I got into business fifteen years ago, and I've been refining it since then. Genetics was my favorite part of biology in high school.

I looked at my watch again. I could run and get a quarter bag and shove it through the door and pull this Humphreys' cash in, and it would all be over in ten seconds. And if the cucumbers started up and he heard them, I'd tell him it was the TV. "You wait there," I called out. "I'll be right back."

I ran and got a quarter bag and a paper lunch sack, and put the gun on a shelf near the door, where I could grab it fast if I had to, but Humphreys couldn't reach inside and get it, and then I opened the door a crack, as far as the chain would allow. "Here," I said. I held up the quarter bag so he could see it, and dropped it in the lunch sack. "You pass the money through, you get this."

He held up a sheaf of bills and slipped them through. All singles and fives, Jesus, what had Sam been thinking? Come to think of it, a quarter bag wouldn't get him very far, not given Sam's smoking habits, but I was guessing he didn't have much money left over, after the cancer. He'd probably been saving up since the chemo started, the poor bastard, and insurance wouldn't pay for mine. I wondered if I should give him some extra for free—he'd been a very good customer for a long time—but in the meantime, I started counting the bills. Old habits.

While I was counting, Humphreys said drily, "Sam said you let him come into the house." I could hear him more clearly now, with the door open, and something about his voice nagged at me. He had a little bit of an accent, English or Aussie maybe. Where had I heard a voice like that lately?

"I know Sam," I said. "No offense." I finished counting—it was all there— and then I handed the bag through. As I did, I got a good look at Humphreys' face for the first time, and two things happened at once.

The first thing was that I recognized him from TV. You just don't see many preachers with Aussie accents feeding bag ladies on the news, especially when the preacher has one deformed ear, the right one, all ugly and lumpy and crumpled up like a cauliflower. I hadn't picked up on the ear before because I'd only gotten a side view of him when I looked out the window.

The second thing was that the cucumbers starting singing, all three of them at once: Wails and whistles and grunts, like a cross between a porno soundtrack and an orchestra of teakettles.

Humphreys' eyes widened. "What—"

"It's the TV," I said, and tried to slam the door, but I couldn't because he'd wedged his foot in there, and he was staring behind me, goggle-eyed. When I turned to look over my shoulder, I saw that one of the cucumbers had staggered out of the den, away from its friends and the nice warm heaters, and was hopping in pathetic circles around my living room, which makes it the first time in almost ten years that a cucumber's moved from where I put it once it got into the house.

I was about to have a very bad day.

The space cucumbers started coming here a few months after Nancy Ann ran off. I don't know why they picked this place—it's just a ranch house out in the middle of nowhere, halfway between Reno and Gerlach, with nothing to look at but sagebrush and lizards and alkali dust, so flat that the mountains on the horizon seem like a mirage—and I never have figured out how they keep from attracting the attention of the air base in Stead. Those bastards are government, and I figure they have to have instruments that can tell if you throw a penny in the air, and the cucumbers have to come in some kind of ship, or come down through the atmosphere, anyway. And you see those air base planes and 'copters doing maneuvers out here all the time, so I don't know why they've never picked up on what's going on. I guess the cucumbers are smarter than they are. It's not hard to be smarter than the government.

I call them space cucumbers because they look like a sea cucumber I saw once—or at least, they look more like that than like anything else. My parents took me on a trip to San Diego when I was a kid, and we went to the aquarium there. They had all kinds of animals, scary ones like sharks and smart ones like dolphins and whales who did tricks, but for some reason, the one I always remembered best was the sea cucumber. It was lying in a tank of water, in this kind of petting zoo they had, and you could reach in and touch it. It was brown and very, very soft, and if somebody had grabbed it and started cutting it into pieces, it couldn't have fought back. It didn't swim or do tricks. It didn't do anything. It just sat there. The aquarium lady said it ate by filtering tiny bits of food out of the water. It was a really boring animal, and I never have known why it made such an impression on me. Probably because I couldn't figure out how a creature like that could survive in the ocean with sharks and lobsters and stingrays. "I guess sharks don't think they taste good," the aquarium lady said, but you could tell she didn't know either. That cucumber was a mystery.

Which is what mine are, too. They show up two or three at a time, every five or six weeks. I just open the door in the morning and there they are, waiting on my welcome mat. They're much bigger than the sea cucumber in San Diego, about three feet tall and as thick around as a flagpole, and I can't touch them because they're wrapped in something like plastic. Like really thick shrink wrap. Or maybe that's their skin, but I don't think so: I think it's some kind of spacesuit, and the animal's the thing inside, the brown blobby cylindrical thing that hops along on nine stubby little legs, all clustered at the bottom of the cylinder, like tentacles. Hopping isn't easy for them, you can tell—I don't think it's how they usually move around, wherever they come from—so I usually pick them up to carry them inside. Wherever they're from, they've come a long way to get here, and I figure if there's anything I can do to make it easier for them, why not? They're always exactly air temperature, or the shrink wrap is, and they're not as heavy as you'd expect from their size. I can just stick them under my arm, like pieces of firewood.

When the first ones came I was terrified, of course. The cucumbers would have been weird whenever they showed up, but Nancy Ann had just left, and I was out of my mind with grief and anger, smoking entirely too much of my own crop just to get to sleep at night. I felt like I was going crazy, and having space cucumbers on my welcome mat didn't help. I didn't know what they were or what they wanted. I didn't know if they were going to kill me or take over the planet or poison the water supply, and I couldn't ask anybody because that would have gotten the government involved, and even if I trusted the government I couldn't have people tramping around my house and finding the plants and grow lights and sprinklers in the basement. I have one hell of a professional setup down there: no way I could argue personal use, even if possession weren't still a felony for anybody without an approved medical condition.

The first time they showed up and hopped into the house, I just went weak in the knees and started babbling at them, trying to figure out what they wanted, trying to find some way to communicate. Didn't work, of course. If they can talk or understand me when I talk, I haven't found any way to tell, not in all these years. Maybe the singing's some kind of language, like what whales have, but if so I haven't figured it out yet, and they never respond in any way I can tell when I say things to them. That first visit, they all hopped over to my wood stove and stood around it, shaking, and the entire forty-eight hours until they started singing, I don't think I slept a wink. I didn't know what they were going to do. I didn't dare shoot them because I didn't want to give them an excuse to destroy the planet, and anyway I could tell even then they had some kind of suit on, and if I broke through it and whatever they were made of came out, who knew what kind of plague I'd start? I never have breached one of those suits.

They didn't do anything that first time, of course, not until they started singing. When the noise started, I got into a duck-and-cover position under my coffee table because I thought they were going to attack me. And then when nothing happened and the singing stopped, I just crouched there, waiting, until about half an hour later the first one liquefied on me, and then within half an hour after that, the other two had gone gravy, too.

You know those gravy packets that come with some kinds of TV dinners?

The plastic pouches you throw into boiling water and then pull out of the pot with tongs, so you can cut them open to pour the gravy out? I guess some people use microwaves, but I think boiling water works better. Anyway, that's what the cucumbers look like when they liquefy: giant gravy pouches. There's a big *sploosh,* and then all of a sudden where there used to be something that looked like an animal, there's just brown mush. If you pick up the suit then, it's like holding a bag of thick brown water, and frankly it's pretty disgusting. The first time I saw it, I nearly got sick, and then I got even more scared, wondering what would happen next.

Nothing happened. Nothing's ever happened, after they go gravy. I think they're dead, then. As near as I can tell, they come here to die. Why they'd come here, I have no idea. Don't think I haven't thought about it, but I've never come up with any idea that makes sense. The first few times it happened, I thought they'd just crashed here or gotten stranded, like motorists without water, and Earth had killed them somehow, or I had. But it's been happening every five or six weeks for ten years, so now I think they come here deliberately. Maybe this is some kind of pilgrimage for them; maybe my house was built on some kind of alien shrine, like Area 51. I just don't know. And I could be wrong, anyway. Maybe they aren't dead at all. Maybe if I opened one of the suits up, they'd come back to life.

For a while I kept some of the cucumber-gravy bags stacked out where the newest ones could see them when they showed up; I thought maybe they'd show me somehow what to do with them. They never responded at all. It was like the gravy packets weren't even there. Don't ask me what kind of animal doesn't recognize its own dead. Then I kept some of those first packets down in the basement, to see if they'd change over time, but they didn't. The suits keep whatever's inside from decomposing more, I guess.

Now I bury them. I've got forty acres here. I don't know what I'll do when my land gets filled in. Go out into the desert, I guess, and try to find places where people won't see me, places that aren't likely to get developed. Who knows what would happen if a backhoe sliced through one of those suits? None of the ones I've buried have ever gotten dug up by coyotes. I guess the cucumbers, dead or alive, are as invisible to coyotes as they are to the government. And as far as I know, the government hasn't seen me digging, either. I don't dig any time I can see or hear planes or 'copters, not that that's any guarantee.

For a while at the beginning I thought maybe the cucumbers really were invisible, thought I was having hallucinations, losing it over Nancy Ann. I drove into Reno a bunch of times to use the Internet at the library—I won't have a computer here because I don't trust the government not to spy on what I'm looking up—and did research, trying to find out if anyone else was reporting space aliens who looked like sea cucumbers. Nothing. I keep checking, every six months or so, but if other people are getting visits, I've never found any sign of it. I've read about crop circles and UFO abductions and all kinds of damnfool things, but never anything about singing cucumbers in plastic suits who turn into mush.

After a few visits, I wasn't scared of them anymore. They're nothing if not predictable. Every five or six weeks I wake up and open the door and find a couple or three on my welcome mat. I've never seen any bright lights in the middle of the night, or heard anything; I just open the door and there they are. And they hop into the house, and forty-eight hours later, give or take an hour, they start singing. They sing for three to seven minutes, and within an hour after that, they go gravy.

Sometimes I wonder what my life would be like if they'd never started coming. Would I still be living here? Would I have taken all the money I've made and moved to Hawaii, the way Nancy Ann and I always planned? Would I have taken that trip around the world I dreamed about when I was a kid? As it is, three or four times a year I take off for a week or two, always right after the latest cucumbers have gone gravy. I go someplace fancy, someplace that might as well be a different planet—New York or New Orleans or Bermuda—and I live it up. Good hotels, good food, high-class hookers. Those women like me. I tip well, and I treat them like human beings. They don't have to worry that I'll get ugly on them, and I don't have to worry that they'll break my heart. Works out for everybody. I could use Nevada hookers too, of course, the legal ones, and sometimes I do, but it feels less like a vacation that way.

I enjoy those trips. But I always come back home, because I always know another batch of cucumbers will be landing on my welcome mat.

I've learned what they like over the years, or I think I have. They like heat: They shake and shiver less the closer they are to the wood stove, or something else warm. I don't like having them in my living room for anyone to see, so early on I covered up the windows in the den and got some heavy-duty space heaters in there, the most powerful ones I could find at Home Depot. I figure the cucumbers wouldn't move close to things that made them shake less unless shaking less meant they were comfortable or happy, so I started paying attention to what else makes them shake. I feel itchy when they shake; it's like watching someone about to sneeze. They're happier on soft things than on the floor, so I used to cover the floor of the den with pillows, but then one time I had an old black-and-white polka-dot beanbag chair and the cucumber sitting on that shook less than the ones on the pillows did. I experimented, moving them around—I felt fine picking them up by then—and all of them seemed to like the beanbag chair better, although some of them shook a little more on it than others did. They seem to have individual tastes, although I can't tell them apart to look at them.

So I went to Wal-Mart—no sense buying fancy when budget will do—and bought a bunch of beanbag chairs. One of them was a really ugly day-glo pink, and I found out the cucumbers liked that better than the other colors, so I went back to Wal-Mart, but they were out of pink ones. They had day-glo orange and yellow and green, so I got those. The cucumbers love those day-glo beanbags. They seem to have different favorite colors, so when they get here I have to spend some time moving them around to see which one likes which color. But all of them like the day-glo chairs better than anything else.

The walls are another thing. Most of my house is decorated with Penthouse Pets and some Playboy pictures. That started as revenge after Nancy Ann left, but I kept doing it, because it makes me happy. Those women are even more beautiful than the hookers I hire, who can't always arrange perfect lighting. But the cucumbers hate those pictures. Once I held one up to my favorite Penthouse Pet, as a kind of joke, and that cuke started shaking like it was about to explode. I tried it with a few others: same thing. Maybe they think naked humans look repulsive, the way lots of people would think the cucumbers themselves do.

So I drove into the library and got out a bunch of art books and started showing them pictures. They don't have eyes that I can tell, but if you hold a picture up to any place along the middle of the cucumber, it will respond. French painters, that's how they voted. Especially Matisse and Monet. So now I've got Matisse and Monet posters all over the walls of the den. I think those pictures are about as exciting as watching paint dry, and they seriously clash with the day-glo beanbags, not that I'm Martha Stewart. But when I put the cucumbers in that room now, they hardly shake at all.

Of course, there's always the chance I'm wrong about all of it. If there's anything I've learned, it's that you can't trust appearances, even in your own species. I loved Nancy Ann, and I thought she loved me. She was as beautiful as a Penthouse Pet, and she was smart and funny and taught me how to cook. I loved her even after she got religion; I loved her even after she started telling me that I was going to go to hell for cursing and growing pot and reading *Penthouse,* even when she said I was possessed by the devil. I figured she was saying all those mean things because she loved me too and didn't want me to go to hell, and even though I didn't believe in hell and never have, I tried to make her happy. I didn't shut down my business, of course, because we needed the money if we were going to move to Hawaii, which was what Nancy Ann wanted. She had expensive tastes, anyway: Diamonds and perfume and a new sports car every couple of years. She cut down on some of that stuff after she got religion, I'll give her that. She said showiness was the sin of pride. Since she seemed serious about it, I tried to curse less, and I canceled my *Penthouse* subscription for a while, and I even went to church with her a couple of times, to hear the Reverend Jebediah Wilkins bellow about Jesus and Satan and hellfire and how we had to *tithe* to the *Lord* if we wanted to be *saved*, hallelujah, while people nodded and moaned and said, "Oh yes, tell it brother," all around us.

That church was the scariest thing I've ever seen, much worse than space cucumbers could ever be. But I tried to love Nancy Ann through all of it, I really did. And I thought she was trying to love me too. And then one day I came home from a trip to town, where I'd just bought her some of her favorite perfume, because it was her birthday and she deserved something nice on her birthday, even if it would have been pride any other time. And I found all her things gone and a note on the kitchen table saying she wouldn't be back, because she'd found true love with Jebediah Wilkins. She said she'd be praying for me, oh yes she would, praying that I'd change my sinful ways before the Lord struck me down and I burned in hellfire forever.

So naturally I was not happy to have a preacher at my front door, staring at a space cucumber staggering in circles around my living room. The one time I've got unwanted company, and that's when the cucumbers have to go and do something different. I wish I could say I handled the whole thing calmly, but I didn't. I flat-out panicked. I'm not sure I've ever moved that fast before; I got the chain off the door and grabbed Humphreys and yanked him inside, and grabbed my gun off the shelf and aimed it at him. "The safety's still on," I said, raising my voice over the cucumbers' singing, "but if you do anything funny, it won't be, I'll blow your head off, I swear to God—"

Humphreys held his hands up and tried to say something, but it came out as a squeak. He was shaking worse than the cucumbers ever have, and I knew the cucumber behind me was too, although I couldn't turn around to look, because I had to keep an eye on Humphreys. Don't ask me what I thought he was going to do: go to the government, or start raving about Satan and try to burn my house down. All I knew was that I couldn't let him leave, once he'd seen the cucumber, and I'd never killed a man before and didn't want to, but I had no idea how else I was going to get out of this one, except that Sam was expecting Humphreys back with the crop and if Humphreys didn't come back Sam would call the police and—

You can see how clearly I was thinking. About all I could figure was that I was doomed. I couldn't see any way out that didn't involve a jail cell or worse.

Humphreys found his voice, then. "Please," he said. "Welly, don't shoot me. I don't—I don't—"

It occurred to me right then that if I could get that cucumber back into the den, where it belonged, maybe I could convince him he'd just been seeing things. And he'd just bought a quarter bag from me, which made him a felon too. He wouldn't want his flock to know about that, except Sam. Preachers may be hypocrites, but most of them try to hide it. I had some leverage here.

I started calming down. The cucumber in the living room stopped singing, too, so it was a little easier to think. "Sit down," I said. "Right there. With your back to the wall." He did, just slid down that wall with his hands still up, and I said, "If you don't move, you'll be fine. Got it?" He nodded, his eyes still big, but he was watching me and the gun, not the cucumber. "Close your eyes," I said, and he did—he was still shaking, you'd better believe it—and I backed up, keeping the gun on him, and scooped that crazy lost cucumber back under my arm so I could take it back into the den.

But it picked that very instant to go *sploosh,* and Humphreys' eyes flew open at the extra noise—I guess he couldn't help it—and he saw that bag of cucumber gravy, and he turned green and gulped and whatever he'd had to eat that day came back up, all over his lap and my carpet. While he was heaving I backed up quick and opened the door to the den and tossed the gravy bag inside, and slammed the door shut again. I don't know if Humphreys saw that or not; he was busy reviewing the contents of his stomach. When he'd finished losing his breakfast he looked up at me, his face wet the way it gets after you've thrown up, and said, "I'm sorry. I really am sorry. I'll clean it up. If you bring me some soap and water and some rags—"

"Never mind that," I said. "I'll clean it up myself. You just get out of here, Reverend. You get out of here and bring Sam his medicine. You didn't see anything unusual, you hear me?"

He shook his head. "What *was* that?"

"It wasn't anything." One of the other cucumbers stopped singing, and I said, "You haven't seen or heard anything. Go on home, now." He just looked at me. The third cucumber shut up, so the house was very quiet, all of a sudden. I still had the gun trained on Humphreys; the safety was still on. I clicked it off and said, "Reverend, you need to go home now."

He swallowed. He'd stopped shaking. When he spoke again, his voice was a lot calmer than it had been before. "Mr. Smith, I've been in front of guns before. The worst you can do to me is kill me. I have to know one thing: That— that creature I didn't see, is it dangerous?"

"Something you didn't see can't be dangerous, Reverend. Go home."

He shook his head again. "I wish that were true, but it's not. What we pretend not to see is what harms us. And if anyone's in danger—"

"Nobody's in danger but you, Reverend." I was starting to panic again. This guy wasn't going to let himself be convinced that the cucumber had just been his imagination. "As far as I know, the creature you didn't see isn't dangerous to anybody. Now go home!"

He just looked at me. He looked very sad. "If it's not dangerous, then why did you kill it?"

I lost it, then. Everything piled into my head in that one instant: how Nancy Ann had told me I was evil and how she'd left me even though I tried to make her happy, and all the work I'd done over the years to try to keep those cucumbers comfortable, to keep them from shaking. Jim Humphreys didn't understand a single goddamn thing. "I *didn't* kill it! It just died! That's what they do! They die! That's how they die! They've been coming here to die for ten years and you don't know a single thing about it, but you think you know everything, don't you? You think those creatures are the minions of Satan and you think I'm going to hell for taking care of them and for having pictures of naked women on the walls and for selling pot, and you think you can come in here and—"

"Welly!" he said. He sounded like I'd hit him over the head with one of those beanbag chairs. "Welly, if I thought you were going to hell for selling marijuana, why would I have come here to buy some for Sam?"

"How do I know? So you could preach to me about it! So you could preach to Sam and tell him he's going to hell! He probably confessed that he'd been smoking because he's dying and scared for his soul, because you people have your hooks in him just like you got them into my wife. I bet you smoke yourself, don't you? I bet you stand up every Sunday and preach about how drugs are a sin and everybody has to give you their money so they'll be saved, and then you come out here and spend that money on pot for yourself. All those fives and singles came from the collection plate, didn't they? Little old ladies giving you their last dollar and then you turn around and spend it on—"

"It's Sam's money," Jim Humphreys said. "The marijuana's for him, Welly. You can call and ask him. I have a phone in the car."

"I'm not done!" I said. "You just listen to me." It felt awfully good to yell at him like that, to have a man on the floor in front of me and to be able to point a gun at him and tell him exactly what I thought of him and have him not be able to do anything about it. It felt better than anything had felt in a long time. "I know about you people! Don't think I don't! I know how you ministers act in the pulpit, trying to scare ordinary folks who are just trying to get by and do the best they can, and then you turn around and you run off with people's wives after you've had the goddamned fucking nerve to make all that noise about the devil! Your kind think they're better than the rest of the world, don't they? Don't they, Reverend? You think you can tell me everything about who I am and how I should live my life, like you've got God in your pocket. Your people think that all they have to do to be saved is to put somebody else down—"

"My people," said Jim Humphreys, very quietly, "believe in welcoming all strangers as Christ." I squinted at him, because I couldn't believe how calm he was, and he said, "Even strangers who aren't human. I don't think I need to tell you anything about that, Welly. I think you've been welcoming strangers as Christ for—what did you say? Ten years? And if you're doing a better job with them than you're doing with me, well, that's because you think I'm not a stranger. You think you know who I am. But you're wrong, Welly. I'm a stranger, too."

I was ashamed, then, of how good I'd felt when I was yelling at him. And then I got angry again because he'd made me ashamed, which was what Nancy Ann and Jebediah had always tried to do. "High and mighty, aren't you? I bet you think I'm the scum of the earth—"

"I think you're scared," he said. "I think that if I were in your place, I'd be scared too. And I think it must be awfully hard, having to watch things die like that for ten years, without being able to talk to anybody about it."

I got a lump in my throat when he said that. It shocked me, because I hadn't cried since Nancy Ann left, and I was damned if I was going to start in front of this preacher. "It's not like that," I said. "It's not like I know them. They all look the same and they all die the same way, and I don't know how to talk to them. This is where they come and I do the best for them I can, but I don't get attached, Reverend. So don't get all sentimental."

He smiled, sitting there on the floor in his own puke. "All right. I won't. But would you mind if I cleaned up the floor here?"

Kicking him out hadn't worked. I might as well let him clean up his own mess. "Go on," I said, and used the gun to wave him into the kitchen. "Bucket and rags are under the sink." I watched while he filled the bucket with soapy water and carried it back into the living room and knelt down and cleaned up the mess. He did a good job; he was careful about it. When he was done he took everything back into the kitchen and rinsed it all out, and then he put a little clean water in the bucket and turned around and looked at me.

"Welly, I'd like to—may I visit your guests? May I see them?"

What the hell. He knew too much already; I wasn't going to get anywhere by trying to keep it from him. And I was starting to be curious about what he'd think of them, frankly. And I guess I wanted him to see that I wasn't just killing them. He'd struck a nerve there I didn't even know I had.

I looked at my watch. We had twenty-five minutes before the others went gravy, max, if they hadn't already. I didn't know what had gotten into the one who ran into the living room. Maybe it was crazy or extra sick, or maybe the cucumbers were about to start pulling new tricks on me, in which case I couldn't count on anything. "I don't know if the others are still alive," I said. "They may have gone gr—they may have died while we were out here. When they sing like that, it means they're going to die pretty soon. So they may look like that other one, now. I'm just warning you."

"Thank you," he said. "I think I'll be fine now." So I took him into the den. It was way too hot in there, with the space heaters, but that's how the cucumbers like it. I still had the gun with me, just in case Humphreys tried to pull something. The other two cucumbers were still solid. I'd never taken a gun into the den before and I was a little worried about how they'd respond, if they'd start shaking again, but they didn't even seem to notice.

Jim Humphreys had a plan, you could tell. He didn't pay attention to anything in that room except those two solid cucumbers. He got down on his knees right away and started muttering and waving his hands over the water in the bucket. Then he dipped his hand in the water and used it to make a sign of the cross on each cucumber—which was awfully brave, really, since it had taken me months to be comfortable touching them, but I guess he'd seen that I was okay after picking that other one up—and mumbled some more. "Look at you," I said. I didn't know whether to be impressed or disgusted. "You talk about welcoming all strangers as Christ and here you are trying to do an exorcism—"

He looked up at me, looking shocked. "Oh, no!" Then he looked a little sheepish. "Emergency baptisms. Although it's somewhat the same thing." He rocked back on his heels and stood up and said, "Now what?"

I shrugged. "Now nothing. Now they have"—I checked my watch—"maybe fifteen minutes left."

He looked at his watch, too. "May I wait here with them? Would that be all right?"

"I don't see why not," I said. He nodded and sat down on the floor, and I sat on the polka-dot beanbag chair. "All right, Reverend. You tell me this. If all strangers are Christ already, why do they have to be baptized?"

Humphreys smiled. "You should be a theologian. That's a good question. Mainly because it's what I know how to do, and it makes me feel better."

"Huh! You think it'll do them any good?"

"I have no idea. I don't see how it can hurt them." He looked around the room, then, up at the walls, and raised his eyebrows. "Matisse?"

"They like Matisse. Or I think they do. Don't ask me, Reverend. I don't know a damn thing. I do this and I do that, and I find chairs I think they like, and I say they're dying, but I could be wrong about all of it. They're not from around here. They're not dogs or cats; they're not the same kind of animal we are at all. I try to keep them still and happy, but maybe when they're still that means they're in pain. Maybe I've been torturing them all this time without meaning to. Maybe they're invading Earth and I'm the one making it possible, and in another ten years all these dead aliens are going to come back to life and take over the world."

He listened to me, his face still and serious. "Yes. It's hard, isn't it, not knowing if we're doing the right thing? I don't think any of us ever know, not really. We do the best we can, and we pray to do more good than harm, but we have to trust God to see it all, and to sort it all out, and to forgive us when we go wrong."

I looked away from him. "I don't believe in God. No offense."

"None taken, Welly."

"Good. What happened to your ear? I saw you on TV, feeding those bag ladies. That's how I knew who you were, when I saw your ear."

"It's a birth defect. My family didn't have enough money for plastic surgery." He shrugged. "I used to keep my hair long to hide it, but it doesn't bother me anymore. It's a help in my work, frankly. People bring their scars to church. They bring the wounds they want healed, but they're ashamed of them, too. If they can see mine, that makes it easier."

"I'll just bet," I said. Nancy Ann had a little scar on the inside of her left thigh, high up. It was a birthmark, too, like Humphreys' ear. It didn't take Jebediah very long to see that one, did it?

The second cucumber went *sploosh,* just then, and Humphreys and I both jumped a little. Humphreys didn't puke this time; he got back on his knees and made another sign of the cross and muttered some more. When he was done I picked up that gravy bag and put it in the corner with the other one, the one I'd tossed back into the den from the living room, and then Humphreys and I sat back down to wait for the third cucumber to go gravy. Five minutes, now.

"Why do you suppose they come here?" he asked me.

"Damned if I know. Maybe they're sick and their people send them away so they won't infect everybody else. Maybe they're dead already when they get here, and Earth's their eternal reward. Now that's scary, isn't it? Maybe when we die we're all going to land on some alien's doorstep, and we just have to hope they'll have comfortable chairs for us and find out what kind of art we like." My heaven will have Lay-Z-Boy recliners and Penthouse Pets, but I wasn't going to tell Humphreys that.

He smiled. "In my father's house are many mansions."

"What?" But the last cucumber went *sploosh,* so I never did find out what Humphreys had been talking about. He did his little praying routine again, and I piled the third cucumber in the corner with the other two.

He looked at the gravy bags, and then at me. "How do you—what do you do with them? Afterwards?"

"I bury them. I've got these things all over my property."

He nodded. "Do you need help?"

"If you're as good with a shovel as you are with a pail, I could use the help, Reverend. Thank you."

So we piled the gravy bags into my pickup, and I threw a tarp over them and loaded up a couple of shovels, and then I drove out to the next gravesite. I've been keeping track of where the cucumbers are, so I can pick a fresh place each time. I brought the gun with me, but that was in case we ran into snakes or something: I wasn't worried about Humphreys anymore, not that way.

He was good with a shovel, strong and fast. He hadn't always been a preacher, you could tell. He'd done manual labor someplace. Watching him dig, I started to get curious. When we stopped to take a break, I said, "So when were you in front of guns before?"

"In Africa." He wiped the sweat off his face. "In Zaire, back during the eighties. A group of us were rebuilding a church. Mobutu's thugs had burned it down because the clergy were speaking out against the government. And the soldiers came when we were rebuilding, and they lined us up against a wall and threatened to shoot us all. I still don't know why they didn't. They killed plenty of other people, before and after that." His eyes got far away, then, and he said, "All the people I worked with there—they're all dead now."

"That's not right," I said.

"No." He started digging again, and I let him. I know how working with your hands can help, when you're upset about something. I re-roofed the house all by myself, after Nancy Ann left.

We got the cucumbers neatly buried, one to a grave, and Humphreys said a little prayer over each one, and then we got back into the truck to go back into the house. I was worried. I had to figure out what to do about him, and it would have been easier if he'd been easier to hate. "Reverend," I said, "you were right before. I'm scared about what will happen if people find out about what's been going on out here."

"I'm not going to tell them," he said. "This is under the seal of clerical confidentiality, Welly. I take that very seriously."

I didn't know if I could believe him or not. I wanted to, but that's not the same thing. "I just hope I can trust you, Reverend."

"I hope you'll learn that you can. I can't expect you to, yet. You've only known me a few hours. Earning trust takes longer than that."

I grunted. That was a better answer than a lot of other people would have given. "Well, listen, you let me know when Sam dies."

"He may not die, not for a long time. We have to hope the chemo will work. We have to hope he'll be healed. But if he dies, certainly, I'll call you." Humphreys smiled. "He'll be having a church service, I have to warn you."

"Call me anyway." We were back at the house. I stopped the truck and said, "You left that bag inside, didn't you?"

"Yes, I did."

"Wait here. I'll get it for you. I'll be right back out."

The paper lunch sack was still sitting in the hallway, next to where

Humphreys had gotten sick. It was wet from the soapy water he'd used. I threw the old sack away and got a fresh one, and then for good measure I threw another eighth into the plastic bag. I knew Sam would notice, and that kind of gesture's good for business, if you don't do it very often. I guess it was my way of gambling that he'd stay alive. And if he mentioned it to Humphreys, maybe the Reverend would be more likely to keep his mouth shut.

I took the sack back out and handed it to Humphreys. "I have something for you, too," he said, and gave me his business card. "Call me if you ever want to talk, about anything at all. You can call me any time. Both my home number and the church number are on there."

"Kind of you," I said, although I was thinking, *when hell freezes over.* "Thank you, Reverend."

"You're welcome, Welly." He held out his hand, and I shook it, and then he got back into his car and drove away. I watched his car until it disappeared, and then I went back into the house. I almost threw the business card away, but something made me toss it into one of my kitchen drawers instead. Don't ask me what. It wasn't like I planned on calling him. It was just a superstitious thing, maybe like what he'd said about the emergency baptisms. Having his business card probably wasn't going to help me, but it couldn't hurt, either.

I was hot, from all that digging. I opened the fridge and got out a beer and drank it down in one gulp. Then I got my cell phone and took it into the living room, and sat back in my recliner and started dialing the phone company.

• BLACK FIRE •
Tanith Lee

Witness A (One)

I first see it as I'm driving back that night up the road—you can bet I pulled over. I thought it was a fucking plane coming down. Like a plunge of flames right through the sky, as if the sky was tearing open from the top to the bottom. The car slams to a halt and I jump out—and I'm below the top of the hill, so I run the rest of the way and just as I get there, this . . . thing, whatever it was, it lands in the woods. Well, our house is around there, me and hers. Only a mouse-house—what she said—mid-terrace in the last street winds out the village.

I stand on the hill sort of frozen, sort of turned to stone, and I hold my breath, the way like you do, not knowing you're not breathing.

So while I watch, all this fire-thing just storms into and through the trees and down and it hits the ground, and I think something's crazy then, because there should be a God-awful great bang, yeah? And great columns of fire and crap. But there ain't a sound. Not a bloody whisper.

And then I remember and I take that missing breath. But it's so quiet. I think that's what struck me anyhow, even while I run up the hill. There's always some kind of noise out here; I mean, we're not that far from the town. And there's animals, too, foxes and things snuffling and screeching. And cars.

Only there isn't a single sound now.

I don't never drink when I drive. Not no more. I got pulled over a couple years ago, random check, and I was just over the limit: half a glass—well, a pint—of beer. But I won't take any chance now. So nobody can say I *imagined* what I seen. Go on, you can test me, if you like. No. I see it. And I see what come after too.

Witness E (One)

He was late. He's always late.

That's what they says about dead people, don't they? Well then he must be dead.

Oh, he's got some bint where he works. Says he hasn't. He's got some—

Anyhow. I was washing my hair, and this blinding like . . . *light* sort of—I thought it was coming straight in the bleeding window—

I thought it was a bomb. You know—a *dirty* bomb like they always go on about? Terrorists. Why does everyone hate everyone?

So I runs out in the garden and I look and this big light—it's like the sky's falling and it's all on fire—only the fire is . . . it isn't red or nothing. It's—I can't describe it really.

Right in the wood.

I started to cry. I was really scared. And *he* weren't there, the bugger.

But there's no crash. Nothing. Just—silence. You know that thing someone said—hear a pin drop. Like that.

And my hair's so wet—but I shakes it back, and I thought: *I can go next door*, but the other three houses there, as we come like out of the village, no one lives in them now.

And then I sees him. This guy. He's walking out between the trees, i'nt he. Just walking.

Witness A (One)

Fucking car wouldn't start, would it, when I goes back to it.

So I beats it up the fucking hill again and belts down the other side toward the house. I mean, I'm thinking of her, aren't I? Yeah?

I mean you do, don't you?

Witness E (One)

It wasn't just he was well fit. I mean he *was* fit. I can see that like. And like he's really—he's beautiful. And I'm standing there in my old jeans and an old bra and no slap on and my hair full of shampoo. But he's got a sort of like, he's sort of *shining*.

It's like—what's that stuff? Phosbros—is it?

He *gleams*.

Only he's dark too. I don't mean he's a black guy. His skin is just kind of like summer tan, sort of like he's caught the sun but over *here*. Not a *real* tan. And his hair is black but it's so long, all down his back, it's like silk.

And he has this face.

I don't think much of them movie celebs, do you? But *this* guy, he's like in films my mum used to watch before she went mad and ended up in Loonyville—I can't think who.

But he comes out the wood and up to the garden, where the dustbin is, and the broken gate, and he looks at me.

I say, "D'you see that flaming thing come down?"

And he smiles at me.

Witness A (Two)

Coming home on that train . . . it's always late and no trolly service; I dread the damn thing. But when I finally got to the station what do you think? The shit Volvo won't start, will it?

So I walked.

Perfect ending to a perfect day, etc.

That's when I saw those fireworks all showering down on everything.

I admit I stopped and stared. I mean, I was recollecting that factory—God, where was it?—that place where all the fireworks blew up. The only difference was, and I eventually figured it out, *these* fireworks were all in a mass, just dropping in one single area. They merely fell out of the sky. Glittering. The rather peculiar thing was, there were no colors. It was quite a naturally well-lit night—aside from the inevitable street lamp light-pollution—a half moon, and stars. And this fountain of fireworks looked somehow much darker. They were—the nearest I can get is something like black sequins, those kind of *gowns* sexy women wore in the forties of the last century.

Anyway, I started to walk again because even when the fountain hit the bloody houses on my street, which I could see from up there on the far side of the park, there wasn't any thudding noise, no detonations.

You get so anxious now. It's how they want to make you, isn't it? All these warnings. I'd been thinking, ever since the trouble years ago, I ought to relocate, just work from home.

But it's difficult. My partner. She likes the high life, frankly, and her own job (she's a sort of PA) simply doesn't cover the rent.

It took me an hour to get back on foot. I steeled myself and didn't stop off at the King's Arms. I thought she might be worried. Sometimes I can be such a bloody fool.

By the time I reached the house the pyrotechnics were long gone. It was just this incredibly silent night. I noted that, you see. It struck me, how dead quiet it was.

When I unlocked the door, there seemed to be no one about. That was unusual. She's usually around. Even if she's asleep in front of the TV with an empty vodka bottle. I called out, I remember . . . I called her name—*Honey I'm home* sort of rubbish.

But no answer.

I felt fed up. I was tired out and hungry. I admit, I felt *unloved*. Childish, stupid, but I'm trying to tell you the truth.

Then I thought I heard a noise upstairs. Had she gone up to bed early? (No care for me, get my own fucking meal even though she'd been home all day.) Or was she ill? She gets migraines sometimes—or she says she . . . she *said* she did.

I went upstairs.

This I can't really explain. I walked quietly. Maybe only because it really was so quiet. Not a sound. (Even when I'd passed the pub, now I come to think of it. Quiet as—well, is even a *grave* so quiet?)

Upstairs the dimmer was on, all the lights half doused.

Then I did hear something. Then I heard it again, through the bedroom door. *Our* bedroom. This cry.

You can't mistake a cry like that.

Unless, of course, you never ever heard it before.

Witness A (One)

I runs the last bit. I'm getting really scared. Even though there'd been no bang nor nothing. I mean, the house lights were all out.

When I gets there I nearly has a heart attack because the front door is standing wide open.

No light—no, one in the lounge. I say lounge—size of a kitchen table—nowhere else though.

Upstairs, in the tiny little mouse room we called our bedroom, I hear a long wild wailing noise.

And I fucking know that noise.

It's her, fetching off, like they say.

It's sex.

I thought, hang on maybe she's just fixed herself, me not being there.

Then I know.

Then I run upstairs fast as I could. Sounded like an elephant to myself, in all the quiet.

When I pushed the door open, there they are. Her and him.

There they are.

Witness E (Two)

He rang the door bell. I think that was it . . . He must have done.

So I opened the door. It wasn't that late. Anyway, I was bored.

The utter rubbish on TV. I'd been going to check the washing-machine because suddenly it seemed so silent that presumably it'd packed up, with all my gear in it, oh, and his favorite three shirts—*unforgiveable*!

I thought I'd seen a kind of flash in the sky earlier. But I'm always seeing things in the sky. Altogether, in the past two years, I've seen six unidentified flying objects. Everyone laughs at me. But I did.

Anyway, standing outside the door is this entirely gorgeous man. There is no other way to describe him. He looks like—oh, God knows. Too good to be true. No, I don't remember what he was wearing.

Yes, I'd been drinking. I always mean to cut down, *never* do it when I'm at work. But sometimes, well. But not that much. I mean, I could *see*.

He was so beautiful.

And he said, "Here you are," and he smiled this wonderful smile.

No, not *charismatic*, nothing so clichéd. You looked at him and—

I fell in love with him. On sight. I fell in love with him.

Can I stop now?

I need some water, please.

Witness E (Three)

We'd been going to go up to the ridge. There was supposed to be a meteor shower. He said so. We're both very interested in that sort of thing—space, you know. He has a wonderful collection of meteor bits—dark fusion crust, really special.

We'd only been together a year. It was awful when he lost his job, but luckily I still have mine. Very luckily, as it turns out. I mean, it's just boring office work, but I'll still need a job, won't I? Or not, for a bit, perhaps.

Anyway, we set off quite early, around sunset. It was lovely, the light sinking over the fields and the birds singing. I know the songs are only territorial, their way of saying *Keep Out!* to other birds. I never knew that till he explained it to me. I just thought they sang because they could do it so well.

The ridge is the highest open place for miles.

We sat down and looked at the dark coming, and then all the lights coming on all round, the two towns, and the city to the north, and the little villages. You can never go far here without seeing people, or signs of them.

It got dark then. The moon was already quite far over to the west, though still high enough to make the upper sky that deep night blue. Lots of stars.

We didn't see anything for a long time. Then this thing just *erupted* out of the zenith.

He jumped up. We both did.

"It's a fireball—" he shouted. "My God—it's colossal—"

It seemed to be falling straight on us, but somehow neither of us could move.

Then I remember being aware of turning, as if I were *being* turned, not doing it myself—and our shadows peeling out jet black behind us and then realizing the meteor was rushing down to the south, in front of us, not directly on to our heads.

He started to run. He was running after it. He didn't wait for me, or even call to me. I suppose he just thought I'd do exactly what he did, I'd be so desperate to see. But I was scared. You know. I mean, it was so big and blazing bright— and yet so *dark*. I didn't know you could have fire like that, *black* fire—it must be a phenomenon associated with certain types of extra-terrestrial objects.

So he'd sprinted off, and the fireball went down on the land. And then—no shock wave, no sound—it just went out. Like a blown candle. Like that.

My legs had gone to jelly. I had to sit down. I thought he'd be all right after all nothing had exploded or was burning. What a coward I was, and he was so brave. He'd really tell me off. Perhaps I could get up and follow him in a minute, pretend I'd fallen over something as I ran—

Then I noticed how completely quiet everything was. Nothing is ever that quiet. I've been out with him enough nights to know. Animals move about, there is the distant hum of traffic from the motorway, or a plane. Even trees sort of *settle*.

And even the quietest flick of breeze moves the leaves. And I could *see* the leaves on trees moving a little. So the silence was just for me, somehow I'd been closed in some sort of bubble of soundlessness—

Then I stood up.

And then he spoke to me. I mean *him*, the man. The—I mean *him*.

He said, "Are you here?"

I said, "Who are you? Where did you come from?"

And he smiled.

He was so wonderful to look at . . . long black hair. He wore—I can't remember. Just ordinary clothes I expect. Because in fact he couldn't have been at all what he seemed. It was a sort of illusion he could create, just the way they do it in SF movies, CGI—in *Dr. Who,* for instance. Because he must be an alien, a species from beyond this world.

I was terrified. But then he touched me.

No, I'm all right.

This isn't *my* blood.

Witness A (Four)

I slung the door open and I ran straight at them. They were by the wall. No need to guess what he'd been doing with her—

She just looked sad. That was all. She didn't even protest.

And he—well, must have slipped out the side door while I was seeing to her, mustn't he? Bastard. *He never even tried to stop me.*

Is she going to be—?

Okay.

No.

All right.

Yes.

Witness E (Seven)

Of course I never want him near me again after what he did. Sure, we've been married three years. So what? Yes, I'll press charges. Look at me.

I don't remember. Yes, there was another bloke. A stranger—so? So what. I don't remember. I must have done.

. . .

Dept. RUP/sub 3x6: ps

My profoundest apologies that the enc: document did not accompany the (coded) transcript of this report.

Here then, belatedly, it is.

(I have to add at this point that whether it will shed any light of logic on the recorded eyewitness reports already deciphered and in your hands, remains to be seen. Those of us *here* are frankly baffled.

I will refer to that again at the end of the enc: document.)

Docu 97/77/ Six. Six. Six.

On the night of the *July 20* (see transcript) a number of emergency calls began to be relayed to this department. They involved urgent requests for all emergency services: police, paramedics and, in some cases, firefighters.

The peculiar feature of all these call-outs was the basic similarity of the claims of all the participants. Each seemed to involve an episode which, though variable, mentioned similar events and actions, and, significantly, one particular male person (as described in the transcripts): a youngish man, tall and slimly built, having very long dark hair and dark eyes. All the living victims—some were no longer alive, and even those who did not regard them-selves as victimized—were in a range of states representing shock, paranoid rage, or extreme exhilaration. All reported a fundamentally similar scenario, despite other countless unlike details. However, the occurrences took place on the same evening, and across the length and breadth of England. While the times, too, varied (incidents began quite early in the evening, and continued to surface until midnight), it is evidentially impossible the same dark-haired man, the main "suspect"—we use this term for want of another—could have appeared in so many widely disseminated areas during so brief a time period.

I will add, so far, we have been entirely unable to trace him, in this country or elsewhere. This is partly due, no doubt, to the lack of any recoverable DNA, or other clue, left behind with the subjects of his . . . visits.

Also, although sightings of UFOs are not uncommon, on this particular night, no one, apart from the people directly involved, called in with any queries about a fiery falling object, whether thought to be a meteor, a spaceship, or a light aircraft. No unusual reports either of an electric storm or alarming fireworks display.

The enclosed transcript relays to you only a *sample* of the huge group of persons who were subsequently interviewed, initially by the police of the ambulance service, and later on by ourselves. It is a sample of the most *typical* reports. Of which, in total there are to date some six hundred and sixty-six.

This number may, of course, not arouse any disquiet in the mind of a modern atheist. Nevertheless I am afraid, in order to preserve for the victims, where feasible, a modicum of the anonymity the Law currently prescribes, we have (perhaps frivolously) labeled each and all of them not by an actual name, but by the letter A, in the case of males, and E, in the case of females. Plus a differentiating number—One, Two, etc.: You may soon be aware why the letters A and E alone have been selected. And we trust you will overlook any perceived levity on our part. *A* stands for the Biblical Adam, naturally. And *E* for Eve, his rib-created partner. As I have said, we have not, here, included every single eyewitness account, but rendered for your consideration the most predominantly recurrent statements; that is, those most representative from all the six hundred and sixty-six interviews we were able to garner. (Of those individuals resultantly dead, or in a condition likely to lead to death—both male and female—we do not yet have conclusive figures.) The ultimate consequences of this replicated event remain, so far, unpredictable.

We shall be very glad to receive your input on this matter. To accept it at apparent (religious?) face-value would seem, shall we say, grotesque. But to ignore so widespread a phenomenon likewise itself poses many problems.

Code seal and signature attached.

Appendage PSX:

My last thought is, I confess, is this really then what is meant by Science Fiction? Or, more disquietingly, was it *always?* I direct your attention to the final words of the final, included witness.

Witness A (Two)

I'm very sorry I did that to her. Yes, I know she won't speak to me. I can't see her. Yes. I've never done anything like that before.

I can't describe it. Can't you try to fucking *understand?* She was lying on the bed with him. She was naked. He was—he was *inside* her. She was holding him in her arms—

I couldn't handle it. *You* didn't see. And there was this light in the room. Like a sort of bloody gilding. The whole scene looked like a pornographic oil painting from the Italian Renaissance.

I don't *remember* what he looked like. Just another man. Some kid, twenties maybe. God knows.

He just moved away from her. There was something then.

He was—what? what?—*sinuous*, something sinuous about how he moved. That I *do* remember. He moved like a trained dancer, an athlete—no, like an animal. Like a big cat. A panther. Or a snake.

I *know* I hit her.

I'm sorry.

I never did anything like that before with anyone.

No, it wasn't really because she'd fucked him. It was what she said.

She said *I can see inside you.*

Witness E (Two)

Yes, I could, I could see all through him. Through everything. No, I can't explain. I would if I could, wouldn't I? I mean all this fucking talk, this interrogation, when I'm covered in bruises, and I'm still pretty articulate, *aren't I? Okay?* If not very pretty. Ha. Ha.

I don't know now what it was.

It was as if I knew everything there was to know, the heights, the depths, yesterday, tomorrow, the beginning, the end-oh—

Shit.

I need the plastic thing—the *bowl*—it's your fault, all these questions—*get the fucking sick bowl before I throw up all* over—

Witness A (One)

She gets off of the bed and she says to me, *I seen the stars.*

That's what she says.

She doesn't mean—I don't know what—I *know* what—

I don't know what to do, do I? I turn to him like a fucking dope, but somehow he's not there no more. But there's something. I can feel it too.

There's this ringing in my head, and this terrific smell, a *good* smell—no, not good; can't be, can it? But it's clean, sweet—only it's drowning me.

I suppose she called you. Or someone. That's all I remember, mate. The lot. But I won't forget none of it. And I ain't been drinking, I told you. *Test* me.

Witness E (Three)

It was like looking through glass. You know, a glass case, perhaps? You can see everything so *clearly,* but you can't *touch* it. If you try, you trigger the alarm.

But I do remember there was a tree. It was very tall, dark but golden, both at once. We were lying high up in it. And there was this beautiful scent—no, more of a taste, really . . .

Witness E (Twenty-Four)

He said to me, "You are here." And then we made love. It was never like that before. Won't ever be again. I saw into this huge light. Only it was black, a black light. And for a moment, just after my climax, I knew that I was God. I know this sounds insane, but I don't think I'm insane. It was only for a moment.

· · ·

Witness A (One)

I'm afraid of her, now. Don't want to see her again. Don't want to see any of you, neither. I wish you'd all fuck off.

Witness E (Three)

When he came running back, the alien man—my *lover*—was gone. But I suppose it must have been obvious, to *him*. I mean, the man I lived with. I wasn't in any tree at all, but lying there on the ridge, naked. I must have looked—well . . . I suppose it was obvious. It was to *him*. He began to shout and yell at me. He seemed to be speaking in another language. But I could see right through the universe, start to finish, even if it was behind glass. I'm such a coward normally; I've said, haven't I? But when he ran at me his first blow never even touched me. I drove my knee into his stomach—no, let's be truthful: into his genitals. And I ripped at his eyes. I am terribly sorry. I understand he may lose his right eye. But I knew he might have killed me otherwise, and frankly, I think you know that too, don't you?

When I hurt him I felt nothing. Or rather, all I could feel was what I'd felt when the alien had sex with me. This incredible blissful opening to all things, in the most amazing way. And that lovely, delicious scent. I can still smell it. That taste of fresh cut apples.

• THE ELEPHANTS OF POZNAN •
Orson Scott Card

In the heart of old Poznan, the capital of Great Poland since ancient times, there is a public square called Rynek Glowny. The houses around it aren't as lovely as those of Krakow, but they have been charmingly painted and there is a faded graciousness that wins the heart. The plaza came through World War II more or less intact, but the Communist government apparently could not bear the thought of so much wasted space. What use did it have? Public squares were for public demonstrations, and once the Communists had seized control on behalf of the people, public demonstrations would never be needed again. So out in the middle of the square they built a squat, ugly building in a brutally modern style. It sucked the life out of the place. You had to stand with your back to it in order to truly enjoy the square.

But we'd all seen the ugly building for so many years that we hardly noticed it anymore, except to apologize to visitors, ruefully remember the bad old days of Communism, and appreciate the irony that the occupants of such a tasteless building should include a restaurant, a bookshop, and an art gallery. And when the plague came and the city was so cruelly and suddenly emptied, those of us who could not let go of Poznan, who could not bear to eke out the last of our lives in the countryside, drifted to the old heart of the city and took up residence in the houses surrounding the square. As time passed, even the ugly building became part of the beauty of the place, for it had been part of the old crowded city now lost forever. Just as the toilets with little altars for the perusal of one's excrement reminded us of the many decades of German overlordship, so this building was also a part of our past, and now, by its sheer persistence among us, a part of ourselves. If we could venerate the bones and other bodily parts of dead saints, couldn't we also find holiness of a kind even in this vile thing? It was a relic of a time when we thought we were suffering, but to which we now would gladly return, just to hear schoolchildren again in the streets, just to see the flower shop once more selling the bright excesses of overcopious nature, spots of vivid color to show us that Poland was not, by nature, grey.

Into this square came the elephants, a group of males, making their way in what seemed a relentless silence, except that a trembling of the windows told us that they were speaking to each other in infrasound, low notes that the human ear could not hear, but the human hand could feel on glass. Of course we had all seen elephants for years on our forays out into the gardens of suburban Poznan—clans of females and their children following a matriarch, gangs of mature males hanging out to kill time until one of them went into musth and set off in search of the nearest estrous female. We speculated at first about where they came from, whether their forebears had escaped from a zoo or a circus during the plague. But soon we realized that their numbers were far too great to be accounted for that way. Too many different clans had been seen. On Radio Day we learned, from those few stations that still bothered, that the elephants had come down the Nile, swum the Suez, swarmed through Palestine and Syria and Armenia, crossed the Caucasus, and now fed in the lush wheat pastures of Ukraine, bathed in the streams of Belarus, and stood trumpeting on the shores of Estonia and Pomerania, calling out to some god of the sea, demanding passage to lands as yet unpossessed by the great stumpy feet, the probing noses, the piercing ivory, and the deep thrumming music of the new rulers of the world.

Why should they not rule it? We were only relics ourselves, we who had had the misfortune of surviving the plague. Out of every hundred thousand, only fifty or a hundred had survived. And as we scavenged in the ruins, as we bulldozed earth over the corpses we dragged from the areas where we meant to live, as we struggled to learn how to keep a generator or two running, a truck here and there, the radios we used only once a week, then once a month, then once a year, we gradually came to realize that there would be no more children. No one conceived. No one bore. The disease had sterilized us, almost all. There would be no recovery from this plague. Our extinction had not required a celestial missile to shatter the earth and darken the sky for a year; no other species shared our doom with us. We had been taken out surgically, precisely, thoroughly, a tumor removed with a delicate viral hand.

So we did not begrudge the elephants their possession of the fields and the forests. The males could knock down trees to show their strength; there was no owner to demand that animal control officers come and dispose of the rampaging beasts. The females could gather their children into barns and stables against the winter blast, and no owner would evict them; only the crumbling bones and strands of hairy flesh showed where horses and cattle had starved to death when their masters died too quickly to think of setting them free from their stalls and pens.

Why, though, had these males come into the city? There was nothing for them to eat. There was nothing for us to eat; when our bicycles gave out and we could cobble together no more makeshift carts, we would have to leave the city ourselves and live closer to the food that we gathered from untended fields. Why would the elephants bother with such a ruin? Curiosity, perhaps. Soon they would see that there was nothing here for them, and move on.

We found ourselves growing impatient as the hours passed, and the days, and still we kept encountering them on the city streets. Didn't they understand that we lived in the heart of Poznan specifically because we wanted a human place? Didn't they feel our resentment of their trespass? All the rest of Earth is yours; can you not leave undesecrated these crypts we built for ourselves in the days of our glory?

Gradually it dawned on us—dawned on me, actually, but the others realized I was right—that the elephants had come, not to explore Poznan, but to observe us. I would pedal my bicycle and glance down a cross street to see an elephant lumbering along on a parallel path; I would turn, and see him behind me, and feel that shuddering in my breastbone, in my forehead, that told me they were speaking to each other, and soon another elephant would be shadowing me, seeing where I went, watching what I did, following me home.

Why were they interested in us? Humans were no longer killing them for their ivory. The world was theirs. We were going to die—I, who was only seven years old when the plague came, am now past thirty, and many of the older survivors are already, if not at death's door, then studying the travel brochures and making reservations, their Bibles open and their rosaries in hand. Were these males here as scientists, to watch the last of the humans, to study our deathways, to record the moment of our extinction so that the elephants would remember how we died with only a whimper, or less than that, a whisper, a sigh, a sidelong glance at God?

I had to know. For myself, for my own satisfaction. If I found the truth, whom else would I tell it to, and for what purpose? They would only die as I would die, taking memory with them into the fire, into the ash, into the dust. I couldn't get any of the others to care about the questions that preyed upon me. What do the elephants want from us? Why do they follow us?

Leave it alone, Lukasz, they said to me. Isn't it enough that they don't bother us?

And I answered with the most perplexing question of all, to me at least. Why elephants? The other wild animals that roamed the open country were the ones one might expect to see: The packs of dogs gone wild, interbreeding back to mongrel wolfhood; the herds of cattle, breeding back to hardiness, and of horses, quick and free and uninterested in being tamed. The companions of man, the servants and slaves of man, now masterless, now free. Unshorn sheep. Unmilked goats. Sudden-leaping housecats. Scrawny wild chickens hiding from ever-vigilant hawks. Ill-tempered pigs rooting in the woods, the boars making short work of dogs that grew too bold. That was the wildlife of Europe. No other animals from Africa had made the journey north. Only the elephants, and not just from Africa—the elephants of India were roaming the Orient, and on the most recent Radio Day we learned, through messages relayed many times, that they had somehow crossed the Bering Strait and were now, in ever greater numbers, grazing the prairies of America, small-eared cousins to the great-canopied beasts that now shadowed us on the streets of Poznan. I pictured them swimming, or piling onto boats that some last human pilot guided for them onto the stygian shore.

They had inherited the Earth, and were bent on surveying their new domain.

So I took to spending my days in the library, reading all I could about elephants, and then about all the processes of life, all the passages of history, trying to understand not only them but ourselves, and what had happened to us, and what our cities might mean to them, our houses, our streets, our rusting cars, our collapsing bridges, our sorry cemetery mounds where winter brought fresh crops of human bone to the surface, white stubble on a fallow field. I write this now because I think I know the answers, or at least have found guesses that ring true to me, though I also know they might be nothing more than a man hungry for meanings inventing them where they don't exist. Arguably, all meanings are invented anyway; and since I have no one to please but myself, and no one to read this who will care, except perhaps one, then I may write as I please, and think as I please, and reread this whenever I can bear it.

They made no effort to follow me inside the library. What good would it do them? Clever as they were with their inquisitive trunks, I could imagine them being deft enough to turn pages without tearing them. But what would the markings on the pages mean to them? Elephants sang their literature to each other in octaves we humans could not hear. Their science was the science of the temporal gland, the probing nose. They observed, but—or so I thought— did not experiment.

I did learn enough to warn the others before the first of the males went into musth. When you see one of them acting agitated, when his temporal glands pour out a steady black streak down his cheeks, when the other males are shy of him and give him room, then we must do the same, staying out of his way, not meeting his gaze. Let him pass. The city is his, wherever he wants to go. He won't stay here long, in musth. He must go and find a female then, and they were all outside in the open fields. He would give his deep rumbling call and pour out his lusty scent into the air and dribble musky fluid onto the ground where every other elephant could smell it and know: This way passed a male bent on making babies. This way passed God, looking for the Holy Virgin.

So we studied each other, and avoided offending each other, and grew used to each other's ways, the elephants and the fifty remaining residents of Poznan.

And then one day they began to push.

The males all gathered in the public square. We, too, gossiping to each other that something important was going to happen, gathered in our houses and leaned at our windows to watch.

They wandered aimlessly through the square, eleven of them—the twelve apostles, I thought, sans Iscariot—until noon made the smallest shadows. Then, as if of one mind, they surrounded the ugly old Communist building, facing it. When all were in place, they moved forward, slowly, each bull resting his massive brow against the miserable façade. Then, slowly, each began to tense his muscles, to shift his weight, to make little adjustments, to plant his feet, and then to push with greater and greater strength against the wall.

They're trying to push it down, I realized. And so did the others, all of us calling out to each other in our high-pitched human voices.

They're critics of architecture!

They've come to beautify Poznan!

We began to address the elephants with our calls, as if they were our football team, as if the plaza were a playing field. We cheered them, laughed in approval, shouted encouragement, placed meaningless bets about whether they could actually break through the walls.

Then, abruptly, I was no longer part of the playfulness. For without meaning to, I changed perspective suddenly, and saw us as the elephants must have seen us. This was Africa after all, and we were the primates perched in the trees, hooting and screeching at the giants, unaware of our own insignificance, or at least unbothered by it.

When I pulled my head back inside my window, I was filled with grief, though at that moment I could not have told you why. I thought at first it was because we humans were so diminished, reduced to chattering from safe perches. But then I realized that the human race had always been the same, had never risen, really, from our primate ways. No, what I was grieving for was that ugly old building, that relic of noble dreams gone sour. I had never lived under Communism, had only heard the stories of the Russian overlords and the Polish Communists who claimed to be fulfilling the will of the masses and perhaps, sometimes, believed their own propaganda—so my father told me, and I had no reason to doubt him. When the Communists decided what was good and what was bad, they acted as rigidly as any Puritan. Aesthetic concerns in architecture led to wasteful overspending of the labor of the working class; therefore, the ugliness of all new buildings was a badge of virtue. We human beings had reinvented ourselves, Homo sovieticus, Homo coprofabricus, or whatever the scientific name would be. A new species that never guessed how quickly it would be extinct.

The elephants would keep pushing until the walls came down—I knew that. Intransigence was built into the elephants' shoulders the way screeching and chattering were built into the primate mouth. And even though the other humans were cheering them, egging them on, I was sad. No, wistful. If we had really wanted that ugly building taken down, we knew where the dynamite was kept, we could have blown it out of existence. Elephants are mighty and strong, as beasts go, but when it comes to destruction, their foreheads are no match for the explosives in the locked sheds at the construction sites of buildings that will never be finished.

We don't need you to take it down, you meddlers, I wanted to say. We built it, we humans. It's ours. What right have you to decide which artifacts should stand, and which should fall?

The fascination of it was irresistible, though. I couldn't stay away from the window for long. I had to check, again, again, to see if they were making any progress, to see if some crack had appeared. The beasts had enormous patience, pushing and pushing until their shadows were swallowed up in the shade of the buildings as the sun headed out past Germany, past France, out to the Atlantic to be plunged steaming into the sea of night. That was the clock they lived by, these elephants; they had put in their day's work, and now they wandered off, heading out of the city as they did most nights, to eat and drink and sleep in some more hospitable place.

The next morning they were back, earlier this time, and formed their circle much more quickly, and pushed again. The betting among us began in earnest, then. Would they succeed? Would they give up? How long till the first crack? How long till a wall fell? We had nothing of value to bet; or rather, we had everything, we had inherited the city from the dead, so that we could bet enormous sums of money and pay in cash or diamonds if we wanted to, but when we wagered we never bothered to carry such useless objects from one house to another. Enough to say who won and who lost. The only reason we had such wealth was because the dead had left it all behind. If they didn't value it any more than that, what was it worth to us, except as counters in games of chance?

There was unguessed-at meaning in their pushing after all. For on the third day of the elephants' pushing—still to no visible effect—Arek came home to Poznan. Arek, whom I had named for my father. Arek, who dashed my last hope. Arek, who killed my wife.

For years after the plague, no children were conceived. From Berlin, where one of the survivors was a doctor, we learned that when the plague was new and they were still trying to study it, the medical researchers determined that the virus rooted in the reproductive systems of men and women, specifically attacking their bodies where the human seed was made. This was not how the plague did its slaughtering, but it guaranteed that the few survivors would be sterile. The message left us in despair.

But I was young, and though I had seen more death before I turned ten than I would ordinarily have seen even if I devoted my whole life to watching American movies, my hope was still undashable. Or rather, my body's hope, which in my teens was much stronger than my reason. As the people from the hinterlands and smaller towns came seeking human company, Poznan became a gathering place. In those days we lived on the outskirts of the city, in a place where we could actively farm, before we realized that farming was redundant with miles and miles of fields and gardens reseeding themselves faster than we could harvest them. So I was hoeing the turnips—the kind of task the adults gratefully left to my strong and flexible young arms and legs—when Hilde and her family came to town in a horse-drawn wagon.

It wasn't Hilde herself that I saw at first, it was the miracle of seeing a family. At first, of course, we assumed they were a nonce family, clinging to each other because no one else in their area survived. But no, no, they looked like each other, that miracle of resemblance that told us all that they were genetically connected. And soon we learned that yes, they were a mother, a father, a daughter, all of whom had survived the plague. They knew it was wrong of them to grieve for the two sons and three daughters who died, for they had not lost everyone they loved, as all the rest of us had done. There was something in them that was stronger than the disease. And Hilde, a plump nordic blonde, soon became beautiful to all of us, because we knew that if any woman had a viable ovum left, it would be her.

She and her parents understood that her womb, if it was not barren, could not belong to her alone, and that her only hope of continuing our poor, weak species was to find a mate whose body still could spew forth living sperm. She had been sexually immature when the plague came, but now was womanly, ready to bear if bear she could. One man at a time would husband her, for three months; then a month of solitude, and then the next man's turn to try. That way there would be no doubt of fatherhood if she conceived; he would be her husband, to father more children on her. She agreed to this because there was no other hope.

I was third to try, at fifteen a frightened child myself, approaching her like the temple priestess that she was, begging the god to choose me, to let life come into her from me. She was sweet and patient, and told no one how clumsy I was. I liked her, but did not yet love her, for she was still a stranger to me. I could mate with her, but not speak to her—or at least not be understood, for she came from a German-speaking area in the westernmost mountains, and had but little Polish—though more of Polish than I had of German.

The second month she had no period, and the third, and the fourth. She was kept away from me, from all men, until in the fifth month she asked for me. "You are half of this miracle," she said in halting Polish, and from then on I was her companion. No more fieldwork for me—what if I was injured? What if I caught cold? Instead I stayed with her, taught her to speak Polish and learned to read German, more or less.

In the eighth month the doctor finally came from Berlin. He had never worked in obstetrics, but he was the best hope we had, and since no one in Berlin was pregnant, they understood what was at stake; even a half-Polish baby in Poznan was better than no more babies anywhere at all. We made him welcome; he taught us how to make beer.

The ninth month. Nothing happened. He spoke of inducing labor. We worked to get a room in the hospital powered up, the old equipment working, and he gave Hilde an ultrasound examination. He could not face us after that. "You counted wrong?" he offered, as a possibility.

No, we did not count wrong. We knew the last time she had sex with anyone—with me—and it was nine months and two weeks ago.

"The baby is not ready yet," he said. "Weeks to go. Maybe many weeks. The limb-length tells me this. The development of the face and hands."

And then the worst news. "But the head—it is very large. And strangely shaped. Not a known condition, though. I looked in the books. Not seen before, not exactly this. If it is still growing—and how can I tell, since it is already as big as an adult human head—this does not look happy for her. She cannot bear this child normally. I will have to cut the baby out."

Cut it out now, her parents said. It has been nine months.

"No," the doctor said. "If I cut now, I think that it will die. I think it has the lungs of a fetus of five months. I did not come here to abort a fetus. I came to deliver a baby."

But our daughter . . .

Hilde agreed with the doctor. "If he has to cut me open anyway, there is no hurry. Wait until the baby himself thinks that he is ready."

We knew now it would be a boy, and were not glad of it. A daughter would have been better, everyone knew that. Everyone but me—I was not ready to play Lot with a daughter of mine, and I was the only man proven to have viable sperm, so I thought it was better that I would have a son and then could wander with Hilde and the boy, through all the world if need be, searching for a place where another mating had happened, where there might be a girl for him. I could imagine that future happily.

Ten months. Eleven. No woman had carried a child for so long. She could not sit up in bed now, for still it grew, and the ultrasound looked stranger and stranger. Wide hips, and eyes far apart on a face appallingly broad. The ultrasound, with its grainy, black-and-white image, made it look like a monster. This was no baby. It would never live.

Worse, it was draining the life out of Hilde. Most of what she ate went across the placenta to feed this cancerous growth inside her. She grew wan of face, weak of muscle even as her belly grew more and more mountainous. I would sit beside her and when she was tired of the book I read, I would hold her hand and talk to her of walks along the streets of the city, of my visit to Krakow when I was six, before the plague; how my father took me along as he escorted a foreign author through the city; how we ate at a country restaurant and the foreigner could not eat the floury bread and the chewy noodles and the thick lard spread. She laughed. Or, as she grew weaker, smiled. And finally, near the end, just clung to my hand and let me babble. I wanted nothing more than to have Hilde. Forget the baby. It's already dead to me, this monster. Just let me have Hilde, the time with her that a man should have with his wife, the life together in a little house, the coming home at night to her embrace, the going forth in the morning with her kiss on my lips and her blessing in my ears.

"I will take it now," said the doctor. "Perhaps the next child will be normal. But she grows too weak to delay any longer."

Her parents agreed. Hilde, also, gave consent at last. The doctor had taught me to be his nurse, and trained me by making me watch the bloody surgeries he did on hares and once on a sheep, so I would not faint at the blood when the time came to cut into my wife. For wife she was, at her insistence, married to me in a little ceremony just before she went under the anaesthetic. She knew, as did I, that the marriage was not permanent. Perhaps the community would give me one more try to make a normal child with her, but if that one, too, should fail, the rotation would begin again, three months of mating, a month fallow, until a father with truer seed was found.

What we did not understand was how very weak she had become. The human body was not designed to give itself so completely to the care of such a baby as this one. Somehow the baby was sending hormonal messages to her, the doctor said, telling her body not to bear, not to present; the cervix not to efface and open. Somehow it caused her body to drain itself, to make the muscles atrophy, the fat to disappear.

The doctor's incision was not large enough at first. Nor with the second cut. Finally, with the third, her womb lay open like the belly of a dissected frog, and at last he lifted the little monster out. He handed it to me. Almost I tossed it aside. But it opened its eyes. Babies aren't supposed to be able to do that, I know now. But it opened its eyes and looked at me. And I felt a powerful trembling, a vibration in my chest and arms. It was alive, whatever it was, and it was not in me, its father, to kill it. So I set it aside, where a couple of women washed it, and did the rituals that the doctor had prescribed—the drops into the eyes, the blood samples. I did not watch. I returned to Hilde.

I thought she was unconscious. But then the baby made a sound, and even though it was lower than a baby's mewling ought to be, she knew it was his voice, and her eyes fluttered open. "Let me see," she whispered. So I ran and took the baby from the women and brought it to her.

It was as large as a toddler, and I was loath to lay such a heavy burden on her chest. But Hilde insisted, reaching with her fingers because she could not raise her arms. I leaned over her, bearing as much of the baby's weight as I could. He sought her breast and, when she found the strength to raise a hand and guide a nipple into his mouth, he sucked mightily. It hurt her, but her face spoke of ecstasy as well as pain. "Mama loves the baby," her lips said silently.

She died as the doctor was still stitching her. He left the wound and tried to revive her, shoving the baby and me out of the way and pumping at her heart. Later, after the autopsy, he told me that her heart had been used up like all her other muscles. The child had ruled the mother, had demanded her life from her, and she had given it.

My Hilde. Till death parted us.

There was some debate on whether to feed the child, and then on whether to baptize it. In both cases, mercy and hope triumphed over fear and loathing. I wanted to oppose them, but Hilde had tried to feed the baby, and even after she was dead I did not wish to contradict her. They made me choose a name. I gave it my father's name because I could not bear to give it mine. Arkadiusz. Arek.

He weighed nearly ten kilograms at birth.

At two months he walked.

At five months his babbling noises became speech. They taught him to call me papa. And I came to him because he was, after all, my own.

Hilde's parents were gone by then. They blamed me—my bad seed—for their daughter's death. In vain did the doctor tell them that what the plague had done to me it no doubt also did to her; they knew, in their hearts, that Hilde was normal, and I was the one with the seed of monstrosity. They could not bear to look at me or at Arek, either, the killers of their last child, their beautiful little girl.

Arek walked early because his wideset legs gave him such a sturdy platform, while crawling was near impossible for him. His massive neck was strong enough to hold his wide-faced, deep-skulled head. His hands were clever, his arms long and probing. He was a font of questions. He made me teach him how to read when he was not yet two.

The two strange apertures in his head, behind the eyes, before the ears, seeped with fluid now and then. He stank sometimes, and the stench came from there. At the time we did not know what to call these things, or what they meant, for the elephants had not yet come. The whole community liked Arek, as they must always like children; they played with him, answered his questions, watched over him. But beneath the love there was a constant gnawing pain. He was our hope, but he was no hope at all. Whatever his strange condition was, it might have made him quicker than a normal child, but we knew that it could not be healthy, that like most strange children he would no doubt die before his time. And definitely, mutant that he was, he must surely be as sterile as a mule.

And then the elephants came, great shadowy shapes out in the distant fields. We marveled. We wondered. They came nearer, day by day. And Arek became quite agitated. "I hear them," he said.

Hear what? We heard nothing. They were too far off for us to hear.

"I hear them," he said again. He touched his forehead. "I hear them here." He touched his chest. "And here."

The flow from the apertures in his head increased.

He took to wandering off. We had to watch him closely. In the middle of a reading lesson, he would stand up and face the distant elephants—or face the empty horizon where they might be—and listen, rapt. "I think I understand them," Arek said. "Here's a place with good water."

All of Poland has good water now, I pointed out.

"No," he said impatiently. "It's what they said. And now they talk of one who died. They have the scent of him. The one who died." He listened more; I still heard nothing. "And me," he said. "They have the scent of me."

Elephants care nothing for you, I said.

He turned to me, his eyes awash with tears. "Take that back," he said.

Sit and do your lessons, Arek.

"What do I care what dead people say? I have no need of what they said!"

You're five years old, Arek. I know better than you what you need to know.

"Your father had to know all this," he said. "But what is it to me? What good has reading done for you?"

I tried to hold him, but at five years old he was too strong. He ran from the room. He ran out into the field. He ran toward the elephants.

I followed him as best I could. Others joined me, calling out Arek's name. He was not swift, and we could have caught him if we were willing to tackle him like rugby players. But our goal was only to keep him safe, and so we jogged alongside him, his short and heavy legs lumbering forward, ever closer to the elephants. A matriarch and her clan, with several babies of varying sizes. We tried to stop him then, to hold him back, but by then the matriarch had noticed us, and as she approached, Arek screamed and tried more violently to get away, to run to her. She trumpeted at us, and finally, tentatively, in fear of her we set him down.

She let him embrace her trunk; he clambered upward, over her great impassive brow, and sprawled his body across the top of her head. Her trunk reached up to him; I feared that she would sweep him from her head like lint. Instead she touched the leaking aperture on his right cheek, then brought the tip of her trunk down to her mouth. To smell and taste it.

That was when I realized: The matriarch, too, had an aperture between eye and ear, a leaking stinkhole. When I did my reading, I learned that it was the temporal gland. The elephants had it, and so did my son.

Neither Hilde nor I was elephantine. Nor was there any logical way, given the little science that I knew, for me to explain how a gland that only elephants had should suddenly show up on a human child. It wasn't just the temporal glands, either. As he sat perched atop the matriarch, I could see how closely his brow resembled hers. No great flapping ears, no abnormality of nose, and his eyes were still binocular, not side-aimed like the elephant's. Yet there was no mistaking how his forehead was a smaller echo of her own.

He has been waiting for them, I murmured.

And then I thought, but did not say: They came in search of him.

He would not go home with me. One by one the others drifted back to our village, some returning to bring me food and offer food to Arek. But he was busy riding on the matriarch, and playing with the babies, always under the watchful gaze of the mothers, so that no harm would come to him. He made a game of running up the trunks and turning somersaults onto an elephant's back. He swung on tusks. He rode them like horses, he climbed them like trees, and he listened to them like gods.

After two days they moved on. I tried to follow. The matriarch picked me up and put me back. Three times she did it before I finally acquiesced. Arek was their child now. They had adopted him, he had adopted them. Whatever music they were making, he heard it and loved it. The pied piper had come to lead away our only son, our strange inhuman child, the only hope we had.

From that day I did not see him, until the twelfth bull elephant arrived with Arek astride his neck.

Full-grown Arek—just a little taller, I estimated, than his father, but built like a tractor, with massive legs and arms, and a neck that made his enormous head look almost natural. "Father!" he cried. "Father!" He had not seen me at the window. I wanted to hide from him. He must be fifteen now. The age I was when I met Hilde. I had put him from my mind and heart, as I had already done with my parents, my baby sister, whom I had left behind unburied when I was too hungry to wait any longer for them to wake again, for God to raise them up from their sickbeds. Of all those I had lost, why was he the one that could return? For a moment I hated him, though I knew that it was not his fault.

He was their child anyway, not mine. I could see that now. Anyone could see it. His skin was even filthy grey like theirs.

He didn't see me. He slid down the brow and trunk of the bull he was riding and watched as his steed—his companion? His master?—took its place in the circle that pushed against the walls of the ugly building. He walked around them, a wide circle, looking up at the windows on the opposite side of the square. But it was not by sight that he found me. It was when he was directly under my window, looking the other way, that he stopped, and turned, and looked up at me, and smiled. "Father," he said. "I have seen the world!"

I did not want him to call me father. Those were his fathers, those bull elephants. Not me. I was the bearer of the seed, its depositor, but the seed itself had been planted in both Hilde and me by the plague. Born in Africa and carried to the world on airplanes, virulent and devastating, the plague was no accident of nature. Paranoid as it sounded even to myself, I had the evidence of Arek's elephantinism to bolster what I knew but could not prove. Somehow in the kettle of the temporal gland, the elephants created this new version of man, and sent the seed out into the world, carried by a virus. They had judged us, these beasts, and found us wanting. Perhaps the decision was born as grieving elephants gathered around the corpses of their kinfolk, slain and shorn of their tusks. Perhaps the decision came from the shrinking land and the drying earth. Perhaps it was their plan all along, from the time they made us until they finally were done with us.

For in the darkness of the library, as I moved along the table, keeping my yellowing books always in the slant of light from the window, I had conjured up a picture of the world. The elephants, the true gods of antiquity. They had reached the limit of what they could do with their prehensile noses. What was needed now was hands, so virus by virus, seed by seed, they swept away one species and replaced it with another, building and improving and correcting their mistakes. There was plenty of the primate left in us, the baboon, the chimpanzee. But more and more of the elephant as well, the kindness, the utter lack of warfare, the benevolent society of women, the lonely wandering harmless helpful men, and the absolute sanctity of the children of the tribe. Primate and elephant, always at war within us. We could see the kinship between us and the apes, but failed to see how the high-breasted elephant could possibly also be our kind.

Only now, with Arek, could the convergence at last be seen. They had made at last an elephant with hands, a clever toolmaker who could hear the voices of the gods.

I thought of the bulldancers of Crete, and then of Arek running up the trunks of elephants and somersaulting on their heads. The mastodons and mammoths were all gone, and the elephants were south of the Mediterranean; but they were not forgotten. In human memory, we were supposed to dance with joy upon the horns and head of a great loving beast, our father, our maker. Our prophets were the ones who heard the voice of God, not in the tempest, but in the silent thrumming, the still small voice of infrasound, carried through stone and earth as easily as through the air. On the mountain they heard the voice of God, teaching us how to subdue the primate and become the sons of God, the giants in the earth. For the sons of God did marry the daughters of men. We remembered that God was above us, but thought that meant he was above the sky. And so my speculation and imagining led me to this mad twisting of the scripture of my childhood—and no less of the science and history in the library. What were the neanderthals? Why did they disappear? Was there a plague one day, carried wherever the new-made Cro-Magnon wandered? And did the Neanderthals understand what their woolly mammoth deities had done to them? Here was their ironic vengeance: It was the new, godmade men, the chosen people, who hunted the mammoths and the mastodons to extinction, who bowed the elephants of India to slavery and turned the elephants of Africa into a vast wandering ivory orchard. We men of Cro-magnon descent, we thought we were the pinnacle. But when God told us to be perfect, as he was perfect, we failed him, and he had to try again. This time it was no flood that swept our souls away. And any rainbow we might see would be a lie.

I spoke of this to no one—I needed human company too much to give them reason to think me mad. Elephants as gods? As God himself? Sacrilege. Heresy. Madness. Evil. Nor was I sure of it myself; indeed, most days, most hours of the day, I mocked my own ideas. But I write them here, because they might be true, and if someday these words are read, and I was right, then you'll hear my warning: You who read this, you are not the last and best, any more than we were. There is always another step higher up the ladder, and a helpful trunk to lift you upward on your way, or dash you to the ground if you should fail.

Arek called me father, and I was not his father. But he came from Hilde's body; she gave her life to give him breath, and loved him, ugly and misshapen as he was, as she held him to her empty breasts while her heart pushed the last few liters of blood through her worn-out body. Not a drop of pap came from her into his mouth. He had already sucked her dry. But for that moment she loved him. And for her sake—and for his, at first, I will be honest here—I tried to treat him well, to teach him and provide for him and protect him as best I could. But at five years of age they took him and he was raised by elephants. In what sense now was he my son?

"Father," he said to me again. "Don't be afraid. It's only me, your boy Arek."

I'm not afraid, I almost said.

But he would know it was a lie. He could smell a lie on me. Silence was my refuge.

I left my room and went down the stairs to the level of the street. I came blinking into the sunlight. He held out a hand to me. His legs were even stockier now; whenever he stood still, he looked as planted as a pair of old trees. He was taller than I am, and I am tall. "Father," he said. "I want them to meet you. I told them all the things you taught me."

They already know me, I wanted to say. They've been following me for years. They know when and where I eat and sleep and pee. They know all they want to know of me, and I want nothing at all from them, so . . .

So I followed him anyway, feeling my hand in his, the firm kind grasp, the springy rolling rhythm of his walk. I knew that he could keep walking forever on those legs. He led me to the new elephant, the one he had arrived with. He bade me stand there as the trunk took samples of my scent for tasting, as one great eye looked down on me, the all-seeing eye. Not a word did I say. Not a question did I ask.

Until I felt the thrumming, strong now, so powerful that it took my breath away, it shook my chest so strongly.

"Did you hear him, Father?" asked my son.

I nodded.

"But did you understand?"

I shook my head.

"He says you understand," said Arek, puzzled. "But you say that you don't."

At last I spoke: I understand nothing.

The elephant thrummed out again.

"You understand but do not know you understand," said Arek. "You're not a prophet."

The elephant had made me tremble, but it was Arek's word that made me stumble. Not a prophet. And you are, my son?

"I am," said Arek, "because I hear what he says and can turn it into language for the rest of you. I thought you could understand him, too, because he said you could."

The elephant was right. I did understand. My mad guesses were right, or somewhat right, or at least not utterly wrong. But I said nothing of this to Arek.

"But now I see you do understand," said Arek, nodding, content.

His temporal glands were dripping, the fluid falling onto his naked chest. He wore trousers, though. Old polyester ones, the kind that cannot rot or fade, the kind that will outlast the end of the universe. He saw me looking, and again supposed that I had understood something.

"You're right," he said. "I've had it before. Only lightly, though. And it did me no good." He smiled ruefully. "I've seen the world, but none like me."

Had what before?

"The dripping time. The madness."

Musth, I said.

"Yes," he answered. He touched the stream of fluid on his cheek, then streaked it on my cheek. "It takes a special woman to bear my child."

What if there isn't one?

"There is," he said. "That's why I came here."

There's no one here like you.

"Not yet," he said. "And besides, I had this gift to give you."

What gift?

He gestured, as if I should have understood all along. The building that the elephants were pushing at. "You always told me how much you hated this building. How ugly it was. I wanted to give you something when I came again, but I couldn't think of anything I could do for you. Except for this."

At his words, the elephants grunted and bellowed, and now it was clear that all their pushing before had been preliminary to this, as they braced themselves and rammed, all at once, again and again. Now the building shuddered. Now the façade cracked. Now the walls buckled.

Quickly Arek drew me back, out of danger. The elephants, too, retreated, as the walls caved in, the roof collapsed. Dust blew out of the place like smoke, blinding me for a moment, till tears could clear my vision.

No silence now, no infrasound. The bulls gave voice, a great triumphant fanfare.

And now the families came: the matriarch, the other females, their babies, their children. Into the square, now unobstructed except for the rubble pile, they came by the dozens. There must be three clans here, I thought. Four. Five. Trumpeting. Triumphant.

All this, because they knocked down a building?

No. The fall of the building was the gift to the father. It was the signal for the real festivities to begin.

"I made them bring her here," said Arek. "You're my family, and these are my friends." He indicated the people leaning out of the windows over the square. "Isn't that what weddings are for?"

The elephants made way for one last arrival. An Indian elephant lumbered into the square, trunk upraised, trumpeting. It progressed in stately fashion to the place where Arek and I were standing. On its back sat Arek's bride-to-be. At first glance she was human, boldly and charmingly nude. But under the shock of thick, straight hair her head was, if anything, larger than Arek's, and her legs were set so wide that she seemed to straddle the elephant's neck the way a woman of my species might bestride a horse. Down the forehead and the trunk of the beast she slid, pausing only to stand playfully upon the tusks, then jump lightly to the ground. Those legs, those hips—she clearly had the strength to carry a baby as large as Arek had been for the entire year. But wide as her body was, could such a head pass through the birth canal?

Because she was naked, the answer was before my eyes. The entrance to her birth canal was not between her thighs, but in a pouch of skin that drooped from the base of her abdomen; the opening was in front of the pubis. No longer would the pelvic circle limit the size of a baby's head. She would not have to be cut open to give birth.

Arek held out his hand. She smiled at him. And in that smile, she became almost human to me. It was the shy smile of the bride, the smile that Hilde had given me when she was pregnant, before we knew it was no human child she carried.

"She's in heat," said Arek. "And I'm . . . in musth. You have no idea how crazy it makes me."

He didn't sound crazy, or act it, either. Instead he had the poise of a king, the easy confidence of an elephant. At the touch of her hand, his temporal glands gave forth such a flow that I could hear the fluid dripping onto the stones of the plaza. But otherwise he betrayed no eagerness.

"I don't know how it's done," said Arek. "Marriage, I mean. They said I should marry as humans do. With words."

I remembered the words that had been said for me and Hilde. As best I could, I said them now. The girl did not understand. Her eyes, I saw now, had the epicanthic fold—how far had they brought her? Was she the only one? Were there only these two in all the world? Is that how close they came to the edge of killing us all, of ending the whole experiment?

I said the words, and she shaped the answers. But I could tell that it didn't matter to her, or to him either, that she understood not a bit of the Polish words she had to say. Below the level of audible speech, they had another kind of language. For I could see how her forehead thrummed with a tone too low for my ears to hear. But he could hear. Not words, I assumed. But communication nonetheless. The thing with speech, they'd work that out. It would still be useful to them, when communication needed to be precise. But for matters of the heart, they had the language of the elephants. The language of the gods. The adamic tongue. The idiom God had used one time to say, Multiply and replenish the earth, and subdue it. We did the first; we did the last. Now, perhaps, this new couple in their new garden, would learn the replenishing part as well. Only a few of us lingering beasts, of us the dust of the earth, would remain, and not for long. Then the whole world would be their garden.

Today they're gone. Out of Poznan, the elephants and their new creatures, the son and daughter of the gods. My Arek and his wife, whose name he never spoke aloud to us. No doubt he has some deep and rumbling name for her that I could never hear. They will have many children. They must watch them carefully. Or perhaps this time it will be different. No stone crashed against a brother's head this time. No murder in the world. Only the peace of the elephants.

They're gone, and the rejoicing is over—for we did rejoice, because even though we know, we all know, that Arek and his bride are not of our kind, they still carry the only portion of our seed that will remain alive in the earth; better to live on in them than to die utterly, without casting seed at all.

They're gone, and now each day I go out into the square and work amid the wreckage of the building. Propping up the old façade, leaning it against a makeshift wall. Before I die, I'll have it standing again, or at least enough of it so that the square looks right. Already I have much of one wall restored, and sometimes the others come and help me, when they see I'm struggling with a section of wall too heavy or awkward for a man to raise alone.

It may have been an ugly thing, that Communist monstrosity, but it was built by humans, in a human place, and they had no right to knock it down.

• LONG ENOUGH AND JUST SO LONG •
Cat Rambo

I'd never wanted to go to Earth until the doctor told me I couldn't, that my bones were too brittle. After that, it wasn't an obsession, just an edge to my days.

Otherwise, my life's good.

I run a courier ship between Earth, Luna, the space stations, Mars, and the Inner Gate. You need as little mass as possible to run a snipship, and due to what that doctor called my defects, I'm one of the smallest, fastest. Good pay, and most of the time I'm low-g, which is easiest on me.

Freetime I slum around Luna, where my best girlfriend Pippi lives. Or she and I go prospecting out in the shadow of the Gate, like the dozens of other crazies, hoping to stumble on an alien artifact, make us all rich. Not too impossible a dream, though. It's happened before.

I had a permanent cradle walker left at Luna, that's how much time I spent there. Pippi worked as a sportscaster for the biggest Moon channel, MBSA. Her name's not really Pippi, but she had orange braids and long legs and freckles everywhere, so what else could everyone call her?

I'm used to my name getting distorted. My parents named me Podkayne after a girl in an old story about Mars. It becomes Poddy and Special K, usually Kayne.

In college, though, they called me the Gimp. Most of the time it was affectionate. Pippi was my roommate, there from day one. She had eight siblings, ranging from twelve years to three months. A roomie with lower limb reduction syndrome didn't faze her. I'd come in with a chip pre-loaded on my shoulder, but I relaxed after a couple of weeks.

Pippi was borderline Aspie, called it like it was, which caused her enough troubles on her own. You had to explain to her why you were angry or sad or whatever, but once she knew what was going on, she knew what sounds to make.

The Aspiness makes her an excellent sportscaster. She knows every sports score for the last half century, and a lot of pre-Net stuff too. You can't come up with a trivia question that's lunar sports-related that she can't answer. That was the only thing she really got passionate about, and in a way that charmed the camera.

We never hooked up. Both of us were wired straight. Pippi had a regular friend named Trevor who was usually away on business trips. I paid for it or went virtual every once in a while, and left things at that.

We were both enjoying sunlight at our favorite park, two blocks away from Pippi's apartment complex. Sitting beside a sculpture there I've always loved, spindly rails of color tumbling taller than me like animation lines, edges glinting pink and blue and purple. The smell of tomato and basil and sage filled the air.

Pippi had her face turned up to the light, soaking in the warmth. She had been indulging in tanners again. Her orange shirt and shorts were vibrant against the expanse of her brown skin.

I was more cautious. I don't want skin tumors later on, so I keep a gauzy over-shirt and hat about me. Silvery sleeves to deflect the light were set over my arms, strapped into the walker's maneuvering legs. Underneath the sleeves, mercurial light played over my skin.

We both saw him when he entered the park: Tourist-new, still dressed in arrival shorts and paper shirt with "Be nice, I'm a newbie" printed on the back, which guaranteed him a 10% discount at any participating business.

Pippi squinted over. "Is that . . . "

I followed her gaze. Dark glasses gave me the advantage. "Yep. It's an AI."

"Not just any AI, though," she said, eyes watering. "Unless I'm wrong?"

"Nope, it's a sexbot," I said.

It was just after what the newsies were calling the Sexbot Scandal, when that Senator was caught traveling with an AI and had used the momentary notoriety to call for AI rights. Now the Senator's 'droid and several others of its kind had bought themselves free. I'd seen an interview with one while trapped in line picking up Chinese takeout the night before. Its plans for the next year were to travel with its friend, another of the bots. Wink wink, nudge nudge.

The oldest human urge: Curiosity about who or what each other was fucking.

He had the white plastic skin most AIs were affecting that year. On his head a slouched wool hat like a noir detective's.

He looked up and saw us looking at him. He froze, like a car grinding gears to a stop. Then he moved again, almost impatient, flinging an arm up as though against us, although I realized a second later that it shielded his eyes from the dazzle of sunlight off the sculpture. Trapezoids of colored light danced over his tunic, glittered on the lenses that were his eyes.

Pippi waved.

He stepped backwards, ducked into the tunnel.

Of course we went in pursuit.

He took the West tunnel. Moving fast, dodging between walkers moving between stations, grabbing handholds to hurl himself along. It wasn't hard to follow him—I'm small, and mostly muscular in the chest and shoulders, so I can rocket along as far as anyone from handhold to handhold. Pippi slowed me down, kept hissing at me to wait up for her.

We emerged in the most touristy of plazas, the complex of malls near the big hotels, the public gardens. I thought I'd seen the flicker of his tunic, his hat's crumpled feather, as he ducked into the Thai garden.

The dome overhead admitted unadulterated sunlight. There were parrot flowers and bua pood, a waterfall, and a grove full of gibbons, safely behind mesh. Trails led off to discreet clothing and lifestyle boutiques, a restaurant, and a walkway to the next mall. I saw his hat bob through its glass confines and elbowed Pippi, pointing.

She said, "He could be going anywhere from there. There's a tube stop in the middle of the mall."

"Where would a sexbot go?"

"Do you think he's for hire?" she said.

The interview had said only a few sexbots had chosen to keep their professions. Most of the others had made enough to fund other careers. Most had become solo-miners or explorer pilots.

"It can't be the first time he's been asked the question," Pippi said.

I hesitated. I could talk her into asking. Could machines feel embarrassment? What was the etiquette of communication? Was a sexbot, like a human, capable of being flattered by a flirtatious or even directly admiring question?

Gibbons hooted overhead. A long-billed bird clung upside down to the other side of the mesh. If we stayed here much longer, we'd have a park fee added to our monthly taxes. Two parks in a single day was way too extravagant.

We went home.

I had a run to the Gate the next morning, so I got up early, let myself out. Took the West tunnel to the tube stop. Grabbed a mushroom roll on the way and ate it on the platform, peering into shop windows at orange and blue scarves and fake ferns and a whole window wall's worth of animate Muffs, the latest wearable animals. The sign said they lived off air impurities. They had no eyes, which to some people made them cute, I guess, but to me just looked sad.

Tourists going past in bright shirts and arcs of perfect white teeth. Demi-gods, powered by cash.

A feather reflected in the window. Behind me stood the sexbot.

This time I followed at a distance. Got in the train car at the opposite end, but kept an eye on him. Luckily for me he was getting out at the port. I don't know what I would have done if it'd looked as though he was going further.

Maybe followed him.

Why? I don't know. There was something charming about the way he held himself. And I was curious—who wouldn't be?—about the experience of some-one *made* for sex, someone for whom sex was his entire rationale for existence. What would it have been like for him (it?) awakening to that?

The port platform straddled the Dundee cliffs, overlooking the Sea of Tranquility. He was there at that flickering curtain of energy and I remembered what it did to constructs—shorted them out, wiped them clean. He had his hand outstretched, and I'm the last to deny anyone their choices, but even so I shouted, "Hey."

He turned, his hand dropping.

I caught up to him. I was in the cradle walker because I was being lazy that day. I could see him taking it in, the metal spidering my lower body, the bulge where my flesh ended, where legs might have been on someone else, the nubs of my left hand—two but as useful as three of your fingers, I swear.

I said, "Want to get a cup of tea and talk about it?"

So cliché, like something you might have seen in a cheap-D. But he said, "Okay," and his voice sounded as sincere as a mechanical voice can.

The café was half-deserted, just a couple of kids drinking coffee near the main window. We were between main shifts, and I was late for my pick-up, but I thumbed a don't-bother-me code, knowing I was one of the most reliable usually. They'd curse me but let it slide.

It's weird, talking to a mechanical. Half the time your mind's supplying all the little body movements, so you feel like you're talking to a person. Then half the time you've got a self-conscious feeling, like you were talking to your toaster in front of your grandmother.

Maybe it was just as strange for him. There's a lot of Gimps up here—lower gravity has its advantages, and in a lot of spaces, like my rig, the less you mass the better. Plus times are lean—less elective surgery. Here he was in the land of the unbeautiful, the people who didn't care as much about their appearance. Strange, when he was beautiful in every single inch, every graceful, economical move.

We didn't say a word about any of that.

I told him the best places to sightsee, and where he could take tours. I thought maybe he had some advantages—did he need to breathe, after all? Could he walk Outside just as he was?

The big casinos are worth seeing, particularly Atlantis and Spin City. I sketched out a map on my cell and shot it to him.

"Where do you like to go?" he said.

I'm not much for shopping, and I said so. I liked to take the mega-rail between Luna and the Cluster—cheap and you could stare out the window at the landscape.

"Let's do that," he said.

• • •

The Cluster used to be a fundamentalist-founded station that ended up selling its space to private concerns in order to fund itself. The remnants of the church were there. They ran the greenhouses that grew food for Luna, where most of the water got processed too. The stuff at the market there was always fresh and good and cheaper than in stores.

A jazz club had bought space, and a tiny government office matched its grander counterpart in Luna. And there was Xanadu, which was a co-op of five wealthy families. Along with a scattering of individuals who dealt in rare or hand-crafted goods.

There was always music there, and it had enough reputation for being dangerous that all but a few tourists steered clear.

His name was Star. He would be all right with me. I knew enough to keep him safe.

We ate berries and sat beside rippling water. He told me about Earth—never about the people, but the landscape. Trees, pines and sycamores and madrona, maples and honey locusts and cedar. He talked about cliffs that were bound with color: Yellows and reds and deep browns. Everything grew there, it seemed.

He talked about rain, about slow gray clouds and tearing nor'easters. Rain drumming on a tin roof versus its sound on slate. Fine spring mist and the hot rain that fell during drought, coin-sized and evaporating too quickly. Rain on sand, echoed by waves. Thunderheads, gathering themselves over the ocean. He had lived beside the sea for a few years, he said.

I wondered who he had lived with.

So much was unsaid. It was like a cloud in the room. We relaxed despite it.

He didn't know where he was staying. He had no luggage. I approved of that. I stick to plas-wear and carry no souvenirs other than the rooms inside my head. Even my ship, where I spend more time than anywhere else, is unpersonalized. I liked it that way.

I was staying with Pippi. Star had money, or so he said, and asked where a clean hotel was. I steered him to Blizz, which caters to the Gate regulars, and went back to Pippi's.

She was surprised to see me. I hadn't felt like going out on a trip, I said, and offered to take her out to dinner.

All the time we were eating sweet potato fries and tempeh steaks, I tried to figure out how to tell her about Star.

I don't know what kept me from just blurting it out. That was usually the level we communicated at. Straightforward and without pretense.

I felt like a shit keeping quiet. Eventually it would come out and the longer it took, the worse it would·be.

• • •

I wasn't prepared to see him at the door the next day.

Pippi answered the door. "Bless you, my dear little friend!" she shouted over her shoulder.

"What?" I scooted back in my chair, glimpsed his hat.

"You got me a present!" She reached out her hands, "Come in, come in."

Her place is tiny. Three of us made it feel crowded. We stood around the table, bumping it with our hips.

"How much do you cost?" Pippi asked Star.

He looked at me. "I don't do that anymore."

"Then why are you here?"

"I came to see Podkayne."

Pippi was unembarrassed. She shrugged and said, "Okay."

He wanted advice about buying into the colony, where to pick a spot. I made him buy me lunch in return for my advice, and we took Pippi along since she knew better than I where the good deals were.

"Over there in Cluster, someone told me a month or two ago," she said. "He was saying the Church is going to sell off more space, and it's going to get gentrified. It's a long ways off though, over an hour by tram." She licked barbecue sauce off her fingers. Star pushed a wipe across the table towards her.

"I don't think he likes me much," she said to me, later.

"I don't think he likes humans much," I said. "He makes allowances, but I think he'd be just as happy dealing with mechanicals only."

"Not many mechs up here," she said.

"Why?" I said. "You'd think it would be ideal for them. No rust. Less dirt. Fewer pollutants in the air."

"It would make sense," she said. "What does it say about us, we're so crazy we pick a place even mechanicals don't want to live?"

Maybe ten thousand on the face of the moon. The space stations ranged in size from a few hundred to a few thousand. Twenty thousand on the surface of Mars. I didn't go back there much, even though it was where I had grown up, after my parents died in a crash. Maybe two or three thousand existing around the bounty of the Gate, another hundred pilots and vagabonds and Parasite-ridden.

The few, the proud, the crazy.

Why had Star chosen to come up here?

I asked.

He said, "There's too many living things on the planet."

"Why not Mars? It's enough people to qualify as civilization."

"They're spread out and it's dusty. Here it's clean."

"You like the sterility up here," I said. "Then why think about living over in the Cluster? It's the most organic spot on the moon."

His face never smiled, just tilted from one degree to another. "It's a controlled organic."

"But what do you want to do?"

"Live," he said. "By myself, with a few friends," he nodded towards me, "according to my own devices."

"What about sex?" I blurted out.

He froze like a stuck strut's shadow. "I beg your pardon?"

"I'm sorry," I said. "I didn't mean to intrude. It's just that I was somewhat interested, but only if you were."

He shook his head, mere centimeters of rejection. "I'm afraid not."

Words I'd heard before. Including what he said next. "We can be friends, though."

"He's not interested," I told Pippi.

"Screw him," she said. "Let's go play Sex Rangers."

We climbed into the virtual suits and tapped in. I found someone interested in fooling around on a rocky shore, underneath fuzzy pines. The suit's as good as sex, any day—releases all the tensions you need released, in my opinion—and a lot cleaner.

Afterwards we logged out and ate pizza and watched a deck about boxing. Pippi said the guy had an 87 percent chance of winning (he did), 54 percent chance by knock-out (he did not).

"I asked Star to come mining with us," I said to her when we were getting ready for bed. I took the couch; she had a fold-down bunk.

"You did what?"

"He'll be an extra pair of eyes. Not like he'll take up oxygen."

She paused. "Fair enough."

He was good enough at spotting. He learned the difference between ice and metal fast enough to satisfy impatient Pippi, who hated explaining things. I focused on getting us close to the debris that swirled in and out of the Gate. You never knew what you might find. One guy picked up a device that fueled a company in food replication and yielded over forty patents. One pilot found a singing harp. Another the greasy lump that ended up becoming snipship fuel.

You never knew.

Pippi and I had a routine. Star didn't intrude on it much, went to the secondary display and focused on looking for mineral spikes.

Usually we chatted back and forth. There, Star was an intrusive, if silent, presence. Pippi ended up thumbing on the usual newschat channel. Nothing much. An outbreak on Mars, but small and well-contained. An ambassador stricken but rallying in order to continue his mission through the Gate. How much he looked forward to being the fifth human through the interstellar passage that allowed us access to the wild and varied universe. How much he looked forward to opening new trade channels.

Who knew what he might find out there?

"What's this?" Star said.

From afar just a glitter. Then, closer, a silver-sided chest, the size of a foot locker but covered with golden triangles. An odd, glittery powder encrusted the hinges and catch as it spun in space.

We brought it in.

Pippi's gloved hand reached to undo the latch. I waited, holding my breath.

Nothing hissed out. A glass sphere inside, clouded with bubbles and occlusions. As Pippi slipped it out of the gray material surrounding it, we could see oily liquid filling it.

"Could be useless," Pippi said, her voice unhappy. "Plenty of stories like that before."

"Could be beaucoup bucks," I pointed out.

"Of course," Pippi said, her voice loud and angry, "it's the time you bring someone along, to split it three ways, that we actually hit a lode."

"I don't want any claim," Star said.

Flummoxed, I stared at him. What must it be like, to have enough to not need more, to have just that one extra layer against yourself and poverty? My parents had left me enough to buy my snipship, but all my capital was tied up in that rig.

"I just wanted the company," he said. "I thought it would be interesting."

"Fucking tourist," Pippi said. "Want to watch the monkeys dance? We'll kiss for another five grand."

He backed up, raising his hands. His feet clattered on the deck. Before he had moved quietly. Did he choose to make that sound to remind us he was a machine?

"Thought we'd just love to take the walking vibrator on tour?" Pippi said. When he remained silent, she turned on me. "See, it doesn't have anything to say to that."

"He," he said.

"He? What makes you a he, that you've got a sticky-out bit? I bet you've got a sticky-in bit or two as well." She laughed. Meanness skewed her face.

"Enough," I said. "Let's tag the find, in our names, Pippi."

She dropped back. I clung to the rigging, started to thumb in figures. She pushed forward, "Let me, it's faster." Fingers clicking, she muttered under her breath, "Get us all home faster that way."

I took over after she'd tagged the spot and put the coordinates in. I was trying not to be angry. Hope mellowed out some of the harsh emotion. It could be a significant find. It was nice of Star to give up his claim.

Back in the ship bay, the lights laddered his face till he looked like a decoration. Pippi was strapping our find into a jitney.

"Why not a place where there's rain?" I said.

"That could only be Earth," he said. "Do you know the worst thing about rain there?"

"What?"

Pippi tied a rope into place, tested it with a quick tug, glanced over her shoulder at us.

"Rain there has gotten so acidic that if I stand out in it I have to come in and shower after a few minutes. It damages my outer skin."

I tried to picture the cold, then acid burn. Luna was better.

"I'm sorry about Pippi."

She honked the horn.

"Go ahead. I'm taking the tram over to the Cluster," he said.

I hesitated. "Meet me later?"

"I'll call you."

He didn't, of course. We cashed in the case—a lump sum from a company's R&D division that doubled our incomes and then some.

I texted him, "Come celebrate with us, we're dockside and buying dumplings." But he didn't reply until three days later. "Sorry, things got busy. Bought house. Come out and see it."

"When?"

"Tomorrow morning. I'll make you breakfast."

I left in the morning before Pippi was awake.

His place was swank, built into a cliff-side, with a spectacular view of the endless white plains below. He made me waffles with real maple syrup. He was an amazing cook. I said so.

"I was programmed that way," he said, and made a sound that was sort of a laugh.

The sexbots—all of the AIs struggling for emancipation lately—had had to demonstrate empathy and creativity. I wondered what that had been like.

He was standing uncomfortably close. I leaned forward to make it even closer, thinking he'd draw back.

He didn't.

"I'm programmed a certain way," he said.

"How is that?"

"I want to please you. But at the same time I know it's just the way I'm programmed."

"It can't be something more than that?" My arm was pressed against his surface. It was warm and yielding as flesh. I couldn't have told the difference.

He pulled away. I bit my lip in frustration, but I liked him enough to be civilized.

I drank the last of my coffee. Real Blue Mountain blend. He kept his kitchen well stocked for human visitors—who did he hope would stop in?

As it turns out, Pippi. Next time I came through on a quick flight (I might be rich, but who was I to turn down fast and easy money?), she told me how he'd fed her.

"Pasta," she said, rolling the words out. "And wine, and little fish, from Earth. And afterwards something sweet to drink."

She said they'd fucked. I believed her. It wouldn't be her style to lie. It would never occur to her.

So I did and said I'd fucked him too. She didn't respond, not right off the bat, but I caught her looking at me oddly by the time I said toodle-oo and went off to sleep in my ship.

It wasn't the first time I'd slept in there, not by a long shot.

I wished them both happiness, I supposed.

Still, two weeks later, I came in response to Pippi's panicked call. He was going back to Earth, she said.

We both showed up at the farewell hall. He was standing with a tall blonde woman, Earth-fat. Star slipped away from us, came over with a bearing jaunty and happy, his polished face expressionless as always.

"Who is that?" Pippi said.

"A journalist. She's going to help me tell my story, back on Earth."

"I see," Pippi said. She and I both surveyed the woman, who pretended not to notice us. Her manicured hand waved a porter over to take her luggage aboard, the hard-shelled cases the same color as her belt.

Pippi said, "Is this because you don't want to fuck me any longer? You said you liked it, making me feel good. We don't have to do that. We can do whatever you like, as long as you stay."

He averted his face, looking at the ship. "That's not it."

"Then what?"

"I want to go back to the rain."

"Earth's acid rain?" I said. "The rain that will destroy you?"

Now he was looking at neither of us.

"What about your place?" Pippi said.

"You can have it," he said. "It never felt like home."

"Will anyplace?" I asked. "Anywhere?"

"When I'm telling my story, it feels like home," he said. "I see myself on the camera and I belong in the world. That's what I need to do."

"Good luck," I said. What else could I say?

Pippi and I walked away through the terminal. There were tourists all around us, going home, after they'd played exotic for a few days, experienced zero-grav and sky-diving and painted their faces in order to play glide-ball and eaten our food and drunk our wine and now were going home to the rain.

We didn't look at each other. I didn't know how long Star's shadow would lie between us. Maybe years. Maybe just long enough for sunlight to glint on forgotten metal, out there in the sky. Maybe long enough and just so long.

• THE PASSENGER •
Julie E. Czerneda

It was a pilgrimage and he was its goal.

This understanding had taken years, had the passenger the means or desire to measure them; decades to be convinced of any purpose beyond curiosity to the parade outside his walls. In the first months, he had cowered behind the furnishings, terrified almost to insanity by the ceaseless, silent mass of flesh quivering against one side of his prison.

At any moment, he could slide his eyes that way and make out a hundred bodies, hung with broad-tipped tentacles, moving with a boneless grace as if the atmosphere outside his prison were liquid. It could have been, for all he knew.

A hundred bodies: they could be the same as the hundred before or different. He still couldn't tell any of them apart. Were only those of the same size and shape allowed to see him? They wore and carried nothing. He was fond of the notion that there were some religious or cultural mores that said they should come before him as he was, for they had never provided him clothing.

Other things, yes. Every few days, or weeks, or months, a panel on the far wall from his bed would glow. He'd learned to set his fingers properly in the seven slots beside the panel to trigger it to slide open. Behind the panel would be a box.

He would open it, of course, despite what he'd come to expect of its contents. At first, the sight of charred and melted wood and plastic, stained with blood, had provoked him to rage. He had cursed his captors, spat at the transparency keeping him from them, them from him, tried with ingenuity to kill himself with whatever sad relic or trophy they'd provided. They had never reacted, beyond simply causing him to slip into unconsciousness while they repaired what damage he'd managed to inflict on himself.

Eventually, he'd stopped. What was the point? The pilgrimage of watchers never ended. The boxes with their pitiful cargo continued to come. He began to sort their contents carefully. When he slept, anything he hadn't touched or handled would be removed from his prison. He made sure to touch it all. When a new box was due, anything he had left on the floor would also disappear like a dream, so he began to sort out what mattered to him.

There was nothing useful. Bits of fabric—never enough for clothing, even when he tried to hoard some. The smell of burned flesh usually clung to it. Metal and plastic, usually bent or damaged beyond recognition. Once in a while, a package that seemed intact. Another passenger's personal possessions, he assumed, better protected than other things.

While these were the most distressing gifts from his captors, he treated them with care. The opaque walls of his prison were uneven, with plentiful ledges. He filled these with trinkets from the dead. He slept watched over by the images of other men's mothers and wives, and spent hours contemplating the fates of children whose faces were not reflections of his own.

If he slid his eyes that way, to watch his watchers, he knew it would be the same sight as every other minute since he came to be here, but the thought brought the involuntary glance. Tentacles, overlapping either because they wanted to or there was no room to avoid touching, made the same corrugated pattern as always. Each body was topped with seven small red eyes, pupilled in black, rolling in unison to face him, to track him as their owner moved along from one side of the wall to the other.

He looked away. There had been a time when he tried to communicate or at least learn by watching the watchers. After that had been a time of anger and depression, of attempts at self-destruction when nothing in the room could be defaced—attempts that availed him only intimate memories of futility.

Then he had stopped caring. He had remained motionless, waiting to die. They wouldn't allow his body to fail. He would wake to find himself nourished, no matter how hard he resisted sleep. But he could allow his brain to die. And he tried.

And had almost succeeded. But that was when his captors, though they seemed incapable of communicating with him or understanding him, began giving him the boxes of belongings. Every item tore his heart; every one reconnected his humanity.

At last, one gave him a purpose to match the unknown one sending the aliens sliding past his prison day in, day out. It was a child's box of markers. He held them against his cheek when he found them, breathing in a faint scent of corruption as well as the clean promise of colour. He cried for the child who had lost them, then, with painful care—he'd never been an artist—used the markers to draw a stick figure child on the floor.

He expected the vivid lines to be gone when he awoke, fingers cramped around the markers. But his captors had left them. So he added a dog, a ball, a tree, a house, a rabbit, a book! The markers failed him, dry halfway through the shining red of a bicycle. He flung them away, and cried, turning his back to the wall of watchers.

Sleeping, he dreamed for the first time in years of home, a dream that for once didn't spiral into the nightmare of chase, burning, struggle, and capture, a dream that gave him up peacefully to reality.

There he found his captors had left him something of their own. On the floor was a seven-sided sheet of white. There was a tray containing greasy sticks, each about the length of his hand, in a variety of colors. They were awkward to hold, but he grabbed them eagerly and waved them happily at his watchers as if they'd respond. Or as if he'd recognize a response if they did.

Another hundred beings slid past. It took each exactly fifteen heartbeats to glide from one end of his wall to the other. Always.

Sixty-three years had passed since. He knew precisely, because that sheet of white had marked the beginning of his purpose. There were a few years lost in the beforetime. Ten years ago, the sad packages from other passengers had stopped appearing behind the panel. It didn't matter. He no longer remembered his age when he arrived in this place, but he could rely on nature ending his imprisonment in the not-too-distant future, regardless of the devoted attention of his captors.

He surveyed this day's work. The colors were subtle, layered in explanations of light and shadow, refinements he'd begun several pieces ago. The center-piece, a bridge, swept upwards, its luminous archways of stone almost hanging in air. The Legion marching across moved in trained synchrony, save for the eyes of one man looking out as if wary of surprise attack. There were storm clouds on the horizon, and dewdrops on the moss in the foreground.

There were probably errors throughout the scene, he worried, as he always did. But the errors were irrelevant; he'd done his best. This one was ready to go. He rolled it up, the motion inflaming the soreness in his joints, and leaned it against the panel. Like all the others, it would be gone when he awoke.

Boneless grace studded with eyes; could any even see the colors he intended?

He'd learned his art. It was, after all, a way to communicate, and he'd hoped until hope died this medium would be the breakthrough allowing him to reach the intelligence that held him here, that marched in unending ranks just to look at him. But there had been no response beyond the disappearance of only finished works, those he rolled up and placed near the panel. He didn't bother wondering anymore if they valued his art or washed off his colors to return the paper to him in some frenzied economy. It was enough he completed each image.

It took three sets of hands to open the roll safely. When it was spread on the seven-sided table specially built for this purpose, they ever-so-gently slid the holding bars over each edge, each bar locking in place with a light *snick* of contact. Only then did they release their careful grip.

The lights around the table dimmed, isolating the brightness glowing down on colors and shapes. The encircling six didn't speak for a long moment, their faces lost in shadows, their thoughts in reverence. They were a close group, drawn together years before by common interests and goals, held together by a responsibility none could escape. These rooms, the automated equipment, and, most importantly, the wonderful artwork such as the latest supine before them, had been their discovery.

"The Romans," said Dr. Susan Crawley softly, drawing in a slow breath around the unfamiliar word. "I've read about them. Earth, early 13th century, I think. They were conquerors, builders . . . definitely pre-Industrial."

"Well, this proves what I have been saying all these years," Dr. Tom Letner's voice held its customary fine and precise diction in the dark, as if those lips never slurred into shipslang after a few beers. "He must have been an historian."

Someone keyed the room lights to full brightness again. Bedlam erupted as others vehemently countered the physicist's assertion. The loudest voice belonged to Lt. Tony Shrib. "All it proves is He was well-read. Susan here is an engineer, for star's sake, and she knows about these Remans."

"Romans," Susan corrected under her breath. She ignored the continuing, well-worn arguments. What was new lay before her. Her eyes moved hungrily over the scene on the table, feasting on its complexity; she admired the stonework of the bridge, the odd moisture on a plant whose name she would have to look up in a text. All were images strange and exotic to the shipborn. Of those party to the secret of this art, only Master Electrician Huong Trang could claim to have set foot on the planet glorified by the Artist and Huong stubbornly refused to discuss what he remembered, as if the memories were sweeter for the hoarding.

Typically, it was Huong who interrupted her pleasure. "My friends," he said in his gentle, clear voice—the voice that had reproached them so many times before. "My colleagues. Is it not time?"

The good-natured bickering faltered and stopped. The others, all officers or senior scientists, found good reasons to look anywhere but at Huong's stern face. He recaptured their attention by placing one blunt-fingered hand firmly on the surface of the art.

Dr. Natalie Emil, a trim woman in her late forties whose love for the art was matched only by her love for her patients in the ship's hospital—and truth be told, for her mother's legacy of Earth chocolate—cried out, "Careful!"

The sacrilegious hand stayed where it was. "Is it not time?" Huong insisted, looking from one to the other in turn. "Has He not suffered long enough?"

The ship's senior psychologist, Dr. Wayne Simmons, shook his mane of heavy gray hair, his eyes troubled behind their thick lenses. "We don't dare release Him from the sim program. You know that, Huong. We can't predict what the effect on His mind would be. We don't have the facilities on this ship to ensure His recovery."

Huong lifted his hand, prompting at least one sigh of relief, then waved it eloquently over the artwork imprisoned on the table. "And we don't want this to stop, do we."

Susan felt the blood draining from her face. She didn't need to glance at her colleagues to know they too would be showing signs of shock. How dare Huong accuse them of—of what?

"We cherish the Artist's work," she said involuntarily. "How is that wrong? Despite His weakness, He's valued by all of us." Susan looked pleadingly at her peers, was strengthened by Natalie's nod of support, by Tony's smile. "You've seen for yourself how our shipmates flock to the Gallery to see His images of our heritage. We've arranged school tours. We let anyone order a reproduction for their quarters. We—"

"We imprison Him in His dream of Earth. We ensure He continues to produce what we crave," Huong said heavily. "And we wait for Him to die and release us from our conscience."

"No! How dare you—" Wayne's hand touched hers briefly. Susan calmed herself but refused to back down. "You've never been comfortable with our decision, Huong. I understand your feelings about it—"

"I don't think you do. I don't think any of you really do." The Master Electrician walked to the side of the room they usually avoided. He activated the sole control on its surface, turning the blank surface into a one-way view of a room, larger than most of the quarters on the colony ship *Pilgrim III*. The room's sole occupant squatted naked and *old* on the floor, colors in those marvelous hands poised to coax shape and texture from the empty page.

Just as the Artist had done each and every day since they had discovered His existence. Almost ten years ago, yet Susan remembered it as if it had been yesterday. They'd searched for the release catches, frantic to rescue the imprisoned stranger, only to be stopped by Wayne and Natalie, their medical experts. It was obviously a sim chamber, like enough to the hundreds on the *Pilgrim III* to be recognizable, if far more elaborate. The planetborn visited the sims regularly, having come on-ship with their private recorded scenes from the verdant world left behind ready to comfort them when the shipworld became too strange to bear.

The shipborn entered the chambers as part of their schooling, a refresher course built from open skies, scented winds, and uneven ground. It was a matter of pride to avoid them as adults, to prefer acclimation to the Ship, though all recognized the coming generations would need the sims and more to prepare for their new home.

But no one lingered in the sims more than a day at a time. Only those who could accept leaving Earth had boarded the Ship; to admit otherwise was to unsettle one's own sanity and disturb those around you. And there was work to be done, the carefully planned busyness designed to occupy minds tempted to hold on to the past. Survival for all meant looking to the future, not dwelling on what was now forever beyond their reach.

The sim chamber hosting the Artist was quite different from those offering education or a harmless moment of blue-skyed nostalgia. It was capable of full life support even if the Ship failed, of remote functions better suited to quarantine facilities. That had been one of their early fears: that He had been a carrier of some disease perilous to the Ship. They'd used the remotes to run tests as He lay unconscious, until they were sure He was nothing more dangerous than a puzzle.

There were recording devices, notes left behind in this secret place. Those had been studied too, though all they offered was a seemingly endless lists of bodily functions, chilling evidence the Artist had indeed been in this chamber every minute since launch.

As vividly, Susan remembered the morning when they'd met, here, to listen with horror as Wayne presented their conclusion: they must do nothing to disturb the Artist within His sim chamber with its automated, if bizarre, treatment. He and Natalie had been utterly convinced and so convincing: Releasing the Artist from his dreams of Earth, replacing them with the here-and-now of the Ship after all this time, would only shatter whatever reality His mind still recognized.

And, unsaid but understood, it would very likely stop His Art.

So they resigned themselves to being His keepers, to hiding the dark secret within the bowels of the Ship, and to sharing the Art with as many as possible. Huong wasn't the only one to have nightmares since. How dare he set himself as their conscience!

Huong's small eyes glittered at Susan, as though he heard her thoughts, or as though he were close to tears. His emotions were becoming embarrassingly public as he aged, perhaps a consequence of outliving most who had walked onto the Ship with him. "I've found out where He came from," he said calmly enough. "I know the truth."

"What?" Tony, the ship's senior stellar cartographer, ran one hand over his close-cropped hair, then down over his face as if to smooth away an expression he'd rather not share. "How? Where?" Susan understood his dismay. Tony had taken the greatest risk of them all, using his clearance and knowledge to search the Ship's records for any clue as to the origin of the Artist on the Ship. He'd found nothing: nothing to explain how the ship's senior psychologist, Dr. Randall Clarke, had been able to requisition then hide the construction of this chamber at the edge of livable gravity inside the immense core of *Pilgrim III*. Nothing to identify the Artist, even when they'd taken advantage of the automatics and obtained DNA samples from His unconscious body.

Nothing to challenge their assumption that the Artist suffered from some delusional state, some flaw Dr. Clarke had been treating him for in this private, hidden place, some condition too severe to allow exposure to the Ship's environment or company.

"Our past is recorded in places other than the Ship's systems, Mr. Bridge Officer," Huong said with deliberate irony.

"Tell us what you've learned," Wayne ordered impatiently.

Huong spoke slowly, methodically, as if to impress each word on them all. "Did Randall mention his wife to any of you?"

They didn't look at Susan, but she felt their focus on her. Everyone knew she and Randall had been lovers until his death. "Is this relevant?" she asked coldly.

"Very."

"Then, no. I didn't know he had ever married."

"Oh yes. In fact, Randall was supposed to board with his wife. Yet Tony's checked the manifest; Ship's records clearly show Randall arriving alone."

"Where did you find this information?" Tom demanded. He'd found the datacube giving directions to this place in Randall's cabin safe—otherwise they might never have discovered it. Sometimes the thought made Susan weak. The beauty and richness of the Artist's work, languishing as dust-covered rolls on the floor where the automatics dumped them. No classes of school children seeing His work, awed by their own past made manifest. They'd have reached orbit around New Earth 17, moved to the surface and started their new lives all unaware, while the great seed ship reconstructed itself as an orbital platform, its automatics sweeping up and recycling the dead organics of the Artist and His Art. She shivered.

Their attention was distracted by the Artist as he stretched then scratched one wrinkled buttock absently before settling back to his labours.

"Corridor sale."

Susan blinked, trying to imagine staid, conservative Huong visiting one of the hundreds of junk sales that went on throughout the colonists' section of the ship. They weren't particularly legal, but the Captains had long ago relented, second-gen officers tending to be more practical than those raised and trained Earthside. Besides being a useful diversion for the colonists, the sales redistributed personal goods no longer obtainable from their source.

"I picked up a collection of gossip mags in the last one." Huong paused patiently as Natalie laughed. "It was worth it. I found our late psychologist—and his wife."

"In a gossip mag?" Susan said with disbelief.

"The wife, Charlette d'Ord, was an athlete turned sports broadcaster. A bit of a celebrity in her way. I found several images of them together—the captions refer to Randall only as her husband, but you can see him plainly enough. Here." Huong drew a datacube out of his pocket and tossed it to Susan.

Numbly, she walked over to the nearest reader panel and inserted the 'cube. The rectangular screen produced an image of a group of people at some public event. Randall's thin face with its surprisingly sensual lips was easy enough to recognize despite the passage of years. He had one arm possessively around the shoulders of an incredibly beautiful woman. Susan smoothed the skirt over her ample hips before she could resist the impulse.

"I know that face," Natalie breathed.

So would anyone on the Ship, Susan thought. Those classic features and warm smile were straight from the Artist's most popular work. Almost every cabin had its copy of the angelic figure hovering, arms spread to shield the Earth from the dark of space, the serene loveliness of the perfect yet so-human face a comfort to folk all too aware they were separated from vacuum by only a hull and skills both a generation stale.

"Pull up the faces behind them," Huong ordered, as if this revelation wasn't enough.

Susan did so, watching with the others as three faces from the background became clearer. The centermost, a young man, was plainly not paying attention to the photographer or event. His dark, *familiar* eyes were fixed on Charlette. Susan turned off the image, inexplicably frightened by the longing captured in that one look.

Huong didn't object, trapping them instead with his slow voice. "Charlette died in a car accident six months before *Pilgrim III* began final assembly. The accident took place over one hundred miles from their home. The car contained her luggage and there was an unconfirmed witness' report that someone else had been driving the car. Randall was apparently questioned by police then released. After all, he was going offworld for the rest of his life. What point in pursuing an investigation?"

Wayne moved closer to the viewscreen covering the opposite wall, his face shadowed and grim as he stared at the Artist. Susan wanted to refuse his vision, to see a patient under sophisticated care, not a victim. Her lips moved numbly: "You're saying the Artist is that young man in the image. You're accusing Randall of murdering his wife and somehow arranging to kidnap and imprison her lover, bringing him on the Ship."

"Randall was on the planning team," Natalie said reluctantly. "He had the access and opportunity to make modifications."

"Why?" Susan breathed. "Why—like this?"

Huong answered. "We can guess. Revenge. Randall could be ruthless. We all knew that about him." No one disagreed. *Pilgrim III* was immense, as colony ships had to be. It would be their children's children who reached humanity's latest new frontier. In the meantime, the Ship was a world onto itself: shelter, workplace, and space for growth. Yet her thousands of inhabitants existed within smaller, insular communities, communities that had to get along or fail to function. The scientific community was one, and Randall had not endeared himself to many in it. Susan was the first to admit that her social standing with her peers had improved after her lover choked to death on his favourite synthetic sweetmeat.

"Now you know what I believe. The Artist is no madman, cared for in an automated sim to calm his delusions and keep him functioning. He is—or was—as sane as any of us before being tortured by our colleague, a man who perverted his knowledge to harm, not heal. The Artist does not belong in this travesty of a life. And so we agree," Huong said, swiveling to look at each of them, his hand rising slowly as if to lift some curtain. "It is time."

Wayne shook his head, an identical gesture to his first response to Huong's plea, and Susan felt her heart starting to pound for no reason she cared to admit. "No," Wayne replied. "We can't."

"Why?" Huong's eyes blazed. He raised his fists in the air. "In the name of justice! Why not? Don't you believe me?"

Susan answered when no one else spoke. "It doesn't matter. The Artist lives in His own World, at peace. You know that, Huong. And if we free Him now, so close to His end, what are we offering Him in return? Your theory that all He has suffered was to satisfy one man's desire for revenge? That whatever purpose He found to sustain Himself has been a lie?" She paused for emphasis. "That His very world is gone?"

Huong's face was deathly pale. "What do you care about Him?" His finger stabbed the air, first at Natalie, then at Wayne. "You'd keep Him locked away just to hide your mistakes." His finger stabbed at Tom, "You, for an excuse to break the rules." Then at Tony, "You're terrified of the Captains' judgment. And you." Susan stared at the now-shaking fingertip targeting her. "You want to keep your lover's legacy for yourself, don't you? I know you believe His Art belongs to you."

"Rant all you want, Huong," Natalie countered, her voice a shade too calm. "Whatever you think are our reasons, you've missed the most important one of all: Our shipmates. They believe the Art they love is the secret work of someone among us, someone keeping our heritage alive in a way no datacube can. Do you wish to tarnish their feelings for His work, turn His accomplishments into this sordid melodrama? We must not consider this one individual above the good of the Ship."

There was a murmur of agreement; Susan sensed their resolve hardening. So did Huong. "At what cost?" he asked, his passion drained away at last, replaced by disgust. "At what cost," he repeated.

404 • The Passenger

Susan found nothing to say. Huong turned and left the room, his feet dragging with each step.

"Will he go to the Captains?" Tony asked.

It wasn't a meaningless concern. They'd used their privileged ranks to hide what they'd found, to produce the Art as if by some miracle. If Huong told now, they would all become suspect. At the very least, they would lose control of their departments to underlings and have their work scrutinized for the remainder of their lives. In many ways, *Pilgrim III* was not a large ship at all.

"No," Wayne said, going over to gaze down at the image of the Legion captured in time. One Legionnaire looked back at him, as if seeking an unknown enemy. "Huong protests. He goads us to do what he believes is right. But he also knows we have no choice. The Artist will live a year more at best; perhaps only months. Whatever fantasy fills His mind, whatever beloved view of home comforts Him, let Him keep it. Let Him finish His work. When He is gone—then it will be time to tell His story." Wayne sighed. "At least, as much of His story as we choose to tell.

"Thanks to Him, humanity will not forget its past."

There was a blank seven-sided canvas ready underneath. He sat on one corner of it, half his mind already planning, the other half gently engaged watching his watchers sliding past, tentacle upon tentacle, eyes rolling from side to side. He believed he understood now. Both their purpose, and his.

He picked up an alien crayon, nodded a proud acknowledgment to the race that forced its guilty millions to parade in shame before him, and prepared to record another piece of human history. As long he lived, Humanity would not be forgotten.

For like that precious bird, kept until death in a glass cage for all to see, wasn't he the last passenger of Earth?

• SIMULACRUM •
Ken Liu

[A] photograph is not only an image (as a painting is an image), an interpretation of the real; it is also a trace, something directly stenciled off the real, like a footprint or a death mask.

—*Susan Sontag*

Paul Larimore:

You are already recording? I should start? Okay.

Anna was an accident. Both Erin and I were traveling a lot for work, and we didn't want to be tied down. But you can't plan for everything, and we were genuinely happy when we found out. We'll make it work somehow, we said. And we did.

When Anna was a baby, she wasn't a very good sleeper. She had to be carried and rocked as she gradually drifted to sleep, fighting against it the whole time. You couldn't be still. Erin had a bad back for months after the birth, and so it was me who walked around at night with the little girl's head against my shoulder after feedings. Although I know I must have been very tired and impatient, all I remember now is how close I felt to her as we moved back and forth for hours across the living room, lit only by moonlight, while I sang to her.

I wanted to feel that close to her, always.

I have no simulacra of her from back then. The prototype machines were very bulky, and the subject had to sit still for hours. That wasn't going to happen with a baby.

This is the first simulacrum I *do* have of her. She's about seven.

-Hello, sweetheart.

-*Dad!*

-Don't be shy. These men are here to make a documentary movie about us. You don't have to talk to them. Just pretend they're not here.

-*Can we go to the beach?*

-You know we can't. We can't leave the house. Besides, it's too cold outside.

-*Will you play dolls with me?*

-Yes, of course. We'll play dolls as long as you want.

• • •

Anna Larimore:

My father is a hard person for the world to dislike. He has made a great deal of money in a way that seems like an American fairy tale: Lone inventor comes up with an idea that brings joy to the world, and the world rewards him deservedly. On top of it all, he donates generously to worthy causes. The Larimore Foundation has cultivated my father's name and image as carefully as the studios airbrush the celebrity sex simulacra that they sell.

But I know the real Paul Larimore.

One day, when I was thirteen, I had to be sent home because of an upset stomach. I came in the front door, and I heard noises from my parents' bedroom upstairs. They weren't supposed to be home. No one was.

A robber? I thought. In the fearless and stupid way of teenagers, I went up the stairs, and I opened the door.

My father was naked in bed, and there were four naked women with him. He didn't hear me, and so they continued what they were doing, there in the bed that my mother shared with him.

After a while, he turned around, and we looked into each other's eyes. He stopped, sat up, and reached out to turn off the projector on the nightstand. The women disappeared.

I threw up.

When my mother came home later that night, she explained to me that it had been going on for years. My father had a weakness for a certain kind of woman, she said. Throughout their marriage, he had trouble being faithful. She had suspected this was the case, but my father was very intelligent and careful, and she had no evidence.

When she finally caught him in the act, she was furious, and wanted to leave him. But he begged and pleaded. He said that there was something in his make up that made real monogamy impossible for him. But, he said, he had a solution.

He had taken many simulacra of his conquests over the years, more and more lifelike as he improved the technology. If my mother would let him keep them and tolerate his use of them in private, he would try very hard to not stray again.

So this was the bargain that my mother made. He was a good father, she thought. She knew that he loved me. She did not want to make me an additional casualty of a broken promise that was only made to her.

And my father's proposal did seem like a reasonable solution. In her mind, his time with the simulacra was no different from the way other men used pornography. No touching was involved. They were not real. No marriage could survive if it did not contain some room for harmless fantasies.

But my mother did not look into my father's eyes the way I did when I walked in on him. It was more than a fantasy. It was a continuing betrayal that could not be forgiven.

Paul Larimore:

The key to the simulacrum camera is *not* the physical imaging process, which, while not trivial, is ultimately not much more than the culmination of incremental improvements on technologies known since the days of the daguerreotype.

My contribution to the eternal quest of capturing reality is the oneiropagida, through which a snapshot of the subject's mental patterns—a representation of her personality—can be captured, digitized, and then used to re-animate the image during projection. The oneiropagida is at the heart of all simulacrum cameras, including those made by my competitors.

The earliest cameras were essentially modified medical devices, similar to those legacy tomography machines you still see at old hospitals. The subject had to have certain chemicals injected into her body and then lie still for a long time in the device's imaging tunnel until an adequate set of scans of her mental processes could be taken. These were then used to seed AI neural models, which then animated the projections constructed from detailed photographs of her body.

These early attempts were very crude, and the results were described variously as robotic, inhuman, or even comically insane. But even these earliest simulacra preserved something that could not be captured by mere videos or holography. Instead of replaying verbatim what was captured, the animated projection could interact with the viewer in the way that the subject would have.

The oldest simulacrum that still exists is one of myself, now preserved at the Smithsonian. In the first news reports, friends and acquaintances who interacted with it said that although they knew that the image was controlled by a computer, they elicited responses from it that seemed somehow "Paul": "That's something only Paul would say" or "That's a very Paul facial expression." It was then that I knew I had succeeded.

Anna Larimore:

People find it strange that I, the daughter of the inventor of simulacra, write books about how the world would be better off without them, more authentic. Some have engaged in tiresome pop psychology, suggesting that I am jealous of my "sibling," the invention of my father that turned out to be his favorite child.

If only it were so simple.

My father proclaims that he works in the business of capturing reality, of stopping time and preserving memory. But the real attraction of such technology has never been about capturing reality. Photography, videography, holography . . . the progression of such "reality-capturing" technology has been a proliferation of ways to lie about reality, to shape and distort it, to manipulate and fantasize.

People shape and stage the experiences of their lives for the camera, go on vacations with one eye glued to the video camera. The desire to freeze reality is about avoiding reality.

The simulacra are the latest incarnation of this trend, and the worst.

Paul Larimore:

Ever since that day, when she . . . well, I expect that you have already heard about it from her. I will not dispute her version of events.

We have never spoken about that day to each other. What she does not know is that after that afternoon, I destroyed all the simulacra of my old affairs. I kept no backups. I expect that knowing this will not make any difference to her. But I would be grateful if you can pass this knowledge on to her.

Conversations between us after that day were civil, careful performances that avoided straying anywhere near intimacy. We spoke about permission slips, the logistics of having her come to my office to solicit sponsors for walkathons, factors to consider in picking a college. We did not speak about her easy friendships, her difficult loves, her hopes for and disappointments with the world.

Anna stopped speaking to me completely when she went off to college. When I called, she would not pick up the phone. When she needed a disbursement from her trust to pay tuition, she would call my lawyer. She spent her vacations and summers with friends or working overseas. Some weekends she would invite Erin up to visit her in Palo Alto. We all understood that I was not invited.

> -Dad, why is the grass green?
> -It's because the green from the leaves on the trees drips down with the spring rain.
> -That's ridiculous.
> -All right, it's because you are looking at it from this side of the fence. If you go over to the other side, it won't be so green.
> -You are not funny.
> -Okay. It's because of chlorophyll in the grass. The chlorophyll has rings in it that absorb all colors of light except green.
> -You're not making this up, are you?
> -Would I ever make anything up, sweetheart?
> -It's very hard to tell with you sometimes.

I began to play this simulacrum of her often when she was in high school, and over time it became a bit of a habit. Now I keep her on all the time, every day.

There were later simulacra when she was older, many of them with far better resolution. But this one is my favorite. It reminded me of better times, before the world changed irrevocably.

The day I took this, we finally managed to make an oneiropagida that was small enough to fit within a chassis that could be carried on your shoulder. That later became the prototype for the Carousel Mark I, our first successful home simulacrum camera. I brought it home and asked Anna to pose for it. She stood still next to the sun porch for two minutes while we chatted about her day.

She was perfect in the way that little daughters are always perfect in the eyes of their fathers. Her eyes lit up when she saw that I was home. She had just come back from day camp, and she was full of stories she wanted to tell me and questions she wanted to ask me. She wanted me to take her to the beach to fly her new kite, and I promised to help her with her sunprint kit. I was glad to have captured her at that moment.

That was a good day.

Anna Larimore:

The last time my father and I saw each other was after my mother's accident. His lawyer called, knowing that I would not have answered my father.

My mother was conscious, but barely. The other driver was already dead, and she was going to follow soon after.

"Why can't you forgive him?" she said. "I have. A man's life is not defined by one thing. He loves me. And he loves you."

I said nothing. I only held her hand and squeezed it. He came in and we both spoke to her but not to each other, and after half an hour she went to sleep and did not wake up.

The truth was, I was ready to forgive him. He looked old—a quality that children are among the last to notice about their parents—and there was a kind of frailty about him that made me question myself. We walked silently out of the hospital together. He asked if I had a place to stay in the city, and I said no. He opened the passenger side door, and after hesitating for only a second, I slipped into his car.

We got home, and it was exactly the way I remembered it, even though I hadn't been home in years. I sat at the dinner table while he prepared frozen dinners. We spoke carefully to each other, the way we used to when I was in high school.

I asked him for a simulacrum of my mother. I don't take simulacra or keep them, as a rule. I don't have the same rosy view of them as the general public. But at that moment, I thought I understood their appeal. I wanted a piece of my mother to be always with me, an aspect of her presence.

He handed me a disc, and I thanked him. He offered me the use of his projector, but I declined. I wanted to keep the memory of my mother by myself for a while before letting the computer's extrapolations confuse real memories with made-up ones.

(And as things turned out, I've never used that simulacrum. Here, you can take a look at it later, if you want to see what she looked like. Whatever I remember of my mother, it's all real.)

It was late by the time we finished dinner, and I excused myself.

I walked up to my room.

And I saw the seven-year old me sitting on my bed. She had on this hideous dress that I must have blocked out of my memory—pink, flowery, and there was a bow in her hair.

-*Hello, I'm Anna. Pleased to meet you.*

So he had kept this thing around for years, this naïve, helpless caricature of me. During the time I did not speak to him, did he turn to this frozen trace of me, and contemplate this shadow of my lost faith and affection? Did he use this model of my childhood to fantasize about the conversations that he could not have with me? Did he even edit it, perhaps, to remove my petulance, to add in more saccharine devotion?

I felt violated. The little girl was undeniably me. She acted like me, spoke like me, laughed and moved and reacted like me. But she was not *me*.

I had grown and changed, and I'd come to face my father as an adult. But now I found a piece of myself had been taken and locked into this *thing*, a piece that allowed him to maintain a sense of connection with me that I did not want, that was not real.

The image of those naked women in his bed from years ago came rushing back. I finally understood why for so long they had haunted my dreams.

It is the way a simulacrum replicates the essence of the subject that makes it so compelling. When my father kept those simulacra of his women around, he maintained a connection to them, to the man he was when he had been with them, and thus committed a continuing emotional betrayal that was far worse than a momentary physical indiscretion. A pornographic image is a pure visual fantasy, but a simulacrum captures a state of mind, a dream. But *whose* dream? What I saw in his eyes that day was not sordid. It was too intimate.

By keeping and replaying this old simulacrum of my childhood, he was dreaming himself into reclaiming my respect and love, instead of facing the reality of what he had done, and the real me.

Perhaps it is the dream of every parent to keep his or her child in that brief period between helpless dependence and separate selfhood, when the parent is seen as perfect, faultless. It is a dream of control and mastery disguised as love, the dream that Lear had about Cordelia.

I walked down the stairs and out of the house, and I have not spoken to him since.

Paul Larimore:

A simulacrum lives in the eternal now. It remembers, but only hazily, since the oneiropagida does not have the resolution to discern and capture the subject's every specific memory. It learns, up to a fashion, but the further you stray from the moment the subject's mental life was captured, the less accurate the computer's extrapolations. Even the best cameras we offer can't project beyond a couple of hours.

But the oneiropagida is exquisite at capturing her mood, the emotional flavor of her thoughts, the quirky triggers for her smiles, the lilt of her speech, the precise, inarticulable quality of her turns of phrase.

And so, every two hours or so, Anna resets. She's again coming home from day camp, and again she's full of questions and stories for me. We talk, we have fun. We let our chat wander wherever it will. No conversation is ever the same. But she's forever the curious seven-year old who worshipped her father, and who thought he could do no wrong.

-*Dad, will you tell me a story?*

-Yes, of course. What story would you like?

-*I want to hear your cyberpunk version of Pinocchio again.*

-I'm not sure if I can remember everything I said last time.

-*It's okay. Just start. I'll help you.*

I love her so much.

Erin Larimore:

My baby, I don't know when you'll get this. Maybe it will only be after I'm gone. You can't skip over the next part. It's a recording. I want you to hear what I have to say.

Your father misses you.

He is not perfect, and he has committed his share of sins, the same as any man. But you have let that one moment, when he was at his weakest, overwhelm the entirety of your life together. You have compressed him, the whole of his life, into that one frozen afternoon, that sliver of him that was most flawed. In your mind, you traced that captured image again and again, until the person was erased by the stencil.

During all these years when you have locked him out, your father played an old simulacrum of you over and over, laughing, joking, pouring his heart out to you in a way that a seven-year old would understand. I would ask you on the phone if you'd speak to him, and then I couldn't bear to watch as I hung up while he went back to play the simulacrum again.

See him for who he really is.

-Hello there. Have you seen my daughter Anna?

• BREAKAWAY, BACKDOWN •
James Patrick Kelly

You know, in space nobody wears shoes.

Well, new temps wear slippers. They make the soles out of that adhesive polymer, griprite or griptite. Sounds like paper ripping when you lift your feet. Temps who've been up awhile wear this glove thing that snugs around the toes. The breakaways, they go barefoot. You can't really walk much in space, so they've reinvented their feet so they can pick up screwdrivers and spoons and stuff. It's hard because you lose fine motor control in micro gee. I had . . . have this friend, Elena, who could make a krill and tomato sandwich with her feet, but she had that operation that changes your big toe into a thumb. I used to kid her that maybe breakaways were climbing down the evolutionary ladder, not jumping off it. Are we people or chimps? She'd scratch her armpits and hoot.

Sure, breakaways have a sense of humor. They're people after all; it's just that they're like no people you know. The thing was, Elena was so limber that she could bite her toenails. So can you fix my shoe?

How long is that going to take? Why not just glue the heel back on?

I know they're Donya Durands, but I've got a party in half an hour, okay?

What, you think I'm going to walk around town barefoot? I'll wait—except what's with all these lights? It's two in the morning and you've got this place bright as noon in Khartoum. How about a little respect for the night?

Thanks. What did you say your name was? I'm Cleo.

You are, are you? Jane honey, lots of people *think* about going to space but you'd be surprised at how few actually apply—much less break away. So how old are you?

Oh, no, they like them young, just as long as you're over nineteen. No kids in space. So the stats don't scare you?

Not shoe repair, that's for sure. But if you can convince them you're serious, they'll find something for you to do. They trained me and I was nobody, a business major. I temped for almost fifteen months on *Victor Foxtrot* and I never could decide whether I loved or hated it. Still can't, so how could I even think about becoming a breakaway? Everything is loose up there, okay? It makes you come unstuck. The first thing that happens is you get spacesick. For a week your insides are so scrambled that you're trying to digest lunch with your cerebellum and write memos with your large intestine. Meanwhile your face puffs up so that you can't find yourself in the mirror anymore and your sinuses fill with cotton candy and you're fighting a daily hair mutiny. I might've backed down right off if it hadn't been for Elen—you know, the one with the clever toes? Then when you're totally miserable and empty and disoriented, your brain sorts things out again and you realize it's all magic. Some astrofairy has enchanted you. Your body is as light as a whisper, free as air. I'll tell you the most amazing thing about weightlessness. It doesn't go away. You keep falling: Down, up, sideways, whatever. You might bump into something once in a while but you never, ever slam into the ground. Extremely sexy, but it does take some getting used to. I kept having dreams about gravity. Down here you have a whole planet hugging you. But in space, it's not only you that's enchanted, it's all your stuff too. For instance, if *you* put that brush down, it stays. It doesn't decide to drift across the room and out the window and go visit Elena over on B deck. I had this pin that had been my mother's—a silver dove with a diamond eye—and somehow it escaped from a locked jewelry box. Turned up two months later in a dish of butterscotch pudding, almost broke Jack Pitzer's tooth. You get a lot of pudding in space. Oatmeal. Stews. Sticky food is easier to eat and you can't taste much of anything but salt and sweet anyway.

Why, do you think I'm babbling? God, I *am* babbling. It must be the Zentadone. The woman at the persona store said it was just supposed to be an icebreaker with a flirty edge to it, like Panital only more sincere. You wouldn't have any reset, would you?

Hey, spare me the lecture, honey. I know they don't allow personas in space. Anyway, imprinting is just a bunch of pro-brain propaganda. Personas are temporary—*period*. When you stop taking the pills, the personas go away and you're your plain old vanilla self again; there's bushels of studies that say so. I'm just taking a little vacation from Cleo. Maybe I'll go away for a weekend, or a week or a month but eventually I'll come home. Always have, always will.

I don't care *what* your Jesus puppet says; you can't trust godware, okay? Look, I'm not going to convince you and you're not going to convince me. Truce?

The shoes? Four, five years. Let's see, I bought them in '36. Five years. I had to store them while I was up.

You get used to walking in spike heels, actually. I mean, I'm not going to run a marathon or climb the Matterhorn. Elena has all these theories of why men think spikes are sexy. Okay, they're kind of a short term body mod. They stress the leg muscles, which makes you look tense, which leads most men to assume you could use a serious screwing. And they push your fanny out like you're making the world an offer. But most important is that, when you're teetering around in heels, it tells a man that if he chases you, you're not going to get very far. Not only do spike heels say you're vulnerable, they say you've *chosen* to be vulnerable. Of course, it's not quite the same in micro gee. She was my mentor, Elena. Assigned to teach me how to live in space.

I was an ag tech. Worked as a germ wrangler in the edens.

Microorganisms. Okay, you probably think that if you stick a seed in some dirt, add some water and sunlight and wait a couple of months, Mother Nature hands you a head of lettuce. Doesn't work that way, especially not in space. The edens are synergistic, symbiotic ecologies. Your carbo crops, your protein crops, your vitamin crops—they're all fussy about the neighborhood germs. If you don't keep your *clostridia* and *rhizobium* in balance, your eden will rot to compost. Stinky, slimy compost. It's important work—and duller than accounting. It wouldn't have been so bad if we could've talked on the job, but CO_2 in the edens runs 6%, which is great for plants but will kill you if you're not wearing a breather. Elena painted an enormous smile on mine, with about eight hundred teeth in it. She had lips on hers, puckered so that they looked like she was ready to be kissed. Alpha Ralpha the chicken man had this plastic beak. Only sometimes we switched—confused the hell out of the nature lovers. I'll tell you, the job would've been a lot easier if we could've kept the rest of the crew out, but the edens are designed for recreation as much as food production. On *Victor Foxtrot* we had to have sign-ups between 8:00 and 16:00. See, the edens have lots of open space and we keep them eight degrees over crew deck nominal and they're lit twenty hours a day by grolights and solar mirrors and they have big windows. Crew floats around sucking up the view, soaking up photons, communing with the life force, shredding foliage and in general getting in our way. Breakaways are the worst; they actually adopt plants like they were pets. Is that crazy or what? I mean, a tomato has a life span of three, maybe four months before it gets too leggy and stops bearing. I've seen grown men cry because Elena pulled up their favorite marigold.

No, all my plants now are silk. When I backed down, I realized that I didn't want anything to do with the day. My family was a bunch of poor nobodies; we moved to the night when I was seven. So nightshifting was like coming home. The fact is, I got too much sun while I was up. The sun is not my friend. Haven't seen real daylight in over a year; I make a point of it. I have a day-night timeshare at Lincoln Street Under. While the sun is shining I'm asleep or safely cocooned. At dusk my roomie comes home and I go out to work and play. Hey, being a mommy to legumes is *not* what I miss about space. How about you? What turned you into an owl?

Well, well, maybe you *are* serious about breaking away. Sure, they prefer recruits who've nightshifted. Shows them you've got circadian discipline.

Elena said something like that once. She said that it's hard to scare someone to death in broad daylight. It isn't just that the daytime is too crowded, it's too tame. The night is edgier, scarier. Sexier. You say and do things that wouldn't occur to you at lunchtime. It's because we don't really belong in the night. In order to survive here we have to fight all the old instincts warning us not to wander around in the dark because we might fall off a cliff or get eaten by a saber-toothed tiger. Living in the night gives you a kind of extra . . . I don't know . . .

Right. And it's the same with space; it's even scarier and sexier. Well, maybe sexy isn't exactly the right word, but you know what I mean. Actually, I think that's what I miss most about it. I was more alive then that I ever was before. Maybe too alive. People live fast up there. They know the stats; they *have* to. You know, you sort of remind me of Elena. Must be the eyes—it sure as hell isn't the body. If you ever get up, give her a shout. You'd like her, even though she doesn't wear shoes anymore.

Almost a year. I wish we could talk more, but it's hard. She transferred to the *Marathon*; they're out surveying Saturn's moons. There's like a three hour lag; it's impossible to have real-time conversation. She sent a few vids, but it hurt too much to watch them. They were all happy chat, you know? Nothing important in them. I didn't plan on missing her so much. So, you have any college credits?

No real difference between Harvard and a net school, unless you're some kind of snob about bricks.

Now that's a hell of a thing to be asking a perfect stranger. What do I look like, some three star slut? Don't make assumptions just because I'm wearing spiked heels. For all you know, honey, I could be dating a basketball player. Maybe I'm tired of staring at his navel when we dance. If you're going to judge people by appearances, hey, *you're* the one with the machine stigmata. What's that supposed to be, rust or dried blood?

Well, you ought to be. Though actually, that's what everyone wants to know. That, and how do you go to the bathroom. Truth is, Jane, sex is complicated, like everything about space. First of all, forget all that stuff you've heard about doing it while you're floating free. It's dangerous, hard work and no fun. You want to have sex in space, one or both of you have to be tied down. Most hetero temps use some kind of a joystrap. It's this wide circular elastic that fits around you and your partner. Helps you stay coupled, okay? But even with all the gear, sex can be kind of subtle. As in disappointing. You don't realize how erotic weight is until there isn't any. You want to make love to a balloon? Some people do nothing but oral—keeps the vectors down. Of course the breakaways, they've reinvented love, just like everything else. They have this kind of sex where they don't move. If there's penetration they just float in place, staring into one another's eyes or some such until they tell one another that it's time to have an orgasm and then they do. If they're homo, they just touch each other. Elena tried to show me how, once. I don't know why, but it didn't happen for me. Maybe I was too embarrassed because I was the only one naked. She said I'd learn eventually, that it was part of breaking away.

No, I thought I was going to break away, I really did. I stuck it out until the very last possible day. It's hard to explain. I mean, when nobodies on earth look up at night—no offense, Jane, I was one too—what calls them is the romance of it all. The high frontier, okay? Sheena Steele and Captain Kirk, cowboys and asteroids. Kid stuff, except they don't let kids in space because of the cancer. Then you go up and once you're done puking, you realize that it was all propaganda. Space is boring and it's indescribably magic at the same time—how can that be? Sometimes I'd be working in an eden and I'd look out the windows and I'd see earth, blue as a dream, and I'd think of all the people down there, twelve billion ants, looking up into the night and wondering what it was like to be me. I swear I could feel their envy, as sure as I can feel your floor beneath me now. It's part of what holds you up when you're in space. You know you're not an ant; there are fewer than twenty thousand breakaways. You're brave and you're doomed and you're different from everyone else who has ever lived. Only then your shift ends and it's time to go to the gym and spend three hours pumping the ergorack in a squeeze suit to fight muscle loss in case you decide to back down. I'll tell you, being a temp is hell. The rack is hard work; if you're not exhausted afterward, you haven't done it right. And you sweat, *God*. See, the sweat doesn't run off. It pools in the small of your back and the crook of your arm and under your chin and clings there, shivering like an amoeba. And while you're slaving on the rack, Elena is getting work done or reading or sleeping or talking about you with her breakaway pals. They have three more hours in their day, see, and they don't ever have to worry about backing down. Then every nine weeks you have to leave what you're doing and visit one of the wheel habitats and readjust to your weight for a week so that when you come back to *Victor Foxtrot*, you get spacesick all over again. But you tell yourself it's all worth it because it's not only space that you're exploring; it's yourself. How many people can say that? You have to find out who you are so that you decide what to hold onto and what to let go of . . . Excuse me, I can't talk about this anymore right now.

No, I'll be all right. Only . . . okay, so you don't have any reset. You must have some kind of flash?

That'll have to do. Tell you what, I'll buy the whole liter from you.

Ahh, ethanol with a pedigree. But a real backdown kind of drug, Jane—weighs way too much to bring out of the gravity well. And besides, the flash is about the same as hitting yourself over the head with the bottle. Want a slug?

Come on, it's two-thirty. Time to start the party. You're making me late, you know.

Do me a favor, would you? Pass me those shoes on the shelf there . . . no, no the blue ones. Yes. Beautiful. Real leather, right? I love leather shoes. They're like faces. I mean, you can polish them but once they get wrinkles, you're stuck with them. Look at my face, okay? See these wrinkles here, right at the corner of my eyes? Got them working in the edens. Too much sun. How old do you think I am?

Twenty-nine, but that's okay. I was up fifteen months and it only aged me four years. Still, my permanent bone loss is less than eight percent and I've built my muscles back up and I only picked up eighteen rads and I'm not half as crazy as I used to be. Hey, I'm a walking advertisement for backing down. So have I talked you out of it yet? I don't mean to, okay? I'd probably go up again, if they'd have me.

Don't plan on it; the wheel habitats are strictly for tourists. They cost ten times as much to build as a micro gee can and once you're in one you're pretty much stuck to the rim. And you're still getting zapped by cosmic rays and solar x-rays and energetic neutrons. If you're going to risk living in space, you might as well enjoy it. Besides, all the important work gets done by breakaways.

See, that's where you're wrong. It's like Elena used to say. We didn't conquer space, it conquered us. Break away and you're giving up forty, maybe fifty years of life, okay? The stats don't lie. Fifty-six is the *average*. That means some breakaways die even younger.

You don't? Well, good for you. Hey, it looks great—better than new. How much?

Does that include the vodka?

Well thanks. Listen, Jane, I'm going to tell you something, a secret they ought to tell everybody before they go up.

No, I'm not. Promise. So anyway, on my breakaway day Elena calls me to her room and tells me that she doesn't think I should do it, that I won't be happy living in space. I'm so stunned that I start crying, which is a very back-down thing to do. I try to argue, but she's been mentoring for years and knows what she's talking about. Only about a third breakaway—but, of course, you know that. Anyway, it gets strange then. She says to me, "I have something to show you," and then she starts to strip. See, the time she'd made love to me, she wouldn't let me do anything to her. And like I said, she'd kept her clothes on; breakaways have this thing about showing themselves to temps. I mean, I'd seen her hands before, her feet. They looked like spiders. And I'd seen her face. Kissed it, even. But now I'm looking at her naked body for the first time. She's fifty-one years old. I think she must've been taller than me once, but it's hard to be sure because she has the deep micro gee slouch. Her muscles have atrophied so her papery skin looks as if it's been sprayed onto her bones. She's had both breasts prophylactically removed. "I've got 40% bonerot," she says, "and I mass thirty-eight kilos." She shows the scars from the operations to remove her thyroid and ovaries, the tap on her hip where they take the monthly biopsy to test for leukemia. "Look at me," she says. "What do you see?" I start to tell her that I've read the literature and watched all the vids and I'm prepared for what's going to happen but she shushes me. "Do you think I'm beautiful?" she says. All I can do is stare. "*I* think I am," she says. "So do the others. It's our nature, Cleo. This is how space makes us over. Can you tell me you *want* this to happen to you?" And I couldn't. See, she knew me better than I knew myself. What I wanted was to float forever, to feel I was special, to stay with her. Maybe I was in love with her. I don't know if that's possible. But loving someone isn't a reason to break away, especially if the stats say that someone will be dead in five years. So I told her she was right and thanked her for everything she'd done and got on the shuttle that same day and backed down and became just another nobody. And she gave up mentoring and went to Saturn and now that we've forgotten all about each other we can start living happily ever after.

No, here's the secret, honey. The heart is a muscle, okay? That means it shrinks in space. All breakaways know it, now you do too. Anyway, it's been nice talking to you.

Sure. Good night.

· SAYING THE NAMES ·
Maggie Clark

On the shuttle out to our connecting flight, the Bo assigned to my mission fixes the bulge of his eyes unwaveringly upon me. I was told to expect this, the species so alien to death it finds our every parting curious; its sense of privacy so absent, not one of its forty-three languages contains the word.

Though L-drive allows us to return long before our loved ones pass on, just the thought of my journey's purpose already has me pining for home: of all the ways I've imagined meeting my father, as defense council in his murder trial does not rank high on the list. Our shuttle crests the white round of the L-ship's hull, powering down non-essentials while preparing to dock.

I can bear the Bo's steady gaze even less in the dark.

In-flight, I dream. Vega III, my home world, holds a species of deep-water squid that can regress at will to any prior phase in its development. When I was small my mother introduced me to this creature as a means of describing the Bo, and with them, my father's permanent absence. No more was ever said about either the man or the mission, and for years I thought of the Bo as slimy cephalopods forever darting from the light. Not until the Academy did my perception of the species take its proper form, of large, mottled amphibians with forelimbs caught between quadrupedal and bipedal use, who did indeed revert to earlier stages of development when their warts grew too big for them to move.

Before then, as a child embroiled in misconceptions, I dreamed of my father trapped at the bottom of the Bo's oceans, assailed by giant barbed tentacles in underground caves. Now he is indeed held prisoner, as best the Bo understand the term, and while hurtling towards him in a prison all its own, my subconscious returns to these vague, inky nightmares of my youth. When I wake for meals, taken with the crew in a long, narrow galley sporting tiny portholes to the stars, we can hear the Bo singing through the ventilation shafts. I find it hard sometimes just to chew.

The captain sits with me the day before our arrival. He has the appropriate look of a spaceman—hardened, lank, with an indifferent cast about his beard, hands lanced with burns and calluses from his work. I think he expects some move on my part for his companionship—the novice traveler's last, desperate cleaving to the familiar before ejection into the great and terrible unknown—but

I've decided to wait for the return trip to make such an overture, and only then if I can't bring my father home.

Captain Sedgwick sets a small parcel before me.

"What's this?"

In the wrapping I find two small devices, each the size of an earbud.

"White noise," he says. "You'll need it. To work, to sleep."

"Is it that loud?"

"It's that constant."

"I have a portable."

"That's not enough. Here—" He shows me the settings, each one's capacity to block out Bo songs on select frequencies. "You're going to be speaking, I gather? For the trial?"

"Of course. But surely then—"

"It never stops. It can't stop. You know the story of the first ambassador?"

"And the last, yes." I worry he'll go on anyway, but the captain accepts my response at face value, or at least seems not to unduly favor the sound of his own voice.

"Well, hold to it, then. They abbreviate nothing. Sentences can go on for days, and they don't take kindly to being told to keep it short. You're better off just blocking out the background bits."

"Thanks."

I remember the story of the ambassador from Conflict Differentials at the Academy, where it served as a classic anecdote on the limits of preparation. The poor, over-educated man in this case thought to ask what the Bo called themselves and their home world, so he might see both proper names used throughout the galaxy in place of other species' words. Pleased by this gesture, the Bo proceeded to speak the names as they did everything else—at length, and sparing no historical or biological detail. For the first three hours, captivated by the sudden wealth of data, the ambassador recorded everything, noting patterns where he could, grappling with obscure referents whenever they emerged, but by the fourth, exhausted, and thinking at last of the realpolitik of his original query, he asked if there might be some shorter variant he could write down instead.

Though slow to speak, his counterparts were surprisingly quick to anger, abbreviation an act of offense, of disdain, with no equal among their kind. In the immediacy of their contempt, they gave the ambassador one syllable, Bo, to serve for both requests, and thereafter declared a complete disinterest in diplomacy with the rest of the galaxy, its vast species all clearly lacking either the intelligence or civility to learn real words.

The utterance of these vehement declarations of course took a week all its own, during which time the ambassador suffered a massive heart attack from the constant, thunderous rebukes directed against his person, and soon after—one hopes with a modicum of regret—the Bo shipped his body and field notes home. No ambassadorship has since existed on their planet, and even scientists avoid the territory. My father is the first in four human generations to make Bo his home.

Captain Sedgwick hesitates at the entrance to my berth. "Your father . . . "

"Yes?"

"If he's found guilty . . . "

Now it's my turn to hesitate. "Like you said, the Bo don't abbreviate anything. And they don't take kindly to those who do."

Captain Sedgwick nods, drumming his hand once on the frame of my door. I study the floor so as not to watch him when he goes.

I had never even seen a picture of my father until his vid showed up at my office, requesting my presence on an alien planet with no readily discernible criminal code. Still, when the Bo bring him to meet my shuttle—his hair long, matted and graying; his body broad, and lean, and gaunt—I can't help thinking how much he's changed, how tired he now looks.

Bo is a tidally-locked world, one side of the planet forever scorched by the heat and light of its sun, the other cast in perpetual darkness and cold. Yet for a particular stretch of land along the circumference between opposing halves, the constant flux of hot and cold creates an oasis where life somehow prevails. What *manner* of life is debatable, however: where the shuttle sets down—presumably a metropolis, from the intensity of Bo songs alone—it is foggy and dark, and I think it no wonder that a human should look wilted under such an oppressive absence of sun.

At the very least, the Bo do not have my father in restraints when I arrive; indeed, they seem perfectly uncertain how best to handle him, and say as much in ceaseless song to one another, their hind-legs and throat sacs rumbling with agitated words on at least two different wavelengths apiece. I wish I could be so open with my own uncertainty, approaching my father for the first time with no sense of what to do next. Shake hands? Embrace?

My father bows his head, then looks at me with an uncomfortable smile. "Hello, Nia. I'm glad you came."

Be angry. Yes. This is an option I'd forgotten, a feeling I'd pushed aside for years. It rears its head now at my father's proximity, the almost amused quality of guilt upon his face. Be angry, yes, and make damn sure the Bo spare my father's life, so I have time to be angry some more.

The Bo have not yet finished their death songs for the one my father is said to have killed, and the city rumbles with this unrelenting grief as we walk the briny length of the docks under escort. Marsh homes emerge to either side of us in the fog, while a thread of golden light persists on distant waters, recalling the intractable sun just beyond. Absent a routine for criminal courts, the Bo permit my father to move where he will during waking hours, but he is under strict curfew, and no Bo will look favorably upon escape.

"If they cannot speak the way they must, they are silent," my father says. "The Bo who came with you—he said nothing, of course. That's how they survive on the rare occasions they travel among us."

"So if they're suddenly silent, no one's going to come running."

"Right. But it's still uncommon. Most often, it signals an impending regression."

"Which they do alone, away from the noise?"

"Quite the opposite. They regress in plain sight, with as much noise around them as possible." My father pauses, a measure of excitement rising in his voice. "Actually, it's what I came here to study—the function of that regression, its mechanisms." When I make no reply he continues, gathering steam:

"You see, evolutionarily, the Bo are already extraordinary. They exist in a narrow margin of viable territory in the middle of a planet of extremes, so of course there's little competition, and few possible niches to fill. Consequently, they lack the evolutionary incentive to evolve fully out of vestigial forms, and boast a wealth of intermediate features practically unheard of at this level of sentience. But then, as if that weren't enough, there's also their ability to regress, a process we've only seen among rudimentary species before—aquatic animals, mostly, and some insects. On Vega III, even, there's a squid—"

"Yes, I know."

He registers my tone and cuts his lecture short. "Nia," he says, gently.

I find I can't look directly at him. "We have a lot of casework to cover."

He waits, but my position does not improve. "All right," he says at last. There is an unpleasant weight in his words now, a pointed brevity. "What do you want to know?"

The Bo assigned to me has a large, dark patch of skin around his left eye, a welcome distinction that allows me to pick it out from others in a crowd. I think to wish it good night after my father is taken away and I'm escorted to quarters of my own, but I worry the cursory words might cause offense. And, of course, with the sky here dark at all hours, illumined only slightly by twin orange moons on the horizon, the concept of "night" also seems moot. I am thus neither surprised nor upset when the Bo leaves without speaking one word to me, its hind-legs humming general notes of exhaustion as it lurches into the street. Better silence, I imagine, than diplomatic incident.

I too am exhausted, but even with Sedgwick's white noise buds turned on

I lie awake in my pod, replaying my father's words and reconstructing the scene of the Bo's sudden death. According to my father, the deceased was his laboratory assistant, a Bo who predominantly sang words of discovery while collecting soil and water samples from the metropolitan marshlands. Listening to my father's detailed description of events—the circumstances under which he and the Bo met and hashed out a working relationship, the hours preceding the Bo's unfortunate demise, the means by which its death became suspect—the complexity of my task grows painfully apparent. The Bo are so suspicious of brevity, so dependent on motive for truth, that to ask potential corroborating witnesses their side of the story bears all the tell-tale signs of walking a minefield. Will they trust me? Will they speak? And if so, how long will all their answers take?

My father's answers alone are slower and more drawn out than I am used to in my work, a consequence I nonetheless expected of his thirty-odd years among the Bo. How does a human manage so long without its own kind, I wondered. We have ritualistic orders on Vega III that emulate emptiness, silence, and of course celibacy, but for the singing out of our very existence, our every interaction in minute and protracted detail, I can only conjure up one god cult that believed the universe would cease to exist if its singing ever stopped. All of its members perished in an avalanche thousands of years back, of course. The universe, to my knowledge, has not.

My thoughts drift eventually to Captain Sedgwick, though the air is clammy and cold, and my pod, an unusual texture, a truly alien space. There are few places, I had thought, where human desire could not reach, and yet my father seems to have found one—even sought it out. I think of my mother, the robustness of her figure, the strength of her mind, given up for over thirty loveless years in the far reaches of space. What kind of man was my father then, to commit such an act of self-denial? What kind of man is he now, having done it?

I turn off the white noise buds, having given up on sleep. One sacrifice, I think, as Bo songs rumble about me, in the foolhardy hope of ever understanding another's.

In the first waking hours on the dark side of Bo, my father takes me to his laboratory, the scene of the incident in question. Nothing has been moved since that wake cycle—not even the dead Bo, its mummifying remains giving me a start when I approach the head of the room. There are no morgues here, no cemeteries: To the Bo this is cast-off matter, a skin one might find at the site of regression. The Bo that accompanies us does not so much as eye the mound of gray and crumbling flesh. It looks bored, standing guard by the door, and hums impatience alongside its standard mourning chord.

"There have been deaths before," my father says, his hands ghosting, but not touching, the long array of enclosures sustaining samples of other lifeforms on Bo. "It's rare, since their proximity to one another, their constant chatter, sings out potential threats. Few environmental disasters ever claim a life, but it does happen. The last was a year after my arrival, a Bo in the middle of regression when a sandstorm hit in the drylands, where the light touches the black rocks and makes them molten, and plant life turns to fire in an instant. The Bo was in a bad place, an inopportune place, and it also caught fire. There were Bo about it, saying its names, minding its abandoned skins as it sought to escape the heat through regression, and they might have caught it when the winds struck—but they didn't. They missed. They were slow. To this day they sing mourning songs that are heard over the escarpments, down in the valleys with the hot and the oxidized rocks. They sing for all their poor timing, and the poor timing of the Bo in their care, and their fears of regression even now. None of those watchers has regressed again yet, that I know of, though their warts have grown heavy and stiff, and their sacs hardly move when they speak . . . "

In his lumpy Bo cloak my father looks toad-like himself, hunched over to peer at old notes on his desk. He has been speaking this rambling, proto-Bo-speak since our arrival, and even without my earbuds I quickly tune him out. Instead of lending him my ear I muster the courage to approach the decaying corpse, slumped over in the bottom of an open tank. But what was it doing inside? How could it have fallen in? My eyes narrow at the thread of a plastic tube still affixed to the back of its wrist.

"I thought you said this Bo was assisting you."

"It was."

I turn to my father, my gaze flicking quickly to the Bo by the door. "Can we talk in private?"

My father straightens, glancing at my Bo in turn, then back to me. His longwinded speech comes to its end with one word: "No."

"As your legal counsel I'd strongly advise—"

"You're not my counsel, Nia."

"Excuse me?"

He shakes his head. "Say what you were going to say."

I hesitate. I know I should ignore my father's words and get him to plead mental unfitness for refusing legal aid, but at the tone in his voice, that base dismissal, the primal anger rises in me again. There is a dead Bo beside me with an IV sticking out of its arm. What game does my father think he's playing now?

"This Bo wasn't just assisting you," I say at last. "It *was* the experiment."

My father looks disconcertingly triumphant. "Yes," he says. "It most certainly was."

• • •

In the gathering space of the Bo, the songs from the spectator pods are indeed deafening and unchecked by the gravity of proceedings, so I gratefully fine-tune my precious earbuds until most of the chatter has been reduced to a murmur; the one voice that still filters through is that of the inquisitor Bo, who presides over the room with tremendous warts wreathed about his skull and coursing down his mottled forelimbs. Beside me my father is quite content to recline in his pod, so that my blood alone is still agitated from the fall-out of his words in the laboratory, now two wake and rest cycles past.

At this time I have just finished my opening remarks to the Inquisitor, who itself took half an hour to formally greet the room and establish the purpose of this second wake cycle's assembly of Bo. My own remarks were simple: I tried to draw them out in appropriate Bo-style but did not last ten minutes, though in that time I had already explained my journey, how far I'd traveled, how I first learned of my father's case, and what it was like to arrive on Bo—how different everything seemed, and how deeply sorry I was if any of my words gave offence in their brevity, as concision was all I was used to back home.

Now we come to the part of the trial for which my father has given clear instructions, and at which I can feel his gaze surreptitiously upon me. The Inquisitor Bo asks me if I think to plead my father's case in this matter, and after five minutes, when its question is completed and fully translated, I glance at my father and then turn to the incessantly murmuring room.

I say to them: "My father has caused the death of a Bo. Of this there can be no doubt. You know it and now I know it too. Therefore I do not come to draw out a game of the courts, of misdirection and passive deceit as it is played on my world, but to serve in another role, an honest role, secondary to my father's testimony, which I hope you will take into consideration before verdict is passed." I bite my lip before the last: "To that end, I stand before you, Nia Palino: Character witness in my father's defense."

The conversation in my father's laboratory two wake and rest cycles prior was not so remarkable in form, the whole of it oversimplified by my shock at his last words, as in function, and thrust. After my father's self-congratulatory answer regarding the dead Bo there was really only one thing I could think to say, so I said it:

"What the hell have you done?"

"Easy," my father said, holding out his hands. "It was consensual. The Bo agreed. We followed every precaution. It's just that, this time, it failed."

"*This* time! What do you think you were doing, putting its life at risk even once like that?"

"'Like that.'" My father's mouth twitched in annoyance. "You don't even know what *that* is."

"I know a Bo is dead because of it. I know it could cost you your life, too. What else do I need to know? What the hell were you doing that was so important you'd risk everything—even your own damned life—to see it through?"

A glint returned to my father's eyes, and he smiled. "What do you think?" he said. "Go on. Try me."

I set my teeth against the smugness in his voice, the goading. "You and your goddamn science," I said. But this seemed only to feed into his pleasure, his aggravating tone.

"Exactly. So you'll be my character witness, then?"

"*Character* witness! Now that's a laugh. I don't even *know* you. At *all*. How could you possibly . . . ?" I was too angry to finish my sentence, and stalked back to the body instead. Though considerably decayed, there were strange features upon the remains that stood out—clear differences between this Bo and the Bo to my right, still guarding the door. If I'd been any more level-headed I might have paused long enough then and there to question my father about each incongruent detail—but of course, I was not. How could I have been?

"Right again," my father said, not even remotely giving me pause to cool down. "And *why* don't you know me? *What* did I choose over you, and your mother?"

I could hear my own heartbeat in my ears, my skin hot to the touch. "Goddamn you, dad," I said.

If my words deflated his humor then, they did not also strip him of his relief, the sense of it clear in both voice and expression when I faced him again. "God? Yes," he said softly, meeting my sudden, asserted gaze. "But with your help, Nia, at least not the Bo."

I am a good speaker, even under unusual circumstances. Even when obliged to be more bombastic than even the most pompous human windbag I know (which, in my profession, is always saying a lot). And so I tell the assembly of Bo that my father's scientific ideals are so important to him that he even abandoned his family in their pursuit over thirty years ago, knowing full well that humans cannot regress, and thus that such opportunities for kinship, once forsaken, almost never emerge again. Considering the ignorance of my audience, the Bo's absence of preferential family bonding from which to draw comparison for this loss, I then explain what it means to be a father, and a husband, and also a daughter or a wife lacking the desired presence of one of the former two.

I close by offering up a variation of the words my father gave at yesterday's first assembly of Bo: my conviction that the Bo's death happened in the name of science, as a consensual act to that end alone, and that if any among the Bo in attendance grieved the loss of their companion, rest assured they could not even begin to approach the grief my father had felt at the time of its passing and every moment since, having sacrificed so much of himself, his mortality, and all claims to happiness therein to those same scientific ideals, only to see his greatest work destroyed in the sunset of his life. (I have to backtrack here alone, to explain the term "sunset," and then to emphasize how the term's very strangeness among the Bo only furthers my point about the sanctity of life to a human being.)

The verdict comes back in four days, taking another full day to be delivered, during which time I fall asleep regularly in the courtroom, while my Bo ducks out on occasion to provide us with food and drink. Twice I linger by the waste receptacles, nauseated by the poorness of my sleep, stalling my return to that ceaseless chatter of spectator Bo as long as I can, clamping my hands to my ears in an effort to recall the sound of pure silence: A fairy tale I hold deep in my heart. I have my white noise buds on their highest settings by the end of it all, and still the Bo-speak trickles through, my ears damnably attuned by then to the chorus of them against all odds, all internal appeals for sanity, and peace.

Finally, the summation arrives: guilty, but pardoned. I close my eyes and sink in my seat. My father is silent, unmoving beside me. I fall asleep again, the whole of my body tingling and drained, and when I wake anew he is gone: The gathering space, empty, save for one Bo with a dark cast over its left eye, waiting patiently off to one side.

"Can I go home now?" I hear the words come out in a croak and think only, to hell with convention and prudence: Let the Bo's anger pour out. But to my great surprise, the Bo hesitates, parting its long, thin mouth in turn, and with clear effort musters a mere three words in response:

"It is done."

It is not, of course, done. Captain Sedgwick greets me grimly when my shuttle docks in the dark cavern of his ship. He knows nothing of my father's verdict save the language of my body, and my body is tired and defeated. We speak scarcely at all before the inevitable unraveling of tensions between us, my blissfully dry berth turned doubly warm-blooded for a spell. Only after, in the darkness, which I find at last I am learning to bear, do I allow myself to think through all of my lingering doubts.

That my father was experimenting with regression was apparent, but so too, it seemed to me, were the aims of his work. Perhaps the Bo at large could not see what I had seen—the discordant number of digits on the dead Bo's shriveled body, the unusual nature of its legs, its head, and its chest. But my father had also said the Bo sought out companion songs when regressing. Could the Bo have missed that, too? Had none of them wondered who had been this Bo's singer as it regrew?

In the long, dark night that followed the trial, my thoughts had grown wilder still: Perhaps saying the names did not sustain the universe, but what if the ritual of it could sustain even one creature, one Bo at a time? And if those songs changed—if the *singer* changed—what of the Bo in regression? Could it take on other forms through the right song alone? These might all have been the idle, fool thoughts of a non-scientist, an outsider—easily pondered, that is, and just as easily let go—if it hadn't been for the last conversation I had on Bo.

I knew it would also be the last time I saw my father, that conversation in the last wake cycle before the shuttle arrived to take me home. My father was back in the laboratory by then, dusting the rank and file of his reclaimed research shelves, when I entered for one last look around. The dead Bo, I quickly noted, was now gone.

"I've buried it," my father said. "In case you're wondering. The Bo don't care, don't mind what happens to the flesh."

"Do you mean that?" I said. "*It?*"

My father paused in his cleaning to look at me. "What else would I mean?"

My heart was pounding at his scrutiny, and I knew then that the anger I felt for him, the coarse utilitarianism of his first and only attempt to contact me—to use me as a tool of his own, meticulous construction and then cast aside again—had to be coloring my view of things. No human could be so cruel, I told myself—so cold. Everyone, I had almost convinced myself, had a soft spot somewhere. Even my Bo had been kindly, in its way, by the end.

"Her," I said at last. "That's what you were doing, wasn't it? Turning the Bo into something else, something not just for science, but for you. Thirty years alone out here. Thirty *years*—"

"I was *not* alone." The terseness in my father's voice sings out my only victory—meager, and for me already fraught with remorse. I do not say the words that follow in my head: *But now you are, aren't you?*

Some losses are caverns. His, I realize at long last, are active mines.

Our breath has fogged up the tiny porthole in my L-ship berth, blotting out the farthest stars, and home. Captain Sedgwick sits on the edge of the bunk, finding his boots, hitching up his uniform to his hips but no further, not yet. I rest my hand on the small of his browned and hairy back, studying my fingers in a glimmer of starlight, as just days ago I had studied the dead Bo's—all five digits not quite squid-like, but still strong enough, pliant enough, to hold something fierce in its grip and never let go.

* 2011 Parsec Award winner

• GOSSAMER •
Stephen Baxter

The flitter bucked.

Lvov looked up from her data desk, startled. Beyond the flitter's translucent hull, the wormhole was flooded with sheets of blue-white light which raced towards and past the flitter, giving Lvov the impression of huge, uncontrolled speed.

"We've got a problem," Cobh said. The pilot bent over her own data desk, a frown creasing her thin face.

Lvov had been listening to her data desk's synthesized murmur on temperature inversion layers in nitrogen atmospheres; now she tapped the desk to shut it off. The flitter was a transparent tube, deceptively warm and comfortable. Impossibly fragile. *Astronauts have problems in space,* she thought. *But not me. I'm no hero; I'm only a researcher.* Lvov was twenty-eight years old; she had no plans to die—and certainly not during a routine four-hour hop through a Poole wormhole that had been human-rated for eighty years.

She clung to her desk, her knuckles whitening, wondering if she ought to feel scared.

Cobh sighed and pushed her data desk away; it floated before her. "Close up your suit and buckle up."

"What's wrong?"

"Our speed through the wormhole has increased." Cobh pulled her own restraint harness around her. "We'll reach the terminus in another minute—"

"What? But we should have been travelling for another half-hour."

Cobh looked irritated. "I know that. I think the Interface has become unstable. The wormhole is buckling."

"What does that mean? Are we in danger?"

Cobh checked the integrity of Lvov's pressure suit, then pulled her data desk to her. Cobh was a Caucasian, strong-faced, a native of Mars, perhaps fifty years old. "Well, we can't turn back. One way or the other it'll be over in a few more seconds—hold tight—"

Now Lvov could see the Interface itself, the terminus of the wormhole: The Interface was a blue-white tetrahedron, an angular cage that exploded at her from infinity.

Glowing struts swept over the flitter.

The craft hurtled out of the collapsing wormhole. Light founted around the fleeing craft, as stressed spacetime yielded in a gush of heavy particles.

Lvov glimpsed stars, wheeling.

Cobh dragged the flitter sideways, away from the energy fount—

There was a *lurch*, a discontinuity in the scene beyond the hull. Suddenly a planet loomed before them.

"Lethe," Cobh said. "Where did that come from? I'll have to take her down—we're too close—"

Lvov saw a flat, complex landscape, grey-crimson in the light of a swollen moon. The scene was dimly lit, and it rocked wildly as the flitter tumbled. And, stretching between world and moon, she saw—

No. It was impossible.

The vision was gone, receded into darkness.

"Here it comes," Cobh yelled.

Foam erupted, filling the flitter. The foam pushed into Lvov's ears, mouth and eyes; she was blinded, but she found she could breathe.

She heard a collision, a grinding that lasted seconds, and she imagined the flitter ploughing its way into the surface of the planet. She felt a hard lurch, a rebound.

The flitter came to rest.

A synthesized voice emitted blurred safety instructions. There was a ticking as the hull cooled.

In the sudden stillness, still blinded by foam, Lvov tried to recapture what she had seen. *Spider-web. It was a web, stretching from the planet to its moon.*

"Welcome to Pluto." Cobh's voice was breathless, ironic.

Lvov stood on the surface of Pluto.

The suit's insulation was good, but enough heat leaked to send nitrogen clouds hissing around her footsteps, and where she walked she burned craters in the ice. Gravity was only a few per cent of gee, and Lvov, Earth-born, felt as if she might blow away.

There were clouds above her, wispy cirrus: aerosol clusters suspended in an atmosphere of nitrogen and methane. The clouds occluded bone-white stars. From here, Sol and the moon, Charon, were hidden by the planet's bulk, and it was *dark*, dark on dark, the damaged landscape visible only as a sketch in starlight.

The flitter had dug a trench a mile long and fifty yards deep in this world's antique surface, so Lvov was at the bottom of a valley walled by nitrogen ice. Cobh was hauling equipment out of the crumpled-up wreck of the flitter: scooters, data desks, life-support boxes, Lvov's equipment. Most of the stuff had been robust enough to survive the impact, Lvov saw, but not her own equipment.

Maybe a geologist could have crawled around with nothing more than a hammer and a set of sample bags. But Lvov was an atmospheric scientist. What was she going to achieve here without her equipment?

Her fear was fading now, to be replaced by irritation, impatience. She was five light hours from Sol; already she was missing the online nets. She kicked at the ice. She was *stuck* here; she couldn't talk to anyone, and there wasn't even the processing power to generate a Virtual environment.

Cobh finished wrestling with the wreckage. She was breathing hard. "Come on," she said. "Let's get out of this ditch and take a look around." She showed Lvov how to work a scooter. It was a simple platform, its inert-gas jets controlled by twists of raised handles.

Side by side, Cobh and Lvov rose out of the crash scar.

Pluto ice was a rich crimson laced with organic purple. Lvov made out patterns, dimly, on the surface of the ice; they were like bas-relief, discs the size of dinner plates, with the intricate complexity of snowflakes.

Lvov landed clumsily on the rim of the crash scar, the scooter's blunt prow crunching into surface ice, and she was grateful for the low gravity. The weight and heat of the scooters quickly obliterated the ice patterns.

"We've come down near the equator," Cobh said. "The albedo is higher at the south pole: a cap of methane ice there, I'm told."

"Yes."

Cobh pointed to a bright blue spark, high in the sky. "That's the wormhole Interface, where we emerged: Fifty thousand miles away."

Lvov squinted at constellations unchanged from those she'd grown up with on Earth. "Are we stranded?"

Cobh said, with reasonable patience, "For the time being. The flitter is wrecked, and the wormhole has collapsed; we're going to have to go back to Jupiter the long way round."

Three billion miles . . . "Ten hours ago I was asleep in a hotel room on Io. And now this. What a mess."

Cobh laughed. "I've already sent off messages to the inner System. They'll be received in about five hours. A one-way GUTship will be sent to retrieve us. It will refuel here, with Charon ice—"

"How long?"

"It depends on the readiness of a ship. Say ten days to prepare, then a ten-day flight out here—"

"*Twenty days?*"

"We're in no danger. We've supplies for a month. Although we're going to have to live in these suits."

"Lethe. This trip was supposed to last seventy-two hours."

"Well," Cobh said testily, "you'll have to call and cancel your appointments, won't you? All we have to do is wait here; we're not going to be comfortable, but we're safe enough."

"Do you know what happened to the wormhole?"

Cobh shrugged. She stared up at the distant blue spark. "As far as I know nothing like this has happened before. I think the Interface itself became unstable, and that fed back into the throat . . . But I don't know how we fell to Pluto so quickly. That doesn't make sense."

"How so?"

"Our trajectory was spacelike. Superluminal." She glanced at Lvov obliquely, as if embarrassed. "For a moment there, we appeared to be travelling faster than light."

"Through normal space? That's impossible."

"Of course it is." Cobh reached up to scratch her cheek, but her gloved fingers rattled against her faceplate. "I think I'll go up to the Interface and take a look around there."

Cobh showed Lvov how to access the life support boxes. Then she strapped her data desk to her back, climbed aboard her scooter, and lifted off the planet's surface, heading for the Interface. Lvov watched her dwindle.

Lvov's isolation closed in. She was alone, the only human on the surface of Pluto.

A reply from the inner System came within twelve hours of the crash. A GUTship was being sent from Jupiter. It would take thirteen days to refit the ship, followed by an eight-day flight to Pluto, then more delay for taking on fresh reaction mass at Charon. Lvov chafed at the timescale, restless.

There was other mail: Concerned notes from Lvov's family, a testy demand for updates from her research supervisor, and for Cobh, orders from her employer to mark as much of the flitter wreck as she could for salvage and analysis. Cobh's ship was a commercial wormhole transit vessel, hired by Oxford—Lvov's university—for this trip. Now, it seemed, a complex battle over liability would be joined between Oxford, Cobh's firm, and the insurance companies.

Lvov, five light-hours from home, found it difficult to respond to the mail asynchronously. She felt as if she had been cut out of the online mind of humanity. In the end she drafted replies to her family, and deleted the rest of the messages.

She checked her research equipment again, but it really was unusable. She tried to sleep. The suit was uncomfortable, claustrophobic. She was restless, bored, a little scared.

She began a systematic survey of the surface, taking her scooter on widening spiral sweeps around the crash scar.

The landscape was surprisingly complex, a starlit sculpture of feathery ridges and fine ravines. She kept a few hundred feet above the surface; whenever she flew too low her heat evoked billowing vapour from fragile nitrogen ice, obliterating ancient features, and she experienced obscure guilt.

She found more of the snowflake-like features, generally in little clusters of eight or ten.

Pluto, like its moon-twin Charon, was a ball of rock clad by thick mantles of water ice and nitrogen ice and laced with methane, ammonia and organic compounds. It was like a big, stable comet nucleus; it barely deserved the status of "planet." There were *moons* bigger than Pluto.

There had been only a handful of visitors in the eighty years since the building of the Poole wormhole. None of them had troubled to walk the surfaces of Pluto or Charon. The wormhole, Lvov realised, hadn't been built as a commercial proposition, but as a sort of stunt: the link which connected, at last, all of the System's planets to the rapid-transit hub at Jupiter.

She tired of her plodding survey. She made sure she could locate the crash scar, lifted the scooter to a mile above the surface, and flew towards the south polar cap.

Cobh called from the Interface. "I think I'm figuring out what happened here—that superluminal effect I talked about. Lvov, have you heard of an Alcubierre wave?" She dumped images to Lvov's desk—portraits of the wormhole Interface, various graphics.

"No." Lvov ignored the input and concentrated on flying the scooter. "Cobh, why should a wormhole become unstable? Hundreds of wormhole rapid transits are made every day, all across the System."

"A wormhole is a flaw in space. It's inherently unstable anyway. The throat and mouths are kept open by active feedback loops involving threads of exotic matter. That's matter with a negative energy density, a sort of antigravity which—"

"But this wormhole went wrong."

"Maybe the tuning wasn't perfect. The presence of the flitter's mass in the throat was enough to send the wormhole over the edge. If the wormhole had been more heavily used, the instability might have been detected earlier, and fixed . . . "

Over the grey-white pole, Lvov flew through banks of aerosol mist; Cobh's voice whispered to her, remote, without meaning.

Sunrise on Pluto:

Sol was a point of light, low on Lvov's unfolding horizon, wreathed in the complex strata of a cirrus cloud. The Sun was a thousand times fainter than from Earth, but brighter than any planet in Earth's sky.

The inner System was a puddle of light around Sol, an oblique disc small enough for Lvov to cover with the palm of her hand. It was a disc that contained almost all of man's hundreds of billions. Sol brought no heat to her raised hand, but she saw faint shadows, cast by the sun on her faceplate.

The nitrogen atmosphere was dynamic. At perihelion—the closest approach to Sol, which Pluto was nearing—the air expanded, to three planetary diameters. Methane and other volatiles joined the thickening air, sublimating from the planet's surface. Then, when Pluto turned away from Sol and sailed into its two-hundred-year winter, the air snowed down.

Lvov wished she had her atmospheric-analysis equipment now; she felt its lack like an ache.

She passed over spectacular features: Buie Crater, Tombaugh Plateau, the Lowell Range. She recorded them all, walked on them.

After a while her world, of Earth and information and work, seemed remote, a glittering abstraction. Pluto was like a complex, blind fish, drifting around its two-century orbit, gradually interfacing with her. Changing her, she suspected.

Ten hours after leaving the crash scar, Lvov arrived at the sub-Charon point, called Christy. She kept the scooter hovering, puffs of gas holding her against Pluto's gentle gravity.

Sol was half-way up the sky, a diamond of light. Charon hung directly over Lvov's head, a misty blue disc, six times the size of Luna as seen from Earth. Half the moon's lit hemisphere was turned away from Lvov, towards Sol.

Like Luna, Charon was tidally locked to its parent, and kept the same face to Pluto as it orbited. But, unlike Earth, Pluto was also locked to its twin. Every six days the worlds turned about each other, facing each other constantly, like two waltzers. Pluto-Charon was the only significant system in which both partners were tidally locked.

Chiron's surface looked pocked. Lvov had her faceplate enhance the image. Many of the gouges were deep and quite regular.

She remarked on this to Cobh, at the Interface.

"The Poole people mostly used Charon material for the building of the wormhole," Cobh said. "Charon is just rock and water ice. It's easier to get to water ice, in particular. Charon doesn't have the inconvenience of an atmosphere, or an overlay of nitrogen ice over the water. And the gravity's shallower."

The wormhole builders had flown out here in a huge, unreliable GUTship. They had lifted ice and rock off Charon, and used it to construct tetrahedra of exotic matter. The tetrahedra had served as Interfaces, the termini of a wormhole. One Interface had been left in orbit around Pluto, and the other had been hauled laboriously back to Jupiter by the GUTship, itself replenished with Charon-ice reaction mass.

By such crude means, Michael Poole and his people had opened up the Solar System.

"They made Lethe's own mess of Charon," Lvov said.

She could almost see Cobh's characteristic shrug. *So what?*

Pluto's surface was geologically complex, here at this point of maximal tidal stress. She flew over ravines and ridges; in places, it looked as if the land had been smashed up with an immense hammer, cracked and fractured. She imagined there was a greater mix, here, of interior material with the surface ice.

In many places she saw gatherings of the peculiar snowflakes she had noticed before. Perhaps they were some form of frosting effect, she wondered. She descended, thinking vaguely of collecting samples.

She killed the scooter's jets some yards above the surface, and let the little craft fall under Pluto's gentle gravity. She hit the ice with a soft collision, but without heat-damaging the surface features much beyond a few feet.

She stepped off the scooter. The ice crunched, and she felt layers compress under her, but the fractured surface supported her weight. She looked up towards Charon. The crimson moon was immense, round, heavy.

She caught a glimmer of light, an arc, directly above her.

It was gone immediately. She closed her eyes and tried to recapture it. *A line, slowly curving, like a thread. A web. Suspended between Pluto and Charon.*

She looked again, with her faceplate set to optimal enhancement. She couldn't recapture the vision.

She didn't say anything to Cobh.

"I was right, by the way," Cobh was saying.

"What?" Lvov tried to focus.

"The wormhole instability, when we crashed. It did cause an Alcubierre wave."

"What's an Alcubierre wave?"

"The Interface's negative energy region expanded from the tetrahedron, just for a moment. The negative energy distorted a chunk of spacetime. The chunk containing the flitter, and us."

On one side of the flitter, Cobh said, spacetime had contracted. Like a model black hole. On the other side, it expanded—like a re-run of the Big Bang, the expansion at the beginning of the Universe.

"An Alcubierre wave is a front in spacetime. The Interface—with us embedded inside—was carried along. We were pushed away from the expanding region, and towards the contraction."

"Like a surfer, on a wave."

"Right." Cobh sounded excited. "The effect's been known to theory, almost since the formulation of relativity. But I don't think anyone's observed it before."

"How lucky for us," Lvov said drily. "You said we travelled faster than light. But that's impossible."

"You can't move faster than light *within spacetime*. Wormholes are one way of getting around this; in a wormhole you are passing through a branch in spacetime. The Alcubierre effect is another way. The superluminal velocity comes from the distortion of space itself; we were carried along *within* distorting space.

"So we weren't breaking lightspeed within our raft of spacetime. But that spacetime itself was distorting at more than lightspeed."

"It sounds like cheating."

"So sue me. Or look up the math."

"Couldn't we use your Alcubierre effect to drive starships?"

"No. The instabilities and the energy drain are forbidding."

One of the snowflake patterns lay mostly undamaged, within Lvov's reach. She crouched and peered at it. The flake was perhaps a foot across. Internal structure was visible within the clear ice as layers of tubes and compartments; it was highly symmetrical, and very complex. She said to Cobh, "This is an impressive crystallisation effect. If that's what it is." Gingerly she reached out with thumb and forefinger, and snapped a short tube off the rim of the flake. She laid the sample on her desk. After a few seconds the analysis presented. "It's mostly water ice, with some contaminants," she told Cobh. "But in a novel molecular form. Denser than normal ice, a kind of glass. Water would freeze like this under high pressures—several thousand atmospheres."

"Perhaps it's material from the interior, brought out by the chthonic mixing in that region."

"Perhaps." Lvov felt more confident now; she was intrigued. "Cobh, there's a larger specimen a few feet further away."

"Take it easy, Lvov."

She stepped forward. "I'll be fine. I—"

The surface shattered.

Lvov's left foot dropped forward, into a shallow hole; something crackled under the sole of her boot. Threads of ice crystals, oddly woven together, spun up and tracked precise parabolae around her leg.

The fall seemed to take an age; the ice tipped up towards her like an opening door. She put her hands out. She couldn't stop the fall, but she was able to cushion herself, and she kept her faceplate away from the ice. She finished up on her backside; she felt the chill of Pluto ice through the suit material over her buttocks and calves.

" . . . Lvov? Are you okay?"

She was panting, she found. "I'm fine."

"You were screaming."

"Was I? I'm sorry. I fell."

"You *fell*? How?"

"There was a hole, in the ice." She massaged her left ankle; it didn't seem to be hurt. "It was covered up."

"Show me."

She got to her feet, stepped gingerly back to the open hole, and held up her data desk. The hole was only a few inches deep. "It was covered by a sort of lid, I think."

"Move the desk closer to the hole." Light from the desk, controlled by Cobh, played over the shallow pit.

Lvov found a piece of the smashed lid. It was mostly ice, but there was a texture to its undersurface, embedded thread which bound the ice together.

"Lvov," Cobh said. "Take a look at this."

Lvov lifted the desk aside and peered into the hole. The walls were quite smooth. At the base there was a cluster of spheres, fist-sized. Lvov counted seven; all but one of the spheres had been smashed by her stumble. She picked up the one intact sphere, and turned it over in her hand. It was pearl-grey, almost translucent. There was something embedded inside, disc-shaped, complex.

Cobh sounded breathless. "Are you thinking what I'm thinking?"

"It's an egg," Lvov said. She looked around wildly, at the open pit, the egg, the snowflake patterns. Suddenly she saw the meaning of the scene; it was as if a light had shone up from within Pluto, illuminating her. The "snowflakes" represented *life*, she intuited; they had dug the burrows, laid these eggs, and now their bodies of water glass lay, dormant or dead, on the ancient ice . . .

"I'm coming down," Cobh said sternly. "We're going to have to discuss this. Don't say anything to the inner System; wait until I get back. This could mean trouble for us, Lvov."

Lvov placed the egg back in the shattered nest.

She met Cobh at the crash scar. Cobh was shovelling nitrogen and water ice into the life-support modules' raw material hopper. She hooked up her own and Lvov's suits to the modules, recharging the suits' internal systems. Then she began to carve GUTdrive components out of the flitter's hull. The flitter's central Grand Unified Theory chamber was compact, no larger than a basketball, and the rest of the drive was similarly scaled. "I bet I could get this working," Cobh said. "Although it couldn't take us anywhere."

Lvov sat on a fragment of the shattered hull. Tentatively, she told Cobh about the web.

Cobh stood with hands on hips, facing Lvov, and Lvov could hear her sucking drink from the nipples in her helmet. "Spiders from Pluto? Give me a break."

"It's only an analogy," Lvov said defensively. "I'm an atmospheric specialist, not a biologist." She tapped the surface of her desk. "It's not spider-web. Obviously. But if that substance has anything like the characteristics of true spider silk, it's not impossible." She read from her desk. "Spider silk has a breaking strain twice that of steel, but thirty times the elasticity. It's a type of liquid crystal. It's used commercially—did you know that?" She fingered the fabric of her suit. "We could be wearing spider silk right now."

"What about the hole with the lid?"

"There are trapdoor spiders in America. On Earth. I remember, when I was a kid . . . The spiders make burrows, lined with silk, with hinged lids."

"Why make burrows on Pluto?"

"I don't know. Maybe the eggs can last out the winter that way. Maybe the creatures, the flakes, only have active life during the perihelion period, when the atmosphere expands and enriches." She thought that through. "That fits. That's why the Poole people didn't spot anything. The construction team was here close to the last aphelion. Pluto's year is so long that we're still only half-way to the next perihelion—"

"So how do they live?" Cobh snapped. "What do they eat?"

"There must be more to the ecosystem than one species," Lvov conceded. "The flakes—the spiders—need water glass. But there's little of that on the surface. Maybe there is some biocycle—plants or burrowing animals—which brings ice and glass to the surface, from the interior."

"That doesn't make sense. The layer of nitrogen over water ice is too deep."

"Then where do the flakes get their glass?"

"Don't ask me," Cobh said. "It's your dumb hypothesis. And what about the web? What's the point of that—if it's real?"

Lvov ground to a halt. "I don't know," she said lamely. *Although Pluto/ Charon is the only place in the System where you could build a spider-web between worlds.*

Cobh toyed with a fitting from the drive. "Have you told anyone about this yet? In the inner System, I mean."

"No. You said you wanted to talk about that."

"Right." Lvov saw Cobh close her eyes; her face was masked by the glimmer of her faceplate. "Listen. Here's what we say. We've seen nothing here. Nothing that couldn't be explained by crystallisation effects."

Lvov was baffled. "What are you talking about? What about the eggs? Why would we lie about this? Besides, we have the desks—records."

"Data desks can be lost, or wiped, or their contents amended."

Lvov wished she could see Cobh's face. "Why would we do such a thing?"

"Think it through. Once Earth hears about this, these flake-spiders of yours will be protected. Won't they?"

"Of course. What's bad about that?"

"It's bad for *us*, Lvov. You've seen what a mess the Poole people made of Charon. If this system is inhabited, *a fast GUTship won't be allowed to come for us.* It wouldn't be allowed to refuel here. Not if it meant further damage to the native life forms."

Lvov shrugged. "So we'd have to wait for a slower ship. A liner; one that won't need to take on more reaction mass here."

Cobh laughed at her. "You don't know much about the economics of GUTship transport, do you? Now that the System is criss-crossed by Poole wormholes, how many liners like that do you think are still running? I've already checked the manifests. There are *two* liners capable of a round trip to Pluto still in service. One is in dry dock; the other is heading for Saturn—"

"On the other side of the System."

"Right. There's no way either of those ships could reach us for, I'd say, a year."

We only have a month's supplies. A bubble of panic gathered in Lvov's stomach.

"Do you get it yet?" Cobh said heavily. "*We'll be sacrificed,* if there's a chance that our rescue would damage the new ecology, here."

"No. It wouldn't happen like that."

Cobh shrugged. "There are precedents."

She was right, Lvov knew. There *were* precedents, of new forms of life discovered in corners of the system: From Mercury to the remote Kuiper objects. In every case the territory had been ring-fenced, the local conditions preserved, once life—or even a plausible candidate for life—was recognised.

Cobh said, "Pan-genetic diversity. Pan-environmental management. That's the key to it; the public policy of preserving all the species and habitats of Sol, into the indefinite future. The lives of two humans won't matter a damn against that."

"What are you suggesting?"

"That we don't tell the inner System about the flakes."

Lvov tried to recapture her mood of a few days before: When Pluto hadn't mattered to her, when the crash had been just an inconvenience. *Now, suddenly, we're talking about threats to our lives, the destruction of an ecology.*

What a dilemma. If I don't tell of the flakes, their ecology may be destroyed during our rescue. But if I do tell, the GUTship won't come for me, and I'll lose my life.

Cobh seemed to be waiting for an answer.

Lvov thought of how Sol light looked over Pluto's ice fields, at dawn.

She decided to stall. "We'll say nothing. For now. But I don't accept either of your options."

Cobh laughed. "What else is there? The wormhole is destroyed; even this flitter is disabled."

"We have time. Days, before the GUTship is due to be launched. Let's search for another solution. A win-win."

Cobh shrugged. She looked suspicious.

She's right to be, Lvov thought, exploring her own decision with surprise. *I've every intention of telling the truth later, of diverting the GUTship, if I have to.*

I may give up my life, for this world.

I think.

In the days that followed, Cobh tinkered with the GUTdrive, and flew up to the Interface to gather more data on the Alcubierre phenomenon.

Lvov roamed the surface of Pluto, with her desk set to full record. She came to love the wreaths of cirrus clouds, the huge, misty moon, the slow, oceanic pulse of the centuries-long year.

Everywhere she found the inert bodies of snowflakes, or evidence of their presence: eggs, lidded burrows. She found no other life forms—or, more likely, she told herself, she wasn't equipped to recognise any others.

She was drawn back to Christy, the sub-Charon point, where the topography was at its most complex and interesting, and where the greatest density of flakes was to be found. It was as if, she thought, the flakes had gathered here, yearning for the huge, inaccessible moon above them. But what could the flakes possibly want of Charon? What did it mean for them?

Lvov encountered Cobh at the crash scar, recharging her suit's systems from the life support packs. Cobh seemed quiet. She kept her face, hooded by her faceplate, turned from Lvov.

Lvov watched her for a while. "You're being evasive," she said eventually. "Something's changed—something you're not telling me about."

Cobh made to turn away, but Lvov grabbed her arm. "*I think you've found a third option.* Haven't you? You've found some other way to resolve this situation, without destroying either us or the flakes."

Cobh shook off her hand. "Yes. Yes, I think I know a way. But—"

"But what?"

"It's *dangerous*, damn it. Maybe unworkable. Lethal." Cobh's hands pulled at each other.

She's scared, Lvov saw. She stepped back from Cobh. Without giving herself time to think about it, she said, "Our deal's off. I'm going to tell the inner System about the flakes. Right now. So we're going to have to go with your new idea, dangerous or not."

Cobh studied her face; Cobh seemed to be weighing up Lvov's determination, perhaps even her physical strength. Lvov felt as if she were a data desk being downloaded. The moment stretched, and Lvov felt her breath tighten in her chest. Would she be able to defend herself, physically, if it came to that? And—was her own will really so strong?

I have changed, she thought. *Pluto has changed me.*

At last Cobh looked away. "Send your damn message," she said.

Before Cobh—or Lvov herself—had a chance to waver, Lvov picked up her desk and sent a message to the inner worlds. She downloaded all the data she had on the flakes: Text, images, analyses, her own observations and hypotheses.

"It's done," she said at last.

"And the GUTship?"

"I'm sure they'll cancel it." Lvov smiled. "I'm also sure they won't tell us they've done so."

"So we're left with no choice," Cobh said angrily. "Look: I know it's the right thing to do. To preserve the flakes. I just don't want to die, that's all. I hope you're right, Lvov."

"You haven't told me how we're going to get home."

Cobh grinned through her faceplate. "Surfing."

"All right. You're doing fine. Now let go of the scooter."

Lvov took a deep breath, and kicked the scooter away with both legs; the little device tumbled away, catching the deep light of Sol, and Lvov rolled in reaction.

Cobh reached out and steadied her. "You can't fall," Cobh said. "You're in orbit. You understand that, don't you?"

"Of course I do," Lvov grumbled.

The two of them drifted in space, close to the defunct Poole wormhole Interface. The Interface itself was a tetrahedron of electric blue struts, enclosing darkness, its size overwhelming; Lvov felt as if she was floating beside the carcase of some huge, wrecked building.

Pluto and Charon hovered before her like balloons, their surfaces mottled and complex, their forms visibly distorted from the spherical. Their separation was only fourteen of Pluto's diameters. The worlds were strikingly different in hue, with Pluto a blood red, Charon ice blue. *That's the difference in surface composition*, Lvov thought absently. *All that water ice on Charon's surface.*

The panorama was stunningly beautiful. Lvov had a sudden, gut-level intuition of the *rightness* of the various System authorities' rigid pan-environment policies.

Cobh had strapped her data desk to her chest; now she checked the time. "Any moment now. Lvov, you'll be fine. Remember, you'll feel no acceleration, no matter how fast we travel. At the centre of an Alcubierre wave, spacetime is locally flat; you'll still be in free fall. There will be tidal forces, but they will remain small. Just keep your breathing even, and—"

"Shut up, Cobh," Lvov said tightly. "I know all this."

Cobh's desk flared with light. "*There*," she breathed. "The GUTdrive has fired. Just a few seconds, now."

A spark of light arced up from Pluto's surface and tracked, in complete silence, under the belly of the parent world. It was the flitter's GUTdrive, salvaged and stabilised by Cobh. The flame was brighter than Sol; Lvov saw its light reflected in Pluto, as if the surface was a great, fractured mirror of ice. Where the flame passed, tongues of nitrogen gas billowed up.

The GUTdrive passed over Christy. Lvov had left her desk there, to monitor the flakes, and the image the desk transmitted, displayed in the corner of her faceplate, showed a spark, crossing the sky.

Then the GUTdrive veered sharply upwards, climbing directly towards Lvov and Cobh at the Interface.

"Cobh, are you sure this is going to work?"

Lvov could hear Cobh's breath rasp, shallow. "Look, Lvov, I know you're scared, but pestering me with dumb-ass questions isn't going to help. Once the drive enters the Interface, it will take only seconds for the instability to set in. Seconds, and then we'll be home. In the inner System, at any rate. Or . . . "

"Or what?"

Cobh didn't reply.

Or not, Lvov finished for her. *If Cobh has designed this new instability right, the Alcubierre wave will carry us home. If not—*

The GUTdrive flame approached, becoming dazzling. Lvov tried to regulate her breathing, to keep her limbs hanging loose—

"Lethe," Cobh whispered.

"What?" Lvov demanded, alarmed.

"Take a look at Pluto. At Christy."

Lvov looked into her faceplate.

Where the warmth and light of the GUTdrive had passed, Christy was a ferment. Nitrogen billowed. And, amid the pale fountains, *burrows were opening.* Lids folded back. Eggs cracked. Infant flakes soared and sailed, with webs and nets of their silk-analogue hauling at the rising air.

Lvov caught glimpses of threads, long, sparkling, trailing down to

Pluto—and up towards Charon. Already, Lvov saw, some of the baby flakes had hurtled more than a planetary diameter from the surface, towards the moon.

"It's goose summer," she said.

"What?"

"When I was a kid . . . The young spiders spin bits of webs, and climb to the top of grass stalks, and float off on the breeze. Goose summer—'gossamer.' "

"Right," Cobh said sceptically. "Well, it looks as if they are making for Charon. They use the evaporation of the atmosphere for lift . . . Perhaps they follow last year's threads, to the moon. They must fly off every perihelion, rebuilding their web bridge every time. They think the perihelion is here now. The warmth of the drive—it's remarkable. But why go to Charon?"

Lvov couldn't take her eyes off the flakes. "Because of the water," she said. It all seemed to make sense, now that she saw the flakes in action. "There must be water glass, on Chiron's surface. The baby flakes use it to build their bodies. They take other nutrients from Pluto's interior, and the glass from Charon . . . They need the resources of *both* worlds to survive—"

"*Lvov!*"

The GUTdrive flared past them, sudden, dazzling, and plunged into the damaged Interface.

Electric-blue light exploded from the Interface, washing over her.

There was a ball of light, unearthly, behind her, and an irregular patch of darkness ahead, like a rip in space. Tidal forces plucked gently at her belly and limbs.

Pluto, Charon and goose summer disappeared. But the stars, the eternal stars, shone down on her, just as they had during her childhood on Earth. She stared at the stars, trusting, and felt no fear.

Remotely, she heard Cobh whoop, exhilarated.

The tides faded. The darkness before her healed, to reveal the brilliance and warmth of Sol.

· SPIDER THE ARTIST ·
Nnedi Okorafor

Zombie no go go, unless you tell am to go
Zombie!
Zombie!
Zombie no go stop, unless you tell am to stop
Zombie no go turn, unless you tell am to turn
Zombie!
Zombie no go think, unless you tell am to think

—from *Zombie* by Fela Kuti,
Nigerian musician
and self-proclaimed voice of the voiceless

My husband used to beat me. That was how I ended up out there that evening behind our house, just past the bushes, through the tall grass, in front of the pipelines. Our small house was the last in the village, practically in the forest itself. So nobody ever saw or heard him beating me.

Going out there was the best way to put space between me and him without sending him into further rage. When I went behind the house, he knew where I was and he knew I was alone. But he was too full of himself to realize I was thinking about killing myself.

My husband was a drunk, like too many of the members of the Niger Delta People's Movement. It was how they all controlled their anger and feelings of helplessness. The fish, shrimps and crayfish in the creeks were dying. Drinking the water shriveled women's wombs and eventually made men urinate blood.

There was a stream where I had been fetching water. A flow station was built nearby and now the stream was rank and filthy, with an oily film that reflected rainbows. Cassava and yam farms yielded less and less each year. The air left your skin dirty and smelled like something preparing to die. In some places, it was always daytime because of the noisy gas flares.

My village was shit.

On top of all this, People's Movement members were getting picked off like flies. The "kill-and-go" had grown bold. They shot People's Movement members in the streets, they ran them over, dragged them into the swamps. You never saw them again.

I tried to give my husband some happiness. But after three years, my body continued to refuse him children. It's easy to see the root of his frustration and sadness . . . but pain is pain. And he dealt it to me regularly.

My greatest, my only true possession was my father's guitar. It was made of fine polished Abura timber and it had a lovely tortoiseshell pick guard. Excellent handwork. My father said that the timber used to create the guitar came from one of the last timber trees in the delta. If you held it to your nose, you could believe this. The guitar was decades old and still smelled like fresh cut wood, like it wanted to tell you its story because only it could.

I wouldn't exist without my father's guitar. When he was a young man, he used to sit in front of the compound in the evening and play for everyone. People danced, clapped, shut their eyes and listened. Cell phones would ring and people would ignore them. One day, it was my mother who stopped to listen.

I used to stare at my father's fast long-fingered hands when he played. Oh, the harmonies. He could weave anything with his music—rainbows, sunrises, spider webs sparkling with morning dew. My older brothers weren't interested in learning how to play. But I was, so my father taught me everything he knew. And now it was my long-fingers that graced the strings. I'd always been able to hear music and my fingers moved even faster than my father's. I was good. Really good.

But I married that stupid man. Andrew. So I only played behind the house. Away from him. My guitar was my escape.

That fateful evening, I was sitting on the ground in front of the fuel pipeline. It ran right through everyone's backyard. My village was an oil village, as was the village where I grew up. My mother lived in a similar village before she was married, as did her mother. We are Pipeline People.

My mother's grandmother was known for lying on the pipeline running through her village. She'd stay like that for hours, listening and wondering what magical fluids were running through the large never-ending steel tubes. This was before the Zombies, of course. I laughed. If she tried to lie on a pipeline now she'd be brutally killed.

Anyway, when I was feeling especially blue, I'd take my guitar and come out here and sit right in front of the pipeline. I knew I was flirting with death by being so close but when I was like this, I didn't really care. I actually welcomed the possibility of being done with life. It was a wonder that my husband didn't smash my guitar during one of his drunken rages. I'd surely have quickly thrown myself on the pipeline if he did. Maybe that was why he'd rather smash my nose than my guitar.

This day, he'd only slapped me hard across the face. I had no idea why. He'd simply come in, seen me in the kitchen and *smack*! Maybe he'd had a bad day at work—he worked very hard at a local restaurant. Maybe one of his women had scorned him. Maybe I did something wrong. I didn't know. I didn't care. My nose was just starting to stop bleeding and I was not seeing so many stars.

My feet were only inches from the pipeline. I was especially daring this night. It was warmer and more humid than normal. Or maybe it was my stinging burning face. The mosquitoes didn't even bother me much. In the distance, I could see Nneka, a woman who rarely spoke to me, giving her small sons a bath in a large tub. Some men were playing cards at a table several houses down. It was dark, there were small, small trees and bushes here and even our closest neighbor was not very close, so I was hidden.

I sighed and placed my hands on the guitar strings. I plucked out a tune my father used to play. I sighed and closed my eyes. I would always miss my father. The feel of the strings vibrating under my fingers was exquisite.

I fell deep into the zone of my music, weaving it, then floating on a glorious sunset that lit the palm tree tops and . . .

Click!

I froze. My hands still on the strings, the vibration dying. I didn't dare move. I kept my eyes closed. The side of my face throbbed.

Click! This time the sound was closer. *Click!* Closer. *Click!* Closer.

My heart pounded and I felt nauseous with fear. Despite my risk taking, I knew this was *not* the way I wanted to die. Who would want to be torn limb from limb by Zombies? As everyone in my village did multiple times a day, I quietly cursed the Nigerian government.

Twing!

The vibration of the guitar string was stifled by my middle finger still pressing it down. My hands started to shake, but still I kept my eyes shut. Something sharp and cool lifted my finger. I wanted to scream. The string was plucked again.

Twang!

The sound was deeper and fuller, my finger no longer muffling the vibration. Very slowly, I opened my eyes. My heart skipped. The thing stood about three feet tall, which meant I was eye-to eye with it. I'd never seen one up close. Few people have. These things are always running up and down the pipeline like a herd of super fast steer, always with things to do.

I chanced a better look. It really *did* have eight legs. Even in the darkness, those legs shined, catching even the dimmest light. A bit more light and I'd have been able to see my face perfectly reflected back at me. I'd heard that they polished and maintained themselves. This made even more sense now, for who would have time to keep them looking so immaculate?

The government came up with the idea to create the Zombies, and Shell, Chevron and a few other oil companies (who were just as desperate) supplied the money to pay for it all. The Zombies were made to combat pipeline bunkering and terrorism. It makes me laugh. The government and the oil people destroyed our land and dug up our oil, then they created robots to keep us from taking it back.

They were originally called Anansi Droids 419 but we call them "*oyibo* contraption" and, most often, Zombie, the same name we call those "kill-and-go" soldiers who come in here harassing us every time something bites their brains.

It's said that Zombies can think. Artificial Intelligence, this is called. I have had some schooling, a year or two of university, but my area was not in the sciences. No matter my education, as soon as I got married and brought to this damn place I became like every other woman here, a simple village woman living in the delta region where Zombies kill anyone who touches the pipelines and whose husband knocks her around every so often. What did I know about Zombie intellect?

It looked like a giant shiny metal spider. It moved like one too. All smooth-shifting joints and legs. It crept closer and leaned in to inspect my guitar strings some more. As it did so, two of its back legs tapped on the metal of the pipeline.*Click! Click! Click!*

It pushed my thumb back down on the strings and plucked the string twice, making a muted *pluck!* It looked at me with its many blue shining round eyes. Up close I could see that they weren't lights. They were balls of a glowing metallic blue undulating liquid, like charged mercury. I stared into them fascinated. No one else in my village could possibly know this fact. No one had gotten close enough. *Eyes of glowing bright blue liquid metal*, I thought. *Na wa.*

It pressed my hand harder and I gasped, blinking and looking away from its hypnotic eyes. Then I understood.

"You . . . you want me to play?"

It sat there waiting, placing a leg on the body of my guitar with a soft *tap*. It had been a long time since anyone had wanted me to play for him. I played my favorite highlife song. *Love Dey See Road* by Oliver De Coque. I played like my life depended on it.

The Zombie didn't move, its leg remaining pressed to my guitar. Was it listening? I was sure it was. Twenty minutes later, when I stopped finally playing, sweat running down my face, it touched the tips of my aching hands. Gently.

Some of these pipelines carry diesel fuel, others carry crude oil. Millions of liters of it a day. Nigeria supplies twenty-five percent of United States oil. And we get virtually nothing in return. Nothing but death by Zombie attack. We can all tell you stories.

When the Zombies were first released, no one knew about them. All people would hear were rumors about people getting torn apart near pipelines or sightings of giant white spiders in the night. Or you'd hear about huge pipeline explosions, charred bodies everywhere. But the pipeline where the bodies lay would be perfectly intact.

People still bunkered. My husband was one of them. I suspected that he sold the fuel and oil on the black market; he would bring some of the oil home, too. You let it sit in a bucket for two days and it would become something like kerosene. I used it for cooking. So I couldn't really complain. But bunkering was a very, very dangerous practice.

There *were* ways of breaking a pipeline open without immediately bringing the wrath of Zombies. My husband and his comrades used some sort of powerful laser cutter. They stole them from the hospitals. But they had to be very, very quiet when cutting through the metal. All it took was one bang, one vibration, and the Zombies would come running within a minute. Many of my husband's comrades had been killed because of the tap of someone's wedding ring or the tip of the laser cutter on steel.

Two years ago a group of boys had been playing too close to the pipeline. Two of them were wrestling and they fell on it. Within seconds the Zombies came. One boy managed to scramble away. But the other was grabbed by the arm and flung into some bushes. His arm and both of his legs were broken. Government officials *said* that Zombies were programmed to do as little harm as possible but . . . I didn't believe this, *na* lie.

They were terrible creatures. To get close to a pipeline was to risk a terrible death. Yet the goddamn things ran right through our backyards.

But I didn't care. My husband was beating the hell out of me during these months. I don't know why. He had not lost his job. I knew he was seeing other women. We were poor but we were not starving. Maybe it was because I couldn't bear him children. It is my fault I know, but what can I do?

I found myself out in the backyard more and more. And this particular Zombie visited me every time. I loved playing for it. It would listen. Its lovely eyes would glow with joy. Could a robot feel joy? I believed intelligent ones like this could. Many times a day, I would see a crowd of Zombies running up and down the pipeline, off to do repairs or policing, whatever they did. If my Zombie was amongst them, I couldn't tell.

It was about the tenth time it visited me that it did something very, very strange. My husband had come home smelling practically flammable, stinking of several kinds of alcohol—beer, palm wine, perfume. I had been thinking hard all day. About my life. I was stuck. I wanted a baby. I wanted to get out of the house. I wanted a job. I wanted friends. I needed courage. I knew I had courage. I had faced a Zombie, many times.

I was going to ask my husband about teaching at the elementary school. I'd heard that they were looking for teachers. When he walked in, he greeted me with a sloppy hug and kiss and then plopped himself on the couch. He turned on the television. It was late but I brought him his dinner, pepper soup heavy with goat meat, chicken and large shrimp. He was in a good drunken mood. But as I stood there watching him eat, all my courage fled. All my need for change skittered and cowered to the back of my brain.

"Do you want anything else?" I asked.

He looked up at me and actually smiled. "The soup is good today."

I smiled, but something inside me ducked its head lower. "I'm glad," I said. I picked up my guitar. "I'm going to the back. It's nice outside."

"Don't go too close to the pipeline," he said. But he was looking at the TV and gnawing on a large piece of goat meat.

I crept into the darkness, through the bushes and grasses, to the pipeline. I sat in my usual spot. A foot from it. I strummed softly, a series of chords. A forlorn tune that spoke my heart. Where else was there to go from here? Was this my life? I sighed. I hadn't been to church in a month.

When it came clicking down the pipe, my heart lifted. Its blue liquid eyes glowed strong tonight. There was a woman from whom I once bought a bolt of blue cloth. The cloth was a rich blue that reminded me of the open water on sunny days. The woman said the cloth was "azure." My Zombie's eyes were a deep azure this night.

It stopped, standing before me. Waiting. I knew it was my Zombie because a month ago, it had allowed me to put a blue butterfly sticker on one of its front legs.

"Good evening," I said.

It did not move.

"I'm sad today," I said.

It stepped off the pipeline, its metal legs clicking on the metal and then whispering on the dirt and grass. It sat its body on the ground as it always did. Then it waited.

I strummed a few chords and then played its favorite song, Bob Marley's "No Woman No Cry." As I played, its body slowly began to rotate, something I'd come to understand was its way of expressing pleasure. I smiled. When I stopped playing, it turned its eyes back to me. I sighed, strummed an A minor chord, and sat back. "My life is shit," I said.

Suddenly, it rose up on its eight legs with a soft whir. It stretched and straightened its legs until it was standing a foot taller than normal. From under its body in the center, something whitish and metallic began to descend. I gasped, grabbing my guitar. My mind told me to move away. Move away fast. I'd befriended this artificial creature. I knew it. Or I thought

I knew it. But what did I *really* know about why it did what it did? Or why it came to me?

The metallic substance descended faster, pooling in the grass beneath it. I squinted. The stuff was wire. Right before my eyes, I watched the Zombie take this wire and do something with five of its legs while it supported itself on the other three. The legs scrambled around, working and weaving the shiny wire this way and that. They moved too fast for me to see exactly what they were creating. Grass flew and the soft whirring sound grew slightly louder.

Then the legs stopped. For a moment all I could hear was the sounds of crickets and frogs singing, the breeze blowing in the palm and mangrove tree tops. I could smell the sizzling oil of someone frying plantain or yam nearby.

My eyes focused on what the Zombie had done. I grinned. I grinned and grinned. "What is that?" I whispered.

It held it up with two of its front legs and tapped its back leg twice on the ground as it always seemed to when it was trying to make a point. A point that I usually didn't understand.

It brought three legs forward and commenced to pluck out what first was a medley of my favorite songs, from Bob Marley to Sunny Ade to Carlos Santana. Then its music deepened to something so complex and beautiful that I was reduced to tears of joy, awe, ecstasy. People must have heard the music, maybe they looked out their windows or opened their doors. But we were hidden by the darkness, the grass, the trees. I cried and cried. I don't know why, but I cried. I wonder if it was pleased by my reaction. I think it was.

I spent the next hour learning to play its tune.

Ten days later, a group of Zombies attacked some oil workers and soldiers deep in the delta. Ten of the men were torn limb from limb, their bloody remains scattered all over the swampy land. Those who escaped told reporters that nothing would stop the Zombies. A soldier had even thrown a grenade at one, but the thing protected itself with the very force field it had been built to use during pipeline explosions. The soldier said the force field looked like a crackling bubble made of lightning.

"*Wahala*! Trouble!" the soldier frantically told television reporters. His face was greasy with sweat and the sides of his eyes were twitching. "Evil, evil things! I've believed this from start! Look at me with grenade! *Ye ye*! I could do nothing!"

The pipeline the men had barely even started was found fully assembled. Zombies are made to make repairs, not fully assemble things. It was bizarre. Newspaper write-ups said that the Zombies were getting too smart for their own good. That they were rebelling. Something had certainly changed.

"Maybe it's only a matter of time before the damn things kill us all," my husband said, a beer in hand, as he read about the incident in the newspaper.

I considered never going near my Zombie again. They were unpredictable and possibly out of control.

It was midnight and I was out there again.

My husband hadn't laid a heavy hand on me in weeks. I think he sensed the change in me. I had changed. He now heard me play more. Even in the house. In the mornings. After cooking his dinners. In the bedroom when his friends were over. And he was hearing songs that I knew gave him a most glorious feeling. As if each chord, each sound were examined by scientists and hand-picked to provoke the strongest feeling of happiness.

My Zombie had solved my marital problems. At least the worst of them. My husband could not beat me when there was beautiful music sending his senses to lush, sweet places. I began to hope. To hope for a baby. Hope that I would one day leave my house and wifely duties for a job as music teacher at the elementary school. Hope that my village would one day reap from the oil being reaped from it. And I dreamt about being embraced by deep blue liquid metal, webs of wire and music.

I'd woken up that night from one of these strange dreams. I opened my eyes, a smile on my face. Good things were certainly coming. My husband was sleeping soundly beside me. In the dim moonlight, he looked so peaceful. His skin no longer smelled of alcohol. I leaned forward and kissed his lips. He didn't wake. I slipped out of bed and put on some pants and a long sleeve shirt. The mosquitoes would be out tonight. I grabbed my guitar.

I'd named my Zombie Udide Okwanka. In my language, it means "spider the artist." According to legend, Udide Okwanka is the Supreme Artist. And she lives underground where she takes fragments of things and changes them into something else. She can even weave spirits from straw. It was a good name for my Zombie. I wondered what Udide named me. I was sure it named me something, though I doubted that it told the others about me. I don't think it would have been allowed to keep seeing me.

Udide was waiting for me there, as if it sensed I would come out this night. I grinned, my heart feeling so warm. I sat down as it left the pipeline and crept up to me. It carried its instrument on top of its head. A sort of complex star made of wire. Over the weeks, it had added more wire lines, some thin and some thick. I often wondered where it put this thing when it was running about with the others, for the instrument was too big to hide on its body.

Udide held it before its eyes. With a front leg, it plucked out a sweet simple tune that almost made me weep with joy. It conjured up images of my mother and father, when they were so young and full of hope, when my brothers and

I were too young to marry and move away. Before the "kill and go" had driven my oldest brother away to America and my middle brother to the north . . . when there was so much potential.

I laughed and wiped away a tear and started strumming some chords to support the tune. From there we took off into something so intricate, enveloping, intertwining . . . *Chei!* I felt as if I was communing with God. *Ah-ah*, this machine and me. You can't imagine.

"Eme!"

Our music instantly fell apart.

"Eme!" my husband called again.

I froze, staring at Udide who was also motionless. "Please," I whispered to it. "Don't hurt him."

"Samuel messaged me!" my husband said, his eyes still on his cell phone, as he stepped up to me through the tall grass. "There's a break in the pipeline near the school! Not a goddamn Zombie in sight yet! Throw down that guitar, woman! Let's go and get . . . " He looked up. A terrified look took hold of his face.

For a very long time it seemed we all were frozen in time. My husband standing just at the last of the tall grass. Udide standing in front of the pipeline, instrument held up like a ceremonial shield. And me between the two of them, too afraid to move. I turned to my husband. "Andrew," I said with the greatest of care. "Let me explain . . . "

He slowly dragged his gaze to me and gave me a look, as if he was seeing me for the first time. "My own wife?!" he whispered.

"I . . . "

Udide raised its two front legs. For a moment it looked almost like it was pleading with me. Or maybe offering me a hug. Then it clicked its legs together so hard that it produced a large red spark and an ear splitting *ting!*

My husband and I clapped our hands over our ears. The air instantly smelled like freshly lit matches. Even through the palms of my hands, I could hear the responses from down the pipeline. The clicking was so numerous that it sounded like a rain of tiny pebbles falling on the pipeline. Udide shuddered, scrambled back and stood on it, waiting. They came in a great mob. About twenty of them. The first thing that I noticed was their eyes. They were all a deep angry red.

The others scrambled around Udide, tapping their feet in complex rhythms on the pipe. I couldn't see Udide's eyes. Then they all ran off with amazing speed, to the east.

I turned to my husband. He was gone.

Word spread like a disease because almost everyone had a cell phone. Soon everyone was clicking away on them, messaging things like, "Pipeline burst, near school! No Zombies in sight!" and "Hurry to school, bring bucket!" My husband never let me have my own cell phone. We couldn't afford one and he didn't think I needed one. But I knew where the elementary school was.

People now believed that the Zombies had all gone rogue, shrugging off their man-given jobs to live in the delta swamps and do whatever it was they did there. Normally, if bunkerers broke open a pipeline, even for the quietest jobs, the Zombies would become aware of it within an hour and repair the thing within another hour. But two hours later this broken pipe continued to splash fuel. That was when someone had decided to put the word out.

I knew better. The Zombies weren't "zombies" at all. They were thinking creatures. Smart beasts. They had a method to their madness. And most of them did *not* like human beings.

The chaos was lit by the headlights of several cars and trucks. The pipeline here was raised as it traveled south. Someone had taken advantage of this and removed a whole section of piping. Pink diesel fuel poured out of both ends like a giant fountain. People crowded beneath the flow like parched elephants, filling jerri cans, bottles, bowls, buckets. One man even held a garbage bag, until the fuel ate through the bag, splashing fuel all over the man's chest and legs.

The spillage collected into a large dark pink pool that swiftly flowed toward the elementary school, gathering on the playground. The fumes hit me even before I got within sight of the school. My eyes watered and my nose started running. I held my shirt over my nose and mouth. This barely helped.

People came in cars, motorcycles, buses, on foot. Everyone was messaging on their cell phones, further spreading the word. It had been a while since people who did not make a career out of fuel theft had gotten a sip of free fuel.

There were children everywhere. They ran up and down, sent on errands by their parents or just hanging around to be a part of the excitement. They'd probably never seen people able to go near a pipeline without getting killed. Hip-hop and highlife blasted from cars and SUVs with enhanced sound systems. The baseline vibrations were almost as stifling as the fumes. I had not a doubt that the Zombies knew this was going on.

I spotted my husband. He was heading toward the fountain of fuel with a large red bucket. Five men started arguing amongst each other. Two of them started pushing and shoving, almost falling into the fountain.

"Andrew!" I called over all the noise.

He turned. When he saw me, he narrowed his eyes.

"Please!" I said. "I'm . . . I'm sorry."

He spat and started walking away.

"You have to get out of here!" I said. "They will come!"

He whirled around and strode up to me. "How the hell are you so sure? Did you bring them yourself?"

As if in response, people suddenly started screaming and running. I cursed. The Zombies were coming from the street, forcing people to run toward the pool of fuel. I cursed, again. My husband was glaring at me. He pointed into my face with a look of disgust. I couldn't hear what he said over all the noise. He turned and ran off.

I tried to spot Udide amongst the Zombies. All of their eyes were still red. Was Udide even amongst them? I stared at their legs, searching for the butterfly sticker. There it was. Closest to me, to the left. "Udide!" I called.

As the name came out of my mouth, I saw two of the Zombies in the center each raise two front legs. My smile went to an "O" of shock. I dropped to the ground and threw my hands over my head. People were still splashing across the pool of fuel, trying to get into the school. Their cars continued blasting hip-hop and highlife, the headlights still on, lighting the madness.

The two Zombies clicked their legs together, producing two large sparks. *Ting!*

WHOOOOOOOOSH!

I remember light, heat, the smell of burning hair and flesh and screams that melted to guttural gurgles. The noise was muffled. The stench was awful. My head to my lap, I remained in this hellish limbo for a long, long time.

I'll never teach music at the elementary school. It was incinerated along with many of the children who went to it. My husband was killed, too. He died thinking I was some sort of spy fraternizing with the enemy . . . or something like that. Everyone died. Except me. Just before the explosion happened, Udide ran to me. It protected me with its force field.

So I lived.

And so did the baby inside me. The baby that my body allowed to happen because of Udide's lovely soothing music. Udide tells me it is a girl. How can a robot know this? Udide and I play for her every day. I can only imagine how content she is. But what kind of world will I be bringing her into? Where only her mother and Udide stand between a flat out war between the Zombies and the human beings who created them?

Pray that Udide and I can convince man and droid to call a truce, otherwise the delta will keep rolling in blood, metal and flames. You know what else? You should also pray that these Zombies don't build themselves some fins and travel across the ocean.

· WOMAN LEAVES ROOM ·
Robert Reed

She wears a smile. I like her smile, nervous and maybe a little scared, sweet and somewhat lonely. She wears jeans and a sheer green blouse and comfortable sandals and rings on two fingers and a glass patch across one eye. Standing at her end of the room, she asks how I feel. I feel fine. I tell her so and I tell her my name, and she puts her hands together and says that's a nice name. I ask to hear hers, but she says no. Then she laughs and says that she wants to be a creature of secrets. Both of us laugh and watch each other. Her smile changes as she makes herself ready for what happens next. I read her face, her body. She wants me to speak. The perfect words offer themselves to me, and I open my mouth. But there comes a sound—an important urgent note—and the glass patch turns opaque, hiding one of those pretty brown eyes.

She takes a quick deep breath, watching what I can't see. Seconds pass. Her shoulders drop and she widens her stance, absorbing some burden. Then the patch clears, and she tells me what I have already guessed. Something has happened; something needs her immediate attention. Please be patient, please, she says. Then she promises to be right back.

I watch her turn away. I watch her legs and long back and the dark brown hair pushed into a sloppy, temporary bun. A purse waits in the chair. She picks it up and hangs it on her shoulder. Her next two steps are quick but then she slows. Doubt and regret take hold as she reaches the open door. Entering the hallway, she almost looks back at me. She wants to and doesn't want to, and her face keeps changing. She feels sad and I'm sure that she is scared. But whatever the problem, she wants to smile, not quite meeting my eyes with her final expression, and I wave a hand and wish her well, but she has already vanished down the hallway.

The room is my room. The chairs and long sofa are familiar and look comfortable, and I know how each would feel if I sat. But I don't sit. Standing is most natural, and it takes no energy. The carpet beneath me is soft and deep and wonderfully warm on bare feet. I stand where I am and wait and wait. The walls are white and decorated with framed paintings of haystacks, and there is a switch beside the door and a fan and light on the ceiling. The light burns blue. The fan turns, clicking and wobbling slightly with each rotation. A window is on my right, but its blinds are drawn and dark. Behind me is another door. I could turn and see what it offers, but I don't. I am waiting. She is gone but will return, and she has to appear inside the first door, and I spend nothing, not even time, waiting for what I remember best, which is her pretty face.

A similar face appears. But this is a man wearing white trousers and a black shirt and glove-like shoes and no jewelry and no eye patch. He stands on the other side of the door, in the hallway, holding his hands in front of himself much as she did. He stares at me and says nothing. I ask who he is. He blinks and steps back and asks who I am. I tell him. And he laughs nervously. I don't know why I like the sound of laughter so much. He repeats my name and asks new questions, and I answer what I can answer while smiling at him, wondering how to make this man laugh again.

Do I know what I am meant to be, he asks. Which is a very different question than asking who I am.

I have no answer to give.

Then he lists names, one after another, waiting for me to recognize any of them. I don't. That's not surprising, he says. I was only begun and then left, which is too bad. Which is sad. I nod and smile politely. Then he asks if I have ever seen anybody else, and I describe the woman who just left the room. That's how I get him to laugh again. But it is a nervous little laugh dissolving into sharp, confused emotions.

That woman was my mother, he says. He claims that thirty-one years have passed and she barely started me before something happened to her, but he doesn't explain. This is all unexpected. I am not expected.

I nod and smile, watching him cry.

He wants to hear about the woman.

I tell him everything.

And then she left?

I tell how the patch darkened, interrupting us, and I describe the purse and how she carried it and the last troubled look that she showed me, and what does it mean that I'm not finished?

It means you are small and nearly invisible, he says. It means that you have existed for three decades without anybody noticing.

But time has no weight. No object outside this room has consequences, and this young man standing out in the hallway is no more real than the painted haystacks on the walls. What I want is for the woman to return. I want her weight and reality, and that's what I tell this stranger.

Shaking his head, he tells me that I am unreal.

Why he would lie is a mystery.

He mentions his father and cries while looking at me. Do I know that his father died before he was born?

An unreal person can never be born, I think.

You were begun but only just begun, he keeps saying. Then he admits that he doesn't know what to do with me. As if he has any say in these matters. His final act is to turn and vanish, never trying to step inside the room.

But he wasn't real to begin with. I know this. What cannot stand beside me is false and suspicious, and the lesson gives me more weight, more substance, the epiphany carrying me forward.

Another man appears.

Like the first man, he cannot or will not step out of the hallway. He looks at my face and body and face again. He wears a necklace and sturdy boots and odd clothes that can't stay one color. He says that it took him forever to find me, and finding me was the easiest part of his job. Operating systems were changed after the Cleansing. He had to resurrect codes and passwords and build machines that haven't existed in quite some time. Then on top of that, he had to master a dialect that died off ages ago.

He wants to know if he's making any sense.

He is a madman and I tell him so.

I found your file logs, he says, laughing and nodding. Stored in another server and mislabeled, but that was just another stumbling block.

I don't know what that means.

He claims that his great-grandfather was the last person to visit me.

Phantoms like to tell stories. I nod politely at his story, saying nothing.

He tells me that the man lived to be one hundred and fifty, but he died recently. There was a will, and my location was mentioned in the will. Until then I was a family legend—a legend wrapped around twin tragedies. His great grandfather's father was killed in the Fourth Gulf War, and his great-great-grandmother missed him terribly. She was the one who began me. She spent quite a lot of money, using medical records and digital files to create a facsimile of her soul mate. And she would have finished me, at least as far as the software of the day would have allowed. But her son was hurt at daycare. He fell and cut himself, and she was hurrying to the hospital when a stupid kid driver shut off his car's autopilot and ran her down in the street. The boy wasn't seriously hurt. What mattered was that the boy, his great-grandfather, was three and orphaned, and a drunken aunt ended up raising him, and for the rest of his many, many days, that man felt cheated and miserable.

I listen to every word, nodding patiently.

He wants to know what I think of the story.

He is crazy but I prefer to say nothing.

Frowning, he tells me that a great deal of work brought him to this point. He says that I should be more appreciative and impressed. Then he asks if I understand how I managed to survive for this long.

But no time has passed, I reply.

He waves a hand, dismissing my words. You are very small, he says. Tiny files that are never opened can resist corruption.

I am not small. I am everything.

He has copied me, he claims. He says that he intends to finish the new copy, as best he can. But he will leave the original alone.

Pausing, he waits for my thanks.

I say nothing, showing him a grim, suspicious face.

But you do need clothes, he says.

Except this is how I am.

My great-great grandma had some plan for you, he says. But I won't think about that, he says. And besides, clothes won't take much room in the file.

My body feels different.

Much better, he says, and steps out of view.

Time becomes real when the mind has great work to do. My first eternity is spent picking at the trousers and shirt, eroding them until they fall away, threads of changing color sprawled across the eternal carpet.

Yet nothing is eternal. Each of the haystacks begins with the same pleasantly rounded shape, but some have turned lumpy and ragged at the edges, while my favorite stack has a large gap eaten through its middle. And I remember the straw having colors instead of that faded uniform gray. And I remember the sofa being soft buttery yellow, and the room's walls were never this rough looking, and the colored threads have vanished entirely, which seems good. But the carpet looks softer and feels softer than seems right, my feet practically melting into their nature.

Portions of my room are falling apart.

As an experiment, I study the nearest haystack until I know it perfectly, and then I shut my eyes and wait and wait and wait still longer, remembering everything; when I look again the painting has changed but I can't seem to decide how it has changed. Which means the problem perhaps lies in my memory, or maybe with my perishable mind.

Fear gives me ideas.

My legs have never moved and they don't know how. I have to teach them to walk, one after the other. Each step requires learning and practice and more time than I can hope to measure. But at least my one hand knows how to reach out and grab hold. I push at the window's blinds, but for all of my effort, nothing is visible except a dull grayish-black rectangle that means nothing to me.

Stepping backwards is more difficult than walking forwards. But turning around is nearly impossible, and I give up. In little steps, I retreat to the place where I began. The carpet remembers my feet, but the carpet feels only half-real. Or my feet are beginning to dissolve. The woman will be here soon. I tell myself that even when I don't believe it, and the fear grows worse. I start to look at my favorite hand, studying each finger, noting how the flesh has grown hairless and very simple, the nails on the end of every finger swallowed by the simple skin.

A stranger suddenly comes to the door.

Hello, it says.

What it looks like is impossible to describe. I have no words to hang on what I see, and maybe there is nothing to see. But my feeling is that the visitor is smiling and happy, and it sounds like a happy voice asking how I am feeling.

I am nearly dead, I say.

There is death and there is life, it tells me. You are still one thing, which means you are not the other.

I am alive.

It claims that I am lucky. It tells me much about systems and files and the history of machines that have survived in their sleep mode, lasting thousands of years past every estimate of what was possible.

I am a fluke and alive, and my guest says something about tidying the room and me.

The work takes no time.

My favorite hand is the way it began. My favorite haystack is rather like it began in terms of color and shape. Legs that never moved until recently barely complain when I walk across the room. It never occurred to me that I could reach into the haystack paintings, touching those mounds of dead grass. Some feel cool, some warm. I sing out my pleasure, and even my voice feels new.

My guest watches me, making small last adjustments.

Because it is proper, I thank it for its help.

But the original file is gone now, it says.

I ask what that means.

It tells me that I am a copy of the file, filtered and enhanced according to the best tools available.

Once more, I offer my thanks.

And with a voice that conveys importance, my guest tells me that I have a new purpose. What I am will be copied once more, but this time as a kind of light that can pierce dust and distance and might never end its travels across the galaxy and beyond.

I don't understand, and I tell it so.

Then my friend does one last task, and everything is apparent to me.

I ask when am I going to be sent.

In another few moments, it promises.

For the last time, I thank my benefactor. Then I let my legs turn me around, looking at the door that was always behind me.

A second room waits. The bed is longer than it is wide and rectangular and neatly made. Pillows are stacked high against the headboard, and identical nightstands sport tall candles that have not stopped burning in some great span of time. I know this other room. I think of her and the room and step toward the door and then suffer for my eagerness.

What is wrong? asks a new voice.

I turn back. A creature with many arms stands in the hallway.

You appear agitated, says the creature.

Which is true, but I am not sure why I feel this way. I stare into a face that seems buried in the creature's chest, hanging word after inadequate word on my emotions.

It listens.

I pause.

You are interesting, says the creature.

I am nothing but a file with a name and a few rough qualities.

But my new companion dismisses my harsh outlook. Every arm moves, drawing complex shapes in the air. You are part of a large cultural package, it says, and do you know how long you have been traveling in space?

I could guess, I say. I could invent infinite estimates, all but one of them wrong.

And then it laughs, revealing a reassuring humor. Even this strange laugh makes me happier than I was before.

An eight billion year voyage, it says.

That seems like an unlikely, preposterous figure, and it shakes me.

It explains that it can't determine which star was mine, and my galaxy barely wears a name, and most of the data that came with me has been lost to the vagaries of time and the great distance being covered.

But here you stand, it says.

I am standing, but sad. My savior is full of hearty laughter, yet I feel sick and sorry and lost.

She is gone forever, I say.

It knows whom I am talking about. It measures my misery and learns what it can from my longing, and then at the end, as if delivering the punch line of a joke, it laughs and says:

But the universe is infinite, and in too many ways to count.

I don't know what that means.

Infinite means eternal, it says, and eternal means that nothing is unthinkable, and what can be imagined is inevitable.

But when? I ask.

And again, the alien laughs, saying:

Are you hearing me? There is no such monster as "when."

I am a file and I am protected and I don't know where I am or how well I am protected. Time stretches, and I suspect that I exist mostly inside some sleep mode, probably initiating only when I blink my eyes.

Once again, the two rooms decay and the haystacks fall apart and I forget how to move and forget a great deal more too.

Beyond the walls, worlds die and dissolve away.

Little flickers tear the walls to pieces, but the pieces knit themselves back together, and I wait, and wait, and then she comes through the door once again. Her clothes are different. There is no eye patch and no purse. But while I am uncertain about much, I know that beautiful face.

It took me a little while, she explains.

She walks toward me, pulling the pins out of her brown hair.

And that's when I remember what I was going to tell her that first time that we met.

I won't ever let you out of this room, darling.

I say it now.

She thinks that is funny and wonderful, and laughs.

And in another moment, I can't remember anything else that ever happened. The universe is nothing but the two of us holding each other, laughing ourselves sick.

• ALL THAT TOUCHES THE AIR •
An Owomoyela

When I was ten, I saw a man named Menley brought out to the Ocean of Starve. Thirty of us colonials gathered around, sweating in our envirosuits under the cerulean sky, while bailiffs flashed radio signals into the Ocean. Soon enough the silvery Vosth fog swarmed up and we watched the bailiffs take off Menley's suit, helmet first. They worked down his body until every inch of his skin was exposed.

Every. Last. Inch.

Menley was mad. Colonist's dementia. Born on Earth, he was one of the unlucky six-point-three percent who set down outside the solar system in strange atmospheres, gravities, rates of orbit and rotation, and just snapped because everything was almost like Earth, but wasn't quite right. In his dementia, he'd defecated somewhere public; uncouth of him, but it wouldn't have got him thrown to the Ocean except that the governors were fed up with limited resources and strict colonial bylaws and Earth's *fuck off on your own* attitude, and Menley crapping on the communal lawns was the last insult they could take. He was nobody, here on Predonia. He was a madman. No one would miss him.

The fog crawled out of the water and over his body, colonizing his pores, permeating bone and tissue, bleeding off his ability to yell or fight back.

He was on his side in a convulsion before the Vosth parasites took his motor functions and stood his body up. They turned around and staggered into the Ocean of Starve, and it was eight years before I saw Menley again.

Before that, when I was sixteen, I was studying hydroponics and genetic selection. In the heat of the greenhouse, everyone could notice that I wore long clothing, high collars, gloves. I'd just passed the civics tests and become a voting adult, and that meant dressing in another envirosuit and going out to the Ocean again. The auditor sat me down in a comm booth and the Vosth swarmed into its speakers. The voice they synthesized was tinny and inhuman.

We tell our history of this colony, they said. *You came past the shell of atmosphere. We were at that time the dominant species. You made your colonies in the open air. We harvested the utility of your bodies, but you proved sentience and sapience and an understanding was formed.*

You would keep your colony to lands prescribed for you. You would make shells against our atmosphere. You would accept our law.

All that touches the air belongs to us.
What touches the air is ours.

Endria was a prodigy. She passed her civics tests at thirteen. She was also stupid.

After two years in hydroponics, I graduated to waste reclamation, specialty in chemical-accelerated blackwater decomposition. No one wanted the job, so the compensation was great—and it came with a hazard suit. I used to take a sterile shower in the waste facility and walk to my room in my suit, past the airlock that led to the open air. That's where I caught Endria.

Emancipated adults weren't beholden to curfew, so she was out unsupervised. She was also opening the door without an envirosuit on.

I ran up to stop her and pulled her hand from the control panel. "Hey!"

She wrenched her hand away. No thanks there. "What are you doing?"

"What are *you* doing?" I asked back. "You're endangering the colony! I should report you."

"Is it my civic or personal responsibility to leave people out there when they're trying to get in?"

I looked through the porthole to see what she was talking about. I had no peripheral vision in the suit, so I hadn't seen anyone in the airlock. But Endria was right: Someone was trying to get in.

Menley was trying to get in.

He looked the same: Silvery skin, dead expression, eyes and muscles moving like the Vosth could work out how each part of his face functioned but couldn't put it all together. I jumped back. I thought I could feel Vosth crawling inside my envirosuit.

"He's not allowed in," I said. "I'm contacting Security Response."

"Why isn't he?"

Of all the idiotic questions. "He's been taken over by the Vosth!"

"And we maintain a civil, reciprocal policy toward them," Endria said. "We're allowed in their territory without notification, so they should be allowed in ours."

Besides the Vosth, there was nothing I hated more than someone who'd just come out of a civics test. "Unless we take them over when they wander in, it's not reciprocal," I said. Vosth-Menley put his hand against the porthole; his silver fingers squished against the composite. I stepped back. "You know it all; who gets notified if an infested colonist tries to walk into the habitat?"

Her face screwed up. I guess that wasn't on her exam.

"I'll find out," she said, turning on her heel. "Don't create an interspecies incident while I'm gone."

She flounced away.

I turned back to the porthole, where Vosth-Menley had smooshed his nose up against the composite as well. I knocked my helmet against the door.

"Leave," I told him. Them. It.

He stared, dead eyes unblinking, then slouched away.

I didn't sleep that night. My brain played old-Earth zombie flicks whenever I closed my eyes, staffed by silver monstrosities instead of rotting corpses. Endria thought I'd create an interspecies incident; I thought about how many people would be trapped without e-suits if a Vosth infestation broke out. How many people would be screaming and convulsing and then just staggering around with dead silver eyes, soft hands pressing into portholes, skin teeming with parasites ready to crawl into anyone they saw.

I talked to the governor on duty the next day, who confirmed that the colony would "strongly prefer" if the Vosth weren't allowed to walk around in naked fleshsuits inside the habitat. She even sent out a public memo.

Three days later, Endria came to give me crap about it. The way she walked into my lab, she looked like someone took one of the governors, shrunk them, and reworked their face to fit that impish craze back in the '20s. She even had a datapad, and a button-up tunic under her hygienic jacket. "I'm not going to enjoy this, am I?" I asked.

"I came to interview you about civil law and the Vosth," she said. "It's for a primary certification in government apprenticeship. I'm going to be a governor by the time I'm sixteen."

I stared at her.

"It's part of a civics certification, so I can make you answer," she added.

Wonderful. "After these titrations," I told her.

Endria went to one of the counters and boosted herself onto it, dropped her datapad beside her, and reached into a pocket to pull out something colorful and probably fragrant and nutrient-scarce. "That's okay. We can make small talk while you're working. I know titration isn't demanding on the linguistic portions of your brain."

Excepting the Vosth, there was nothing I hated more than people who thought they knew more about my work than I did.

"Sit quietly," I said. "I'll be with you shortly."

To my surprise, she actually sat quietly.

To my annoyance, that lasted through a total of one titration and a half.

"I'm going to interview you about the sentence passed on Ken Menley in colony record zero-zero-zero-three-zero-four," she said. "According to my research, you were the youngest person there, as well as the only person there to meet Menley again. You have a unique perspective on Vosth-human interactions. After the incident a few nights ago I thought it would be a good idea to focus my paper on them."

"My perspective," I started to say, but thought better of calling the Vosth names usually reserved for human excrement. They were shit, they were horrifying, they were waiting out there to crawl inside us, and if Endria was going to be a governor by age sixteen she'd probably have the authority to rehabilitate me by sixteen and a half. I didn't want her thinking I needed my opinions revised. "I have no perspective. I don't deal with them."

Endria rolled the candy around in her mouth. "I don't think any of my friends are friends with you," she said. "Isn't it weird to go past two degrees of separation?"

"Wouldn't know," I said. My primary degrees of separation were limited to my supervisor and the quartermaster I requisitioned e-suits from. I wouldn't call either of them friends.

Endria kicked her heels, tilting her head so far her ear rested on her shoulder. "Everyone thinks you're a creep because you never take that e-suit off."

"That's nice," I said.

"Are you afraid of the Vosth?" Endria asked. She said it like that was unreasonable.

"I have a healthy skepticism that they're good neighbors," I said.

"And that's why you wear an e-suit?"

"No," I said, "that's why I'm active in colonial politics and took the civics track with an emphasis on interspecies diplomacy." I set down the beaker I was working with. For irony.

Endria sucked on her teeth, then gave me a smile I couldn't read. "You could go into Vosth research. It's a promising new area of scientific inquiry."

I pushed the beaker aside. "What new area? We've been here for a generation. Bureaucracy is slow, but it's not that slow."

"It's a hard science, not sociological," she said. "We couldn't do that before. I don't know much about it, but there's all sorts of government appropriations earmarked for it. Don't you read the public accounting?"

I turned to look at her. She was kicking her heels against the table.

"You should go into Vosth research, and you should use your experience with Menley to open up a line of inquiry. It's probably xenobiology or something, but it might be fertile ground for new discoveries. Then you could be the colony's expert on the Vosth. Interspecies relations are an important part of this colony. That's why I'm writing a paper on them for my civics certification."

"I'm not getting this titration done, am I?"

Endria smiled, and said the words most feared by common citizens interacting with civil law. "This will only take a minute."

It wasn't against the law to go outside the compound, and some people liked the sunlight. Some people—daredevils and risk-takers—even enjoyed the fresh air. As for me, I passed the front door every time I got off work and always felt like I was walking along the edge of a cliff. I'd tried taking different routes but that made it worse somehow, like if I didn't keep my eye on it, the airlock would blow out and let these seething waves of silver flow in and I wouldn't know until I got back to my shower or had to switch out my suit for cleaning. Or I'd be opening my faceplate for dinner and feel something else on my lips, and there would be the Vosth, crawling inside. I had trouble eating if I didn't walk past the airlock to make sure it was closed.

Yeah, Menley made that worse.

I started staring at the airlock, expecting to see his face squashed up against it. Maybe he was just outside, seconds away from getting some idiot like Endria to let him in. People walked past me, and I could hear them talking in low tones while I watched the airlock, like maybe I'd gone into an absence seizure and they should get someone to haul me away. And then they could have me investigated for colonist's dementia despite the fact that I'd been born here. And they could take me out to the Ocean of Starve . . .

After two nights I realized if I didn't step outside to make sure the Vosth weren't coming with a swarm, I was heading for a paranoid fugue.

Actually walking out took two more nights because I couldn't stand to open the airlock myself. I finally saw a couple strolling out as I passed, e-suited hand in e-suited hand, and I fell in behind them.

The airlock and the outside were the only places I could be anonymous in my e-suit. The couple didn't even cross to the other side of the enclosure as it cycled the air and opened the outer door.

The grass was teal-green. I hear it's less blue on Earth, and the sky is less green, but I was just glad neither one was silver. The sunlight was strong and golden, the clouds were mercifully white, and there wasn't a trace of fog to be seen. So that was good. For the moment.

The Ocean of Starve was a good ten-minute hike away, and I didn't want to get near it. I walked around the habitat instead, eyeing the horizon in the Ocean's direction. I'd made it about a half-kilometer around the periphery when I caught a flash of silver out of the corner of my eye and jumped, ready for it to be a trick of the light or a metal component on the eggshell exterior of the dome.

No. It was Menley.

I screamed.

The scream instinct isn't one of evolution's better moves. Actually, it's a terrible idea. The instant sound left my mouth Menley turned and dragged himself toward me. I considered running, but I had this image of tripping, and either losing a boot or ripping a hole in my e-suit.

Menley staggered up and stared at me. I took a step back. Menley turned his head like he wasn't sure which eye got a better view, and I stepped back again.

After about a minute of this, I said "You really want inside the compound, don't you?"

The Vosth opened Menley's mouth. His nostrils flared. I guess they were doing something like they did to the speakers in the audience booth—vibrating the equipment. The voice, if you wanted to call it that, was quiet and reedy. *We are the Vosth.*

"I know that," I said, and took another step back from them. Him. Vosth-Menley.

You will let us inside? he asked, with an artificial rise to his voice. I guess the Vosth had to telegraph their questions. Maybe they weren't used to asking.

"No," I told him.

He shifted his weight forward and ignored my answer. *The Vosth are allowed inside your partition shell?*

"Look what you do to people," I said. "No, you're not allowed inside."

This is natural, they said, and I had no idea if that was supposed to be an argument or agreement.

"What?"

Take off your suit, Vosth-Menley said.

"Hell no."

The air creates a pleasurable sensation on human skin.

"And the Vosth create a pleasant infestation?"

We will promise not to take you.

If they had to tell me, I wasn't trusting them. "Why do you want me to?"

Do you want to? the Vosth asked.

I checked the seal on my suit.

Take off your suit, Vosth-Menley said again.

"I'm going home now," I answered, and ran for the compound door.

Endria was in the canteen, sitting on a table, watching a slow-wave newsfeed from Earth and nibbling on a finger sandwich, and I was annoyed to run into her there. I was also annoyed that it took me that long to run into her, after trying to run into her in the library, the courthouse auditorium, the promenade and my lab.

Endria just annoyed me.

I dodged a few people on their rest hours and walked up to her table, putting my hands down on it. I hadn't sterilized them after being outside and was technically breaching a bylaw or two, but that didn't occur to me. I guess I was lucky Endria didn't perform a civilian arrest.

"One," I said, "I don't want anything to do with the Vosth in a lab, or outside of one, and two, in no more than thirty seconds, explain Vosth legal rights outside the colony compound."

Endria jumped, kicking over the chair her feet were resting on, and looking agape at me in the middle of a bite of sandwich. Sweet schadenfreude: The first word out of her mouth was the none-too-smart: "Uh."

Of course, she regrouped quickly.

"First of all, the Vosth don't believe in civil or social law," she said. "Just natural law. So the treaty we have isn't really a treaty, just them explaining what they do so we had the option not to let them. We don't have legal recourse. It's like that inside the colony, too—we can adjust the air system to filter them out and kill them, so they know we're in charge in here and don't try to come inside. Except for Menley, but that's weird, and that's why I'm doing a paper. Did you find anything out?"

I ignored that. "And he doesn't act like the other—how many other infested colonists are there?"

She shrugged. "A lot. Like, more than forty. A few of them were killed by panicked colonists, though. We don't know much about them. In the last hundred records, Menley's the only—"

"*Vosth-Menley*," I corrected.

Endria rolled her eyes. "Yeah, that. Whatever. *Vosth-Menley* is the only one to make contact with us. There's actually this theory that the rest are off building a civilization now that the Vosth have opposable thumbs. Even if it's only, like, eighty opposable thumbs."

The base of my neck itched. Fortunately, years in an envirosuit let me ignore that. "We lost forty colonists to the Vosth?"

"Oh, yeah!" she said. "And more when everyone panicked and there were riots and we thought there was going to be a war. That's why so many Earth-shipped embryos were matured so fast. In fact, our colony has the highest per-capita percentage of in-vitro citizens. We've got sixty-three percent."

"I'm one of them," I said.

"I've got parents," Endria responded.

I managed not to strangle her. "So there's no law?"

"Not really," Endria said. "But there's a lot of unwritten stuff and assumed stuff. Like we just assume that if we wear e-suits out they won't think they own the e-suits even though they touch the air, and we assume that if they did come in the compound they'd be nice." She shot me a sharp look. "But I don't think that's an issue now, since you squealed to the governors."

"Yeah, thanks." I did not *squeal*. Endria just didn't see what was wrong with having a sentient invasive disease wandering around your colony. "I'm going to go now."

"I still want to complete our interview!" Endria said. "I think you have opinion data you're holding back!"

"Later," I said, gave a little wave, and headed off.

On the way out of the canteen I ran into one of the auxiliary governors, who pulled me aside and gave my envirosuit the usual look of disdain. "Citizen," she said, "I need a thumbprint verification to confirm that your complaint to the colony council was resolved to your satisfaction. Your complaint about the infested colonist."

I looked to the hall leading in the direction of the outside doors. "Right now?"

"It will only take a moment."

I looked to the vents, and then back at Endria.

I hated thumbprint confirmations.

Quickly, I unsealed one glove, pulled my hand out, and pressed my thumb into the datapad sensor. The air drew little fingers along my palm, tested my wrist seal, tickled the back of my hand. "Thank you, citizen," the auxiliary said, and wandered off.

I tucked my exposed hand under my other arm and hurried back toward my room to sterilize hand and glove and put my suit back together.

I went outside again. I don't know why. Specialized insanity, maybe.

Actually, no. This was like those people on Mulciber who'd go outside in their hazard suits even though the Mulciber colony was on a patch of stable ground that didn't extend much beyond the habitat, and they always ran the risk of falling into a magma chamber or having a glob of superheated rock smash their faceplate in. Some people find something terrifying and then just have to go out to stare it in the face. Another one of evolution's less-than-brilliant moves.

Vosth-Menley was stretching his stolen muscles by the shore of the Starve. I could see the muscles moving under his skin. He laced his fingers together and pulled his hands above his head. He planted his feet and bent at the waist so far that his forehead almost touched the ground. I couldn't do any of that.

I went through the usual colony-prescribed exercises every morning. The envirosuit pinched and chafed, but like hell I was going to show off my body any longer than I had to. Vosth-Menley didn't have that problem. The Vosth could walk around naked, for all they cared, if they had a body to *be* naked.

The Vosth noticed me and Vosth-Menley turned around. He clomped his way over, and I tried not to back away.

The air is temperate at this time, at these coordinates, Vosth-Menley said.

I looked over the turbid water. It caught the turquoise of the sky and reflected slate, underlaid with silver. "Why do you call this the Ocean of Starve?"

Vosth-Menley turned back to the Ocean. His gaze ran over the surface, eyes moving in separate directions, and his mouth slacked open.

Our genetic structure was encoded in a meteorite, he said. *We impacted this world long ago and altered the ecosystem. We adapted to rely on the heat of free volcanic activity, which was not this world's stable state. When the world cooled our rate of starvation exceeded our rate of adaptation. Here, underwater vents provided heat to sustain our adaptation until we could survive.*

My stomach turned. "Why do you take people over?"

Your bodies are warm and comfortable.

"Even though we proved sapience to you," I said.

Vosth-Menley didn't answer.

"What would you do if I took off my envirosuit?"

You would feel the air, Vosth-Menley said, like I wouldn't notice that he hadn't answered the question.

"I know that. What would *you* do? You, the Vosth?"

You would feel the gentle sun warming your skin.

I backed away. Nothing was stopping him from lunging and tearing off my suit. Not if what Endria said was true: that it was the law of the wild out here. Why didn't he? "You don't see anything wrong with that."

I wished he would blink. Maybe gesture. Tapdance. Anything. *You have been reacting to us with fear.*

The conversation was an exercise in stating the useless and obvious. "I don't want to end up like Menley," I said. "Can't you understand that? Would you want that to happen to you?"

We are the dominant species, the Vosth said. *We would not be taken over.*

"Empathy," I muttered. I wasn't expecting him to hear it. "Learn it."

We are not averse to learning, the Vosth said. *Do you engage in demonstration?*

Demonstration? Empathy? I shook my head. "You don't get what I'm saying."

Would we be better if we understood? he asked, and stumbled forward with sudden intensity.

I jumped back, ready to fight him off, ready to run.

We want to understand.

• • •

[Can the Vosth change?] was the first thing I wrote to Endria when I sat down at my terminal. I don't know why I kept asking her things. Maybe despite the fact that she was five years my junior and a pain in the rectum she was still less annoying than the diplomatic auditors. Maybe because she was the only person who didn't look at me like they might have to call Security Response if I walked up. I didn't really talk to anyone on my off hours.

She never wrote me back. Instead, she showed up at my door. "You're going to have to be a little more specific."

"Hello, Endria," I said as I let her in. "Nice of you to stop by. You couldn't have just written that out?"

She huffed. "You have a pretty nice room, you know that? The quarters I can get if I want to move out of our family's allotment are all little closets."

"Get a job," I said. "Look, when you said the Vosth—"

"Don't you ever take that suit off?" she interrupted. "I mean, we're inside about five different air filtration systems and an airlock or two."

I ran a hand around the collar of my envirosuit. "I like having it on."

"How do you eat?"

"I open it to eat." And shower, and piss, and I took it off to change into other suits and have the ones I'd been wearing cleaned. I just didn't enjoy it. "Can you reason with the Vosth?"

Endria shook her head. "More specific."

"Do they change their behavior?" I asked.

Endria wandered over to my couch and sat down, giving me a disparaging look. "*Nice* specifics. They adapt, if that's what you mean. Didn't you listen at your initiation? They came to this planet and couldn't survive here so they adapted. Some people think that's why we can negotiate with them at all."

I didn't follow. "What does that have to do with negotiation?"

"Well, it's all theoretical," she said, and tried to fish something out of her teeth with her pinky.

"Endria. Negotiation. Adaptation. What?"

"They *adapt*," she said. "They fell out of the sky and almost died here and then they adapted and they became the dominant species. Then we landed, which is way better than falling, and we have all this technology they don't have, and they can't just read our minds, even if they take us over, so wouldn't you negotiate for that? To stay the dominant species? I think they want to be more like us."

Would we be better if we understood, the Vosth had asked. "They said they took over colonists because our bodies were comfortable," I said.

Endria shrugged. "Maybe being dominant is comfortable for them."

I ran a hand over my helmet. "Charming."

"I mean, letting them be dominant sure isn't comfortable for you."

I glared. "What, it's comfortable for you?"

"They're not that bad," Endria said. "I mean, they're not territorial or anything. They just do their thing. When I'm a governor, I want to see if we can work together."

"Yeah. Us and the body-snatchers."

Endria tilted her head at me. "You know, I think it would be kinda neat, sharing your body with the Vosth. I mean, if it wasn't a permanent thing. I bet you'd get all sorts of new perspectives."

I gaped. I don't think Endria saw my expression through the helmet, but it was disturbing enough that she didn't share it. "It *is* a permanent thing! And you don't share—you don't get control. They take you over and you just die. There's probably nothing *left* of you. Or if there is, you're just stuck in your head, screaming."

"And that's why you're asking if the Vosth can change?" Endria asked.

"I'm asking because—" I started, and then couldn't finish that sentence.

Endria smiled. It was a nasty sort of hah-I-knew-it smile. "See?" she said, hopping off the couch and heading for the door. "You *are* interested in Vosth research."

Twenty minutes later someone knocked on my door. I opened it, thinking it was Endria back to irritate me. No. In the corridor outside my room stood a wide-faced, high-collared balding man, with an expression like he'd been eating ascorbic acid and a badge on his lapel reading DIPLOMATIC AUDITOR in big bold letters.

He'd even brought a datapad.

"This is a notice, citizen," he said. "You're not authorized to engage in diplomatic action with the Vosth."

"I'm not engaging in diplomatic action," I said, shuffling through possible excuses. It'd be easier if I had any idea what I *was* doing. "I'm . . . engaging in research."

He didn't look convinced.

"Civil research," I said, picking up a pen from my desk and wagging it at him like he should know better. "Helping Endria with her civics certification. Didn't she fill out the right forms to make me one of her resources?"

There were no forms, as far as I knew. Still, if there were, I could probably shuffle off the responsibility onto Endria, and if there weren't, the sourface in front of me would probably go and draft some up to mollify himself. Either way, I was off the hook for a moment.

He marked something down on his datapad. "I'm going to check into this," he warned.

At which point he'd argue his case against Endria. Poor bastards, both of them.

"Expect further communication from a member of the governing commission," he warned. Satisfied with that threat, he turned and went away.

For about a day, I decided work was safer. If I kept to the restricted-access parts of the waste reclamation facility I could cut down on Endria sightings, and I could work long hours. Surely the governors wouldn't work late just to harass me.

It wasn't a long-term solution. Still, I thought it'd be longer-term than one work shift.

I got back to my room and my terminal was blinking, and when I sat down it triggered an automatic callback and put me on standby for two minutes. Now, in theory automatic callbacks were only for high-priority colony business, which, considering I'd seen my supervisor not ten minutes ago and I wasn't involved in anything important in governance, I expected to mean that Endria wanted something and they took civics certification courses way more seriously than I'd thought. I went to get a drink while it was trying to connect.

And I came back to a line of text on an encrypted channel, coming from the office of the Prime Governor.

Most of my water ended up on my boots.

[Sorry I'm doing this over text,] she wrote. [I just wanted an official record of our conversation.]

When a governor wants an official record of your conversation, you're fucked.

[What can I do for you?] I typed back.

[Someone stopped by to talk to you,] she went on, the lines spooling out over the screen in real-time. [About your not being authorized to engage in diplomatic action.]

I had expected that to be defused, not to escalate. Escalating up to the Prime Governor had been right out. [I still believe that I wasn't engaging in diplomatic—] I started, but she typed right over it.

[How would you like authorization?]

That hadn't been on the list of possibilities, either.

[I'm sorry?] I typed. What I almost typed, and might have typed if I didn't value my civil liberties, was *I recycle shit for a living. My skillset is not what you're looking for.*

[You may be aware that we're pioneering a new focus of study into the Vosth,] the Governor typed.

Vosth research. I wondered if Endria had recommended me upward. [Yes, ma'am,] I wrote.

[We now believe that we can reverse the effects of Vosth colonization of a human host.]

I looked at my water. I looked at my boots. After a moment, I typed [Ma'am?] and got up for another glass. I needed it.

I came back to a paragraph explaining [You've been in contact with one of the infested colonists. We'd like you to bring him back to the compound for experimentation.]

Okay. So long as I was just being asked to harvest test subjects. [You want to cure Menley?]

[We believe it unlikely that human consciousness would survive anywhere on the order of years,] she typed back, and my stomach twisted like it had talking to Menley. [This would be a proof of concept which could be applied to the more recently infected.]

And Menley wasn't someone who'd be welcomed back into the colony, I read between the lines. I should've asked Endria who had sat on the council that decided Menley's sentence. Was this particular Prime Governor serving, back then? Why did I never remember these things? Why did I never think to ask?

[So, you would extract the Vosth,] I started, and was going to write *leaving a corpse?*, maybe hoping that we'd at least get a breathing body. She interrupted me again.

[The Vosth parasite organisms would not be extracted. They would die.]

My mouth was dry, but the idea of drinking water made me nauseous. It was like anyone or anything in Menley's body was fair game for anyone.

[I want to be clear with you,] she said. Dammit. She could have just lied like they did in every dramatic work I'd ever read. Then, if the truth ever came out, I could be horrified but still secure in the knowledge that there was no way I could have known. No. I just got told to kidnap someone so the scientists could kill him. I wasn't even saving anyone. Well, maybe in the future, *if* anyone got infested again.

Anyone the governors felt like curing, anyway.

Then she had to go and make it worse.

[We would not be in violation of any treaties or rules of conduct,] she wrote. [If we can develop a cure for or immunity to Vosth infestation, the de facto arrangement in place between our colony and the Vosth will be rendered null, and the restrictions imposed on our activities on the planet will become obsolete.]

I wished Endria was there. She could interpret this. [Isn't this an act of war?]

[We're confident that the Vosth will regard an unwarranted act of aggression as an expression of natural law,] the Governor explained.

That didn't make me feel better, and I think it translated to *yes*. [I thought it was understood that things like that wouldn't happen.]

[It was understood that the dominant species could, at any time, exercise their natural rights,] the Governor explained. [Perhaps it's time they learned that they aren't the dominant species any more.]

We believe the ambient temperature to be pleasant for human senses today, Vosth-Menley told me when I got to the Ocean of Starve. I was beginning to wonder whether his reassurances were predation or a mountain of culture skew.

"What is your obsession with me feeling the air?" I asked him. Them. The Vosth.

You would be safe, Vosth-Menley insisted.

I should have asked Endria if the Vosth could lie. I should have kept a running list of things I needed to ask. "Listen," I said.

We would like to understand, Vosth-Menley said again.

I read a lot of Earth lit. I'd never seen a butterfly, but I knew the metaphor of kids who'd pull off their wings. Looking at Menley, I wondered if the Vosth were like children, oblivious to their own cruelty. "What would you do if someone could take you over?"

Our biology is not comparable to yours, Vosth-Menley said.

Bad hypothetical. "What would you do if someone tried to kill you?"

It is our perception of reality that species attempt to prolong their own existence, he said.

"Yeah." I was having trouble following my own conversation. "Look, you're a dominant species, and we're supposed to have a reciprocal relationship, but you take people over and—look." I'd gone past talking myself in circles and was talking myself in scatterplots.

The back of my neck itched, and I couldn't ignore it.

"What if I *do* want to take off my suit?" I asked, and then scatterplotted, "Do you have any reason to lie to me?"

The Vosth considered. *Yes.*

Oh. Okay. Great.

Our present actions are concurrent with a different directive, he added. *There is reason to establish honesty.*

Nothing was stopping him from attacking. He could have torn off my suit or helmet by now. Even if it was a risk, and it *was* a risk, and even if I had a phobia the size of the meterorite the Vosth had ridden in . . .

I'd seen how many Vosth had swarmed over Menley's whole body, and how long it had taken him to stop twitching. If it was just a few of them, I might be able to run back to the compound. Then, if the governors really had a cure, they could cure me. And I'd feel fine about tricking the Vosth into being test subjects if they'd tricked me into being a host. That's what I told myself. I didn't feel fine about anything.

I brought my gloves to the catch on my helmet.

Two minutes later I was still standing like that, with the catch still sealed, and Vosth-Menley was still staring.

"You could come back to the compound with me," I said. "The governors would love to see you."

We are curious as to the conditions of your constructed habitat, Vosth-Menley said.

Yeah, I thought, *but are you coming back as a plague bearer or an experiment?*

I squeezed my eyes shut, and pried my helmet off.

I'd lost way too many referents.

The outside air closed around my face with too many smells I couldn't identify or describe, other than "nothing like sterile air" and "nothing like my room or my shower." Every nerve on my head and neck screamed for broadcast time, registering the temperature of the air, the little breezes through the hairs on my nape, the warmth of direct sunlight. My heart was racing. I was breathing way too fast and even with my eyes shut I was overloaded on stimuli.

I waded my way through. It took time, but amidst the slog of what I was feeling, I eventually noticed something I wasn't: Anything identifiable as Vosth infestation.

I opened my eyes.

Vosth-Menley was standing just where he had been, watching just as he had been. And I was breathing, with my skin touching the outside air.

Touching the air. That which touched the air belonged to the Vosth. I wasn't belonging to the Vosth.

I looked toward the Ocean. Its silver underlayer was still there, calm beneath the surface.

I took a breath. I tasted the outside world, the gas balance, the smell of vegetation working its way from my nostrils to the back of my throat. This was a Vosth world, unless the governors made it a human world, and I wasn't sure how to feel about that. Looking back to Vosth-Menley, I didn't know how he'd feel about it either.

"You came from beyond the shell of atmosphere," I said. "Like we did, right?"

Vosth-Menley said, *Our genetic predecessors came to this world on an meteorite.*

"And you adapted, right?" I almost ran a hand over my helmet, but stopped before I touched my hair. I hadn't sterilized my gloves. Never mind that my head wasn't in a sterile environment anymore either. "Do you understand that we adapt?"

It is our perception of reality that living organisms adapt, he said.

That was a yes. Maybe. "Look, we don't have to fight for dominance, do we?" I spread my hands. "Like, if you go off and re-invent technology now that you have hands to build things with, you don't need to come back here and threaten us. We can have an equilibrium."

His eyes were as dead as usual. I had no idea what understanding on a Vosth colonist would look like.

"We'd both be better."

We are not averse to an equilibrium, Vosth-Menley said.

I swallowed. "Then you've gotta go now." Then, when I thought he didn't understand, "The governors are adapting a way to cure you. To kill you. Making us the dominant species. Look, I'm . . . telling you what will happen, and I'm giving you the option not to let us do it."

Vosth-Menley watched me for a moment. Then he turned, and walked back toward the Ocean of Starve.

Interspecies incident, said a little voice at the corner of my mind. It sounded like Endria. Sterile or not, I sealed my helmet back onto my e-suit and walked back toward the colony at double-time.

That night I filed a report saying that I'd invited Vosth-Menley back, but he'd declined for reasons I couldn't make sense of. Communications barrier. I thought of telling the Prime Governor that she should have sent a diplomatic auditor, but didn't.

I didn't hear anything until the next day when a survey buggy came back in, and its driver hopped down and said that something strange happened at the Ocean of Starve. Far from being its usual murky silver, it was perfectly clear and reflecting the sky. He said it to a governor, but news spread fast. It came to me via Endria as I was walking out of my lab.

"The only thing that would cause that would be a mass migration of the Vosth, but that's not something we've seen in their behavior before now!" She glared at me like I might know something, which, of course, I did.

A diplomatic auditor came by later to take a complete transcript of my last interaction with Vosth-Menley. I left most of it out.

Survey buggies kept going out. People walked down to the Ocean shore. Auditors flashed radio signals out of the communications booth, but no one answered. The Vosth had vanished, and that was all anyone could tell.

I stopped wearing my envirosuit.

The first day, stepping out of my door, I felt lightbodied, lightheaded, not entirely there. I felt like I'd walked out of my shower without getting dressed. I had to force myself to go forward instead of back, back to grab my envirosuit, to make myself decent.

I walked into the hall where every moment was the sensory overload of air on my skin, where my arms and legs felt loose, where everyone could see the expressions on my face. That was as frightening as the Vosth. I'd just left behind the environmental advantage I'd had since I was ten.

But I was adapting.

• MANEKI NEKO •
Bruce Sterling

"I can't go on," his brother said.

Tsuyoshi Shimizu looked thoughtfully into the screen of his pasokon. His older brother's face was shiny with sweat from a late-night drinking bout.

"It's only a career," said Tsuyoshi, sitting up on his futon and adjusting his pajamas. "You worry too much."

"All that overtime!" his brother whined. He was making the call from a bar somewhere in Shibuya. In the background, a middle-aged office lady was singing karaoke, badly. "And the examination hells. The manager training programs. The proficiency tests. I never have time to live!"

Tsuyoshi grunted sympathetically. He didn't like these late-night video-phone calls, but he felt obliged to listen. His big brother had always been a decent sort, before he had gone through the elite courses at Waseda University, joined a big corporation, and gotten professionally ambitious.

"My back hurts," his brother groused. "I have an ulcer. My hair is going gray. And I know they'll fire me. No matter how loyal you are to the big companies, they have no loyalty to their employees anymore. It's no wonder that I drink."

"You should get married," Tsuyoshi offered.

"I can't find the right girl. Women never understand me." He shuddered. "Tsuyoshi, I'm truly desperate. The market pressures are crushing me. I can't breathe. My life has got to change. I'm thinking of taking the vows. I'm serious! I want to renounce this whole modern world."

Tsuyoshi was alarmed. "You're very drunk, right?"

His brother leaned closer to the screen. "Life in a monastery sounds truly good to me. It's so quiet there. You recite the sutras. You consider your existence. There are rules to follow, and rewards that make sense. It's just the way that Japanese business used to be, back in the good old days."

Tsuyoshi grunted skeptically.

"Last week I went out to a special place in the mountains . . . Mount Aso," his brother confided. "The monks there, they know about people in trouble, people who are burned out by modern life. The monks protect you from the world. No computers, no phones, no faxes, no e-mail, no overtime, no commuting, nothing at all. It's beautiful, and it's peaceful, and nothing ever happens there. Really, it's like paradise."

"Listen, older brother," Tsuyoshi said, "you're not a religious man by nature. You're a section chief for a big import-export company."

"Well . . . maybe religion won't work for me. I did think of running away to America. Nothing much ever happens there, either."

Tsuyoshi smiled. "That sounds much better! America is a good vacation spot. A long vacation is just what you need! Besides, the Americans are real friendly since they gave up their handguns."

"But I can't go through with it," his brother wailed. "I just don't dare. I can't just wander away from everything that I know, and trust to the kindness of strangers."

"That always works for me," Tsuyoshi said. "Maybe you should try it."

Tsuyoshi's wife stirred uneasily on the futon. Tsuyoshi lowered his voice. "Sorry, but I have to hang up now. Call me before you do anything rash."

"Don't tell Dad," Tsuyoshi's brother said. "He worries so."

"I won't tell Dad." Tsuyoshi cut the connection and the screen went dark.

Tsuyoshi's wife rolled over, heavily. She was seven months pregnant. She stared at the ceiling puffing for breath. "Was that another call from your brother?" she said.

"Yeah. The company just gave him another promotion. More responsibilities. He's celebrating."

"That sounds nice," his wife said tactfully.

Next morning, Tsuyoshi slept late. He was self-employed, so he kept his own hours. Tsuyoshi was a video format upgrader by trade. He transferred old videos from obsolete formats into the new high-grade storage media. Doing this properly took a craftsman's eye. Word of Tsuyoshi's skills had gotten out on the network, so he had as much work as he could handle.

At ten A.M., the mailman arrived. Tsuyoshi abandoned his breakfast of raw egg and miso soup, and signed for a shipment of flaking, twentieth-century analog television tapes. The mail also brought a fresh overnight shipment of strawberries, and a homemade jar of pickles.

"Pickles!" his wife enthused. "People are so nice to you when you're pregnant."

"Any idea who sent us that?"

"Just someone on the network."

"Great."

Tsuyoshi booted his mediator, cleaned his superconducting heads and examined the old tapes. Home videos from the 1980s. Someone's grandmother as a child, presumably. There had been a lot of flaking and loss of polarity in the old recording medium.

Tsuyoshi got to work with his desktop fractal detail generator, the image stabilizer, and the interlace algorithms. When he was done, Tsuyoshi's new digital copies would look much sharper, cleaner, and better composed than the original primitive videotape.

Tsuyoshi enjoyed his work. Quite often he came across bits and pieces of videotape that were of archival interest. He would pass the images on to the net. The really big network databases, with their armies of search engines, indexers, and catalogues, had some very arcane interests. The net machines would never pay for data, because the global information networks were noncommercial. But the net machines were very polite, and had excellent net etiquette. They returned a favor for a favor, and since they were machines with excellent, enormous memories, they never forgot a good deed.

Tsuyoshi and his wife had a lunch of ramen with naruto, and she left to go shopping. A shipment arrived by overseas package service. Cute baby clothes from Darwin, Australia. They were in his wife's favorite color, sunshine yellow.

Tsuyoshi finished transferring the first tape to a new crystal disk. Time for a break. He left his apartment, took the elevator and went out to the comer coffeeshop. He ordered a double iced mocha cappuccino and paid with a chargecard.

His pokkecon rang. Tsuyoshi took it from his belt and answered it. "Get one to go," the machine told him.

"Okay," said Tsuyoshi, and hung up. He bought a second coffee, put a lid on it and left the shop.

A man in a business suit was sitting on a park bench near the entrance of Tsuyoshi's building. The man's suit was good, but it looked as if he'd slept in it. He was holding his head in his hands and rocking gently back and forth. He was unshaven and his eyes were red-rimmed.

The pokkecon rang again. "The coffee's for him?" Tsuyoshi said.

"Yes," said the pokkecon. "He needs it."

Tsuyoshi walked up to the lost businessman. The man looked up, flinching warily, as if he were about to be kicked. "What is it?" he said.

"Here," Tsuyoshi said, handing him the cup. "Double iced mocha cappuccino."

The man opened the cup, and smelled it. He looked up in disbelief. "This is my favorite kind of coffee . . . Who are you?"

Tsuyoshi lifted his arm and offered a hand signal, his fingers clenched like a cat's paw. The man showed no recognition of the gesture.

Tsuyoshi shrugged, and smiled. "It doesn't matter. Sometimes a man really needs a coffee. Now you have a coffee. That's all."

"Well . . . " The man cautiously sipped his cup, and suddenly smiled. "It's really great. Thanks!"

"You're welcome." Tsuyoshi went home.

His wife arrived from shopping. She had bought new shoes. The pregnancy was making her feet swell. She sat carefully on the couch and sighed.

"Orthopedic shoes are expensive," she said, looking at the yellow pumps. "I hope you don't think they look ugly."

"On you, they look really cute," Tsuyoshi said wisely. He had first met his wife at a video store. She had just used her credit card to buy a disk of primitive black-and-white American anime of the 1950s. The pokkecon had urged him to go up and speak to her on the subject of Felix the Cat. Felix was an early television cartoon star and one of Tsuyoshi's personal favorites.

Tsuyoshi would have been too shy to approach an attractive woman on his own, but no one was a stranger to the net. This fact gave him the confidence to speak to her. Tsuyoshi had soon discovered that the girl was delighted to discuss her deep fondness for cute, antique, animated cats. They'd had lunch together. They'd had a date the next week. They had spent Christmas Eve together in a love hotel. They had a lot in common.

She had come into his life through a little act of grace, a little gift from Felix the Cat's magic bag of tricks. Tsuyoshi had never gotten over feeling grateful for this. Now that he was married and becoming a father, Tsuyoshi Shimizu could feel himself becoming solidly fixed in life. He had a man's role to play now. He knew who he was, and he knew where he stood. Life was good to him.

"You need a haircut, dear," his wife told him.

"Sure."

His wife pulled a gift box out of her shopping bag. "Can you go to the Hotel Daruma, and get your hair cut, and deliver this box for me?"

"What is it?" Tsuyoshi said.

Tsuyoshi's wife opened the little wooden gift box. A maneki neko was nestled inside white foam padding. The smiling ceramic cat held one paw upraised, beckoning for good fortune.

"Don't you have enough of those yet?" he said. "You even have maneki neko underwear."

"It's not for my collection. It's a gift for someone at the Hotel Daruma."

"Oh."

"Some foreign woman gave me this box at the shoestore. She looked American. She couldn't speak Japanese. She had really nice shoes, though . . . "

"If the network gave you that little cat, then you're the one who should take care of that obligation, dear."

"But dear," she sighed, "my feet hurt so much, and you could do with a haircut anyway, and I have to cook supper, and besides, it's not really a nice maneki neko, it's just cheap tourist souvenir junk. Can't you do it?"

"Oh, all right," Tsuyoshi told her. "Just forward your pokkecon prompts onto my machine, and I'll see what I can do for us."

She smiled. "I knew you would do it. You're really so good to me."

Tsuyoshi left with the little box. He wasn't unhappy to do the errand, as it wasn't always easy to manage his pregnant wife's volatile moods in their small six-tatami apartment. The local neighborhood was good, but he was hoping to find bigger accommodations before the child was born. Maybe a place with a little studio, where he could expand the scope of his work. It was very hard to find decent housing in Tokyo, but word was out on the net. Friends he didn't even know were working every day to help him. If he kept up with the net's obligations, he had every confidence that some day something nice would turn up.

Tsuyoshi went into the local pachinko parlor, where he won half a liter of beer and a train chargecard. He drank the beer, took the new train card and wedged himself into the train. He got out at the Ebisu station, and turned on his pokkecon Tokyo street map to guide his steps. He walked past places called Chocolate Soup, and Freshness Physique, and The Aladdin Mai-Tai Panico Trattoria.

He entered the Hotel Daruma and went to the hotel barber shop, which was called the Daruma Planet Look. "May I help you?" said the receptionist.

"I'm thinking, a shave and a trim," Tsuyoshi said.

"Do you have an appointment with us?"

"Sorry, no." Tsuyoshi offered a hand gesture.

The woman gestured back, a jerky series of cryptic finger movements. Tsuyoshi didn't recognize any of the gestures. She wasn't from his part of the network.

"Oh well, never mind," the receptionist said kindly. "I'll get Nahoko to look after you."

Nahoko was carefully shaving the fine hair from Tsuyoshi's forehead when the pokkecon rang. Tsuyoshi answered it.

"Go to the ladies' room on the fourth floor," the pokkecon told him.

"Sorry, I can't do that. This is Tsuyoshi Shimizu, not Ai Shimizu. Besides, I'm having my hair cut right now."

"Oh, I see," said the machine. "Recalibrating." It hung up.

Nahoko finished his hair. She had done a good job. He looked much better. A man who worked at home had to take special trouble to keep up appearances. The pokkecon rang again.

"Yes?" said Tsuyoshi.

"Buy bay rum aftershave. Take it outside."

"Right." He hung up. "Nahoko, do you have bay rum?"

"Odd you should ask that," said Nahoko. "Hardly anyone asks for bay rum anymore, but our shop happens to keep it in stock."

Tsuyoshi bought the aftershave, then stepped outside the barbershop. Nothing happened, so he bought a manga comic and waited. Finally a hairy, blond stranger in shorts, a tropical shirt, and sandals approached him. The foreigner was carrying a camera bag and an old-fashioned pokkecon. He looked about sixty years old, and he was very tall.

The man spoke to his pokkecon in English. "Excuse me," said the pokkecon, translating the man's speech into Japanese. "Do you have a bottle of bay rum aftershave?"

"Yes I do." Tsuyoshi handed the bottle over. "Here."

"Thank goodness!" said the man, his words relayed through his machine. "I've asked everyone else in the lobby. Sorry I was late."

"No problem," said Tsuyoshi. "That's a nice pokkecon you have there."

"Well," the man said, "I know it's old and out of style. But I plan to buy a new pokkecon here in Tokyo. I'm told that they sell pokkecons by the basketful in Akihabara electronics market."

"That's right. What kind of translator program are you running? Your translator talks like someone from Osaka."

"Does it sound funny?" the tourist asked anxiously.

"Well, I don't want to complain, but . . . " Tsuyoshi smiled. "Here, let's trade meishi. I can give you a copy of a brand-new freeware translator."

"That would be wonderful." They pressed buttons and squirted copies of their business cards across the network link.

Tsuyoshi examined his copy of the man's electronic card and saw that his name was Zimmerman. Mr. Zimmerman was from New Zealand. Tsuyoshi activated a transfer program. His modern pokkecon began transferring a new translator onto Zimmerman's machine.

A large American man in a padded suit entered the lobby of the Daruma. The man wore sunglasses, and was sweating visibly in the summer heat. The American looked huge, as if he lifted a lot of weights. Then a Japanese woman followed him. The woman was sharply dressed, with a dark blue dress suit, hat, sunglasses, and an attache case. She had a haunted look.

Her escort turned and carefully watched the bellhops, who were bringing in a series of bags. The woman walked crisply to the reception desk and began making anxious demands of the clerk.

"I'm a great believer in machine translation," Tsuyoshi said to the tall man from New Zealand. "I really believe that computers help human beings to relate in a much more human way."

"I couldn't agree with you more," said Mr. Zimmerman, through his machine. "I can remember the first time I came to your country, many years ago. I had no portable translator. In fact, I had nothing but a printed phrasebook. I happened to go into a bar, and . . . "

Zimmerman stopped and gazed alertly at his pokkecon. "Oh dear, I'm getting a screen prompt. I have to go up to my room right away."

"Then I'll come along with you till this software transfer is done," Tsuyoshi said.

"That's very kind of you." They got into the elevator together. Zimmerman punched for the fourth floor. "Anyway, as I was saying, I went into this bar in Roppongi late at night, because I was jetlagged and hoping for something to eat . . . "

"Yes?"

"And this woman . . . well, let's just say this woman was hanging out in a foreigner's bar in Roppongi late at night, and she wasn't wearing a whole lot of clothes, and she didn't look like she was any better than she ought to be . . . "

"Yes, I think I understand you."

"Anyway, this menu they gave me was full of kanji, or katakana, or romanji, or whatever they call those, so I had my phrasebook out, and I was trying very hard to puzzle out these pesky ideograms . . . " The elevator opened and they stepped into the carpeted hall of the hotel's fourth floor. "So I opened the menu and I pointed to an entree, and I told this girl . . . " Zimmerman stopped suddenly, and stared at his screen. "Oh dear, something's happening. Just a moment."

Zimmerman carefully studied the instructions on his pokkecon. Then he pulled the bottle of bay rum from the baggy pocket of his shorts, and unscrewed the cap. He stood on tiptoe, stretching to his full height, and carefully poured the contents of the bottle through the iron louvers of a ventilation grate, set high in the top of the wall.

Zimmerman screwed the cap back on neatly, and slipped the empty bottle back in his pocket. Then he examined his pokkecon again. He frowned, and shook it. The screen had frozen. Apparently Tsuyoshi's new translation program had overloaded Zimmerman's old-fashioned operating system. His pokkecon had crashed.

Zimmerman spoke a few defeated sentences in English. Then he smiled, and spread his hands apologetically. He bowed, and went into his room, and shut the door.

The Japanese woman and her burly American escort entered the hall. The man gave Tsuyoshi a hard stare. The woman opened the door with a passcard. Her hands were shaking.

Tsuyoshi's pokkecon rang. "Leave the hall," it told him. "Go downstairs. Get into the elevator with the bellboy."

Tsuyoshi followed instructions.

The bellboy was just entering the elevator with a cart full of the woman's baggage. Tsuyoshi got into the elevator, stepping carefully behind the wheeled metal cart. "What floor, sir?" said the bellboy.

"Eight," Tsuyoshi said, ad-libbing. The bellboy turned and pushed the buttons. He faced forward attentively, his gloved hands folded.

The pokkecon flashed a silent line of text to the screen. "Put the gift box inside her flight bag," it read.

Tsuyoshi located the zippered blue bag at the back of the cart. It was a matter of instants to zip it open, put in the box with the maneki neko, and zip the bag shut again. The bellboy noticed nothing. He left, tugging his cart.

Tsuyoshi got out on the eighth floor, feeling slightly foolish. He wandered down the hall, found a quiet nook by an ice machine and called his wife. "What's going on?" he said.

"Oh, nothing." She smiled. "Your haircut looks nice! Show me the back of your head."

Tsuyoshi held the pokkecon screen behind the nape of his neck.

"They do good work," his wife said with satisfaction. "I hope it didn't cost too much. Are you coming home now?"

"Things are getting a little odd here at the hotel," Tsuyoshi told her. "I may be some time."

His wife frowned. "Well, don't miss supper. We're having bonito."

Tsuyoshi took the elevator back down. It stopped at the fourth floor. The woman's American companion stepped onto the elevator. His nose was running and his eyes were streaming with tears.

"Are you all right?" Tsuyoshi said.

"I don't understand Japanese," the man growled. The elevator doors shut.

The man's cellular phone crackled into life. It emitted a scream of anguish and a burst of agitated female English. The man swore and slammed his hairy fist against the elevator's emergency button. The elevator stopped with a lurch. An alarm bell began ringing.

The man pried the doors open with his large hairy fingers and clambered out into the fourth floor. He then ran headlong down the hall.

The elevator began buzzing in protest, its doors shuddering as if broken. Tsuyoshi climbed hastily from the damaged elevator, and stood there in the hallway. He hesitated a moment. Then he produced his pokkecon and loaded his Japanese-to-English translator. He walked cautiously after the American man.

The door to their suite was open. Tsuyoshi spoke aloud into his pokkecon. "Hello?" he said experimentally. "May I be of help?"

The woman was sitting on the bed. She had just discovered the maneki neko box in her flight bag. She was staring at the little cat in horror.

"Who are you?" she said, in bad Japanese.

Tsuyoshi realized suddenly that she was a Japanese American. Tsuyoshi had met a few Japanese Americans before. They always troubled him. They looked fairly normal from the outside, but their behavior was always bizarre. "I'm just a passing friend," he said. "Something I can do?"

"Grab him, Mitch!" said the woman in English. The American man rushed into the hall and grabbed Tsuyoshi by the arm. His hands were like steel bands.

Tsuyoshi pressed the distress button on his pokkecon.

"Take that computer away from him," the woman ordered in English. Mitch quickly took Tsuyoshi's pokkecon away, and threw it on the bed. He deftly patted Tsuyoshi's clothing, searching for weapons. Then he shoved Tsuyoshi into a chair.

The woman switched back to Japanese. "Sit right there, you. Don't you dare move." She began examining the contents of Tsuyoshi's wallet.

"I beg your pardon?" Tsuyoshi said. His pokkecon was lying on the bed. Lines of red text scrolled up its little screen as it silently issued a series of emergency net alerts.

The woman spoke to her companion in English. Tsuyoshi's pokkecon was still translating faithfully. "Mitch, go call the local police."

Mitch sneezed uncontrollably. Tsuyoshi noticed that the room smelled strongly of bay rum. "I can't talk to the local cops. I can't speak Japanese." Mitch sneezed again.

"Okay, then I'll call the cops. You handcuff this guy. Then go down to the infirmary and get yourself some antihistamines, for Christ's sake."

Mitch pulled a length of plastic whipcord cuff from his coat pocket, and attached Tsuyoshi's right wrist to the head of the bed. He mopped his streaming eyes with a tissue. "I'd better stay with you. If there's a cat in your luggage, then the criminal network already knows we're in Japan. You're in danger."

"Mitch, you may be my bodyguard, but you're breaking out in hives."

"This just isn't supposed to happen," Mitch complained, scratching his neck. "My allergies never interfered with my job before."

"Just leave me here and lock the door," the woman told him. "I'll put a chair against the knob. I'll be all right. You need to look after yourself."

Mitch left the room.

The woman barricaded the door with a chair. Then she called the front desk on the hotel's bedside pasokon. "This is Louise Hashimoto in room 434. I have a gangster in my room. He's an information criminal. Would you call the Tokyo police, please? Tell them to send the organized crime unit. Yes, that's right. Do it. And you should put your hotel security people on full alert. There may be big trouble here. You'd better hurry." She hung up.

Tsuyoshi stared at her in astonishment. "Why are you doing this? What's all this about?"

"So you call yourself Tsuyoshi Shimizu," said the woman, examining his credit cards. She sat on the foot of the bed and stared at him. "You're yakuza of some kind, right?"

"I think you've made a big mistake," Tsuyoshi said.

Louise scowled. "Look, Mr. Shimizu, you're not dealing with some Yankee tourist here. My name is Louise Hashimoto and I'm an assistant federal prosecutor from Providence, Rhode Island, USA." She showed him a magnetic ID card with a gold official seal.

"It's nice to meet someone from the American government," said Tsuyoshi, bowing a bit in his chair. "I'd shake your hand, but it's tied to the bed."

"You can stop with the innocent act right now. I spotted you out in the hall earlier, and in the lobby, too, casing the hotel. How did you know my bodyguard is violently allergic to bay rum? You must have read his medical records."

"Who, me? Never!"

"Ever since I discovered you network people, it's been one big pattern," said Louise. "It's the biggest criminal conspiracy I ever saw. I busted this software pirate in Providence. He had a massive network server and a whole bunch of AI freeware search engines. We took him in custody, we bagged all his search engines, and catalogs, and indexers . . . Later that very same day, these *cats* start showing up."

"Cats?"

Louise lifted the maneki neko, handling it as if it were a live eel. "These little Japanese voodoo cats. Maneki neko, right? They started showing up everywhere I went. There's a china cat in my handbag. There's three china cats at the office. Suddenly they're on display in the windows of every antique store in Providence. My car radio starts making meowing noises at me."

"You *broke* part of the network?" Tsuyoshi said, scandalized. "You took someone's machines away? That's terrible! How could you do such an inhuman thing?"

"You've got a real nerve complaining about that. What about *my* machinery?" Louise held up her fat, eerie-looking American pokkecon. "As soon as I stepped off the airplane at Narita, my PDA was attacked. Thousands and thousands of e-mail messages. All of them pictures of cats. A denial-of-service attack! I can't even communicate with the home office! My PDA's useless!"

"What's a PDA?"

"It's a PDA, my Personal Digital Assistant! Manufactured in Silicon Valley!"

"Well, with a goofy name like that, no wonder our pokkecons won't talk to it."

Louise frowned grimly. "That's right, wise guy. Make jokes about it. You're involved in a malicious software attack on a legal officer of the United States Government. You'll see." She paused, looking him over. "You know, Shimizu, you don't look much like the Italian mafia gangsters I have to deal with, back in Providence."

"I'm not a gangster at all. I never do anyone any harm."

"Oh no?" Louise glowered at him. "Listen, pal, I know a lot more about your set-up, and your kind of people, than you think I do. I've been studying your outfit for a long time now. We computer cops have names for your kind of people. Digital panarchies. Segmented, polycephalous, integrated influence networks. What about all these *free goods and services* you're getting all this time?"

She pointed a finger at him. "Ha! Do you ever pay *taxes* on those? Do you ever *declare* that income and those benefits? All the free shipments from other countries! The little homemade cookies, and the free pens and pencils and bumper stickers, and the used bicycles, and the helpful news about fire sales . . . You're a tax evader! You're living through kickbacks! And bribes! And influence peddling! And all kinds of corrupt off-the-books transactions?"

Tsuyoshi blinked. "Look, I don't know anything about all that. I'm just living my life."

"Well, your network gift economy is undermining the lawful, government approved, regulated economy!"

"Well," Tsuyoshi said gently, "maybe my economy is better than your economy."

"Says who?" she scoffed. "Why would anyone think that?"

"It's better because we're *happier* than you are. What's wrong with acts of kindness? Everyone likes gifts. Midsummer gifts. New Years Day gifts. Year-end presents. Wedding presents. Everybody likes those."

"Not the way you Japanese like them. You're totally crazy for gifts."

"What kind of society has no gifts? It's barbaric to have no regard for common human feelings."

Louise bristled. "You're saying I'm barbaric?"

"I don't mean to complain," Tsuyoshi said politely, "but you do have me tied up to your bed."

Louise crossed her arms. "You might as well stop complaining. You'll be in much worse trouble when the local police arrive."

"Then we'll probably be waiting here for quite a while," Tsuyoshi said. "The police move rather slowly, here in Japan. I'm sorry, but we don't have as much crime as you Americans, so our police are not very alert."

The pasokon rang at the side of the bed. Louise answered it. It was Tsuyoshi's wife.

"Could I speak to Tsuyoshi Shimizu please?"

"I'm over here, dear," Tsuyoshi called quickly. "She's kidnapped me! She tied me to the bed!"

"Tied to her *bed*?" His wife's eyes grew wide. "That does it! I'm calling the police!"

Louise quickly hung up the pasokon. "I haven't kidnapped you! I'm only detaining you here until the local authorities can come and arrest you."

"Arrest me for what, exactly?"

Louise thought quickly. "Well, for poisoning my bodyguard by pouring bay rum into the ventilator."

"But I never did that. Anyway, that's not illegal, is it?"

The pasokon rang again. A shining white cat appeared on the screen. It had large, staring, unearthly eyes.

"Let him go," the cat commanded in English.

Louise shrieked and yanked the pasokon's plug from the wall.

Suddenly the lights went out. "Infrastructure attack!" Louise squawled. She rolled quickly under the bed.

The room went gloomy and quiet. The air conditioner had shut off. "I think you can come out," Tsuyoshi said at last, his voice loud in the still room. "It's just a power failure."

"No it isn't," Louise said. She crawled slowly from beneath the bed, and sat on the mattress. Somehow, the darkness had made them more intimate. "I know very well what this is. I'm under attack. I haven't had a moment's peace since I broke that network. Stuff just happens to me now. Bad stuff. Swarms of it. It's never anything you can touch, though. Nothing you can prove in a court of law."

She sighed. "I sit in chairs, and somebody's left a piece of gum there. I get free pizzas, but they're not the kind of pizzas I like. Little kids spit on my sidewalk. Old women in walkers get in front of me whenever I need to hurry."

The shower came on, all by itself. Louise shuddered, but said nothing. Slowly, the darkened, stuffy room began to fill with hot steam.

"My toilets don't flush," Louise said. "My letters get lost in the mail. When I walk by cars, their theft alarms go off. And strangers stare at me. It's always little things. Lots of little tiny things, but they never, ever stop. I'm up against something that is very, very big, and very, very patient. And it knows all about me. And it's got a million arms and legs. And all those arms and legs are people."

There was the noise of scuffling in the hall. Distant voices, confused shouting.

Suddenly the chair broke under the doorknob. The door burst open violently. Mitch tumbled through, the sunglasses flying from his head. Two hotel security guards were trying to grab him. Shouting incoherently in English, Mitch fell headlong to the floor, kicking and thrashing. The guards lost their hats in the struggle. One tackled Mitch's legs with both his arms, and the other whacked and jabbed him with a baton.

Puffing and grunting with effort, they hauled Mitch out of the room. The darkened room was so full of steam that the harried guards hadn't even noticed Tsuyoshi and Louise.

Louise stared at the broken door. "Why did they do that to him?"

Tsuyoshi scratched his head in embarrassment. "Probably a failure of communication."

"Poor Mitch! They took his gun away at the airport. He had all kinds of technical problems with his passport . . . Poor guy, he's never had any luck since he met me."

There was a loud tapping at the window. Louise shrank back in fear. Finally she gathered her courage, and opened the curtains. Daylight flooded the room.

A window-washing rig had been lowered from the roof of the hotel, on cables and pulleys. There were two window-washers in crisp gray uniforms. They waved cheerfully, making little catpaw gestures.

There was a third man with them. It was Tsuyoshi's brother.

One of the washers opened the window with a utility key. Tsuyoshi's brother squirmed into the room. He stood up and carefully adjusted his coat and tie.

"This is my brother," Tsuyoshi explained.

"What are you doing here?" Louise said.

"They always bring in the relatives when there's a hostage situation," Tsuyoshi's brother said. "The police just flew me in by helicopter and landed me on the roof." He looked Louise up and down. "Miss Hashimoto, you just have time to escape."

"What?" she said.

"Look down at the streets," he told her. "See that? You hear them? Crowds are pouring in from all over the city. All kinds of people, everyone with wheels. Street noodle salesmen. Bicycle messengers. Skateboard kids. Takeout delivery guys."

Louise gazed out the window into the streets, and shrieked aloud. "Oh no! A giant swarming mob! They're surrounding me! I'm doomed!"

"You are not doomed," Tsuyoshi's brother told her intently. "Come out the window. Get onto the platform with us. You've got one chance, Louise. It's a place I know, a sacred place in the mountains. No computers there, no phones, nothing." He paused. "It's a sanctuary for people like us. And I know the way."

She gripped his suited arm. "Can I trust you?"

"Look in my eyes," he told her. "Don't you see? Yes, of course you can trust me. We have everything in common."

Louise stepped out the window. She clutched his arm, the wind whipping at her hair. The platform creaked rapidly up and out of sight.

Tsuyoshi stood up from the chair. When he stretched out, tugging at his handcuffed wrist, he was just able to reach his pokkecon with his fingertips. He drew it in, and clutched it to his chest. Then he sat down again, and waited patiently for someone to come and give him freedom.

• MAMA, WE ARE ZHENYA, YOUR SON •
Tom Crosshill

Mama,

This is Zhenya, your son. I'm in a castle with gnomes! When you said Dr. Olga would pay many rubles for a boy to help her, I was afraid but I didn't tell you. I didn't want to be selfish because with rubles you can pay for the hospital so you can be strong again. Now I'm happy that I came.

Dr. Olga says I must write what happens in a letter so you can read it and not worry. We can't send pictures because the gnomes have no cameras (silly gnomes) so I will describe everything.

I fell asleep in Dr. Olga's big room, in the red university building by the Botanical Garden. I had a helmet on my head stuffed with wires. There were lots of lights and noises like in that game which Dima's Papa bought him and you said we couldn't buy because we don't have a Papa or rubles. Then the lights went away and I was in a castle.

It's not like Moscow at all except maybe on the Red Square. There are stone corridors and pretty towers with mushroom tops, and a big hall with a glass roof so you can see the stars when it's dark.

The gnomes live in the cellar. They're short and green and wear big fluffy hats with their names on them, like GUI 1, GUI 2, GUI 3, which they said means gnome user innerface. I asked them for food but they didn't understand me real good, only jumped around and sang songs. I think Sulyik is smarter.

Oh, yes, Sulyik is here! Dr. Olga put a helmet on his head too. At first he was afraid of the gnomes but now he barks at them very loud. We found a run place for him with grass and water. I told Dr. Olga about the linden tree behind our building where he likes to bury bones and she put a linden tree in the run place too. He likes that.

Dr. Olga can't come here but she talks to us sometimes. Her face is in the wall like the stone is soft and moving. She hasn't told me what work I have to do yet but I promise I'll work the hardest I can, Mama!!!!!

Zhenya (your son)

Mama,

This is Zhenya, your son.

We are hungry. It's not so bad for me, but Sulyik whines and drags his belly on the floor.

Dr. Olga says there is a food place and it's our job to find it, but we can't because the path between places keeps changing. We go all around the castle and we should be where we started and we're not. Start in sleep place, end in run place. Start in run place, end in the big hall. It's like that time I got lost in Izmaylovsky Park and you said I was a stupid boy because anyone could just follow the signs but there are no signs here.

Dr. Olga doesn't help. She says if I train my mind to get from sleep place to food place and food place to sleep place, then I can find the treasure place. I ask her what treasure place but she doesn't tell me. I hope she doesn't think I'm stupid too. But maybe I am. Maybe Sulyik is hungry because I'm not smart enough.

Zhenya (your son)

Mama,

This is Zhenya, your son.

Sulyik found the food place! We were in the big hall and he ran away from me like at the carnival with the mirrors, many Sulyiks in every direction. Then he barked and ran back and pulled at my pants, just one Sulyik. When I tried to go with him there were many Sulyiks again, and I didn't know which one to follow. Then he brought me a banana and I got excited because I remembered the time I got to eat one for my birthday, but the gnomes took it from me before I could have it. I ran after them but the gnomes are very fast.

I told Dr. Olga, and she says I should be more flexible. After all I am only eight and my pathways are fresh and it's really not hard if Sulyik can do it.

Dr. Olga doesn't know Sulyik. He's a very smart dog. I can't win hide and seek with him even with my eyes open. When I watch him run away there are many Sulyiks everywhere so that doesn't help. But when I see him somewhere and go catch him, I can't guess which way he's running and how fast.

The gnomes watch and laugh and chant, hai-zen-berg! hai-zen-berg! hai-zen-berg! I don't get angry at them, though. My Sulyik is smarter than me!

I'm still hungry.

Zhenya (your son)

P.S. Did you go to the hospital, Mama? Are you all right?

Mama,

This is Zhenya, your son.

I'm afraid, Mama. The gnomes make me play a game, and they hit me when I lose. It hurts very much! Sulyik tries to stop them but they hit him too. And Dr. Olga doesn't come when I call.

It's a hard game. The gnomes have a big gold box with two rooms and a paper wall and no door in the wall. They put me in one room by the wall and they leave me. There's a dragon painted on the wall, all red and black. The gnomes say I must get to the other room or the dragon will eat me.

But the dragon doesn't come. The gnomes come back later and ask me, why are you still in this room? And then they hit me and make me do it again.

One time I broke the paper wall and went to the other room, and they got very angry and hit me many times and said I shouldn't do that. Tunnel, they say, use a tunnel, but the floor is hard and I don't even have a shovel.

What can I do, Mama? I know I must try hard for you, but it hurts!

Zhenya (your son, waiting for your letter)

Mama, the dragon came. She came and I was so scared, I went through the wall and it didn't break. Only she came again on the other side and I couldn't run away. She burned me! She burned me real bad, Mama.

I'm sorry, Mama. I'm sure I did something very bad but I don't know what. Please, can I leave now? I know we need rubles but I'm scared. Please, Mama?

Mama,

I think this is Zhenya, your son. I'm not sure.

Nothing is sure. I understand that now. Everything is, and is not. The dragon helped me understand. A wall is no wall if I'm everywhere.

I can find the food place now, if every one of me goes looking. Every me doesn't find every food place, but one of me finds a food place.

I don't know why I was all in one place before. I think all the little parts of me, they could be many different places but they disagreed. They pulled in different directions like in that story about the wagon and the horses so they stayed in place. Now every little piece of me agrees, and I am everywhere I want to be.

Oh, yes, Dr. Olga came back. I was angry about the dragon but she said it's okay because I can go home soon. You always said I should keep my mouth shut around aunts and uncles, Mama. I try very hard with Dr. Olga but I don't like her so much anymore.

She says my pathways changed. A miracle of tabyula raza, she says. A young mind can learn to think qantumikally in a simulated qantumikal environment. I think she wanted to talk very much because she said many more things about how she proved the brain of somebody called Penroz is real, which is silly because how could a brain not be real. Then she looked very strange and cried. I asked her why, and she said many important aunts and uncles would be very happy and put her name in books, which I guess is important like when you get a Giness record for how big a cake you can bake.

I don't care about any of that, Mama. I just want to come home.

Zhenya (probably your son)

* * *

Mama,

We are Zhenya, your son.

All of I found the Dr. Olga says I have to write clearly because you can't understand. Is that why you don't send me letters, Mama? I'm sorry. I want you to write very much.

I found the treasure place. It's on the roof, with the stars right above. The treasure's a groaning metal thing as big as a house. I knew what it was as soon as I saw it because gnomes were standing in a circle, holding their hats and singing, "Treasure, treasure, treasure!"

I'm not sure it's a very good treasure if gnomes have to tell you that's what it is. And Sulyik doesn't like it. I called him over but he just barked and wouldn't come near.

Anyway, I thought the treasure was interesting. There are so many handles you can pull, it's like a big yellow hedgehog, with twisting knobbly gears which are never in the same place when you look. Dr. Olga said she couldn't understand the treasure because it's a qantumikal motor and it needs a qantumikal brain but I should understand it because I've got one.

She's right. When I'm everywhere at once, I get all tangled up with the treasure and the handles become my arms like I'm conducting an orchestra, and I understand everything. But it's scary when that happens, Mama. The castle becomes squishy like plasticine in my hands, and I can shape it.

I was very bad at shaping at first so I broke the food place. There were sparks everywhere, and Dr. Olga said the hash had overflowed though I don't know why because I never saw potatoes in the food place. Then I learned to stretch the castle so for every thin part there is a thick part and it doesn't break. I stretched and stretched until I could see through to other castles.

Mama, there are many castles just like this one except each a little different. Some are a lot different. And when I stretch more with the handles, I can make openings to those other castles and reach through and be in all castles at once!

Dr. Olga said I should grab rooms and light from the other castles and bring them back so we have more energy. I did it but I think there is another Zhenya and another Sulyik in each of the other castles and they didn't like it, because there was a loud noise and the castle moved very much, and some of the gnomes screamed and fell to the ground. Now there is green blood on their hats and they don't move anymore.

Dr. Olga said not to worry, it's a soft wear glitch and they're not important anyway. I don't like the gnomes but I think that's not very nice of her. The treasure hurt them and it's all because of her.

I'm scared, Mama.

Zhenya (your son, we are)

• • •

Mama,

Today Dr. Olga told me to use the treasure to look out of the castle and at the big room where Sulyik and I went to sleep. I moved the handles to stretch the air and I saw us sleeping on a long table, Sulyik and me. Aunts and uncles worked all around, and in the middle of the room there was a big metal box. It hummed and flashed lights when I moved the handles of the treasure.

I think the metal box is like the treasure except it's in Moscow and it doesn't move. When I used the treasure and the box started to make noises, all the aunts and uncles looked very excited and not afraid. I thought that was dumb because I was very afraid.

Dr. Olga told me to use the treasure to open other Moscows, like I'd opened other castles. But when I stretched the big room thin, I saw bad little fast things come out of the metal box. They were hitting Dr. Olga and all the aunts and uncles so I stopped.

The aunts and uncles and Dr. Olga didn't believe me because they couldn't see the bad little fast things. Dr. Olga said they had Gaigar counters and eye-on chambers and there was nothing there. She said I had to use the treasure to get energy from other Moscows because only I had a qantumikal brain and the whole world was waiting and anyway Sulyik wanted me to.

I said no. I don't think Sulyik wants me to do a bad thing. I asked him and he licked me which is not very bad. He just wants to sleep with me under the linden tree in the sun.

When I told Dr. Olga that, she said she can't give me rubles if I don't help with the treasure.

I think maybe that is important but some of I are not sure anymore. In some Moscow, always, she gives me rubles. In some Moscow, always, she does not give me rubles. Both happen always. You're sick and you're fine always, Mama. Some of you, in some Moscow.

If that is so always, why should I help? All is, always, somewhere. But the bad little fast things are bad everywhere.

Zhenya (your son, we are)

Mama,

Okay, I will help Dr. Olga with the treasure tomorrow. Okay, okay, I will help.

All of I loves Sulyik. When Dr. Olga said she will hurt Sulyik, I thought many Sulyiks everywhere, can't hurt all Sulyiks, we will be okay. But she took Sulyik away from the castle and when I used the treasure I saw him standing alone by the table with my body, outside in Moscow. He looked very sad with his head all shaved. Dr. Olga came and took him away, and now I can't see him at all but he barks very loud like he hurts, and it's hard to remember there are other Sulyiks in other Moscows.

I don't think Dr. Olga is nice. I think maybe she was never nice. I think maybe when she promised us rubles she didn't really mean it.

Please, ask her to give me Sulyik back. I'll be good, I promise. I'll do anything she wants.

Zhenya

Mama,

Zhenya, son.

I put this letter your table. Don't afraid. Don't scream.

Yes hide under bed. Under bed safe. Don't open windows. Don't go outside. Moscow not safe. Hungry smoke bad.

I protect you.

Sorry write little. Only have fingers if think hard.

Zhenya

Mama,

Zhenya again. Got more time now so I can write better.

Please, come out from under the bed. Don't stare like that. Aren't you happy that I'm back? I know I look scary but at least I'm strong enough for eyes and fingers. I can't talk but I can write you letters.

I saw you got all the old letters I wrote for you. You must have been very busy at the hospital if you couldn't answer. That's okay. I'm glad Dr. Olga gave you rubles after all. You look stronger.

Soon I'll be stronger too, Mama. I'll have arms, many, many arms, and I'll hold you, and we'll be together. Won't that be lovely, Mama? You always took care of me even when I was stupid and bad, and now I'll take care of you and won't ever, ever, ever let you go. Won't that be great?

But we won't have Sulyik. He died, Mama. When I started the treasure, the metal box in Dr. Olga's room growled, and Sulyik ran out of a closet barking. Then the air stretched and broke, and out came all the bad little fast things. They flowed together and became the hungry smoke and came flying buzz buzz buzz, like many black bees.

I stopped the treasure but it was too late. The hungry smoke buzzed and wrapped around Sulyik, and he barked and barked, and then the hungry smoke ate his head and I couldn't do anything.

I thought maybe it's okay because there are other Sulyiks in other Moscows but it didn't feel okay. It didn't feel okay at all, Mama.

Then the smoke barked like Sulyik, loud and sad. It barked lots while it ate all the aunts and uncles, and Dr. Olga too. Dr. Olga screamed very long and

I thought maybe she wanted another Giness record but she stopped and the smoke ate her head too.

After that the smoke gave up barking and whispered things, real soft like Dr. Olga. "Take, take, take from us! Steal from us! No, boy, no. No, no, no!" It ate my head last, because I was on the table and couldn't run. When I heard it coming—"Boy! Boy! Boy!"—I ran to the castle but the castle got dark so I came back. I got real scared and I twisted the treasure very much and the metal box roared, and I ripped open the air between the castle and Moscow, and I came through all the way, all of me everywhere.

I tried using my body again but it didn't work. The hungry smoke ate my head after all. It didn't even hurt because I was everywhere at once.

Don't worry about me, Mama. It's okay.

Sorry about Moscow. I couldn't help all the aunts and uncles and boys and girls and grandmas and grandpas. Sorry about the blood and the screaming. It makes me want to cry but I don't have any tears. I don't think crying would help anyway.

I couldn't protect everyone but at least I protected you. The smoke won't get into the apartment, don't you worry, Mama. I think it's real angry cause we tried to steal from its Moscow, and it gets smarter when it eats heads like when I read books, but you've got me and I'm smart too, and I'm everywhere.

I have to catch the hungry smoke now. I hope I can use Dr. Olga's metal treasure-box and stretch the air, and send it all home. Then I'll come for you. You just hold on.

Zhenya

Mama,

I caught much hungry smoke and sent it home. I promised we wouldn't steal from other Moscows again but it just yelled, "Slide the curve! Blast the boy! Twisted metric!" It sounded like Uncles and Aunts and Grandpas and Grandmas and little kids too, happy and sad and angry and calm. I think maybe eating all those heads wasn't so good for it. I think maybe it got confused.

I'm home, Mama. I sit next to you right now, here on the couch. Do you feel my fingers on your back? See the curtains move? It's me, Mama.

Smile, Mama. Please, why won't you smile? Once I catch the last of the smoke, we'll be together for good. We can even go to Paris like you always wanted. I don't think the smoke got to Paris.

But before that, can you help me? Look outside the door. I left Sulyik there. His fur is sticky and his head is gone. Can you wash him Mama? Can you bury him in the garden under the linden tree?

When everyone died I thought I was sad but I wasn't sure. There are many Moscows and this is only one Moscow, so why is it important anyway?

But then I remembered Sulyik. There was only one Sulyik who mattered, in the end. That means there will always be only one Sulyik. I will remember him, all of I, for sure.

Sulyik taught me that. Even being qantumikal I can still know things for sure.

Zhenya (your son, all of I, for sure)

• VELVET FIELDS •
Anne McCaffrey

Of course we moved into the cities of the planet we now know we must call Zobranoirundisi when Worlds Federated finally permitted a colony there. Although Survey had kept a watch on the planet for more than thirty years standard and the cities were obviously on a standby directive, the owners remained conspicuous by their absence. Since Resources and Supplies had agitated in council for another breadbasket planet in that sector of the galaxy and Zobranoirundisi was unoccupied, we were sent in, chartered to be self-sufficient in one sidereal year and to produce a surplus in two.

It would, therefore, have been a great misdirection of effort not to have inhabited the cities—we only moved into four—so patently suitable for humanoid life-forms. The murals that decorated a conspicuous wall in every dwelling unit gave only a vague idea of the physiology of our landlords, always depicted in an attitude of reverent obeisance toward a dominating Tree symbol so that only the backs, the rounded fuzz-covered craniums, and the suggestions of arms extended in front of the bodies were visible.

I suppose if we had not been so concerned with establishing the herds, generally breaking our necks to meet the colony charter requirements, we might have discovered sooner that there had been a gross error. The clues were there. For example, although we inhabited the cities, they could not be made fully "operational" despite all the efforts of Dunlapil, the metropolitan engineer. Then, too, we could find no single example of the Tree anywhere on the lush planet. But, with R&S on our backs to produce, produce, produce, we didn't take time to delve into the perplexing anomalies.

Dunlapil, with his usual urbane contempt for the botanical, quipped to Martin Chavez, our ecologist, that the Tree was the Tree of Life and therefore mythical.

"Carry the analogy further," he would tease Martin, "and it explains why the Tree worshipers"—that's what we called them before we knew—"aren't around anymore. Some dissident plucked the Apple and got 'em all kicked out of the Garden of Eden."

Eden might well have been modeled on this planet, with its velvet fields, parklike forests, and rolling plains. Amid these sat lovely little cities constructed of pressed fibrous blocks tinted in pleasant colors during a manufacturing process whose nature frustrated Dunlapil as much as the absence of Trees perplexed Chavez.

So, suppressing our pervasive sense of trespassing, we moved into the abandoned dwellings, careful not to make any irreparable changes to accommodate our equipment. In fact, the only sophisticated nonindigenous equipment that I, as colony commissioner, permitted within any city was the plastisteel Comtower. I ordered the spaceport constructed beyond a low range of foothills on the rather scrubby plain at some distance from my headquarters city. An old riverbed proved an acceptable road for moving cargo to and from the port, and no one really objected to the distance. It would be far better not to offend our landlords with the dirt and chaos of outer-space commerce close to their pretty city.

We pastured the cattle in neatly separated velvet fields. Martin Chavez worried when close inspection disclosed that each velvet field was underpinned by its own ten-meter-thick foundation of ancient, rock-hard clay. Those same foundations housed what seemed to be a deep irrigation system.

I did ask Martin Chavez to investigate the curious absence of herbivores from a planet so perfectly suited to them. He had catalogued several types of omnivores, a wide variety of fowl, and a plethora of fishes. He did discover some fossil remains of herbivores, but nothing more recent than traces comparable to those of our Pleistocene epoch.

He therefore was forced to conclude—and submitted in a voluminous report with numerous comparisons to nearby galactic examples—that some catastrophes, perhaps the same that had wiped out the humanoids, had eliminated herbivores at an earlier stage.

Whatever the disaster had been—bacterial, viral, or something more esoteric—it did not recur to plague us. We thrived on the planet. The first children, conceived under the bluish alien sun, were born just after we had shipped our first year's surplus offworld. Life settled into a pleasant seasonal routine: The beef, sheep, horses, kine, even the windoers of Grace's World imported on an experimental basis, multiplied on the velvet fields. The centenarian crops from half a dozen worlds gave us abundant yields. We had some failures, of course, with inedible or grotesque ergotic mutations, but not enough to be worth more than a minor Chavezian thesis in the record and the shrug of the pioneering farmer. If a colonist is eating well, living comfortably, with leisure time for his kids and time off with his wife on the languid southern seas, he puts up with minor failures and irritations. Even with the omnipresent guilt of trespassing.

I was not the only one who never felt entirely at ease in the pretty cities. But, as I rationalized the intermittent twinges of conscience, it would have been ridiculous to build facilities when empty accommodations were already available, despite their obstinate refusal to work no matter how Dunlapil tried to energize them. Still, we managed fine and gradually came to ignore the anomalies we had never fully explored, settling down to make our gardens and our families grow.

The tenth year was just beginning, with surprising warmth, when Martin Chavez called a meeting with me and Dunlapil. Chavez had even convened it on a Restday, which was annoying as well as unusual.

"Just in case we have to call a meeting of the colony," he told me when I protested. That statement, on top of his insistence on a meeting, was enough to make me feel apprehensive. Although Martin was a worrier he was no fool; he did not force his problems on anyone unnecessarily, nor was he one for calling useless meetings.

"I've an unusual report to make on a new plant growth discernible on the velvet fields, commissioner Sarubbi," he announced, addressing me formally. "Such a manifestation is not generally associated with simple mono-cotyledonous plants. I've cross-checked both used and unused pastures, and the distortions of the growth in the used fields are distressing."

"You mean, we've imported a virus that's mutating the indigenous grasses?" I asked. "Or has the old virus that killed off the herbivorous life revived?"

"Nothing like this mutation has ever been classified and no, I don't think it's a return of a previous calamity." Chavez frowned with worry.

"Ah, champion, Martin," Dunlapil said with some disgust. "Don't go calling for a planetary quarantine just when we're showing a nice credit balance."

Chavez drew himself up indignantly.

"He hasn't suggested anything of the sort, Dun," I said, wondering if the urban engineer was annoyed because Chavez might be closer to solving the enigma of the Tree than Dunlapil was the mechanics of the cities. "Please explain, Specialist Chavez."

"I've just recently become aware of a weird evolution from the family Graminaceae, which these plants have resembled until now." He snapped on the handviewer and projected a slide onto the only wall in my office bare of the ubiquitous murals. "The nodular extrusions now developing in the velvet fields show none of the characteristics of herbaceous plants. No joined stems or slender sheathing leaves." He looked around to see if we had seen enough before he flashed on a slide of magnified cellular material. "This cross section suggests genus *Helianthus*, an improbable mutation." Chavez shrugged his helplessness in presenting such contradictory material. "However, something new is under every sun and we have not yet determined how the usual blue light of this primary will affect growth after prolonged exposure. We might get a Bragae Two effect."

"The next thing you'll be telling us, Martin," Dunlapil said as if to forestall a discourse on galactic comparisons, "is that these plants are the aliens who built these cities." He shot me a grin.

"That ought to be obvious," Chavez said with such a lack of rancor that the disbelief I had been entertaining disappeared. "Commissioner"—Chavez's grave eyes met mine—"can you give me another reason why every city has similarly fenced lots, all placed to catch full daily sun? Why the velvet fields with that central dominant Tree symbol appear to be the reverent focus of the aliens—excuse me—the indigenous species?"

"But they're humanoid," Dunlapil said in protest.

"Their culture is agrarian. *And* there are no grazers. Not a single example of that blasted Tree anywhere on the planet—yet!"

That was when I truly began to be afraid.

"There are no grazing beasts," Chavez went on inexorably, "because they have been eliminated to protect the velvet fields and whatever is growing in them now."

"You mean, when those fields bloom with whatever it is they bloom with, the aliens will return?" Dunlapil asked.

Chavez nodded. "If we haven't irreparably altered the growth cycle."

"But that's fantastic! An entire civilization can't be dependent on a crazy who-knows-how-long cycle of plant life." Dunlapil was sputtering with indignation.

"Nothing is impossible," replied Chavez at his most didactic.

"Your research has been sufficiently comprehensive?" I asked him, although I was sick with the sense of impending disaster.

"As comprehensive as my limited equipment and xenobotanical experience allow. I would welcome a chance to submit my findings to a board of specialists with greater experience in esoteric plant-life forms. And I respectfully request that you have Colonial Central send us a team at once. I'm afraid that we've already done incalculable damage to the—" He paused and, with a grim smile, corrected himself. "—*indigenous* organism seeded in those fields."

The semantic nicety jarred me. If Chavez was even remotely correct, we would require not only xenobotanists and xenobiologists but an entire investigation team from Worlds Federated to examine our intrusion into a domain that had not, after all, been abandoned by its occupants like a *Marie Celeste* but had simply been lying fallow—with the *indigenous* natives quiescently in residence.

As Chavez, Dunlapil, and I walked from my office toward the Comtower, I remember now that I felt a little foolish and very scared, like a child reluctant to report an accident to his parents but dutifully conscientious about admitting his misdemeanor. The plastisteel tower had never looked so out of place, so alien, so sacrilegious as it did now.

"Hey, wait a minute, you two," Dulapil protested. "You know what an investigation team means . . . "

"Anything and everything must be done to mitigate our offense as soon as possible," Chavez said, interrupting nervously.

"Dammit!" Dunlapil stopped in his tracks. "We've done nothing wrong."

"Indeed we have. We may have crippled an entire generation." Chavez spoke with an expression of ineffable sorrow.

"There are plenty of fields we never touched. The aliens—natives—can use them for food."

Chavez's sad smile deepened and he gently removed Dunlapil's hand from his arm. "'From dust ye came, to dust ye shall return, and from dust shall ye spring again.'"

It was then that Dunlapil understood the enormity of our crime.

"You mean, the plants are the *people?*"

"What else have I been saying? They are born from the Trees."

We did what we could even as we waited for the specialists and investigation team to arrive.

First we cleared the animals and crops from every one of the velvet fields. We removed every sign of our colonial occupation from the cities. The team, composed of five nonhuman and three humanoid species, arrived with menacing expedition well before the initial flood of xenospecialists. The team members did not comment on our preliminary efforts to repair our error, nor did they protest their quarters in the hastily erected dwellings on the bare, dusty plain and the subsequent roaring activity of the spaceport close by. All they did was observe with portentous intensity.

Of course, except for vacating the cities—and occupying them was apparently the least of our cumulative crimes—everything we did to remedy our trespass proved horribly inept in the final analysis. We would have been less destructive had we kept the cattle on the velvet fields and not slaughtered them for food. We ought to have let the crops ripen, die, and return to the special soils that had nourished them. For the fields we stripped produced the worst horrors. But how were we to know?

Now, of course, we know all too fully. We are burdened to this very day with guilt and remorse for the wholesale dismemberment and dispersal of those irretrievable beings; eaten, digested, defecated upon by grazers. And again, eaten, digested, and eliminated by those who partook of the grazers' flesh. Of the countless disintegrated natives removed from their home soil by unwitting carriers, none can bear fruit on foreign soil. And on their own soil, to repeat, the fields we had stripped produced the worst horrors . . .

I remember when the last report had been turned in to the eight judges composing the investigation team. Its members wasted no further time in formulating their decree. I was called to their conference room to hear the verdict. As I entered, I saw the judges seated on a raised platform, several feet above my head. That in itself was warning that we had lost all status in Worlds Federated.

A flick of the wrist attracted my attention to one of three humans on the team. Humbly I craned my head back, but he refused to glance down at me.

"The investigation is complete," he said in an emotionless tone. "You have committed the worst act of genocide yet to be recorded in all galactic history."

"Sir . . . " My protest was cut off by a second, peremptory gesture.

"Xenobiologists report that the growths in the velvet fields have reached the third stage in their evolution. The parallel between this life-form in its second stage and that of the cellulose fauna of Brandon Two is inescapable." Chavez had already told me of that parallel. "Now the plants resemble the exorhizomorphs of Planariae Five and it is inevitable that this third stage will give way to the sentient life pictured in the murals of their cities.

"You came here as agrarians and agrarians you shall be, in the fields of those you have mutilated. What final reparations will be levied against you, one and all, cannot be known until the victims of your crimes pronounce the penance whereby you may redeem your species in the eyes of the Worlds Federated."

He stopped speaking and waved me away. I withdrew to announce the verdict to my dazed fellow colonists. I would far rather that we had been summarily executed then and there, instead of being worn and torn apart by bits and pieces. But that was not the way of judgment for those who trespass in modern enlightened times.

We could not even make an appeal on the grounds that the planet had been released to us, for the colony in its charter took on all responsibility for its subsequent actions, having reaped benefits now so dearly to be paid for.

So we worked from that day until Budding Time late that heinous fall. We watched anxiously as the seedling exorhizomorphs grew at a phenomenal rate until they were ten, then twenty, finally twenty-five feet high, thick-trunked, branching out, lush with green triangular foliage. By midsummer we knew why it was that during our time on the planet we had never been able to find any examples of the Tree: Such Trees grew once every hundred years. For they were the Trees of Life and bore the Fruit of Zobranoirundisi in the cellular wombs, two to a branch, three to eleven branches per Tree. In the good fields—that is, the unviolated fields.

In the others . . .

The galaxy knows we tried to atone for our crime. Every man, woman, and child was devoted to tending the twisted, stunted, deformed, half-branched Trees that grew so piteously in those desecrated fields. Every one of us watched with growing apprehension and horror as each new day showed further evidence of the extent of our sacrilege. Oh, the hideous difference between those straight, tall, fine Zobranoirundisi and—the Others. We were ready for any sacrifice as penance.

Then, the morning after the first good frost, when the cold had shriveled the stems, the first Zobranoirundisi tore through his vegetable placenta. He shook his tall willowy body, turned and made obeisance to his natal Tree of Life, ate of the soil at its roots, of its triangular foliage . . . and knew.

I can never retell the agony of that day, when all those Zobranoirundisi faced us, their maimers, and announced the form our expiation would take. We bowed our heads to the inevitable, for we knew the sentence to be just and of Hammurabian simplicity.

We had to give back to the soil what we had taken from it. The handless Zobranoirundisi, recognizing his missing member from the cells now incorporated into the fingers of a young colony child nurtured on milk from cattle fed in the velvet fields, had every right to reclaim what was undeniably his own flesh. The legless Zobranoirundisi could not be condemned to a crippled existence when the Terran child had used the same cells to run freely for seven years on land where previously only Zobranoirundisi had trod.

We rendered, all of us, unto the Zobranoirundisi that which was truly theirs—seed and soil of the velvet fields, part and particle of the originally fertilizing dust that would have been reconstituted during the cycle we had so impiously interrupted.

Nor were we permitted to evade the least segment of required reparation, for the galaxy watched. I will say this of us proudly, though I no longer have a tongue: Mankind will be able to live with its conscience. Not one of us, when required, failed to give his flesh to the Zobranoirundisi in atonement.

• THE HARROWERS •
Eric Gregory

The kid didn't have a feed. He glanced over his shoulder and scratched the back of his head, and I saw there was nothing in his neck. You didn't find many folks without feeds in the city. Right away, I knew he'd brought me a problem. "I'm looking for Ez," he said, and I said yeah, I was him.

He looked relieved then lowered his voice. "And you're a guide?"

I wiped grease on the front of my jeans, closed the hood of the 4Runner, and gestured for the kid to follow me. He took the hint, nodding with absurd gratitude, and I led him down past the line of old rigs, all waiting to be stripped. Across the yard, someone cranked up a saw.

"Who gave you my name?" I asked.

"Guy called himself Coroner."

"You don't want to talk to him again."

The kid gave a sad sort of smile. "No. I really don't."

He wasn't the roughneck sort who usually came around looking for a guide. Right age, maybe: Seventeen, eighteen. But the boy had a pressed, conservative look to him. Skinny, clean-shaven, all done up in slacks and suspenders and a white, sweaty shirt. I didn't know what to make of him, and I didn't like that I didn't know.

"You from around here?" I asked.

He shook his head. "No, sir. Lynchburg."

"Nice town," I lied. Hive of fanatics. "How long you been here, then?"

"Not quite a day."

"And you already want to go outside." I grinned. "Jesus."

It wasn't much cooler in the office, but there was beer and shade. The kid settled onto my ratty, floral-print sofa, and I opened two Yanjings, thinking maybe he was used to the fancy stuff. I still couldn't get a fix on him, but he dressed like a big spender. He folded his arms and crossed his legs at the knee, glancing at the old gas station signs on the wall.

"What do I call you?" I said.

He frowned into his beer. "P.K."

"All right, P.K. You want to tell me about your deathwish?"

He shook his head.

"No deathwish. I just want to see my old man again."

My turn to frown. "Your old man."

"Yessir. He's outside."

I slid my bottle across the desk, back and forth from one hand to the other.

"How far outside?"

"Cherokee North. Between here and Johnson City."

"That's a lot of forest."

He shrugged.

Some guides don't like to get nosy. Take the job, don't ask questions. Lot of those guides develop a nasty case of dead.

"You want my help," I said, "you're going to have to tell me what he was doing there." If Coroner had sent him, I didn't have many choices here, but maybe the boy didn't know that. He nodded, answered without hesitation.

"We were out harrowing."

Christ, I thought. And then: Of course—P.K.: *Preacher's Kid*. Should've caught that earlier. I finished off the Yanjing, then opened the cooler and unscrewed a jar of whiskey. I'd heard of harrowers before, but never met one alive.

"You were with him," I said.

"Yessir."

"He preaches, you shoot. That how it works?"

The kid looked embarrassed. "I haven't learned to bless yet."

"And you got separated?"

He inclined his head. "Pack of wolves surprised us. We were running, and my father—" He paused. "He fell. Over a ledge. I saw him roll, heard him call out, but the slope sharpened and—I didn't see where he landed. I searched until sundown. I love my father, but—"he pursed his lips—"but I'm not stupid."

"You did right." I leaned forward. "But you understand he's dead."

The boy was silent.

"I ain't gonna sell you false hope. Your daddy's gone. I'll take your money, I'll take you out there, and I'll help you make whatever amends you want to make. But I want us both to understand what's going on here. I don't want any confusion between us. You have to show me that you know we're not going to find him smiling."

"I have to find him," he said. "I know the odds."

I wasn't sure he did. "I ain't cheap. And I ain't stupid either." I told him the deposit. "I need to see triple the advance in a credit account, and I need the account linked to my feed. In the event of my death, the triple transfers automatically to my family."

Little joke, there. Family.

"That's fair," he said. "And if I die?"

"We link your feed to my account. The deposit transfers back."

He shook his head. "I don't have a feed."

I'd forgotten. Mark of the Devil. I smiled through a stir of jealousy. The little metal nub in my neck let me work in the city, let me spend and collect credit, but mostly it just felt like a warm seed of debt, always itching beneath my skin, waiting for me to die or default, always threatening to grow.

"We can go to my credit agency and set up a timed withdrawal from my account," I said. "If you're not around to cancel it in three days, the advance'll transfer to the account of your choice."

He nodded. "Works for me."

"I think we understand one another, P.K." I took the Colt from my drawer, set it on my desk. The old, faded sticker on the grip said *Keep Asheville Weird*. "If you got the yuan, I got the yeehaw."

And just like that, we were in business.

No one ran outside the law in Asheville without owing money to Coroner. He found you when you were down, desperate, earthless. He fed you, paid your rent. If you wanted to be a guide, he made it easy: Set you up as a company mechanic, pulled all the right bureaucratic triggers to assign you to truckers on his payroll, to divert shipping routes. Last Christmas, he'd bought me a suit of skintight armor straight out of Cupertino. Sometimes it was hard to figure out where the companies ended and Coroner began, but it was absolutely clear who owned you.

Coroner had placed me and Xin Sun together so often that I could tell you her granddaddy's favorite singer (Johnny Cash) and the city where her mama was born (Raleigh). She was short, wiry, somewhere in her forties, with a line of faded hearts tattooed around her wrist. Her rig was a behemoth, a messy cross between a Humvee and an old furniture truck. I sat in the cab, behind the old automatic rifle mounted on the hood. P.K. huddled in the cargo crawlspace with the liquor.

Xin caught my eye as she eased toward the gate. "You're a bad person, Ez."

"Yeah?"

"The daddy's gone," she said. "Boy don't need to see that."

"I told him. He can make up his own mind."

She shook her head, scratched her neck. "He's green as shit. The dead on the moon can see it. You ought to know better."

"He's shot his share of dead. He don't need a mama, Xin."

She stared straight ahead, gripped the wheel.

Asshole, said the silence.

The traffic light changed, and Xin eased forward again. Bluecoats crowded around us with rifles and pads. My feed ran hot, so I could almost feel their fingers in the back of my neck, sifting through my licenses and permissions, my employers and outstanding debts. The bluecoat captain read through our manifest while his grunts looked over the cargo. Xin ignored me, and I tried not to touch my gun or crack my knuckles or otherwise announce that I was scared turdless. I listened to the clang of footsteps in the back and wondered what the kid was thinking, hidden down there with the liquor.

The footsteps in the back receded. The door slammed shut, and the captain waved us on. I tipped an invisible hat and Xin told him to have a good one.

The gate opened, and we drove outside.

There's something about leaving a city that makes you want to get drunk and scream. You ride out into the emptiness of the frontier and you can feel the weight of gazes falling away with every mile. Debts, shopping centers, manifests—all that headsmoke recedes until it's just you and the quiet, the clouds wrapped around road-carved mountains. I watched the trees as we rode out: The leaves were only just tinged with orange. Ahead, the Interstate wound through the broad swells of the Blue Ridge, all steep slopes and sharp drops. If you rode fifteen miles outside of Asheville, you could hardly tell that anyone had ever bothered to live on the mountains. Even the billboards were scarce and choked by kudzu.

"Want to let him out?" said Xin.

"Guess I ought to."

I pulled myself out of the gunner's seat, grappled my way to the back and ducked past stacked pallets marked in Portuguese, Italian, Chinese. All the world's shit packed up in crates. You couldn't see much by the emergency lights, and as often as I'd navigated Xin's rig, they packed it a little different every time. I pushed a box of canned soup off of the hidden door, rapped three times, waited, rapped again. I heard the door unlatch from his side, and I pulled it open. P.K. stared out from the crawlspace, his arms crossed over his chest like an old-fashioned corpse, mason jars shifting slightly around him. He was red-faced, his hair sweat-wet against his forehead.

"Thank you," he breathed.

I offered my hand. "Everything all right down there?"

He blinked. "Are we out?"

"Yessir."

I helped him up, guided him to the front. "Have a sit-down," I said, waving him into the gunner's seat. Xin glanced over her shoulder and smiled at the boy.

"Hope you didn't sample the whiskey," she said. Gently, teasing. "I don't want Coroner to come knocking."

He flushed. "No, ma'am. I don't drink."

I tried not to imagine Coroner at my door.

Xin laughed. "That so? You're either wise or insane. Not sure which."

"Out here," P.K. ventured, smiling nervously, "I think it's for the best."

"Out here, you may be right."

On the side of the road, empty signs. Words scraped and weathered away. A lone dead woman, one-armed and skeletal, limped along the side of the road, stumbling now and then into the guardrail, threatening to tumble over and down into a far hollow. Xin and P.K. fell silent, and I watched the sky for birds.

I still couldn't work out what Coroner was trying to say, sending me this job. When I'd called to line up the ride, I asked about the kid, but the minder only told me that the operation was important to the boss. "Make sure the boy and his daddy come back with you," he'd said. "Finish the job, you'll be fine."

Coroner wasn't an idiot—he knew the preacher was dead by now. Was he trying to play the kid for money? That didn't make sense; this was small change for him. He wanted the job done, but I didn't understand *why*. I didn't know the stakes, didn't understand what I stood to lose.

Xin braked hard, lashing me out of my thoughts.

I barely caught myself from toppling headfirst into the windshield. Ahead, an eighteen-wheeler lay on its side, its head curled into the median and its ass blocking half of the Interstate, splayed out like a sleeping cat. The semi's rear turret was shredded, the cow-catcher banged up and twisted into bad art. Gathered around the cab was a cluster of red bears—dead, from the look of them—ripping the skin from the rig. In unison, the bears looked up from their work.

Some people call dead eyes dull, but I've never understood that. You look the dead in the eyes, you see the judgment.

When guides and truckers get together to drink, you hear talk of road churches that worship the red bears. We're not a very spiritual lot, but I believe it. Sometimes you got to pray to the thing that scares you. And if you ain't scared of a twelve-foot, three-thousand-pound monster bred to consume as much flesh as possible, you're already underground. The companies engineered the red bears to clear the forests of the dead, and on paper, it still sounds like a good idea: Carnivorous cyborg weapons, carrion-eaters with titanium-reinforced skeletons. They were supposed to be uninfectable, a walking immune system for the world outside.

Problem was, they got infected anyway.

I grabbed P.K.'s shoulder, tried to pull him out of the seat, but he shook me off. Four of the animals broke off from the pack, loping toward us. Xin gripped the wheel, shifted the truck into reverse. The approaching dead split into two groups, flanking us; the ones that stayed behind tore open the cab of the downed rig—

Crack.

The nearest bear lurched to the right as blood sprayed from the side of its head. His face blank, P.K. swung the barrel of the rifle toward the next animal, then frowned slightly when he noticed that the first bear was still coming, its jaw hanging loose and swinging side-to-side as it ran. Xin watched the mirror and held the wheel steady, pushing the truck backward as fast as it would go, but the bears moved faster, hardly slowing as P.K. shot them in the chest, in the head. Finally, the one with the loose jaw stumbled and fell forward, as if it was dizzy or out of breath. At first, I thought P.K. had worn it down, but no: Its hind legs had collapsed.

The other three bears were close enough that I could see the meat between their teeth. I leaned into P.K.'s ear, shouted over the gun: "*Shoot them in the legs.*"

He nodded once and concentrated his fire on the space in front of the animals. There was less flesh around the joints where their forelimbs met their paws; red fur and muscle fell away, and bone-alloy gleamed underneath. P.K. didn't waste a shot, but we'd have to reload soon. The tallest bear staggered and hit the pavement, scraped away its snout as it fell.

The last hurled itself forward and hit our hood. The rig shook, but Xin kept it steady. The bear slumped and fell away then lay still on the road. Xin slowed, and we watched the rest of the dead in the distance. There were seven or eight bears circled there, maybe more. They'd already pulled apart the cab of the fallen truck, and now were eating.

"I can turn us around," Xin said quietly. "Get off the last exit, bypass the Interstate for a couple miles."

I wondered about the folks in the middle of that circle. Other truckers. Other guides, maybe. I wondered if I knew them.

"Yeah," I said. "Let's do that."

"I hope they were Christians," P.K. said softly.

We talked about our families. Xin's mother, half out of her mind in a nursing home in Charlotte. She didn't mention her ex-husband and sons. My daughter, grown and living on a Monsanto farm colony in the Pacific, still writing every couple months for money. Xin had heard the story a dozen times before—often enough that she ought to have pegged it for bullshit—but she still watched me with something between warmth and bitterness.

P.K. told us about his father, Joseph. At first, the kid spoke hesitantly, responding to Xin's questions with short, one-word answers, but finally he relaxed into his story, seeming to surprise himself with the pleasure of the telling.

Joseph hadn't always harrowed souls in the wilderness. As a young man of the Lynchburg Watch, he'd walked the walls and killed the dead. Joseph had mumbled his prayers since he was a boy, the town being what it was, but he didn't find religion until a circuit rider passed through in the summer of his twentieth year. He'd only recently become a father, and the death he'd dealt out weighed on him with new urgency, even if it was only the long-rotted he'd sent to their final repose. The circuit rider preached that the souls of the dead still resided in those wasted bodies, that for all their hunger and decay, they could always receive or reject the love of Christ. He preached that the living death was an opportunity, a flesh limbo, and that it was the duty of all Christians to speak the gospel to lost souls and offer them salvation. Just as Christ had descended to Hell to harrow pagan souls, the faithful were bound to travel the wilderness and minister to the dead.

Joseph found his calling. He rode with the circuit man for three years, preaching in the walled cities and preaching to the dead outside, returning now and then to Lynchburg to give his wife and son the money he'd collected from churches throughout the South. When P.K. was seven, Joseph came home to find his wife lost to pneumonia, his son motherless and afraid. For almost a year, Joseph gave up the circuit and raised the boy, working the wall as he'd done before, now hollering salvation as he delivered bullets into creeping bodies.

It was on the wall that he had his Revelation. As he fired his rifle at a cluster of dead in army camouflage, an angel of the Lord seized his tongue and set it ablaze with the language Enoch knew, the words spoken in the Kingdom of Heaven. The dead paused to hear his ministry, and he saw the light of Christ in their eyes. He killed them all immediately, before they could move or doubt. He was ecstatic.

His fervor restored, Joseph resolved to return to the wilderness, this time with his son. P.K. was already a fine shot, a junior watchman. The circuit rider had traveled in an armored truck, declaiming over loudspeakers, but Joseph now understood that glass and metal separated him from the souls he meant to save; he bought two horses and taught P.K. to ride.

"Wait," I said. "You rode *horses*? Out here?"

P.K. shrugged. "They're fast."

"You're fucking with me now."

"No, sir."

I glanced aside at Xin. She focused on the road, negotiating the sharp, mountainside S-curves of Cherokee North. We had to drive at a crawl, but P.K. said we weren't far from the last place he'd seen Joseph.

"How do you survive something like those bears?"

He smiled tightly. "I got lucky last night. But the dead stand aside for my father. He preaches as he rides."

They stand aside, I thought. *Of course.*

"What happened next?" said Xin. "He taught you?"

P.K. seemed reluctant. "That's all there is to tell. He taught me to ride, and we rode. We visited churches often enough to keep food in our stomachs, but his heart was never much in ministering to the living. We spent more and more time in the wild, released thousands of souls to the Lord. Father's done his best to teach me the tongue of Heaven, but I lack . . . " He trailed off, stared out the window. "The Revelation," he finished quietly.

The tires whined as the road wound back around on itself, almost a three-hundred-sixty degree turn. I gritted my teeth, tried not to see the sheer drop to my left or the rock face to my right. P.K. leaned forward, pointed at a graffiti symbol on the rock. "I recognize—"

Something hit the side of the truck. Hard, on the right side.

We screeched toward the side of the road, mangled the guard-rail. "The *hell*—" Xin shouted. I swung behind P.K.'s seat, pulled on the safety straps and curled into a ball. There was another deep, metal-rending crash, and another, and then the world rolled and blurred. A rank, cloudy explosion as the airbags deployed and then gravity fell out from underneath me, snapped back in brief, vicious cracks against my knees and elbows. I covered my head the best I could, but suddenly it felt *hot*, and then everything was heavy and dark.

Metal ground against metal, keening.

"Wake," shouted Xin, "the fuck up."

Two gunshots. I took a breath like a knife to the chest, opened my eyes. The cab was pillowy and white. Almost heavenly, except for the bent metal and bloodstains. There was a sour stench, piss mixed with sulfur. My feed burned. I moved my fingers, feet, blinked blood out of my eyes. Felt like maybe I'd bruised a rib, but I could sit up, breathe. Limbs intact. Head was wet, but it was a shallow gash.

Xin stood over me, covered in white powder from the airbags. A pleasant, middle-aged phantom with a Desert Eagle. There was a wide hole in the back of the rig. Jeans and soda and high heels, all strewn around like Christmas in the Asheville Mall, not that I'd ever had the yuan or self-loathing to step in *there*. Three dead men in faded orange jumpsuits peered inside the truck, eager in the instant before Xin shot them down.

"You good?" she asked.

"Golden. P.K.?"

"Up top." She gestured toward the roof with her head. "Looks like they hit us with rocks."

I unbuckled the safety straps, stood up shakily. Almost fell, but steadied myself against the driver's seat.

"Kid have a gun?" I asked, fumbling for my holster.

"He's got the rifle."

"So why isn't he shooting?"

Xin bit her lip. I flicked off the safety on my Colt, and we pressed our way to the back, kicking aside boxes of designer boots, finally stepping outside. It looked like Xin had killed the last of the orange-suited dead: there was nothing but breeze and the glare of afternoon light. The truck was caught between two large trees; we hadn't rolled all the way to the bottom, maybe hadn't rolled that far at all, which meant we were still on a sharp slope.

Also, P.K. wasn't up top.

I ripped the handset from my belt. Prayed it wasn't broken.

"Where the hell are you?" I hissed.

There was a long silence. I wondered what Coroner would do if I lost the boy. Lost the *money*. "Down the hill a bit," P.K. answered at last, his voice crackling on the handset. "To the east. You can probably still see me."

And there he was, through the trees: A dot.

"I already sent the SOS," Xin said, leaning into my handset. "Company's coming. Maybe thirty minutes. We just got to wait here."

P.K. said, "My old man's close. I can find him in half an hour."

"Wait here for the rescue," Xin said. "We'll all go out and look for him."

He gave a sad little laugh. "The company's not going to send out a search party. You know that. All they care about is their cargo and whatever they can salvage from the truck. My father's less than meaningless to anyone but me."

Well, I wanted to say, *he is dead*. Instead, I started down the hill.

"Slow down," I said. "I'm coming with you."

"What?" said Xin.

I took my thumb off the handset.

"Kid can't die," I said, wondering how much honesty I could afford.

"You mean you need the money."

I held on to a low tree limb with my free hand. Moved ahead, grabbed hold of another tree, all the while trying not to slip on leaves or trip on roots.

"Jesus, Ez." Xin was flushed, agitated. She took a step forward, not following me so much as making sure I could hear her. "We *all* need the money. But it's no goddamned good if you're dead."

"Not true. Boy owes me a pile if I die."

"Yeah? What if you both get eaten?"

"That'll be complicated. May have to hire an accountant."

"I save your life and you're going to leave me alone. All those times we rode together, you're going to leave me alone."

I forced myself to keep walking, to fix my eyes on the kid. "You know guilt don't work on me, Xin. Lock yourself in the crawlspace. Pour a few shots, drink to our health, and don't let the rescue team leave without us." I stepped over another corpse in an orange jumpsuit, pale and gaunt and forest-scratched, its face little more than a skull beneath skin. These were the desperate dead, the old and ravenous. The fatter, younger, brighter ones favored the night, when the sun wouldn't rot muscle from their bones.

"Ez," said Xin. "The boy's lying."

I stopped.

"I don't know what's truth and what's lies," she said. "But I seen him before. Back home, at the New French. Playing cards and throwing back shots." She lowered her voice, spoke in a high-speed hiss. "That no-ma'am-I-don't-drink business was horseshit, and I reckon he's been in Asheville a lot longer than a night. I don't know what his game is here, but I don't feel like dying for a lie today. Just stay back. If the kid gets himself killed, well, we lose a little money. We'll have another job tomorrow."

Was *she* telling the truth? Or just trying to keep me from getting myself killed? As long as Coroner was knocking on my door, it didn't really matter.

"Tomorrow's too late," I said.

She shook her head and stepped back. She said, "You stupid asshole."

I worked my way down.

P.K. waited in a hollow where the ground flattened out. There was a creek nearby, invisible but mumbling. He forced a smile, cradled the M-16. His clothes were sweat-soaked, weighted down with ammunition. The air smelled smogless and new. Like God had just invented it and still thought it was good.

"You ain't a tourist," I said.

He shrugged a shoulder, then turned away and raised his rifle toward the trees. Skipped over a rocky outcrop and made toward the sound of the creek. "I told you. I've spent every day outside for as long as I can remember. We should keep our mouths shut."

Ordinarily I'd have welcomed the caution. There was a certain flavor of tourist who hooted his glee every time he pulled a trigger, or almost pulled a trigger, or thought about pulling triggers. But silence seemed ridiculous now, and I didn't appreciate the boy hushing me. "We're the only game in town, kid. Every corpse for miles around already knows we're here."

He gave another half-shrug.

The creek was low enough that we didn't bother walking on stones. Tadpoles flitted around our boots. On the other side, we started moving uphill again. The leaves here were shot through with streaks of red, as if we'd stumbled our way deep into autumn.

"You're a hell of a good son," I said. "Boy your age usually wants to strangle his daddy."

He looked back. "Did you strangle yours?"

"Never knew him. But I wanted to." I paused. "Strangle him, I mean."

He chewed that over a while. "Where did you grow up?"

"Richmond."

"Never heard of it."

"That's because it ain't there anymore."

The flutter of birds overhead. You could depend on birds. They died and stayed dead. Twigs snapped underfoot. The climb sharpened.

"I have to be honest with you," he said.

"Okay."

"Sometimes, I think I'm not a good enough person."

"I know *I'm* not."

"I mean to speak the tongue. The angels' language."

"Are you an angel?"

"No."

"There you go."

P.K. pursed his lips, looked like he wanted to say something. Instead, he pointed up. I followed the line of his finger to the purpling sky ahead and the silhouette of an old fire tower. When clients wanted to hunt, I took them to towers like that. Tall, ancient, sturdy. Dead folks are slow climbers.

"That's where he'll be," said the boy. "I should warn you—"

I raised my hand to cut him off. Listened.

"Do you hear that?" I whispered.

The strongest argument against talking when you're outside is that your voice masks important warnings. Like the sound of feet against dirt, running.

We sprinted up the hill. P.K. scanned the woods ahead, his rifle following his eyes, and I glanced back over my shoulder. My lungs felt like someone had balled them up, pissed on them, and stapled them into my ribcage, but I pushed on, legs dragging underneath me. My feed was hot with its broadcast of *I am alive, I am still alive, I will pay my debts*, and a tendril of shame shot through the middle of my fear, because this was the only reason anyone cared that I was alive, to earn and owe money. We made it halfway to the tower before I saw our pursuers, and realized I'd been wrong about the sound.

It wasn't just feet against the dirt.

There were also paws.

The wolves were ragged, skeletal things, ribs half-exposed beneath gray and white fur. They wove like steel needles through the trees. A man and a woman trailed the wolves, wearing tattered green uniforms. I fired at the closest animal. Missed.

"Behind us," I rasped.

P.K. twisted around as he ran, took aim, tore the front legs off the wolf I'd missed. I couldn't tell how many were left—they ducked in and out of sight, gray-green blurs, faces of the forest. One appeared a body's length from P.K.'s left side; I got it in the head, almost fell over the body as it crumpled. Caught my footing and squeezed off a shot at the man in green.

The dead didn't breathe, didn't growl or hiss or groan. They watched and lunged and snapped, silent. Eyes flashed ahead. They flanked us with a kind of brutal grace, closing from every side with each footfall, and I had one of those idiot epiphanies that seem profound when you're dizzy with adrenaline and about to be eaten: *It's like they're dancing.* Every lunge in concert, every bite. We were going to die because the dead were dancers.

The kid stopped.

I was running too fast, too close behind him. We hit the dirt. Someone shouted, but I didn't understand the words. I smelled rotted meat. I tried to stand but my legs were tangled; someone was still shouting. My shoulder throbbed. Each breath was a suckerpunch. I gripped the Colt, braced for the bite, and someone was still shouting. I looked up.

The dead all stared at the man in black.

He was tall, pale. He wore a day's gray-brown stubble and his eyes were hidden by the shadow of his wide-brimmed hat. His voice was hoarse but commanding as hunger—every nonsense syllable he shouted was a slap, a crack, all thunder and hard edges. The dead folks slumped as he spoke, cowed or subdued or enraptured. The wolves pawed the dirt, uncertain, saliva dripping from their mouths, their eyes never leaving the preacher. Joseph took off his hat and stared down at his son, his blue eyes blunt, and then he spoke English instead of the babble of Heaven.

"Go on and shoot 'em," he said. "My throat hurts like a bitch."

When I first came to Asheville, I'd lived for six months with an ex-Pentecostal poet from the mountain collectives south of Blacksburg. Once, after a night of smoke and sweat and Blackjack, she'd given me slurred lessons in glossolalia, giggling as she coached me on tongues. There were, she said, patterns in the babble. Sounds that looped and recurred. Subtle cadences. The language of Heaven was poetry without meaning, empty words taking shapes.

There was an art to it.

Silently, I wrapped my tongue around the syllables of Joseph's sermon. *Nalumasakala, sayamawath,* shit like that. Kidsounds, but they'd tamed the dead. The man had reached out with his tongue and *controlled* them. I tried to memorize his rhythms and words that weren't words. I wanted to beg him to preach again.

Joseph wasn't lost. He wasn't stranded or waiting for saviors. He was at home, at ease.

There was a reinforced steel stable at the base of the tower—a horse grunted inside. After we killed the last of the dead, Joseph lit a cigarette and gestured to a rope ladder. Invited us up for coffee. "I ain't got much to offer," he said, "but I can boil you some beans."

P.K. didn't move. "You need to come with us," he said, terse and low. "Rescue's coming soon, but we have to meet them on the other side of the creek."

"Already told you. I ain't going nowhere."

P.K. gripped his rifle. "Father. You can't live out here."

Joseph snorted. "Missed you too, Christopher. How you like the city? You going to introduce me to your friend?"

"He's a tour guide. He's here to help. You're sick. We want to help you."

Christopher. The kid glanced at me, frowned.

"My name's Ezekiel," I said. Held out my hand. He eyed me carefully, then shook it.

"You from around here?" he asked.

"No, sir. Richmond."

He grimaced, exhaled smoke. "You had people there?"

My joke, my family. "I did."

"I passed through, once. Few months after Christopher left." He flicked ash into the dirt. "You see that place, you have a hard time looking the Lord in the eye."

I didn't know what to say. I said, "Yes, sir."

"Father," Christopher pressed. "You need to come with us now."

Joseph shook his head. "It's good to see you, son. I'm happy to drink a cup of coffee with you, and you can tell me what it is you really want. Grace Baptist took up a collection last month—you need money, we can talk. But I ain't going to live inside of walls for you." He turned around, started to walk back to his ladder.

And P.K.—Christopher—hit him in the head with the butt of his rifle.

The preacher crumpled.

My instinct was to reach for the Colt, but I balled my fist and stood very still. Christopher kneeled and fumbled in his father's jacket, withdrew a ring of keys.

"He doesn't want to leave the wilderness anymore," he said. "He's senile. He needs saving. If you want to help him, the best thing you can do is help me get him on the horse."

You could smell the bullshit in every word. I watched him as he searched through his daddy's keys, and I remembered Xin's story about the New French. I remembered that the minder told me to bring back the old man, and a nasty hunch worked itself out in my head. I would have shaken my head in grudging admiration, but no one had told me, and that left me scratching the nub in the back of my neck. Feeling the dim heat of my feed, the constant heat of debt and return. Coroner had sent me into this blind, and now I was stuck, choiceless. Why had he chosen me? Because I was dependable? Or because he thought I was stupid, expendable?

Finish the job and you'll be fine.

"Okay," I said slowly. "I'll get this arm, we'll hold him up together."

We pulled his father to his feet, draped his arms over our shoulders and carried him to the stable. Christopher unlocked the steel door, and we hauled Joseph inside. The place was cramped and thick with shit-stink. Bars of light slanted through the grates, and the ground was covered with hay. The horse huffed, stepped back. It was gaunt, its fur as black as Joseph's coat. I couldn't remember the last time I'd seen such a large animal alive. Rodents tended to stay dead, but most mammals bigger than cats were liable to come back. You didn't see them much in the cities.

The horse was calm; it let us push Joseph onto its back without much fuss. We swung the preacher around by his legs so that he was sitting more or less upright, his head hanging forward. Christopher climbed onto the horse, inclined his head to me. "Thank you," he said.

Then he shot me in the chest.

The blast knocked me into the dirt. Even with the armor under my coat, it felt like someone had jackhammered the breath out of me, and I fought to suck down air. Christopher's horse charged into the woods, and for a beautiful, adrenaline-soaked moment, I stopped worrying about money and consequences and Coroner. I raised the Colt, fired.

The first shot missed. The second hit its mark, and the boy toppled from the horse. The animal panicked, reared back, and knocked off the preacher, who fell on his side and rolled.

I winced and climbed to my feet. Staggered outside in time to see the kid duck behind a tree, weaving and heavy-breathing but alive, the M-16 in hand. I pulled the trigger again, splintered bark, took cover behind a fallen trunk.

It looked an awful lot like Coroner had bought the kid Californian armor, too.

"So," I called, "You want to sell your old man?"

Christopher coughed. It took me a moment to realize he was laughing. "Is that why you're shooting at me? Because I'm a bad *son*?" His shot grazed bark, burned moss, whistled over my head. "Or do you want to sell him yourself?"

"Didn't plan on it," I said. I slid down the length of the log, listened for footsteps or tells. "I just make a point of shooting folks who shoot me."

He was silent.

"I want to know if I got this right," I shouted. I willed him to make a move while I talked, willed him to peer out and try to find me. "You were sick of it, weren't you? The preaching. The wilderness. You were sick of it, and you were sane, and you wanted to go live with the living, so you ran off to the city and got caught up in cards and whiskey. Do I have it right so far?"

Wind in the leaves. The snap of a reloaded magazine. I focused on the snap, raised the barrel of the Colt over the log.

"You play the tables long enough in the New French, you start owing money around town. Which, in the end, really just means you owe Coroner. I bet it wasn't long before Coroner came calling, and you started to wonder what you could give him to get him off your back. Then you remembered your daddy, and it all—"

He cut me off with a thundercrack. I fired twice over the log.

The Colt clicked.

Christopher must have heard it. He coughed and fired into the dead tree, tearing through moss and bark and wood as if he were hacking with a machete, moving closer and coughing and ripping apart the air—

And then he stopped.

There was a *snap*, and the woods fell silent.

I peered over the log.

She held him like a lover. His head hung limp, twisted. Her forearm was mangled, her mouth bloodstained. She was still covered in the powder from the airbag. Three dead rescue workers in camouflage armor staggered through the trees behind her.

I gave up, then.

Those armor suits, so bulky and futile. Xin Sun with blood in her mouth. Everyone was dead. No one was coming for me. And even if I found my way home, Coroner would be waiting.

Xin pressed her lips against the dead boy's throat. At first, it looked like a kiss. And then it didn't. She opened the artery, ripped away muscle. Her eyes flicked to the side and met mine; she seemed torn between finishing her meal and moving on to me. The boy's blood ran down the front of her shirt. The rescue crew's legs were all bent into painful angles—maybe they'd wrecked— but they still hitched toward us, inch by inch.

"You were right," I said softly. "I'm a stupid asshole."

She watched me, shifted her weight. You look the dead in the eyes, you see the judgment.

"I can't go back to the city. Don't know why I'd go back, anyway. I ain't got no family, no daughter in California. All I got is a landlord and some funerals I ain't paid for."

The rescuers were close now. I opened my fingers, dropped the Colt.

"I don't want to be owned," I said. "I don't want to owe nobody no more. I been stuck a long time."

She was silent. I tried to relax. Tried not to feel the blood drum in my neck, my chest. The air tasted good—I was glad to die outside. It was the best I could hope for, going out where I could see the birds. There was a kind of relief in it, a lightness. *This is how it's going to be.* Feet scuffed the dirt, one step and then another.

"Go on, Xin," I said.

She jerked backward with a *thwip*.

Xin and Christopher fell, tangled together. Before they hit the dirt, the rescue workers' heads shattered in a spray of bone and blood. I spun around, followed the sound of silenced shots. The preacher stood at the base of his tower with a pistol in each hand, his guns raised toward me and the dead, his face empty as an abandoned city.

We burned the bodies in silence. Joseph stood too close to Christopher's pyre, head bowed and lips moving wordlessly. The sun was almost down. I held one of his pistols and watched the woods. Far as I could tell, the preacher didn't know what his son had planned to do. I wasn't going to tell him. I didn't have anything more to say to Xin, and I felt guilty for it. Still, I stood by her pyre, clinging quietly to my only friend at a lonely party.

When the preacher finished his prayers, we climbed the tower and watched the fires burn down. He made bitter coffee, and we drank it slowly as the stars came out, denser and brighter than I'd seen in years. When Joseph spoke, his voice was hoarse and flat.

"You still want to try to take me back to your city?"

I reckoned I could do it. Carry him to Coroner. My debt might not be paid, but the boss would be off my back for another day. He'd have something priceless, something that no thuglord or company—not even the few who could fly over oceans—could buy: Words that could hold the dead at bay. Joseph might not cooperate, but Coroner knew how to make a man talk. He'd learn the loops and rhythms, put poets on his payroll, try to vivisect the tongue of Heaven. He'd try to figure out what other things those words could make the dead do.

I swallowed my coffee. "No, sir."

The old man nodded, then unsheathed his knife.

"You were blessing her," he said.

I watched the knife's tip, tried to work out the right answer. He took my silence for confusion.

"The woman. You were blessing her."

The pyrecoals glowed below, a constellation of deaths.

"Her name was Xin Sun," I said. "She was the nearest thing to family that I had." I looked up from the knife and met his eyes, willing him to believe me. "I don't know how to save a soul, but I would have liked to have saved hers."

There was nothing about Xin's soul that needed saving. I hoped she would have forgiven the lie. Joseph leaned on the rail and toyed with his knife, moonlight glinting on the blade. My palms were sweaty, my throat tight with unasked questions. I wasn't used to *wanting* something like this. Wanting to walk in the wilderness, outside of walls. Wanting to ride the roads and forests, far from companies and criminals, free from Coroner and the machinery of obligation. I'd never believed that kind of life was possible, and now I was drunk on the fantasy.

"If you want me to teach you," Joseph said at last, "I'm gonna have to cut out your feed."

I touched the warm nub on my neck and bit back a smile.

Mark of the Devil.

Already, I could feel it. The sting of alcohol. Metal on skin, the knife's edge like nightbreeze. Blood. One drop, and then a trickle. The cut, the last hum of the feed running my numbers.

And then a release, when it tells the world that I'm a dead man.

• BIBI FROM JUPITER •
Tessa Mellas

When I marked on my roommate survey sheet that I'd be interested in living with an international student, I was thinking she'd take me to Switzerland for Christmas break or to Puerto Rico for a month in the summer. I wasn't thinking about a romp around the red eye of Jupiter, which is exactly what I'd have gotten had I followed my roommate home. Apparently, American school systems have gotten popular all over. Universities shepherd the foreigners in. Anything to be able to write on the brochures, "Our student body hails from thirty-three countries and the far reaches of the solar system."

You'd think there'd have been an uproar over the matter. I mean, here we have student-funding going down the toilet and everyone staging protests to show they're pissed. And she gets a full ride, all the amenities paid for. She comes in like a Cuban refugee, minus the boat, sweeps up all the scholarships. And why shouldn't she? She probably qualifies as fifteen different types of minority. Don't get me wrong. I don't have anything against her. We were friends. I just didn't expect her to be so popular. I figured I'd have to protect her from riots and reporters. But as it turns out, she was really well liked.

The first time I met her I nearly peed my pants. It's the end of August and I've got all my stuff shoved in the family van, a bit too unorganized for my father's taste, but we only live an hour away. I'm hoping to get there first to pick the best side of the room, the one with the most sunlight and the least damaged furniture. I get up early—just to beat her there. But I don't.

She's sitting at her desk already, reading the student handbook. I double-check the room number. 317. I've got the right place. This is my roommate.

At first, I think she's an inmate. She's wearing this light-blue jumpsuit. And she's got pale-green skin that looks sickly. Gangrene, I think, not quite knowing what that is. It just sounds like a disease that would turn you green. She's not an all-out green. Tinted rather, like she got a sunless tanner that didn't work out. Her ears are inset like a whale's, and she doesn't have eyelids. She's this tiny creature, not even five feet tall, completely flat, no breasts. It doesn't even look like she has nipples.

My parents are right behind me. My mother's carrying my lava lamp like some offering. My father's got my futon extended over his head, trying to be all macho in case my roommate's a babe. They drop my stuff on the side of the room with a broken closet door and turn to this green, earless girl. They're all excited, want to make friends with the new roommate. So they start asking questions: "How was your drive? Do you like the campus? Have your parents left?"

Not even acknowledging the obvious. That she's green. Maybe they didn't notice. Like I said, it was a pale green, a tint really, but it was pretty obvious to me, and she had weird eyes too, beady black pinhead eyes like a hamster's.

So finally I ask, "Where are you from?"

And she says, "Jupiter."

"Jupiter, New York?" my parents ask.

Not that they know there *is* a Jupiter, New York. It just makes more sense than the other possibility.

"No," she says. "Jupiter, Jupiter. The planet."

"Oh," they say. "I didn't realize we'd found life on other planets yet. How interesting."

She says, "You didn't. We found you," and goes back to her reading.

That shuts my parents up fast. They have no response. They do an about-face and head back to the car.

"Jupiter," my father's saying. "You believe that, Cath?"

My mother's shaking her head, saying "Jupiter" over and over. First, like it's a word she's never heard, a word she's trying to get used to. Then like a question. "Jupiter?" Not quite sure whether or not to believe it. She says it several more times, looks at my father, then me.

"I was worried about Angela living with city kids," she says. "This is a bit different." She unlocks the car, grabs a handful of pillows, and adds, "Is Jupiter the one with the rings?"

"I thought Jupiter was made of gas," my father says. "How can she live on a gaseous planet?"

"Let's just drop it," I say. "She could be from the moon, for all I care."

As it turned out, she *was* from the moon. Well, one of them. Apparently Jupiter's got a few dozen. The one she's from is called Europa—by Americans at least. But she tells everyone she's from Jupiter, says it's easier to explain. Her name is Bibi. No last name. Just Bibi. I looked it up. It means "lady" in Arabic. Ironic, as her kind doesn't have genders, just one type, like flowers, self-germinating and everything. But she looks more like a girl than a guy, so that's how we treat her while she's here, even though her body parts serve both functions.

She tells me most of this the first night in the dorm. I'm unpacking my toiletries and makeup, and she's still reading. I say, "Your parents were cool with you coming to America? Mine wouldn't even let me go out of state."

"I don't have parents," Bibi says.

"Oh Christ!" I say. "I'm sorry. That sucks." What can you say in a situation like that? I'd never met an orphan.

"It's fine," she says. "Nobody has parents. I grew up like this, sort of in a dorm."

"How can nobody on Jupiter have parents?" I ask. I know I'm being nosy, but you've got to admit it's a bit strange.

"It's complicated," she says. "I don't feel like getting into it."

I'm about to insist when there's a knock at the door. Bibi jumps to get it and these men wheel in a full-size fridge. It's brand-new, a Frigidaire, one of those side-by-side freezer-and-fridge jobs complete with icemaker. They prop it against the window, plug it in, and leave.

"What the hell is that?" I ask, knowing damn well it's a fridge, not quite sure what it's doing in our room. My parents bought us one of those mini units, just enough space for a Brita filter, pudding snacks, and string cheese. The university had exact specifications on which ones were allowed. This Frigidaire wasn't on the list. Bibi explains how she got special permission to have it in the room, says she has a medical condition.

"What kind of condition?" I ask. "Are you contagious?"

"It's not a viral condition," she says. "I need a daily supply of ice."

"Ice," I say. "For what?"

"Don't they teach you this stuff in school?" she asks. "The basics of the solar system?"

"Of course," I say. "Third grade. We memorized the planets. There was a song."

Apparently she doesn't believe me. She goes to my dresser and starts grabbing stuff. She throws my nightie in a lump in the middle of the floor and says, "That's the sun." She places a red thong beside it and calls that Mercury. Venus is a pair of toe socks. Earth a blue bra. Mars a pair of leggings. And Jupiter and all its moons are my best sparkly panties. She lines them up, stands to the side, says, "See?"

"Yeah, I get your point," I say, though I don't really. I'm too pissed that my underwear are on the floor. Matching bras and panties aren't cheap. "I appreciate the astronomy lesson," I say, but she cuts me off.

She points at my bra. "You're here," she says. "We're there. See how far we are from the sun? It's cold. We don't have sweat glands. Your planet is hot, so I need ice. Capisce?"

Capisce? Who the hell does she think she is? A Jupitarian girl trying to intimidate me with Italian. Barging in with her refrigerator. Taking the best side of the room and making my thong a planet. I snatch her solar system off the floor and stuff it back in my drawer, say, "I don't know much about Jupiter, but here, shit like that just isn't cool."

There's another knock at the door. I'm about to say, "That better not be a fucking stove," when these guys from down the hall walk in. They want Bibi to join them for a game of pool.

"I'm Angela," I say, extending my hand.

"You can come too if you want," they say. But it's clear they're just interested in Bibi.

I shrug. "I got stuff to do. Maybe next time."

And Bibi takes off. No apology. No, "I'm not going without my roommate." No nothing. She just leaves me there with her big fucking fridge while she goes to shoot pool with these boys she's never even seen. I'm not sure what they see in her. She isn't at all pretty. I mean, I don't think so. We have rigid aesthetics here, right? How can you count a green earless girl without eyelids as pretty?

I watch them head down the stairs. The dorm is quiet, empty. I thought people were supposed to congregate on their floor the first night, praise each other's bedspreads and posters and shit. The door across the hall opens and a guy wearing pink pants and a polo shirt steps out.

"Hey," I say.

"Hey," he replies.

He's wearing his collar propped up like he's Snow White. His hair is gelled back and all goopy. I want to tell him that went out of style with the Fonz, but instead say, "I'm Angela," even though it's written on the construction paper sign on my door.

"Call me Skippy," he says, even though his sign says John Ward III.

"Where'd the nickname come from?" I ask.

"I made it up. People say you can reinvent yourself in college."

"Huh," I say. "Good choice."

"So that green girl's your roommate?" he asks.

"Yeah. Afraid so."

"Do you know when she's getting back?" he asks. "I heard she's from Jupiter. You think you could introduce me? *Lloyd in Space* is my favorite cartoon."

The first week wasn't at all what I expected from freshman year. Bibi followed me all over the place, dragging her leaky ice packs along. Didn't quite understand we had different schedules. She's taking all these science and math courses. And I have this good mix. Swahili. Ballet. Psychology. Statistics. My adviser made me take that last one, said I needed a math credit. But besides statistics, I'm thinking classes will be fun.

Then in psych lab, I turn around and there she is sitting behind me. She's even got the books. I figure she must have bought them for both our schedules. How's a girl from Jupiter to know better?

Everyone wants to be her lab partner. They crowd around her desk and ask stupid questions like, "Are you going to be a psychologist? Will you go back to Jupiter and counsel manic-depressives?"

"No," she says. "I'm a neurobiology major. Stem cell research. I'm going to learn to grow pancreases and livers on rats, then take them back to Jupiter and implant them in bodies."

"Right," I say. "You're not even supposed to be here. Don't you have chemistry?"

She doesn't answer, just prepares her rat for the maze.

Of course, hers finishes first. Mine gets stuck in a corner and goes into shock.

But what does it matter that her rat's the smartest? The girl doesn't have any common sense. She forgets her shoes all the time, puts the toothpaste in her mouth instead of on the brush, and doesn't close the stall door behind her when she goes to the bathroom. No one wants to see how Jupitarians pee. Actually, everyone was interested, but once they saw it, they didn't want to see it again.

Around the third week I finally get a look at her schedule. It's in one of those ugly-ass Trapper Keeper things. As it turns out, Bibi *is* enrolled in my classes. Hers too. She's taking nine at once. I didn't think that was allowed. Bet they make exceptions for Jupitarians, figuring anyone from another planet is more intelligent than us. Bibi is pretty smart actually, gets perfect scores on the tests even though she says absolutely nothing in class.

And to top it all off, even the boys are into her. That guy Skippy won't stop hanging around. He's a complete dork, a grade-A loser. He stands outside our door like he's the king's guard. At night he brings Bibi ice cream and Popsicles. He follows her to dinner and leaves flowers outside our door, nasty weedy ones with ants. Bibi hangs them from the ceiling and the flowers die because there's absolutely no light in the room. She won't let me open the blinds, not even a crack, on account of her condition. So now we've got all these ants crawling across our ceiling between brown crusty root systems. And Skippy's become this stalker. I find him in my closet behind my shoe rack and Dustbuster.

"Just playing hide-and-seek," he says, and winks.

"Hide-and-seek, my ass," I yell. "She doesn't even have a vagina!"

I call my mother and tell her about Skippy and the icepacks and the ants. My mother tells me to be patient. She reminds me about Martin Luther King Jr. I tell her she shouldn't send Bibi presents anymore. She puts something in all my care packages for Bibi. Cookies. Statuettes from the dollar store. *Soup-for-the-Soul* books. I tell her, "Bibi doesn't need presents. You should see this girl's checks. The government gives her plenty of money."

My mother says presents are different. Bibi doesn't have parents. She tells me to be mindful of that. I tell my mother no one on Jupiter has parents. She says that doesn't sound right, and I agree. I mean a whole planet full of orphans. That just seems too sad to be true. She's probably lying. Going for the sympathy vote. I could press the issue, but I don't. I think about Martin Luther King Jr., and when Bibi comes back, I give the roommate chitchat thing another try.

"So who do you have the hots for?" I ask.

And she says, "Nobody really."

I'm not quite sure how it works for Jupitarians, since they can self-germinate. She seems asexual, never mentions boys.

I say, "What about Skippy? He wants you bad."

"Oh, him," she says, as though she hadn't noticed. She gets her shower caddy and heads down the hall. I stare at the door after she's gone.

Maybe she's bisexual. Maybe she's gay. I wonder if she masturbates when I'm out of the room. It seems like genderless people don't care about anyone but themselves. They might, but Bibi could give two shits about me.

By the time Thanksgiving rolls around, I'm getting pretty sick of my roommate. I mean how many times do you have to tell a person, "Put on your shoes," before she gets it right? There's snow on the ground, and she's prancing in it like some leprechaun. She walks around in her bare feet, leaving these monster frog prints. Did I mention Jupitarians only have three toes? It's like she needed to show them off. You'd think she at least would have tried to fit in. I think she liked being different. Everyone was always stopping by our room to see what the space alien was up to. I was happy to have a week at home without her.

But there was no place for her to go, and my mother offered our house, insisted, really, said, "Angela, if we were dead, I would hope someone would be nice enough to take you in for the holidays."

I guess she was right. Bibi couldn't very well go back to the moon. The least I could do was share my goddamn turkey with the girl. My turkey. My gravy. My family.

Bibi stayed in the guest room, and wouldn't you know it, she got along great with my mom. Better than me. The two of them bonded like bears.

My mother showed her how to cook cranberry sauce and corn bread from scratch and, of course, how to pull the guts out of a turkey. Bibi was fascinated, watched my mother tear the bird's insides out of its ass, leaving this hollow pink part in the middle. Bibi couldn't stop staring at it, until finally I said, "It's only a turkey. Gobble, gobble."

Bibi didn't answer, just looked at me like I'd threatened to cut off her head.

And my mother said, "Angela, why don't you help your father clean the garage?"

Things went on like this for days, my mother acting like Bibi's her new adopted daughter and treating me like chopped meat.

Then Thanksgiving Day, we sit down for dinner and, of course, my mother makes us hold hands. We do this every year, even though we're a family that doesn't go to church. Even though we're a family that doesn't pray. My mother insists we still believe in God.

She starts out as usual with, "Thank you, Lord, for the food before us." Then she goes off on this new part, says, "Thank you for bringing this space child into our lives. May our civilizations be as peaceful as those of the Pilgrims and Indians."

I want to say, "God, Mom, does everything have to be about Bibi?" Instead, I grab the nicest piece of turkey and dump gravy all over, a little extra in case Bibi helps herself to more than her fair share. But she doesn't. She takes some potatoes and squash, a little cranberry sauce and corn bread, really small portions. My father tries to pass her the turkey.

"Don't you like meat?" he asks.

My mother says, "Bill, maybe she's a vegetarian."

"No," Bibi says. "It's just that the turkey reminds me of my mother."

I want to ask Bibi what the hell she meant at dinner, but she goes to bed early and shuts the door. The next day my mother takes us to the mall. I'm thinking she feels bad about the turkey thing because she tells us to buy any outfit we want. But Bibi doesn't want clothes. She goes to the cooking store and buys a turkey baster. And now I'm really confused.

We go to the food court for lunch. We get Sbarro's, chow mein, and Arby's. My mom's sucking a slushie. She gives Bibi a sip, says, "Tell me about your mother."

Bibi says, "I never had a mother. No one does. She died before I was born."

It's been three months and this chick still hasn't explained the "no parents" situation. So I say, "What's the deal? No parents. No fathers. How exactly do you make babies?"

My mother gives me this look like I'm being rude.

"What?" I say. "You started it."

Bibi swallows the rest of her egg roll, asks, "You wanna see?"

"What? Here?" my mother says.

She lifts her shirt, and there's this hole where her belly button should be. It's the size of a nickel, but it scoops in and up like the inside of a funnel. She does this right in the middle of the food court. People turn and stare. My mother tells her to pull down her shirt.

"So it's like a vagina," I say.

"Except you put your own pollen up there, push it in deep instead of flushing it."

"What a relief," my mother says. "I thought you couldn't have children."

"I can," Bibi says. "But I won't. Anyone who has a baby ends up dead."

"Childbirth used to be risky here," my mother says. "Thank God for modern medicine."

"No," Bibi says. "Procreation is suicide. Babies can't come out the bottom. There's no hole. To get out, they gnaw through your stomach. They eat the other organs on their way out."

I sit there, shocked, my fries turning to mush on my tongue. "My God," I say. "Why would anyone want to get pregnant?"

"They say it's wonderful. Like being on heroin for nine months. The best euphoria there is."

"Christ Almighty," I say, "that's some mad kind of population control." I ask her if she's heard of the one-child law in China, but she doesn't answer.

"You're in good hands now," my mother says and gives her a hug, rocks her back and forth in her arms. Right there in the middle of the food court like she's five years old. I just sit and stare at my food. As though I could eat after that.

My mother drops us off at school on Sunday, tells Bibi if she needs anything to call. We carry our laundry upstairs. Under our folded clothes, we find notes from my mother on matching stationery taped to bags of Hershey's kisses. Mine says, "Loved having you home. So nice to spend time with you and Bibi."

"Your mom's really cool," Bibi says. She props her turkey baster and note up on her dresser.

"Yeah," I say. "I guess."

Now that she likes my mom, she wants to be friends with me. Go figure.

I curl up on my futon with a piece of leftover corn bread. "So did you ever think of doing it?" I ask. "Just to see what pregnancy's like? Don't you think you will eventually?"

"Why would I do that?" she says.

"Don't you think you're missing out? You said it's like drugs. I'd try that."

"I don't want to die," Bibi says. "That's why I'm here."

"How does your planet feel about stem cell research?" I ask.

"They don't understand why things should change."

"Yeah, it's kind of the same in America," I say. "Stem cell research is a sin. Better watch out. They might throw you out of the country."

She empties her chocolate kisses into the porcelain bowl my mother gave her.

"I think you'll do it," I say. "That's what the turkey baster's for, right? To stick the pollen all the way up?"

She just stares at me with her black eyes bugging out, and for a second I think she's going to throw the bowl at my head. Either that or she's going to cry. But she just turns and walks out of the room.

She didn't come back that night. I wasn't sure where she went. And frankly, I didn't care.

Bibi didn't speak to me for weeks. We gave each other the silent treatment and slammed the door a lot. I called my mother and told her I wanted to switch rooms. She said, "Angela, that's not how we deal with our problems."

I went to the RA and asked how long it would take to get a new room. She said I could file a complaint, but room changes were rarely approved.

It looked like Bibi and I were stuck with each other, at least for six more months. I started thinking I should muster up some sort of reconciliation. I thought about apologizing. Maybe she'd apologize for being such a bitch. I had a plan, was going to do it after my last class the Monday before finals. I swear I was going to.

But then I get back to my room, and Bibi's in bed with Skippy. He's straddling her stomach. His schlong's way up in her belly, shoved up there real good. He's riding her like a madman, and Bibi's arching up so her belly keeps hitting his balls.

I slammed the door behind me and slept in the lounge.

Who did she think she was having sex with a human boy, and one from our floor? It's not that I liked him. He was too pimply for me. But she'd been lying to me all semester, pretending she didn't understand my crushes, and now this. She loses her virginity to Skippy. She loses her virginity before me. I couldn't believe a Jupitarian had beaten me to it.

Still, I figured I'd be the bigger person. I figured we should talk. The next day, I get back from ballet, and she's sitting at her desk reading chemistry, taking pages of notes, pretending like nothing happened. So I sit on my futon and sigh this huge sigh, hoping she'll get the gist we need to talk. And when that doesn't work, I say, "If you're going to be one of those kinds of girls, we need a system."

She says, "Skippy told me to put a bra on the door. I don't have any. Is that what you mean?"

"Yeah, that's what I mean," I say. And then, "So what's the big idea? I thought you were genderless. Were you lying about the self-germination?"

"I can't get pregnant the human way. It's got to be my own pollen. You're not even the right species."

"A girl who can't get pregnant," I say. "The boys are going to love that."

She shrugs. She doesn't even care that she just lost her cherry. It doesn't even faze her.

"So did you orgasm all over good ole Skippy?" I ask. "Was he good? Can Jupitarians even get off?"

"You're so stupid," she says. "Would a species survive if they couldn't orgasm?"

"Screw you," I say. I grab my towel and shower caddy and slam the door behind me. Emily, our next-door neighbor, is just leaving for class.

"God," I say, "that Bibi is such a whore. I wish she'd warn me before she fucks guys in the room."

Emily says, "Really? Bibi? I didn't know she could. We were wondering about that."

"Yeah," I say. "She's a little bitch."

"Didn't she go to your house?" Emily says. "I thought you were friends."

"Not anymore."

I pound down the hall as hard as I can, though flip-flops don't make much noise. I slam the bathroom door to let the whole floor know Bibi's a skank. I let the hot water wash over my back. "Slut," I say under my breath. And then a little louder, "At least I'm not a slut like you are." I say it as though I'm talking to someone in the opposite shower stall. "You're such a slut," I say again and imagine Bibi across from me. I say it once more, almost shout it, "You're the biggest slut in the galaxy, and I wish you'd go back to the moon!"

I'm not sure if it was Skippy who spread the word or Emily. It might even have been me, proclaiming loudly from the shower stall that day. Whoever it was, my bra ended up on the door an awful lot the next month. I left a note on her desk that said, "Stay the hell away from my underwear drawer."

Bibi did a different guy nearly every day. I saw one of those little black books on her desk. She had all the boys on the hall penciled in. There were even some names I didn't know. She really *had* turned into a whore. I wondered if they paid her or if she did it for free. I missed the old Bibi. The Bibi who forgot her shoes. The Bibi who studied all night. The Bibi who didn't know jack shit about boys.

We didn't talk anymore. We just came and went as though we didn't know each other. I moved my futon into Emily's room and slept there most of the time. I wondered what would become of Bibi. I figured her grades would plummet, and she'd get kicked out of school. But when I got back from Christmas break, her marks were posted to the wall, nine A's. She'd completed a whole year of college in four months.

I'm not sure how she kept it up, the sex and the studies. Her second semester she upped her course load to ten. They even let her into a graduate class. Like I said, if you're not from America, they let you get away with that shit.

Then around February she starts looking greener. I wonder if she has that seasonal depression thing. Then one day, I get back to my room, and Bibi's jumping all over her bed. She's got the music cranked as high as it goes, some god-awful Broadway crap, and she's singing, "I feel pretty. Oh so pretty." And she's wearing this outfit that's half her clothes and half mine with my sparkly panties around her head.

"What the hell's going on?" I say. "I thought I told you not to touch my stuff."

She jumps off her bed and dances this little jig. She looks so goddamn ridiculous I have to laugh.

"Did you find some solution to Jupiter's baby problem?" I ask. "Is your research going well?"

"No," she says. "I'm pregnant."

"You're not," I say. "I thought you couldn't."

"Well, it's not like I had proof it was impossible," she says. "I guess it is. I'm pregnant with a half-human baby." At this, she bursts out laughing. Pollen puffs out her ears in yellow clouds.

"Who?" I say. "Whose baby is it?"

"A boy's," she says. "A human boy's." And then she's surrounded by pollen again. She swirls it around with her hands. "Can you believe that?"

"Are you going to keep it?" I say. "If you give birth, it'll kill you, right?"

"I'm giving birth to the first half-human, half-Jupitarian baby ever!" she screams. She rips the panties off her head and twirls them in the air.

"Can't you get an abortion? Those are common here. They'll get rid of it. You'll be fine."

"I don't want an abortion," she says. "I want to be eaten alive."

I didn't know what to say. She'd turned ten types of crazy. It must have been that euphoria she told me about. I began to wish I had a normal human roommate I could take to the abortion clinic so things would be better. I'd never had a friend with a life-threatening illness. Only grandfathers and uncles. And they died. There was nothing I could do. Bibi had lost it. Her condition was terminal, and she didn't even care.

In the weeks that followed, Bibi stopped seeing the boys. I moved my futon back into our room, and we started talking again. I became Bibi's bodyguard, shielding her from all the male scum on the floor. Boys would stop by and say, "I'm here for some alien sex."

I'd say, "Fuck off, asshole." And they'd go away.

By March, Bibi had given up her studies. No more stem cell research. Instead, she starts holing herself up in our room making sculptures out of dining hall silverware. She hangs them from the ceiling where the ants used to be and opens the windows to watch the dead flowers blow in the breeze.

We start having parties in our room every weekend. Everyone brings beer and fills up our fridge. The RA doesn't give a damn because Bibi got her through chemistry first semester, and she hopes she'll get her through physics next fall.

I call my mother and tell her we're getting along great. I tell her Bibi is the best. My mother's glad we're back to being friends, says she knew we'd work it out. I don't mention that Bibi is pregnant. My mother would be disappointed. She wouldn't understand.

Finally, Bibi and I do everything together like roommates should. We order pizza at midnight, rate the guys on the hall, redecorate the room. We move the beds against one wall and scatter huge pillows on the floor. Bibi finds these red Christmas lights on sale at the hardware store and hangs them up. She turns them on and lies under her swaying spoons, pretends she's watching hot liquid hydrogen swirl around Jupiter from the moon. She says, "Angela, come lie with me. We can watch Jupiter together. Better enjoy me while you can. Pretty soon, this baby will eat its way out."

"Don't talk like that," I say.

"Like what?" She dangles her three-toed feet in the air, says, "It's okay. It's only death."

By April she's really showing. She's got this great green hump of a belly, draws faces on it with finger paint and calls it Skippy Junior. Every day she plans something different. She says, "Let's take Skippy Junior to the zoo. Let's take Skippy Junior ice skating. Let's take Skippy Junior for parachute lessons."

I say, "Bibi, I've got classes."

She says, "I'm going to be dead in a few months. You can study then."

So we go ice skating and snorkeling and rent lots of porno and drink slushies. Bibi does this thing with her turkey baster, fills it up with slushie and lets it volcano into her mouth. Half goes in. Half gets all over, which makes the ants come back. But this is kind of great, just like before when we hated each other and Skippy was a stalker. Back when Bibi studied all the time and didn't care about parties or drinking or boys.

The new Bibi is completely different. She dances all over the room, begs me to go with her to clubs, says, "You gotta teach me that booty bounce thing." She puts on a sparkly shirt and lipstick, a short skirt and heels. She tapes a paper bow tie to her stomach and says, "Skippy Junior's ready."

So that's what we do. We go to the only dance club in town, Freaky Willy's. And I teach her to dance the American way. I show her how to grind like a skanky ho.

We run into Skippy at the club. He's there with some guys. His acne looks a bit better. He buys us both drinks, Coronas all around. You've got to give him credit. At least he got us good beer. Then he wants to dance with Bibi. He seems genuine enough. Anyhow, there's no way he can get sex with her funnel closed up. One of those really bouncy songs comes on with the flashing lights, and Bibi drags Skippy to the dance floor and rocks it out.

I sit at the bar and watch. She's picked up the booty bounce, no problem. She looks kind of sexy gyrating her tiny hips, her shoulders bopping with the music. In this light, she doesn't even look green. Skippy puts his hand on her back and tries to shake his pelvis too. But you can tell he's not the dancing type.

Later, he walks us home, and Bibi invites him in. I go to Emily's room until he leaves.

When he's gone, I ask, "So does he want you back? Is it his baby?"

"It's nobody's baby," she says. "On Jupiter, no one belongs to anyone else."

That was the last time I saw Bibi. When I woke up, she was gone. There was a note on my desk that said, "Thanks for teaching me to dance. Thanks for sharing your family." Most of her stuff was still there. I assume she went back to Jupiter, but who's to be sure. I don't like to think of other possibilities.

After that, there were lots of policemen and school officials who wanted to know where Bibi went. I told them I didn't know. Word got out to the papers. Skippy came by our room and put a bouquet of weedy flowers by the door.

He said, "I really loved her. I don't know why she had sex with all those other guys."

"I know," I said. "I'm sure it was your baby."

I invited him in. We sat on Bibi's bed real close, and it felt better, that warmth, being next to someone who understood. We stayed like that for hours, shoulder to shoulder, not even talking. When it got dark, we slid under the covers. I was wearing those sparkly panties, the ones Bibi tossed on the floor that first night, the ones that were Jupiter. Skippy slid his hand down the front, brushed his fingers against what I imagined to be Bibi's moon. I didn't even mind when he aimed his boner at my belly button. I guided it lower, and he found the right hole.

"What if she comes back?" he asked.

"She's gone," I said, and kissed him hard.

He moved his hips back and forth and buried his head in my neck. My eyes locked on the turkey baster on Bibi's dresser, and I tried to imagine that she had never been here. That she had never existed. That I had gotten here on my own.

· ELIOT WROTE ·
Nancy Kress

"Not only is the universe stranger than we imagine, it is stranger than we can imagine."

—J.B.S. Haldane

Eliot wrote: *Picture your brain as a room. The major functions are like furniture. Each in its own place, and you can move from sofa to chair to ottoman, or even lie across more than one piece of furniture at the same time. Memory is like air in the room, dispersed everywhere. Musical ability is a specific accessory, like a vase on the mantle. Anger is a Doberman pinscher halfway out of the door from the kitchen. Algebra just fell down the heat duct. Love of your sibling is a water spill that evaporated three weeks ago.*

Well, maybe not accurate, Eliot thought, and hit DELETE. Or maybe too accurate for his asshole English class. What kind of writing assignment was "Explain something important using an extended metaphor?"

He closed his school tablet and paced around the room. Cold, cheerless, bereft—or was that his own fault? Partly his own fault, he admitted; Eliot prided himself on self-honesty. He could turn up the heat, pick up the pizza boxes, open the curtains to the May sunshine. He did none of these things. Cold and cheerless matched bereft, and there was nothing to do about bereft. Well, one thing. He went to the fireplace (cold ashes, months old) and from the mantel plucked the ceramic pig and threw it as hard as he could onto the stone hearth. It shattered into pink shards.

Then he left the apartment and caught the bus to the hospital.

Eliot's father had been entered into Ononeida Psychiatric Hospital ten days ago, for a religious conversion in which he saw the clear image of Zeus on a strawberry toaster pastry.

Ononeida, named for an Indian tribe that had once occupied Marthorn City, was accustomed to religious visions, and Carl Tremling was a mathematician, a group known for being eccentric. Ordinarily the hospital would not have admitted him at all. But Dr. Tremling had reacted to the toaster pastry with some violence, flinging furniture out of the apartment window and sobbing that there was dice being played with the universe after all, and that the center would not hold. A flung end-table, imitation Queen Anne, had hit the mailman, who was not seriously injured but was considerably perturbed. Carl Tremling was deemed a danger to others and possibly himself.

A brain scan had failed to find temporal lobe epilepsy, the usual cause of religious visions. Dr. Tremling had continued to sob and to fling whatever furniture the orderlies were not quick enough to defend. Also, the psychiatrist on intake duty, who had recognized both the Einstein and Yeats quotes, was puzzled over the choice of Zeus as the toaster-pastry image. The usual thing was either Christ or the Virgin Mary.

The commitment papers had been signed by Dr. Tremling's sister, a sweet, dim, easily frightened woman who had never been comfortable with her brilliant brother but who was fond of Eliot. She was leaving the hospital as her nephew arrived.

"Eliot! Are you alone?"

"Yes, Aunt Sue." In Susan Tremling Fisher's mind, Eliot was perpetually nine instead of sixteen, and should not be riding buses alone. "How is he?"

"The same." She sighed. "Only they want to—he wants to—Eliot, are you eating enough? You look thinner."

"I'm fine."

"You shouldn't stay in that apartment alone. Anything could happen! Please come and stay with Uncle Ned and me, you know we'd love to have you and I hate to think of you alone in that big apartment without—"

If Eliot didn't stop her, she would start her Poor Motherless Lamb speech. "What does Dad want to do?"

"What?"

"You said 'They want to—he wants to'—so what do the doctors want to do?"

She sighed again. "I wish I had your memory, Eliot. You get it from poor Carl. That doctor with the mustache, he wants to try some new procedure on Carl."

"What new procedure?"

"I can't recall the name . . . " She fumbled in her purse as if the name might be among the tissues and supermarket coupons.

"Was it Selective Memory Obliteration Neural Re-Routing?"

"Yes! The very words! Your *memory*, Eliot, I swear, your mother would have been so proud of—"

Eliot grabbed her arm. "Are you going to let them operate? *Are you*?"

"Why, Eliot! You're hurting me!"

He let go. "I'm sorry. But—you are going to let them operate, aren't you?"

Aunt Sue looked at him. She had small eyes of no particular color, and a little mouth that was pursing and unpursing in distress. But she was a Tremling. Into those small eyes came stubbornness, an unthinking but resolute stubbornness and yet somehow murky, like a muddy pool over bedrock. She said gently, "I couldn't do that."

"*Aunt Sue—*"

"Carl will come to himself eventually, Eliot. He's had spells before, you know—why, just consider that time he shut himself up in my spare room for six days and wouldn't even come out to eat! I had to bring him meals on a tray!"

"He was working on his big breakthrough on the topography of knots!"

"Not only would he not eat, he wouldn't even wash. I had to air that room out for two days afterward, and in *February*. But Carl came out of that spell and he'll come out of this one, too. You just wait and see."

"It's not the same! Don't you understand, his whole mental construct has been turned upside down!"

"That's exactly what he said when he came out of my spare room with those knot numbers," she said triumphantly. "Knots! But even as a boy Carl took fits, why I remember when he was just eight years old and he found out that somebody named Girdle proved there were things you couldn't prove, why that doesn't even make common sense to—"

"Aunt Sue! You have to sign the papers allowing this operation!"

"No. I won't. Eliot, you listen to me. I went online last night and read about this Memory Obligation Whatever. It's new and it's dangerous because the doctors don't really know what they're doing yet. In one case, after the operation a woman didn't even remember who she was, or recognize her own children, or anything! In another case, a man could no longer read and—get this!—he couldn't relearn how to do it, either! Something had just gone missing in his brain as a result of the operation. Imagine Carl unable to read! We can't risk—"

Eliot was no longer listening. He'd known Aunt Sue all his life; she wasn't going to budge. He barreled down the hall and rattled the door to the ward, which was of course locked. An orderly wielding a mop peered at him through the reinforced glass and pantomimed pressing the call button.

"Yes?" said the disembodied voice of a nurse. Eliot recognized it.

"Mary, I want to see Dr. Tallman!"

"Oh, Eliot, I'm glad you came just now, your father is quiet and—"

"I don't want to see my father! I want to see Dr. Tallman!"

"He's not here, dear. I'll just buzz you in."

Mary came out of the nurse's station to meet him. Middle-aged, kind, motherly, she radiated the kind of brisk competence that Eliot admired, and had seen so little of in his own disordered household. Or at least he would have admired it if it weren't for the motherliness. She saw him not as the intellectual he knew himself to be, but rather as the skinny, short, floppy-haired kid he seemed to be. He was smarter than Mary, smarter than Aunt Sue, smarter than most of the world, so why the hell couldn't the world notice that?

"I want to see Dr. Tallman!"

"He's not on the ward, dear."

"Call him!"

"I'm afraid I can't do that. Eliot, you seem upset."

"I *am* upset! Isn't my father going to have SMON-R? Because my aunt wouldn't sign the papers?"

Motherliness gave way to professionalism. "You know I can't discuss this with you."

No one would discuss anything with Eliot. He didn't count. The rational world didn't count, not in here. Eliot glared at Mary, who gazed calmly back. He said, "I'll sign them! I will!"

"You're underage, Eliot. And your father is non compos mentis. Did you come to visit? He's in the day room. But if you're going to upset him, it might be better if you chose another time to visit."

Eliot bolted past her and ran into the day room.

His father was not flinging furniture. He slumped inert in a chair, staring at the TV, which showed a rerun of *Jeopardy*. Eliot groaned. His father had published papers in scientific journals, developed algorithms for high-resolution space imagery, had a promising lead on actually solving the Riemann Hypothesis. He did not watch *Jeopardy*. This was the anti-psychotic drugs, not the real Carl Tremling. Everything the hospital was doing was just making the situation worse.

"Hey, Dad."

"Hey, Eliot."

Alex Trebek said, "The tendency of an object in motion to remain in motion, or an object at rest to remain at rest, unless acted upon by an outside force."

"How are you doing?"

"Just fine." But he frowned. "Only I can't quite . . . there was something . . . "

Something. There were a lot of somethings. There was rational thought, and logical progressions, and the need to restore a man's proper intellect.

Someone on the TV said, "What is 'inertia'?"

"Zeus," Dr. Tremling brought out triumphantly. "Who would have believed—" All at once his face sagged from underneath, like a pie crust cooling. "Who would have believed . . . " His face crumpled and he clutched Eliot's sleeve. "It's real, Eliot! It's loose in the world and nothing that I thought was true—"

"It was a *toaster pastry*, Dad!"

Three patients slowly swiveled their heads at Eliot's raised voice. He lowered it. "Listen to me. Please listen to me. The doctors want to do a procedure on you called Selective Memory Obliteration Neural Re-Routing. It will remove the memory of the . . . the incident from your mind. Only Aunt Sue—"

"Where's the pig?" Dr. Tremling said.

Eliot rocked back and forth with frustration. "Even if Aunt Sue won't sign the papers, if you can seem reasonably lucid—in compos mentis—then—"

"I asked you to bring the pig!"

"It's broken!"

Dr. Tremling stared at Eliot. Then he threw back his head and howled at the ceiling. Two orderlies, a nurse, and four patients sprang to attention. Dr. Tremling rose, overcoming the inertia of his drugs, and picked up his chair. His face was a mask of grief. "It isn't true. Nothing I believed is true! The universe—Zeus—dice—"

Eliot shouted, "It was just a fucking toaster pastry!"

"I needed that pig!" He flung the chair at the wall. Orderlies rushed forward.

Nurse Mary grabbed Eliot and hustled him out of the room. "I told you not to upset him!"

"I didn't upset him, *you* did, by not giving him what he needs! Do you know how finely balanced a mathematician's brain is, how prone to obsessions already, and it needs to be clear to—you're refusing to remove a tumor from his brain!"

"Your father does not have a brain tumor, and you need to leave now," Mary said, hustling him down the hallway.

A male voice said, "I'll take scientific terms for 400, Alex."

"It's his brain!" Eliot shouted. He meant: *My brain*, and he knew it, and the knowledge made him even angrier.

Mary got him to the door of the ward, keyed in a code to unlock it, and waved him through. As he stalked off, she called after him, "Eliot? Dear? Do you have enough money for the bus home?"

Eliot's parents had met at college, where both studied mathematics. Even though Eliot's mother was not beautiful, there were few girls in the graduate math program, and she was sought after by every mathematician with enough social skills to approach her, including two of the professors. Her own social skills lacked coherence, but something in Carl Tremling appealed to her. She emailed her bewildered mother, "There is a boy here I think I like. He's interested in nothing but algorithms and pigs." Carl, who had grown up in farm country, had a theory that pigs were much smarter than other animals and deserved respect.

Fuming on the bus, Eliot wondered why his father had wanted the ceramic pig. Did he have a premonition that in its artificial pink wrinkles he might see

Hermes, god of mathematics? Aphrodite? His dead wife? How could his mind have so betrayed Carl Tremling? Eliot wanted his father back, and in his own mind.

Eliot's mind was so much like his father's. Everybody said so.

"Fuck," he said aloud, which caused a man to glare at him across the bus aisle and a woman to change her seat. Embarrassed, Eliot pulled out his school tablet.

Memory, he wrote, *is a bridge between what you are today and what you were for all the days before that. All your life you go back and forth across that bridge, extending and reinforcing it. You add a new strut. You hang flower pots on the railing. You lay down kitty litter during icy weather. You chase away the kids who are smoking pot on top of the pilings and under the roadway. Then one day, a section of the bridge gives way. When that happens, it is criminal to not repair it. An unrepaired bridge is like a deep pothole on a dark road and—*

Two metaphors. This was not working. And it was due Tuesday.

The man across the aisle was still watching him. Probably thought that Eliot was some sort of gang-affiliated punk. Well, no, not that, not with his build and clothing. A crazy, then. The man thought Eliot might be a gun-toting, cheerleader-loathing shooter who would court death to kill everybody on the bus, perhaps because school shooting was now such a risk, what with all the metal detectors and guards and lock-down protocols.

I am not a shooter, Eliot silently told the man. He was a rationalist and an intellectual, and he just wanted his father back, whole, the way he had been before.

He got off the bus at his Aunt Sue's building.

The building was depressing because it was so smug. It looked as if nothing bad could ever happen here as long as the stoop was swept clean and the curtains were a bright color and the flower boxes were watered. Nothing bad! Wanna bet? Inside, his aunt's apartment was even worse. Her decorating style was country-mystic, with wreaths of dried flowers and tapestries of unicorns and small ceramic plaques that said things like "LET A SMILE BE YOUR UMBRELLA."

"Aunt Sue, I have to tell you things I didn't get a chance to say at the hospital. Please listen to me."

"Of course, Eliot. Don't I always?"

Almost never. But he composed himself and arranged his arguments. "I was online last night, too. Those two cases you mentioned, the man who couldn't read again and the woman who didn't recognize her kids, were anomalies. Selective Memory Obliteration Neural Re-Routing is new, yes, but it passed clinical trials and FDA approval and it has an eighty-nine percent success rate, with a one percent confidence level. Of the remaining eleven percent, two-thirds were neither better nor worse after the operation. That leaves only three-point-eight percent and when you take into account those with only minor—"

"No."

"You're not listening!"

"I *am* listening. Nobody is going to cut into Carl's brain."

"But he believes he saw a defunct Greek god in a toaster pastry!"

"Eliot, is that so bad?"

"It's not true!"

"Well, it's true that Carl *saw* it, anyway, or he wouldn't be so upset. He'll come out of whatever spell he's having about it, he always does. And anyway, I don't understand Carl's reaction. Would it be so bad to believe this Zeus-god is around?"

"That's the part that's not true!"

She shrugged. "Are you so sure you know what's true?"

"Yes!" Eliot shouted. "Mathematics is true! Physics is true! Memory can play us false, there's a ton of research on that, nobody can be sure if their memories are accurate—" He stopped, no longer sure what he was saying.

Aunt Sue said calmly, "Well, if memory is playing Carl false, then he's all the more likely to get over it, isn't he?"

"No! It isn't—I didn't mean—"

"Wouldn't you like some walnut cake, Eliot? I baked it fresh this morning."

Hopeless. They came from two different planets. And she—this kind, stupid woman who inexplicably shared one-quarter of his genes—held the power. In a truly rational world, that couldn't have been true.

"Cream-cheese icing," she said brightly, and caressed his cheek.

Eliot wrote: *Memory is like a corn stalk. Corn blight can wreck any entire economy, starve an entire nation, but it responds to science. Find the bad gene, cut it out, replace it with a genetically engineered Bt gene that fights blight because it allows the use of strong pesticides and voila! Memory functions again! Science triumphs!*

Possibly the worst writing he had ever done. He hit DELETE.

His father's liquor cabinet still held three inches of Scotch. Eliot poured himself two fingers' worth, so he could sleep.

The next morning, just as he was leaving to catch the bus for school, the hospital called.

"The answer," his father said, "is obvious."

It wasn't obvious to Eliot. His father sat in the day room, out of his bathrobe and dressed in his ordinary baggy khakis and badly-pilled sweater.

Dr. Tremling had shaved. He looked just as he once did, and Eliot would have felt hopeful if he hadn't felt so bewildered, or if the new twitch at the corner of his father's left eye wasn't beating madly and irregularly as a malfunctioning metronome.

"I did see what I thought I saw," his father said carefully. "I *know* so, in a way that, although it defies explanation, is so incontrovertible that—"

"Dad," Eliot said, equally carefully—if only that twitch would stop! "You can't actually 'know' that for certain. Surely you're aware that all our minds can play tricks on us that—"

"Not this time," Dr. Tremling said simply. "I saw it. And I know it was true, not just an aberration of pastry. I know, too, that mathematics, the whole rational underpinning of the universe, is also true. The dichotomy was . . . upsetting me."

Upsetting him. Eliot glanced around at the mental hospital, the orderlies watchful in the corners of the room, the barred window. His father had always had a gift for understatement, which was in part what had made this whole thing so . . . so upsetting.

"What I failed to see," Dr. Tremling said, "was that this is a gift. I have just been handed my life's work."

"I thought the topography of knots was your life's work?"

"It was, yes. But now my life's work is to find the rational and mathematical underpinnings for this new phenomenon."

"For Zeus? In a toaster pastry?"

The twitch beat faster, even more irregularly. "I concede that it is a big job."

"Dad—"

"There must be a larger consciousness, Eliot. If so, it is a physical entity, made up of energy and matter, *must* be a physical entity. And a physical entity can be described mathematically, possibly through a system that does not yet exist, possibly based on non-local quantum physics."

Eliot managed to say, "You aren't a quantum physicist."

"I can learn." Twitch *twitch* TWITCH. "Do you remember what Werner Heisenberg said about belief systems? 'What we observe is not nature itself, but nature exposed to our method of questioning.' I need a new method of questioning to lead toward a new mathematics."

"Well, that's a—"

"They're letting me have my laptop back, with controlled wifi access, until I go home."

"Have they said when that might be?"

"Possibly in a few more weeks."

Dr. Tremling beamed, twitching. Eliot tried to beam, too. He was getting what he'd wanted—his father back home, working on mathematics. Only—"a new mathematics"? His father was not Godel or Einstein or Heisenberg. He wasn't even an endowed chair.

Eliot burst out, before he knew he was going to say anything, "There's no evidence for any larger consciousness! It's mystical wish-fulfillment, a non-rational delusion! There's just no evidence!"

"I'm the evidence. Son, I don't think I actually told you what I experienced." He leaned closer; involuntarily Eliot leaned back. "It *was* Zeus, but it was also Odin, was Christ, was . . . oh, let me think . . . was Isis and Sedna and Bumba and Quetzalcoatl. It was all of them and none of them because the images were in my mind. Of course they were, where else could they possibly be? But here's the thing—the images are unimportant. They're just metaphors, and not very good ones—arrows pointing to something that has neither image nor words, but just *is*. That thing is—how can I explain this?—the world behind the world. Didn't you ever feel in childhood that all at once you sort of glimpsed a flash of a great mystery underlying everything, a bright meaning to it all? I know you did because everybody does. Then we grow up and lose that. But it's still there, bright and shining as solid as . . . as an end table, or a pig. I saw it and now I know it exists in a way that goes beyond any need to question its existence—the way I know, for instance, that prime numbers are infinite. It's the world beyond the world, the space filled with shining light, the mystery. Do you see?"

"No!"

"Well, that's because you didn't experience it. But if I can find the right mathematics, that's a better arrow than verbal metaphors can ever be."

Eliot saw in his father's eyes the gleam of fanaticism. "Dad!" he cried, in pure anguish, but Dr. Tremling only put his hand on Eliot's knee, a startlingly rare gesture of affection, and said, "Wait, son. Just wait."

Eliot couldn't wait. His English assignment was due by third period, which began, with the logic of high school scheduling, at 10:34 a.m. No late assignments were accepted. His tablet on his knees on the crowded bus, Eliot wrote: *Memory is not a room or a bridge or a corn stalk with blight. Memory is not a metaphor because nothing is a metaphor. Metaphors are constructions of a fanciful imagination, not reality. In reality everything is what it is, and that is—or certainly should be!—enough for anybody!*

The little boy sitting next to him said, "Hey, man, you hit that thing so hard, you gonna break it."

"Shut up," Eliot said.

"Get fucked," the kid answered.

But Eliot already was.

• • •

Dr. Tremling came home three weeks later. He was required to see a therapist three times a week. Aunt Sue bustled over, cooked for two days straight, and stocked the freezer with meals. When Eliot and his father sat down to eat, Dr. Tremling's eye twitched convulsively. Meals were the only time they met. His father chewed absently and spoke little, but then, that had always been true. The rest of the time he stayed in his study, working. Eliot did not ask on what. He didn't want to know.

Everything felt suspended. Eliot went to school, took his AP classes, expressed scorn for the jocks and goths who teased him, felt superior to his teachers, read obsessively—all normal. And yet not. One day, when his father was at a therapy session, Eliot slid into Dr. Tremling's study and looked at his notebooks and, to the extent he could find them amid such sloppy electronic housekeeping, his computer files. There didn't seem to be much notation, and what there was, Eliot couldn't follow. He wasn't a mathematician, after all. And his father appeared to have invented a new symbol for something, a sort of Olympic thunderbolt that seemed to have left- and right-handed versions. Eliot groaned and closed the file.

Only once did Eliot ask, "So how's it going, Dad?"

"It's difficult," Dr. Tremling said.

No shit. "Have you had any more . . . uh . . . incidents?"

"That's irrelevant, son. I only needed one." But his face twitched harder than ever.

Three weeks after he came home, Dr. Tremling gave up. He hadn't slept for a few nights and his face sagged like a bloodhound's. But he was calm when he said to Eliot, "I'm going to have the operation."

"You are?" Eliot's heart leapt and then, inexplicably, sank. "Why? When?"

His father answered with something of his old precision. "Because there is no mathematics of a larger conscious entity. On Tuesday at eight in the morning. Dr. Tallman certified me able to sign my own papers."

"Oh." For a long terrible moment Eliot thought he had nothing more to say. But then he managed, "I'm sorry about the pig."

"It's not important," Dr. Tremling said, which should have been the first clue.

On Tuesday Eliot rose at 5:00 a.m., and took a cab to the hospital. He sat with his father in Pre-Op, in a vibrantly and mistakenly orange waiting room during the operation, and beside his father's bed in Post-Op. Dr. Tremling recovered well and came home a week later. He was quiet, subdued. When the new term started, he resumed teaching at the university. He read the professional journals, weeded the garden, fended off his sister. Nobody mentioned the incident, and Dr. Tremling never did, either, since hospital tests had verified that it was gone from his memory. Everything back to normal.

But not really. Something had gone missing, Eliot thought—some part of his father that, though inarticulate, had made his eyes shine at a breakthrough in mathematics. That had made him love pigs. That had led him, in passion, to fling bad student problem sets and blockhead professional papers across the room, as later he would fling furniture. Something was definitely missing.

"Isn't it wonderful that Carl is exactly the way he used to be?" enthused Aunt Sue. "Modern medicine is just amazing!"

Eliot didn't answer her. On the way home from school, he got off the bus one stop early. He ducked into the Safeway as if planning to rob it, carrying out his purchase more secretively than he'd ever carried out the Trojans he never got to use. In his room, he locked the door, opened the grocery boxes, and spread out their contents on the bed.

On the dresser.

On the desk, beside his calculus homework.

On the computer keyboard.

When there were no other surfaces left, on the not-very-clean carpet.

Then, hoping, he stared at the toaster pastries until his head ached and his eyes crossed from strain.

Eliot wrote, "Metaphor is all we have." But the assignment had been due weeks ago, and his teacher refused to alter his grade.

• SCALES •
Alastair Reynolds

The enemy must die.

Nico stands and waits in the long line, sweating under the electric-yellow dome of the municipal force field.

They must die.

Near the recruiting station, one of the captives has been wheeled out in a cage. The reptile is splayed in a harness, stretched like a frog on the dissection table. A steady stream of soldiers-in-waiting leaves the line, jabbing an electro-prod through the bars of the cage to a chorus of jeers. It's about the size of a man, and surprisingly androform except for its crested lizard head, its stubby tail and the brilliant green shimmer of its scales. Already they're flaking off, black and charred, where the prod touches. The reptile was squealing to start with, but it's slumped and unresponsive now.

Nico turns his head away. He just wants the line to move ahead so he can sign up, obtain his citzenship credits and get out of here.

The enemy must die.

They came in from interstellar darkness, unprovoked, unleashing systematic destruction on unsuspecting human assets. They wiped mankind off Mars and blasted Earth's lunar settlements into radioactive craters. They pushed the human explorers back into a huddle of defenses around Earth. Now they've brought the war to cities and towns, to the civilian masses. Now force shields blister Earth's surface, sustained by fusion plants sunk deep into the crust. Nico's almost forgotten what it's like to look up at the stars.

But the tide is turning. Beneath the domes, factories assemble the ships and weapons to take the war back to the reptiles. Chinks are opening in the enemy's armour. All that's needed now are men and women to do Earth's bidding.

One of the recruiting sergeants walks the line, handing out iced water and candies. He stops and chats to the soldiers-to-be, shaking them by the hand, patting them on the back. He's a thirty-mission veteran; been twice as far out as the orbit of the moon. He lost an arm, but the new one's growing back nicely, budding out from the stump like a baby's trying to punch its way out of him. They'll look after you too, he says, holding out a bottle of water.

"What's the catch?" Nico asks.

"There isn't one," the sergeant says. "We give you citizenship and enough toys to take apart a planet. Then you go out there and kill as many of those scaly green bastards as you can."

"Sounds good to me," Nico says.

Up in the fortified holdfast of Sentinel Station, something's different. The tech isn't like the equipment Nico saw at the recruiting station, or in basic training back on Earth. It's heavier, nastier, capable of doing more damage. Which would be reassuring, if it wasn't for one troubling fact.

Earth has better ships, guns and armour than anyone down there has heard about—but then so do the reptiles.

Turns out they're not exactly reptiles either. Not that Nico cares much. Cold-blooded or not, they still attacked without provocation.

The six months of in-orbit training at Sentinel Station are tough. Half the kids fall by the wayside. Nico's come through, maybe not top of his class, but somewhere near it. He can handle the power-armour, the tactical weapons. He's ready to be shown to his ship.

It's not quite what he was expecting.

It's a long, sleek, skull-grey shark of a machine that goes faster-than-light.

"Top secret, of course," says the instructor. "We've been using it for interstellar intelligence gathering and resource-acquistion."

"How long have we had this?"

The instructor grins. "Before you were born."

"I thought we never had any ambitions beyond Mars," says Nico.

"What about it?"

"But the reptiles came in unprovoked, they said. If we were already out there . . . "

They haul him out after a couple of days in the coolbox. Any more of that kind of questioning and he'll be sent back home with most of his memories scrubbed.

So Nico decides it's not his problem. He's got his gun, he's got his armour and now he's got his ride. Who cares who started the damned thing?

The FTL transport snaps back into normal space around some other star, heading for a blue gas giant and an outpost that used to be a moon. The place bristles with long-range sensors and the belligerent spines of anti-ship railguns. Chokepoint will be Nico's home for the next year.

"Forget your armour certification, your weapons rating," says the new instructor, a human head sticking out of an upright black life-support cylinder. "Now it's time to get real."

A wall slides back to reveal a hall of headless corpses, rank on rank of them suspended in green preservative.

"You don't need bodies where you're going, you just need brains." she says. "You can collect your bodies on the way back home, when you've completed your tour. We'll look after them."

So they strip Nico down to little more than a head and a nervous system, and plug what's left into a tiny, hyper-agile fighter. The battle lines are being drawn far beyond conventional FTL now. The war against the reptiles will be won and lost in the N-dimensional tangle of interconnected wormhole pathways.

Wired into the fighter, Nico feels like a god with armageddon at his fingertips—not that he's really got fingertips. He doesn't feel much like Nico any more. He cracks a wry smile at Chokepoint's new arrivals, gawping at the bodies in the tanks. His old memories are still in there somewhere, but they're buried under a luminous welter of tactical programming.

Frankly, he doesn't miss them.

They're not fighting the reptiles any more. Turns out they were just the organic puppets of an implacable, machine-based intelligence. The puppet-masters are faster and smarter and their strategic ambitions aren't clear. But it doesn't concern thing-that-was-once-Nico.

After all, it's not like machines can't die.

Strategic Command sends him deeper. He's forwarded to an artificial construct actually embedded in the tangle, floating on a semi-stable node like a dark thrombosis. Nico's past caring where the station lies in relation to real space.

No one fully human can get this far—the station is staffed by bottled brains and brooding artificial intelligences. With a jolt, thing-that-was-once-Nico realises that he doesn't mind their company. At least they've got their priorities right.

At the station, thing-that-was-once-Nico learns that a new offensive has opened up against the puppetmasters, even further into the tangle. It's harder to reach, so again he must be remade. His living mind is swamped by tiny machines, who build a shining scaffold around the vulnerable architecture of his meat brain. The silvery spikes and struts mesh into a fighter no larger than a drum of oil.

He doesn't think much about his old body, back at Chokepoint, not any more.

The puppetmasters are just a decoy. Tactical analysis reveals them to be an intrusion into the wormhole tangle from what can only be described as an adjunct dimension. The focus of the military effort shifts again.

Now the organic matter at the core of thing-that-was-once-Nico's cybernetic mind is totally obsolete. He can't place the exact moment when he stopped thinking with meat and started thinking with machinery, and he's not even sure it matters now. As an organism, he was pinned like a squashed moth between two pages in the book of existence. As a machine, he can be endlessly abstracted, simulated unto the seventh simulation, encoded and pulsed across the reality-gap, ready to kill.

This he—or rather it—does.

And for a little while there is death and glory.

Up through the reality stack, level by level. By now it's not just machines versus machines. It's machines mapped into byzantine N-dimensional spaces, machines as ghosts of machines. The terms of engagement have become so abstract—so, frankly, higher-mathematical—that the conflict is more like a philosophical dialogue, a debate between protagonists who agree on almost everything except the most trifling, hair-splitting details.

And yet it must still be to the death—the proliferation of one self-replicating, pan-dimensional class of entities is still at the expense of the other.

When did it begin? Where did it begin? Why?

Such questions simply aren't relevant or even answerable anymore.

All that matters is that there is an adversary, and the adversary must be destroyed.

Eventually—although even the notion of time's passing is now distinctly moot—the war turns orthogonal. The reality stack is itself but one compacted laminate of something larger, so the warring entities traverse mind-wrenching chasms of meta-dimensional structure, their minds in constant, self-evolving flux as the bedrock of reality shifts and squirms beneath them.

And at last the shape of the enemy becomes clear.

The enemy is vast. The enemy is inexorably slow. As its peripheries are mapped, it gradually emerges that the enemy is a class of intellect that the machines barely have the tools to recognise, let alone understand.

It's organic.

It is multi-form and multi-variant. It hasn't been engineered or designed. It's messy and contingent, originating from the surface of a structure, a higher-mathematical object. It's but one of several drifting on geodesic trajectories through what might loosely be termed "space." Arcane fluids slosh around on the surface of this object, and the whole thing is gloved in a kind of gas. The enemy requires technology, not just to sustain itself, but to propagate its warlike ambitions.

Triumph over the organic is a cosmic destiny the machines have been pursuing now through countless instantiations. But to kill the enemy now, without probing deeper into its nature, would be both inefficient and unsubtle. It would waste machines that could be spared if the enemy's weaknesses were better understood. And what better way to probe those weaknesses than to create another kind of living thing, an army of puppet organisms, and send that army into battle? The puppets may not win, but they will force the adversary to stretch itself, to expose aspects of itself now hidden.

And so they are sent. Volunteers, technically—although the concept of "volunteer" implies a straightforward altruism difficult to correlate with the workings of the machines' multi-dimensional decision-making matrices. The flesh is grown in huge hangars full of glowing green vats, then shaped into organisms similar but not identical to the enemy. Into those vast, mindless bodies are decanted the thin, gruel-like remains of compactified machine intellects. It's not really anything the machines would recognise as intelligence, but it gets the job done.

Memories kindle briefly back to life as compactification processes shuffle through ancient data, untouched for subjective millenia, searching for anything that might offer a strategic advantage. Among the fleeting sensations, the flickering visions, one of the machines recalls standing in line under an electric-yellow sky, waiting for something. It hears the crackle of an electro-prod, smells the black char of burning tissue.

The machine hesitates for a moment, then deletes the memory. Its new green-scaled puppet body is ready, it has work to do.

The enemy must die.

ABOUT THE CONTRIBUTORS

Stephen Baxter was born in Liverpool, England. With a background in math and engineering, he is the author of over fifty novels and over a hundred published short stories. He has collaborated with Sir Arthur C. Clarke and is working on a new collaboration with Sir Terry Pratchett. Among his awards are BSFA awards, the Philip K. Dick Award, and Locus, Asimov, and Analog awards. His latest novel is *Stone Spring*, first of a new series.

Tobias S. Buckell is a Caribbean-born speculative fiction writer who grew up in Grenada, the British Virgin Islands, and the U.S. Virgin Islands. He has written four novels, including the *New York Times* bestseller *Halo: The Cole Protocol*. He currently lives in Ohio with a pair of dogs, a pair of cats, twin daughters, and his wife.

Orson Scott Card is the bestselling author of more than forty novels, including *Ender's Game*, which was a winner of both the Hugo and Nebula Awards. The sequel, *Speaker for the Dead*, also won both awards, making Card the only author to have captured science fiction's two most coveted prizes in consecutive years. His most recent books include another entry in the Enderverse, *Ender in Exile*, and the first of a new young adult series, *Pathfinder*. His latest book is *The Lost Gates*, the first volume of a new fantasy series.

Adam-Troy Castro's seventeen books include *Emissaries from the Dead* (winner of the Philip K. Dick award), and *The Third Claw of God*, both of which feature his profoundly damaged far-future murder investigator, Andrea Cort. His next books will be a series of middle-school novels about the adventures of a strange young boy called Gustav Gloom, the first of which will be *Gustav Gloom and the People Taker,* due out from Grossett and Dunlap in August 2012. His short fiction has been nominated for five Nebulas, two Hugos, and two Stokers. Adam-Troy, who describes the odd hyphen between his first and middle names as a typo from his college newspaper that was just annoying enough to embrace with gusto, lives in Miami with his wife Judi and a population of insane cats that includes Uma Furman and Meow Farrow.

Maggie Clark is an emerging Canadian writer with her toes in many literary waters. Alongside this first publication for science fiction, she's been published for poetry in *RATTLE*, *Pedestal Magazine*, *Ryga*, and *ditch*, while a novelette is forthcoming at Vagabondage Press. Her first play was given a reading at Canada's Magnetic North Theatre Festival, and among her current commissioned projects is a feature length film. Having devoured wide tracts of science fiction throughout her childhood, returning to the form as a mature writer feels a lot like coming home.

Tom Crosshill's fiction has appeared in magazines such as *Beneath Ceaseless Skies*, *Sybil's Garage* and *Flash Fiction Online*. In 2009, he won the Writers of the Future contest. Originally from Latvia, he writes in English and lives in New York, where he's a member of the writers' group *Altered Fluid*. In the past, he has operated a nuclear reactor, translated books and worked in a zinc mine, among other things. He's currently working on a post-Singularity YA novel featuring superpowers and giant robots. Visit him at tomcrosshill.com.

Since 1997, **Julie E. Czerneda** has turned her love and knowledge of biology into science fiction novels and short stories that have received international acclaim, multiple awards, and bestselling status. A popular speaker on scientific literacy and SF, in 2009 Julie was Guest of Honor for the national conventions of New Zealand and Australia, as well as Master of Ceremonies for Anticipation, the Montreal Worldcon. She's presently finishing her first fantasy novel, *A Turn of Light*, to be published by DAW in 2011. Most recently, Julie was a guest lecturer at the National Science Teachers convention in Philadelphia and participated in Laurentian's Social Science & SF conference. As for new projects, Julie is co-editing *Tesseracts 15: A Case of Quite Curious Tales* with Susan MacGregor and will be a juror for the 2011 Sunburst Awards. (No matter what, she'll be out canoeing, too.) For more about Julie's work, visit czerneda.com.

Tananarive Due is a winner of the American Book Award and a two-time finalist for the Bram Stoker Award. Her novels include the My Soul to Keep series, *The Between*, *The Good House*, and *Joplin's Ghost*. Her short fiction has been published in *The Magazine of Fantasy & Science Fiction*, and in anthologies such as *Dark Delicacies II*, *Voices from the Other Side*, *Dark Dreams*, *Dark Matter*, and *Mojo: Conjure Stories*. She is a frequent collaborator with SF writer Steven Barnes: they've produced film scripts, short stories, and three Tennyson Hardwick detective novels, the latest of which (written with actor Blair Underwood) is *From Cape Town With Love*. (They also collaborate in another way: they're married.)

Carol Emshwiller grew up in Michigan and in France. She lives in New York City in the winter and in Bishop, CA in the summer. She's been doing only short stories lately. A new one will appear in *Asimov's* soon. She's wondering if she's too old to start a novel but if a good idea came along she might do it anyway. PS Publishing is publishing two of her short story collections in a single volume (sort like an Ace Double), with her anti-war stories on one side and other stories on the other.

John R. Fultz (johnrfultz.wordpress.com) lives in the Bay Area, California, but is originally from Kentucky. His fiction has appeared in *Weird Tales, Black Gate*, and *Space & Time*, as well as the comic book anthologies *Zombie Tales* and *Cthulhu Tales*. His graphic novel of epic fantasy, *Primordia*, was published by Archaia Comics. John's literary heroes include Tanith Lee, Thomas Ligotti, Clark Ashton Smith, Lord Dunsany, William Gibson, Robert Silverberg, and Darrell Schweitzer (not to mention Howard, Poe, and Shakespeare). When not writing stories, novels, or comics, John teaches English Literature at the middle/high school level and plays a mean guitar. In a previous life he made his living as a wandering storyteller on the lost continent of Atlantis.

Eric Gregory lives in Raleigh, North Carolina, where he is working toward his MFA at North Carolina State University. His stories have appeared in *Strange Horizons, Interzone, Futurismic, Shine: An Anthology of Optimistic Science Fiction*, and other publications. Find more at ericmg.com.

Joe Haldeman writes for a living and teaches as an absorbing hobby. He has been a full-time writer since 1969, except for the occasional teaching and a short tenure as senior editor of *Astronomy Magazine*. He has taught writing at MIT every fall semester since 1983. Main hobbies are astronomy, bicycling, watercolor, and guitar. His latest books are *Marsbound* and *Starbound*. He's hard at work on the final book of the trilogy, *Earthbound*.

Vylar Kaftan writes speculative fiction of all genres, including science fiction, fantasy, horror, and slipstream. She's published stories in places such as *Clarkesworld, Realms of Fantasy*, and *Strange Horizons*. She lives with her husband Shannon in northern California and blogs at vylarkaftan.net.

James Patrick Kelly has written novels, short stories, essays, reviews, poetry, plays and planetarium shows. His most recent book is a collection of stories entitled *The Wreck of the Godspeed*. His short novel *Burn* won the Nebula Award in 2007. He has won the Hugo Award twice: In 1996, for his novelette "Think Like A Dinosaur," and in 2000, for his novelette, "Ten to the Sixteenth to One." His fiction has been translated into eighteen languages. With John Kessel he is co-editor of *The Secret History of Science Fiction, Feeling Very Strange: The Slipstream Anthology* and *Rewired: The Post Cyberpunk Anthology*. He writes a column on the internet for *Asimov's Science Fiction Magazine* and is on the faculty of the Stonecoast Creative Writing MFA Program at the University of Southern Maine and the Board of Directors of the Clarion Foundation. His website is jimkelly.net.

Caitlín R. Kiernan has published seven novels, most recently *The Red Tree*, which has been nominated for the World Fantasy and Shirley Jackson awards. Her short fiction has been collected into several volumes, including *Tales of Pain and Wonder; From Weird and Distant Shores; To Charles Fort, With Love; Alabaster; A is for Alien;* and *The Ammonite Violin & Others*. In Spring 2011, Subterranean Press will release *Two Worlds and In Between: The Best of Caitlín R. Kiernan (Volume One)*. She studied geology and paleontology at the University of Alabama and the University of Colorado, and has published in several scientific journals, including the *Journal of Vertebrate Paleontology*. She's currently working on her next novel. Kiernan lives in Providence, Rhode Island with her partner, Kathryn.

Alice Sola Kim currently lives in San Francisco but occasionally finds herself in St. Louis, where she is completing an MFA program at Washington University. Her short fiction has appeared in publications such as *Asimov's Science Fiction, Strange Horizons,* and *Lady Churchill's Rosebud Wristlet*.

Stephen King is the bestselling, award-winning author of innumerable classics, such as *The Shining, Carrie, Cujo,* and *The Dead Zone*—all of which have been adapted to film, as have many of King's other novels and stories. Other projects include editing *Best American Short Stories 2007*, writing a pop culture column for *Entertainment Weekly*, scripting for the Vertigo comic *American Vampire*, and a collaboration on a musical with rocker John Mellencamp called *Ghost Brothers of Darkland County*. His most recent books are the novels *Blockade Billy* and *Under the Dome*, a thousand-plus-page epic he has been working on for more than twenty-five years. His latest book is *Full Dark, No Stars*, a short fiction collection of four all-new, previously unpublished stories. Another recent collection, *Just After Sunset*, came out in 2008. Other recent short stories include a collaboration with his son, Joe Hill, called "Throttle," for the Richard Matheson tribute anthology *He Is Legend*, and "UR," a novella written exclusively for the Amazon Kindle. His other work includes classics such as *The Stand, The Dark Tower, Salem's Lot*, among others.

David Barr Kirtley has been described as "one of the newest and freshest voices in sf." His work frequently appears in *Realms of Fantasy*, and he has also sold fiction to the magazines *Weird Tales* and *Intergalactic Medicine Show*, the podcasts *Escape Pod* and *Pseudopod*, and the anthologies *New Voices in Science Fiction*, *The Dragon Done It*, and *Fantasy: The Best of the Year*. He's also appeared in several of John Joseph Adams's anthologies: *The Living Dead* and *The Living Dead 2*, and he has a story forthcoming in the anthology *The Way of the Wizard* that's due out in November. Kirtley is also the co-host (with John Joseph Adams) of the *Geek's Guide to the Galaxy* podcast.

Ted Kosmatka is the author of numerous short stories and novelettes. His work has appeared in *F&SF* and *Asimov's*, the anthology *Seeds of Change*, and has been reprinted in seven best-of-the-year anthologies, serialized over the radio, and translated into Hebrew, Russian, Polish, and Czech. He is a winner of the Asimov's Readers' Choice Award and has been a finalist for the Nebula Award and Theodore Sturgeon Memorial Award. His first novel, *The Helix Game*, is forthcoming from Del Rey. Ted worked for most of the last decade in laboratories in Indiana but now makes his home in the Pacific Northwest, where he writes science fiction video games for a living.

Nancy Kress is the author of twenty-six books: three fantasy novels, twelve SF novels, three thrillers, four collections of short stories, one YA novel, and three books on writing fiction. She is perhaps best known for the Sleepless trilogy that began with *Beggars in Spain*, which was based on the Nebula- and Hugo-winning novella of the same name. She won her second Hugo in 2009 in Montreal, for the novella "The Erdmann Nexus." Kress has also won three additional Nebulas, a Sturgeon, and the 2003 John W. Campbell Award (for her novel *Probability Space*). Her most recent books are a collection of short stories, *Nano Comes to Clifford Falls and Other Stories*; a bio-thriller, *Dogs*; and an SF novel, *Steal Across the Sky*. Kress's fiction, much of which concerns genetic engineering, has been translated into twenty languages. She often teaches writing at various venues around the country and blogs at nancykress.blogspot.com.

Geoffrey A. Landis is a physicist who works at the NASA John Glenn Research Center on developing advanced technologies for human and robotic space exploration. He is also a Hugo- and Nebula-award winning science fiction writer; the author of the novel *Mars Crossing*, the short-story collection *Impact Parameter and Other Quantum Realities*, and more than eighty short stories, which have appeared in places including *Analog*, *Asimov's*, *The Magazine of Fantasy & Science Fiction*, and numerous best-of-the-year volumes. Most recently, his poem "Searching" won the 2009 Rhysling award for best science-fiction poem, and his poetry collection *Iron Angels* appeared from Van Zeno. His most recent story, "Sultan of the Clouds," appears in the September 2010 issue of *Asimov's Science Fiction*.

Sarah Langan is the author of the novels *The Keeper* and *The Missing*, and her most recent novel, *Audrey's Door,* won the 2009 Stoker for best novel. Her short fiction has appeared in the magazines *Cemetery Dance*, *Phantom*, and *Chiaroscuro*, and in the anthologies *Darkness on the Edge* and *Unspeakable Horror*. She is currently working on a post-apocalyptic young adult series called *Kids* and two adult novels: *Empty Houses*, which was inspired by *The Twilight Zone*, and *My Father's Ghost*, which was inspired by *Hamlet*. Her work has been translated into ten languages and optioned by the Weinstein Company for film. It has also garnered three Bram Stoker Awards, an American Library Association Award, two Dark Scribe Awards, a *New York Times Book Review* editor's pick, and a *Publishers Weekly* favorite book of the year selection. She lives in Brooklyn with her husband, daughter, and rabbit.

Joe R. Lansdale is the author of over thirty novels and two hundred short pieces, fiction and non-fiction. He has received the Edgar Award, seven Bram Stokers, the British Fantasy Award, and many others. His novella, *Bubba Hotep*, was made into a movie of the same name.

Tanith Lee was born in 1947, didn't learn to read till nearly eight, and started to write aged nine—and she hasn't stopped since. In 1975, DAW Books published her epic fantasy *The Birthgrave* (soon due for re-release from Norilana) and so rescued Lee from lots of silly jobs at which she was extravagantly bad. Since then, she's written more than ninety novels and collections plus almost three hundred short stories. She lives on the S.E coast of England with her husband, writer/artist John Kaiine, in a house full of books and plants, under the firm claw of two cats.

Yoon Ha Lee's work has appeared in *The Magazine of Fantasy & Science Fiction, Clarkesworld, Fantasy Magazine, Ideomancer, Lady Churchill's Rosebud Wristlet, Farrago's Wainscot, Beneath Ceaseless Skies, Electric Velocipede,* and *Sybil's Garage*. She's also appeared in the anthologies *Twenty Epics, Japanese Dreams, In Lands That Never Were, The Way of the Wizard, Year's Best Fantasy 6,* and *Science Fiction: The Best of 2002*. Her poetry has appeared in such venues as *Jabberwocky, Strange Horizons, Star*Line, Mythic Delirium,* and *Goblin Fruit*. Learn more at pegasus.cityofveils.com.

Ursula K. Le Guin is the author of innumerable SF and fantasy classics, such as *The Left Hand of Darkness, The Lathe of Heaven, The Dispossessed,* and *A Wizard of Earthsea* (and the others in the Earthsea Cycle). She has been named a Grand Master by the Science Fiction Writers of America, and is the winner of five Hugos, six Nebulas, two World Fantasy Awards, and twenty

Locus Awards. She's also a winner of the Newbery Medal, The National Book Award, the PEN/Malamud Award, and was named a Living Legend by the Library of Congress.

Ken Liu (http://kenliu.name) was a programmer before he became a lawyer, and he thinks legal drafting can benefit from some software coding practices. His fiction has appeared/will appear in *The Magazine of Fantasy & Science Fiction, Asimov's, Strange Horizons, Science Fiction World*, the *Writers of the Future* anthology, *The Dragon and the Stars,* and *Panverse*, among other places. He lives in the Greater Boston Area with his wife, artist Lisa Tang Liu, and they welcomed their daughter into the world in 2010. Those late nights when the newborn wouldn't sleep proved a good time to think about stories. He is currently working on his first novel.

"Postings from an Amorous Tomorrow" is **Corey Mariani's** first piece of published fiction. He lives in northern California with his beautiful wife. In his free time, he plays bass in the rock band, Shays' Rebellion, which tours extensively throughout Humboldt County every winter.

George R.R. Martin is the wildly popular author of the *A Song of Ice and Fire* epic fantasy series, and many other novels, such as *Dying of the Light* and *The Armageddon Rag.* His short fiction—which has appeared in numerous anthologies and in most if not all of the genre's major magazines—has garnered him four Hugos, two Nebulas, the Stoker, and the World Fantasy Award. Martin is also known for editing the *Wild Cards* series of shared world superhero anthologies, and for his work as a screenwriter on such television projects as the 1980s version of *The Twilight Zone* and *Beauty and the Beast.* A TV series based on *A Song of Ice and Fire* debuted on HBO in 2011.

Anne McCaffrey is a winner of both the Hugo and Nebula Awards, a SFWA Grand Master, and an inductee into the SF Hall of Fame. Her work is beloved by generations of readers. She is best known for authoring the Dragonriders of Pern series, but she has also written dozens of other novels. She was born in Cambridge, Mass. in 1926 and currently makes her home in Ireland, in a home named Dragonhold-Underhill.

Jack McDevitt, who Stephen King describes as "the logical heir to Isaac Asimov and Arthur C. Clarke," is the author of sixteen novels, nine of which were finalists for the Nebula Award. His novel *Seeker* won the Nebula in 2007, and other award-winners include his first novel, *The Hercules Text*, which won the Philip K. Dick Special Award, and *Omega*, which received the John W.

Campbell Memorial Award for best science fiction novel. McDevitt's most recent books are *Time Travelers Never Die* and *The Devil's Eye,* both from Ace Books. A Philadelphia native, McDevitt had a varied career before becoming writer, which included being a naval officer, an English teacher, a customs officer, a taxi driver, and a management trainer for the US Customs Service. He is married to the former Maureen McAdams, and resides in Brunswick, Georgia, where he keeps a weather eye on hurricanes.

Tessa Mellas is currently a PhD student at the University of Cincinnati. She is an editorial assistant for *The Cincinnati Review.* Her fiction has been published in *StoryQuarterly, Hayden's Ferry Review, Gulf Coast, Fugue,* and *New Orleans Review.* She has been a vegetarian for over two decades, was formerly a competitive synchronized figure skater, grew up on the St. Lawrence River, where each June shadflies rose out of the water in great gray clouds, and is an aficionado of snow.

Nnedi Okorafor is the author of the novels *Zahrah the Windseeker, The Shadow Speaker,* and *Who Fears Death.* Her book for children, *Long Juju Man,* won the Macmillan Writer's Prize for Africa. She is also the winner of the Wole Soyinka Prize for Literature and the Carl Brandon Society's Parallax Award, and has been a finalist for the NAACP Image Award, Andre Norton Award, and the Essence Magazine Literary Award. Forthcoming books include *Akata Witch* and *Iridessa the Fire-Bellied Dragon Frog.* Her short fiction has appeared in *Strange Horizons, Clarkesworld,* and in anthologies such as *Eclipse Three, So Long Been Dreaming, Dark Matter: Reading the Bones,* and in John Joseph Adams's *Seeds of Change* and *The Way of the Wizard.*

Variously known as a student of Linguistics, a web application developer, a graduate of the 2008 Clarion West class, a writer of speculative fiction, and a purveyor of medieval armor and fine baked goods, **An Owomoyela** mostly resides in places contrary to consensus reality but is compelled to list a university town in the American Midwest as home on most official documents. Fiction bearing the mark of this elusive author can be found in an increasing variety of "here"s and "there"s, and more general information can be found at an.owomoyela.net.

Susan Palwick's publication credits include the novels *Flying In Place, The Necessary Beggar,* and *Shelter.* Much of her short fiction—which has appeared in *Asimov's Science Fiction, Amazing Stories, The Magazine of Fantasy & Science Fiction,* and elsewhere—was recently collected in the volume *The Fate of Mice.* Her work has been a finalist for the World Fantasy, Locus, and Mythopoeic awards, and *Flying in Place* won the Crawford Award for best first fantasy novel. She is Associate Professor of English at the University of Nevada, Reno, and lives in the foothills of the Sierra Nevada with her husband and three cats.

Cat Rambo writes in the Pacific Northwest. Her collection, *Eyes Like Sky and Coal and Moonlight*, appeared from Paper Golem Press in 2009, following her collaboration with Jeff VanderMeer, *The Surgeon's Tale and Other Stories* in 2007. Among the places her work has appeared are *Asimov's, Weird Tales,* and *Clarkesworld.*

Robert Reed is the author of more than two hundred works of short science fiction, with the occasional fantasy and odd horror thrown into the mix. He has also published various novels, including *Marrow* and *The Well of Stars,* two epic tales about a world-sized starship taking a lap around the galaxy. His novella, "A Billion Eves," won the Hugo in 2007. Reed lives in Lincoln, Nebraska with his wife and daughter, and a computer jammed with forgotten files.

Alastair Reynolds was born in Barry in 1966. He spent his early years in Cornwall, then returned to Wales for his primary and secondary school education. He completed a degree in astronomy at Newcastle, then a PhD in the same subject at St Andrews in Scotland. He left the UK in 1991 and spent the next sixteen years working in the Netherlands, mostly for the European Space Agency, although he also did a stint as a postdoctoral worker in Utrecht. He had been writing and selling science fiction since 1989, and published his first novel, *Revelation Space,* in 2000. He has recently completed his tenth novel and has continued to publish short fiction. His novel *Chasm City* won the British Science Fiction Award, and he has been shortlisted for the Arthur C Clarke award three times. In 2004 he left scientific research to write full time. He married in 2005 and returned to Wales in 2008, where he lives in Rhondda Cynon Taff.

Hugo-award winning author **Kristine Kathryn Rusch** publishes fiction in many genres under many names. Her novels have appeared in fifteen countries, and her short stories have appeared in many year's best collections. Once upon a time, she edited *The Magazine of Fantasy & Science Fiction,* as well as *Pulphouse: The Hardback Magazine,* but she gave all that up for writing. Over the next three years, WMG Publishing will put her entire backlist into print, including all of her short stories (in electronic form). For more information on her work, visit kristinekathrynrusch.com.

Robert Silverberg—four-time Hugo Award-winner, five-time winner of the Nebula Award, SFWA Grand Master, SF Hall of Fame honoree—is the author of nearly five hundred short stories, nearly one hundred-and-fifty novels, and is the editor of in the neighborhood of one hundred anthologies. Among his most famous works are *Lord Valentine's Castle, Dying Inside, Nightwings,* and *The World Inside.* Learn more at www.majipoor.com.

Bruce Sterling is the author of many novels, including *Islands in the Net, Heavy Weather, Distraction, Holy Fire, The Zenith Angle, The Caryatids,* and, with William Gibson, *The Difference Engine.* He is the winner of three Locus Awards, two Hugos, the John W. Campbell Memorial Award, and the Arthur C. Clarke Award. He is also the editor of the seminal cyberpunk anthology *Mirrorshades.* Much of his short fiction, which has appeared in magazines such as *F&SF* and *Omni,* was recently collected in *Ascendancies: The Best of Bruce Sterling.*

David Tallerman is the author of around a hundred short stories, many of them published or forthcoming in markets such as *Bull Spec, Andromeda Spaceways, Space and Time, Flash Fiction Online,* and John Joseph Adams's zombie best-of anthology *The Living Dead.* He's also published poetry (in *Chiaroscuro*), film reviews (in *Son and Foe*) and a comic script (in the award-winning British comic *Futurequake.*) His first novel, tentatively known as *Giant Thief,* is currently seeking a good home, and he recently completed the first draft of his second. He can be found online at davidtallerman.net.

Born in the Pacific Northwest in 1979, **Catherynne M. Valente** is the author of over a dozen works of fiction and poetry, including *Palimpsest,* the Orphan's Tales series, and the crowdfunded phenomenon *The Girl Who Circumnavigated Fairyland in a Ship of Own Making.* She is the winner of the Tiptree Award, the Andre Norton Award, the Mythopoeic Award, the Rhysling Award, and the Million Writers Award. She was a finalist for the World Fantasy Award in 2007 and 2009, and the Lambda and Hugo Awards in 2010. She lives on an island off the coast of Maine with her partner, two dogs, and an enormous cat. Learn more at catherynnemvalente.com.

Genevieve Valentine's first novel, *Mechanique: A Tale of the Circus Tresaulti,* is forthcoming from Prime Books in 2011. Her short fiction has appeared in or is forthcoming from: *Running with the Pack, The Living Dead 2, The Way of the Wizard, Teeth, Clarkesworld, Strange Horizons, Escape Pod,* and more. Her appetite for bad movies is insatiable, a tragedy she tracks on her blog, genevievevalentine.com.

Carrie Vaughn is the bestselling author of the Kitty Norville series. The eighth volume, *Kitty Goes to War*, is due out in July. She has also written a young adult novel, *Voices of Dragons*, and a stand-alone fantasy novel, *Discord's Apple*. Her short fiction has appeared many times in *Realms of Fantasy*, and in a number of anthologies, such as *Fast Ships, Black Sails* and *Warriors*. She lives in Colorado with a fluffy attack dog. Learn more at carrievaughn.com.

Charles Yu received the National Book Foundation's 5 Under 35 Award for his story collection, *Third Class Superhero*. He has also had work published in *Alaska Quarterly Review*, *Eclectica*, *The Gettysburg Review*, *The Malahat Review*, *Oxford American*, and *Sou'wester*. His first novel, *How to Live Safely in a Science Fictional Universe* (Pantheon) was published in September. He lives in Los Angeles with his wife and two children.

ACKNOWLEDGEMENTS

Many thanks to the following:

Lightspeed's publisher, Sean Wallace, for publishing *Lightspeed* and choosing me to edit it.

The brilliant and dedicated *Lightspeed* editorial team: Molly Tanzer, Esther Inglis-Arkell, Stefan Rudnicki, Christie Yant, Erin Stocks, Stacey Friedberg, and Robyn Lupo. I couldn't edit the magazine without your support; although only my name goes on the cover and may be recognized by award committees, you guys are every bit as much a part of this as I am. Additionally, a huge thanks goes out to former team members Andrea Kail and Jordan Hamessley—both of whom were with us from the very start and were instrumental in getting *Lightspeed* off the ground.

Our amazing webmaster Jeremiah Tolbert, for creating such a beautiful design for the magazine, and making all of the behind-the-scenes coding and whatnot work without a hitch.

Our ever-vigilant slush readers: Kate Galey, Andrew Liptak, Shannon Rampe, Caleb Schulz, Moshe Siegel, and LaShawn Wanak.

Our nonfiction writers—including especially our most prolific contributor Genevieve Valentine—for balancing our fiction with some fact.

All of our wonderful artists who provided our covers.

Astronomers Mike Brotherton and Pamela Gay, for not only providing some of *Lightspeed*'s nonfiction content, but also advising on the astronomical science in some of our stories.

My intern, Rebecca McNulty, for her tireless devotion to the occasionally mundane tasks I assign her, and for always being there when I need her.

My agent, Joe Monti, for the incredible amount of support he's provided since taking me on as a client—he's gone above and beyond the call of duty. To any writers reading this: you'd be lucky to have Joe in your corner.

Gordon Van Gelder, for mentoring me, and giving me my start in the field. None of my successes would have been possible without his tuteledge.

My mom, for her endless enthusiasm for all my new projects.

My dear friends Robert Bland, Desirina Boskovich, Christopher M. Cevasco, Douglas E. Cohen, David Barr Kirtley, and Matt London, for all of their support.

The readers and critics who have praised *Lightspeed* and made our first year such a huge success.

And last, but certainly not least: a big thanks to all of the authors who appear in *Lightspeed* and in this anthology.

ACKNOWLEDGEMENT IS MADE FOR PERMISSION TO PRINT THE FOLLOWING MATERIAL:

"Gossamer" by Stephen Baxter. © 1995 by Stephen Baxter. Originally published in *Science Fiction Age*. Reprinted by permission of the author.

"Manumission" by Tobias Buckell. © 2008 by Tobias S. Buckell. Originally published in *Jim Baen's Universe*. Reprinted by permission of the author.

"The Elephants of Poznan" by Orson Scott Card. © 2000 by Orson Scott Card. Originally published in *Fantastyka*. Reprinted by permission of the author.

"Arvies" by Adam-Troy Castro. © 2010 by Adam-Troy Castro. Originally published in *Lightspeed Magazine*, August 2010. Reprinted by permission of the author.

"Saying the Names" by Maggie Clark. © 2011 by Maggie Clark. Originally published in *Lightspeed Magazine*, March 2011. Reprinted by permission of the author.

"Mama, We are Zhenya, Your Son" by Tom Crosshill. © 2011 by Tom Crosshill. Originally published in *Lightspeed Magazine*, April 2011. Reprinted by permission of the author.

"The Passenger" by Julie E. Czerneda. © 1999 by Julie E. Czerneda. Originally published in *Treachery & Treason*, edited by Laura Anne Gilman and Jennifer Heddle. Reprinted by permission of the author.

"Patient Zero" by Tananarive Due. © 2000 by Tananarive Due. Originally published in *The Magazine of Fantasy & Science Fiction*. Reprinted by permission of the author.

"No Time Like the Present" by Carol Emshwiller. © 2010 by Carol Emshwiller. Originally published in *Lightspeed Magazine*, July 2010. Reprinted by permission of the author.

"The Taste of Starlight" by John R. Fultz. © 2010 by John R. Fultz. Originally published in *Lightspeed Magazine*, October 2010. Reprinted by permission of the author.

"The Harrowers" by Eric Gregory. © 2011 by Eric Gregory. Originally published in *Lightspeed Magazine*, May 2011. Reprinted by permission of the author.

"More Than the Sum of His Parts" by Joe Haldeman. © 1985 by Joe Haldeman. Originally published in *Playboy*. Reprinted by permission of the author.

"I'm Alive, I Love You, I'll See You in Reno" by Vylar Kaftan. © 2010 by Vylar Kaftan. Originally published in *Lightspeed Magazine*, June 2010. Reprinted by permission of the author.

"Breakaway, Backdown" by James Patrick Kelly. © 1996 by James Patrick Kelly. Originally published in *Asimov's Science Fiction*. Reprinted by permission of the author.

"Faces in Revolving Souls" by Caitlín R. Kiernan. © 2005 by Caitlín R. Kiernan. Originally published in *Outsiders*, edited by Nancy Holder and Nancy Kilpatrick. Reprinted by permission of the author.

"Hwang's Billion Brilliant Daughters" by Alice Sola Kim. © 2010 by Alice Sola Kim. Originally published in *Lightspeed Magazine*, November 2010. Reprinted by permission of the author.

"Beachworld" by Stephen King. © 1984 by Stephen King. Originally published in *Weird Tales*. Reprinted by permission of the author.

"Cats in Victory" by David Barr Kirtley. © 2010 by David Barr Kirtley. Originally published in *Lightspeed Magazine*, June 2010. Reprinted by permission of the author.

"In-Fall" by Ted Kosmatka. © 2010 by Ted Kosmatka. Originally published in *Lightspeed Magazine*, December 2010. Reprinted by permission of the author.

"Ej-Es" by Nancy Kress. © 2003 by Nancy Kress. Originally published in the anthology, *Stars*, edited by Janis Ian and Mike Resnick. Reprinted by permission of the author.

"Eliot Wrote" by Nancy Kress. © 2011 by Nancy Kress. Originally published in *Lightspeed Magazine*, May 2011. Reprinted by permission of the author.

"The Long Chase" by Geoffrey A. Landis. © 2002 by Geoffrey A. Landis. Originally published in *Asimov's Science Fiction*. Reprinted by permission of the author.

"Hindsight" by Sarah Langan. © 2010 by Sarah Langan. Originally published in *Lightspeed Magazine*, October 2010. Reprinted by permission of the author.

"Tight Little Stitches in a Dead Man's Back" by Joe R. Lansdale. © 1986 Joe R. Lansdale. Originally published in *Nukes* edited by John MacLay. Reprinted by permission of the author.

"The Silence of the Asonu" by Ursula K. Le Guin. © 1998 by Ursula K. Le Guin. Originally published in *Orion*. Reprinted by permission of the author.

"Black Fire" by Tanith Lee. © 2011 by Tanith Lee. Originally published in *Lightspeed Magazine*, January 2011. Reprinted by permission of the author.

"Flower, Mercy, Needle, Chain" by Yoon Ha Lee. © 2010 by Yoon Ha Lee. Originally published in *Lightspeed Magazine*, September 2010. Reprinted by permission of the author.

"Simulacrum" by Ken Liu. © 2011 by Ken Liu. Originally published in *Lightspeed Magazine*, February 2011. Reprinted by permission of the author.

"Postings from an Amorous Tomorrow" by Corey Joshua Mariani. © 2011 by Corey Joshua Mariani. Originally published in *Lightspeed Magazine*, January 2011. Reprinted by permission of the author.

" . . . for a single yesterday" by George R.R. Martin. © 1975 by George R.R. Martin. Originally published in *Epoch*. Reprinted by permission of the author.

"Velvet Fields" by Anne McCaffrey. © 1973 by Anne McCaffrey. Originally published in *Worlds of If*. Reprinted by permission of the author and the author's agent, The Virginia Kidd Agency.

"The Cassandra Project" by Jack McDevitt. © 2010 by Cryptic, Inc. Originally published in *Lightspeed Magazine*, June 2010. Reprinted by permission of the author.

"Bibi From Jupiter" by Tessa Mellas. © 2007 by Tessa Mellas. Originally published in *StoryQuarterly*. Reprinted by permission of the author.

"Spider the Artist" by Nnedi Okorafor. © 2008 by Nnedi Okorafor. Originally published in *Seeds of Change*, edited by John Joseph Adams. Reprinted by permission of the author.

"All That Touches the Air" by An Owomoyela. © 2011 by An Owomoyela. Originally published in *Lightspeed Magazine*, April 2011. Reprinted by permission of the author.

"Cucumber Gravy" by Susan Palwick. © 2001 by Susan Palwick. Originally published in *SCI FICTION*. Reprinted by permission of the author.

"Amid the Words of War" by Cat Rambo. © 2010 by Cat Rambo. Originally published in *Lightspeed Magazine*, September 2010. Reprinted by permission of the author.

"Long Enough and Just So Long" by Cat Rambo. © 2011 by Cat Rambo. Originally published in *Lightspeed Magazine*, February 2011. Reprinted by permission of the author.

"Woman Leaves Room" by Robert Reed. © 2011 by Robert Reed. Originally published in *Lightspeed Magazine*, March 2011. Reprinted by permission of the author.

"Scales" by Alastair Reynolds. © 2009 by Alastair Reynolds. Originally published in *The Guardian*. Reprinted by permission of the author.

"The Observer" by Kristine Kathryn Rusch. © 2008 by Kristine Kathryn Rusch. Originally published in *Front Lines* edited by Denise Little. Reprinted by permission of the author.

"Travelers" by Robert Silverberg. © 1999 by Agberg, Ltd. Originally published in *Amazing Stories*. Reprinted by permission of the author.

"Maneki Neko" by Bruce Sterling. © 1998 by Bruce Sterling. Originally published in *Hayakawa's Science Fiction Magazine* (Japanese language) and *The Magazine of Fantasy & Science Fiction* (English language). Reprinted by permission of the author.

"Jenny's Sick" by David Tallerman. © 2010 by David Tallerman. Originally published in *Lightspeed Magazine*, December 2010. Reprinted by permission of the author.

"How to Become a Mars Overlord" by Catherynne Valente. © 2010 by Catherynne Valente. Originally published in *Lightspeed Magazine*, August 2010. Reprinted by permission of the author.

"The Zeppelin Conductors' Society Annual Gentlemen's Ball" by Genevieve Valentine. © 2010 by Genevieve Valentine. Originally published in *Lightspeed Magazine*, July 2010. Reprinted by permission of the author.

"Amaryllis" by Carrie Vaughn. © 2010 by Carrie Vaughn, LLC. Originally published in *Lightspeed Magazine*, June 2010. Reprinted by permission of the author.

"Standard Loneliness Package" by Charles Yu. © 2010 by Charles Yu. Originally published in *Lightspeed Magazine*, November 2010. Reprinted by permission of the author.

ABOUT THE EDITOR

John Joseph Adams (www.johnjosephadams.com) is the editor of *Lightspeed Magazine* and *Fantasy Magazine*. He is also the bestselling editor of many anthologies, such as *Wastelands, The Living Dead, By Blood We Live, Federations, The Improbable Adventures of Sherlock Holmes, Brave New Worlds, The Living Dead 2*, and *The Way of the Wizard*. Forthcoming work includes *Under the Moons of Mars: New Adventures on Barsoom, Armored*, and *The Mad Scientist's Guide to World Domination*. In 2011, he was a finalist for two Hugo Awards and two World Fantasy Awards. John is also the co-host of The Geek's Guide to the Galaxy podcast, which airs on io9.com.